The Riddell Diaries
1908–1923

The Riddell Diaries

1908–1923

*Edited and with an Introduction
by J.M. McEwen*

Foreword by John Grigg

**The Athlone Press
London and Atlantic Highlands, NJ**

First published in Great Britain in 1986
by The Athlone Press
44 Bedford Row, London WC1R 4LY
and 171 First Avenue,
Atlantic Highlands, NJ 07716

Copyright © 1986 John M. McEwen
Copyright © 1986 Foreword, John Grigg

British Library Cataloguing in Publication Data
Riddell, *Sir*, George
  The Riddell diaries 1908–1923.
  1. Riddell, *Sir*, George
  I. Title.   II. McEwen, John M.
  941.083'.092'4   DA566.9.R5

  ISBN 0–485–11300–7

Typesetting by The Word Factory, Rossendale, Lancashire
Printed in Great Britain at the University Press, Cambridge

Contents

Foreword

Anyone interested in the political history of the first quarter of this century, and more especially in the ministerial career of David Lloyd George, has long been indebted to the three volumes of diary extracts published by Lord Riddell towards the end of his life, which have the crucial merit of recording conversations with and between leading politicians. But Riddell left out much good material to avoid, for instance, giving offence to other newspaper magnates. The full text was deposited at the British Museum with instructions that it be reserved from public use until fifty years after his death (in 1934).

Now that the close season is at an end we have, at last, the authentic text of the Riddell diary, edited, in a single volume, by Professor J. M. McEwen; and it seems to me that he has done a superb job. If his scholarly labours have caused some of the diary, as originally published, to be disqualified as later addition, he can justly claim that the material now appearing for the first time more than makes up for what he has had to reject.

His notes are very helpful, and the commentary leading into chapters sets the stage very well. Above all, his introduction gives an excellent sketch of Riddell's personality and career. Though in some ways a rather repulsive character, Riddell was a very shrewd observer and certainly no sycophant. As Professor McEwen says, as a diarist he cannot be compared with Boswell or Pepys, but he performed, nevertheless, a great historical service, which can now be appreciated to the full with Professor McEwen's expert assistance.

JOHN GRIGG

Acknowledgments

I wish to thank the British Library for permission to examine Lord Riddell's manuscript diaries and use hitherto unpublished material. In particular I am grateful to Dr A. N. E. D. Schofield of the Department of Manuscripts for his assistance on more than one occasion. Nor can I omit to mention the unfailing courtesy of the staff of the Manuscripts Room. Also in the public domain, the Public Trustee as surviving executor and trustee of the will of Lord Riddell helped me with advice on the status of the diaries.

News Group Newspapers Limited kindly granted me permission to read an unpublished biography of Riddell by Mr Stafford Somerfield and to draw freely upon that material in preparing my Introduction. I was greatly assisted in this by the Chief Librarian of the firm, Mr George Oliver. To Victor Gollancz Limited and The Hamlyn Publishing Group Limited, publishers of two of Riddell's volumes, acknowledgment is made for their help in clarifying the position with regard to copyright. The Walton Heath Golf Club furnished me with interesting information about that famous institution, and I express my thanks to the secretary, Mr W. E. McCrea.

I am indebted to Mr John Grigg for reading the typescript and writing a Foreword to this volume. On the publishing side, I record my thanks to Mr Brian Southam for his suggestions and sage advice. My research task would have been much harder without a grant from the Social Sciences and Humanities Research Council of Canada to help defray the costs of several months in London. I acknowledge also my obligation to Brock University for granting me leave of absense from teaching duties at the right moment, and for providing assistance towards the costs of publication.

It only remains to acknowledge the invaluable support of my wife and family, who encouraged me in this work.

Editor's Note

Editing the diaries of Lord Riddell presented some unusual problems. Readers of his published volumes probably assumed that the words were transcribed directly (and accurately) from the manuscripts. This was not so. The original diaries, now in the British Library (Add. MSS 62955–68), consist of fourteen volumes of manuscript. Mostly they are in Riddell's hand, but a small amount near the end is typewritten or in the hand of an amanuensis. For several reasons they are difficult to read. Riddell wrote on loose sheets of paper, often folded so that the order is not clear, and sometimes he inserted entries out of chronological order. Occasionally he added passages hours or days later as he recalled belatedly some extra things he wished to record, again interfering with the chronological order. Nor are matters made easier by his difficult, one might almost say execrable, handwriting.

When Riddell decided to publish selected passages his secretaries prepared a typed copy of the original diaries. This too is now in the British Library (Add. MSS 62969–90). The work was not altogether free from error. As an example, the entry for 4 December 1916, the eve of the fall of the Asquith government, reads: 'Saw LG at the War Office. Found him reading War Office papers.' But the manuscript has 'Found him packing War Office papers', which conveys a quite different picture. Names also were sometimes wrongly transcribed, as in the entry for 9 July 1912 describing the Naval Review, where the name of Sir Edward Carson was included. In the manuscript this reads 'Sir Edward Cassell', which of course should be 'Sir Ernest Cassell'. Other variations from the original were caused by Riddell's tampering with the text as typed for him, making a second stage where errors occurred. Sometimes he deleted or altered certain words he had used too frequently ('very' and 'that' were regular offenders). Sometimes he altered a passage to tone it down or clarify the meaning. Sometimes he inserted matter not in the manuscript. And, it must be admitted, sometimes he improved a little on the original where his own remarks were concerned. Another serious blemish in the published volumes is the many times Riddell failed to indicate by three or four dots that the manuscript contained material he had not included for publication.

I have attempted to correct all of these mistakes so that the present volume accords with the original manuscript. However, as Riddell often wrote hurriedly and with scant regard for punctuation or paragraph structure, it has been necessary occasionally to impose a more orderly division of words, without in any way altering the meaning.

Another problem concerns entries that were wrongly dated. Luckily these were usually easy to spot and correct, although a number of entries give only the month and the year. In default of other evidence they have been inserted at the place where they are found in the manuscript. With the exception of a few letters, Riddell's papers, which might have been used to supplement the diaries and confirm the accuracy of dates, have not survived.

A vexing problem for an editor is what to include and what to omit. The guiding principles were as follows. First, to select the most important passages – from a historian's point of view – used in the published volumes, and correct them to agree with the manuscript diaries. Next, to incorporate hitherto unpublished material that sheds fresh light on people and events. And lastly, to eliminate all that seemed of ephemeral interest or was too trivial to deserve survival, saving only a few of the choicer anecdotes. In the last resort the selection has had to be a personal one, reflecting the editor's interests.

One or two final points. Abbreviations present few difficulties. Most are obvious – 'K' for Kitchener, 'LG' for Lloyd George, 'N' for Northcliffe, etc. Some refer to offices – 'CIGS' for Chief of the Imperial General Staff, 'LCJ' for Lord Chief Justice, 'QMG' for Quartermaster-General, etc. The titles of Riddell's published volumes are given in full in the Introduction but thereafter reduced to *More Pages*, *War Diary* and *Intimate Diary*.

Biographical details of persons fall into two categories. At the beginning is a list of 'Important Persons', people whose names figure prominently in the diaries. Others mentioned less often in the text are usually identified in a Note where the name first appears. The remaining Notes are deliberately brief, intended only for cross reference or to clarify points which may be obscure to a general reader.

As Riddell remains a comparatively unknown figure, notwithstanding the frequency with which his name is invoked by other writers, it seemed appropriate to include a short biographical essay as an 'Introduction'.

Important persons
(and principal offices between 1908 and 1923)

AITKEN, William Maxwell (1879–1964), Unionist MP, Chancellor of Duchy of Lancaster and Minister of Information 1918, created Baron Beaverbrook.

ASQUITH, Herbert Henry (1852–1928), Liberal statesman, Prime Minister 1908–16, acting Secretary for War, March–August 1914, November 1915 and June–July 1916, created Earl of Oxford and Asquith.

BALFOUR, Arthur James (1848–1930), Unionist statesman and former Prime Minister, First Lord of Admiralty 1915–16, Foreign Secretary 1916–19, Lord President of Council 1919–22, created Earl of Balfour.

BUCKMASTER, Stanley Owen (1861–1934), Liberal Minister, Solicitor-General 1913–15, Lord Chancellor 1915–16, Director of Press Bureau 1914–15, created Viscount Buckmaster.

CARSON, Edward Henry (1854–1935), Ulster Unionist leader, Attorney-General 1915. First Lord of Admiralty 1916–17, Minister without Portfolio with seat in War Cabinet 1917–18, created Baron Carson.

CECIL, Lord Edgar Algernon Robert (1864–1958), Unionist Minister, Parliamentary Under-Secretary for Foreign Affairs 1915–16, Minister of Blockade 1916–18, created Viscount Cecil of Chelwood.

CHAMBERLAIN, Joseph Austen (1863–1937), Unionist Minister, Secretary for India 1915–17, Minister without Portfolio with seat in War Cabinet 1918–19, Chancellor of Exchequer 1919–21, Lord Privy Seal 1921–2.

CHURCHILL, Winston Leonard Spencer (1874–1965), Liberal Minister. President of Board of Trade 1908–10, Home Secretary 1910–11, First Lord of Admiralty 1911–15, Chancellor of Duchy of Lancaster 1915, Minister of Munitions 1917–19, Secretary for War 1919–21, Colonial Secretary 1921–2.

DALZIEL, James Henry (1868–1935), newspaper proprietor and Liberal MP, created Baron Dalziel of Kirkcaldy.

DERBY, 17th Earl of (1865–1948), Unionist Minister, Director-General of Recruiting 1915, Parliamentary Under-Secretary for War 1916, Secretary for War 1916–18, Ambassador to Paris 1918–20.

DONALD, Robert (1861–1933), Editor of *Daily Chronicle* 1902–18, a director at Department of Information 1917.

FISHER, John Arbuthnot (1841–1920), Admiral of the Fleet, First Sea Lord 1904–10 and 1914–15, created Baron Fisher.

FRENCH, John Denton Pinkstone (1852–1925), Field-Marshal, Chief of Imperial General Staff 1912–14, Commander-in-Chief of British Forces in France 1914–15, Lord Lieutenant of Ireland 1918–21, created Earl of Ypres.

GEDDES, Eric Campbell (1875–1937), Unionist Minister, Inspector-General of Transportation 1916–17, First Lord of Admiralty 1917–19, Minister of Transport 1919–21.

GREY, Edward (1862–1933), Liberal statesman, Foreign Secretary 1905–16, created Viscount Grey of Fallodon.

HAIG, Douglas (1861–1928), Field-Marshal, Commander-in-Chief, British Expeditionary Force, 1915–19, created Earl Haig.

HALDANE, Richard Burdon (1856–1928), Liberal Minister, Secretary for War 1905–12, Lord Chancellor 1912–15, created Viscount Haldane.

HARMSWORTH, Alfred Charles William (1865–1922), newspaper proprietor, owner of *The Times*, *Daily Mail*, etc; headed special War Mission to United States 1917, Director of Propaganda in Enemy Countries 1918, created Viscount Northcliffe.

HARMSWORTH, Harold Sidney (1868–1940), newspaper proprietor, owner of *Daily Mirror* and *Sunday Pictorial*, Minister for Air 1917–18, created Viscount Rothermere.

ISAACS, Rufus David (1860–1935), Liberal Minister, Solicitor-General 1910, Attorney-General 1910–13, Lord Chief Justice of England 1913–21, Viceroy of India 1921–6, created Marquess of Reading.

KERR, Philip Henry (1882–1940), private secretary to Lloyd George 1916–21, 11th Marquess of Lothian.

KITCHENER, Horatio Herbert (1850–1916), Field-Marshal, Secretary for War 1914–16, created Earl Kitchener of Khartoum and of Broome.

LAW, Andrew Bonar (1858–1923), Unionist statesman, Colonial Secretary 1915–16, Chancellor of Exchequer with seat in War Cabinet 1916–19, Lord Privy Seal 1919–21, Prime Minister 1922–3.

LAWSON, Harry Lawson Webster Levy- (1862–1933), newspaper proprietor, owner of *Daily Telegraph*, Unionist MP, created Viscount Burnham.

LLOYD GEORGE, David (1863–1945), Liberal statesman, President of Board of Trade 1905–8, Chancellor of Exchequer 1908–15, Minister of Munitions 1915–16, Secretary for War 1916, Prime Minister 1916–22, created Earl Lloyd-George of Dwyfor.

McKENNA, Reginald (1863–1943), Liberal Minister, President of Board of Education 1907–8, First Lord of Admiralty 1908–11, Home Secretary 1911–15, Chancellor of Exchequer 1915–16.

MASTERMAN, Charles Frederick Gurney (1874–1927), Liberal Minister, Parliamentary Under-Secretary to Home Office 1909–12, Financial Secretary to Treasury 1912–14, Chancellor of Duchy of Lancaster 1914–15.

MILNER, Alfred (1854–1925), Unionist Minister, Minister without Portfolio with seat in War Cabinet 1916–18, Secretary for War 1918–19, Colonial Secretary 1919–21, created Viscount Milner.

MONTAGU, Edwin Samuel (1879–1924), Liberal Minister, Chancellor of Duchy of Lancaster 1915 and 1916, Minister of Munitions 1916, Secretary for India 1917–22.

MURRAY, Alexander William Charles Oliphant, the Master of Elibank (1870–1920), Liberal Chief Whip 1910–12, created Baron Murray of Elibank.

NICOLL, William Robertson (1851–1923), Editor of the *British Weekly* 1886–1923.

ROBERTSON, William Robert (1860–1933), Chief of Imperial General Staff 1915–18, Field-Marshal.

RUNCIMAN, Walter (1870–1949), Liberal Minister, President of Board of Education, 1908–11, President of Board of Agriculture 1911–14, President of Board of Trade 1914–16, created Viscount Runciman of Doxford.

SAMUEL, Herbert Louis (1870–1963), Liberal Minister, Chancellor of Duchy of Lancaster 1909–10 and 1915–16, Postmaster-General 1910–14 and 1915–16, President of Local Government Board 1914–15, Home Secretary 1916, created Viscount Samuel.

SIMON, John Allsebrook (1873–1954), Liberal Minister,

Solicitor-General 1910–13, Attorney-General 1913–15, Home
Secretary 1915–16, created Viscount Simon.

SMITH, Frederick Edwin (1872–1930), Unionist Minister, Solicitor-
General 1915, Attorney-General 1915–19, Lord Chancellor
1919–22, created Earl of Birkenhead.

SMUTS, Jan Christian (1870–1950), South African statesman,
Minister without Portfolio with seat in War Cabinet 1917–19, later
Prime Minister of South Africa.

Introduction

Historically-minded people with an interest in the First World War era have long been indebted to George Allardice Riddell, first (and last) Baron Riddell of Walton Heath.[1] For half a century his published works have provided informed and sometimes entertaining comment on the inner workings of British politics during the Asquith and Lloyd George years – that is, from 1908 to 1922. On the face of it this seems highly improbable. Riddell held no political office and therefore was not present at Cabinet meetings or conferences where great issues were being discussed and decided. Nor was he an important figure in Downing Street or Whitehall, a mandarin with access to state and other secrets and perhaps even with a little influence. His habitat was Fleet Street, or to be more precise, Bouverie Street. But in an age of the great Press lords like Northcliffe and Rothermere, Burnham and Beaverbrook, to say nothing of editors as eminent as J. L. Garvin, C. P. Scott and J. A. Spender, to name only a few, ownership of a popular Sunday newspaper such as Riddell's *News of the World* scarcely made him a person of importance, save perhaps in the matter of circulation figures.

Riddell's stature in his own day and later was owing to other reasons. First, he became a close friend of David Lloyd George early in the century, and as a result of that friendship he met and talked with many of the leading figures of the time, not just politicians. Of course they were foremost, including Prime Ministers past and future (A. J. Balfour, Neville Chamberlain, Winston Churchill, Andrew Bonar Law, Ramsay MacDonald) as well as leaders of the two great republics (Presidents Wilson and Harding, Prime Ministers Clemenceau and Briand). There were also famous women (Nancy Astor, the Duchess of Atholl, Elinor Glyn, Lily Langtry, Mrs Pankhurst), and other personalities as diverse as Sir J. M. Barrie, Bernard Baruch, Field-Marshal Lord Kitchener, Dr W. G. Grace and Sir William Orpen. The list was long and extraordinarily interesting. Secondly, it was well understood that Riddell's role was primarily that of the rich man who could afford to be a good host and a good listener. He was not a participant, hence not a colleague or potential rival, nor did he aspire

1

to be a maker of public opinion. Consequently many things were said in his presence which otherwise would not have been divulged to one beyond the small circle of men possessing or seeking power. And finally, Riddell was obsessed by an almost unnatural craving to learn as much as he possibly could about everybody who mattered and many who didn't. This drove him to record in his own hand (though later he dictated), usually within hours of acquiring such knowledge, those items of news and details about persons which seemed to him important in building a complete picture. Indeed, very often they *were* important, as those who seek to understand the period have reason to appreciate.

Riddell died in late 1934, but two years previously he decided to publish some of the copious notes he had made over a decade and a half. Three volumes appeared in rapid succession. First came *Lord Riddell's War Diary, 1914–1918* (1933),[2] by all odds the most valuable of the three as a contribution to historical knowledge. It was clear at the outset that these were not diaries in the ordinary sense. The reader learnt next to nothing about Riddell himself, for true to the habits of a lifetime the man and his work remained in the background, if not out of sight altogether. Only an evident interest in money matters betrayed something of the writer's character and tastes. On the other hand the book constituted a remarkable record of conversations with, often between, famous men and women, while the next volume would also include some perceptive accounts of great events. *The Times* commented that the *War Diary* was 'of the utmost historical value, and Lord Riddell has wisely printed his impressions without attempting to harmonise their occasional discrepancies'.[3]

Spurred on by favourable reviews and private congratulations, and suspecting that he had not long to live, he brought forth the second volume a few months later: *Lord Riddell's Intimate Diary of the Peace Conference and After, 1918–1923* (1934).[4] This too was well received by critics in the Press, one reviewer venturing to say: 'As a diary Lord Riddell's second volume is even better than his first.'[5] It is now recognised that this was a mistaken judgment, though Volume Two was not without merit, for the very good reason that Riddell was in the wings during most of the post-war conferences and busily making notes at the end of each day. Finally there appeared *More Pages from My Diary, 1908–1914* (1934),[6] the least substantial of the three volumes yet containing informative detail about such matters as the miners' strike of 1912, the Lloyd George–Winston Churchill relationship, and problems within the Asquith Cabinet. By now, however, Riddell was too near death to take any further interest in his belated venture in publishing.

Not unnaturally, those familiar with the turbulence of British politics whilst Lloyd George was at centre stage wondered if Riddell had told all he knew. Lord Beaverbrook, upon reading the *War Diary*, wrote to him: 'My only complaint with the book is that you have not been indiscreet enough. What a lot of things you must have omitted to tell – or cut out after you had told them!' His letter continued: 'I hope you have left an unbowdlerised manuscript lying in some place of safety so that posterity may not be cheated of the key, which you alone possess, to innumerable incidents in history. You have a duty to the poor devils who will be alive a hundred years hence.' Riddell replied: 'You are quite right. I have had to expurgate a great deal. After all, one must live! Nevertheless, I am preserving the deleted parts. They may, as you imply, create fresh interest later on!'[7]

This was no idle remark to titillate Beaverbrook. Riddell did preserve the manuscript diaries and left instructions that they were not to be opened until long after his death. Accordingly they were deposited in the British Museum by the Public Trustee in February 1935, 'to be reserved from the Public use for fifty years'.[8] Only now has it been possible to examine them and compare the published with the unpublished version. This was a challenging task. The three published volumes totalled 1,012 pages of text, whereas the material in the British Library comprises thirty-six volumes. The size of the latter is due to duplication, fourteen volumes being the original diaries, partly autograph or in the hand of an amanuensis, a small amount typewritten. The other twenty-two volumes are typewritten copies of the first fourteen, not perfectly accurate. By rough calculation the number of words which Riddell set down on paper is somewhere upwards of 650,000. A little further arithmetic suggests that rather less than half the original total was published in the three volumes to appear in 1933 and 1934. But before proceeding to the diaries themselves it may be useful to say something of Riddell's life, hitherto very much a closed book.[9]

Some men who have risen from modest beginnings are understandably reticent about their origins. Others, Prime Ministers not least, glory in the fact of comparatively humble birth and spin romantic tales. Riddell belonged in the first category, going to great, even absurd, lengths to hide the facts about his birth and childhood. There seems to have been a pathological fear, perhaps of being laughed at, possibly that the path to riches and power might be made more difficult if the truth were known. Or it may be that the inwardness of the solitary child became a habit too strong to be broken. This remained unchanged to the end. Just before he died he instructed his wife and his literary secretary to ensure that all his papers would be destroyed, save for the diaries. His confidential clerk not only carried out these instructions to the letter, but over-zealous assistants went so far as to burn some *News of the World* records as well. In addition, pages containing his name were removed from books of reference. It was as if Riddell had determined that all traces of himself should be removed from Bouverie Street. Such precautions notwithstanding, there remained on the premises some evidence that he had in fact existed. The small Christmas bonus to *News of the World* staff continues to be paid to long-serving members these many years after his death. And a bronze bust would occupy a place of honour in the directors' corridor on the second floor. It remained there until quite recently, by which time the newspaper had entered upon a new era of ownership. *Autre temps, autres moeurs.*

In truth there was little in Riddell's background of which he had reason to feel ashamed. And yet by his strange sensitivity on the subject, he allowed all sorts of rumours to gain currency, not least that he was illegitimate. It was also widely believed in Fleet Street and beyond that he was born in Scotland, a myth which Riddell encouraged. Though his forbears were Scottish, in fact his paternal grandfather removed from Berwickshire to London in the early 1800s. It was into a respectable, lower-middle-class Brixton family that George Allardice Riddell was born, in wedlock, on 25 May 1865, only a few days prior to the birth of the future King George V, before whom he was destined to kneel twice. The father, James Riddell, nominally a photographer, was not a success in the various occupations he attempted, and he died before his infant son reached the age of two. Thus did Riddell join the large company of eminent men who have made their way in the world without benefit of a father's presence.[10] There is a rather pathetic touch of fantasy in the fact that, on the occasion of his second marriage, he entered the word 'gentleman' on the marriage certificate after his father's name.

Upon the mother, whose maiden name was Isobel Young, fell the burden of rearing this child, though not without help. After the death of her husband she returned to the home of her parents, strong

Presbyterians, where the young George was raised in a stern and narrow tradition. Isobel taught him to read at an early age and, as might be expected, placed great emphasis upon study of the Bible. There followed some years at a Church school in South London, a period in his life of which the mature Riddell never spoke. He was neither outgoing nor good at games, sufficient reasons for a boy who was not very muscular to wish to obliterate that experience. Despite the cheerlessness of school and long evenings of study under the watchful eyes of mother and grandfather, it was not a totally bleak existence for a child lacking brothers and sisters. The Youngs were a large family and the household an active place, though Isobel and her son were cast in the role of poor relations. And if luxuries were quite unknown, there was nothing like hardship by the standards of those days. The older members of the family observed how George was able to master his lessons with considerable ease, aided by a memory that even then was deemed phenomenal. Such qualities greatly impressed his uncle, D. W. Allardice, who determined that the boy should have a chance to make his way in the world. At age seventeen he went to work with the firm of Octavius Wooler, solicitors, of Bedford Row, and shortly afterwards he passed the preliminary examinations for the Law Society. Riddell was articled in August 1883 and there began five years of hard study during which time he had little diversion of any sort.

The fierce determination with which he pursued his studies brought its reward: first-class honours and the Law Society's Prize for the year. It was now that Riddell began to display those other qualities destined to bring him riches early and a measure of fame later in life. His gaunt appearance, grim visage and black clothes caused people to mistake him for a Methodist preacher, though he was only twenty-three. The resemblance ended there. Riddell's god was wealth and he pursued it to the exclusion of all else. Lacking capital of his own, he resorted to a time-honoured method. His marriage to Grace Williams, of a Welsh family settled in London, brought him sufficient money to join two other young solicitors in purchasing the London office where he had been articled (Wooler's being a Darlington firm). Before the end of the year 1888 he was head of a new firm of solicitors: Riddell, Vaizey & Smith. During the next fifteen years he sacrificed nearly all the pleasures of life – domestic bliss, the society of friends, entertainment of any kind, even his health – in order to make his affairs prosper. At this stage it was truly said of Riddell that he 'lived only to work'. Inevitably the firm did well and within a few years he had a considerable income, largely because of his astuteness in property transactions. Among his early clients was the impresario Sir Oswald Stoll, whom Riddell encouraged to buy a chain of music halls in London and sought appropriate sites. Not content with buying property for others, he was soon acquiring premises for himself and harvesting regular profits at little risk. Speculation on the Stock Exchange was something to be avoided because of the possibility of loss, and Riddell never took unnecessary chances where money was concerned.

Few marriages could have withstood the strain Riddell imposed upon his union with Grace Williams. He did provide her with a modest home by prevailing upon his mother to leave the house in Finsbury Park which they had shared for some years, the aging widow going off to rooms in Kilburn. But his work habits continued unchanged and Grace seldom saw him from early in the morning until late at night. Saturdays and Sundays were no different from week days. It seems that the unhappy woman took to drink (we only have Riddell's version of this) and within five years the marriage had broken down irreparably. Riddell walked out, arranged for her to receive a small allowance and ordered her to stay away from his office. His wife countered by going to court and in August 1893 Mr Justice Barnes (later first Baron Gorell) ordered her husband to return home within a fortnight 'and render to her conjugal rights'. Riddell neither appeared in court nor complied with the order and nothing more was heard of the matter for seven years.

By then both Riddell and Grace wished to marry again, making necessary the formality of a divorce. On 2 April 1900, Mr Justice Barnes again spoke, declaring the marriage dissolved 'by reason that since the celebration thereof the said respondent Riddell had been guilty of adultery and non-compliance with a decree for restitution of conjugal rights'. Again Riddell did not appear and he was ordered to pay costs; seven months later the decree was made absolute. The manner in which this marriage ended would loom large at a later date when he wanted a peerage. Both parties were now free to wed again and did so promptly. Within four days Riddell married his cousin Annie Allardice, a nurse in her mid-thirties, at All Saints Marylebone. The service was performed according to the rites of the Church of England notwithstanding that he was the guilty party in a divorce case. Grace continued to receive the allowance of £300 which Riddell had paid her annually since their separation, and this amount remained constant down the years, even when he was a millionaire.

Before the completion of these changes in his domestic arrangements Riddell had started down another path. The Wooler firm had had interests in South Wales in connection with the *Western Mail*. This influential daily newspaper was founded in 1869 by the third Marquess of Bute as part of his great scheme to develop the region around Cardiff. Local people had to be won over, and Bute brought in the young Lascelles Carr as 'producer' of the paper. It was an inspired choice. Cecil Rhodes is supposed to have remarked: 'Give me Lascelles Carr in South Africa and I will rule the world.' This man now became Riddell's first acquaintance in the realm of newspapers and he was properly impressed. Doubtless he was equally impressed by the commercial possibilities in the burgeoning South Wales of that day, where there was a good chance of making even more money. By 1891 he had acquired a small interest in the *Western Mail* and when the firm was incorporated a few years later he became a director. From 1901 to 1916 Riddell was chairman and managing director, although curiously there is no record of his appointment. He was now favourably placed to meet men in public life, one in particular.

Prior to that event, however, his newspaper interests had broadened. In 1891 Lascelles Carr and his partner Daniel Owen consulted Riddell about buying the *News of the World*, then an ailing Sunday newspaper with a circulation of less than 50,000. The owners, Walter John Bell and Adolphus William Bell, were in financial difficulties and only too happy to be rid of the property. Carr and Owen soon completed the purchase, the company was reorganised, and Riddell became secretary and legal adviser. A few months later he added the managing-directorship to his duties and began to build up his holdings in the company. From a modest beginning of 192 ten-pound shares, accepted in lieu of fees as solicitor, Riddell steadily acquired additional stock until by 1904 he owned the second largest number of both preference and ordinary shares. But it was not until 1925 that he became principal shareholder, although he had been chairman for many years previously. As the paper prospered – circulation passed 100,000 in 1896 and a million in 1906; debts were paid off by 1901 – the value of *News of the World* shares soared. Though still a comparatively young man, Riddell found himself in the possession of wealth beyond his dreams, certainly far in excess of anything he might have earned as a solicitor.

Immense effort and long hours of toil had gone into making the *News of the World* a success whilst at the same time keeping up his practice as a solicitor, and Riddell paid a heavy price in terms of health and happiness. Many years later he told a story about returning home late one night, weary and jaded, when suddenly there came the realisation that he was missing much in life. At once he decided to drop the solicitor's work and lead a more leisurely existence as a newspaper proprietor. Perhaps Riddell remembered from Sunday school days the story of Saul on the road to Damascus. Of course his tale was fabrication, a romantic fiction glossing over the more prosaic truth. The fact was that in the early years of the new century his health gave way. Riddell was what we would term a 'workaholic', which aggravated his chronic indigestion to the point where doctors refused to be responsible unless he changed his habits. A period in a nursing home under the shadow of becoming an invalid drove him reluctantly to the conclusion that he must choose between his two careers. So he opted for the *News of the World*, but did not quite shut the door on the legal work. As a form of insurance he continued in good standing as a solicitor should it ever become necessary to resume the practice of law.

Fortunately his domestic life had entered tranquil waters. Annie was a woman of some taste and with a little money of her own, hence her demands on Riddell were minimal. He needed even less from her. They had few interests in common, leaving him free to indulge such fancies as travelling at top speed in a chauffeur-driven open motor car, with a fine disregard for pedestrians, other traffic and even weather conditions. On one project they found common ground, for he acquired a fine residence in Westminster, which the new Mrs Riddell furnished quite elegantly and hired a suitable staff to run. Soon also Riddell took up the game of golf, and this became one of the few passions in a hitherto pleasureless life. Before long the house at 20 Queen Anne's Gate[11] and the golf course at Walton Heath in Surrey were to become meeting-places for famous people.

It was through the Welsh connection that Riddell became acquainted with the man who was to have the greatest influence upon his life – Lloyd George. Though the *Western Mail* was not a Radical paper, Lloyd George knew and admired Lascelles Carr for supporting the claims of Welsh miners and dockworkers to receive a better deal. Carr introduced Riddell to Lloyd George in Cardiff, and the two men were to meet again in London, sometimes in the company of Carr's nephew Emsley, now and for many years to come the editor of the *News of the World*. Unlike in nearly every respect, the politician and the newspaper proprietor were attracted to each other. Almost the only things they had in common were similarities in age and background – each had been left fatherless as a child, but with a strong-willed uncle to provide education and guidance; each had chosen the profession of solicitor and struggled hard in the early years; neither regarded marital fidelity as of great consequence. As a rising Liberal MP whose wife disliked living in London, Lloyd George welcomed Riddell's friendship. This blossomed into something more when Lloyd George became a Cabinet Minister and occasionally needed to entertain in the evening or perhaps dine quietly with one or two acquaintances. Riddell saw to it that Queen Anne's Gate was available at such times and without ostentation he slipped into the role of political host on a small scale. It only remained to introduce Lloyd George to the pleasures of golf and Riddell moved into an even stronger position on the fringe of high politics.

Golf was a popular pastime with politicians of the Edwardian age, something Riddell appreciated and exploited. Shortly after the founding of the golf club at Walton Heath he became a director, which enabled him to purchase at favourable prices certain building sites alongside the links. He had little difficulty persuading Lloyd George that a busy Cabinet Minister needed recreation in the invigorating air of the North Downs, particularly when his car was always ready at short notice to provide transport from Westminster. Lloyd George took to the game with enthusiasm since it enabled him to relax and at the same time talk politics in seclusion with a few chosen companions. Some time later Riddell provided a house for him to live in for little or no rent, but eventually made an outright gift of the property. Whether Lloyd George was wise to accept such largesse is matter for debate, but it suited both him and Riddell well enough at the time.

Where Lloyd George went, others were likely to follow. Soon such Liberal Ministers as Rufus Isaacs, Reginald McKenna, Sir John Simon, and Charles Masterman, along with the editor of the *Daily Chronicle*, Robert Donald, were also showing interest in residing at Walton Heath. This prompted Lloyd George to jest that Riddell was becoming a modern-day Wilberforce with his own band of 'Saints'. Another enthusiastic golfer of pre-war days was Winston Churchill, with whom Riddell played regularly at one stage. Occasional players were Bonar Law and Colonel J. E. B. Seely, while other politicians came to watch and talk. Not content with a poor standard of golf, Riddell frequently went round with the club professional, the famous James Braid, and there exists a painting of a Walton Heath foursome that includes Lloyd George, Riddell and Braid, along with some under-sized caddies. In Riddell's will Braid received a small legacy 'for his discretion'.[12] It goes without saying that the many references to golf at Walton Heath, which are to be found in the diaries and elsewhere, testify to the importance of this kind of matchmaking.

None of these activities interfered with Riddell's work as a newspaper proprietor, rather they supplemented it. From conversations in the relaxed atmosphere of Walton Heath he heard interesting talk and gleaned information of a confidential character, morsels of which appeared discreetly in the *News of the World* column 'Gossip of the Day', sometimes written by the editor Emsley Carr, sometimes by Riddell himself. It is doubtful if more than a handful guessed the significance of what they were reading. The *News of the World*, whose circulation passed the two million mark in 1914, existed primarily to edify the masses on Sunday mornings. The standard fare was 'Crime', 'Sport', 'News of the Day', 'Marital Woe' and 'Politics', possibly in that order. Regardless of censorious critics, the paper was a great success commercially. Riddell's mind was always open to any scheme that might increase sales and revenue. Fleet Street liked to recall how at one time he would stuff his pockets with handbills and scatter them in hotels, railway carriages, cabs, anywhere they might catch the eye of a prospective subscriber or, better still, advertiser.

The business side of newspaper-owning led Riddell into allied operations in publishing and printing. As if in search of the respectability which the *News of the World* did not confer, he became chairman of *Country Life* and *John O'London's Weekly*, of which he was very proud. Bernard Falk, among others, noted Riddell's fondness for telling a story of a dream in which he knelt before the Recording Angel and pleaded that his connection with these two journals should lighten his punishment for the *News of the World*.[13] Less happy was his brief association with the *Church Family Newspaper*, from which he withdrew to the echo of sardonic laughter from other newspapermen, something Riddell did not relish. In addition there were directorships of such other concerns as George Newnes Limited, which he joined in 1906, as well as C. Arthur Pearson Limited and the Caxton Publishing Company. It was through the last-named that Riddell came up against a tough adversary in the person of the governing director of the firm, Hedley Le Bas.

For some years these two men got along well as fellow directors, indeed they became friends. They were not business competitors and frequently played golf together or in the company of others at Walton Heath. Each had risen from obscurity as a result of hard-headedness and determination to succeed. But friendship perished abruptly when, on the occasion of Le Bas being proposed for a knighthood in late 1915, Riddell thoughtlessly, or perhaps a little maliciously, revealed some details about the other's background, including such items as that Le Bas had at one time peddled books from door to door and worked in a billiards saloon. Le Bas and his wife were furious, believing that they and their children had been held up to ridicule. So they struck back. Shortly before the war Riddell had paid Le Bas £500 towards publication costs of a biography of Lloyd George which had not yet appeared, and when Riddell unwisely accused Le Bas of fraud in connection with this transaction the latter promptly began an action. Riddell was forced to back down, which he did most reluctantly and with ill grace.

Any chance of reconciliation between the two men became impossible when Le Bas let it be known that the Press might be interested in some facts about Riddell's own past – meaning, presumably, his divorce. This fuelled ill feeling to explosive proportions, for Riddell feared what such a disclosure might mean for his position. There is a story, impossible to confirm, that they chanced to meet on the clubhouse veranda at Walton Heath and exchanged strong words, whereupon Le Bas seized Riddell and pitched him unceremoniously into some rose bushes. Whether or not it happened quite like that, Riddell's rancour towards Le Bas was undiminished years afterwards. Eventually the other directors of George Newnes Limited prevailed upon Le Bas to leave the board of that company and in return Riddell withdrew from the Caxton. Though he tried to persuade himself otherwise, Riddell had been bested and he never forgave or forgot. All this might seem comparatively trivial had it not been that Hedley Le Bas was close to the Chancellor of the Exchequer, Reginald McKenna, who had become Lloyd George's *bête noire*, and vice versa. In such odd ways were relations made worse between two leading members of the war-time Cabinet.

There was more to Riddell's life than this might suggest. During the period before 1914 when his friendship with Lloyd George was developing, his interests broadened beyond the *News of the World*. People, especially people in high places, fascinated him, and he was eager to learn as much as possible and to record the political machinations of those days. While there was nothing discreditable about this, it is pleasanter to note that he displayed a genuine sympathy for the problems of ordinary working-class people. This can be traced to his association with Lascelles Carr in South Wales. Miners in particular interested Riddell, and he was anxious to use in their behalf his considerable knowledge of their wages and conditions. As a result he played an important role in helping settle the 1912 coal strike and fashioning the Miners' Minimum Wage Act. Thereafter, until Lloyd George's fall from power a decade later, Riddell's advice and assistance would be sought whenever trouble threatened in the pits.

Meanwhile, in Fleet Street, he acquired a certain standing among his fellow proprietors. By 1914 he was vice-chairman of the Newspaper Proprietors' Association, an important body headed by Lord Burnham of the *Daily Telegraph*. With the coming of war it was only logical that he should become a member of the Admiralty, War Office and Press Committee, which was charged with the task of establishing proper liaison between Government and Press. J. R. Scott in the *Manchester Guardian* obituary called Riddell the 'dominating influence' on this committee,[14] and Riddell's diaries confirm that this was so. As well he helped create the Press Bureau, the body responsible for preventing newspapers from publishing matter that might give aid or comfort to the King's enemies. Therefore, to dismiss Riddell as a mere sycophant whose importance derived from proximity to Lloyd George is a superficial judgment. After the war he came to be recognised by a larger public as a figure in his own right, and for good reason. As principal liaison officer between the British delegation and the Press at the Paris Peace Conference, he carried out a difficult job not merely adequately but with distinction. It is true he owed his appointment to his friend the Prime Minister, but he remained his own man. What happened next was perhaps inevitable. Riddell noted with growing concern Lloyd George's increasingly anti-French and anti-Turk bias. The overburdened statesman was steadily becoming more autocratic and had little patience with anyone who ventured to disagree with him, even an old crony. Doubtless, too, Riddell was growing to think of himself as more important than he was. So they grew apart, until in the last months of Lloyd George's premiership there only remained a shadow of the earlier intimacy. But contrary to popular belief, a final and irrevocable break never took place.

In the course of their friendship Lloyd George was instrumental in gratifying Riddell's craving for recognition, not once but three times. As usual where honours are concerned, there was a certain amount of pretending all round. With regard to the first occasion, Riddell published this somewhat laconic entry for 25 June 1909: 'My knighthood announced – recommended by Asquith and Pease. Of course I received the usual letter from Mr A several days ago. LG surprised.'[15] Riddell got his knighthood all right, but this version is fiction; the manuscript diary contains nothing for that day. Even if the entry had been genuine, it is hard to see why Lloyd George should have been surprised – clearly no one else was responsible. A little light is shed on secret processes by the diary of the Liberal Chief Whip, J. A. Pease, who some months earlier had noted that Asquith 'sent for me and told me' that Riddell 'wanted a knighthood'. Money was not mentioned, of course, but Asquith reckoned that in return for the honour Riddell 'might help a hospital, and use his paper in our favour'.[16] To J. A. Spender of the *Westminster Gazette*, Asquith feigned ignorance of Riddell, but in fact he had been briefed by him when the two were practising law and could hardly have forgotten. Whatever passed between Bouverie Street and Downing Street and the Whips' Office, Riddell duly became 'Sir George' and at a touch of the sword attained greater respectability, certainly in his own eyes.

Nine years elapsed before the next step up, although Riddell's name is to be found in the list of prospective Liberal peers prepared in 1911 to confront the intransigence of the House of Lords. By now he had performed valuable war-time service in smoothing difficulties between the civil and military authorities and Fleet Street. In 1918 honours were raining down on all sorts of people, often for payment, but again it is not clear what happened in Riddell's case. Lloyd George was Prime Minister and a baronetcy for his companion surprised no one even if it did annoy some observers. Riddell is supposed to have remarked: 'And next I shall have a peerage.' Probably he used such words, and with reason, for his services to Lloyd George seemed a sure ticket to the House of Lords in the near future. One day towards the end of 1919 he was asked to call at Downing Street. 'When I arrived Miss Stevenson handed me a letter stating that the PM had decided to offer me a peerage.'[17] Significant choice of words, which would not have amused the Palace. Yet it summed up the realities of the situation, for the King and his entourage were appalled at the thought of a guilty party in a divorce case being elevated to the peerage. Though they might fume, they were overborne by Lloyd George's insistence on having his own way in this as in so many other matters. Riddell at once set out for Criccieth in North Wales to thank Lloyd

George in person, and was told: 'My dear boy, it has been a pleasure to be able to do it for you.' But one puzzle remains: Did Riddell pay, and if so, how much? By whatever means, he had arrived.

To conclude the story of the Riddell – Lloyd George friendship, it must be asked how solid was its foundation. Undoubtedly the person best qualified to judge was Frances Stevenson, the statesman's secretary and mistress. For more than a dozen years she was exceptionally well placed to observe both men. Her passionate attachment to Lloyd George is well known, but how did she appraise Riddell? In 1921 Frances Stevenson published a little book entitled *Makers of the New World. By One Who Knows Them*,[18] and had this to say of him:

> He is no partisan, seeing only on one side of the fence, and content that the other should be debarred from him except as a trespasser. He likes to roam on both sides of the fence, taking a keen and intimate interest in what is happening in every direction. Not the smallest detail escapes his attention, for he is essentially and amazingly inquisitive and acquisitive. His curiosity is remarkable and is his outstanding characteristic. He has a natural aptitude for acquiring news; he thinks in paragraphs.[19]

And there was this entry in her diary for 6 December 1934: 'A mournful day, with news of Riddell's death. He was such a very good friend to me – kind, understanding, shrewd and always helpful.'[20] Can one detect here a hint of relief that Riddell's recently published volumes were wonderfully discreet about her relationship with Lloyd George? Years afterwards, when Lloyd George too was dead and Frances Stevenson his widow, she spoke in a more critical vein about Riddell. Admitting all that he had done for her husband by way of houses, cars, holidays, entertainment, etc, she flatly rejected the idea that it might have been a somewhat one-sided arrangement. She repeated what Lloyd George frequently had said to her: 'Riddell doesn't lose by it!' By this he meant such things as titles, scoops for *News of the World*, choice items for the 'Gossip of the Day' column, to say nothing of the chance to mingle with the famous. She added cryptically: 'He also knew when big events were about to take place, and how to take advantage of them.'[21] Since Riddell never speculated on the Stock Exchange, financial gain of that sort is ruled out. What it seems to imply is that Riddell used such knowledge to place himself as near the forefront as possible on great occasions, so impressing the world with his importance. Even when acknowledging that she and Lloyd George owed much to Riddell's generosity and discretion, there is a certain diffidence in Frances Stevenson's words. It was as if she never felt wholly comfortable when he was present.

What one cannot find in her writings is anything to suggest real warmth in the feelings Lloyd George and Riddell had for each other. Perhaps that is why she took little trouble to explain how the friendship declined. Her diary for 6 December 1934 continued:

> It was a pity he and D [Lloyd George] parted company, but after the Paris Peace Conference, when D became so bitterly anti-French, there was a rift between him and Riddell, who was pro-French and pro-Turk. There was an angry scene at Lucerne in 1920, when D at the lunch-table openly called Riddell unpatriotic because he took a pro-French view. Riddell left for London the next day. . . .

This was only partly true. She stated correctly that they had a sharp exchange over foreign policy, but Riddell remained in Lucerne for several days longer, had further conversations with Lloyd George, and was present when the Prime Minister entertained the Mayor and Mayoress of Lucerne to dinner. And there were many amicable meetings between the two men after July 1920, though they were not so frequent as formerly.[22] Possibly their mutual disenchantment was largely due to Lloyd George's anti-French bias after the war, of which Riddell's diaries provide much evidence, and doubtless their differences over Greece and Turkey in 1922 worsened matters. But Riddell was also alienated by what he conceived to be Lloyd George's failure to sympathise fully with the urban working classes, whilst Lloyd George may have begun to suspect that Riddell was a fair-weather friend who soon would bolt, a notion which Beaverbrook spread. Then too there may have been other, more frivolous, reasons for the gulf to widen. Various writers tell the story, with suitable embellishments, how Riddell went to visit Lloyd George at Churt one day and was terrorised by a large black chow. For more than an hour the hapless peer suffered until Lloyd George returned from a stroll and ended the ordeal. What was worse, Lloyd George thought the situation immensely funny and did not scruple to tell it as a good joke. Riddell is supposed to have departed in a rage, muttering that the dog was as vicious as its master. From Lloyd George's side Riddell committed the unpardonable sin of throwing the support of the *News of the World* behind Bonar Law at the 1922 general election. Perhaps the honours were even.

For nearly a decade the two men saw little of each other, but towards the end there was a reconciliation of sorts. In 1933 both were about to publish on the war years. Riddell sent Lloyd George the proofs of his *War Diary*, saying: 'Privately, I think you will like the Diary. I am told it gives a wonderful account of you and the splendid work you did during the war.' When the book appeared, Lloyd George wrote: 'Your book seems to have made a great sensation. I congratulate you heartily in scoring such a triumph.' He added: 'When are you coming down to see us here?' A few weeks later Riddell was able to return the compliment on the publication of the first volume of Lloyd George's *War Memoirs*. He sent a rather fulsome letter about how the book 'has proved so fascinating that it has interfered with my work!' adding: 'Before long I shall make another descent on you, if you will allow me.' In October 1934, on the occasion of a third volume of the *War Memoirs*, Riddell wrote another warm letter of thanks and congratulations. It ended with these words: 'I am rather lame, but propose to offer myself for a short visit one day. I often think of you.'[23] The visit never took place. Riddell died in early December.

The Riddell diaries themselves are a storehouse of information. He was no Pepys, not even a Boswell, but he was an assiduous collector of detail about the thoughts and actions of important people. One not very attractive personal trait aided him in this endeavour. He was a teetotaller, not out of conviction that drink was evil, rather because he believed that alcohol was a loosener of tongues. Others could grow garrulous over their brandy whilst he listened with a clear head for revealing phrases or possible indiscretions. Of course the instances of this were exceptional; enough was said by sober men to fill his pages and more. So it was that the many hundreds of thousands of words Riddell consigned to paper became an important record of the times. His long years as a solicitor had sharpened an ingrained love of detail and precision, and as far as possible he tried to keep his own likes and dislikes from slanting the record (save where Hedley Le Bas was concerned). It was an achievement, if not unique, at least remarkable for the breadth of the stage and the cast of characters. In the course of seventeen years of this kind of bookkeeping he recorded something like eleven hundred conversations with, or between, nearly two hundred persons, few of them unimportant. Some names appear only once or twice, others regularly. Bonar Law's words, for example (other than brief exchanges), are quoted thirty-two times, and Reginald McKenna's forty-nine. Winston Churchill is even more in evidence, figuring in, or dominating, seventy-four conversations. But the statistics on Lloyd George leave no doubt as to the central figure in the diaries. On nearly seven hundred occasions Riddell was in Lloyd George's company to listen, to stimulate talk, and afterwards to record. The subject matter included in the pages that follow speaks for itself.

The rest of Riddell's career after Lloyd George's fall is unimportant. The *News of the World* continued to grow as it satisfied the appetites of Sunday-morning newspaper readers. Like most other proprietors in Fleet Street he did his best to hinder the development of broadcasting, but to his credit he encouraged the Press not to be the pawn of bellicose Cabinet Ministers during the General Strike of 1926. Like Press lords before and since, he appeared in the House of Lords but seldom and said little. His last years seem to have been spent largely on such matters as a new building for the *News of the World*, sitting on various hospital boards, and finally preparing excerpts from his diaries for publication.

Riddell's character and personality were not of a kind to win him a wide circle of friends or admirers. His view of humanity, certainly of the upper and middle classes, was too inclined to be narrow and unsympathetic, the product of a cold, even cynical, mind. Remarks attributed to him have a chilling quality – 'Nothing is ever what it seems to be'; 'In this world money means power'; 'Experience has taught me that every man has a price' – seldom redeemed by light and witty touches, except inadvertently. Whilst yet a young man he came dangerously near to matching Dickens's classic description of another man of property, Ebenezer Scrooge. Moreover, he played up this trait – dressing shabbily, denying himself most pleasures in life, eating sparsely and without enjoyment, sleeping in a bare room at Walton Heath and under the eaves at Queen Anne's Gate. From what can be learnt about his relations with the other sex, modern feminists would have deemed him a prize specimen of all that they abhor. Men grew to respect him because of his wealth and power; few women cared for him with anything like affection.

But there was another worthier side to Riddell that cannot be overlooked. He seems to have had a genuine feeling for the poor and disadvantaged, and it cannot be denied that he used much of his great wealth for the benefit of hospitals and clinics. For this philanthropy many had cause to be grateful, as did the numerous people who benefited from his will. These things notwithstanding, it was perhaps inevitable that few tears were shed when he died, although a memorial service was held in St Bride's, attended by Lloyd George and many others. In accordance with his wishes his body was cremated and the ashes scattered on the golf course at Walton Heath, some say at the eighth hole.

Whatever the image of the man that emerges from this sketch, Lord Riddell's usefulness to those who seek to understand the era of the First World War is beyond question. For that alone there is reason to be grateful for his existence, and we continue to go back to his diaries for information not available anywhere else.

1908–1911

The first volume of Riddell's diaries begins with the following entry, undated but clearly written some time after he had begun to keep a record of his conversations with important people:

> Note: These notes have been made usually immediately after the interview recorded. They must be pieced together with the notes on separate sheets. If published they should not be made public until a proper interval has elapsed between the events recorded and the date of publication. They may be of interest years hence as they deal with historical characters and important events. *But in no case must they be published until publication can be made without causing annoyance to any person referred to in the notes.*

Riddell began to keep some kind of personal journal in October 1908, but not for three or four years could it be likened to a diary in the normal sense. Irregular and largely anecdotal, the early entries serve only as an introduction to some of the personalities who were to figure so largely in the pages to come. They are of little historical interest and for the most part have not been included here. Exceptions are those occasions or incidents or conversations where Lloyd George and Winston Churchill are the central characters, with a few tit-bits about such others as Bonar Law, A. J. Balfour, John Morley, J. A. Spender and Sir William Robertson Nicoll. The worth of these items lies chiefly in the way Riddell depicts the relationship between the great war-time leaders. Churchill obviously has a healthy respect for Lloyd George's powers and wishes to work with him for a 'constructive social policy'. Lloyd George on the other hand qualifies his admiration for Churchill with remarks about his recklessness and tells Riddell one or two stories which tend to denigrate Churchill.

As yet Riddell was not going about the task of keeping a journal in any systematic way. Frequently there are long intervals between diary entries, and sometimes his words were written long after the event, which of course diminishes their value. The most notable instance of this concerns Lloyd George's celebrated Mansion House speech of warning to Germany in July 1911. In *More Pages* (pp 21–2) Riddell contrived to make it appear that he wrote of this on the same day. In fact he was writing in November from memory. Towards the end of 1911 the entries are becoming more regular as Riddell developed the habit of recording immediately what Lloyd George and others had said in his presence. Subjects of importance include German naval building, National Insurance, manhood suffrage and suffragette activities.

1908

17 October[1]   [. . .] Lloyd George told me that he had never met anyone with such a passion for politics as Winston Churchill. He said that after his marriage he commenced talking politics to him in the vestry and was quite oblivious of the fact that he had to take out the bride [. . . He also] told me that Balfour was the first prominent politician to take notice of him; that he went to John Morley[2] and Harcourt[3] and told them that when the Radicals came into power they must give that young man office, and high office.

28 October   Robertson Nicoll showed me a long letter from Runciman, Minister of Education,[4] protesting against criticism on the part of Dissenters at the delay in settling the Education Question, stating that he was negotiating for a settlement, and that he hoped to bring his negotiations to a successful conclusion; that anyone could beat the newspaper drum, and that he was working quietly, etc, etc, and thought it very hard that he should be subjected to adverse criticism. I thought the letter a very weak one for a Cabinet Minister to write to a newspaper editor who had criticised him. [. . .]

I had a long talk with Lloyd George in regard to the unemployment question. He said that his idea was to form a Board in each trade which would make a levy in prosperous times upon employers and workmen, and that the sums contributed would be applied by the Board in times of depression in alleviating distress. [. . . He] seemed very pleased with his plan. His suggestion was that the Board should be formed partly of employers and partly of workmen with an independent Chairman. [. . .]

When I was staying at Walton, Lloyd George sent his secretary, Rowland, to me in great haste to ask me to advise him concerning a paragraph which appeared in the *Bystander*, which implied that he was likely to be a co-respondent in a divorce case. I went to town and saw

Lloyd George who seemed very much agitated. He said that there was not a word of truth in the story, and vowed vengeance against the editor. I subsequently saw the proprietor of the *Bystander*, and eventually it was agreed at an interview at Downing Street that they should publish an apology and contribute three hundred guineas to the Carnarvon Infirmary. I asked them what evidence they had to go on. They said that apparently the writer of the paragraph had been guided by idle gossip.[5]

29 October[6] Willie Davies (editor of the *Western Mail*) has been up in town seeing Lloyd George. He had a long chat with him in his room at the House of Commons. Bonar Law was there. He made a bet (£5) with Lloyd George that the Government would be out in two years. They discussed the office which Bonar Law would get if the Conservatives came in. BL said that the Board of Trade would have to deal with the tariffs, but LG pointed out that this would be a matter for the Treasury, and that Bonar Law would have to get that office if he wished to deal with the subject. BL spoke well of Austen Chamberlain, but LG thought him a poor thing. (He expressed the same opinion to me several times.) BL intimated that he feared that Balfour would endeavour to bring back all the old gang. [. . .]

30 October Breakfasted with LG at Downing Street. [. . .] We discussed Winston Churchill. He [LG] said that he was inclined to be reckless, but was always kept back by fear of his father's fate. [. . .]

We talked of Balfour. He said, 'I could work with Balfour, but the trouble with him is his underlying sense of class superiority. He is kind and courteous, but you feel that he feels that he is a member of a superior class. This makes him unpopular with his own people like Bonar Law, Carson, etc.' [. . .]

He told me that John Morley was the most interesting person to talk to in the House of Commons, and that his prophecies concerning the future of the various members had invariably proved correct. He said that Balfour had described McKenna as 'an able accountant and there he ends', implying that he had the accountant's strength and weakness – viz. accuracy on the one hand and lack of executive power on the other.

2 November [. . .]Donald of the *Daily Chronicle* told me today that he was breakfasting with Sir Edward Grey, the Foreign Minister, tomorrow. It is curious how much attention the members of this Government pay to the Press. I doubt whether such frequent and intimate relations have ever existed before between so many Ministers and so many newspaper editors. Spender,[7] editor of the *Westminster Gazette*, has been in the closest communication with Sir Edward Grey and other members of the Cabinet during the recent Eastern crisis.

6 November   Lloyd George told me a good story about Chamberlain.[8] Chamberlain said to Goulding,[9] MP, 'That fellow Harmsworth came to see me. He said, "What will kill your policy (Tariff Reform), Mr C, is *anno domini*."' Chamberlain remarked, 'But you see, I am still here!' Very pathetic in a way, as Chamberlain's jaw is twisted by paralysis and his speech rather indistinct, but his mind quite clear.

The Tariff Reform people are busy. Bonar Law says, 'They have put certain questions to Balfour, who has replied satisfactorily.' But from what I hear, there is a movement against him in the party. On Wednesday, Goulding, who is said to be Joe's 'jackal', invited thirty journalists who are said to be staunch on Tariff Reform to dinner at the St Stephen's Club. Long, Bonar Law and Austen Chamberlain were there, I believe. [. . .]

24 November   Breakfasted with LG, who did not seem at all disturbed by the fate of the Licensing Bill. He said that a thanksgiving service would take place in the Treasury at 10.30, as he was looking forward to taxing the trade. He ridiculed the rumour that the Peers would or could interfere with or reject the Budget. [. . .]

27 November   Breakfasted again with LG, and played golf with him all day. [. . .] He spoke in high terms of Asquith, and said that he had a remarkably clear and forcible mind, and that his only defects were due to his legal training, which had curbed his imagination and vivacity. [. . .]

10 December   Fuller,[10] the Junior Whip, told me today that three members of the Cabinet are in favour of an early dissolution, amongst them Lloyd George and Winston Churchill. He said that the Cabinet meeting yesterday was very gloomy, and that Asquith is much distressed concerning the Education Bill.

12 December   Sir George Newnes has made a sad hash of his affairs. It is curious that such an able man should have acted so foolishly.[11] [. . .]

The Liberal Party owe him a good deal for having founded the *Westminster Gazette*, which cost him £180,000. When he sold it in October last for £40,000 and £20,000 shares [in a new company] it was losing £10,000 per annum. The sale was arranged through the Liberal Whips, as Sir George could afford to carry it on no longer. [. . .]

Massingham,[12] editor of the *Nation* and formerly editor of the *Daily Chronicle* and *Daily News*, told Robertson Nicoll on Friday that Mond,[13] Chairman of the new company which owns the *Westminster Gazette* (a wealthy Jew manufacturer), is interfering considerably with Spender's editorial policy, that Spender was in favour of advocating the postponement of dissolution for two or three years, but that Mond had pressed him to take up a very strong line concerning the House of Lords and advocating an early appeal to the country. Massingham said that Spender had told him that although his pecuniary conditions were improved – he now gets £2,000 per annum as against £1,500 and has a ten years' contract – he found his position very difficult and irksome and that he was not nearly so happy as under the old regime. The hand behind the throne is very potent and the public have very little idea of the forces which really influence newspapers. [. . .]

17 December [. . .] These Labour men beat ordinary politicians in being able to work harder and longer without feeling the strain. They have wonderful digestions and never seem to require holidays, but they just lack a something which prevents them from being first-class. They always remain working men underneath the surface. Then again, they are nearly always short of money, and to be short of small sums is a trying ordeal for a public man.

1909

25 March I have written little lately, having been very busy. The Naval Scare is at its height. I had a long chat with Lloyd George. We spent the day together. He said that Sir John Fisher is a very clever man and very persuasive. When he wants to carry a point he always gives technical details which seem to be overwhelming. [. . .] LG says that Fisher is a great man, but too prone to be always making the pace, so that other nations are urged on to do more than they would otherwise. [. . .]

1911

March [n.d.]   Winston did not attend the Asquith lunch at the Opera House. The Prime Minister felt hurt that all his political family were not there. LG discussed the subject with Winston, who said, 'If I had known it was to be a sort of Lord's Supper, I would have attended.' LG replied, 'Yes. Even Judas Iscariot was present at the Lord's Supper!'[14]

Winston, LG and Niel [*sic*] Primrose were dining together, Winston being the host. The evening was passing pleasantly when Niel Primrose said, 'That's no argument!' Winston's face became over-clouded, and he at once called for the bill and broke up the party. LG said to him when they were driving home, 'What's wrong? What has happened?' Winston replied, 'I was annoyed that a boy like that should speak to me in that manner.'[15]

June [n.d.]   Winston describes LG as the greatest political genius of the day. He says LG has more political insight than any other statesman. He told me that he and LG had resolved upon the necessity for a constructive social policy, and that LG had selected and 'imported' with great skill four units: (1) the labour exchanges, (2) the sweated trades wages scheme, (3) the Insurance Bill, (4) the Unemployment Bill. [. . .]

August [n.d.]   Winston told me that in the night it had occurred to him that our ammunition stores were practically unprotected and that he had telephoned to the War Office giving instructions that they should be guarded by military. Curious that no one should have thought of this. [. . .]

November [n.d.]   I have not written anything for a very long time, but the events of the past few months have been so important that they warrant a few notes.

I have seen a great deal of Lloyd George and Winston Churchill and for the past twelve months have usually played golf with Winston on one or two days each week. [. . .] Many people think that he and Lloyd George are only veiled friends, but this is not the case. They act in the closest co-operation and are obviously impressed with each other's powers. [. . .] There is no doubt that he [Winston] pays a great deal of attention to Lloyd George's advice. Lloyd George frequently makes good-humoured comments on his contemporaries. About Winston he said, 'Very often I hear him come stalking down the hall at Downing Street, and then I see him put his head inside the door and look round the room. I know from his face that something has happened, and I always say, "What's wrong now?"' [. . .]

During the period of the strikes, Winston had a very difficult job. He started out by being perhaps too lenient, and was gradually forced into a very awkward and difficult position in relation to the working classes. I could see that the situation was weighing upon him very seriously and that his position at the Home Office was gradually becoming intolerable to him. It was obvious that he was gradually setting his teeth, and being a soldier he would be likely to act in a thorough and drastic manner in the event of further labour troubles. [. . .]

The situation was obviously causing anxiety to the Prime Minister and Lloyd George. I had many talks with the latter and with Masterman [. . .] on the subject, and could see that they were very apprehensive. [. . .]

I said, 'How did you persuade McKenna to move?' Lloyd George laughed and said, 'By peaceful picketing!'

The newspapers were very ill-informed as to the reasons for the change, and all sorts of wild speculations were rife as to the cause. Some of the papers suggested that the new First Lord [Churchill] had been appointed for the purpose of economy, others because the Navy had been found to be inefficient during the recent German crisis. Very few of them even hinted at the real reason. [. . .][16]

Touching the German crisis, I was playing golf with Winston on the day when Lloyd George made his celebrated speech at the Mansion House. He told me that the Chancellor of the Exchequer was to make a big declaration. I had an invitation to the dinner so hurried back. Lloyd George kept the Lord Mayor waiting nearly half an hour. The delay was due, as he told me afterwards, to consideration of the precise terms of the speech by certain members of the Cabinet. The speech was written but caused comparatively little notice at dinner. Alec Murray, the Chief Whip, was there and was very enthusiastic over the speech. I congratulated LG and told him that he had performed a great national service as the speech would show the Germans that Radicalism was not inconsistent with nationalism. He seemed very pleased.

A few days afterwards I was at the Prime Minister's garden party. I again congratulated Lloyd George on his speech. He then took me aside and told me that the German Government had endeavoured to get him dismissed or 'Delacassed'[17] because of his speech, and that the German Ambassador had been very much surprised when he was told that the speech was the speech of the Cabinet and not Lloyd George. Lloyd George was evidently very angry at the action of the Germans.

On the following day, I called at Downing Street. He was busy in his garden holding a conference over the Insurance Bill. Ramsay MacDonald,[18] the Labour leader, with some Government officials, were seated with him under a tree. It was a very hot day. I asked him to give me a few minutes. I then said, 'Can we make public the facts as to your attempted dismissal?' He said, 'Yes, it is just as well that the nation should know what the German attitude of mind is. The policy of the jackboot won't do for us. I am all for peace, but I am not going to be jackbooted by anybody.' [. . .]

Early in November   I had lunch with Alec Murray, when we had a long talk over the political situation. [. . .] On the following day came the announcement by the Prime Minister as to manhood suffrage. I at once called on the Chief Whip and congratulated him upon what had taken place. [. . .] He then told me that the matter had been much discussed and that the Prime Minister had not really made up his mind until he heard Silvester Horne's arguments. Silvester Horne[19] was the leader of the deputation. I subsequently saw Lloyd George, who confirmed what the Master of Elibank had told me. He said that the whole of the Prime Minister's training made it difficult for him to take such a step, and that while he was heartily in sympathy with the people, yet he had the lawyer's fears of the uneducated. Lloyd George added, 'This will be one of the greatest changes which has taken place for many years.' I gathered from what he said that the Prime Minister had deliberated a great deal, and that up to the last moment Lloyd George and Alec Murray were doubtful whether he would take the plunge.

A few days afterwards, I again saw Lloyd George. Meanwhile Balfour's resignation had been announced. I mentioned that the papers attached more importance to this than to manhood suffrage, but that the one was a mere event of only temporary importance, while the other would affect the country in a marked degree for all time. I also pointed out how curious it was that the proposed addition of 4,500,000 voters should have attracted so little comment. Lloyd George said that he quite agreed but added that no one could forecast the result of the addition to the electorate, but it was obvious that in future what are called 'the lower classes' were going to exercise more power than they have done. As he put it, 'The future lies with them.' [. . .]

We discussed the appointment of Bonar Law as leader of the Conservative Party. I told Lloyd George that I had been to see Bonar Law and had had a long talk with him, and I commented upon his modest and kindly ways. Lloyd George said, 'The Conservatives have done a wise thing for once. They have selected the very best man – the only man. He is a clever fellow and has a nice disposition, and I like him very much. He has a good brain.'

A few days previous to Bonar Law's appointment he drove me home in his motor. [. . .]

On the Saturday when his appointment was provisionally announced, I called upon him. He lives quietly, just off Kensington High Street. [. . .]

We discussed the relations between political leaders. He said. [. . .] 'I like Lloyd George. He is a nice man, but the most dangerous little man that ever lived.' [. . .]

Winston is very fond of discussing military subjects. He is evidently a soldier at heart. He has often told me there is nothing like war. [. . .] He said that if the country were engaged in a great war he would throw up his position as Home Secretary and go to the front. He said that a great war should be carried on by a joint ministry, and that if such an event took place during the present Liberal administration, Balfour and several more prominent Conservatives should be invited to join the Government.

2 December I discussed with LG the violent oppositon to the Insurance Bill, and he said that he had never been daunted or frightened by opposition from his opponents. [. . .]

He was very angry regarding the misrepresentation in the *Daily Mail*. He said it seemed to him they were making a personal attack upon him. He said he should retaliate if need be. Curiously enough Caird, the night editor of the *Daily Mail*, was in the next room. I had a long talk with him about the attack on the Bill. He said that LG had made a grossly unfair statement about the *Mail* and they meant to smash him and his Bill. [. . .]

7 December [. . .] Drove home from the Other Club with Winston C and Seely.[20] Winston said, 'Grey had to omit from his speech on the

German question the only important thing, viz. that so long as Germany continues her shipbuilding programme, so long shall we regard her with distrust and suspicion. Naval supremacy is essential to our very existence. We feel that Germany wishes to be in a position to challenge it and we act accordingly. Our alliance with France is our only possible course under the circumstances.' [. . .]

9 December   I told LG of my conversation with Winston on the 7th. He said he quite agreed with what he had said. LG spoke in bitter terms regarding the German attitude. [. . .]

I hear Jacky Fisher has been constantly with Winston on the Admiralty yacht, and that the new Admiralty appointments have been instigated by him. If Beresford[21] learns this he will alter his attitude to Winston very quickly. I mentioned the matter to LG and Masterman. LG evidently thought the rumour correct. He said that Fisher was not a very safe adviser and that Winston would have to be cautious.

12 December   [. . .] Nicoll and I spent three days at Hythe with LG. [. . .] He was full of his insurance scheme, which he roughly outlined to us and was working on and off with his two assistants, one Braithwaite,[22] a nice man who had worked in the East End amongst the poor and has been to Germany to investigate the working of the German scheme. Personally I don't like the plan, which will involve an enormous amount of officialism and state interference. But I did not argue. LG told me that Asquith had been his chief ally in regard to the Budget. [. . .] LG said that A strongly supported the scheme in the Cabinet, and that to begin with he and Winston were practically his only supporters. [. . .]

17 December   On Saturday LG was violently assaulted by a male suffragette [*sic*]. [. . .]

We subsequently had another chat, in the course of which he referred in bitter terms to the fact that those responsible for financing the suffrage movement were engaging bravoes to effect personal injury upon members of the Government. He said that the people who should be prosecuted were the people who found the money and employed these men. I asked him why he thought the suffragettes were attacking him, as he had declared himself strongly in favour of female suffrage. He said that in his opinion the leaders of the movement, who were being well paid, did not wish any solution, and that they were attacking him 'because they thought he was a little devil who had a knack of getting things through, and that he would really secure the vote for women'. He believed that Mrs Pankhurst[23] was receiving £2,000 per annum. [. . .]

1912

The year of the *Titanic* witnessed increasing turbulence on the domestic scene and a renewed threat that war in the Balkans might engulf Europe. None of Britain's political parties had reason to face the future with equanimity. The governing Liberals were now prisoners of their own Parliament Act, which ensured that Irish Home Rule and Welsh Disestablishment would be delayed two years and more. The Tories had a new and untried leader in Bonar Law, who showed neither the will nor desire to curb the intransigence of Sir Edward Carson and his Ulster Unionists. Labour was making little headway at the parliamentary level but syndicalists were flexing their muscles as a prelude to major industrial conflict. Though Asquith's opponents were unlikely to topple him, he had little cause to be complacent as leader of a party which seemed unsure of its destination. The victory over the House of Lords was history, and the recently passed National Insurance Act had created at least as many enemies as friends. Faced with militant Unionism on one flank and disenchanted working-class voters on another, and embarrassed by the suffragettes, the Liberals badly needed a new war-cry to rally the faithful. Lloyd George, ever fertile with ideas, thought he had the answer in a great campaign to reform land ownership. His colleagues were lacking in inspiration.

From Riddell's pages it is evident that all was not sweetness and light in the Cabinet. In late 1911 Churchill had replaced Reginald McKenna at the Admiralty, where his sudden enthusiasm for a big Navy made him suspect. The political priorities of Churchill and Lloyd George were now quite different, in marked contrast to their recent collaboration on social reforms. They began to grow apart, though still able to agree privately on such a controversial issue as military conscription. The disgruntled McKenna went to the Home Office, where he nursed his grudge against Churchill and at the same time irritated Lloyd George over Welsh affairs. Haldane was only a little less disgruntled than McKenna over the Churchill appointment, believing that he was the right person for the Admiralty. Then there was John Burns, at the Local Government Board a drag on the wheel and thought to be acting disloyally to his colleagues. Before the end of the summer came the resignation of the Chief Whip, the Master of Elibank, a highly skilled political operator, who departed suddenly without making it altogether clear why he was going. The ostensible reason was the parlous state of his family's finances; another reason became apparent the following year with the Marconi affair.

All of these things fascinated Riddell and he determined to learn as much as possible about them. Accordingly he spent more and more time in the company of leading politicians, recording twice as many conversations as in 1911. From the increasing frankness with which they spoke, it appears that he had been accepted as one whose discretion was beyond question. Another stage in Riddell's progress can be seen at the time of the miners' strike in March and April of 1912. For the first time he is more than just a confidant or silent observer. Using his considerable knowledge of miners' conditions and his rapport with such of their leaders as Vernon Hartshorn and Robert Smillie, he provided Asquith and Lloyd George with invaluable assistance in settling the strike and fashioning the Miners' Minimum Wage Act. Whether the knighthood Riddell received in 1909 was deserved or not, he earned it by his liaison work on this occasion.

21 January   Spent the day with Winston. Talked of threats by Orangemen in connection with Winston's visit to Belfast. W said he should pay the visit and make his speech, but should offer to hold meeting in another hall if one were available, as he saw no object in causing a riot in regard to such a trivial matter. He said that the Unionists are anxious to start the anti-Home Rule campaign by bloodshed, and that the Government would be playing into their hands by taking a course which might lead to this. He also said that the Unionists are anxious to show that their threats of civil war are accurate. [. . .]

He told me that there was no truth in the reports as to the condition of the Navy at the time of the German scare, or that he had been appointed to succeed McKenna because he had mismanaged naval affairs. He confirmed what I wrote at the time of the appointment, and said that the Navy had never been in a more efficient state than at the present time. He said that the Germans were going to extend their naval programme, which would make his task easy. [. . .]

2 February   Called to see Winston. Found him dressing. He spoke vehemently regarding his projected visit to Belfast, pointing his observations with his safety razor. He said that the forthcoming session was likely to be one of the most violent on record. He spoke bitterly of Sir Edward Carson and said he had been doing his best to bring about a serious breach of the peace. [. . .]

10 February   LG and Masterman talked of John Burns'[1] disloyalty to his colleagues, and said that all the rumours as to conspiracies to displace Asquith, etc, etc, can be traced to JB's imprudent statements at the National Liberal Club. [. . .] Donald of the *Chronicle* said that JB should be corrected and made to mind his p's and q's, but evidently this did not meet with LG's approval. [. . .] Any such proceedings might bring about a Cabinet catastrophe of some sort, as it would confirm the popular impression – a wrong impression – that the Cabinet are disunited. [. . .]

Winston has returned from Belfast – got back at 6 a.m. I breakfasted with Lloyd G and Donald. LG said Winston had rung him up already to ask what he thought of his speech at Glasgow (advocating a strong Navy and calling the German Navy a luxury).

LG said I told him most imprudent and calculated to ruin Haldane's mission to Germany, which was on a fair way to success. LG added, 'Winston did not reply, but I could see his face.'

I suggested that the speech might be useful to Haldane as showing that British overtures are not due to cowardice or unreadiness, and that British naval developments are the natural outcome of a long-settled policy extending over the past 200 years, and are not directed against Germany and German aspirations.

LG would not agree to this view. [. . .]

15 February   Other Club Dinner. [. . .] Winston said what impressed him most on his visit to Scotland was the unfriendly and disaffected attitude of the working classes. He said they evidently mean trouble. LG said he thought progress in ameliorating the conditions of the people would be slow. I said the joint stock system is chiefly to blame, and instanced the huge sums representing capitalised goodwill – very often the goodwill of the workers' labour, upon which dividends are expected.

I asked him if he thought an attempt would be made to regulate wages by Act of Parliament. He said he thought this would be the trend of the Labour movement, but did not believe in the practicability of the scheme.

F. E. Smith waxed very angry on the suffrage question, and said that he, Austen Chamberlain and Walter Long[2] had told Bonar Law that they would resign from any Government which proposed to give the franchise to women. FES said to me, why don't you take the matter up and strongly oppose the movement? No paper has done it. It would be very popular.

17 February Donald told LG and me that he had received a letter from John Burns vilifying LG and all his doings. LG took Donald on one side and asked him to let him have the letter on Monday. I suppose he wants to show it to Asquith. [. . .]

22 February Long and interesting talk with Masterman; Sir Henry Dalziel, editor of *Reynolds* and MP for Kirkcaldy; Hills,[3] Conservative MP for Durham; Percy Illingworth,[4] one of the Liberal Whips; and Astor,[5] son of the American millionaire, MP for Plymouth. [. . .]

M contended that the Labour Party would make but little progress politically, and that the working classes would continue to vote Liberal. [. . .]

Dalziel said that Labour would be the predominating political force in ten years, either under the name of the Liberal Party or some other name. He instanced the enormous growth of trade unionism in his own constituency and the improved organisation of trade unionism all over the country. Masterman and the others seemed rather staggered and Masterman said, 'We are talking like the people must have talked before the French Revolution.' [. . .]

25 February Saw LG and discussed the impending coal strike.[6] He said that the men had presented their case well at the conference, but he felt that the men's delegates, with the exception of [Robert] Smillie,[7] the Scotch representative, were not now the real active forces of the movement, and that the activist fighters were the younger men such as Hartshorn.[8] I told him of Hartshorn's article in the *Clarion.* He asked me to send him the paper so that he might read the article before the adjourned conference on Monday, when the younger leaders are to be present. I told LG of my talk with Masterman, Dalziel and the others. He said Masterman had already told him about it, and that he thought Dalziel exaggerated the strength of the Labour Movement.

LG said, 'I wonder.' He is evidently intent upon schemes such as the Insurance Act, and does not want to recognise the strength of the movement for more wages. He finds it hard to believe that the mass of the people do not care for the Party propaganda – Home Rule, Disestablishment and the like. [. . .]

27 February   Met the Archbishop of Canterbury[9] and Sir George Askwith[10] [the Industrial Commissioner] at lunch. We talked of the coal strike. Sir G had come straight from the conference between masters and men. He said he doubted a settlement. The Archbishop said he was engaged to speak at Derby during the next few days, but thought he would cancel the fixture as he did not like speaking at such a time. [. . .]

2 March   Went to Downing Street. Found LG at breakfast with the Attorney-General [Sir Rufus Isaacs], Harold Spender[11] and P. W. Wilson[12] of the *Daily News*. They asked me what I thought of the strike. I said, 'The biggest thing that has taken place for years – the beginning of an economic and industrial revolution.' They said the men had put themselves in the wrong by declining to return to work now that the principle of the minimum wage had been conceded. I replied that the men say they mean to settle first and return to work afterwards, that they did not intend to be jockeyed as the railway-men were jockeyed in August.

LG said, 'I did not jockey them. Henderson[13] jockeyed them.'

I added, 'We live in stirring times. The people mean to have a greater share of the profits of industry.'

LG: 'I for one am not sorry. But they have no leaders. Smillie, the Scotch miners' leader, is a clever man, but too hot-tempered for a great leader. *Asquith's declaration for a minimum wage sounded the death-knell of the Liberal Party in its old form.*'[14] [. . .]

NB – This strike has evidently staggered the Cabinet. They have never believed that Labour would assert itself in this way. They have helped to uncork the bottle containing the *djinn*, thinking they could control and direct the 'spirits' when released. But the 'spirits' have their own ideas and will not be led or kept quiet by Government doles. They want more money, which means more freedom [. . .]

3 March   It is curious to see how all the newspapers express the same note regarding the strike position and the refusal of the miners to depart from their demands. The public little understand that there exists at the House of Commons a group of journalists who are on the terms of closest intimacy, and who represent all the leading journals and news agencies. They meet daily and communicate news and information freely to each other. The information is treated differently in different newspapers according to their political or social complexion, but the atmosphere is the same. The plants have been grown in the same hot-house but developed in different ways to suit different markets.

6 March   Coal strike in full swing. Had Hartshorn, the Welsh miners' leader, to dinner. Long and interesting talk. Very nice man. Not at all violent.

7 March   By request of Sydney Buxton,[15] President of the Board of Trade, called on him regarding the coal strike. Saw him, Sir H. Llewellyn Smith[16] and Sir George Askwith. All very pleasant, particularly Buxton. They struck me as very incompetent to deal with such a situation. They did not seem to realise the serious character of the position, and are evidently dealing with the subject in the usual formal and official way. It is terrible to think of a great national crisis being handled in such a feeble manner. I wrote to Buxton pointing out that if the principle of the minimum is conceded, the men will no doubt discuss the schedule of wages, but that they decline to enter upon such a discussion until they know exactly how the S. Wales and Scotch areas are to be dealt with. Buxton replied that he saw my point, but that in effect could do nothing. LG says that the matter is being badly handled by the Board of Trade, but that the P. Minister is doing well, and that he quite affected the men when he described the perils and dangers of the miner's life. LG says that the PM is becoming more kindly and genial every day, and that they are the very best of friends. He spoke bitterly of John Burns, who is evidently very disloyal to his colleagues and very unpopular.

14 March   LG telephoned asking me to go and see him immediately. Found him in his bedroom evidently very unwell and much worried. He said that he thought things were going badly in reference to the strike, and that some effort must be made on other lines to bring about a settlement and said that he had told the Premier that the whole Trinity would not persuade the Scotch and Welsh mine-owners to settle, and that the only chance of a settlement was to arrange matters with Smillie the Scotch leader and Hartshorn, and that he had suggested that I should see the latter. I sent for him, and he came to my house in Queen Anne's Gate at 9 o'clock. He told me that the conference had been engaged in the hopeless task of investigating wage schedules and that the investigation would take months. After considerable discussion, at 1 a.m. I sat down and wrote a memorandum embodying proposals for a settlement of the dispute and setting forth reasons for breaking up the conference and dealing with the matter by legislation. Hartshorn said he would support the scheme, and thought the other leaders would do the same.

(Later on it was embodied in the Miners' Minimum Wage Act, with certain additions.)

15 March Took memorandum to LG. Found him in bed very feverish and unwell. He said he had been ordered away by the doctor. I read the memorandum to him. He said it was splendid and that he would take it to the Prime Minister at once. I went off to Walton Heath, but was telephoned for, as the Prime Minister wished me to be in attendance. I found LG at lunch. He said the PM was delighted with the memorandum, and had had it typed and circulated and he was going to act on it. [. . .]

Waited at Downing Street till the evening when the Premier made a statement that he would on Tuesday introduce a Bill substantially in accordance with memorandum prepared by me. Hartshorn came to see me again and I spent several hours with him. He said that the Bill must provide for a *5s* minimum wage, subject to increase by the local wage boards. He asked me to communicate this to the Government, which I did by letter the following day. As he went away he said, 'The only thing I envy you people with money is a good cigar. Has it occurred to you that during the two nights I have spent at your house I have smoked a day and a half's miner's minimum wage at the rate of *7s* per day? That makes you think, doesn't it?' [. . .] He said that his grandfather had been a miner for sixty-five years, from 5 years of age to 70, and that his father had also been a miner, but being a very hard worker, had broken down at 45. He said with pride that he himself had been the best workman in the colliery where he worked, and that when he became a check weigher he earned more money than any other check weigher in the coalfield.[17]

18 March LG and Hartshorn met at my house. We had a long discussion on the situation. Hartshorn pressed very strongly that the

Government should include in the Minimum Bill a definite proposal that *5s* and *2s* should be paid as an absolute minimum. LG said the Cabinet could not agree to this.[18] Hartshorn said that the conference would not pass the Bill unless it contained this provision. If they did the men would not return to work.

LG stayed until nearly 12 o'clock. Hartshorn then stayed on and said that the masters and men could hold out longer than the country, that in three weeks' time there would be something like a revolution, and that the men would then decline to return unless the schedules were included in the Bill in their entirety. He seemed very gloomy about the position. I discussed with him the other strikes which were threatened, and the fact that the Government were taking no steps to deal with labour unrest, not only in the collier trade but in other trades.

19 March I called on LG. I found Rufus Isaacs awaiting him. I pointed out that the Bill as outlined in the morning papers seemed to be a mere pious expression on the part of Parliament that a minimum should be paid. [. . .] [LG] agreed as to the serious character of the situation.

Later I had a long talk with LG and told him what Hartshorn had said as to the *5s* and *2s*. I pointed out that if the Bill were passed and the men did not return, the Government would be in a serious position. He said, 'If that happens, we shall use every means at our disposal. We shall declare strike pay illegal, and if necessary imprison the leaders.' I said I thought this would be the end of the Liberal Government. [. . .] I also told him of the serious position in reference to Labour generally, and urged that it was the duty of the Government to put aside the legislative proposals in which they were engaged and in which the people were really not interested for the purpose of dealing in a statesmanlike manner with the condition of affairs. [. . .] He said he would communicate this to the Prime Minister. He said he could work up no enthusiasm about Home Rule or Welsh Disestablishment. [. . .] His whole mind was now bent on the Labour question, which had developed in an alarming and unexpected fashion.

24 March This has been one of the most exciting weeks that I remember. Public feeling regarding the coal strike has been worked up to the highest pitch of excitement. The Government began with the Minimum Wage Bill but sadly bungled on Friday by refusing to include an absolute minimum of *5s* and *2s*, with the result that the Bill has been held up and no one knows what will happen on Monday.

On Thursday I called and saw the Prime Minister. I told him plainly that the Bill would not go through unless the *5s* and *2s* were included. [. . .] [He] said he would see what could be done regarding the *5s* and *2s*. He seemed worried, and walked rapidly up and down the room. He was, however, genial and kind. I apologised for troubling him, but he said he was much indebted, etc, etc.

On Friday I wrote to LG proposing that the difficulty should be met by referring the *5s* and *2s* question to a Committee or the Board of Trade, who could then issue some paper early next week which with the Bill would satisfy the minds of the men. I sent the letter to the House of Commons. LG showed it to Asquith and Sir Ed[ward] Grey, but the former would not give way. He says it is a question of principle. [. . .]

Yesterday I lunched with LG, Rufus Isaacs, Masterman and Harold Spender. All terribly worried about the mess over the coal strike. LG said that he had strongly supported the inclusion of the *5s* and *2s*. [. . .] LG looked worn out, physically and mentally. He said he would like to postpone the Budget until after Easter. He will have to take care or he will break down altogether. Masterman told me that McKenna was opposed to the insertion of the minimum *5s* and *2s* because he thought it would lead to competition between Parliamentary candidates in mining districts at election times, and that the votes would go to the candidate who made the hightest bid for increasing the wage. Masterman added, 'McKenna's is a mining constituency, and we have twenty more.'

I said, 'It is scandalous that such a consideration should have weight at such a time of national peril, with half the people on the brink of starvation.' I meant of course the personal and party aspect. The objections to Parliamentary interference with wages are only too obvious. But we are in for a new era and we must make the best of it. [. . .]

LG said, 'The Prime Minister would not have proposed the Minimum Bill had he not done so hurriedly. I got up, put on my dressing-gown and slippers and went into the Prime Minister's house (there are private doors between the two houses) and gave him your memorandum. He adopted it at once. During the past week all sorts of influences have been brought to bear upon him, and having gone seven-eighths of the way, he has stopped short.'

Masterman made the same remark as we drove away.

I said the PM did the same with regard to Manhood Suffrage. He hurriedly came to a decision at the instance of the Master of Elibank and afterwards endeavoured to explain away and curtail what he had said. He is in a false position. He is really an old-fashioned Radical of the Manchester school, who is leading a heterogeneous band of followers in which the more active groups are bent on breaking up the traditions and ideas of his party. [. . .]

27 March   Walked with LG and the Attorney-General in St James's Park. They both agreed that a serious mistake had been made in not inserting the *5s* and *2s* in the Minimum Wage Bill. They were evidently much perturbed regarding the new situation created by the modern labour movement. LG said, 'I am afraid this may be the knell of the old Liberal Party. It has done splendid work, and although the counsels of its wealthier members may have been allowed to prevail too much, yet [. . .] I do not know whether the Party which will succeed it will not possess defects of a more dangerous and serious character.' [. . .]

LG asked me to use my influence with the men to get them back to work. He said that the South Wales mine-owners had acted badly. He complained of the manner in which the men had acted, but said the Government had offered to insert the *5s* and *2s* if the men would undertake to return to work, but they had declined to give this undertaking.

Later in the day I saw Hartshorn, who told me this was not correct, and that the men had not understood the Government's proposals, which had been inadequately explained by Enoch Edwards.[19] He said that the conference had passed a resolution which had annoyed the Premier, who in a hasty moment had made a statement in the House of Commons from which he could not withdraw with dignity, and that this had occasioned the whole of the trouble. He said that the result of the ballot was very doubtful.

(The Cabinet declined to include the *5s* and *2s* minimum. The whole story appears in the newspapers, so I will not repeat it here.)

30 March   Long talk with Masterman. Asked him how Ramsay MacDonald had done during the coal strike. He said 'Not very well. He is a nerveracked man. It is a tragedy that the lives of three of the men who have been facing each other day after day during the crisis have been saddened by the same cause – the death of a wife – Bonar Law, Sir Edward Grey and Ramsay MacDonald. I have watched them.

They are all obviously miserable and struggling with an ever-present sorrow.' [. . .]

Masterman said that Winston had been violent against the men and had been causing much trouble at Cabinet discussions on the subject. He added, 'Winston seems to be quite unsympathetic towards the working classes.' M told me that Bonar Law had come to Lloyd George's room during the crisis and told him and Masterman that he would support the Bill, because if the Government and the country objected to the miners striking, the necessary consequence was that Parliament should secure the men fair wages.

Telephoned to Lloyd George at Folkestone, telling him result of the miners' ballot to date. Also pressed upon him the importance of securing appointment of a suitable independent chairman. On Thursday, March 28th, the Prime Minister telephoned asking me to use my influence to get the men to return to work. I said I would do what I could. Also received letter from Percy Illingworth, the Whip, making the same request. On Friday, 29th, I wrote to the Prime Minister urging him to see that proper persons were appointed as Chairmen of the District Boards and indicating serious consequences which would result if awards were unsatisfactory. [. . .] I suggested that the Prime Minister should endeavour to induce Lord St Aldwyn[20] (Hicks Beach) to act in S. Wales, as he was the best of all trade arbitrators and rarely gave dissatisfaction to either side.

31 March Spent the afternoon with Winston. He said stories of a breach between him and LG are all lies. [. . .] He said, 'I feel that no one can do my job (the Navy) properly. It is too big and difficult, but I feel that owing to my experience as a soldier and politician I can do it better than anyone else. I love the work.' He said he had knocked Germany 'sprawling' in the matter of naval construction, and that she had not realised the expense and small satisfaction which result from being a 'second-rate' naval power. [. . .]

14 April Talked with Bonar Law. He said the session will be a stormy one. 'We shall oppose the Home Rule Bill by every means in our power. The Lords will not pass it, and in order to force an election they may decline to pass any legislation. It all turns on Ulster. The demonstration last week was a great surprise to me. It may seem strange to you and me, but it is a religious question. These people are in serious earnest. They are prepared to die for their convictions. If

Ulster, or rather any county, had the right to remain outside the Irish Parliament, for my part my objection would be met.' I said, 'Ulster say they will fight. Whom are they going to fight? They cannot form an Army and march on the rest of Ireland.' He said, 'They will decline to pay their taxes and will resist their collection by force of arms.' [. . .]

He is a nice straightforward man – very unassuming and earnest – not a deep or subtle thinker. Just the opposite to Arthur Balfour. I said to Bonar Law, 'I don't envy the task of whoever has to govern this country during the next five years. The social outlook is stormy.' He replied, 'I quite agree, we are in for troublous times.'

17 April Called on LG at 10 p.m. Found him at supper with his daughter. He told me that the Cabinet have appointed a committee to investigate the Labour question and that he has been appointed chairman. He said that the Committee intend to interview the Labour leaders and the employers. He does not know who is now the recognised leader of the sailors. [. . .] He said he wanted to find some man thoroughly in touch with the Labour Movement, and did not believe that Ramsay MacDonald possessed the necessary information. He asked if I knew anyone. I said I would think it over. I said that the continuance of Labour troubles might seriously prejudice our international trade. He agreed and said that he thought that in future Labour would co-operate on international lines to secure international increases in wages. I said that this might be so but that for present purposes we must deal with things as they are. [. . .]

27 April Masterman said today, 'The alliance between LG and Winston has broken up. They are still as friendly as ever, but are not concerting joint plans of action as formerly.' He added, 'LG and Edward Grey have now joined hands. That is the new alliance. It dates from the coal strike. They are in sympathy regarding the Labour question and foreign policy.' From my own observation I think this is correct. I told Masterman that Winston was keen to get the sailors more money, and that while he had no strong sympathy with working men in general, yet he was very anxious to improve the position of 'his boys' in the Navy because they were 'his boys' – just in the same way as he was generous to his servants and those in personal touch with him. Masterman agreed. [. . .]

Masterman is chairman of the Insurance Commissioners. I asked him how he was getting on. He said, 'It is a stupendous task. The Act is

a mere skeleton. All the work has to be done. I doubt if the scheme will
ever be popular. I think the people will come to tolerate it, but they will
never bless the Liberal Party for it as LG thought they would. He said
that LG was a great natural force. He had raised the Welsh Disestablishment debate out of the mud by the fine fighting speech he delivered two or three days ago. He said that there was an organised
attempt by the Tories to barrack the chief Liberal speakers and that
LG was the only one who could really tackle that sort of opposition.
'But,' he said, 'LG does not attempt to administer his department. He
never reads any papers.' (Winston made the same comments to me
some time ago.) He spoke highly of Bonar Law's Home Rule speech.
He said it was a fine fighting speech. McKenna's speech on the Welsh
Disestablishment Bill was a wretched effort. [. . .]

28 April [. . .] LG and Masterman to dinner. Talked of Asquith. LG
said he was a most loyal colleague. M said he sometimes wondered
how Mr A had become leader of the Liberal Party.

   LG: He is like a great counsel in whom solicitors and clients have
faith. The party feel that the matter is in his hands and that he will see
it through satisfactorily. He has splendid judgment and, as a rule, deals
with great subjects, in council and in the H of C, in the same
imperturbable manner as small ones. It, however, remains to be seen
how he will conduct himself if he has to fight a failing cause. Arthur
Balfour made a marvellous fight. Single-handed he carried on the
battle in the country and in the House. Physically broken, he displayed
undaunted courage. Always on the spot, and sometimes so dextrous in
his controversy that one almost thought he was going to win. The
question is whether Asquith has the same first-class courage. That has
yet to be proved.

2 May Other Club dinner. [. . .] F. E. Smith said, 'I will bet £100 that
the Home Rule Bill in its present form never becomes law.' No one
would take the bet. Winston said he was in favour of special treatment
for Ulster. He saw no reason why Ulster should not be excluded from
the operation of the Bill. Buckmaster said this was impracticable.
Winston: 'It is better than riots or shooting. We are not going to have
any shooting.'

16 May [. . .] Drove Winston to the House of Commons. J. L.
Garvin,[21] editor of the *Observer*, came with us. [. . .]

[Speaking of the Navy] Garvin said to Winston, 'I cannot support you, but I can always call for something *more* than you are doing, so that I shall in effect give you support.'

Winston asked me about the working of the Shops Act. I said it was a popular and beneficial measure, although no doubt it required some small amendments to meet unforeseen conditions. He seemed very pleased, and said, 'I should like the people to know that I did accomplish a practical and beneficial piece of social legislation. It was a troublesome job.' [. . .]

19 May   Met Donald of the *Daily Chronicle*. Told him that I heard Harold Harmsworth was to get a peerage. He was furious and commented severely upon action of Master of Elibank, whom he described as being 'too slim'. [. . .]

27 May   [. . .] *Important.* – LG said, 'I am convinced that the land question is the real issue. You must break down the remnants of the feudal system. I have a scheme. I propose that a land court should be established to fix fair rents and tenures. [. . .] You need not be surprised if you hear one day that I have retired from the Cabinet to devote myself to carrying on this land movement . . .'

R: [. . .] Is it necessary to take such a drastic step as resignation? There are causes which warrant great personal sacrifices. Is this one of them?

LG: Well, one would not go to the stake for land reform, but there are times when Radicalism needs a great stimulus – when the Radical cause has fallen into the abyss of respectability and conventionality. Something must be done to put fresh life into the dry bones. I feel that the land and the agricultural labourer are at the root of the whole social evil. [. . .]

LG [. . .] is the only leading man who has the courage to attack the rich and powerful. All other leading politicians deal with the stock political commodities, such as Home Rule, Disestablishment, Tariff Reform. They do not deal with the real issues – privilege and the division of the profits of industry. LG says what the mass of the people feel but cannot express. When he comes to definite proposals his defect is that he usually wants to invent some new scheme full of intricacies and which is indirect in its action. [. . .]

28 May   [Conversation with Lloyd George] [. . .] We also talked of the important changes in the newspaper world. I again told him of the sale of

Kennedy Jones'[22] and Harold Harmsworth's interest in the *Daily Mail*, and alluded to the rumoured peerage for the latter. LG said very sharply, 'He is not going to be made a peer – at least not now. Murray wanted to give him a peerage, but (pointing towards Asquith's house) he will not agree.'[23] [. . .]

1 June Talked with Bonar Law. We spoke of Arthur Pearson,[24] who has become completely blind, and is in a bad state of health. It is rumoured also that his finances are none too good. [. . .] I said I had heard that the [Conservative] Party had bought or were about to buy the *Express*. BL said this was not true. The proposal had been made, but he had vetoed it, as the effect would be to create hostility on the part of the Harmsworth faction, and possibly on the part of the Lawsons[25] and other proprietors of Conservative newspapers. I told him I thought he had come to a wise decision. [. . .]

6 June [. . .] I talked alone with Elibank. He said, 'We are in for a new political situation. When Home Rule and Welsh Disestablishment have been disposed of, we shall have to face a great economic problem. The Labour question is the question of the future. How things will shape I cannot say.' [. . .]

15 June Spent the day with Masterman. Referring to the appointment of Haldane as [Lord] Chancellor in place of Loreburn,[26] who resigned on Monday week, he said that Rufus Isaacs has been furious at being passed over, as he considered that as Attorney-General he was entitled to the office. Masterman said that on Friday and Saturday he had 'gone for' LG and Elibank and on Monday for Asquith, but that he had been appeased by Elibank's device of making him a member of the Cabinet.

I said, 'Lloyd George and Winston do not seem to be as intimate as they were.'

Masterman replied, 'Personally they are as close friends as ever, but they are drifting wide apart on principles.' [. . .]

I said, 'LG is evidently growing out of sympathy with the other members of the Cabinet.'

Masterman: Quite correct. He is very restless. He said to me the other day when he came from a Cabinet meeting at which he had been trying to do something for the poor dockers, 'I don't know exactly what I am, but I am sure I am not a Liberal. They have no sympathy with the people.'

R: LG is beginning to understand town dwellers better than he did.

Masterman agreed, adding: That used to be the difficulty. LG is a country lad. All his early experiences were in an agricultural community.

I said, to carry out his present-day policy he will have to come to the Minimum Wage, which he wishes to enforce by round-about methods, which will not produce the result. [. . .]

19 June LG, Masterman and Robertson Nicoll came to dinner. Long and interesting talk. [. . .]

We discussed the political situation. LG, turning to me, said, 'I have told the Prime Minister [about my plans]. He has given his consent. As I have told you before, the old boy has always treated me extremely well.' LG then stated his new land policy as already detailed in these notes:

(1) The breaking down of the 'relics of feudalism'. (2) The creation of land courts to fix fair rents and tenure for agricultural land. (3) The creation of courts to fix fair terms for leaseholders who desire to improve the demised premises. (4) (And this is new), the creation of tribunals to fix agricultural wages in the various districts. (5) The establishment of a rule that in fixing agricultural rents regard must be had not to wages paid but to wages which should be paid and which are to be ascertained under (4), [. . .]

He said, 'First of all we shall make an investigation to ascertain the facts accurately. That will cost money.' Then, turning to me, 'I shall want some money from you.'[27] He said he proposed to start the campaign in September. I said, 'Take the case of a mixed farm of 500 acres, rent £500. Would the reduction of £100 in rent be sufficient to materially improve the position of labourers working on the farm?' LG then took an envelope out of his pocket, and after some discussion as to the number of men who would be employed upon such a farm, he made a calculation that a £100 reduction would enable each man on a farm to receive an extra *2s* per week in wages. As he was figuring away on his envelope, I was thinking of the great issues depending upon these and similar calculations.

28 June Saw LG at the request of one of the employers concerned in the dock strike, and put before him certain proposals [. . .] He went and saw the Prime Minister, and it was arranged that Wedgwood Benn,[28] one of the Junior Whips, should see Gosling,[29] the men's leader. But I am doubtful if anything will come of it. LG said Gosling was a very nice man with fine manners, and that he had created a most favourable impression at the conferences. [. . .]

2 July   Lloyd George told me that yesterday he sat next to Elizabeth Asquith, the Prime Minister's youngest daughter, at lunch. She made some remark concerning McKenna, whereupon LG replied, 'He is a very nice man. He does not always do himself justice.' The young lady then observed, 'His faults are on the surface. You don't have to dig them up. Winston digs his faults up for you. He saves you the trouble. In your case (LG himself), I should think you would have to dig pretty deep to discover yours.' She further observed, 'McKenna is a calico man. You can measure him out by the yard – all the same. He is like the small boxes of paints we had when we were children – red, green and blue, all the same size, each in its little compartment. You knew just what you had to expect. You (LG), on the other hand, resemble the small tubes of paint which one has to squeeze. You never know exactly how much or how little will appear, or whether the paint will be thick or thin, or, if you have lost the label, what the colour will be.' LG was highly amused and diverted at these pleasantries.[30] [. . .]

I commented upon the Prime Minister's action on the previous night in regard to the Labour motion in reference to the dock strike. (The PM had said that the Government would leave members to vote as they thought fit.) I remarked that this seemed a weak policy.

LG: I think so too. I would not be a party to it. [. . .] The duty of a government is to govern. He said, 'I have told Sir Edward Grey of my land policy. He seemed favourable. I have also told Winston. He has become quite a Tory. He has changed immensely. I have also mentioned it to Runciman. As Minister of Agriculture, he might feel he had a grievance if he had not been told. When starting a new policy, it is always well to consult your colleagues beforehand, otherwise they may become opponents out of mere pique.' I said, 'I suppose Runciman, Hobhouse[31] and Co. don't really matter.' 'No,' said he. [. . .] He continued, 'Some time ago I thought the whole matter out. I said to Winston, 'I have two alternatives to propose – the first to form a coalition, settle the old outstanding questions, including Home Rule, and govern the country on middle lines which will be acceptable to both parties but providing measures of moderate social reform. The other, to formulate and carry through an advanced land and social reform policy.' Mrs Winston, who was there, said, 'I am for the second.' Winston replied, 'I am for the first!' LG said to me, 'I shall never forget the incident. We were playing golf at Criccieth. Winston forgot all about the game and he has never forgotten our conversation.' [. . .]

6 July   Spent the day with LG and Seely, new Minister for War. [. . .]

It is evident from what LG said today that the fight between the Liberal and Labour Parties is pretty bitter. It is quite clear that the Liberals would like to wipe out the Labour Party, and that, failing this, they are most anxious to keep it 'in its place'. The truth is that the aims and objects of these two parties differ far more than those of the moderate Liberals and Conservatives, both of whom are pledged to improve the condition of the people, but who shrink from drastic action directed against the commercial classes. [. . .]

9 July   Naval Review. Winston very kindly sent me a ticket for the Admiralty yacht *Enchantress*. The party on board consisted of the Prime Minister, Mrs Asquith, Winston, four Canadian Cabinet Ministers, Buckle,[32] Editor of *T. Times*, Marlowe[33] ditto *Daily Mail*, Donald ditto *Chronicle*, Gardiner[34] ditto *Daily News*, Blumenfeld[35] ditto *Daily Express*, General French and Sir Edward Cassell [*sic*].[36] The PM stood on the bridge nearly all day taking great interest in the proceedings. [. . .]

14 July   [. . .] Talked with Bonar Law. [. . .] BL spoke of Lloyd George. He said that a prominent member[37] of the Liberal Party in close touch with the Government had asked him whether he was friendly with the little man. BL had replied, 'I like him personally, but, as I am attacking him, think it wiser and more proper to avoid him.' The prominent member had replied, 'Well, even we find him a little trying sometimes.' He spoke of Winston, and asked me if I thought that the alliance between him and LG was at an end. I said, with caution, 'They are still personal friends, but Winston's whole attention is now directed to the Navy.'

BL: But I am sure he finds time to think of Winston a little. I sometimes wonder why he shows Arthur Balfour so much attention nowadays. He seems very anxious to heal the breach between them. Balfour tells me all about it. Winston is the only Machiavelli in politics nowadays. I wonder whether he believes that a coalition may come, as I believe it may, and that he will get what he wants by lying dormant for the time being. [. . .]

27 July   Spent the day with Lloyd George. Winston called on him in the morning. They walked up and down the garden in Downing Street for half an hour in close conversation. LG said Winston has now turned his attention to the land question. [. . .] He said further that he believed that Winston had been meditating during the last few weeks going over to the other side, but that he had now abandoned the idea. [. . .]

We spoke of the suffragettes. He said Mrs Asquith had told him that the attacks had quite unnerved the Prime Minister. I could see they have made LG himself rather shaky. . . . He said, 'The suffragettes have lost their opportunity. They have ruined their cause for the time being. A poll would show three out of four against them.' He said that Mrs Pankhurst is a clever woman, but spoke in slighting terms of the ability of Christabel.[38] [. . .]

28 July   Spent the afternoon with Seely. He had been with the King all the morning, and was late. [. . .] Seely again spoke highly of Asquith. He said that he manages Cabinet meetings with much skill, and composes differences with much tact and dexterity. He inferred [*sic*] that there had been a difference of opinion regarding the Mediterranean question (the Naval force to be kept there, etc). He said Asquith works hard. He gave us an instance. The other day it was absolutely necessary for him (Seely) to see the PM on an urgent matter. He went to Asquith at 6 o'clock. He said, 'I must go into the House now to speak. Then I have to see the King. At eight I have to receive a deputation. Come to my house at 8.30.' Seely went, but the PM had not returned. Mrs A asked S to dine, which he did. At 9.15 in came Mr A. Dinner was nearly over. He bolted some food and a glass of wine, and at 9.30 signalled to Mrs A to take the family away. By 9.45 he had settled the problem – a troublesome one – and was on his way back to the House of Commons. The opposition were calling out, 'Where's Asquith?' He made no explanation as to the cause of his detention but went calmly on with the business. [. . .]

LG and Masterman came to dinner. Long talks on the latter's speech on insurance tomorrow. [. . .] He [LG] seemed uneasy about Winston, and it is obvious that their relations are not quite what they were. [. . .]

31 July   Spent the morning talking with Hartshorn. He says the syndicalists are working to capture the men's organisation by an alteration in the rules which would take away all power from the leaders, who would become merely the instruments of the men to carry out their resolutions. He spoke bitterly of the syndicalist movement, which has for its object the overthrow of the existing order. He wants to improve the position of the workers on existing lines. He said that he feared that LG's land policy would cause much class hatred. Introduced Hartshorn to the future Marquess of Winchester.[39] Curious to see how much interested they were in each other. They investigated as if they were meeting a new animal for the first time. They got on well. The aristocracy have the game in their hands if they like to be pleasant and sociable with the people. [. . .]

4 August   Spent the day with Seely at Seaford. He spoke in doubting terms regarding the new Land Campaign. He said, 'Why not go straight out for an increase in the super-tax and a free breakfast table?' [. . .]

10 August   [See Appendix for Riddell's letter of 10 August 1912 to Sir William Robertson Nicoll concerning the Master of Elibank's resigntion as Chief Whip of the Liberal Party.][40]

22 October   Lunched with Mr and Mrs Winston. [. . .] We spoke of Alec Murray. Winston said his action in leaving the party was a tragedy and that he had told Murray that his political life was at an end, and that he would never be able to regain his place. W said that he had begged Murray to reconsider his decision. [. . .]

24 October   Called to see LG at Downing Street. [. . .] He then talked of his house at Walton Heath.[41] He said that Winston, P. Illingworth, the Attorney-General and Masterman all wanted houses there. 'We [LG added] shall be like the Clapham Saints in Wilberforce's time, and as you [R] will be our Patron Saint, our lives no doubt will be equally pure and exemplary.' [. . .]

26 October   Spent the afternoon with LG, Col. Seely and Masterman. We talked of Lord Roberts's[42] speech as to the necessity for universal military service. LG said, 'Within the four corners of this room I may say I am in favour of it.[43] But no party could carry it except in the case of some great national emergency. It should have been proposed immediately after the South African War. Then it might have been carried. It would be a great safeguard of peace. When the conference took place three years ago with the Opposition, I proposed that six things should be carried on non-party lines. That was one of them. But, as you know, the whole thing fell through. Some day the facts will be published.' LG is very anxious to take possession of his house at Walton before Christmas, so that he may spend Xmas there. He asked me to hurry up the builders. [. . .]

2 November   Spent the day with Alfred Lyttelton.[44] [. . .]

We discussed the indifference of public men to criticism. He said Balfour was quite indifferent to what the outer world said of him, but the criticism of his small inner circle of friends affected him most acutely. He asked me about LG. I told him of his love for his children which is rather like the passion of an animal for its young in the case of the dead daughter and little Megan.[45] This seemed to greatly interest him. [. . .]

Lyttelton said, 'Northcliffe's opinion on questions apart from his own business is not worth much. Except to this extent. He is like a jobber on the Stock Exchange. He is clever in divining what the public will think tomorrow. He knows nothing of the real merits of a question; he has no foresight or deep insight. The jobber goes on public opinion, not on the intrinsic merits of the stock. It is dangerous for him to hold a view. His business is to watch and profit by the turn of the market. That is Northcliffe's idea of politics. . . .'

9 November   Spent the day with LG, Masterman and Percy Illingworth at Walton Heath. LG very worried and nervous regarding the Balkan crisis. Said he had slept very badly. Also that outlook very serious, and that war between Austria and Russia, which would involve France and Germany, seemed very probable. He said further that Great Britain might be involved. He pointed to a bank of dark and lowering clouds, and remarked, 'That is emblematic of the situation. It may be a regular Armageddon. It is the most serious situation which has occurred for years. No body of men ever had a greater responsibility than the Cabinet. Sir Edward Grey and the Premier are very anxious.' (I have never seen LG himself so much disturbed.) We drove back to Downing Street to tea. LG sent for the Foreign Office box, which was awaiting him, and read the despatches while we took our meal. When he had finished he seemed somewhat relieved and said the situation was a little more hopeful. He talked of the Army and said we should have a million men at call. He said Winston is too selfish for the Navy. Some portion of the increased expenditure should be devoted to the Army. [. . .]

10 November Spent the morning with Winston and Mrs Winston. He spoke gloomily of the Balkan position. He says it all depends on Austria and Germany. If the former maintains her position regarding Servia, war is inevitable unless Germany declines to support her, which she may do as she has all to lose and nothing to gain. England may be able to keep out of the trouble, but if she stands aloof, and if Germany and Austria are successful in their combat with Russia and France and the Balkan States, we should be left alone in Europe. It might therefore be better for her to join France, Russia and the Balkan States so as to ensure their success. [. . .]

24 November Drove to Walton with Col. Seely. On the road he read his Foreign Office despatches. He said, 'The outlook is gloomy. There may be war at any moment between Austria and Servia and the Allies.' [. . .]

Winston [. . .] confirmed what Seely had said about the international situation. [. . .]

28 November Spent the morning with Winston. Evidently much perturbed.

He said: 'He [LG] beat me yesterday, over a paltry £26,000 per annum for the men. I cannot understand him. I shall not resign over such a matter, strongly as I feel. The £26,000 will just make the difference. It will prevent me from making a handsome addition to the wages of the older section of the men. If this is an earnest of what I am to expect on the estimates, my resignation later on when they are presented is certain. I am quite prepared. I shall then become a voice, and not a functionary. I wonder sometimes whether LG wants to get rid of me, and whether he has used this paltry question to place me in an impossible situation. You never know what he is at.'

I said, 'He always speaks well of you.' Winston replied, 'I hear to the contrary. He knows we are friends, and would be guarded in what he said to you.' I said, 'but did not the PM support you?' 'He agreed with me, I think,' explained Winston, 'But he did not support me.'

(Evidently things are very strained. I notice that both Winston and Masterman have delayed deciding upon their houses at Walton. They evidently feel that there are breakers ahead. [. . .]

We talked of conscription. I said it would be very unpopular. Winston agreed, but added, 'If it was law the people would probably accept it. The Insurance Act shows how law-abiding the British people are. If both parties were agreed, it might come to pass, but the temptation would be too great. One party would be certain to oppose for party purposes.'

I said: LG is privately in favour of some sort of compulsory service, but doubts if such a measure could be carried.

Winston remarked, 'Yes, I know he has been talking in that way. He will have to be careful or what he says will be quoted publicly. It is very indiscreet.'

29 December   Called and had tea with LG at Walton. [. . .]

We talked of journalists. He said, 'Robertson Nicoll is the greatest living journalist from a polemical standpoint. It is a pity he is too old to edit a daily paper. He would make it an enormous power.'

When discussing the food tax agitation in the Conservative Party, he remarked, 'They are making too much fuss. They should let the matter drop. They attach too much importance to what journalists and politicians are saying and thinking. [. . .] A party should put its house in order privately.'

1913

In some respects this was a year of marking time, yet divisive forces were at work both at home and abroad. Riddell's diaries have very little to say about Ireland, although storm clouds were fast gathering over Ulster. There is even less about foreign affairs, the Balkans notwithstanding. The important entries for 1913 concern those areas which were of intimate concern to Lloyd George and Winston Churchill in particular. From mid-July onwards the land campaign was uppermost in Lloyd George's mind, and Riddell learnt of his deep concern to secure the solid backing of Cabinet colleagues in this venture. Earlier in the year Churchill showed signs of making national service an issue in the Cabinet, possibly even parting company with the Liberal party, until Asquith effectively closed off discussion of this potentially disruptive subject. This caused Lloyd George to reflect upon Churchill's intentions concerning the Tories, in which he was encouraged to take a dark view by Reginald McKenna who had had a brush with Churchill over Irish policy. By year's end it was evident that a battle was looming over the Navy estimates for 1914. At first it seemed that a bargain had been struck, Lloyd George agreeing to find more money for the Navy if Churchill would support his land policy. But Churchill wanted too much and Lloyd George began to dig in his heels.

By far the most sensational happening of 1913 was the Marconi affair, and Riddell through numerous conversations with Lloyd George and Rufus Isaacs was unusually well placed to hear interesting things. He fully appreciated that the outcome was crucial to the careers of both men, and others too, even to the unity of the Liberal party. Hence he made every effort to acquire information that might illuminate the proceedings. The result gives us some insight into the workings of Lloyd George's mind during this crisis in his affairs. In addition there is added light on Churchill's reasons for working so hard to save Lloyd George from disaster, not least his prevailing upon Lord Northcliffe to take a soft line in his newspapers. Riddell's coolly critical assessment of Northcliffe's motives in this matter is especially noteworthy. Future as well as present press lords come under scrutiny,

as the figure of Sir Max Aitken emerges for the first time, puzzling but
not captivating the diarist. A measure of Riddell's disinterestedness is
seen when, at the end of the Marconi affair, he remarks upon the party
spirit and marvels that never once did he hear Lloyd George or Isaacs
admit the slightest responsibility for their predicament.

4 January   LG much elated at the defeat of the doctors.[1] Winston was
of the party. He said to LG (with whom he is now very friendly again),
'My dear David, I am delighted that you have beaten these fellows.
They have acted very badly. They say you have defeated them by
questionable practices. They might just as well say that if a man comes
to me and says, "You are a blackguard and a swindler, and I am going
to bash you to a jelly," and I in self-defence very mildly hit him on the
nose, that I should be guilty of questionable practices.'
   In talking of negotiations with the doctors, Masterman remarked,
'They have managed things very badly. They would not negotiate.'
Although, he added, negotiating with George is like negotiating with
the Devil. [. . .]
   LG and Ellis Griffith[2] also of the party, very much disturbed by
latter's statement that McKenna intends to provide compensation in
Disestablishment Bill for Welsh curates. LG very angry: 'That is like
McKenna. Why did he not consult me? As a Minister and a Welsh
member I have a right to know of any such proposals and to be heard
upon it.' [. . .]

5 January   Had a chat with Lord Knollys.[3] He spoke in high terms of
Asquith. He said that he liked LG, but that he wished he would not
make those violent speeches, which did great harm. Lady K said, 'He
(LG) uses too much vulgar abuse.' I remarked that Bonar Law was
following in the same track, good or bad. Lord K also spoke very highly
of Sir Edward Grey and Campbell-Bannerman.[4] Lord K is a delightful person, a great gentleman. [. . .]

18 January   Spent the morning with LG, Masterman and Illingworth.
LG was 50 yesterday. [. . .] He is very much elated regarding the
Insurance Act position. P. Illingworth said the Cabinet had stood by
LG in the most loyal manner. None of his colleagues (excepting J.
Burns) had ever wavered in their loyalty. PI added, 'The PM is a
splendid man to work with. When I had that trouble some weeks ago
over that snap division which caused the Government so much

difficulty, he never made use of a word of complaint. The first thing he said was, "I am so sorry for your sake, old man!"' I said, 'He has a wonderful knack of keeping his Cabinet together, and has no jealousy in his disposition.'

P. Illingworth: Yes, you are quite right. He is always glad to learn of their successes. Nothing gives him more pleasure. [. . .]

25 January   LG, Masterman and P. Illingworth.

I asked LG how he got on with the suffragettes at the deputation? He said, 'Not badly.' I said, 'Were you nervous?' 'No,' he replied, 'danger is a curious thing. It has a peculiar attraction. It made me quite look forward to the event.'

I said, 'Don't you think the Tories have made a mistake in endeavouring to smash the Franchise Bill? Is it not a good send-off for the Government in view of the suffrage differences?'

He laughed and said, 'You have hit the nail on the head. This is the second time in two months that they have let us out by a tactical blunder. Bonar Law may talk as his people talk in their clubs. He may reflect the Conservative mind and therefore please his followers in the country, but he does not know the Parliamentary game. He is almost invariably wrong. For real business give me old Arthur Balfour!' [. . .]

7 February   Congratulated Rufus [Isaacs] on result of Marconi enquiry.[5] He said he had read the evidence and was lost in amazement at the whole business. The writers of the articles had not even been tricked. They had based their charges on idle, unverified gossip.

8 February   Spent the evening alone with LG. Long chat. [. . .]

We talked of Winston. I said, 'His career looms large with him.' 'Yes,' said LG, 'more than with any other statesman I know. We are all keen on success, but there is a difference.' I said, 'The absence of the Napoleonic idea.' 'Yes,' replied LG, 'that is what I mean.' [. . .]

In reference to the Marconi libels, LG said that he had taken advice as to instituting proceedings, but F. E. Smith had advised him to do nothing as the defendants would cross-examine him as to the attacks which he had made on other people, and would tell the jury that a person with his record must not be thin-skinned. LG added, 'Perhaps he was right. Joe (Chamberlain) never took any action regarding aspersions on his character – perhaps for the same reason.'

9 February Lunched with Sir Max Aitken at Cherkley Court, Leatherhead, to meet Bonar Law. Spent the afternoon playing golf with him. A nice, kind, simple man.

He said, 'Lloyd George is a dangerous rascal, but a charming man, unspoilt by success.' He told me that he was unmoved by Press criticism, but found that eighty per cent of the party had not the pluck to continue the fight, as they thought they would not be successful in the country. He spoke highly of Austen Chamberlain, whom he described as 'loyal, and straight as a line'. He said that AC had improved as a speaker in a remarkable manner and that now he was an excellent debater. [. . .] He described Asquith as the best debater in the House of Commons. I asked him what he thought of the younger politicians, to which he replied, 'It may seem a large order, but I could form a Government equal to the present one without including a single man now on the Front Bench.' I said, 'I quite agree that it would be a large order – a very large one.' He is very friendly with Sir Max Aitken. His son is in the latter's office. He spoke highly of Aitken's ability as a man of business. No doubt he is a very clever fellow, but he has no knowledge of this country and exhibited great ignorance in the course of our conversation. [. . .] Aitken is said to be very wealthy but he is not a cultured man. He is just a colonial financier who has dumped himself down in London. [. . .]

19 February Early this morning my bedside telephone rang, and a message came through to say that part of the house I am building for LG at Walton Heath had been blown to smithereens by the suffragettes.

(This outrage caused a sensation all the world over. I was inundated with Press cuttings. Speaking at Cardiff the same evening, Mrs Pankhurst admitted that she had incited her followers to commit this outrage and took personal responsibility for the occurrence. She was subsequently tried at the Old Bailey and sentenced to three years' penal servitude. I met her years afterwards [. . .] and had quite a pleasant chat.[6] [. . .])

23 February Had a long talk with General French. He says the Committee of Defence has grown too big and unwieldy, and the preponderance of civilians upon it has become too great. He spoke in high terms of Asquith, and said if he had to face a big war he would rather see him Prime Minister than anyone else. His judgment is so good, and he acts with such calmness and decision. The General said, 'We have had some anxious times during the past few months, and have had to make some most important decisions. Several nights I have been unable to sleep knowing that at any moment I might be called up on the telephone to receive news which would make it necessary for me to mobilise.' He spoke very highly of Colonel Seely, and said he had acted with great judgment and coolness in very trying situations during the crisis. He described him as the right man in the right place. A man with sufficient knowledge of military affairs to enable him to form a sound judgment, but one who did not place too much reliance on his own military experience. The General said that the Germans and Austrians were not ready for war, but that in twelve months' time their position would be much improved. He seemed to regard war as certain in the future.

4 March   LG and Mrs LG and I visited the house at Walton Heath to see the effects of the bomb explosion. LG much interested. Said the facts had not been brought out and that no proper point had been made of the fact that the bombs were concealed in cupboards, which must have resulted in the death of twelve men had not the bomb which first exploded blown out the candle attached to the second bomb, which could not have been discovered, hidden away as it was. He was very indignant and said he should see the Attorney-General at once. [. . .]

19 March   For some days I have known that something serious was about to take place. What, I did not exactly realise. This morning, Masterman sent for me. He told me what I had heard earlier in the day, that in the action for libel brought by Rufus Isaacs and H. Samuel against the *Matin* [. . .] it would be stated [. . .] that Rufus Isaacs had purchased 10,000 shares in the American Marconi Company, of which he had sold 1,000 to Lloyd George and 1,000 to Alec Murray. [. . .] [Masterman said] that this transaction had worried LG and Rufus terribly, and that LG had offered his resignation to Asquith who had ridiculed the idea. He said that LG had wanted to write (yesterday) a long letter to the Press explaining the transaction, but that he (Masterman) had dissuaded him from doing so, saying that the case had better speak for itself. [. . .]

Masterman said that the Prime Minister had counselled silence and was chiefly responsible for the course which had been pursued. [. . .]

Masterman said that the Press had been arranged with [*sic*]. Northcliffe had promised that *The Times* and *Daily Mail* would not be objectionable, and Harry Lawson had agreed to refrain from an attack in the *Telegraph*. Massingham had been very nasty, and they feared an attack in the *Nation*. Gardiner of the *Daily News* and Donald of the *Chronicle* were both friendly. Masterman said that the thing had been like a black cloud hanging over the Ministry, and that at one time he had feared LG would break down. (I am bound to say that he has shown no signs of doing so.)

20 March [Marconi disclosures made today.] . . .] LG and Rufus were evidently very worried. [. . .] [LG] was anxious to know Robertson Nicoll's views. [. . .] I said, 'He is very favourable,' which seemed to please LG. [. . .]

21 March (*Good Friday*) Long and confidential talk with Winston Churchill, with whom I spent the day. He outlined to me his views on national service and other matters. He said that he felt that he must make an early declaration on the subject and proposed to say that while the Navy was thoroughly efficient and while there was no cause for immediate alarm, he could not see his way to oppose a scheme for national service. He continued, 'I shall be perfectly loyal to Asquith, my chief, to whom I owe so much, but I shall take this line without consultation. One must trust in a matter of this sort to one's own flare [*sic*]. I am prepared, when the time comes, to throw my hat over the wall and risk all. I do not want to take any drastic action for another twelve months, not until my work at the Admiralty is finished, which it should be by then. I wish you could find out what the readers of the *N[ews] of the W[orld]* think of National Service.' I said I doubt its popularity. [. . .]

Winston then proceeded to put forward a proposal for a national party. He said, 'The time will soon be ripe for a joinder of the two parties. A national party could secure great aims. The Conservative section in exchange for a system of national service could agree to a minimum wage for agricultural labourers and other trades, and to a reform of the land system. Our national life requires more organisation and more discipline. There is a body of sensible men in both parties who are tired of the existing state of things. In both parties there are fools at one end and crackpots at the other, but the great body in the middle is sound and wise.' I said that I doubted the possibility of forming a national party. The 'haves' must form one party and the 'have nots' another. Their aims and objects were quite at variance. Parties may be readjusted, but the tendency would not be towards a national party, but towards a capital party as opposed to a labour party. To this he replied that his combination would contain all the talents, and would be sufficiently strong to smash all other parties. I said I had my doubts.

He spoke at length regarding the Marconi business. He thought that an earlier disclosure should have been made in the House of Commons, but that the matter would quieten down. He said that he had arranged for the pacific attitude of *The Times* and *Daily Mail*. It is evident that he is in close touch with Northcliffe. [. . .]

He said, 'LG is favourable to national service.' I remarked, 'The people don't like the prospect of compulsion. They don't look forward to life in the barrack square. They never see anything of the bright side of military life. Soldiers, like convicts, are carefully kept apart from the people. . . .' He said, 'We should have to begin gradually, and the proposals would not affect present-day voters – only their sons under twenty-one.' [. . .]

Mrs Churchill [. . .] said that Arthur Balfour had never seen his late secretary, Jack Sandars,[7] since he left him, which showed that AJB was a fish-like person, as he had been on the terms of closest intimacy with Sandars, whose advice he used to seek and who in a measure ran him. Winston retorted, 'His (Sandars) advice was usually bad and many of AJB's worst mistakes were due to that cause. [. . .]

22 March   A large party at Walton Heath. [. . .]

Drove home with LG, who said that Bonar Law had spoken to him in a friendly and manly way regarding the Marconi incident. He said that he was quite sure there had been no moral wrong on LG's part, but that he would have to raise the question in the House. LG offered to produce to him all his private books and papers relating to his own affairs, but BL said there was no occasion for this, as he had no doubt on the subject.

We spoke of the future of parties. LG said that the working classes would never improve their position without the assistance of able men in other walks of life, men trained in business, affairs, controversy. All revolutions had shown this to be true. In the French Revolution the leaders were lawyers and educated men – Robespierre, etc. Asked what he thought about the possibility of national party. He said he thought it impossible, but that it might be practicable to detach from the Tories some of the men with advanced views. [. . .]

Again he reverted to the Marconi question. He said, 'This is the sort of time when one finds out who are one's friends. The Cabinet without exception have treated me in the most considerate and kindly fashion. The same applies to the journalists with the exception of Massingham, who has acted harshly and unkindly. I can never forget it. He and I have always been such friends.' [. . .]

Mrs LG very pleasant. She takes all this Marconi trouble so well – no fuss, always sweet and helpful. LG referred to her today with many expressions of gratitude and affection. [. . .]

23 March [. . .]LG told me last night that the condition of affairs on the Continent is still most serious and that Sir Edward Grey is having an anxious time. Winston said the same thing.

24 March It is obvious to me that LG is very anxious regarding the Marconi matter and very anxious to conciliate the Press. It was amusing to see the attention he paid today to Donald. [. . .] LG was beating the war-drum on Saturday and again today. I mean the real war-drum – serious position on the Continent, etc, etc. [. . .] But he was very dark and gloomy, more so than I have seen him even when he was ill. Mrs LG said he felt this Marconi business very acutely.

28 March[8] [. . .] LG said, 'He [Lord Robert Cecil] knew very well that I should raise the question of the conduct of his brother-in-law, Selborne,[9] who was a Director of the P & O company while a member of the Conservative Government and when that company was making Government contracts.' [. . .]

I told him (LG) that I had just left McKenna, who had spoken very nicely about him and was evidently delighted at the manner in which the examination had gone off. 'Yes,' said LG, 'McKenna has acted like a brick all the time. In fact all my colleagues but one have treated me splendidly. John Burns is the only one who has acted badly. . . .'

30 March [. . .] [Re. Marconi] Winston: It must make a difference to LG. He cannot conduct his land campaign as he otherwise would have done. The upper classes have treated him well over the business. He cannot attack individuals as he has been accustomed to do in the past. [. . .]

1 April   Long talk with Percy Illingworth who told me that the past few months had been an anxious time, and that the consequence of the Marconi scandal might have been very serious. [. . .] Illingworth also told me that the Prime Minister has been very worried about the affair, and that he had taken the, for him, unusual course of writing a letter to Illingworth on Sunday and of forwarding it by special messenger. [. . .]

4 April   Masterman told me that LG had had a letter from Northcliffe regarding the Marconi business, in reply to one from LG thanking him for the manner in which *The Times* and *Mail* had dealt with the issue. Northcliffe said in his letter that he had been glad to be of service, that he had never believed the rumours, and that in view of the condition of Continental affairs he hoped that he and LG might be able to work together for the good of England. I said to Masterman that this confirmed me in thinking that Northcliffe and Winston were working to rope LG into the National Service party. Masterman said he had no doubt that this was the case, and that the letter was a polite reminder that services rendered would have to be remembered in future. [. . .] M added that LG's position with the Tory Press would be very difficult in view of his obligations to Northcliffe and Lawson. [. . .]

12 April   [. . .] Caird[10] of the *Daily Mail* was at Walton. LG was busy coquetting with him. He never misses an opportunity with the Press. The affair Marconi has made him very eager to conciliate newspaper men. [. . .]

13 April   [. . .] After lunch, he [LG] opened the box containing the Budget papers and read to us a remarkable set of figures as to the progress of taxation and population, which he said he intended to use in his speech. We discussed the effect of a general rise in wages of 5s per week per worker. I said the difficulty is that all increases in wages are followed by increases in prices, and I suggested that in the end the only method of protecting the worker would be for the state to appropriate half a man's property on his death, over and above a certain amount, and then treat the amount appropriated as capital. LG said, 'That is Carnegie's[11] idea also.' [. . .]

19 April   [. . .] The national service question is evidently becoming acute. It is plain that wire-pulling is in active operation. LG has stated more than once that he rather favours some form of compulsory service. Masterman said today that if the Government supported the scheme, the result would be to split the Liberal Party. He is a strong opponent. The *Nation* has a violent article denouncing Seely as being weak-kneed on the matter. Winston told me of it today. He seems very angry. He said, 'I think I shall write in reply, pointing out that Massingham (the editor) has fallen foul of almost every member of the Government. The Prime Minister, who has accomplished practically all that he set out to do; Sir Edward Grey, who has prevented a European conflagration; the Chancellor of the Exchequer, who has done more for the working classes than any other statesman; the First Lord of the Admiralty, who has tried, however inefficiently, to do his duty; and now Seely, who is endeavouring in a courageous and able manner to deal with a most difficult situation. In fact from Massingham's point of view, the Liberal Party consists of himself and perhaps Simon and Burns.' [. . .]

26 April Spent the day with LG, McKenna, Rufus Isaacs, Masterman and McKenna's brother. We talked of the movement for national service. LG said that Prince Louis of Battenberg's[12] public statement last Monday to the effect that our present system of national defence was inadequate and that the Navy must be supplemented was most improper. If a public servant desired to make such speeches he should resign his position [. . .] particularly when the matter discussed was under consideration by the Committee of National Defence.

Masterman: Winston is mad on national defence. He was dining with P. Illingworth the other night. Percy said he talked of nothing else.

McKenna: Quite true. It is absurd. [. . .]

We talked of the political situation. They all agreed that good trade is the chief factor in elections.

LG: I think we should go to the country while trade remains good.

Masterman: But we ought to get our Bills through first.

LG: Hang the Bills! We can see to them later.

Riddell: How about plural voting? I suppose the Lords will reject it?

LG: Yes; it cannot become law for two years, but we should have to risk that.

Masterman: A redistribution scheme would be very helpful.

To this they all agreed.

McKenna: I should not mind going out, but I hate to see them come in. [. . .] They have no measures and no men.

LG: I don't agree. They could form a strong Cabinet. Apart from the old gang, they have F. E. Smith, Lord Robert Cecil, Lord Hugh Cecil,[13] Harry Lawson, and several more very competent men. Make no mistake. They could form quite a strong Cabinet. [. . .]

We talked of ages.

LG: 1863 is the great vintage year of the Cabinet. Look up their ages and you will find I am correct.[14]

The changes in Parliamentary associations and friendships and the rise and decline of Ministers is interesting. Two years ago LG and Winston were always together and McKenna was under a cloud. Now LG and Winston *seem very good friends*,[15] but they are not always together as they were formerly. McKenna and LG now seem close allies.

27 April Lunched with LG at his house at Walton. LG, his son, and Megan. Spent the afternoon talking with him alone. A delightful afternoon.

R: I wonder what will be Winston's destination? Do you think that he meditates breaking away?

LG: I think he would like to but does not see his way. He could not go over on the land question. [. . .] He could not go over on Free Trade. Perhaps he might on conscription. [. . .]

R: The South African constitution was the biggest thing established in our day. Who was responsible? C[ampbell]-B[annerman] or Asquith?

LG: Oh, CB! He deserves all the credit. It was all done in a ten minutes' speech at the Cabinet – the most dramatic, the most important ten minutes' speech ever delivered in our time. In ten minutes he brushed aside all the checks and all the safeguards devised by Asquith, Winston and Loreburn. At the outset only two of us were with him, John Burns and myself. But his speech convinced the whole Cabinet. It was the utterance of a plain, kindly, simple man. The speech moved one at least of the Cabinet to tears. It was the most impressive thing I ever saw. [. . .] The result of CB's policy has been remarkable. It captured Gen. Botha[16] by its magnanimity, just as all great men are impressed when you display your confidence in them. If we had a war tomorrow, Botha and 50,000 Boers would march with us side by side. He would, if necessary, drive the Germans out of South Africa. [. . .]

1 May   Spent the day with Northcliffe at Walton Heath. He said,
'The Conservative Party is a party of little men with no policy. I tell
them so and it makes them angry.'

Referring to the Marconi affair, he said, 'Winston telephoned to me
for an interview. I did not know what he wanted. He told me the story
and was much agitated. I did not know until then that he was so much
attached to Lloyd George. I fancy that he must have gone to other
papers.' Northcliffe said, 'This business will draw LG's teeth. He
cannot attack the rich as he has done in the past. He is a man lacking in
the sense of proportion. [. . .] This affair will make his position very
difficult with the governing classes.'

3 May   [. . .] I asked McKenna whether he prepared his speeches. He
said, 'Only in a general way. [. . .] I don't pretend to be a great speaker.
I am not able to do the big Bow-Wow like Asquith. . . .'

4 May   I had a chat with Bonar Law, who told me that the Opposition
intended to raise the Marconi question in the House of Commons. He
said, 'I am sorry for Rufus Isaacs and LG, but one must attack them.
There was no corruption, but they acted imprudently and improperly,
and in a manner unfitting for Cabinet Ministers charged with the
performance of such high functions. That is the line we shall take.' He
added. 'I wonder whether their action is a sign of a general weakening
in the moral fibre of the House of Commons and the nation.' [. . .]

5 May   [. . .] I think Winston's plan regarding National Service has
been knocked on the head by the Prime Minister. Masterman says that
Winston has been told that he must 'shut up'.

7 May   Called on Arthur Pearson. He is quite blind – a sad sight.
Asked me to take over his business. We may come to terms. He said
that the circulation of the morning *Standard* went down as the old
readers died off. Inclement weather brought about an immediate drop
in sales. When he changed the size of the *Evening Standard* and
amalgamated it with the *St James's Gazette* he received a letter from
Lord Knollys asking him to call. Lord Knollys said that the King
(Edward) did not like the change and begged him not to alter his old
friend and companion the *St James's Gazette*. Pearson replied he was
sorry his plans could not be changed, and asked that the King should
read the new paper for six weeks and then let him know his view. Six

weeks later to the day Pearson had a letter from Lord K saying the King had changed his opinion and was now satisfied that the right policy had been pursued. Pearson said the *Daily Express* had broken his health. He spoke cheerfully of the future, but is evidently convinced that he will never be any better but may be much worse.

21 May [At Criccieth. . .] Wet and stormy. The sea rather rough. We walked along the shore and sat for some time on the rocks watching the waves. LG gave me an insight into a curious side of his character. He showed me a letter which he had received from a palmist and soothsayer, in which the writer stated, amongst other things, that LG was beset by many dangers, but that he would be protected by unseen spirits until he had accomplished a great mission which he was destined to perform. LG said, 'That is a remarkable statement, because I am myself convinced that nothing will be allowed to happen to me until I have accomplished some great work for the performance of which I have been singled out. I feel that I shall be quite secure until then.' I said, 'But what is to happen afterwards?' 'Ah,' he replied, 'afterwards! Well, afterwards I suppose I shall share the fate of all other men who have been selected to perform great works. I shall be left to my fate. I shall be deserted.' I said, 'Has this been the fate of other great leaders?' 'Yes,' he replied, 'I think it has. Gladstone, Chamberlain.' I said, 'How about Disraeli?' 'Well,' replied LG, 'he died an unhappy man.' It is quite obvious that LG thinks that he is the subject of special protection on the part of Providence, and that he is destined to perform some great service to humanity. This is what helps to sustain him and give him confidence. Masterman has told me before that LG has this belief, but I have never taken the statement seriously. I now find it to be true. [. . .]

We talked of the Marconi affair.

LG: I am going for them in the debate on the report. I am going to show up Selborne's transactions with the P & 0, of which he was a Director while a member to the Government; Balfour's dealings in Whittaker Wright's[17] shares; Hicks-Beach's sale of his land at an outrageous price to the Government; and Joe's transactions in relation to the Niger Company of which he was a large shareholder. But I don't like to attack Joe. He can't defend himself. If I refer to him I shall do so in a manner to which he could not reasonably object. [. . .]

31 May Very interesting talk with LG and Masterman.

LG: You (turning to me) remember our talk about the date for starting the new campaign.[18] Five men, all representing different phases of thought, have pressed me to begin the campaign at once.

R: Well, why not, if you are ready? But July would be a bad month.

LG: That is the trouble. I am not quite ready. There are certain details to be settled.

Masterman: Early in July would do, but you will have to get the Cabinet's approval.

LG: I shall not trouble about that. I shall get the Prime Minister's approval, and mention the subject to two or three of the others. I am not going to discuss the matter at the Cabinet. What is the use of discussing it with John Burns, who would not understand it?

Masterman: It would be wiser to endeavour to carry them all with you.

LG: You cannot begin a campaign on those lines. [. . .]

4 June   Dined with Robertson Nicoll and Garvin of the *Pall Mall*. He is a clever fellow, but on the mad side, and very vain and self-centred. [. . .]

7 and 8 June   This has been an amazing week. On Thursday came the bombshell that Alec Murray had been investing in American Marconis, both on his own account and on account of 'a trust' – no doubt the party funds, but we shall hear more later. The disclosure owing to the failure and absconding of a stockbroker. [. . .] No one in the Cabinet knew of these dealings, which have caused the direst dismay in the Liberal Party. LG and Rufus were astounded. I met Percy Illingworth at dinner on Thursday, the day of the disclosure. He said, 'Have you heard the news?' I said, 'I have not yet read the account of today's proceedings.' 'Well,' said he, 'you will have something interesting to read. Alec Murray is an amazing fellow. He has spoofed us all. It is a nice mess.' Illingworth seemed very much disturbed. Later on I talked with Winston, who said, 'Murray has acted badly. . . . He has put his friends [LG and Isaacs] in a terrible position. . . .'

On Saturday and Sunday I spent several hours with LG – evidently very depressed but cheered by the verdict in the Chesterton libel case.[19]

LG said: 'I knew nothing of this. Murray never said a word. . . . He believed in the American Marconi as an investment. . . . No doubt he thought he was doing well to invest the party funds in that way, if he did so.'

On Friday I met Donald, of the *Daily Chronicle*, evidently very angry with the Government. [. . .] He told me that he intended to go for the Government. [. . .]

9 June   The murder is out. It now appears that £9,000 of the party funds was invested by Alec Murray in American Marconis, and apparently that Fenner the broker has lost or appropriated £30,000 entrusted to him by Murray as Chief Whip. [. . .] Illingworth has known these facts for some little time. The disclosure has caused a great sensation.

(The party spirit is a curious thing. During all this Marconi discussion I have never heard LG, Rufus or Masterman frankly admit the other point of view. [. . .] Attacks they always describe as 'unscrupulous', 'disgraceful', etc. They never admit that LG and Rufus have brought the attacks on themselves. . . .)

14 June   The Marconi Report is published. Gallons of whitewash! The Chairman, Sir Alfred [*sic*] Spicer,[20] was unable to get his way. His report, not so favourable, was rejected. He is very much annoyed, and says he will stand to his guns whatever may be the effect on his political career. He wrote to Asquith while the enquiry was proceeding, resigning his position on the ground that the information as to the dealings in American Marconis had first been communicated to Faulkener[21] [*sic*] and Booth,[22] instead of to him as Chairman. Asquith saw him and persuaded him to withdraw his resignation as the effect would be disastrous to the Party. [. . .]

Masterman says that if the report had been unfavourable, Rufus Isaacs would have resigned and LG would have followed suit. [. . .]

19 June   Spent the day with Northcliffe at Sutton Place. Talked Marconi.

He said, 'I hope our friends (LG and Rufus) appreciate the action of my papers.'

I said, 'Yes. They say you have acted like a great gentleman.' That evidently pleased him. He said, 'Winston has acted well. He has been very loyal. In great measure they have him to thank for the course I have taken.' [. . .]

[Riddell reflects on Northcliffe:] He has no fixed principles except the desire to have his own way. [. . .] The point is that he has no regard whatever for truth or accuracy. [. . .] He manipulates the facts to suit his mood at the moment. [. . .] Most papers mislead under the influence of party politics. Northcliffe misleads in order to secure *his* own way, be it good or bad. [. . .]

26 June   [. . .] Played with LG, Ramsay MacDonald and Donald of the *Chronicle*. Much talk of LG's speech at the luncheon which is to be given to him and Rufus on Tuesday at the National Liberal Club. LG very strongly for a violent, *tu quoque* attack on the other side.[23] He said, 'I must uncork the bottle. There are many things I feel I must say.' Ramsay MacDonald said, 'Well, I should keep my finger on the neck of the bottle!'

LG: Well, I want to go for the *Morning Post* who are attacking me in the most disgraceful way.

Donald: Newspapers like to be attacked. They live on attacks. I wish Bonar Law would attack the *Daily Chronicle*. It would be worth a lot of money to us.

LG: [. . .] Strachey[24] of the *Spectator* has never got over my sneering reference to him. [. . .]

6 July   [. . .] Seely and I called to see LG at Walton Heath. I complimented him on his speech at the National Liberal Club. I said, 'It was just the right thing. So well graded in all respects.'

LG: I am glad to hear you say that. It was the only course open to me. I am not a white-sheet man. It does not suit me. I got a tremendous reception. [. . .] I must now get to work on my Land Campaign. I shall give them hell. I think it will be well devised to meet the grievances, the terrible grievances, which undoubtedly exist. Fix up that dinner with Robertson Nicoll so that we may have a good talk.

19 July   LG and Megan lunched with me. He said that last night he had entertained some members of the Government at dinner to talk over the land campaign, Crewe[25] and Simon being of the party.

LG: Crewe has the feeling of the territorial magnate strongly developed, and does not wish to lose his privileges. He has a subtle mind, and put the other point of view very well. The landowner likes to walk round his estate and give a tenant a new cow-house, not because he is legally bound to do so, but like the Lord Almighty because he is graciously pleased to confer a benefit. Simon is a clever fellow, clear-headed but pedantic. He wants everything very precise. Sir Edward Grey is with me. He is a kind fellow, the only man I would serve under except Asquith. I would serve under Grey. He sees that you cannot leave the farmer in the cold. If he is paying the full rent, you must put a part or the whole of the increased wages to be paid to the workman on to the landlord. All parties are sympathetic to labour. When I shall have the trouble will be in dealing with the incidence of the increase in wages. Some of my colleagues will kick at the proposal to charge it on the land.

R: How about Winston?

LG: I think he will be all right. He sympathises with the minimum wage, but he won't like the proposal that the land shall bear it. [. . .] He is a fighter and will enjoy the fray.

R: How about Haldane?

LG: Well, I really don't know where he is. I never do know where he is. He is the most muddle-headed clever man I have ever met.

R: Has the Prime Minister agreed?

LG: I have only had one talk with him. He has the papers now. He is a big man. He never initiates anything, but he is a great judge. He brushes aside all small points, and goes straight to the heart of the subject. I prefer to discuss a big project with him rather than with anyone else. That is one of the troubles in the House of Commons. He stands so much above the other side and dominates the situation.

R: He is like a steam roller. He goes straight down the road in a solemn stately way, crushing all the pebbles and small obstacles in his path.

LG: And never stopping until he comes to a great boulder and then he deals with that. [. . .]

9 August   The feeling between the two parties is very bitter. This is due in great measure to the new regime adopted by Bonar Law, who considers social relations between the two parties undesirable. [. . .] There is no doubt that B. Law has been embittered by the somewhat contemptuous way in which he has been treated and spoken of by his opponents. Now it is war to the knife. The Conservatives seem to shun Walton Heath nowadays, no doubt because they do not wish to meet the other side. The Marconi affair has left great bitterness on both sides. Now a fresh cause of friction has arisen in relation to the brothel in Piccadilly which was recently raided by the police. The papers found on the premises contained the names of some of the patrons of the establishment. These have been alleged to include the names of one or more Cabinet Ministers. The Home Secretary has been closely questioned on the subject and has specifically denied the truth of this statement. [. . .] Now it appears that the papers include the names of several Tory peers, including a Duke. [. . .]

26 September   From what McKenna says there is considerable difference of opinion amongst the members of the Cabinet regarding the proposals for a minimum wage and a revision of the system of rating and taxing land. There is no doubt that a large section of the Cabinet do not view the working classes with much favour. [. . .]

29 September   Papers full of visit of Asquith, L. George, Winston, Seely and Attorney-General to P. Illingworth at Isle of Arran. McKenna says that the PM is not at all keen on the new programme, and that LG has undertaken not to launch it until it has been approved by the Cabinet. Also that the PM thinks that the present programme should first be carried out and that the launching of the new one should be deferred for twelve months. McK further says that the visit was arranged some time ago and that he and the others were invited, and that he believes the PM will do his best not to discuss the new proposals. Whether McKenna is correct in all this I rather doubt. [. . .]

McKenna told me of a curious conversation he had had with the King at the time of the *Titanic* disaster. Some reference was made to the criticism that male first-class passengers were preferred when filling the boats to women in the steerage. The King remarked, 'It is ridiculous. Of course if a man pays first-class fare he is entitled to preference!' [. . .]

9 October   Called on LG at Walton. [. . .] He asked me if I had read the speeches of McKenna and Winston on the Ulster question and said that they were inconsistent, which was most unfortunate as it gave the appearance of Cabinet dissension. He also said that he thought they should have left the subject to the PM and Birrell,[26] as it is their job. He told me that Winston had promised to support him on the land question, but had added, 'Don't be too hard on the landlords.' LG remarked, 'I often think he is sorry he came over and would be glad to go back if he could. . . .'

13 October   Long talk with LG. We spoke of his speech at Bedford on Saturday, opening the Land Campaign. [. . .]

The McKennas arrived. We all had tea together – LG, the McKennas and Masterman. [. . .] He [McK] said to me privately that Winston's speech was scandalous. He had no authority to say what he did. 'The PM,' he added, 'is really too easy.' [. . .]

16 October   [. . .] LG had to leave early to go to a Cabinet meeting. He told me that the Government policy on the Irish question had been settled on the previous day, when they determined to let matters take their course and do nothing. He told me that F. E. Smith had been to see him, and that he had said that the opposition were in serious trouble regarding Ulster, and did not know what to do, or something to that effect. [. . .]

17 October   LG in high glee. Yesterday the Cabinet decided on the land policy and authorised him to go ahead. [. . .] The only critic was John Burns. [. . .] He told us that Winston was to announce the minimum wage for agricultural labourers in his speech at Manchester on the morrow. [. . .]

31 October and 1 November   Long talks with LG. Full of spirits regarding his new land scheme. [. . .]

[He said:] Most people have a price of some sort. Very often the price is the support of some policy in which they are much interested. For example: *I have made a bargain with Winston. He has agreed to support my land policy with which he is not in sympathy, and I have agreed to give him more money for the Navy. You may call this a bribe, but I have nothing to gain personally. I am only endeavouring to carry out my scheme of social reform, which I believe is for the good of the people. I am not at all sure that the bargain will meet with the approval of some of our party. Indeed I already see signs that it will not.* [27][. . .]

2 November   Spent the day with Rufus Isaacs. [. . .]

We talked of LG. Rufus said, 'It is quite obvious that he has made a bargain with Winston. Our people are beginning to see it. It will be very unpopular.' (This confirms what LG said himself.)

November [n.d.]   Played golf with Mr and Mrs Winston. Joined by Lloyd George who played with us. A good deal of talk and chaff regarding the Navy estimates. Winston evidently perturbed at the attitude of a large section of the Radicals. He said, 'Why is Donald attacking me in the *Chronicle?*' LG and I replied, 'Not on personal grounds, but because he believes he is voicing the views of the party. He is not against you. He is opposed to your policy.' [. . .]

16 November   [. . .] With LG to Nicoll's house at Hampstead. [. . .]

LG: Haldane is a warm-hearted, kindly man. A big man.

R: He is not very popular. Not so popular as Sir Ed. Grey.

LG: He is more human that Grey. Grey is a fish-like person.

R: Anyway, he appeals to the British people. They like him and trust him.

LG: No doubt they do, but he is a fish. (Evidently Grey has been opposing or criticising LGs land policy!)

LG said that Haldane was a splendid fellow when he took up a scheme. Most helpful. Always endeavouring to be of use. (Evidently he is helping with regard to the land!) [. . .] You will remember what I have always said about the lawyers during a revolution. Never hang or shoot them. Always keep them. The same remark applies to Winston. He is much less dangerous with us than against us. [. . .]

13 December   The Navy estimates and the Ulster question are causing serious differences of opinion in the Cabinet. There is no doubt a strong set against Winston on both. I saw McKenna today. He has been working up the case for reducing the estimates, and is very strong against concessions to Ulster. He was very reserved and dour. Not at all like he usually is. Evidently much worried. Masterman who was with me noticed this also. The story published today as to the dinner at which proposals for a settlement with Ulster were discussed is incorrect. LG was not there. The diners were Winston, Lord Morley, F. E. Smith and Austen Chamberlain. Masterman says the outlook is black. Devlin [28] tells him that the Irish Party will not consent to anything in the nature of exclusion for Ulster, and that the Irish leaders could not, if they would, carry such a proposal with their followers. Ministers (LG, Masterman, McKenna, etc) are talking of civil war as being very possible.

14 December   McKenna referred to his manner yesterday and said he had been very worried and bitter concerning the Navy estimates and Ulster. [. . .] McK has told me (R) several times that LG will not control public expenditure as he should. [. . .]

Later I had a talk with Masterman, who says that Samuel, Hobhouse, Pease[29] and Runciman have formed a combination against Winston and that if McKenna were to join with Harcourt[30] he could bring Winston down.

I then went to LG's house at Walton and had a chat with him. He said, 'I shall be no party to driving Winston out of the Cabinet. I do not agree with some of my colleagues concerning him. I think it is better to have him with us than against us. I shall not be the one to give him the knife if it has to be done.'

R: He was very loyal to you over the Marconi business. [. . .]

LG: Yes, I know, and I never forget an action like that. Of course I have been too easy with him during the past two years regarding the Naval estimates. When he went to the Admiralty I made a bargain with him about the expenditure. He has not kept it. He has been extravagant. He is like a man who buys Rolls Royce motor cars and dines at the Carlton with other people's money. He has not been economical. Because he has been at the Admiralty everything else has had to be sacrificed. Now the feeling against him is very strong. I, however, think he will see the error of his ways and amend his figures to meet the views of the party. [. . .]

18 December   Things are in a very interesting and critical state. There are grave disputes in the Cabinet regarding the Naval estimates. Winston is being bitterly attacked in the Liberal papers. Samuel, Simon and Runciman are doing their utmost to force him out of the Cabinet. Masterman says he thinks he is sure to resign, but whether he will resign over the estimates or Ulster remains to be seen. [. . .]

LG says that the position is very acute. Evidently he sees that the party are strongly against Winston and is reconsidering or has reconsidered. [. . .] Now LG is trimming his sails. He told me today that Samuel, Simon, Runciman and Co. are doing their utmost 'to down Winston' as he stands in their way. Also that the Prime Minister has received strong protests from some of his most influential supporters in the country. He said that Seely had made a sort of 'bleating speech' in Winston's defence, but received no support. Winston had said to him (LG), 'Europe is suffering from a cold fit and I am the victim.'

I said, 'Will Winston resign?'

'Not now,' replied LG, 'but I think he will later on. If he is wise, he will endeavour to fall in with the views of the Cabinet, and if I were you I should advise him to do so. [. . .His Guildhall speech] was a piece of madness. The public will not stand provocative speeches of that sort. They are quite unnecessary. Winston has been a loyal friend to me, but there comes a time when one cannot allow oneself to be influenced by personal considerations of that sort.' [. . .]

Later I called at the McKennas. Saw Mrs McK. She says that McKenna has not joined in the attack on Winston – that he felt he could not do so. That Winston is certain to resign, but will probably go out on Ulster and not over the estimates, which will be a better thing for the party. Seely called upon McKenna last night. He said that he had not seen Winston, but McKenna thought he had come to ascertain how the land lay. Mrs McK told me that the PM is furious about Winston's speech at the Guildhall. That he did not know what he was going to say, and that he was astonished. [. . .]

19 December   Called to see LG at Downing Street. [. . .] I enquired what had been done concerning the Navy estimates.

LG: They have cornered Winston.

R: What line did McKenna take?

LG: He has acted very cleverly.

R: I suppose that he took no active part, but supplied other people with the powder and shot in the shape of technical information?

LG: Yes (with emphasis). . . . His technical information has been very useful.

20 December   Played with Masterman who denies that he is about to enter the Cabinet. He says there is no vacancy. [. . .] He confirms what LG told me regarding the Naval estimates. [. . .]

January–July 1914

(Henceforth chapter divisions are dictated less by the calendar than by great events.) The battle over the Navy estimates continued for several weeks into the new year. Churchill refused to make any cuts and a section of the Cabinet undertook to humble him in hopes of forcing his resignation. Lloyd George chose this moment to launch a peace offensive via the *Daily Chronicle*, with the twofold purpose of reasserting his claim to lead the Radicals and at the same time defeating Churchill's pretensions. Asquith, however, was fully committed to the expenditure on the Navy, and Churchill survived with only minimal damage to his programme. During these weeks while the Cabinet was engrossed with its most difficult member, Riddell had frequent and lengthy conversations with Lloyd George and Churchill, and also with Reginald McKenna and Charles Masterman. From them and others we learn something of the intense feelings generated by this issue.

With the new session of Parliament the problem of Ireland eclipsed other considerations. The diaries add little to our knowledge of events from the 'mutiny' at the Curragh in March to the failure of the Buckingham Palace Conference in late July. One incident, not noted in the latest biography of Lloyd George, nevertheless is of some interest as a harbinger of things to come. The Chancellor of the Exchequer was making heavy weather of the 1914 budget and his prestige with the Liberal Parliamentary Party had declined appreciably. On the occasion of the Lord Mayor's annual banquet to the Bankers of London, Lloyd George had a secret meeting with Lord Northcliffe, whose brother Lord Rothermere acted as go-between. Riddell witnessed the preliminaries to this unusual conclave and concluded that Lloyd George was anxious to make a pact with Northcliffe, or at least square him over the Irish question.

On the eve of war we find Riddell about to undertake a new role which would enhance his importance and give him fresh opportunities to acquire material for his journal. During the war and post-war years he was to be heavily occupied with liaison work between Fleet Street and civil and military authorities.

6 January   Things are in a critical position with the Government. The public suspect, but do not know, the truth. The interview with LG on the Navy published in the *Daily Chronicle*[1] has caused a great sensation. It is regarded by those in the know as a very unnecessary and indiscreet utterance. It is obviously provocative to Winston, who had declined to make any statement 'upon a subject which is being considered by the Cabinet'. [. . .] I hear there was a rather a sharp passage at the last Cabinet between Winston and LG; that the former left without speaking to LG, and that the result is a breach between the two. Until recently LG has been strongly in favour of keeping Winston in the Cabinet. He has often said so to me. Masterman says that when on an Admiralty yacht in the summer, LG said to the PM: 'It pays the Liberal Party to spend an extra £2,000,000 per annum on the Navy to keep Winston.' And the PM replied, 'Do you really think it is worth it?' [. . .]

I had a long talk with McKenna. He takes a gloomy view of the situation, although he has come out on top. He says that the Government may break up on the question of the Navy estimates. He strongly disapproves of LG's interview. He says that Winston has acted very indiscreetly and has managed things badly, but that he has been allowed to go on and make arrangements which have been negatived at the last moment. LG should have taken the question of the estimates in hand months ago, instead of which he took no step until he was forced to do so by his colleagues. Simon and Runciman returned from the North with serious accounts of the state of feeling regarding the Estimates. The PM also received representations from other quarters, with the result he and most of his colleagues put LG in such a position that he was compelled to tackle Winston. [. . .]

McKenna thinks that Winston must resign. Masterman told me today that Sir Ernest Cassell had promised to give him a partnership if he went out of office. This would provide Winston with an income. He (Masterman) also says that Winston wants to go out over Ulster, not the Navy. He spoke of a conversation between Winston and LG, at which he was present, when Winston said, 'You understand that if a shot is fired I shall go out.' LG said, 'Don't be a fool. If we offer reasonable concessions and they won't accept them, you could not reasonably take a course which would be highly prejudicial to yourself and the Government.' [. . .]

9 January   Mrs McKenna told me that Asquith dined with them last night. He is very worried, and says he will require a rest cure. He does not mind Winston resigning so much, but Sir Edward Grey is furious regarding LG's interview in the *Daily Chronicle* and refuses to be placated.

16 January McKenna and his wife dined with us.

He says position very serious. He dined with Winston last night. He says Winston has shown his fangs and they are pretty big fangs. He has cornered the PM, who is committed up to the hilt to all that Winston has done. He has it all down, chapter and verse. McK fears that LG will have to change his attitude, as he also is committed. [. . .]

17 January Golfed with LG. One of the most important and interesting meetings I have had with him. I asked him about the now famous *Daily Chronicle* interview.

He said, 'It contained nothing I have not said before, but, as I have often seen, at one time a statement attracts no attention, while at another the same statement sets the whole world agog.'

Riddell: I suppose you gave the interview without premeditation – probably out of good nature, to help some poor reporter?

LG: That was just what took place. Naylor, a reporter on the *DC*, came to Criccieth and asked me for an interview. He called three times, and at last I gave him something. . . . (Then suddenly looking at me fixedly.) Well, I shall go. I shall not give way.

R: What? You don't mean to say you intend to resign?

LG: Yes, that's what I mean. I am backward in entering upon a quarrel. It was long before I decided to take up my present position, but having entered upon the controversy, I shall pursue my course. Samuel, Runciman and Co., who started the controversy, will probably back out, but I shall not. The PM must choose between Winston and me. Our meeting (LG and Winston) yesterday was quite friendly. Winston began perorating, but I stopped him and said, 'Let us deal with facts.' We came to no agreement. None seems possible. What the issue will be, I don't know. It looks as if either Winston or I will have to go. [. . .] Winston has acted disgracefully. We now ascertain for the first time that he has exceeded the estimates by no less than £5,000,000. He has been guilty of gross negligence and extravagance. [. . .]

[LG. continued:] Winston has acted like an extravagant boy placed in possession of a banking account for the first time. [. . .] I think he wants to get back to the Tory party again. He would no doubt like to form a central party which he would lead, and which would eventually become one of the two great parties. He would also like to see me lead a democratic party.

Mrs Asquith said a clever thing about him recently in a letter. She wrote, 'Winston is staying near here, but I hope he won't come over. He has a noisy mind, which would be too much just now for my poor nerves!' [. . .]

We talked of LG's future if he resigned. I said, 'You need not worry. I will guarantee to get you £1,500 per annum for your literary work.' This seemed to reassure him. [. . .]

18 January   Golfed with Winston. [. . .] As we drove from the Admiralty, he said, 'I don't know how long I shall be here. The position is very acute. I cannot make further economies. I cannot go back on my public declarations, and I cannot pay the bill myself. LG has not acted well. He will find the Cabinet with me. The PM is committed to the expenditure up to the hilt. I can make no further concessions. I cannot agree to any concealment of the actual figures. [. . .] I think I know the English people. I think I have the flair. The old Cromwellian spirit still survives. I believe I am watched over. Think of the perils which I have escaped.' (LG believes the same about himself. If there is a row, it will be interesting to see which guardian angel is the stronger!) [. . .]

In the afternoon I played with McKenna, who said that perhaps the true policy of the Liberal Party should be to adopt Winston's estimates and remove him from the Admiralty as a guarantee for future economy. [. . .]

Later on talked with McK and Masterman, who both strongly commented on Winston's extravagance, Masterman saying that he would have been impeached in former days! They both agree that if LG resigns the result will be the break up of the Party.

23 January   Masterman says that the position is still acute, but that he thinks things will be settled. [. . .] He says that letters which LG has received from his wife and other Welsh people, urging him not to resign for the sake of the Welsh Disestablishment Bill, have been very great factors in the situation. The PM told LG that he would not go on without him and that if he intended to resign he would dissolve at once.[2] Masterman described the attitude of Simon and Samuel as being indecent, their one desire being to hound Winston out of the

Cabinet. He said, 'This is evident from their manner. They cannot conceal it.' He says that Winston has had a shock, as LG has intimated that the Cabinet may adopt his programme but throw him overboard. He had not reckoned on this contingency.

24 January Played with LG, Winston and Donald of the *Daily Chronicle*. LG and Winston in frequent conference. Both evidently much worried. We had tea with McKenna and Masterman and much talk about the estimates. The McKennas are to lunch with LG at Walton tomorrow. I drove home with them. McKenna says that LG will not make up his mind. But that he thinks LG and Winston have come to an arrangement, which may not be acceptable to some of their colleagues. McK told LG that this might place him (LG) in an unfortunate position, as the resignation of a minor member of the Cabinet might be disastrous. [. . .]

25 January Lunched with Mr and Mrs Winston. She told me that he was much worried and sleeping badly.[3] [. . .]

Winston told me that things are still in a serious position. He said, 'LG will not make up his mind to go with me. If he would, we could win easily. "The crew" have no stomach for a fight. I know them! They are a lot of cowards.'

Winston and I went to tea with LG at his house. They had a private talk in a separate room. Scott[4] of the *Manchester Guardian* had been lunching with LG. Scott is very bitter about the estimates. [. . .]

When driving home, Winston said, 'I am nearly at the end of my tether. I can't make David (LG) out. They can't get anyone to do the job better than me. But perhaps they want to get rid of me. I can make no more concessions. . . .'

As we drove into the Admiralty, I said, 'Well, you have one pull over your critics.' 'What is that?' he asked. I said, 'You are only thirty-nine years old!'

He laughed bitterly and said, 'Not too young to wreck a Government!' Previously he had said, 'LG is accustomed to deal with people who can be bluffed and frightened, but he will not bluff or frighten me! He says that some of the Cabinet will resign. Let them resign! What a nice position they will be in if they do.' [. . .]

Called on McKenna, who again referred to LG's inability to make up his mind. [. . .]

I said, 'LG is always for compromise.'

McK: Yes, the sort of compromise in which Winston will get all his own way. . . [5]

31 January   LG says the naval question is not yet settled. 'Winston [. . .] has used money which should have been applied to reduce the expenditure during succeeding years for other purposes. He has been very extravagant and has placed me in a false situation.' LG spoke very bitterly and it is evident that he feels very strongly on the subject. [. . .]

1 February   [. . .] It is evident that strong personal feelings and animosities are involved. The attacking party are out to humiliate Winston. . . .[6]

5 February   [. . .] LG told me that the Navy question was still unsettled and that Winston was becoming very impatient.

6 February   Telephoned Winston and begged him to be patient. Told him I was confident matters would be adjusted satisfactorily in the end. He said he was nearly at the end of his tether, but would do his utmost to abide the result with patience.

7 February   Played with LG, who said, 'Winston will have to give way. They now have their own committee. I have declined to join the hunt. Winston has, however, acted very[7] badly. . . .' LG spoke very strongly.
    Subsequently saw McKenna, who said, 'Winston will have to give way. We have broken with him.'

26 February   The Navy question has been settled. McKenna says, 'We have got off another £1,000,000.[8] We have made Winston give up his manoeuvres and he is to submit his speech to the Cabinet.' McK seemed quite pleased with the result.
    And so ends a great struggle. No resignations and no very drastic revision of the Estimates. What a world it is! Winston is in high spirits, and well he may be.

6 March   Played with LG. Full of the Irish question. He has been conducting the negotiations with the Irish Party. Asquith is to make his statement on Monday. I said, 'I hear you have adopted the principle of the referendum, and that each of the Ulster Counties is to have the option of exclusion from the Home Rule Bill.'

LG: [. . .] The PM is furious. He says that if any member of the Cabinet has made the disclosure he will have to go. [. . .]

Riddell: How is the PM?

LG: Worried, but he does not say much. [. . .] The PM's trouble is that he hates anything unpleasant or in the nature of a row. He hates an unpleasant interview. [. . .]

7 March [. . .] Talked with LG and Masterman concerning the Tories in the House.

LG: They are fools. When they have a good case they spoil it. They let me head them off in an absurd fashion. They rise in an extraordinary way. They make some interruption. I appear to get angry and retaliate. As a rule, they lose sight of the main issue and give me an opportunity of diverting the discussion to some personal question which is more or less irrelevant. The House loves a scene. As a matter of fact, I am rarely angry. In their own interest they ought to be gagged! [. . .]

15 March The Liberal Party are in fine fighting form. Robertson Nicoll told me that the Nonconformist Conference at Norwich was most enthusiastic in favour of the Government. He said, 'We are back again in 1906 so far as concerns the Dissenters.' [. . .]

22 March Great excitement regarding Ulster. Resignation of Army officers reported. [. . .] I asked Mrs McK[enna] how the King was acting. She said very well. He is all right now but at one time threatened to abdicate rather than sign the Home Rule Bill.

24 March A bomb has burst in the form of the extraordinary Seely memorandum. Tremendous excitement. The Radicals furious. Painful scene at the Cabinet when the PM lectured Seely on the enormity of his offence.

29 March [. . .] Long interview with Sir John French, who said that he would like me to state in the *News of the World* tomorrow that his resignation would not be withdrawn, and to give his version of the recent happenings. He added, 'There is no paper so widely read in the Army, and by doing this you will be performing a national service.' [. . .]

30 March   The PM has made the dramatic announcement that Seely, French and Ewart have resigned, and that he will become Minister for War. The Radicals are delighted, and regard this as an intimation that the PM intends to trounce the Army. I am confident that he proposes to do nothing of the sort. There are two opposing sections in the Cabinet [. . . who] hold different views as to recent events. On the one side Haldane, Morley, Grey and Harcourt, and on the other LG, Winston and McKenna. Had the PM appointed someone who was in sympathy with either side trouble would have resulted. He is trusted by both sides, and will do his utmost to avoid friction. He does not believe in a democratic Army, I am quite sure, and will not go further in that direction than is absolutely necessary. He is a crafty old dog.

24 April   [. . .] LG says [. . .] that the PM let Winston down badly last night and that Winston is very much upset. The PM when asked when he first heard of the movements of the Navy towards Ireland replied, 'On the morning of the 21st, and in the afternoon I countermanded the orders.' LG says the other side did not at first see the importance of this reply, but are now on the alert and the result will be to give a fresh impetus to the statements regarding the plot.

LG said, 'The PM ought not to have done this. I have been trying to make peace.' [. . .]

LG says that the Tories are mad with Winston. They think he has betrayed them. That in some way he has learned their secrets and has then made use of the information. There is no doubt they are very bitter against Winston just now.[9]

25 April   LG is in a great rage with Herbert Samuel, who yesterday made a speech in which he prophesied large subventions to the Local Authorities, thus forecasting the Budget. LG says this is a gross breach of confidence and that he has written a strong letter to Samuel. [. . .] LG described Samuel as a greedy, ambitious and grasping Jew with all the worst characteristics of his race. [. . .]

30 April   Spent the day with Seely, who made some surprising statements. He implied that he had been made a scapegoat. [. . .]

17 May   Golfed with LCJ and the McKennas. [. . .] McKenna evidently does not favour the Budget. He does not like the local subventions, and thinks the rating proposals complicated and unworkable. [. . .]

23 May Called to see LG at Walton. He thinks Masterman is certain to be defeated.[10] LG said that Masterman should have attacked the other side and particularly Northcliffe, who has made such a personal attack upon him. At night I telephoned the result to LG. (Masterman badly beaten.) He said he was not surprised and that it would be a severe blow to the Government. [. . .]

13 June Spent the day with LG, Masterman and Donald. Masterman says LG's Budget is unpopular and that he (LG) is in a nervous, troubled state. He did not seem so, however, and was full of fun and good humour. [. . .] He spoke much of Masterman, as did Donald also. LG says he is very unpopular in the House of Commons, that he is neglecting his work, drinking more than is good for him, and looking very unkempt and untidy.[11] [. . .] LG seemed pleased that [Theodore] Roosevelt[12] had asked that he should be invited to meet him. LG, however, expressed a poor opinion of Mr Roosevelt, but spoke highly of Woodrow Wilson.[13] [. . .]

20 June [. . .] We lunched with the McKennas and Masterman. Masterman says that the Budget is going badly and that LG is not pleased. [. . .]

23 June Had a talk with McKenna. (Yesterday the Government jettisoned a great part of the Budget proposals and reduced the income tax by 1*d*.) McK says that the whole thing has been a shocking muddle; that the Budget Committee knew nothing of LG's proposals until their meeting shortly before the introduction of the Budget; and that LG spoke for three hours explaining his scheme, which left no time for any discussion. The Bill as drawn was very complicated, many of its chief provisions being in the schedules. It would have required three months to pass it. LG talked of passing it in a week, which was absurd. The House of Commons is not in the mood for heavy, tedious Bills.

It was evident that McK was not sorry for what had happened. He has all along expressed himself in the same way. There can be no doubt that the Budget was an ill-digested production. LG is a wonderful man for drawing attention to abuses and creating an atmosphere, but his schemes for reform are too complicated. [. . .]

July [n.d.] Went to the Lord Mayor's Banquet to the Bankers. LG made the usual speech. After dinner an interesting incident occurred.

The Lord Mayor told me that LG and Northcliffe wanted to meet and that he was taking them upstairs to a private room. Then Rothermere (Northcliffe's brother) said that he was endeavouring to bring LG and Northcliffe together. Then LG told me that he wanted to see Northcliffe privately. Finally the two of them went upstairs to the Lord Mayor's room. LG evidently very eager for the interview, which I thought strange and imprudent. Evidently he wants to square N over the Irish question. This was on Thursday or Friday, I forget which. On Monday *The Times* and *Mail* came out with the exclusive statement of the conference called by the King. Where they got the news is not definitely known. Perhaps LG may have given N the hint. LG told Donald that N wanted to see him [LG], but it was quite obvious to me that the boot was on the other leg. On the Sunday I had a long talk with LG, who was very reticent as to what had taken place with Northcliffe. The Liberal papers are furious at *The Times* and *Mail* getting this information beforehand. They blame Asquith, who does not hesitate to express his contempt for the Liberal Press and is suspected of leanings to *The Times* as a *gentleman's paper*![14] [. . .]

LG says Balfour describes John Simon as a small man for a big job and a big man for a small job. Not a bad description. He has no breadth of view. The Conference[15] has broken down, as I thought it would. It was doomed to failure. Alec Murray has come on the scene again in some mysterious way. [. . .]

12 July   LG has had a bad week. His stock stands low with the party. The Budget has been a fiasco, and badly managed. He, however, seems in excellent spirits and full of fight. His courage and powers of endurance are wonderful. He must possess a wonderful nervous system. [. . .]

26 July   This evening I telephoned to LG informing him of the Dublin Riots and that several people had been killed by the military. He was much distressed, and said the incident would cause fresh and serious complications. He spoke of the poignant situation. He said that Austria had made demands which no self-respecting nation could comply with, and that such demands, when addressed by a great nation to a small one, were in the nature of bullying threats. He said the situation was serious, but that he thought there would be peace – in fact, he thought so very strongly.

27 July Suddenly called to the War Office to a meeting of the Admiralty, War Office and Press Committee. Most of the members were away from home. Graham Greene,[16] the Secretary of the Admiralty, in the chair. Present: Sir Reginald Brade,[17] Col. Macdonough,[18] H. C. Robbins (representing his father, who was abroad) and myself.

Graham Greene in a halting hesitating sort of way apprised us that the continental situation was becoming very serious. He said that it might be necessary to move troops and ships, that the authorities were anxious to confer with the Committee as to the best method of doing this secretly. After a short conversation I drafted a letter to the Press, writing it out on a stray sheet of paper I found on the table. This was agreed to and issued by Robbins in the name of the Committee, and was the first official intimation to the Press of the impending war. The result was remarkable. No information was divulged, and the Germans were unacquainted with what was being done.[19]

31 July [. . .] LG said, 'I am fighting hard for peace. All the bankers and commercial people are begging us not to intervene. The Governor of the Bank of England said to me with tears in his eyes, "Keep us out of it. We shall all be ruined if we are dragged in!"'

August 1914–May 1915

With the coming of war Riddell's diaries gain considerably in interest. Now he had new opportunities to meet a wider range of important persons and add them to his canvas. He continued to see Lloyd George frequently and was able to assess his transformation from man of peace to man of war. There were occasional but useful conversations with Churchill, McKenna, Reading and Masterman, and soon he would make the acquaintance of A. J. Balfour, a fascinating figure to contemporaries. But it was Riddell's liaison work between Fleet Street and Westminster that opened new doors and widened his perspective. He had a hand at the birth of the Press Bureau, the body charged with the task of ensuring that newspapers did not print information about the Army and Navy which might prove useful to the enemy. As well he became an important member of the Admiralty, War Office and Press Committee, whilst at the same time continuing to be vice-chairman of the Newspaper Proprietors' Association. Few outside the Cabinet and service chiefs had quite the same opportunity to see as much and hear as much.

It must be stated that some of the more colourful entries in the early pages of the *War Diary* do not appear in the manuscript, and therefore were a touch of gloss added later. But the loss of one or two good anecdotes is more than offset by the discovery of material which Riddell felt obliged to excise from his published work. There is, for example, a much fuller account of the hours immediately before and after Lloyd George's famous Queen's Hall speech of 19 September 1914. And we learn something more of the reasons for F. E. Smith's unrelenting hatred of the editor of *The Times*, Geoffrey Robinson. The decline of Churchill in the estimation of his colleagues is a recurring theme, and McKenna emerges looking rather worse than before. Some of the more important entries for these last few months of Liberal government concern the Press censorship question, since Riddell had a good vantage point to study the position adopted by Lord Kitchener at the War Office and Churchill at the Admiralty. Belated credit is given to F. E. Smith's successor as Press Censor, Sir Stanley Buckmaster, who struggled manfully to keep the Press from being muzzled by Kitchener and Churchill, whilst at the same time trying to resist Northcliffe's wild lunges.

By March and April 1915 Riddell senses that a big blow-up is fast approaching, and his conversations with Lloyd George, Churchill, Kitchener and Northcliffe have added piquancy. He was also fortunate at this time in being on fairly close terms with the Permanent Secretary at the War Office, Sir Reginald Brade.

2 August [. . .] Lloyd George, Sir John Simon, Masterman, and Ramsay MacDonald came to dinner at 20 Queen Anne's Gate.[1] LG said he had been at work for eighteen hours, but he seemed wonderfully fresh. I gathered that John Burns had practically resigned, and that Sir John Simon, Beauchamp,[2] Morley, and Mackinnon Wood[3] were considering the advisability of doing so. [. . .]

We had a long discussion regarding the rights and wrongs of the situation. LG [. . .] spoke very strongly regarding the observance of Belgian neutrality. Ramsay MacDonald also agreed that if Belgian neutrality was infringed, this country would be justified in declaring war upon Germany. He said that he and the Labour Party would resolutely oppose intervention on any other grounds. LG strongly insisted upon the danger of aggrandising Russia and upon the future problems which would arise if Russia and France were successful. I said, 'Let the future take care of itself. We have got to think about the present. How shall we feel if we see France overrun and annihilated by Germany?' To this LG replied, 'How will you feel if you see Germany overrun and annihilated by Russia?' [. . .]

Sir John Simon then began to talk about 'precedents', just like a lawyer. 'We have always been wrong when we have intervened. Look at the Crimea. The Triple Entente was a terrible mistake. Why should we support a country like Russia?' [. . .]

When LG came to dinner at night he made some reference as to what was going to be done tomorrow. He said, 'We intend' . . . and then he said, 'that is, if we are governing the country tomorrow, which is very doubtful.' [. . . I said] that if Grey resigns, the country will be horror-stricken. Everyone trusts him.[4]

3 August [. . .] I went off to Hampstead to see Robertson Nicoll and had a long talk with him on the situation. When I saw him last Wednesday, he was about to get the Free Churches to prepare a memorial to the Government against intervention and supporting

Russia. I fully explained the situation to Nicoll. [. . .] Before I left he told me that he thought we had no alternative but to support France, and that we must all stand together and sink differences of opinion. I wrote a note to Masterman saying what Nicoll had told me and suggested that he should show it to LG, which he did with considerable effect. [. . .]

LG said that the action of Germany regarding Belgium had made his decision quite clear, and that he could now support Grey without any hesitation. Burns and Morley have both resigned. Simon is on the fence.

I told LG that if he had resigned he would have inflicted a terrible blow on the country, as it was absolutely necessary that we should all stand together. [. . .]

6 August   Went to dinner at the Other Club in the evening. The first dinner we have had since Marconi days – a remarkable gathering. Kitchener in the chair with Winston opposite to him. A very full attendance. I sat between F. E. Smith and Bonar Law. [. . .]

F. E. Smith has been appointed to supervise matter to be given out to the Press. I had a long talk with him and Kitchener on the subject, and they asked me to see them tomorrow at the War Office.[5]

7 August   [. . .] Called to see LG. Congratulated him on his speeches in the House. [. . .]

Met Seely going into the War Office, and had a long interview with Kitchener, Seely, F. E. Smith and Sir Reginald Brade, secretary of the WO, regarding Press censorship arrangements. Indicated lines on which I thought the Bureau should be organised, and arranged to convene a meeting of newspapers to discuss the matter.

My proposals were confirmed at the meeting, and later in the day I had another interview with Sir Reginald Brade and Mr Robbins of the Press Association, when the circulars were finally drafted embodying the arrangements which had been made.

When discussing with Kitchener this morning the things to be published, he said, 'We must make the English people understand that we are at war, and that war is not pap. At the present moment they do not understand the situation. They ought to act as if we were at war, and give up playing and watching games. War is the game at the moment, and as I have said, war is not pap.'[6]

9 August   [. . .] LG said that the change of opinion during the week had been amazing. On Saturday, 1 August, just before going out to dinner, he had received a letter from Robertson Nicoll saying that he and the Free Churches would strongly oppose any war. LG did not put his dress clothes on again until Friday last, 7 August. When he put his hand into his pocket he found Nicoll's letter. He told his secretary to attach the letter to Nicoll's article in this week's *British Weekly* written on Wednesday, the 5th, in which he strongly supported the war. [. . .]

15 August [. . .] played golf with McKenna. [. . .]

McK: Winston is clever but not really good. Not a man of action. He talks well but has never done anything big. Now he is fighting with my ships – the ships he endeavoured to prevent me from building. He it was who attacked my naval programme so bitterly, and did his best to hound me out of the Admiralty. What a comedy it all is! [. . .]

25 August[7] I think   Spent the evening at LG's, Downing St. Present: LG, the Chief Justice and Attorney-General (Simon). My purpose was to get LG to make a speech explaining the reasons why we were at war and appealing to the patriotism of the people. He said that he did not feel like speaking and expressed himself strongly regarding the conduct of the French generals. . . . I, however, continued to press my point and think he may reconsider his decision.

We had a long talk regarding the war. Simon much to my surprise is still very anti-war, peace at any price. He spoke strongly to this effect. LG made a fine little speech on our duty to small nations, [. . .] concluding, 'I would rather see the British Empire bite the dust than allow poor little Belgium to be crushed by this hectoring bully!' Simon did not like it. He was all against him. [. . .]

The Press is furious regarding the censorship arrangements. The Cable Censor's department is chiefly responsible. It has been created hastily and is officered by half-pay officers, many being of an antiquated type. I am carrying on a campaign for reform and hope to get fresh arrangements made. There has been a great row in the Cabinet, so I am told, regarding suppression of news and delay in publication. Kitchener cannot understand that he is working in a democratic country. He rather thinks that he is in Egypt where the Press is represented by a dozen mangy newspaper correspondents whom he can throw into the Nile if they object to the way in which they are treated. This is F. E. Smith's statement, not mine.

F.E. has had a bad fall regarding an alarmist dispatch which he allowed *The Times* and *W Dispatch* to publish. It turned out to have been a full appreciation. Unfortunately F.E. added words of his own and wrote what he said was a private letter to the editor. When the dispatch was challenged by the PM in the H of C, the *Daily Mail* published the letter by way of justification. F.E. is furious. He says that the editor of *The Times* saw him before he (Smith) made his statement in the House when he exculpated *The Times*. [. . .]

Smith says he has been grossly betrayed and vows vengeance. Northcliffe is a dirty dog. He cannot be trusted. No doubt F.E. was endeavouring to curry favour with him so he has himself to blame. His action was most ill-advised and has caused widespread remark and criticism.[8]

11 September   Having become on friendly terms with Arthur Balfour at meetings of the National Relief Committee, invited him to dinner to meet Robertson Nicoll. Very interesting conversation [about books and speeches]. [. . .]

18 September   LG is to make his big speech tomorrow. We had tea together and a long talk. He said that he was miserable and inert. His brain would not work. [. . .]

19 September   [. . . LG] lunched with me at Queen Anne's Gate. The meeting was at 3 o'clock in the afternoon.[9] He was terribly nervous, feeling, he said, as if he were about to be executed. It was a curious sight to see him lying on the sofa, yawning and stretching himself in a state of high nervous excitement, almost trembling. He spoke well and did not give any sign of perturbation, except [. . .] that his eyes had a peculiar appearance. They looked like two smouldering furnaces. Alec Murray had lunch with us and came to the meeting – evidently very nervous of reappearing in public.[10] A seat had been reserved for him next to LG. Murray took it somewhat reluctantly, so that LG appeared with Murray on his right [. . .] and Rufus Isaacs [on his left, next to the chairman], so that he looked something like our Lord on the Cross between the two thieves. I don't think LG was very pleased. [. . .]

After the meeting we went to tea with the LCJ and dined in the evening with Alec Murray. An interesting party – Crewe, Winston, Garvin, Neil Primrose, Rothermere (Northcliffe's brother), F. E. Smith and the Duke of Marlborough.[11] Much amusing talk, but most amusing of all Rothermere's observations on *The Times'* article which gave rise to the censorship dispute. He said to F. E. Smith, 'You did a patriotic thing to pass that article. I know why you passed it. You wanted to stimulate recruiting.

F.E.: I passed it because I believed it to be true, and that it was in the public interest that it should be published.

Rothermere: But it did not matter whether it was true or not. The object was to get recruits, and you were justified in passing any article, true or untrue, which would have the result.

This disclosure of the Harmsworth ethics evidently caused no little surprise amongst the uninitiated. Rothermere told me that Northcliffe was in an excited state, and that he (N) thinks he is ruined for the time being. There is evidently no love lost between the brothers. R said in effect that N is suffering badly from a swollen head and that he is quite unreliable. The more friendly he is with you, the more likelihood there is that he will suddenly become your violent critic and possibly enemy. [. . .]

21 September LG, Mrs LG, Megan, Masterman and I dined at the Carlton. [. . .] Big disaster in the North Sea just announced.[12] [LG] says he cannot trust Winston – never knows what he may be up to, and afraid to leave town for long for fear Winston may bring forward some dangerous plan. [. . .]

I have seen a good deal of McKenna lately. He hates Winston like poison and cannot conceal his feelings. [. . .]

2 October Received letter today [. . .] regarding output of American munition factories which the Germans are trying to purchase. Showed this to LG, who said he must read it to the Cabinet, where he had already raised the question, which he said was of grave importance. He says the arrangements at the War Office are very bad.

10 October A remarkable conversation.[13] Spent the day with LG, the LC Justice, Mr and Mrs McKenna, Masterman, Donald and Le Bas.[14] At tea we had a remarkable conversation. Antwerp fell yesterday. [. . .] I give the conversation as it occurred. Donald was not at tea.

LG: Our greatest danger is incompetent English junkers. Winston is becoming a great danger. [. . .]

McK: All Winston's great excursions have been most unfortunate. The Antwerp business is a repetition of Sidney Street.

LG: Yes, or the railway strike all over again. [. . .] He makes me very uneasy. His interference with land operations, or for that matter with naval operations, is all wrong. [. . .] Winston is like a torpedo. The first you hear of his doings is when you hear the swish of the torpedo dashing through the water. [. . .]

(I met Buckmaster yesterday. I said, 'How are you getting on?' He replied, 'It is an awful job. How would you like to control an office staffed by men whom you have not appointed, whom you cannot dismiss, and most of whom have been appointed in order to find them jobs at £300 or £400 per annum?'[. . .])

13 October   More about armaments. LG says Kitchener is a big man. He does not resent advice and criticism. Haily and Von Donop[15] who are at the head of the Ordnance know all about guns, but have no wide view of a situation. Already LG has got orders for guns largely increased. There has been no difficulty. The gun-making firms readily took the orders. Von Donop and Haily seemed surprised that they could have any money they required. LG said to them: 'What are ten, twenty, or thirty millions when the British Empire is at stake? This is an artillery war. We must have every gun we can lay hands upon. We are sadly deficient in guns now. You have never asked for more money.' [. . .]

22 October   Violent attacks on Winston Churchill in the *Morning Post*, *The Times* and *Daily Mail*. [. . .] Rang Winston up and said that I wanted to see him. He said, 'Come round now.' This was at 10.30 a.m. I went at 11. Ushered into his bedroom. Found him dressing – in fact just pulling on his underclothes (pink silk as before). Three telephones at his bedside. [. . .]

Winston: [. . .] I have no wish to stay if the Cabinet wish me to go. I would rather be at the Front. [. . .] What do you think about Prince Louis?

R: The feeling is very strong against him.[16] The public says that being a German he must either be false to his nationality or to his employers. [. . .]

Winston: It is a scandalous injustice. [. . .]

25 October   Dined at Masterman's at Walton Health. LG there also. Talked a lot about the war. LG said that Elizabeth Asquith had described Kitchener as 'a big poster' – i.e. 'a large advertisement'.

LG: I think she is right. He is a big man, but he does not understand

English life; and whatever he may have done in the past, he pays no attention to details and does not properly control his staff. He is just a big figurehead. The [War] Office is terribly incompetent. [. . .]

LG and I drove home together. On the way we talked of the Navy. LG said, 'Winston is really dangerous. The PM should speak to him.'

28 October [. . .] A hurriedly convened meeting of the Admiralty, War Office and Press Committee was held today when the Committee were asked to assist in suppressing the information [re. sinking of *Audacious*]. The crew have been landed and the disaster must be well known. I therefore criticised the withholding of the information, saying that the public would thereby be rendered suspicious and unduly apprehensive when the news was disclosed. I also said that the Press is in an irritable and dissatisfied state, and that it was just as well that this be understood by the official members of the Committee. This statement seemed to cause some surprise, except on the part of the Solicitor-General (the Censor), who expressed his agreement. [. . .]

In the evening Robertson Nicoll, LG, McKenna, and Masterman to dinner. LG arrived late. He told me that he had had a row with Kitchener regarding the recruitment arrangements in connection with the Welsh Army Corps, which are notoriously bad, and also in reference to the treatment of Dissenters who are joining the Army. In many recruiting centres they are being insulted. LG looked flushed and rather worried. [. . .]

We had a long chat as to the desirability of suppressing the news of the *Audacious*. LG was strongly opposed to it. He said he had spoken against it in the Cabinet. McKenna was strongly in favour. [. . .]

29 October Great outcry against McKenna for not arresting the Germans.[17] Met him in Parliament Street and walked home with him. He says he is not responsible and that the War Office are at fault. He wants to arrest, but the War Office, whose duty it is to take charge of them, cannot find the necessary accommodation. [. . .] Personally [he added] I am indifferent to any attacks from the Harmsworth papers. I know just what they are worth. The War Office arrangements are quite inadequate. [. . .]

31 October Prince Louis of Battenberg has resigned, as he should have done weeks ago. Fisher is to take his place. McKenna says this will make the King furious, as he hates Fisher. When Fisher retired the King never wrote to him. [. . .] McKenna says he doubts whether Fisher will stand the strain for more than six months. He is considerably over seventy.

LG full of his interview with Kitchener. He greeted me with: 'Look here! Kitchener is a big man. Nothing small and petty about him. Yesterday he sent for me. He said, "I have thought over what you said. There is a good deal of justification for these complaints. Tell me exactly what you want." I said, "That, that, that, and that!" K wrote an appropriate order against each item. He really acted extraordinarily well.' [. . .]

5 November   McKenna, Lord Reading, and Sir William Lever[18] to dinner. McK said that Fisher had found things in an unsatisfactory state at the Admiralty. [. . .]

Rufus met Morley today. R says that he is very sore – feels that he had been jockeyed out of the Government. He is particularly angry with Harcourt and Simon. He thinks they sold him.

Buckmaster tells me that he is heading for a row with Northcliffe, who is becoming more and more impertinent. He has now written demanding an explanation in regard to some matter from Buckmaster and saying that in default he will take such steps as he is advised. Buckmaster is furious. He says he can prove that Northcliffe induced the American papers to attack the Censor so that he (N) may quote their comments in *The Times*. [. . .]

7 November   LG, the McKennas, Masterman, Donald and Gilbert Parker.[19] Devil of a row at the Cabinet yesterday regarding the Press Bureau. Buckmaster attended and addressed them. LG and McK say that Kitchener and Winston treated him very badly, but that he acted like a gentleman. All the other members of the Cabinet with him. [. . .] Apparently Buckmaster's refusal to suppress criticism has annoyed Winston, who, LG says, wants to abolish the Press Bureau and resort to the former practice of censoring Army news at the War Office and naval news at the Admiralty. LG said to me privately, 'You know what that would mean. The publication of what suited Kitchener and Winston and nothing more.' [. . .]

LG is not very keen about attacking the Harmsworth crowd. There is no doubt some sort of understanding between him and Northcliffe, who did a clever thing in not attacking LG about the Marconi business. Then again I have little doubt that LG gave *The Times* the information as to the Home Rule Conference. I have not forgotten the secret meeting at the Mansion House on the night of the Bankers' Dinner.[. . .]

10 November [. . .] A jolly evening at Montagu's. LG, the LCJ, Illingworth, Buckmaster, Bonham Carter[20] (the PM's secretary), Montagu and self. Much talk about the delinquencies of *The Times*. Buckmaster furious. Says that the Cabinet are not supporting him, and that Kitchener and Winston are afraid to court-martial Northcliffe. The Government Departments will persist in showing preference to *The Times*. Bonham Carter says the PM has issued a notice to the Departments warning them to refrain from this practice. [. . .]

LG said that he intended to say some sharp things about the War Office in his speech on Tuesday. He said, 'They are wanted.' McK agreed that they were. [. . .]

16 November The *Pall Mall* and *Observer* have been sold for £100,000 —purchase to be completed in January. The purchaser (Gardner Sinclair, a Scotch printer) showed me a letter from Benson, the banker, offering him £150,000 for the property. A singular transaction.[21]

19 November [. . .] Brade says that K is showing signs of age. He is not the man he was when the war started. The strain has told on him. [. . .] Brade says that he alone was responsible for the idea of an extra half-million men. (LG, McKenna, and others ascribe this to Asquith.)

20 November The Defence of the Realm Acts are being consolidated. The drastic and unique provisions of this legislation have not attracted the attention they deserve. The legislation has taken place so rapidly that the measures have not been properly discussed. The press have been singularly ill-informed and lacking in criticism regarding a law which wipes out Magna Carta, the Bill of Rights, etc, in a few lines. We have got some alterations made, but trial by court martial still stands. A very dangerous innovation. [. . .]

LG told me a few days ago that he had said to Bonar Law that McK was really a nice and able man, but Bonar Law would not have it and replied, 'We all dislike him more than anyone in the Cabinet.' This is all due to his manner. [. . .]

22 November Spent the evening with LG at Walton. He says Grey is very worn out. [. . .] LG added, 'He feels that if things were to go wrong, he would be responsible for the downfall of the British Empire. . . . The old PM does less work that any of us. He has not turned a hair. He is as strong as a horse!'[. . .]

The *Daily Chronicle* has been criticising him [LG] this week. He was evidently annoyed and spoke to Donald on the subject. [. . .]

28 November   Drove with the LCJ to Walton. Horrible day. Called on LG. [. . .]

I told LG and the Chief [Reading] of my meeting with Northcliffe and of his prophecy concerning the war. LG responded that apart from his own business Northcliffe had the worst judgment of any man he knew. [. . .]

We talked of the Defence of the Realm Act. Both LG and the Chief thought this sort of legislation very dangerous and subversive of the best British traditions – an opinion shared by Halsbury,[22] Loreburn, and others. The naval and military authorities are supreme. There is no appeal against them.

6 December   Dined with LG at his house at Walton. [. . .] He does not think much of Sir John French as a strategist. No doubt we have been defeated in the North. Our turning movement has been unsuccessful. [. . .]

LG says Buckmaster is to give up the Censorship. Apparently he and Winston have quarrelled. Winston has proposed Alec Murray. A bad suggestion. [. . .] This situation is evidently the result of the state of feeling between McKenna and Winston. McK wrested the Censorship from the Admiralty and War Office. Now they (or the Admiralty) are fighting to recover it. I suppose that Buckmaster has declined to suppress the criticism of the Navy. The articles in the *Morning Post*, etc. There is evidently a bitter feeling. Buckmaster has really done his job well and is being badly treated. [. . .] He gets all the opprobrium due to the suppression of the news by the Admiralty and War Office, who secretly attack him because he will not suppress criticism and act entirely as their tool. [. . .]

20 December   [. . .] Dined with LG, Mrs LG, and Megan at Walton. [. . .]

Some day [said LG] I will show you (GAR) a paper which I dictated in 1910 at the time of the conference.[23] I thought I had lost it, but old

Sharp at the Treasury had a copy. Had my proposals been adopted, we should have had an army of 1,500,000 men and 1,500,000 rifles. I proposed the Swiss plan. I also proposed to deal with Education, Insurance, Home Rule, the Land, the Drink Question. [. . .] Balfour, Bonar Law, Lansdowne[24] and F. E. Smith were all in favour of my scheme. So were Asquith, Grey, and Birrell. [. . .] Winston of course agreed. He would have done anything to get the other side with us. Balfour at the last moment was afraid of splitting his party. [. . .] Balfour asked me if I would stand out of the Government if he did. I said, yes, I would. Asquith, however, declined to go on without me. He was afraid. At that time I was very strong. The suggestion was that Balfour and I should stand out to balance each other, but that we should support the Government. I suppose Asquith thought the arrangement would break down. I said to Balfour, 'Let us abolish all party controversies for ten years. Let us try to reorganise our national life. Let us endeavour to get something done and done well. After ten years the country will have had enough of us, but we shall have accomplished something. As things are now reforms are difficult.' [. . .]

LG said the PM had been very disappointed that the Navy had not sunk the German ships at Scarborough. He was fully convinced they would. [. . .]

21 December　Lunched with the McKennas. McK very sarcastic about the Navy. Says it was a scandal that the Germans escaped and that the raid was permitted. He cannot understand Fisher. Thinks Winston and he were manoeuvring for a spectacular battle on old-fashioned lines. McK says that we knew on Wednesday that the raid was impending. We might have stopped it. Winston assured the PM that the German ships would be sunk. In the Cabinet his only excuse was that the enemy got away in the fog. [. . .]

1915

2 January　Played and lunched with LG who told me that he had been attending several meetings with Winston and Kitchener at the War Office to discuss various questions relating to the War. He said, 'I think Kitchener likes to have me there as a set-off against Winston. He feels that he requires protection against his eloquence.' LG also told me he was dissatisfied with the progress of the war in the West and was drawing up a memorandum on the subject, which he would circulate amongst his colleagues. He said, 'We really have not much brains at the head of our army in France. General French is a good cavalry leader, but he is not a great strategist or tactician. We are making no progress, and I think the whole situation requires consideration.' [. . .]

4 January   Called to see Winston at the Admiralty. [. . .]

We talked about the war in France. I said, 'I don't think we have any very great generals there. I mean in the army. We have not done very well. Our men have been very brave, but we have not displayed any great skill. We took on the protection of a longer line than we could hold, and consequently lost an enormous number of men.' [. . .]

Winston (hurriedly): 'We were bound to do that or the Germans would have got to Calais.' He spoke so anxiously that it seemed as if he had been partly responsible for the policy. [. . .]

14 January   The McKennas have been staying with the PM at Walmer Castle over the week-end. Mrs McK told me that the PM was in a holiday mood and would not discuss business. [. . .]

Much talk about Northcliffe. I hear on good authority that N is very nervous. He has come badly out of his contest with the *Daily News* arising out of his pretentious pamphlet 'Scaremongering', in which he alleges that the *Daily Mail* foretold the war. To use LG's recent simile, he thought he was picking up a rabbit and found it was a hedgehog. The *Daily News* have retaliated and proved him to be a dishonest liar. [. . .] He is a journalistic monomaniac. [. . .]

17 January   [. . .] LG again represented that he thinks Kitchener a big man and the best for the job. He says K has shown more foresight than any of the other generals. He foresaw that the Germans would take the road which they did take. [. . .]

LG says French has gone back happy and well satisfied. They all treated him very nicely and his confidence was re-established. He had been very suspicious of Kitchener. LG believes that this is due in a great measure to Wilson,[25] who is on French's Staff, who (so Freddie Guest[26] told LG) informed French that when K was in France he had asked the French Generals whether they would like a change in the highest command. LG says that he does not believe K said anything of the sort. If he did, he would not have done so in Wilson's presence, as

Wilson alleged. LG says that Wilson has a clever but wicked face. He does not believe that K wants to go to France. He does not think French a great general, and was much impressed by the fact that when here he seemed to have no plan of action. He thinks that this is a time when the Prime Minister should endeavour to bring about more homogeneity of action between the Departments. The War Office and the Admiralty, etc. The PM is unrivalled in giving accurate and speedy decisions on matters submitted to him, but he has not got the art of probing into things for himself and cleansing and restoring weak places. [. . .]

29 January   Gulland[27] has been appointed Chief Whip. No one seems very pleased. He is not an impressive or attractive person. [. . .] Masterman has had to send in his resignation. Macnamara[28] has been offered the position, but declined unless he could remain at the Admiralty. [. . .] From his own point of view I have no doubt he has done the wrong thing. This is the third time he has missed his chance. Missing chances is dangerous in the greedy game of politics. LG and others describe his conduct as 'heroic'! [. . .]

Called to see LG at Downing Street. I said, 'Well, how is the Bankers' pet?' (The Bankers have been larding him with praise at their annual meetings. One said he ought to be made a Duke!) [. . .]

Donald told me a curious story about the Haldane controversy. The *Daily Express, Globe,* and other papers have been full of bitter attacks on Haldane, who is designated incompetent and pro-German. Donald has published a series of effulgent articles on the other side. On Thursday, Sir George Arthur,[29] one of Kitchener's private secretaries, arrived at the *Daily Chronicle* office. He said that he had noticed that the *Daily Chronicle* was about to publish the articles in pamphlet form, that Lord Kitchener and Sir Edward Grey thought it undesirable to continue the controversy, and that Lord K would be glad if Donald would stop the publication of the pamphlet. Arthur said he had been to the *Express,* who were willing to stop, but that he feared that the pamphlet would start them again. Donald said he could give no such undertaking, and that if the *Express* renewed their attacks he should go for *Herr* Blumenfeld, the editor, who is an American Jew, Donald says, of German origin. Arthur is alleged to have then 'shut up'. Donald showed me a letter from Haldane thanking him for the articles and asking for fifty copies of the pamphlet, so apparently he does not share in the desire for suppression. The question is, did Arthur make the visit on his own initiative, or was he sent by Kitchener, and did Grey approve? [. . .]

30 January   Golfed with LG. He is going to Paris on Monday to attend a financial conference of the Allies. Montagu is to accompany him. Also Professor Keynes,[30] a professor of political economy whom he has engaged at the Treasury. [. . .]

3 February   Lunched at the McKennas to meet Lord Fisher. [. . .] Long and interesting talk with Fisher, who drove me to the Admiralty. [. . .He said]: '[. . .] This war requires one man to manage it. There is no one to keep the threads together. There is no proper cohesion between the different departments. Asquith is good at exposition, but *he is as slow as a slug and as timid as a louse*'[sic][31]. [. . .]

7 February   Lloyd George back from Paris. He telephoned asking me to lunch at Walton. He says that the Conference was most successful, not only from a financial standpoint, but in other respects. [. . .] Prof. Keynes, the Professor of Political Economy, who accompanied LG, was not a success and he [LG] gave up taking him to the conferences. [. . .]

LG visited General French, who is looking well. He also saw Robertson, who he says is the biggest soldier he has met except Kitchener. [. . .]

LG said that he had been so much impressed with Robertson that he had reported in favour of giving him some high command which he did not indicate. I told him that some years ago Winston had asked me if I knew Robertson, and had said that he would rather meet him than any man whom he did not know already. [. . .] I said that this had led me to make inquiries concerning him, and I sketched his career. [. . .] LG was must interested. [. . .]

10 February   Sir Reginald Brade sent for me to the War Office. He asked me to read a memorandum describing proposals for sending out war correspondents on a trip round the British lines and for the issue of periodical bulletins as to the result of military operations in France. At the foot of the memorandum was a letter in Kitchener's handwriting and beginning,

> My Dear Prime Minister,
>
>   I have made the following arrangements with Sir John French. Are they satisfactory?
>
>   Yours very faithfully,
>   Kitchener

The PM had written at the foot, 'Excellent. – HHA'. He had also written the same thing in the left-hand corner of the document and covered his writing with large blots. I said to Brade, 'Evidently the PM was overcome with emotion. Are those tears of joy?' [. . .]

14 February [. . .] When LG went to Paris he was accompanied by Lord Murray, who continues to work underground in the most industrious way. He is a dangerous man, although very pleasant. It is singular that Reading and Murray, the heroes of the *affaire Marconi*, should be so closely identified with the national finances. [. . .]

20 February LG takes a gloomy view of the military situation. He says that the Russians have had a bad defeat and he fears the war may last a long time. [. . .] He however wishes to discuss the matter[32] with Robertson Nicoll and me, and I have arranged to ask Nicoll to dine on Thursday. [. . .]

McKenna told me that [. . .] he proposed Cecil Harmsworth[33] [as Parliamentary Under-Secretary, Home Office]. The PM thought that this would be a good appointment.[34] [. . .] McK said that LG, Masterman and others had objected that the appointment would look like an attempt to conciliate the Harmsworth interest. [. . .]

The talk turned on Sir Henry Dalziel. All present agreed that he was an able man whose career had been spoilt by a bad financial reputation. [. . .]

7 March The Defence of the Realm Amendment Act passed its second reading. The Attorney-General accepted my amendments. [. . .] Amid the clash of this huge war the liberty of the subject seems a small matter, but in reality it is vital. We shall not always be at war, and must try to preserve the precious things which make civilisation worth having. [. . .]

LG: [. . .] The old boy [Haldane] has been terribly upset by the war. I suppose he has felt the attacks upon him. He is quite ineffective now. I am very sorry for him. He has been treated disgracefully by the public, who are firmly convinced that he is a German spy, whereas he is one of the most patriotic persons in the country, which owes him a great deal. It is all due to his having described Germany as his 'spiritual home' and entertained the Kaiser to dinner. [. . .] The public have done poor old Haldane a serious injustice.

R: As a matter of fact, he was for fighting the Germans in 1911. It was he who ousted McKenna from the Admiralty because he would not furnish the ships to take the expeditionary force to France.[35]

LG: Yes, that is correct. In fact the Prime Minister was proposing to make Haldane First Lord of the Admiralty when I happened to appear on the scene. [. . .] I knew Winston was unhappy at the Home Office and I pressed the PM to give him the Admiralty. [. . .]

10 March   Dined as usual with Robertson Nicoll, who is furious at what he describes as the Government betrayal of the Dissenters over the Welsh Church Bill – the operation of which it is proposed to postpone by agreement. Nicoll vows that the Dissenters will not rest under this injustice. He begged me to convey this to Lloyd G.

13 March   Golfed and lunched with LG and the Lord Chief Justice. Drove to Walton with the latter. He told me that he had spent the week-end at Walmer with the PM. He says the PM's great responsibilities sit lightly upon him. Except for two hours when he was dealing with the business upon which the Chief had been called to Walmer, he barely mentioned the war. [. . .]

I again asked LG whether he thought the war was being conducted with sufficient vigour; whether Asquith was not too easy. He answered, 'Things are still very unsatisfactory in that respect. . . .'

We talked of Welsh Disestablishment. LG says that a horrible mess has been made. [. . .]

17 March   The Newspaper Proprietors' Association forwarded to the Cabinet a letter drafted by me at the request of the Council by way of reply to a circular from the Press Bureau complaining that the Press was unduly optimistic. [. . .] I also called on Sir Reginald Brade and showed him the letter which the NPA was issuing. [. . .] I said, 'I do not contend that the authorities should issue depressing news, but they are bound to show both sides of the picture which they do exhibit. They are not justified in claiming great victories unless they let the public know at what cost these have been secured. The man-in-the-street does not know the real facts regarding Neuve Chapelle.[36] If he did, his view of the incident would be very different. The people believe that the war is virtually over and that the Germans are beaten. The result is an altogether wrong tone in the country. Everyone is playing for his own hand. The commercial and industrial situation is very serious. The working classes are teeming with discontent and the result will be most serious unless the country is made to realise the real position and the nature of the task before it.'

Brade agreed and promised to discuss the subject with Kitchener. [. . .]

29 March LG telephoned to me in a state of great anger and excitement regarding a leader in the *Chronicle*,[37] referring to a so-called conspiracy to supersede the Prime Minister. The names of his suggested successors were mentioned, including LG, who described the leader as most injurious and indiscreet. He said he feared it had been inspired by McKenna, and asked me to ascertain if this were so. I spoke to Donald, the editor of the *Chronicle*, who expressed surprise that the leader had caused dissatisfaction, and indirectly repudiated the McKenna story. I communicated this to LG's secretary. At night LG telephoned again – still very angry and upset, and asked me to make more enquiries. Donald again repudiated the statement that McKenna had been the instigator.

30 March By appointment called to see LG at the Treasury, and told him what Donald had said. LG spoke very strongly of Donald's conduct, which he described as that of a silly, indiscreet fool. He said that the Prime Minister is much perturbed. 'The old boy was in tears,' LG continued. 'I shall not let this rest. I still believe that McKenna is responsible. He is obsessed by the fear of a coalition government in which there would, of course, be no place for him. That would be the end of his political career. He is heavy-handed and indiscreet. I have never intrigued for place or office. I have intrigued to carry through my schemes, but that is a different matter. The Prime Minister has been so good to me that I would never be disloyal to him in the smallest detail. I may criticise him amongst ourselves, as no doubt he criticises me, but we are absolutely loyal to each other. I have been very worried by this leader, which is open to the construction that it was inspired by me with a view to giving point to the criticisms in the Tory papers, of which no one is taking any notice.' I strongly advised LG not to allow the subject to worry him. He looked quite ill. He thanked me for my advice and said he had told the Prime Minister he should consult me.

Letter from the Prime Minister inviting the NPA to meet him on Thursday. All the members are going but *The Times*. I spoke to Northcliffe some days ago when he said that he disapproved of any such conference. He spoke in slighting terms of Asquith and said, 'I want nothing from them and shall not go near them.' [. . .]

1 April   The conference [with the Press] took place at 10 Downing Street. Present: The PM, Kitchener, Winston, McKenna, Buckmaster, Swettenham,[38] Sir E. T. Cook, [39] Bonham Carter, and the editors of all the London papers but *The Times*. Harry Lawson stated the case for the Press and the PM made an interesting speech in reply, but said nothing definite. When he had finished I told him that the public were under the impression that the war would be over in two or three months. I asked him whether the Government wished the Press to foster this idea. He said, 'Ask Lord Kitchener.' Kitchener then said, 'The public are very much mistaken if they think that.' We then had a general discussion, as a result of which the PM said that he would always be glad to meet the Press, and the suggestion was made that the Press should appoint someone who could keep in close touch on their behalf with Kitchener and Winston. In the course of the PM's speech he disclaimed having been unduly optimistic and drew a distinction between what he described as true and false optimism. He strongly disclaimed any intention on the part of the Government to interfere with criticism. When he said this I saw Winston and Kitchener look at each other in a very significant way. Evidently they did not approve.

2 April   Dined with LG. [. . .] We had much talk tonight on the drink question. LG spoke in favour of compensating the trade. On Sunday he is to confer with Simon and others. He says that the lack of ammunition is very serious and that drink is largely responsible. He spoke very strongly. I said I thought total prohibition would be very dangerous. He admitted that he did not favour it, but said that the threat would make the trade easier to deal with. [. . .] He said that the PM hates the whole thing, for obvious reasons.[40]

6 April   Harry Lawson wants me to act as the Press representative to meet Kitchener and Winston, but today the Newspaper Proprietors' Association declined to appoint any representative. All the papers but the *Telegraph* are working for their own commerical ends. [. . .]

7 April   [. . .] Called on Bonham Carter [. . .] and strongly urged necessity of early speech by the Prime Minister, supporting my case by reading some notes communicated to me by Hartshorn, the miners' leader [. . .] I showed him [McKenna] a letter from Hartshorn, the miners' leader, in which he says that unless the situation is handled carefully there will be a coal strike in the course of a few months. McKenna treated the letter with indifference. [. . .]

8 April   Called on Winston at the Admiralty when he again strongly urged that the Press should reconsider their decision. He said, 'It would make you better known to Kitchener. It would be most useful. You could keep him acquainted with public opinion, which he does not understand.' I read Winston Hartshorn's notes. These seemed to impress him. [. . .]

9 April   Meeting of the NPA, who reversed their previous decision and decided to appoint a representative to confer with the War Lords. The selection fell upon me. [. . .]

10 April   [. . .] LG: I thought Rosebery [41] looked very old and ill at the wedding (of Neil Primrose). When I went into the vestry they all laughed and greeted me with, 'Here's the man who wants to stop our liquor!' Old Queen Alexandra said in her strange voice, 'Mr Lloyd George, I hear you are wanting to turn us all into teetotallers.' F. E. Smith dined with Kitchener the other night. K said 'Well, here is seltzer, and there is lemonade. Which will you have?' F. E., who likes his champagne dearly, replied, 'Many thanks! I take them mixed!'
   R: This agitation is saturated with humbug and hypocrisy. The working-man is to be reformed and regulated, but most of the reformers are laying in good stocks of liquor to provide against the evil day of prohibition. [. . .]

11 April   Dined with LG and family. [. . .] LG says that Kitchener has agreed to his taking over the supervision of the manufacture of munitions. He again spoke in strong terms of the action or inaction of Von Donop, the MGO. LG thinks the war will last over Christmas. He says that Winston has acted too impetuously regarding the Dardanelles, and that things out there are not going well. [. . .] He is an able fellow, but very dangerous. He will not look at the arguments on the other side. [. . .]

12 and 15 April   Two long interviews with Kitchener, who was very pleasant. [. . .]
   He spoke fully and freely on the subject of Press correspondents and put his position quite well. He said, 'I must be loyal to Joffre. He won't have

correspondents. He is in command. If he changes his rules, I will follow suit. But I will not put the blame on him. I act in conjunction with him.' [. . .] I complained to K of the suppressions of news, and said that every line of French's dispatch regarding Neuve Chapelle spelt excuse or failure if you knew the facts. Kitchener said, '*I have not had time to read his dispatch*,[42] but I think you are putting it too high. It was a victory, but not what it might have been.' [. . .] He talked of war correspondents and their effect on soldiers, which he said was bad. [. . .]

14 April   Called to see McKenna, who I am beginning to think is a wrong-headed, ineffective person. [. . .] His hatred of Winston amounts to an obsession. [. . .] McKenna was treated badly when he was ejected from the Admiralty, but his state of mind is not conducive to the public weal. [. . .] I again warned McK regarding the serious position in the colliery industry. He was not responsive and rather belittled the danger of the situation.

15 April   Long talk with Winston. He spoke at length regarding the position in the Dardanelles. He admitted that we had received a check, but said that the operation would be carried to a conclusion. [. . .] We talked of the campaign in France. I commented on Sir John French's dispatches regarding Neuve Chapelle, just published. Winston said, 'We must stick to French. He is a good fellow.' [. . .] Evidently he has not forgotten that French let him down easily over Antwerp. Winston is most anxious to stand well with the Press. He showed this by his manner. [. . .]

16 April   Sir Reginald Brade sent for me hurriedly today. He said he wanted my advice concerning a dispatch which had been submitted to the Censor by the London News Agency. It had been written by a journalist in the employ of the *Daily Mail*, Mr Valentine Williams,[43] who had been taken by Northcliffe to France, where they stayed with Sir John French. The dispatch contained a description of Neuve Chapelle. It had been revised and altered in pencil by French himself, and the News Agency stated that he had authorised publication. Brade telegraphed to inquire if this was true, to which French had replied in the affirmative, but that he had made the condition that the matter should appear in all newspapers. Brade said that this created a very awkward position in view of Kitchener's arrangements with Joffre,[44] and that he, Brade, proposed to commandeer the article and issue it through the Press Bureau. I strongly advised him to submit the matter to the PM and Kitchener, and suggested that the article should be released through the London News Agency, subject to the condition that all papers should have the option to take it, and that some definite understanding should be arrived at with French.

Later Brade sent for me again, when he said the PM and Kitchener were much disturbed and perplexed. They did not like to stop publication, but thought French had acted indiscreetly. The PM said that Brade could not 'burgle' the article, as he proposed, but agreed to my suggestion, which was to be adopted, and a telegram sent to French pointing out that his action seemed inconsistent with the arrangement with Joffre. Brade showed me the draft cable in which I suggested some changes, which he made. [. . .] It is obvious that French knows there is a movement here which is unfriendly to him, and that he is trying to counter it by cultivating Northcliffe and the other newspaper people. If need be, he (F) is going to appeal to Caesar (the populace).

17 April   Golfed with LG. It appears that on Wednesday he asked the editors of the *Daily News, Daily Chronicle, Manchester Guardian, Liverpool Post,* and *Westminster Gazette* to dinner to discuss the drink question, when he proposed to them a scheme for the purchase of the trade interests by the nation – a small deal amounting to some £300,000,000. With the exception of Donald of the *Chronicle,* the editors appear to have acquiesced. It is a wild cat scheme, and I told LG so. He did not relish my criticism and replied, 'Mr Gladstone tried to deal with the drink question without buying out the trade. Surely we cannot expect to accomplish what he failed to do.' I (Riddell) cannot believe that the Cabinet will sanction such a proposal. The drink trade is on the decline. Why should the State engage in such an enterprise? The prospect is most alarming. [. . .]

18 April   Dined with LG who says that he believes that Kitchener is chiefly responsible for the suppression of news. We had a long talk concerning the drink question. I strongly criticised LG's big scheme. From his manner I should think it was dead. He said, 'I am sure it is the best, but it may be impracticable.' [. . .]

From this I gather that he is preparing a modified scheme on these lines. He is evidently very disappointed that his big scheme has broken down. He said, 'The future of this country depends on what takes place during the next five years – perhaps the next five months. That is why the drink question is so important.'

20 April   Spent an hour with Northcliffe, who spoke in violent and contemptuous terms regarding Asquith and Kitchener. He says that the former is indolent, weak and apathetic. He exercises no control over the various departments. He will never finish the war. LG may be the man. He is the best of the lot. Kitchener's brain is paralysed. He is better than Haldane, but most inefficient. He is also tricky and unreliable. [. . .] K is afraid of the Press. He is lying about the French objection to correspondents. N thinks well of Sir John French. [. . .] N talks in a curious disordered way but he is a good judge of character and sees the weak places. His great defect is vanity and conceit. His opinion of himself is colossal. On the other hand he is a good listener and quick to take a hint. He is very receptive. If he were not so conceited he would be a big man and a useful one. Everything has to go down before his vanity and self-interest.

21 April   Robertson Nicoll is much annoyed with Asquith's Newcastle speech,[45] and says he is disgusted with his management of affairs. His nerveless hand, etc, etc. He says that A puts LG to do all the dirty work and that LG has far too much work in hand.

22 April   Long talk with Kitchener, who said that LG's alleged statement as to the number of troops in France was inaccurate and that what LG had really said was that the number of troops 'overseas' amounted to thirty-six divisions. I referred to the speech, in which the words were 'over there'. K said, 'Well, if he said that he was wrong, and the speech must be put right in Hansard.' He asked Brade to see that this was done.

K commented upon what he called 'Newspaper embroidery' and complained of the criticisms as to the inconsistencies between his statements and those of the PM as to the efficiency of our output of munitions of war. He asked my opinion. I replied that they seemed inconsistent and that this was the general opinion. K said, '*The Times* has been the most virulent critic, I am told, but I never read it.' He asked me to look up the speeches, which I did subsequently, and wrote to him setting out the two passages. He said that Northcliffe was acting very badly and that it was difficult to know how to deal with him. [. . .]

Obviously the relations between K and French are very strained, and he thinks that French is endeavouring to make himself a popular hero. K spoke with emotion of the bravery of the troops in the recent fighting, and of the brutal manner in which the Germans have been treating our men. I said something regarding one of French's dispatches. K replied, 'The truth is, I have not read it.'

Spent an hour with Winston. [. . .] He complained that he had been misrepresented by the Press. He said, 'The Press do not understand that we are gentlemen. We tell the truth. We are entitled to be trusted. We have concealed nothing but the *Audacious* and the loss of some submarines. You know why the *Audacious* was concealed.' He asked me to explain this, and concluded, 'I look to you to see that justice is done to the Admiralty in this matter.' I urged the necessity for war correspondents in France. Winston said, 'Why don't you get a deputation to the Prime Minister? If you do, I will support you. Kitchener is all wrong about this.' [. . .]

23 April Hartshorn, the miners' leader, came to see me. He said that Runciman handled the conference with miners' leaders very badly. They were most dissatisfied and insisted on seeing the PM, who in the first instance tried to evade an interview. Smillie made a good speech and explained that while the men are willing to sacrifice themselves in the national interest, they are not prepared to do so in the interests of the masters, who are making enormous profits. Asquith was apparently impressed and frightened at the prospect of another strike. [. . .]

24 April Played with LG in the morning, and he lunched with me.

Still much talk on the drink question. Evidently his big scheme is definitely abandoned.

In the evening I dined with him and had a long and interesting talk. He spoke strongly regarding the PM's Newcastle speech, which he described as most unfortunate. LG says we are very short of ammunition. We have plenty of explosives but not enough shells. Our organisation has been deplorable, while the French have made the most of their facilities, which are considerably less than ours. The result is that they are turning out four times as many shells as we are doing. [. . .] LG spoke very violently and described the inaction of the War Office as damnable. [. . .]

We talked of the PM. LG said he would not go on without Asquith. He did not wish to be PM. He would hate the ceremonial. He said, 'As it is, I always get my own way unless the circumstances are such that there is really good reason why I should not. The PM has been loyal to me and I am absolutely loyal to him. I am quite happy where I am.' [. . .]

29 April Long talk with Kitchener, who seemed anxious and worried. [. . .]

Winston asked me to lunch. I could not go. Saw him at five o'clock and was with him an hour and a half. He spoke in strong terms of a leading article in *The Times* of today. [. . .] He said that Northcliffe was a danger to the country – jumpy and with bad judgment; vain and conceited. He is under the impression that he is God Almighty. [. . .]

He said, 'I think we [the Dardanelles Expedition] will be successful. [. . .] You cannot win this war by sitting still. [. . .] I am not responsible for the Expedition. The whole details were approved by the Cabinet and Admiralty Board. That can be proved. I do not shirk responsibility, but it is untrue to say that I have done this off my own bat. I have followed every detail, and I think I am the right man for the job. Fisher and I have a perfect understanding. Between us we control the situation. . . .'

1 May LG played golf and lunched. He seemed well and full of spirits, notwithstanding his troubles regarding the drink question. His vitality is remarkable. [. . .]

I feel sure from Fisher's manner today that trouble is brewing. He spoke in a sharp and peremptory way to Winston.

2 May [. . .] Walked with LG. He talked of nothing but the war, which he prophesies will be a long affair. He said, 'I fear that eighteen months or two years hence we shall be in just the same mess – trenches blown up – air raids – destroyers sunk. In fact, I am confident that the war will last a long time. Perhaps three years.' [. . .]

4 May Interesting interview with Northcliffe, who strongly expressed the opinion that reflection had assured him that the war would continue for years. [. . .] He talked in a very bumptious way about himself. He said, 'I am keenly alive to my responsibilities. I am not carrying on *The Times* and *Daily Mail* from a business point of view. I have a huge income, and might spend my time fishing and amusing myself, but I feel my responsibility to the nation. I feel that I must remain to guide and criticise.' After this he made some shrewd and sagacious observations on passing events. His tame leader writer was waiting to take his instructions. Poor creature. Name Sydney Brooks. He has sold himself, body and soul, for £1,500 a year, or thereabouts, so I am told. [. . .]

13 May Long talk with Kitchener, who began by saying, 'I suppose you have come to put me through my weekly cross-examination.' I replied, 'No. I have come to receive such information as you are good enough to impart.' He laughed, and then proceeded to make a long and most interesting statement concerning the political and strategic reasons for the Dardanelles Expedition and American intervention.[46] [. . .]

Brade told me that Repington,[47] *The Times* correspondent, is at French's headquarters. K has never been consulted. This is a distinct breach of the arrangement. French is working for his own hand. Brade spoke strongly on the subject, and well he might. The rest of the newspapers will be furious, and already there are signs of revolt. [. . .]

Long talk with Buckmaster, who told me he had written me a strong letter in reply to one from me criticising certain of the arrangements at the Bureau, a topic which had been discussed at the last meeting of the NPA. [. . .]

16 May Brade came to Walton Heath. He says that French is acting most disloyally to Kitchener. The article by Repington which appeared in *The Times* two or three days ago [. . .] was inspired by French. Brade has no doubt that French is endeavouring to work up a Press campaign in his own favour. He and Northcliffe met in France, and there is no doubt that they came to some arrangement for joint action. French is easily led and seems to be in the hands of the American, Moore, with whom he lives when in London.

(Lord Murray has been the medium of communication with Northcliffe. No doubt he is in N's pay. N told me he had found him very useful in communicating with French and Joffre, and he has done similar jobs before.)

17 May Northcliffe telephoned yesterday asking me to make an appointment for him to see LG today, which I did. Later Northcliffe telephoned saying that he had had an hour's talk with LG, which he (N) described as very useful. He said that LG wanted to see Colonel Repington, and that he, N, had arranged for them to meet at my house. Repington came at 7 o'clock. I was not there. LG sent a messenger to take

R to the H of C, where he had a long talk with him. LG did not tell me what transpired, but I rather suspect that some sort of an understanding was arrived at between himself and N.

18 May   Harry Lawson (*Daily Telegraph*) sent for me. He says that FitzGerald,[48] French's private secretary, has been to see him. [. . .] He explained that he had come because he thought that Lawson might have misunderstood the circumstances under which Repington's article in *The Times* had been written. Repington had been staying with French as his private guest. French had applied to Kitchener for certain percentages of high explosives which had not been supplied. In order to remedy matters, French had given the information to Repington for publication in *The Times*. FitzGerald concluded by inviting Harry Lawson to visit French and by disclaiming on behalf of French and his staff all desire to give preferential treatment to *The Times*. I told Lawson that this was all a bit of bluff. Having done the deed, French, Northcliffe, FitzGerald & Co. are anxious to allay criticism.

The bombshell has fallen. Fisher has resigned. A coalition Government is in the making. [. . . Brade] says that there is another dispatch from Repington which he, Brade, has referred to Kitchener and the Prime Minister, who were considering whether they should permit publication. They did, but the message was severely cut. Brade said he would like to see LG, and I said I would arrange a meeting.

May–December 1915

The first seven months of the Asquith coalition ministry provided Riddell with an unusual variety of subjects for his diary. He recorded much about the formation and early days of the new government, noting especially the depths of Churchill's humiliation and bitterness at being demoted from the Admiralty. In conversations with Riddell, Churchill did not trouble to hide his feelings about Lloyd George and Lord Fisher, whom he held responsible for his fate. The former now had little time to spare for Churchill's problems as he was soon involved in battle with Kitchener and the War Office over munitions production. In early July there was 'a devil of a row' concerning the Royal Arsenal at Woolwich and the delinquencies of the Master-General of the Ordnance. Riddell observed closely Lloyd George's dissatisfaction with the new ministerial regime and his scarcely-concealed determination to find alternative ways of achieving those things he believed necessary for winning the war. One such was closer collaboration with the powerful but dangerous Northcliffe. Another was the threat of resignation, which surfaced before the coalition was a few weeks old and became a recurring theme until Lloyd George superseded Asquith as Prime Minister.

A coal strike in midsummer gave Riddell another opportunity, as in 1912, to assist with negotiations for a settlement and prove again his worth in industrial disputes of this kind. Apart from his comments on this and some acerbic remarks about Sir Hedley Le Bas, he remained the detached observer of the political scene. His notes for the rest of 1915 have two main themes – conscription and military strategy – the great issues facing Britain's leaders in these months. As usual it is Lloyd George's thoughts and words that are of chief interest, and Riddell chronicles his drawing away from old Radical friends as he finds new allies among the Tories. Never content with one source, Riddell sought out Northcliffe from time to time, and he also became acquainted with Lord Derby, now a big figure on account of the famous recruitment scheme. For the first time, too, he met Sir Edward Carson, and there were several interviews with a somewhat un-sympathetic Home Secretary, Sir John Simon, over the issue of Press censorship. By year's end we find Riddell encouraging Lloyd George to take some dramatic steps in order to shake up the Government.

19 May   The Liberal Party looks as if it were dead. I went to the
House of Commons to see LG. Waited in his secretary's room for an
hour. Intense excitement. [. . .]

The main topic, the bombshell and the fate of the Liberal Party.
The Liberals are mad to see the prospect of a Coalition. At last I saw
LG, who had been detained by one Bishop Furse.[1] [. . .]

I told LG that the state of affairs between Kitchener and French was
lamentable, and that Brade thought K had not put his case properly
before his colleagues.

I read LG the Resolution which had been passed by the Newspaper
Proprietors regarding Repington's dispatches. [. . .] LG proposed that
we should dine together, which we did. The Attorney-General came
also. Brade was late. Before he arrived LG described an interview
which he had had with Winston, who had been turned over to him by
the Prime Minister. LG said that Winston came in with a face like the
faces we used to see on old mugs. Winston said that he intended to
make a statement in the House of Commons, and that he had prepared
it. LG told him he could not carry out his intention, as the effect upon
foreign politics would be disastrous, particularly with Italy hanging in
the balance. Winston said, 'You forget my reputation is at stake. I am
wounded.' LG said, 'I read his statement. When I came to the part in
which he referred to his own services, I could see his eyes filling with
sympathy for himself.' [. . .] [LG] persuaded him that the statement
could not be made, and off he went. [. . .]

When Brade arrived we had a long talk on the War Office position.
Brade spoke in high terms of K, who, he said, had suffered from his
loyalty to his colleagues and subordinates. LG said that K had acted
badly in keeping back information and particularly French's demands
for high explosives from the Cabinet and LG as Chairman of the
Munitions Committee. He said that if the facts were stated to the
House of Commons, there would be a terrible row. LG added that he
had got the information from a private source. I fancy from
Northcliffe. Kitchener would have to give up this part of the
organisation. LG intimated that the PM wanted him to become Secretary for War but that he did not feel disposed to accept the position. He
talked with Brade of alternative arrangements. For example, that K
should become Commander-in-Chief. Brade explained the technical
questions involved. I then left LG and Brade together. [. . .]

LG arranged to see Brade again in the morning. I walked home with
LG who said that in view of the position at the Admiralty and War

Office a coalition was the only possible solution. He said that Mrs LG had begged him not to go to the War Office and that Mrs Asquith had done the same. He seemed much amused at Mrs A. He said he did not want to go. I told him that I thought he would do well to leave Kitchener as Sec. of State for War and take over the whole control of the munitions. [. . .] He said that Winston would have to leave the Admiralty. He is a dangerous fellow. He also said that Samuel and Runciman had not done well. Samuel would probably have to go. A place would have to be found for Winston. McKenna, who is *supposed* to have done badly, will stay. (Strange metamorphosis. LG is evidently now working with McKenna, of whom he formerly held the poorest opinion. . . .)

20 May Called to see Winston at the Admiralty. Found him in his room. He looked very worn out and harassed. He greeted me warmly and said, 'I have been stung by a viper. I am the victim of a political intrigue. I am finished!' I said, 'Not finished at forty, with your remarkable powers!' 'Yes!' he said. 'Finished in respect of all I care for – the waging of war; the defeat of the Germans. . . . L George has been partly responsible. Fisher went to him and he told him to resign, or at any rate did not dissuade him. . . .'

'This is a political intrigue. It centres round L George. He thinks he sees his way to go to the War Office. Is he going to be Minister of War? What has he decided?' I said, 'He does not want to go to the War Office.' Winston replied, 'You are wrong. He does!'

Then he went on to speak of Balfour and Bonar Law. He said, 'They insist on high office. Bonar Law also wants the War Office.' I said, 'I think you are wrong.' Winston, however, insisted upon his point. Then he said, 'But today I have received the greatest compliment I have ever had in my life. Sir Arthur Wilson[2] [. . .] has written to the Prime Minister saying that he would serve as First Sea Lord under me, and [. . .] under no one else. He is an honest man, not a traitor like Fisher.' [. . .]

We talked of Kitchener and French. I said, 'Do you think French was justified in causing Repington to write that inspired article regarding shells which appeared in *The Times*? Should he not have written to the Prime Minister?' Winston replied, 'The poor devil is fighting for his life. Had I spent some of my time in lollying the newspapers instead of working here twelve hours a day, I should not be in this plight. This is a Northcliffe Cabinet. He has forced this.'

R: Don't you thing the P Minister has been very weak in the conduct of the war?

Winston: Disgracefully weak – supinely weak. His weakness will be the death of him.

Thus closed a most painful and eventful interview, and I left this broken man pacing up and down his room. [. . .] I wonder whether Winston remembers McKenna's downfall. [. . .]

Brade came to lunch. He says Winston is going – that is certain. After leaving us last night Brade saw Max Aitken, who is acting as jackal for Bonar Law, and ultimately saw Bonar Law himself. Bonar Law is very strongly opposed to Kitchener. Aitken says he has advised Bonar Law not to go to the War Office. I saw Brade later. He has had an interview with Lloyd George, Bonar Law, and McKenna this morning. LG then proposed that K should stay on as Sec. [of State] for War and that he, LG, should take over the munitions. Bonar Law would not agree, nor would he agree that Kitchener should remain in the Cabinet. He said that he must consult his party, as, although the coalition was practically agreed upon, he must consult with his people until the final arrangements had been made.

21 May Violent attack in the *Daily Mail* today upon Kitchener, in which it is alleged that he had neglected the manufacture of high-explosive shells and had supplied the Army with too much shrapnel. Brade sent for me. He said that last night Kitchener had telephoned, asking him to see him at 11, K having just arrived from his visit to the munition areas. K was tired and evidently harassed by the position of affairs. Brade told him of his interview and apologised for interfering. K said he had done the right thing. K proposed that he should remain as Joint Secretary for War, and also that he should be appointed Commander-in-Chief. He, however, intimated that he would not care to act with LG as his colleague. This morning Brade saw Bonar Law at the latter's house, Pembroke Lodge, when BL said that he would not agree to K's proposal that he should act as Joint Secretary and Commander-in-Chief. He proposed that K should accept the latter position without a seat in the Cabinet. BL and Balfour do not believe in K. They think that he has a way of concealing things, etc. Brade then saw K again who said he would retire altogether. He did not want to go on. Brade said this was impossible in the national interest. K then said that if it was insisted upon, he would take the post of Commander-in-Chief as proposed, but that having regard to his relations with French, the arrangements would break down in a week. Ultimately he conveyed to Brade through Fitzgerald, his secretary, that he would be willing to waive the position as Commander-in-Chief and act as Joint Secretary for War. Brade telephoned this to Bonar Law, who said that he would consult his people, and that if they agreed he would send Sir Edward Carson to see Brade in order to ascertain whether it would be possible to define the respective positions of the War Secretaries. There the matter rests, but Brade expects to see Carson this afternoon. Brade says that he has been examining K's case in reply to the *Daily Mail* article, which Brade was perusing for the first time when I arrived at 5 p.m. K had not seen it! No one had brought it to his attention. He does not read newspapers very much. Brade says Von Donop's case is very weak. He admits that instead of preparing the high-explosive material, the shell cases, and the fuses and other details *pari passu*, he had confined himself in the first instance to solving the difficulties as to manufacture of high-explosive material, leaving other difficulties to be dealt with later on. [. . .]

22 May   *Daily Mail* burnt at Stock Exchange, Baltic, etc. Great public indignation at attacks on Kitchener.

The political situation has taken an amazing turn this week. McKenna, who has been the most unpopular member of the Cabinet, and who has never been in the inner circle, has suddenly wriggled his way to a front place. [. . .] Now McKenna seems to have replaced Winston. [. . .]

23 May   Dined with LG at his house at Walton. He says the Cabinet crisis came very quickly. He expected it, and Grey thought it inevitable, but all the same it came like a bombshell. [. . .] On the Sunday or the Monday, Bonar Law came to see LG at the Treasury. He was very excited, and said, 'You know what I have come about. Fisher has resigned. Either I must raise this in the H of C, or we must have a National Government.' Bonar Law went on to propose that LG should be Premier, but he said that he could not accept the position. He could not act in competition with Asquith, who had always treated him well. LG told the PM what Bonar Law had said, but omitting BL's proposal as to the Premiership, as LG said this information might unnerve Asquith in his dealings with the new people. LG. said that Winston had acted badly inasmuch as he had not told the Cabinet that all the Naval Board were of opinion that the Dardanelles operations should be combined sea and land attack. [. . .]

LG said he had fought to get Winston high office – the Colonies, the India Office, the Viceroyalty of India. His colleagues would not, however, agree to his having anything but a minor position. They would not listen to India, where things are in an unsettled state. [. . .] Winston had acted foolishly. He had written some very wild and silly things to the PM, who had been very angry and had written Winston a sharp letter in reply. [. . .] Amongst other things Winston had said no one but I [i.e. himself] can bring the Dardanelles operations to a successful conclusion. [. . .] When any man talks like that he is on the way to a lunatic asylum.[3] [. . .]

LG said he was doubtful how long the new Cabinet would last. [. . . He] spoke strongly regarding Kitchener, who he said had concealed serious things from his colleagues. The PM knew nothing of French's demands for high-explosive shells. The PM told LG that Kitchener had said that French was getting all he wanted and that he (Asquith) had framed his Newcastle speech accordingly. [. . .]

LG continued, 'Kitchener would never act as a subordinate. He wants a tame colleague who will be useful but who will sign what he tells him. [. . .] K is either incompetent or tricky. [. . .] Either he did not know or appreciate what French wanted, or he concealed it.' [. . .]

25 May   Northcliffe telephoned to say that he had heard that Harry Lawson had said that his attack on Kitchener was due to a personal quarrel. N said that he had spoken to H. Lawson on the telephone, and that he [L] had offered to write a letter of apology. N said he did not want this, but wished me to ensure that the statement was not repeated at the NPA Council meeting. N then told me that he had been to see Lloyd George at Walton Heath on Sunday morning (this is Tuesday), and that he had urged LG to go to the War Office. [. . .]

26 May   Called to see Sir Reginald Brade, who told me that last night he had a conference with Bonar Law, Carson and Austen Chamberlain, at Max Aitken's flat, when Kitchener's position was discussed at length. They are not at all friendly to K. Brade says that it was only decided yesterday that LG should take the position of Minister of Munitions, but I doubt whether Brade really knows the facts. He says that the Prime Minister is going to France on Monday to see Sir John French, with the object of preventing a repetition of the recent incident with *The Times* and of endeavouring to establish a satisfactory relationship between French and Kitchener. [. . .]

Called to see LG at Walton. [. . .]

He again remarked that Kitchener had acted badly in withholding information. I repeated what I had said as to the obvious course which French should have taken. LG said, 'Yes, he did the wrong thing, but Northcliffe was right in his facts, and I am not sure that he was wrong in directing public attention to the subject as he did.'

LG did not mention that he had seen Northcliffe again on Sunday, 24th. I have a shrewd suspicion that LG has been a party to the attacks on Kitchener in *The Times* and *Daily Mail* and *Manchester Guardian*. He did not appreciate how powerful Kitchener is in the country, or how much Northcliffe is hated by the Press generally and distrusted by the public. LG is very deep and subtle in his proceedings. He rarely tells me *all* the story.

Called at the Admiralty to see Winston's secretary. Winston came out and took me into his room, and I afterwards walked with him to the Bath Club. As he left the Admiralty he said, 'I leave the nation a Navy in a state of perfect efficiency. I cannot say more. [. . .] Lloyd George is responsible for the coalition government. He has treated me disgracefully. He has no sense of honour. Notwithstanding our former relations, notwithstanding how I stood by him in the Marconi days, he did nothing to help me. He never put out a hand. He acted just as if they had been killing a rat. I will never work with him again. I will never be friends with him again. He never hesitates to sacrifice a friend if he stands in the way of his game. He might act differently with some of his old Welsh friends, but the English are a different race. [. . .] All this is due to Lloyd George's intrigue. [. . .] Fisher has acted like a treacherous devil. His Malay blood has come out.[4] At last he was attacked by nerves. He is suffering from a nervous breakdown. He is an old man. There is that to be said for him. [. . .] This is all for your private ear, but remember what I say regarding LG. Whatever your friendship or relations with him may have been, he will never scruple to sacrifice you without compunction if you stand in the way of his plans.'

27 May Interview with Kitchener and Brade. K said (referring to the attack upon him in the Northcliffe papers), 'This has been a sad and worrying time. It is terrible to think that such a breach of discipline should have taken place in the Army, and that such lies, such damned lies, should have been circulated. Under ordinary circumstances I should have taken measures. But in the face of the Germans, what can I do? [. . .] French has plenty of ammunition at Havre. Why does he leave it there? Here are the figures.' He then read the details from a paper on his table, from which it appeared that French has 689 rounds of high-explosive shells per gun, in addition to shrapnel, etc. K said, 'I am sending him 23,000 rounds tonight, and a consignment is forwarded every night. [. . .] I would rather have been kicked from one end of the country to the other than have had the Army dragged through the mire in this way.' He seemed much worried and upset and evidently feels very strongly regarding French's share in the transaction. [. . .]

29 May Drove LG to Walton, played golf with him and dined with him in the evening. Masterman came to dinner also. [. . .]

LG spoke at length regarding his new position as Minister of Munitions. He said that the arrangements were deplorable and that Von Donop had been guilty of serious mismanagement, for which Kitchener must also be held responsible as he was warned in October that the arrangements were inadequate. [. . .]

LG told me it would be some time before the new organisation could become effective, and that the experiment of getting shells manufactured by firms unaccustomed to that class of work might in the first instance lead to the production of unsuitable and ineffective shells. [. . .]

Masterman and Donald of the *Daily Chronicle* (who played with us in the morning) both took up the position that Asquith had made a mistake in agreeing to the Coalition. LG strongly dissented. [. . .]

3 June Northcliffe telephoned that French was in London and that he wanted to see LG. French had suggested a meeting at Lancaster Gate – the house occupied jointly by Moore and French. N said that LG should not go there and suggested meeting at my house. I promised to communicate with LG's secretary, LG being at Manchester. This I did, and explained the position. Davies, the secretary, said he had instructions to see French and make an appointment. He agreed as to the inadvisability of a meeting at L[ancaster] Gate.

5 June Played with LG and the LCJ. Robertson Nicoll came to Walton to see LG. Northcliffe has written to Nicoll saying that LG will justify his attacks on Kitchener. [. . .]

I spoke at a Printers' Charity Dinner, Northcliffe in the chair. I sat next to him. He spoke to me at length regarding the war. He said that he intended to attack Kitchener again, and also to attack Asquith, of whom he spoke in slighting terms. He also spoke in the same sense of all the Ministers but LG, who, he said, would have to become Premier. I said, 'How about Grey?' N replied, 'He managed the war diplomacy well, but does not understand the war.' N prophesies that the war will last for years and says that very probably none of the Ministers or generals now in power will be permitted by the people to see the war to a conclusion. N made several shrewd observations, but generally speaking talked in a wild way.[5] I said, 'You must give the new Government a chance. You have no one better to suggest.' To this he replied, 'Someone will turn up. The war will disclose a genius,' and so on. He said, 'Kitchener knew that I saw LG last Sunday. He has spies watching me. My letters are opened and my telephone tapped. But I have my spies at the War Office.' [. . .]

Earlier in the day I (R) received four telegrams from Northcliffe asking me to arrange a meeting between him and LG, tomorrow, Sunday. LG appointed 3 p.m. on Sunday afternoon at Walton. [. . .]

6 June Called to see LG at his house at 10 a.m. Told him of my interview with Northcliffe and how I read his intentions. LG thanked me and said, 'I always feel uneasy with him. [. . .] He is now doing harm by his continual criticism, and I shall tell him so. I still think he did the right thing in publishing his first attack in the *The Times*.' [. . .]

LG then proceeded to speak of Kitchener, who, he said again, had acted very badly. He said, 'If I were to show you the figures, you would agree with me. He covered up and distorted the facts. The PM hates unpleasant facts and is always glad of an excuse to disbelieve them. [. . .] When the question of ammunition was raised by me at the War Council, McKenna subsequently brought forward figures which convinced the PM that I was wrong. I am sorry to say that K is a liar. [. . .] The PM made a most unfortunate speech at Elswick. That was on the faith of K's statement that French had written a certain letter stating that he was satisfied with the ammunition, etc. There never was any such letter. The whole thing was a lie. The PM has only now learned the truth.' [. . .]

Saw LG again, when he said that Northcliffe had been with him for an hour and a half, but why he came he (LG) did not know. N said nothing of moment and asked no questions. LG added, 'He is a most extraordinary person. . . .'

9 June Nicoll says that on Saturday LG told him that before accepting the position of Munitions Minister he had stipulated certain conditions which had not been performed, and that he had asked his advice whether he should resign if they were not fulfilled. Nicoll (most unwisely I think) had advised him in the affirmative. LG gave Nicoll, so he said, a most depressing account of the situation, including a statement by the PM to the effect that our trenches were inadequate and not to be compared with those of the French Army. Nicoll has written what I regard as an injudicious article in the *British Weekly*.[6] Whether he has overstated what LG said, I do not know, nor do I know LG's object. It looks as if he wished to lead Nicoll to write an article which would strengthen his hands with his colleagues and which would be quoted in other papers. [. . .]

Nicoll and LG concocted a letter in reply to one from Northcliffe to Nicoll saying that LG would confirm the charges made by *The Times* and *Mail* against K. The reply went on to deprecate the manner of the attack, but I thought the joint concoction a mistake. It is a valuable weapon for Northcliffe.

10 June   Called at the Munitions Department to see LG. [. . .]

R: Nicoll has written an extraordinary article in this week's *British Weekly*. He suggests that you intend to resign unless you get your own terms. I hope that this is not true, and that you don't intend to desert the country at such a time, simply because you cannot get your own way?

LG: You have never known me shirk, have you? I have not read the article, but from what I hear the old man has gone too far.

R: Let me show you what he says. (The paper was lying on his table with others. I showed him the passage.) Nicoll says that you inspired the article when you saw him on Saturday.

I thought LG coloured slightly when I said this. He made no reply. [. . .]

11 June   [. . .] Spender said that the Liberals are very disgruntled with LG. They believe he is going the way of Chamberlain and are much perturbed at a sentence in one of his recent speeches, in which he foreshadowed the extinction of party politics and indicated the possibility of men standing side by side who had hitherto been bitterly opposed to each other. Spender said, 'Our people do not feel like that. They intend that after the war Liberal principles shall be maintained and advocated as strongly as ever.' He asked what scheme I thought LG had in view. I replied that I was not certain. [Perhaps] he was simply drifting on the tide of events. Spender thought he had a scheme in his mind. Murray is a cunning fellow. None of these people seem to have any idea that he is hand in glove with Northcliffe. [. . .]

13 June Northcliffe telephoned to me from Broadstairs saying that he would like to see LG again. I told him LG was still away, but I would see what could be arranged. [. . .]

19 June [. . .] From what Sir Reginald Brade tells me, the differences between the War Office and LG are in train for amicable settlement. The Munitions Department is in a state of the most awful chaos. There is no proper head, and no organisation or appropriation of duties amongst the new officials who have been introduced. Neither LG nor Girouard[7] is an organiser, with the consequence that no one's duties are defined. Stevenson,[8] one of the new men, told LG that he would have to resign unless things were changed. [. . .]

Spent the day with the LCJ. [. . .] Lord and Lady Murray and Lady Lewis[9] and her daughter were there. Murray says that Hobhouse is very sore at having been ejected from the Cabinet and is vowing vengeance on LG, to whom he ascribes his downfall. Murray thinks that Hobhouse may be able to act the part of critic with greater effect than most people give him credit for. [. . .]

22 June Long talk with Kitchener. [. . .] He was very friendly and communicative. [. . .]

My impression of Kitchener was confirmed today. He knows little or nothing of detailed administration. He is not consulted by the officials and he does not probe into their doings. On the other hand, he seems to have an instinct for the trend of the war. He understands the military situation and probabilities better than anyone else whom I meet. [. . .]

26 June [. . .] Played golf with LG and LCJ, McKenna, Le Bas, Masterman and Donald. LG spoke in strong terms of General Von Donop, the Master-General of Ordnance, who, he says, deserves to be shot. LG says he has grossly mismanaged his department and that he must go. LG made some dark suggestions concerning him but said that he had no proofs. He says that the Press should begin the attack on Von Donop and that his removal will thus be rendered easier. He suggested that Donald should commence the campaign in the

Chronicle. Donald said that he would, but subsequently asked me if I did not think such a proceeding would be very dangerous. I replied in the affirmative. Donald put the same question to McKenna, who said that he thought the attack would be most dangerous and that on paper Von Donop could make out a very good case. I thought all this very remarkable. Surely if Von Donop has acted badly the Cabinet should deal with him, not the newspapers. Our Government seems lamentably weak.

29 June Told Sir Reginald Brade that feeling is very strong against Von Donop, and that if Kitchener were wise he would remove him from control of the Ordnance Department. Brade promised to let K know. General French is here and K is very busy, so I could not see him.

1 July I met Freddie Guest as I was leaving the H of C. We had some talk regarding French's action in publishing statement regarding ammunition. I said, 'F acted badly. He should have made statement to Prime Minister.' Guest said he disagreed. *That course was discussed and rejected!*[10] I said, 'F should have told Asquith that he could not get what he wanted, and that unless this state of affairs was remedied he should resign and tell the nation his reason.' [. . .]

Guest (dramatically): How could a general retire in the face of the enemy? [. . .]

(Northcliffe said yesterday in discussing the same subject, 'The disclosure in *The Times* was quite unpremeditated. There was no plan. It was all done on the spur of the moment.' He seemed uneasily anxious to make me believe this. His story does not fit in with Guest's. . . .)

2 July Lunched with Northcliffe at *The Times* office. He rang me up yesterday to request me to urge economy in the newspaper production. We had a long talk extending over two hours. He takes the gloomiest view of the situation and prophesies great disasters which will move the people to fury. [. . .] The Cabinet he described as being full of intrigue. Lloyd George has many enemies who are anxious to accomplish his ruin. Winston is intriguing to get the War Office in the place of K, etc, etc. The PM and family are openly hostile to LG. McKenna and others allege that there is no shortage of ammunition. Generally speaking, we are in an evil plight. Bonar Law is a poor creature, just fit to be McKenna's secretary and McKenna himself is only fit to be a lawyer's managing clerk. Northcliffe thinks, however, that he may be safe in money matters. He would not trust his money to LG, who is too venturesome. LG is a *simple* little man, who may easily be ruined by his enemies and rivals! I ventured to doubt his simplicity, but N persisted in his opinion, so I did not trouble to argue further.

Hulton[11] sent yesterday to say he is respondent in a divorce suit and to beg me not to report the case. He said that Northcliffe had agreed not to do so. I agreed. I could not well do anything else,[12] but the situation is peculiar. Newspaper proprietors will now become a privileged class who can fornicate with comparative impunity. This should increase the value of newspapers! [. . .] Northcliffe had refrained from publicity because he desires to place Hulton under a serious personal obligation which will prevent him from attacking Northcliffe himself. N described Hulton as an ignorant shop-keeper who knows nothing about the war!

N said that his brother Cecil, who has no judgment or brains, is entirely under McKenna's influence, which exemplifies Cecil's stupidity. I however gathered that McK has succeeded in getting at N through the family fool. N wants to see LG and I have promised to endeavour to arrange a meeting for Sunday.

Last night there was a devil of a row in the House of Commons regarding Von Donop and the administration at Woolwich. I called to see Brade, who seemed worried. *He says Kitchener asked the PM what he should do regarding Von Donop, and Asquith replied, 'Leave him where he is!'*[13] It seems there was a row in the Cabinet today in reference to K's failure to reply to a letter written by LG to Kitchener on the subject of taking munition workers from the Army. [. . .] When K returned from the Cabinet he was much upset. Brade says that now things are not working smoothly between K and LG. We discussed the situation at length. I advised Brade to see Kitchener [. . .] and advise him to make an offensive and defensive alliance with LG. Brade agreed. [. . .]

4 July LG asked me to lunch. We lunched alone and had a long talk. He spoke much concerning McKenna, who is busily engaged in denying the statements as to shortage. LG says [. . .] that Asquith will not face inconvenient facts. He hates to have his optimism shaken. LG says that McKenna is busily working the Press! [. . .]

LG says that W[inston] is fully convinced that he [LG] devised and carried through the Coalition. Winston is angry and hurt, but full of admiration for LG's Machiavellian cleverness! [. . .]

Northcliffe arrived at 3 o'clock and stayed for an hour and a half. LG talked very freely. Obviously he has been seeing a good deal of N or hearing a good deal from him. N called LG's attention to an article in the *Westminster Gazette* saying that there was no shortage, etc, etc. LG repeated with violent emphasis that if any of his colleagues made this statement publicly, he would state the facts. Northcliffe said that he wished to urge LG to make plain his own position as Chairman of the Munitions Committee, appointed in October, as people were freely saying that LG was equally responsible, if not more responsible than other Ministers, for any deficiencies of ammunition that may exist. N prophesied, as he did on Friday, that a great national disaster was impending, and that the present Ministry would be swept away. He expressed his anxiety that LG should survive the flood. LG rather avoided a direct answer to this suggestion. [. . .]

5 July   The position in the South Wales coal trade is very serious. Hartshorn and Hodges,[14] two of the leaders, told me that a stoppage is imminent. At their request I saw Runciman and arranged for him to see them privately at my house tomorrow. He says that the coal-owners are a grasping lot, and that F Davies, the Chairman, is an arrogant person who does much to cause trouble. The PM told Runciman that in his opinion Ministers devote too much time to settling Labour disputes, and that Runciman was not to go to Cardiff to the Conference last week. Runciman then talked for nearly an hour regarding the war. He now takes a gloomy view of the situation and yesterday wrote to the PM saying that in his opinion it was most essential to consider the appointment of a new general in the place of Sir John French, of whom Runciman receives the most indifferent accounts. French and Robertson attended the Cabinet meetings on Friday and Saturday. Runciman thinks French is not an able or a strong man. [. . .] Runciman is a nice man – very accessible, and eager to do his job well. But he does not strike me as a heavyweight.

6 July   Lunched with Winston C at 21 Arlington Street. Also present Mrs Churchill and Lloyd George. Main topic of discussion Haldane's speech of yesterday, in which he glorified and defended Von Donop and alleged that the Cabinet Committee, consisting of Kitchener, LG, McKenna, and Winston, were responsible for ordering the munitions and that the shortage was due to contractors' inability to execute orders owing to labour trouble. LG said that he would not sit down under these imputations and intended to make a public statement of the facts, which would show that Von Donop was responsible for watching the contracts. Winston said he thought the matter should first be brought up in the Cabinet. LG replied that he knew this would mean that nothing would be done. [. . .] Both LG and Winston agreed that Haldane's speech was partly due to malice owing to his having been turned out of the Cabinet. [. . .] Both Winston and LG were much amused at Haldane appearing as Von Donop's champion, which would lead the public to think more than ever that Haldane was in sympathy with the Germans.[15] [. . .] LG said he was determined to make a public statement. [. . .]

8 July Northcliffe came to Walton and spent the afternoon with me. Still gloomy. Prophesies Asquith's downfall in six weeks. He says French has sealed his doom. I suppose he has declined to continue his association with Northcliffe. N says the Navy is short of high explosives. He left early to develop his attack on Haldane in tomorrow's *D. Mail*. He says this is a conspiracy to accomplish LG's downfall. He told me that before he left he gave instructions to the *Evening News* to attack Haldane, against whom the Northcliffe campaign commenced with a bitter leader in this morning's *Times*. [. . .]

9 July LG called. [. . .] He is furious with Haldane, and says that his speech is the public evidence of a secret intrigue led by McKenna, and in which Montagu is concerned. LG says that McKenna & Co. are very upset at Haldane's indiscretion, which has delivered the intriguers into LG's hands. He intends to write to the PM protesting against these intrigues and saying he will not allow such a state of things to continue.

10 July McKenna tells me he is satisfied that nothing better could have been done in the past regarding munitions. Our condition is due to the fact that we were not prepared for war. Only an archangel could have been expected to display more foresight last October. [. . .]

Went to Swinley to see the LCJ, with whom I had a long chat on the situation. He says he is anxious regarding LG. The Liberal Party are angry with him. They think he is conspiring with Northcliffe against the PM. The LCJ thinks Haldane should not have made the statements which have led to the controversy. He says Haldane is very bitter. He ascribes his downfall to LG.

Donald is very disgruntled with LG. His hatred of Northcliffe tends
to prejudice his views on the whole question. Evidently Donald is hand
in hand with McKenna. [. . .]

15 July   I had an interesting little chat with Lord K. [. . .] He spoke
strongly in favour of Von Donop and referred to the statements of
excitable Ministers, evidently meaning LG. Altogether his attitude
seemed very bitter.

16 July   [. . .] The coal strike in South Wales looks very serious.
Hartshorn called to see me and gave me a note of the terms on which
he thought the strike might be settled. These I took to Runciman at
10.30 p.m. and stayed with him until 11.30 p.m., discussing the details.
The outlook does not seem hopeful. He was very nice, but rigid except
upon one or two points.

18 July   LG sent for me to discuss the coal strike. I suggested that
certain points should be conceded, that leaders should be told the
amended terms were final, and that in default martial law would be
proclaimed in the coalfield. Later Nicholas, the solicitor to the Miners'
Federation, came to lunch with LG. We had a long talk. N agreed with
my view. LG seemed of the same opinion. He said he thought the PM
would have to see the miners' leaders again. The outlook seems black.

21 July   The coal strike has been settled practically on the terms
which Hartshorn and I drew up on Friday night and which I then
submitted to Runciman and later to LG (on Sunday). This is a great
triumph for LG, and Runciman [. . .] has missed a great opportunity.
[. . .] LG's stock, which has been rather low of late, is now up again,
well above par.

5 August   Winston [. . .] said the new Government is worse than the
old one. The Tories are so glad to be in office again that they are like
sucking doves. They have lost all their sting. There is no effective
opposition and no effective criticism. The House of Commons is
muzzled, and the criticism in the Press[16] is so badly done that it is
ineffective here and most harmful abroad. [. . .]
    Winston then went on to say that he wished I could arrange for him
to meet Robertson Nicoll and Donald of the *Daily Chronicle.* [. . .]

12 and 14 August   [. . . LG and I] had some talk on conscription, which he strongly favours. Donald is strongly opposed to the change. LG said that if he could get 120,000 skilled workers back from the Army he would then have all the men he wants, and that he could only secure the return of the 120,000 by means of conscription, which would enable K to get additional men to replace them. LG is still very gloomy regarding the state of the war and prophesies its continuance for at least twelve months. [. . .]

20 August   LG [. . .] told me that McKenna had been acting very badly. About six weeks ago he strongly opposed LG's proposal to order more big guns, on the ground of expense and because he alleged that Naval requirements would be prejudiced. There was a Cabinet discussion which LG closed by enquiring of the PM whether he was to proceed with his orders or not. The PM then said that he had better go on. McKenna [. . .] is strongly opposed to conscription in any form. [. . .] LG, who strongly favours it, said that before it was raised in the Cabinet the facts should be ascertained, and that it was very important to secure Kitchener's support. If he declares in favour of conscription, opposition would be almost impossible, whereas if he declares against it, the supporters of the policy would have a hard task before them. It was agreed that F. E. Smith should see the Conservative leaders and arrange that they should not raise the question until a Cabinet Committee had reported on the facts, and that FES should also see Kitchener. [. . .]

22 August   LG and I motored to Margate to visit Bonar Law. Winston and F. E. Smith were there. They had a long conference at which I was not present. LG very gloomy. He says that the news regarding Bulgaria is very bad. They are likely to go in against Servia. Bonar Law looked very serious and anxious. [. . .] LG told me this morning *that there is to be a big offensive in the West.*[17] and that he had to scrape up all the ammunition he could find. He bitterly complained that the PM or his secretary had delayed informing him of the fact for two precious days. The letter only reached him last night. [. . .]

26 August   Brade says Kitchener has an enlistment scheme up his sleeve which he meant to produce later, but now his hand has been forced and he will have to declare himself. He also says that Bonar Law, Curzon, Austen Chamberlain, W. Long, and Carson will resign if necessary on the question of National Service.

27 August   Dined with Frederick Guest. Present a curious mixture –
Henry Dalziel, Gwynne [18] of the *Morning Post*, Nicholson[19] of the
Daily News, Wedgwood,[20] MP, Cave,[21] MP, Robert Harcourt,[22] MP,
Ivor Herbert,[23] MP.

Guest says he has returned temporarily to endeavour to carry
through National Service. He denies that he is working with
Northcliffe. He has given a series of dinners of the same kind with a
view to stimulating action. After dinner he read out a very clever
memorandum [. . .] and proposed that it should be signed by a number
of Liberal Members of Parliament and circulated to the remainder of
the Liberal Members. I suggested that this would be dangerous. If
made public the memorandum might do the nation much injury.
Ultimately they determined upon a deputation to the PM.

28 August   Guest played golf with me yesterday. Very anxious for LG
to see his memorandum. Evidently Guest is playing the great game. He
should be at the Front. I have not forgotten our conversation when the
position of Chief Whip was vacant.[24] He is very ambitious. [. . .]

29 August   Lunched with LG at Walton. Long talk over mining
dispute. He agreed that Runciman had acted very foolishly. LG says
he is a small man with narrow views and very obstinate. LG says the
PM will have to assume responsibility, as in default of a settlement
there will be a serious row. I consequently spoke to the leaders and
explained the position.

Long talk with LG on the military position, conscription, etc. He
says that B Law, Curzon, etc are sure to resign unless something is
done. B Law will go, because if he stays and Curzon goes, the latter
will certainly become leader of the Conservative Party. LG says further
that the PM will probably try a compromise by accepting some form of
national service in order to keep himself on the elephant. He added,
'In the howdah.' [. . .]

LG read Guest's memorandum, written, I think, by Philip Carr or
Kerr[25] of the *Round Table*, who I am told is a very clever fellow. LG
was much impressed by the memorandum, but described it as a
dangerous document for publication. He was much interested as to the
amount of support for National Service available amongst Liberal
Members. I said, 'Guest mentioned forty-five.'

LG: That would do it. The PM could not stand against forty-five
members of his own party.

1 September Ellis Griffith, who is to speak at the Demonstration at the Queen's Hall tomorrow in favour of compulsory service, came to consult me regarding his speech. I strongly advised him to abandon the idea of universal service, industrial and military, and to confine himself to the latter. With this he agreed. I also advised him to urge the necessity for more careful selection in recruiting, so as to avoid the depletion of the manufacturing and export industries.

4 September I had a long talk with Captain F. Guest and introduced him to Caird of the *Daily Mail*. Guest strongly urged that the *Mail* should abstain from a violent propaganda in favour of compulsory service, and pointed out that this would be certain to defeat its own object. [. . .] Played golf with LG and Donald. LG very strong on necessity for conscription, but said that arrangements must be carried out by civilians. He told Donald that he was taking up the wrong line and would have to eat his words. [. . .] Donald was obviously very uneasy, but held his ground with feeble arguments which evidently annoyed LG. [. . .]

15 September Le Bas has proved to be a low blackguard. Having offended him over some small matter,[26] he wrote me two blackmailing letters in which he threatened to expose my divorce proceedings, and charged me with obtaining £500 from him by fraud three years ago. The £500 was part of a sum of £1,000 paid to LG in connection with the publication of his 'Life'. I showed the letters to LG who treated me very kindly and said, 'Do not worry. Your friends will stick with you. Le Bas is like a whore who is very pleasant so long as she gets her own way, but when crossed, spits, scratches, and uses vile language. He is a coarse fellow. You can see it in his face. His letters are disgraceful productions.' [. . .] I have never shown more kindness to any man, and have never been so badly treated by anyone.

29 September Sir Reginald Brade, Sir William Lever and Sir Howard Frank[27] to dinner. Brade told me privately that he doubts whether we shall get through the Dardanelles unless the efforts of the Turks can be diverted elsewhere. He says that Kitchener is busily considering various schemes for compulsory service. The War Office believe that it will be impossible to obtain the men required by voluntary effort. He believes that Kitchener favours the quota system. [. . .]

2 October   Drove to Walton with LG. He takes a gloomy view of the offensive in the West and does not believe that the Allies will achieve their object. He says the casualties have been enormous, ours amount to some 80,000 already. He believes that the Bulgarians are certain to side with Germany, and repeated that the negotiations have been badly managed by the Foreign Office. I inquired whether he thought that Kitchener had decided upon some sort of national service, and told him what I had heard from Brade. He gave no direct reply, but said that whatever K's own views might be, he was certain to stick closely to the PM, whom he regards, and perhaps rightly, as his only friend in the Cabinet. LG is of opinion that the Trade Union recruiting campaign will be a failure, as no recruits can be drawn from colliers, engineers, railway men, etc. The classes who can be spared and who have recruited badly are not trade unionists. LG says that Kitchener is most incompetent and that all the Cabinet realise this. There never was, in his opinion, a man who so little deserved his great reputation. He is quite incapable of dealing with his huge responsibilities. LG spoke highly of Carson, but thinks Bonar Law is a weak man. He says that the intrigue against him (LG) has broken down, as he knew it would. [. . .]

October [n.d.]   Dined with LG at Walton. He has not been well, but is better today. He spoke most anxiously of the situation. He says we are making straight for disaster. The situation in the Balkans is most serious. The Foreign Office have muddled the negotiations and the War Office have no plan of action. LG saw the PM today, and remonstrated, but without effect. [. . .]

LG says the PM is hopeless and that the management of affairs is characterised by general ineptitude. Then he exclaimed with great vehemence, 'I think it will be necessary for six or seven of us to resign and tell the country the truth. For a time we should be unpopular. We should be told that we were shaking the confidence of the nation and of our allies, and we should be charged with acting from selfish motives, but later on the public would recognise that we had done the right thing.' [. . .]

16 October   Dined with LG who says that Kitchener has come down definitely on the side of compulsory service. He is very firm and says that he will resign unless his scheme is accepted. The PM is, however, obdurate and obstinate, and appears to be entirely subject to

McKenna's influence. LG thinks the PM would like to get out as he does not care to face the storm. Probably he would ask Arthur Balfour to form a Cabinet in which he would be Lord Chancellor. The PM has been living in a quiet backwater which has suddenly been swept into the raging torrent. LG says that McKenna's advice is bad and dangerous, and that he will land the PM into a morass from which he may be unable to extricate himself. [LG says] Carson is sick to death of the eternal talk and policy of drift. The PM is a great man, but his methods are not suited to war. LG thinks anyone who accepts the Premiership now will be a bold man, as most probably he will have to face months of disaster, which he will not have the means of avoiding. [. . .]

19 October   Went to Strachey's (editor of the *Spectator*) to meet Lord Derby, with whom I spent two hours discussing his new recruiting scheme. He seems an able and energetic man. Very practical and clear. He also seems very cute. [. . .] He wanted to know how to interest the Press. I told him that at first the newspapers would be quite enthusiastic without any stimulus beyond the King's Appeal and Lord D's own letter. I, however, suggested that he should write a personal letter to all editors, which he said he would do. [. . .]

He talked of politics, and said that the war had proved to him that both parties were on the wrong tack. He felt that never again could he work with the Tories. For example the connection between the Tory Party and the liquor trade was, in his opinion, indefensible. [. . .]

21 October   Called on Northcliffe by appointment. Found him still full of prophecies and criticism. I have not seen him for about three months. He is a keen observer, and said many shrewd things. He still considers the Government most incompetent. The management of the Gallipoli campaign has been scandalous. The Balkan negotiations have been muddled, and there is no proper military plan. The defence of London has been neglected and mismanaged. The condition of affairs in Russia is most serious, and in France the recent offensive has been the most costly victory ever secured by British arms. I inquired what course N thought things will take. He replied, 'This Government will be out in three months. It will be succeeded by a Committee of Safety, comprising perhaps five leading men. Later they will probably be turned out, and then there will be a revolution. Another thing that may happen is a public exposure of the state of affairs in my newspapers.[28]

No doubt they may prosecute me, but I shall not mind if they do. When the true story of the Gallipoli campaign is published, the public will be aghast. Carson will probably state the case. He is an able man. He was against me in the soap libel.[29] He has the material for a very strong speech, and I think he will make it. He is a stout-hearted fellow.' [. . .]

23 October Lunched and played golf with LG. [. . .] He is perplexed as to the course he should take. He is convinced that unless our methods are changed we shall have a great disaster in the East, and that we shall ultimately be beaten in the war. He thinks the nation should be told the truth, but on the other hand that that cannot be done without disclosing information which it would be better not to make public. He is evidently pondering alternative courses of action. He does not know how to act. I told him of my conversation with Northcliffe, and in particular of his suggested exposure and subsequent prosecution. [. . .]

As I left LG I said, 'Perhaps it might be well to wait a little before deciding how to act. . . .'

LG laughed, and saying, 'There may be something to be said for a "wait and see" policy,' pulled the shawl over his aching head and composed himself for a nap. [. . .]

29 October LG, Lord Reading and Robertson Nicoll to lunch. We had a long talk extending from 1.30 to 4 p.m. Lord R is to spend the week-end with the PM, who evidently wishes to consult him upon the political situation. LG saw the PM this morning and is to see him again later in the day. LG says the whole Cabinet consider Kitchener incompetent, but that the PM cannot make up his mind to act. [. . .]

Lord Reading said he hoped LG would not resign, as this would be a national calamity. In any event he must base his case on some specific issue. Robertson Nicoll thought he should resign. LG said that he agreed. I said that the specific issue was the military conduct of the war, but that the PM would no doubt institute reforms rather than that LG should resign. LG said that he had not yet threatened resignation. If he resigns he would rather do so alone. Resignation in company with a group of Tory Ministers would lay his action open to misconstruction. He will have to determine how to act before Tuesday, when the PM makes his statement. Nicoll said that unless LG resigns he will be responsible for the mismanagement of affairs. Lord Reading responded, 'He cannot escape responsibility for the past, and it would be a calamity that the nation should be deprived of the services of the only man in the Cabinet with driving force, foresight, and initiative.' LG referred to the written warnings and protests which he had addressed to the PM, but admitted that he could not hope to escape responsibility for what had occurred. [. . .] LG bitterly complained of the attitude of the Liberal papers, which he said was due to McKenna. [. . .] In the early days of the Munitions Department he [McK] had gone about saying it was in a state of chaos and was being seriously mismanaged. LG said of course it was chaotic. How could it be anything else? How could you hope to start a big undertaking without a preliminary period of chaos? 'I started,' said he, 'with a chair and a table in a carpetless room with no staff. The whole fabric had to be created. Had McKenna been my friend he would have replied to criticism instead of encouraging it.'

I had tea at the Home Office with Sir John Simon. We had a long talk regarding the Censorship arrangements, when he outlined certain new proposals. [. . .]

He seemed to think No 1. [that disobedience to a Press Bureau notice would *ipso facto* constitute an offence under the Defence of the Realm Act] would meet with the approval of a large section of the Press. I assured him he was mistaken. The Press might quarrel amongst themselves, but they would all join in opposing any attempt to impose greater restraints or punishments. I also advised him to employ more trained sub-editors at the Bureau and to strengthen the Admiralty, War Office and Press Committee instead of creating a new body. I said that the Committee should meet regularly and frequently and should have a secretary who would keep in touch with the various departments. Sir John thanked me and promised to consider what I proposed. I think, however, that he meditates immediate action and I therefore communicated my suspicions to the most prominent members of the Newspaper Proprietors' Association. The Lord Chancellor, who was formerly director of the Press Bureau [Buckmaster], is said to be very active in his endeavours to tighten the Press shackles. [. . .]

Lord Derby asked me to call to see him.[30] He told me that this week's *Nation* contained a poisonous statement to the effect that he was getting all the recruits he required, and that this inaccurate statement, if repeated in other papers, would probably do his movement serious injury. I advised him to issue a contradiction through the Press Bureau, coupled with a statement that no estimate of the success of his scheme can yet be formed. He agreed to do this, and we drafted a memorandum, but could not complete it as he had no copy of the *Nation*. Lord D said he must keep faith with the married men, who were enlisting more freely than the young unmarried men. The married must not be called out unless the unmarried had enlisted in reasonable numbers. [. . .]

Lord D considers it an amazing sign of weakness that at such a time the Cabinet, feeling as they do, should not have the courage to reform the military administration. They are frightened of the people who believe in K because they do not know the facts.

4 November   Called to see LG at 6 Whitehall Gardens, but found him engaged. I, however, met Northcliffe coming out of his room, who eagerly inquired if I knew who the Cabinet Committee were to be. [. . .] Later Winston arrived looking very gloomy. He said that things are looking very bad. He also told me that he was tired of his present mode of life, and would not stand it much longer. [. . .]

A long interview at the House of Commons with the Home Secretary [Simon] regarding the Censorship. I handed him resolution passed on Wednesday by the Newspaper Conference, submitting that no change should be made without previous discussion with the newspapers. He was obviously much annoyed when I suggested that the Government might be proposing to pass an Order in Council which would make a breach of a Press Bureau notice an offence *ipso facto* under the Defence of the Realm Act. This he did not deny, but was very cool and distant. I told him that however much one section of the Press might criticise the other, the newspapers would unite in opposing any further restrictions. This seemed to surprise him. He told me that he was going to France to inquire into the Censorship arrangements for the Cabinet. I offered to send him my recent correspondence with the War Office. He gladly accepted this proposal. [. . .]

5 November   Talked with PM's secretary regarding alterations in censorship. I repeated what I had said to the Home Secretary. From what the secretary, Davies, told me, the subject has evidently been much discussed. Sir Graham Greene, the Secy for the Admiralty, sent for me and referred to the same question. I told him that the real defect in the system was the manner of censoring military information.

The Press Officers at GHQ are considered unduly restrictive and the military censors at the Bureau do not know their business. The remedy was to alter the policy at GHQ and to employ more sub-editors at the Bureau. I said that there was comparatively little criticism of the Admiralty.

7 November   Dined with L.G. [. . .]

LG: Yes, it has been a big week.

R: Did the PM show much fight?

LG: Yes and no. I saw he was moving, and so *I handed him my resignation last Sunday.*[31] I took a big risk. I might have been outside the Cabinet. However, it turned out all right. Bonar Law would have resigned with me. He was here last Sunday. I had someone down to write my letter and sent it by my messenger. Now the old PM and I have resumed our former relationship. I think from custom the old boy is glad. He had been accustomed to act with me for so long that he missed me. [. . .]

R: I suppose Kitchener will not return to the War Office. (Yesterday it was announced that he had gone to the East to advise the Government.)

LG: No. I am relieved that he has gone. The whole tone of the War Office has changed for the better. Everyone was afraid of him. We could get nothing done. Then again he is a liar. [. . .]

R: Who is going to the War Office?

LG: I think the PM will stay there for the present. He rather likes the job. Haldane will have to stay away. [. . .]

R: Have you heard of the proposals regarding the Censorship?

LG: Yes. Curzon and I are fighting them in the Cabinet. Simon and Buckmaster don't like our opposition. Buckmaster has not been a success. He is a poor Chancellor and does not do well in the Cabinet. [. . .]

LG: I have enjoyed our talk, as I always do. That was a useful chat we had with Rufus and Robertson Nicoll at your house on Friday week. It helped me a great deal in my interviews with the PM. It gave me a line. Perhaps, however, I should have insisted on resigning.

R: You did the right thing. Resignation would have been a mistake. You are more effective in the Government than you would be outside. You have had your way. You are getting things put right. You may have sacrificed yourself, but you have done the best thing for your country.

LG: That is the only thing that matters. I am content, and happier than I have been for months.

And so to bed.

9 November   It is evident that LG is working closely in touch with
Northcliffe, and gradually shedding the sentimental section of the
Radical party – men like Whitehouse,[32] for whom he now has the
heartiest contempt. None of the Radicals in the Cabinet is working
with him. McKenna, Simon, Runciman, McKinnon Wood,
Buckmaster, Harcourt, etc, are bitterly opposed to him. He finds his
supporters amongst the Conservatives. It looks as if he is going the
same road as Chamberlain. LG's attitude to the war makes his
severance from the Radicals inevitable. The force of circumstances is
leading him into the same position as that in which Chamberlain found
himself. Bereft of his associates on the great question of the day, he is
perforce obliged to seek support elsewhere. LG's future is interesting.

11 November   [Brade][33] lunched with me. He says K made no special
remark when he left the War Office. He just said goodbye and that he
would be back in about three weeks or a month. 'And,' added my
friend, 'I believe he means to come back. If he achieves a great success
in the East and decides to return to the WO, they will have a lot of
trouble to turn him out.' [. . .] My friend says that Mr A is easy to do
business with. Very quick and very definite. If any topic requires
prolonged investigation, he puts it aside for consideration and an-
nounces his decision later. [. . .]

November [n.d.]   Several interviews this week with Sir John Simon
regarding the Censorship. His evident anxiety to meet the newspaper
editors is most amusing. He is a sly fellow and eaten up with
ambition. [. . .]

14 November   Dined with LG. Evidently much annoyed that
McKenna has been added to the Cabinet War Committee. [. . .]

26 November   Met Sir Edward Carson for the first time. Much struck
by his gentle manner and kindly ways. He made some humorous
remarks regarding the amount of talking done in the Cabinet; but
spoke highly of Lloyd G. Carson said he was sorry Winston had
resigned,[34] as he was one of the few men of action in the Government.
[. . .] He told me a good story concerning Disraeli and Biggar, who
used to take off his boots during all-night sittings. Disraeli was seated

on the bench in front of Biggar, who placed one of his stockinged feet on the back of the bench on each side of Disraeli's head, with the most comical effect. 'What is happening?' inquired one of Disraeli's friends, who had just entered the House. 'We fear foot and mouth disease,' responded Disraeli in deep sepulchral tones!

28 November LG and I played golf and lunched together. He says things are very unpleasant in the War Council. Chiefly for reasons of personal antagonism. McKenna opposes almost every project which LG suggests or supports. As a result the atmosphere is unpleasant and unfavourable to the transaction of business. [. . .] Kitchener is expected back in a week or ten days. LG says he does not yet know what will happen on his return, i.e. whether he will go back to the WO. Since his departure a wonderful change for the better has taken place. It is now possible to transact business with reasonable facility.[35] [. . .]

I suspect that Masterman is responsible for the mistake made this week by Simon in attacking *The Times* for a paragraph which had appeared in a Russian paper criticising the attitude of *The Times* concerning the war. The paragraph had in fact been cabled to Russia from Paris, and had apparently been written in England. Simon apparently did not know that *The Times* is the English organ of the Russian Government. Of course the editor was easily able to quote the Czar and other distinguished Russians in opposition to the newspaper paragraph. Simon foolishly apologised and this gave *The Times* an opportunity of castigating him.[36]

Masterman & Co. are always endeavouring to make war on the Northcliffe press. The result is that they usually bring trouble on themselves. If they adopted the wiser policy of waiting for a suitable opportunity, they would do better.

30 November Brade lunched with me. He says Kitchener will be back tomorrow, but Brade does not know whether he will return to the War Office.[37] K has had no letters and does not know what has happened in his absence. While he has been away important events have occurred. LG has been very busy taking over the Ordnance Board, etc. He has evidently been most anxious to get the transfer completed before K's return. [. . .] Asquith [. . .] seems to have assisted LG to carry out his plans. [. . .] The position regarding K is amazing. No doubt the PM is between the Devil and the deep sea. If K does not agree to take up other duties, the PM may be faced with the recrudescence of the resignations difficulty in the Cabinet. If K resigns the Government will be much weakened in the country. The people implicitly believe in K and distrust the politicians. [. . .] Brade is looking forward to tomorrow with no little curiosity and evidently some perturbation. He thinks that K will content himself with registering a protest against what has been done in his absence.

5 December   Dined with LG at Downing Street. Donald and Herbert Lewis, MP, also. [. . .]

Herbert Lewis told me as I walked home that the Radicals are very suspicious of LG just now. They suspect him of being in close touch with Northcliffe, their arch-enemy. Herbert Lewis added, 'I don't know if the charge is true or not, but the party are watching their late idol very closely.'

11 December   [. . .] In the evening I dined with LG, Mrs LG, and Olwen. After dinner LG and I had a long private talk. He inquired whether I did not think that the country was becoming very anxious and dissatisfied with the Cabinet, and particularly with the PM. Last night LG dined with Waldorf Astor, who told him that he heard this on all sides. I said that I did the same. Everywhere one goes it is the same story. Everyone is complaining of the Government's indecision and lack of plans. I added, 'The psychological moment is fast arriving for some action on your part.'

LG: [. . .] The situation is serious. The PM cannot make up his mind. Having formed the War Committee, he has rendered it practically useless by bringing in the Cabinet on all important occasions. [. . .]

The wits are calling Asquith 'Old Squiffo', and Asquith and Balfour 'Boozle and Foozle' – very disrespectful. [. . .]

18 December   Dined with LG. [. . .] He is still gloomy about the war. He deplores the lack of co-ordination among the Allies and says the Serbian Army has been sacrificed in consequence. Like a political Mrs Gummidge, he still hankers after Winston. [. . .]

31 December   Lord Derby asked me to call to see him at the War Office. He said he wished to thank me. [. . .] He spoke very kindly and with considerable feeling. He was also good enough to say that I had given him sound advice which he had found most useful. He seemed much perturbed at the suggestion which is being made in Labour circles that he had jockeyed the PM into the pledge to the married men. He said that the PM had rendered him every assistance, and that what Asquith had done had been performed entirely on his own initiative. [. . .]

We talked of K. Lord D said that he did not think that K appreciated that the Cabinet were antagonistic to him. [. . .] He has already had one or two passages with Robertson, the new Chief of Staff, who is a tough nut. [. . .]

The Press are concerned at the growing practice of Cabinet Ministers and other public officials in granting interviews to persons not connected with newspapers and to foreign journalists, regarding important public affairs. At the request of the Conference I addressed a letter to the PM on the subject and also wrote to McKenna, the latest and most pronounced offender. The latter replied expressing regret. The PM is considering the subject.

January–July 1916

After the conscription crisis of late 1915 the first three months of the new year were comparatively tranquil on the home front. Lloyd George was less occupied with departmental matters than in the early days of the Ministry of Munitions, and Riddell saw more of him. His isolated position in the Cabinet encouraged him to make many critical observations on certain colleagues, Asquith not least, and also to hark back more than once to the subject of resignation. Disgruntled with his fellow Ministers, Lloyd George now began to extol the merits of colonial politicians like Hughes of Australia, whom he introduced to Riddell, and Smuts of South Africa. At the same time Northcliffe continued to interest Lloyd George greatly, although he reacted coolly to a trial balloon sent up by Robertson Nicoll of the *British Weekly* that Northcliffe should be made Minister for Air Defence. From January to March, Riddell's source of inside information was limited chiefly to Lloyd George, with Lord Reading being in their company occasionally. He saw nothing of Churchill, who was mostly in France, and conversations with McKenna had ceased altogether. On the other hand his liaison work for the Press brought him into contact with 10 Downing Street. During these weeks the names of prominent news-papermen like Lord Northcliffe, Sir Henry Dalziel, Robert Donald and Sir Robertson Nicoll appear frequently in the diary.

The second quarter of 1916 was anything but calm in Britain. In a period of seven weeks there occurred: (*a*) the final conscription crisis which nearly wrecked the Government; (*b*) the fall of Kut; (*c*) the Easter rebellion in Dublin; (*d*) the death of Lord Kitchener; and (*e*) the battle of Jutland. The battle of the Somme began on 1 July. In consequence Riddell's diary is much fuller, the result of many talks with Lloyd George, chiefly about the minister's future, and other conversations with such figures as A. J. Balfour, Bonar Law, General Robertson and Sir Reginald Brade. The burning issue during the month of June was whether Lloyd George should go to the War Office, and as before he turned to Riddell and Nicoll for advice. A *Daily Chronicle* article on the powers of the Secretary for War angered Lloyd George, and for the first time he began to talk about humbling

Robert Donald and getting control of the paper. This followed logically from his remarks to Riddell a few weeks earlier concerning a new political party under his leadership and financed by wealthy friends.

Meanwhile the stirring events of this quarter kept Riddell busier than usual with his Press liaison work. By the beginning of July we find Lloyd George and Churchill resuming something of their old amicable relationship, with Max Aitken becoming more prominent in the role of go-between.

5 January   Golfed and lunched with LG and the LCJ. The former gave an interesting account of his trip to France last week. He says things are much more business-like than in French's time. There is a new spirit. Haig seems very keen on his job and has a fine staff. LG admits that the Government is showing more grip in all Departments except air-raid defence. [. . .]

I explained to LG a new system of political corruption which is being established. The Government Departments, notably the Treasury and the War Office, are giving out huge amounts of advertising to the Press. No institution can be more readily influenced by a comparatively small expenditure. Unless compelled by strong circumstances, newspapers rarely attack large advertisers. They cannot afford to do so. The Press lives on advertising. The company promoter, bucketshop keeper, and patent medicine dealer who advertises is seldom attacked or criticised. The Government departments are being awakened to the advantages of advertising, the campaign being conducted by McKenna's protégé, my quondam friend Sir Hedley Le Bas. Last week the thrift committee report was issued. This is a Treasury committee of which Le B is a member. The same day the Press was plastered with whole pages of Treasury advertising, and the night before the Editors were canvassed by Le Bas for favourable notices. Obviously this is a most dangerous implement which might lead to widespread corruption. LG was much interested and said he must watch this carefully.

We talked much concerning the Labour situation on the Clyde.[1] Things are going better than was anticipated. The Government have at last laid the seditionists by the heels. [. . .]

I strongly urged LG to attend the Free Church Conference this year. Dr Clifford is anxious that he and Robertson Nicoll should do so. At first LG was doubtful. He said he was not disposed to divert his attention from getting on with the war. I pointed out that the continued support and goodwill of the Dissenters was an important factor. Ultimately he said he thought I was right, and that he would attend. He is to lunch with Nicoll and me on Thursday to discuss the details.

14 January Long and interesting meetings of the Admiralty, War Office and Press Committee, convened to discuss feasibility of devising some method of punishing newspapers which habitually committed minor breaches of regulations of Press Bureau and thus inflicted injury upon their rivals by whom the regulations were observed. I moved a resolution to the effect that it was undesirable to create new methods of punishment or procedure and that the authorities should use the ample powers conferred on them by the Defence of the Realm Act. This was carried unanimously. The authorities enforce the Act in a most unequal and inadequate manner. No steps are taken against papers which habitually publish seditious matter.

15 January Much Labour dissatisfaction with the Conscription Bill. I wrote LG criticising the drafting and pointing out the necessity for amending the Bill so as to preclude the possibility of industrial compulsion. He agreed. I also saw Bonham Carter, the PM's secretary, as to the miners' opposition, which had been explained to me by Hartshorn and other leaders. I suggested that the PM should see representatives of the Miners' Federation. I told Bonham Carter that miners, railway men and transport workers were not acting in conjunction with Henderson and that the miners considered they had been slighted by the Government. [. . .]

Golfed with LG, and LCJ and Donald. LG full of spirits and more optimistic than I have seen him. He is satisfied that the Labour opposition to the Bill will be pacified and ridicules anything in the nature of a strike. [. . .]

16 January Dined with LG. He says McKenna and Runciman are very unhappy regarding their anti-compulsion campaign. The Lord Chief was sure they would resign, but LG offered to bet him they would not. The PM also thought their resignation certain, but LG told him he really need have no fears, and that in any case the Government would not be severely shaken. Simon is very sick that McKenna and Runciman did not stand by him. LG thinks that Simon will not suffer in the long run. [. . .] The PM was irresolute and acted only when he was told that a large section of his Cabinet would resign if he did not fulfill his pledge. The Liberal Members would have acted with him had he determined to ignore it, of course, excluding LG. [. . .] LG does not know what will happen at the War Office. At present the arrangements are very unsatisfactory. K is doing little or nothing. [. . .] The difficulty is to know whom to send to the War Office if K goes elsewhere. [. . .] We had a long talk about labour. He fears trouble in Glasgow, regarding which I have been warning him for months past. He says he intends to take a firm line and would rather have a six weeks' strike now than later on. He excuses the inaction of the Government in reference to sedition by saying that McKinnon Wood and the Lord Advocate[2] are afraid to act. The latter he calls a rabbit. [. . .]

21 January Bonham Carter asked me to call. He said the PM is anxious to explain privately to the Press the principles of the blockade before the debate on Wednesday, and asked my opinion as to the advisability of such a conference. I said some of the editors might decline to attend, e.g. the editors of *The Times, Morning Post,* and *Daily Mail,* but on the whole I thought the conference would be useful. I arranged to call it for Tuesday next. I spoke to Northcliffe, or rather he rang me up on another matter. He said the editors of *The Times* and *Daily Mail* would not attend. He did not approve of conferences. He, however, seemed anxious to know what took place. He says the Government intend to prohibit the import of newspaper and wood pulp, and that a meeting has been, or is about to be, convened at the Board of Trade for the purpose of discussing the subject and if possible of arranging to limit the size of newspapers during the war. He seemed very hostile to the project, and intimated that he and his brother would endeavour to take full advantage of the position in which they were placed by their Newfoundland venture. It is said that the day after the subject was discussed in Cabinet, Rothermere at once bought up all the available supplies of wood pulp. How he heard of the Cabinet decision does not yet appear, but I have my suspicions.[3]

23 January Golfed with LG, who says he has made up his mind to enforce the dilution of labour in Glasgow next week. He expects serious trouble – a prospect confirmed by private letters from Glasgow people who know. These I have been sending him for weeks past. [. . .] He commented upon an article by the Military Correspondent of *The*

Times which appeared on Thursday, in which the writer urged the necessity for concentration on the Western Front, and said it represented the views of the General Staff. He added that during the war the Press had performed the function which should have been performed by Parliament, and which the French Parliament had performed. I did not remind him that in the early part of the war he had been in favour of Parliament being suspended, which I always thought a great error from the national point of view. LG is evidently very close with Northcliffe, no doubt through the medium of Alec Murray. [. . .]

25 January The PM met the Press and made a convincing statement regarding the blockade. Some of the editors criticised the action of the Government, but they cut a poor figure. They should have asked for a half-hour interval, during which they could no doubt have pulverised Mr A with pen and ink. When Steed,[4] the Foreign Editor of *The Times*, was speaking, the PM put two or three artful questions which entirely disorganised Steed's arguments. Lord Robert Cecil, clad in two waistcoats, made quite a good little speech, but too gracious and polite. He evidently wanted to conciliate the Press. Balfour did not speak except to ask in a very loud voice, 'Who is this man?', referring to Steed. [. . .]

Yesterday Runciman outlined his policy in regard to restricted imports of pulp and paper. I spoke for the Press, and the Conference was adjourned till today, when we had another long meeting, one of the most momentous in the history of newspapers. Sizes will have to be reduced, and other economies effected. I have a difficult task. The views of the different proprietors are so divergent. Northcliffe has been in close touch with me, but it is difficult to know what he really wants, except of course to restrict the limitations of imports to the smallest possible dimensions. [. . .] There is going to be a big fight between those who have paper stocks and those who have none. [. . .]

11 February Nicoll has published an absurd article in which he proposes that Northcliffe should be appointed Minister of Air Defence. He suggests that the Government should disarm their chief critic and let him show what he can do. Northcliffe evidently regards the proposal seriously and had sent an emissary in the shape of Leicester Harmsworth[5] to feel Nicoll's pulse, and to intimate that in a leading position the great man might oblige. Nicoll of course speaks for himself alone, and his suggestion is generally regarded with ridicule.

Today LG and Nicoll lunched with me at Queen Anne's Gate. LG soon mentioned N's article with evident curiosity. He said, 'Northcliffe would not be a success. He has no experience of acting with equals. He would be specially handicapped in a Cabinet of twenty-two. He would be overcome by the inertia and combined opposition of his colleagues – trade unionism is strong amongst politicians – that is the trouble during a war like this. Usually a Minister thinks more of defending his own position than he does of the matter in hand. [. . .]'

Returning to Northcliffe, he remarked, 'He is best where he is. . . . A minister cannot threaten resignation every day, and unless he is strong and well supported, no threat would have much effect.' [. . .] Nicoll has made a grave error in starting the idea that N must be bought off with a seat in the Cabinet. [. . .]

17 February Had breakfast with LG. [. . .]

LG thinks Winston should have been made head of the [Air] Department. He says the PM is rattled badly. I remarked that his speech at the opening of Parliament was very slipshod and contained a split infinitive, which the world usually regards as worse than a German victory! LG laughed and agreed. [. . .]

The immediate purpose of our talk was the appointment of a successor to Lord Murray as head of the Labour Department at the Munitions. The preliminary announcement that Sir George Croydon Marks[6] is to succeed him has roused a storm in the Department. [. . .]

These breakfast parties [of LG] are a mistake. Before he starts the work of a day he has talked columns. [. . .] The consequence was that by noon he was feeling tired out and had to telephone for the doctor. [. . .]

26 February Motored to Walton. [. . .] I had a long talk with [LG]. He is perturbed at the progress of the battle at Verdun and thinks the French are losing ground. He is evidently dissatisfied with the condition of affairs here. He says the PM never moves until he is forced, and then it is usually too late. He fears we shall not improve matters until we get another leader. He says that at a time like this the PM should lead, not follow. Mr A has no policy and is always prepared to adopt any change which will enable him to retain his position. In that respect he is growing like Walpole. [. . .]

He considers that Bonar Law is partly to blame, as he does not take a strong line with the PM. He thinks Bonar Law's position difficult, as he has no support in the Cabinet from his own party. Balfour regards him with mild contempt, Curzon[7] and Walter Long hate him, Bob Cecil is opposed to him on most subjects, and Austen Chamberlain is his rival. I inquired whether the time had come when he (LG) should say something publicly. He replied, 'I should have to resign.' I said, 'You would have to explain the reason and give specific causes.' 'That I should be unable to do,' he answered. [. . .]

LG asked me why I thought Northcliffe was adopting this new role of advertising himself. Formerly he kept in the background and only advertised his papers. It was *The Times* or *Daily Mail*. Now it is Northcliffe. [. . .]

10 March   To breakfast at LG's at Downing Street, to meet W. M. Hughes,[8] the Australian Prime Minister. Mrs Hughes, Donald, and Gwynne of the *Morning Post* also of the party. Hughes struck me as an able man. He is very deaf but remarkably acute and direct in what he says; the ablest Colonial politician I have met. [. . .]

11 March   Called for LG. [. . .] He says Winston has made Fisher's return to the Admiralty impossible.[9] LG also thinks it will now be impossible for the Cabinet to make Fisher a member of the War Council. [. . .] He thinks, however, that Winston may retrieve his position. [. . .]

12 March   In the evening I went to LG's to dinner. He told me he was sure the War Office had intended to smash him. [. . .] Haldane's speech in support of Von Donop was made after Haldane *had seen the PM*.[10] LG spoke at length upon the necessity for a constructive agricultural policy and said that after great trouble he had succeeded in getting a Cabinet Committee appointed to investigate the subject. He also referred to the necessity for constructing more lateral lines of railway at the front in France, so as to facilitate the massing of troops, artillery, etc. He added, 'No one deals with these topics in the House of Commons. This makes me feel that perhaps the time has come for me to leave the Government. If I did, I should not attack the Government; I should confine myself to constructive proposals. The war is really being run badly. The nation is not being organised.' [. . .]

'McKenna is now most anxious to be friendly with me (LG). The collapse of Le Bas' attack on you (R) shows that. He is now getting no support from McKenna.'

(Le Bas made an ignominous settlement with me which I did not seek. He has discontinued his libel action, paid the costs, apologised for his rascally letter, retired from the Newnes board, and given me my own terms for my interest in the Caxton.)[11] [. . .]

18 March   Golfed with LG, the LCJ, and Donald. Political atmosphere cloudy. At these times the LCJ always appears on the scene. No doubt as the PM's emissary. The LCJ says Asquith's stock is low just now, but that he will probably revive it by a clever speech. The Chief spoke of him as a wonderful person. [. . .]

19 March   Dined with LG and Mrs LG alone. He told me that Hughes, the Australian PM, had spoken to him of the present unsatisfactory condition of affairs. Hughes said he had seen all sorts of people and was satisfied all was not well and that a change would have to be made. He had suggested that LG should see Bonar Law with a view to closer co-operation. LG remarked that he did not quite see the object in view. He would not be prepared to replace Asquith by Bonar Law. He thinks Asquith much superior to BL in every way – a much bigger man. [. . .] LG thinks Hughes should stay here for at least six months and that other great Colonies should be represented. He would like to see Borden[12] and Botha or Smuts on the Council, particularly Smuts, of whom LG spoke very highly. He said that Asquith held a contemptuous opinion of Smuts at the time of the South African War. Asquith did not appreciate what a remarkable man he was.

LG again referred to Asquith's contempt of the Press. He regards journalists as ignorant, spiteful and unpatriotic. Notwithstanding this, Massingham goes to Downing Street to lunch. LG told Mrs A that Massingham always turned on his friends and will turn on Mr A. 'And,' added LG, 'he is turning already. Have you seen the *Nation* lately?' [. . .] He [LG] says the Government still lacks driving force, initiative, and foresight. Notwithstanding this, he thinks Mr A the best man for Premier, but wishes he would make him, LG, a sort of executive officer charged with the duty of listening to suggestions and exercising general supervision. LG has given up seeing Asquith privately to discuss matters or to urge suggestions.

24 March   [. . .] Sir Henry Dalziel came to lunch. [. . .] Dalziel tells me that he believes LG will be Premier before Christmas, and that Bonar Law has agreed to serve under him.[13] They are all getting sick of Asquith, so Dalziel says. [. . .]

1 April LG [. . .] had dinner with Carson on Friday. LG told me that he is much dissatisfied and thinks he must leave the Cabinet. He feels he is taking part in a fraud which is sacrificing and will sacrifice hundreds of thousands of lives. Mr A has no plan, no initiative, no grip, no driving force. He made a poor show at the Conference. LG thinks he will have to resign soon. The condition of affairs is serious. [. . .] He spoke highly of Dr Addison's[14] management of the Clyde district. He says he is a clever, courageous little man. [. . .]

8 and 9 April LG says Bethmann-Hollweg's[15] speech is most important. It discloses for the first time German plans of territorial settlement after the war. LG thinks the speech able and virile. With the exception of the *Daily News*, the papers have failed to recognise its importance. The political situation here is still disturbed. Derby wants to resign his position as Director of Recruiting. LG has persuaded him not to do so. His appointment was made by Asquith & Co. to ward off conscription. LG favours conscription for all – married and single – but Bonar Law and the Tories funk the situation. Bonar Law told Donald two or three days ago he was not convinced we could spare more men from industrial occupations. LG thinks this statement accurately describes Bonar Law's views. [. . .]

I asked what LG thought of the Budget speech. LG said, 'It was very good – clear and plain – no attempt at oratory.' I said, 'McKenna has altered his tone as to our financial resources. Some months ago he foreshadowed financial ruin. Now he talks in a more optimistic strain.'

LG: Yes, I reminded him of that a few days ago. [. . .]

I enquired what line Northcliffe was taking just now.

LG: I have not discussed the matter with him. He does not know that all depends on Robertson's decision.

R: You must be careful of Northcliffe. He has a dangerous strain. He is apt to want to destroy things in which he is not directly concerned, without providing for reconstruction or replacement. [. . .]

13 April Nicoll and Scott arrived, followed by LG who said he had seen Scott earlier in the day. [. . .]

LG: [. . .] Well, what do you think of the position, Sir William? I have got Scott's opinion and I want yours. We have a Cabinet today to consider the recruiting question. The Army Council have made a strong report. We came to no decision. The discussion is adjourned until Monday. [. . .] Now, Sir William, what is your opinion? Do you think I should go out? [. . .]

Nicoll: May I ask you a question? On what are you thinking of going out? On the enlistment question?

LG: One must have an immediate reason. Enlistment would furnish this, but I should really resign as a protest against the general conduct of the war. We never do anything until we are prodded into doing it, and then we are always too late. [. . .]

Nicoll (after profound meditation): I think you should go out. You will be of more service out than in.

LG: I am glad to hear you say that. That is my opinion, and Scott agrees. What is your view, Riddell?

R: You must consider the effect upon the country and our Allies. Your resignation will cause a shudder. On the other hand, if you feel that the conduct of the war is so inefficient that resignation is the only remedy, I think you should go. [. . .]

Nicoll and Scott: You must remain in the House of Commons and form, not an opposition, but a party of criticism.

Scott: But you must not confine yourself to a destructive policy. You must put forward a constructive policy.

LG: I agree. Carson is improving daily. He is managing his little group with great skill. He is a fine fellow.

Nicoll: He has no following in the country.

LG: Perhaps you are right about that. However, I have quite made up my mind. Unless they accept the Army Council recommendations, I shall go out on Monday. [. . .]

The interview lasted for nearly two hours. LG seemed in good spirits. He went away with Scott. [. . .]

14 April As I anticipated, the LCJ appeared on the scene this morning. He drove down to Walton with LG, lunched, and played golf in the afternoon. He told me that last Sunday he stayed with the PM at his house on the Thames. What happened did not relate, but I have no doubt that wily Henry[16] arranged for tactful Rufus[17] to bring his powers to bear upon LG. The same procedure always happens when LG kicks up his heels. Sometimes it is the LCJ; at others oily Alec Murray; and in cases of dire distress a combined attack. Just now Murray is *hors de combat*. I inquired how the Chief regarded the situation. He replied that he was strongly opposed to LG resigning, as he thought the resignation would have a bad effect on our allies. [. . .]

LG says he doubts if Asquith will give way. Asquith feels he is committed against further conscription. [. . .]

Thus end two exciting days. LG's intentions are not of course surmised by the Press. He may be bluffing to get better terms from the PM, but I think not. As old Nicoll says, 'Whatever happens, it is very interesting.' I wish the conditions were not so serious.

16 April Stamfordham[18] called to see LG with the object of pre-vailing upon him to abandon his intention of resigning. Davies,[19] LG's secretary, tells me that LG remained quite firm and that Stamfordham left evidently surprised and disappointed at the failure of his mission. [. . .]

20 April The political crisis is over. I called to see LG at Downing Street. He was alone, preparing to go to Criccieth for Easter. I said, 'You have had a great victory. It must have been an arduous task.' He replied, walking up and down the room, 'It has been a trying week. I have had a hard fight. I have had to carry it on single-handed almost to the end, except of course for Robertson's assistance. He is a splendid fellow. When the dispute came to a certain point, Bonar Law turned round and made a great show of being firm and courageous. His followers compelled him to take that course. But I am sick of the Cabinet and sorry I am not out of it. They are poor creatures to carry on a great war.' [. . .]

21 April Lunched at Carlton Gardens with Arthur Balfour. Lord Lansdowne called while we were at lunch and joined the party. AJB arrived late, having been detained at the Cabinet. He brought the news that the crisis was over; that a settlement had been reached and that the facts and figures on which it had been based are to be stated in a secret session of Parliament which is to be held on Tuesday. He said that he thought the settlement fair and one which would commend itself to all parties. [. . .]

The conversation turned on the armament firms. I told Balfour and Lansdowne about Zaharoff,[20] the wonderful man who controls Vickers and other armament firms. They had never heard of him, strange to say, and were much surprised and interested. [. . .]

24 April My wife and I dined with Sir Reginald Brade to meet General and Lady Robertson and Bonar Law. Bonar Law talked very freely of the political situation, which he regards as serious. He considers the attack in the *Daily News* on LG vicious and uncalled for.[21] He was evidently anxious to hear whether LG intends to reply to it. I, of course, not knowing, was unable to enlighten him. He said he thought the article was due to political causes. I told him I thought it was due in a great measure to the fact that LG had been acting in conjunction with Northcliffe, whom the *Daily News* people hate with virulent animosity. BL says that Northcliffe is quite unreliable and altogether wanting in stability. He has no principles and is merely an opportunist. BL thinks the Government may break up at any moment. He said that Asquith accepted the new conscription plan because he (BL) and his colleagues from the Tory side would have resigned had he not done so. [. . .]

How many men are available he [Robertson] does not know. That will have to be ascertained. The only method of getting the information is to take compulsory powers. Bonar Law replied, 'You foolish soldiers think that the winning of the war depends only on men. You forget that it depends on money as well.' This rather nettled Robertson, who retorted, 'How about the foolish politicians? Only today I told my people to look out the memoranda I prepared and submitted to the Cabinet some years ago regarding the means of performing our Treaty obligations to Belgium and on Home Defence. They were brushed aside in the most contemptuous way, and what has been the result?'

Bonar Law then discussed the relative demands of trade and the Army, rather insisting upon the former, but ultimately admitted the necessity for compulsion to gather in the 200,000 married men who, it is admitted, can be spared. BL spoke highly of Asquith's judgement, but admitted his lack of grip and driving power. He thinks it would be impossible to replace him, and that if the soliders were asked, they would say that Asquith is the best of the politicians in the War Council. BL turned to Robertson and said, 'Don't you agree?' Robertson did not give a definite reply. [. . .] Bonar Law then turned the conversation to Kitchener, and remarked that our one great mistake in the war had been to appoint him Secretary of State for War. I said, 'He has flashes of genius'; to which BL retorted, 'I am glad to hear he has flashes of anything.' I reminded BL that when K was first appointed his colleagues regarded him almost with awe. [. . .] He thinks that too much blame has been attached to Winston in respect of Gallipoli, and that the failure was really due to the inefficiency of the War Office. BL spoke much of LG. He said that LG recently came to him and remarked that there was no real confidence between them and that he would like a heart-to-heart talk. BL replied. 'I do not confide in you because I do not agree with you.' [. . .]

27 April   Balfour met the Press at the Admiralty. He spoke for an hour and a half and gave an interesting account of the naval situation. He did not mention Fisher or Winston, but gave them some Balfourian thrusts which were not noticed by his hearers, but which conveyed the desired impression in a subtle way. [. . .]

28 April   [. . .] I called to see him [LG] later at his office about 6.30. While I was waiting, in walked Geoffrey Robinson[22] (Editor of *The Times*). He had an interview with LG, who is evidently very close with Northcliffe & Co. LG said to me that the *Daily News* article had really served him a good turn. It had rallied the Conservatives around him and also a number of people who dislike personal attacks. It had also served to cut him off from 'that crowd', by which I suppose he meant the Radical Party. He added, 'One must have friends.' I said, 'I am sorry to say the march of events has justified and will justify your position: the Irish Rebellion; the Fall of Kut, just announced; and the muddle regarding the Recruiting Bill, ignominiously withdrawn last night.' [. . .]

I drove away with LG. As he was leaving the Ministry he met David Davies,[23] the colliery millionaire, with whom he had a short but earnest conversation. LG said, 'David Davies will be useful. If a new political party is to be formed, money will be wanted.[24] You cannot fight an election without an organisation, which means money. I have told Davies that he will have to help and I have received offers from other quarters.'

I then had to leave LG and so heard no more of his plans, but evidently he contemplates a new party. A dangerous experiment at such a time. However, we shall see. I did not tell him how unpopular he is with the working classes, who think he is endeavouring to shackle them. Hartshorn, a good judge, came to see me last night. He says that a Minister should go to Wales to address the miners. Strangely, he proposed Bonar Law. He described LG as 'impossible'. What a change in a few months! [. . .]

29 April   LG came to dinner. [. . .] I warned him that the working classes are not friendly to him at the moment and that he will have to be careful not to antagonise them any further. He said, 'They will come round later on. They like a man.' I agreed, but emphasised the importance of not fanning suspicion and discontent, which are grave national perils. He said that Asquith evidently fears his speech. He has suggested that LG should visit Russia regarding munitions. LG proposes to postpone his temporary disappearance from the scene of action here. His antagonism to his colleagues is becoming more and more marked. [. . .]

4 May Attended deputation to Home Secretary and Attorney-General regarding Defence of the Realm Regulations affecting the Press. I presented the case. The Ministers promised very slight concessions, and I told them plainly we should continue our agitation.

13 May [. . .] Golfed with LG. He wants me to arrange a conference between him and the Press, which I have promised to do. The *Glasgow Herald* has been attacking him. He puts this down to Bonar Law.[25] The consistent attacks upon LG are evidently having their effect. He is becoming more bitter and aggressive. He evidently thinks that his colleagues, including the PM, are anxious for his downfull, and he hails with ill-concealed satisfaction any signs of their waning popularity. [. . .]

This week I presented LG with the house in which he lives at Walton Heath.[26] In acknowledging the deed he wrote me a most charming letter. [. . .] A delightful souvenir of our friendship.

14 May T. P. O'Connor,[27] Joseph Devlin, O'Farrell and Browne, the Irish barrister, arrived at Walton Heath intent upon negotiations for the settlement of the Irish question. They wanted to see LG, so I arranged for them to dine with me. The Irish had a long chat with LG, who ultimately promised to see Carson and Northcliffe. The Nationalists are evidently very anxious for a settlement. [. . .]

15 May LG and I golfed together in the morning. He said that Carson has a great opportunity to make a bargain with the Irish Party. LG doubted, however, whether Carson was an astute bargainer. [. . .] He said it was a pity he was in the Government, as otherwise he would have had the task of making the bargain. From this and other signs I gather that he contemplates being the leader of a new party mainly composed of Conservatives. He said in reply to my inquiry that he doubted whether Asquith had gone to Ireland with any plan. He thinks he went chiefly to avoid a parliamentary difficulty, which is the one sort of difficulty he fears. LG, like all politicians, possesses a firm belief in himself and his power and ability to cope with difficulties. Self-confidence is part of the politician's stock-in-trade. I suppose that without it they could not carry on. [. . .] LG often says Asquith is not a war minister, and although he does not add, as he might well do, that he himself has the capacity, obviously is fully assured he has. [. . .]

As we came in we met Geoffrey Howard,[28] one of the Liberal Whips. LG cut him and said he was a boor, and that Howard had neglected on Saturday to raise his hat when he met LG with two ladies. LG added, 'I won't stand for that!' I wonder whether Howard's close association with the PM and his clique is in any way responsible for LG's anger. [. . .]

21 May A long chat with Sir Reginald Brade. [. . .] Kitchener was going to Russia, but the visit is off for the moment. K is not very happy – rather like a lost soul. [. . .]

LG has gone to spend the week-end with Colonel Lee,[29] who acts as Northcliffe's envoy. [. . .] He is a successful professional husband, having married a wealthy American. There is no doubt that LG and Northcliffe are acting in close concert. The Radicals are wobbly and, as LG says, one must have friends and allies. Hence Northcliffe and [. . .] Lee. LG is obviously most anxious not to offend N. [. . .] N is a wonderful man, but self-centred and unscrupulous. LG is growing to believe more and more every day that he (LG) is the only man to win the war. His attitude to the PM is changing rapidly. He is becoming more and more critical and antagonistic. It looks as if LG and Northcliffe are working to dethrone Mr A. [. . .]

27 May LG called for me this evening and I returned with him for dinner. [. . .]

He spoke highly of Redmond,[30] who, he said, had many of Asquith's qualities, which would have secured him a high position in this country had it not been for his faithful adherence to the Irish cause. [. . .]

We reverted to Asquith's position. I said, 'This appointment gives you the reversion of the Premiership. Mr A and the Cabinet have admitted your position.'

LG: Yes, if I pull it off, it will be a big thing. They have appointed me because I have certain qualities necessary for the task, but as I have said, I believe there were other motives which led them to make the proposal.[31] [. . .]

The plot thickens. LG is very angry with Spender of the *Westminster Gazette*, and is rejoicing in his troubles with his Board, some of whom object to his policy. LG said today, 'Even if the *Westminster* is the Government organ, that is no reason why they should attack me. Am I not a part of the Government?'

LG never mentions to me directly that he sees Northcliffe, but I am sure they are in daily contact. [. . .]

31 May Nicoll tells me that Fisher has written some most incendiary letters to Jellicoe[32] and the Emperor of Russia. [. . .]

1 June Called at Downing Street and warned Bonham Carter concerning Fisher. This in strict confidence, and only because I thought it necessary in the national interest. Bonham Carter seemed concerned, and promised to inform the PM and to make discreet enquiries.

3 June Called to see LG at Walton. Found him very excited regarding naval news.[33] He spoke in strong terms of Balfour and the Board of Admiralty. He said Fisher should have been recalled, but that AB did not like to be surrounded by strong men. [. . .] LG complained that no meeting of the War Council had been called to consider the situation. He said that he did not think it right to play golf and intended to go to London, which he did. He again referred to the serious position of affairs and the PM's neglect to recognise it. [. . .]

LG is evidently very bitter. He said that when he raised the question of postponing the Whitsuntide holiday, Arthur Balfour remarked, 'I agree, but so far as the Admiralty is concerned, there is no necessity!' LG said that Balfour quite failed to recognise the importance of not losing a day in the Admiralty preparations. He added, 'It is interesting that on the same day as we have received the news of what is apparently a naval disaster, the King has conferred the Order of Merit on the First Lord for philosophic and literary research.'

We discussed the Irish settlement. LG intimated that the leaders were favourable, but that they had gone to Ireland to consult the party leaders there. He did not seem very confident of the result. [. . .] He told us he thought the final settlement of the Irish question lies in Imperial Federation and that the Colonies would in future decline to

be committed to a war, in the making of which they had no voice. [. . .]
LG thought an Imperial Parliament practicable. [. . .]

4 June   The Admiralty have adopted the unusual course of getting
Winston to write a semi-official *précis* of the naval battle, based on the
official documents. There is much criticism concerning this novel
departure – no doubt a skilful device on the part of Arthur Balfour to
draw the teeth of his chief potential critic. [. . .]

6 June   Poor old Kitchener has been drowned. [. . .] I have never met
a more uneven and streaky man.[34] [. . .]

8 June   Called to see Arthur Balfour to question him in relation to the
Jutland Dispatch which has caused so much consternation. [. . .] I
asked why the Admiralty did not publish a statement that a battle was
in progress. Balfour replied that he was of opinion that such a
statement would have occasioned unnecessary anxiety. I then inquired
why he published the message which caused so much consternation.
His answer was that he thought it his duty to publish with slight
excisions the telegram received from Jellicoe. Balfour handed me a
copy of this, which I subsequently read privately to the Press Conference. B said that Jellicoe's subsequent telegrams showed that he
considered that the Navy had gained a substantial victory and that the
German Fleet was temporarily *hors de combat*. I got B to dictate a
memorandum to that effect, which I also read to the Conference. B
said that he had an anxious time when waiting for news. I suggested
that in lieu of the telegram which he published he should have issued a
statement that a severe battle had taken place in which both sides had
sustained heavy losses, that the German Fleet was in retreat, and that a
further statement would be published immediately further details had
been received. To this he gave no satisfactory reply. I explained that I
was voicing the views of the whole Press. He commented adversely
upon the action of the evening papers in publishing emasculated
statements, and said that their action showed the inadvisability of
issuing such important statements to the evening press. [. . .]

11 June   Dined with LG. Found him very preoccupied. He said that
he had lunched with Max Aitken at his house, which is about three
miles from Walton. Bonar Law was there. Bonar Law intends to resign
unless LG is appointed Minister for War or he is appointed himself.

LG is not disposed to take the office, and feels that the time has come when he can do greater service by resigning. He is very dissatisfied regarding the conduct of the war, and thinks the situation in France very serious. [. . .] He thinks our failures inexcusable, as we have men, guns and ammunition. He considers that we have no brains at the top, and that Haig is not an able man. He says that Asquith does not want a man at the War Office who will give him trouble. He is very dissatisfied with Mr A and thinks him very tricky. Bonar Law agrees that LG is the most suitable man to go to the War Office. If he does, Bonar Law would take over the Munitions. LG thinks that the War Office is a difficult task [. . .] he might be met with insuperable difficulties. If he were leading the Opposition he could accomplish more. [. . . He said,] 'If I went out I should at once form a great Party organisation. I have promises of all the money necessary.' [. . .]

As we were talking, both *The Times* and *Daily Mail* rang up, and I think, Northcliffe. [. . .] Shortly afterwards, to his [LG's] surprise, Max Aitken. [. . .]

It is notable that LG rarely mentions Northcliffe's name nowadays, and *never* mentions that he is in communication with him. [. . .]

Shortly afterwards Max Aitken arrived. LG went to see him in another room, and after some time came to tell me that Aitken had come full of all sorts of things. I did not wait to hear what they were. [. . .]

15 June LG, Robertson Nicoll and Dr Addison to dine at Queen Anne's Gate at LG's suggestion, so that he might discuss the desirability of accepting the position of Secretary for War. This afternoon I had an interview with Brade, who told me that he feared trouble if any attempt were made to curtail Robertson's powers. He described Robertson as being very stiff and nervous, and said that the Army would support him. Brade said LG had cracked many a tough nut, but would probably find the WO a tougher nut than any he had yet tackled and that he might break his teeth as others had done before him. The position was rendered all the more difficult by reason of the powers conferred upon Robertson by the Order in Council. Brade thinks R will cling tenaciously to these. Brade suggested that I should indicate all this to LG without mentioning the source.

After dinner LG opened the subject of the conferences.

LG: At the risk of appearing egotistical, I now wish to discuss a matter of great importance. I have been offered the position of Secre-

tary for War by the Prime Minister.[35] I have not accepted, as there are
important questions which must first be decided. It was arranged before
he left for Scotland that during his absence we should both think the
matter over. My decision may have a marked effect upon the result and
duration of the War. I saw Northcliffe yesterday, when he said that if I
accept I shall give the Government a new lease of life and that it will be
impossible to turn them out. But I also saw Carson, who said that he
would be glad in one way if I came out. He would like to work with me,
and that together we might bring the Government down and replace it
by a sounder and more energetic body. He, however, thought that I
could render more useful service by going to the War Office, but that I
must stipulate for full powers. [. . .] My own inclination would be to
resign. The Munitions Department is now in full swing, so that my mind
would be easy on that score. The war is being sadly muddled. [. . .] In
short, the question is whether I am in or out?

Nicoll: Mr Minister, I think your position quite clear. You must
accept the office. Do not haggle about powers. You will later on get all
the powers you want. [. . .]

Addison: I agree with much that Sir William Robertson Nicoll has
said, but I think you would place yourself in a false position if you did not
stipulate for full powers. [. . .]

R: It will be a difficult task. I am told the soldiers will oppose any
change in the arrangements.

LG: That is what Brade says. He knows. He is a levelheaded fellow.

R: [. . .] Now is the time to get a proper limitation of your powers; it
will be more difficult later on. The PM cannot afford to let you go. [. . .]

LG: If I do not take the office, Bonar Law thinks he is entitled to it,
but he considers I am the best man for it. If I resign, I think he would
follow suit. The Government would then break up. I, however, think it is
my duty to take the office, subject to my having reasonable powers.[36] I
shall see the PM on his return. [. . .]

16 June Called upon Brade and told him I thought LG would accept
the office subject to having reasonable powers. Brade said that
Robertson was very obdurate and that he (Brade) had no authority from
LG to discuss the matter with him. [. . .] I doubt whether he [Brade]
wants LG at the WO. [. . .]

18 June Brade came to see me at Walton. He has had a long
conference with Robertson, who is very stiff about his powers. [. . .]

Brade then went to see LG, and returned after about an hour and a half saying he had had a long talk with LG but could not understand whether he wanted the position or not. LG telephoned to me to dine with him, which I did. [. . .] I asked LG if he had seen the PM, and he said, 'No, not yet.' I referred to a leader in yesterday's *Daily Chronicle*, in which the writer emphasised the importance of making no change in the War Office arrangements, and said that any such change would be resented by the Army.

LG: Donald is not straight. He poses as a friend but stabs one in the back. He has done this before.[37] He is a blundering fool. The article is most harmful; it will prejudice the negotiations with Robertson. [. . .]

R: I see considerable difficulty in getting Robertson to acquiesce in the revocation of the Order in Council. [. . .]

LG: Yes. It would be difficult to revoke the Order. The question is, as you say, what does it imply? I am told that, as a matter of practice, Kitchener had abdicated all his powers to Robertson. I do not wish to interfere in military operations. That would be absurd, but I must control the administrative departments. That is a *sine qua non*. Otherwise I should be a mere figurehead. [. . .]

19 June   LG telephoned respecting article in the *Daily Chronicle* as to the powers of Secretary of State for War. He described the article as most pernicious, and spoke very angrily concerning Donald's action in publishing it.

21 June   Dined with Nicoll, Paton, Morgan and Donald. Much talk about the peccant articles. Donald's excuse very lame. Nicoll accused him of being prompted by Spender of the *Westminster*. This Donald vehemently denied. [. . .] Personally I doubt whether Spender prompted the article. It was, I think, due to Donald's association with General Robertson and Donald's desire to show his independence.

22 June   Called to see LG at the Munitions Department. Found him still very angry with Donald. LG said that he was treacherous, and that he did not feel inclined to see him. LG asked me to ascertain on what terms the *Chronicle* could be bought, and said that he could find the cash.[38] I gathered that Mond, Henry[39] & Co. are prepared to put up the money. LG said that he must have a Liberal paper. I suggested that it might be best to negotiate through Donald.

LG: I can talk to Donald when I have got the paper.

LG said that McKenna had been working hard to keep him from the WO, and that he knew from Northcliffe that Le Bas had been round Fleet Street trying to get up an agitation against LG. Le Bas had said to Northcliffe that LG could not afford to resign because his means were not large enough. LG very indignant. He described Le Bas as a contemptible jackal. [. . .]

23 June   Saw Sir Reginald Brade at the War Office. He says it is now fairly certain that LG will be the new War Minister. Brade is preparing a memorandum as to the working of the Office. [. . .] Brade said that he really could not understand whether the PM wanted LG to go to the War Office. Mr A is such a foxy old boy that it is often impossible to say what he really means. [. . .]

24 June   [. . .] LG asked me to dinner, but I was unable to go. I went after dinner. I told him I had invited Brade for tomorrow. We talked of the War Office. I urged him to accept, and said that questions as to the limitation of his authority would readily adjust themselves. He agreed, and also that it would be impossible to revoke or alter the Order in Council. [. . .]

2 July   Lunched with Sir Max Aitken at Cherkley Court. Found Winston there painting a landscape. [. . .] He spoke in depreciatory terms of Haig and our generals. Evidently he is in a very unhappy, disgruntled state of mind. [. . .] He talked of nothing but the war, and again developed his theory regarding the mistakes of the Germans and Allies respectively. After lunch he went off in my car to visit LG at Walton, leaving me with our strange host and Sir Reginald Brade, who was staying at Cherkley Court. Aitken is good company, but rather a weird creature. Very natural and unaffected, and I should say not over-scrupulous. [. . .]

Winston was with LG for five hours. He is evidently pushing hard to get back into the Cabinet. LG said he thought Winston would be the best man to succeed him at the Munitions Department, but that the PM would not appoint him. I said I thought the appointment would be most unpopular. LG was afraid it might be. I said, 'Winston's mind is concentrated on the war.' 'Yes,' replied LG, smiling, 'but it is more concentrated on Winston.'

July–December 1916

Churchill's hopes of regaining office at this time were dashed and once again, as in May 1915, Riddell heard an outpouring of bitterness, this time directed against Asquith. Though Lloyd George backed him to succeed at Munitions, that post went to Edwin Montagu, whose behaviour towards his predecessor was marked by duplicity. Lloyd George was now Secretary for War, without conditions, and with the exception of a brief post-script on the failure of the Irish negotiations his preoccupations over the next five months were with military strategy and hard-headed generals. This only served to increase his dissatisfaction with Britain's political leadership. As the failure of the Somme offensive became evident to those with eyes to see, Lloyd George revealed to Riddell his growing isolation and frustration. He made no secret of Asquith's deficiencies and declared his preference for Carson as a war leader. Even Northcliffe was a lost cause, as he had become a generals' man and would hear no criticism of Haig and Robertson. Riddell observed as early as August that it was evident Lloyd George was heading for a big fight with the generals.

Events leading up to the fall of Asquith gathered momentum by the end of September, when Lloyd George gave his famous 'Knock-out blow' interview. This somewhat blunted controversy with the generals, save for Northcliffe and the *Morning Post* persevering in their belief that the Secretary for War was a danger to the military leaders. The gulf between Lloyd George and his Liberal colleagues was now nearly complete, for he suspected them of inclining towards peace talks whereas he had taken his stand uncompromisingly on a fight to the finish. Riddell thought Lloyd George exaggerated his colleagues' disinclination to fight on, but recognised his apprehension concerning the military position. He also observed that in the midst of these grave matters Lloyd George showed a renewed determination to get control of the *Daily Chronicle*. The two men had only two or three conversations in November, in which Riddell found the Minister gloomy and preoccupied, as if a crisis was at hand. Resignation seemed certain, for Lloyd George's mind appeared to be made up at last.

In the days immediately preceding that event Riddell saw Lloyd

George only briefly and the diary entries are correspondingly thin. This changed with the fall of the Asquith Government and Riddell recorded many interesting things from 6 December on. On the 10th, for example, Lloyd George talked at considerable length about his problems in forming a ministry and about his former Liberal colleagues, McKenna in particular. Perhaps even more interesting is a long interview with Winston Churchill on the 11th, when Riddell once more was the recipient of some remarkably frank talk which made clear the other man's state of mind. The last entry for the year was on Christmas Day, which Riddell spent with Lloyd George and had much conversation about the Press, ending with a laughing comment on Max Aitken's peerage.

7 July   Lunched with Winston and Mrs C at 41 Cromwell Road. Long talk extending over three hours. Winston has written four articles for the *Sunday Pictorial* for which he received £1,000. While I was with him he sold the American rights for £300. He asked £400 and drove a hard bargain. [. . .] He spoke fully and freely of his position and prospects. Thus: 'I have left the Army. I was in the trenches for eighty days. [. . .] *I did not see why I should remain at the mercy of some ill-directed shot.*[1] [. . .] Asquith has treated me badly. He has not defended me as he should have done. He shared the responsibility for all that was done, but beyond a general statement that he accepted responsibility – a statement which was calculated to show how magnanimous he is – he never made any case in my favour. I have a complete documentary defence. . . .'

R: What happened regarding the Munitions Department? LG spoke very strongly in favour of your succeeding him.

Winston: Yes, both he and Bonar Law thought I should go. I did not want to join this Government, but felt that I could have rendered useful service in that capacity. The PM, however, would not hear of it, and I am no suppliant for office. The Government is rotten to the core. It is full of personal jealousies and intrigues. [. . .]

R: Do you think the Jutland battle a success? Did Beatty[2] do the right thing?

Winston: Yes, it was a brilliant affair – worthy of the best traditions of the Navy. The public do not understand naval warfare. They criticise naval losses more severely than military losses. The loss of a ship is regarded as a crime. The public do not appreciate that you cannot fight military engagements without a loss.

R: What do you propose to do?

Winston: I shall write to earn my living and I shall go on painting. Painting has been a great solace; it helped me to tide over the horrible time after I left the Admiralty. [. . .]

A visitor was announced, and I left. Winston can, I think, make a good case. Whether this is the time to reopen the question is another matter. The only object is to re-establish Winston's reputation. [. . .]

I was much struck with Winston's ignorance of the feeling with which he is regarded by most of his late colleagues, and the governing classes. [. . .]

15 July   Dined with LG, who presided over the Army Council for the first time today. [. . .] LG said he had dined with Lord French at his house in Lancaster Gate. French had criticised the arrangements for our advance in France. He said the movement had been too freely advertised and too rigidly prepared. LG appeared to agree. I said it might be that French was jealous of Haig, and that the thing had been well planned. LG seemed doubtful. LG thinks it unfortunate that a Jew has been appointed Minister of Munitions.[3] The Russians will not like it.

16 July   Dined with LG. After dinner we walked in the garden for an hour and a half. [. . .]

I inquired the position of the Irish question.

LG: Serious and awkward, Bonar Law is very anxious. He says his people won't have Home Rule.

Evidently the party meeting was very difficult. [. . .] LG said to Bonar Law that if he, Carson and LG stood together, they could pull the thing (Home Rule) through. Bonar Law replied that the position is very serious, as opposition to Home Rule is one of the Party principles.

R: How will it work out? You will bring in the Bill?

LG: Yes, the Cabinet have agreed to that. The difficulty is that it will be debated at length. All sorts of amendments, some of them apparently innocuous, will be proposed. [. . .] However, I have pledged my word to the Irish, and if the pledge is not fulfilled, I shall have to resign. There are certain pledges which leave the person who makes them no alternative. This is one of them. The whole position is most serious and embarrassing in view of the military situation. A break-up of the Cabinet just now would be a misfortune. [. . .]

[LG:] K was a most surprising old boy – in many ways a regular humbug.

R: Yet now and again he had vision concerning big things.

LG: Yes, I think my lighthouse analogy best describes him. A great flash of light across the ocean, and then absolute darkness with no warning as to how long it would continue. [. . .]

19 July Long talk with Sir Reginald Brade regarding newspaper correspondents at GHQ in France. Each paper now wants its own correspondent, in lieu of the present grouping arrangement. Brade thinks the military authorities will raise difficulties.

He says that LG and Robertson are getting on well together. [. . .] A number of generals have been recalled – Hunter Weston, De Lisle, Ivor Phillips and others. They failed to do well in the recent advance.

20 July F.E. Smith, the Attorney-General, made some caustic remarks to me concerning Mr A. F.E. considers Montagu's appointment [as Minister of Munitions] most unfortunate.[4] [. . .]

21 July At the WO met Winston waiting to see LG. [. . .] The Cabinet have decided not to publish the Dardanelles papers. Winston says they have drawn back from their undertaking on the ground that publication will be harmful to the public interest. Winston is very depressed. He says it is hard that he should have to remain under a stigma until after the war. [. . .] I said to him, 'You have had a wonderful life. You are only forty-three. Think what you have done!' 'Yes,' he replied, 'that is all very well, but my life is finished. I only care about the war and I am banished from the scene of action.' Evidently he means to go for the PM. [. . .]

Met Walter Long in St James's Park. We walked together. He says that the PM is terribly lacking in decision, and that it is strange that a man with such a great intellect should be so indecisive. Long considers that the present unfortunate position of the Irish question is due in a great measure to Mr A's failure to bring in the Bill without delay. Long said he thought LG had been mistaken in not bringing the Ulstermen and Nationalists together, and implied that misunderstandings had resulted in consequence of separate negotiations. He described LG as a most attractive fellow and said that he had both the power of decision and the gift of speech. Long does not, however, always agree with his decisions!!! [. . .]

30 July Dined with LG who says he thinks the war will certainly last until next June. He is, however, much more optimistic than he was, and spoke in glowing terms of the Russian victories. He asked my opinion of the result of a General Election in which the issue would be the more vigorous prosecution of the war. The new party to be headed by Carson, whom he described in glowing terms. A man of resolution, good judgment, and inspiring personality. [. . .]

LG: The position would be difficult, I agree, but I think that the nation would prefer Carson to Asquith. The people who go to music halls and cinema shows are more favourable to the former. Mr A gets very few cheers nowadays. But the truth is that if you could get rid of McKenna, the Government would not be a bad Government. [. . .]

R: Would you be willing to serve under Carson? You should be the alternative to Asquith.

LG: I should be glad and proud to serve under him. I think he would do well. My only purpose is to get on with the war. [. . .]

1 August   Griffith, the Assistant Canadian High Commissioner, tells me that Max Aitken is endeavouring to get appointed High Commissioner. [. . .] [Aitken] is good-natured but handicapped by his face, which does not inspire confidence.

2 August   [. . .] Davies, LG's secretary, tells me that he has seen a memorandum prepared by Montagu regarding the vacancy at the War Office due to Kitchener's death. It was evidently written with the object of advising the PM. The memorandum stated that the vacant position was one of the highest importance in the eyes of the public; that before the war, LG was discredited and was floundering in the morass of an ill-devised Budget; that the war had rehabilitated him and that he was now the most popular man, not only with the people but with the Allies; that it would therefore be impossible not to appoint him as Secretary for War; that the position was far less important than it was thought to be by the public; that LG would probably be engulfed by the machine; and finally that it would be desirable to appoint him at once so that he would have the credit for the many casualties which were certain to result from the new offensive which was about to begin. Davies kept no copy of this precious document, nor has he told LG of it.[5] [. . .]

9 August   To breakfast with LG at Downing Street. Found him and Burnham walking together in the garden. LG explained that Burnham's statement to him regarding the offensive in the West had created a flutter in military circles. We then adjourned for breakfast.

LG intimated that he had taken the line that the offensive should not be actively pursued now that we had achieved our object in diverting the Germans from Verdun. [. . .] LG remarked he thought both Robertson and Haig were in a measure relieved that the offensive was not to be actively continued until 1917, when our superiority in guns and ammunition would be more marked. LG then went on to comment on Northcliffe's article in yesterday's *Times*, in which he described the condition of affairs behind the lines as being 'perfect' and expressed the opinion that nothing should be changed. [. . .] LG remarked, 'He is all wrong this time. Things behind the lines require to be vastly improved. . . .'

Colonel Lee shortly afterwards arrived, looking pale and anxious. He brought with him two letters from Northcliffe, dated from Paris. LG read them, evidently with much annoyance. He said that N had been got at, and repeated that he was all wrong. Lee said, 'He is still friendly to you but the soldiers have got at him. There is a movement to undermine your influence. . . .'

LG goes to Paris tomorrow and he asked Lee to write to Northcliffe requesting him to call to see him. LG said, 'I must put him straight.' [. . .]

(It is evident that LG is in for a big fight with the soldiers. He may conciliate them, but they are tough nuts and resent interference. As Brade said today, 'Soldiers are just as much wire-pullers as politicians. They use every weapon at their command.' [. . .]

4 September   Having been away for three weeks, called at War Office to see LG. While I was waiting, Mrs Pankhurst arrived. LG came out to get a paper and took the opportunity to introduce me. [. . .]

19 September   LG back from France, where he has been for nearly a fortnight. I called to see him at the War Office. [. . .] He complained of having to go to Windsor to see the King. He says that although the ostensible object of his visit is to report upon his trip, the K will do all the talking. He talks incessantly, but without point or judgment, just like a boy. [. . .]

LG thinks we are doing well, but that the war may last for a considerable time. The public know only half the story. They read of the victories. The cost is concealed. [. . .]

LG is very angry with Massingham, and meditates an action for libel against him for suggesting that LG arranged for the National Liberal

Club to be taken over by the WO in order that he might break up the organisation of the Liberal Party. [. . .]

20 September Dined with LG. Three of his secretaries – David Davies, MP, Miss Stevenson[6] and Sutherland[7] – were there. Much talk again about the defects of the War Office. But we spent the greater part of the evening in singing Welsh hymns and later old songs such as 'Come into the garden, Maud', 'Cockles and Mussels', etc. LG in great form. [. . .]

21 to 25 September LG, Mrs LG, Megan, Davies the secretary, and I motored to Brighton, where we spent Thursday, Friday, Saturday and Sunday. LG very active all the time. [. . .] Sir Reginald Brade came down on Friday and spent the night. He says LG's position with the soldiers is rather ticklish. They dislike his interference and the intro-duction of civilians and civilian methods. Brade is anxious to keep the peace. LG has appointed Rothermere, Northcliffe's brother, to take charge of the Army Clothing Department. LG asked what I thought of the appointment. I said I thought Rothermere would do the job well, but the public might think it strange to select a newspaper proprietor to run a clothing works.

1 October Dined with LG at Walton. On Thursday [the] *Morning Post* published an attack on him for interfering with the military. On Friday appeared LG's remarkable interview with an American journalist, in which he warned neutrals against interference.[8] It has created an enormous sensation, and has blown LG's enemies sky high. [. . .]

LG: The article in the *Morning Post* was an ill-conditioned thing. If it comes to the point I shall tell the country that when in France I tried to minimise the loss of our brave boys. I enquired how it was that the French achieve more than we do with fewer casualties. I suppose this is what the *Morning Post* referred to. I have had numerous letters from soldiers' relatives thanking me for the interview. That shows the feeling of the country.

R: Did the Foreign Office arrange the interview?

LG: No, they had nothing to do with it. The American journalist came to see me. I said I would not give him an interview then, but I began to talk. [. . .] He went away and wrote out what I had said. He showed it to Northcliffe, who sent a message saying he wished I would allow the thing to be published. I asked to see it, and, after revising it, agreed to allow it to appear. Grey had cold feet about it but Hardinge[9] was delighted. [. . .]

LG: [. . .] If you had to govern this country by a Committee of Six, three from either side, whom would you choose from our side?

R: You, Asquith and Grey.

LG: So should I. On the other side I should choose Balfour, Carson, and I think Curzon. I am disappointed with Bonar. He does not really bring much to council. [. . .]

R: Why Curzon? Is he valuable?

LG: Yes, he is. He has travelled a lot; he knows about the countries of the world. He has read a lot. He is full of knowledge which none of us possesses. He is useful in council. He is not a good executant and has no tact, but he is valuable for the reasons stated.

As to Walter Long and Austen Chamberlain, LG thinks either would be useful in a Council in order to display the point of view of the average man, but that Walter Long would be the better. [. . .]

5 October   Breakfasted with Colonel David Davies, MP, by arrangement, so that LG might meet Burnham of the *Daily Telegraph*. [. . .] Burnham remarked that he was under the impression that LG and Northcliffe were very *épris*.

LG: Oh no! Just now we are like this (crossing his fingers). Northcliffe has been captured by the soldiers. They covered him with attention and adulation when he was at the Front. They took his measure very quickly. [. . .]

7 October   Played golf at Walton with LG. The first time for several months, I think. He says he believes his recent interview was none too soon and that there has been 'peace talk'. Also that Asquith and McKenna are in it, and perhaps Grey. LG thinks it noticeable that the *Spectator* did not applaud the interview, and suggests Strachey is under the influence of the PM and represents his views. I rather pressed for more information as to the reasons for his belief, but got nothing further. His suspicions may have led him to attach too much importance to minor manifestations which really signify nothing more than an attitude of mind on the part of the aforesaid colleagues. [. . .]

8 October   Dined with LG at Walton. Sir Vincent Evans and Colonel David Davies there also. [. . .]

LG is evidently keen to get a daily paper which he can control. He has set Col. Davies, the millionaire, to work. The Colonel asked me to lunch with him and we had a long talk on the subject. He said he would put up £50,000 toward buying the *Daily Chronicle*.

14 October LG, David Davies and Brade lunched with me at the Carlton, after which I drove with LG to Walton. LG says that Northcliffe is taking up a strong line against him and is endeavouring to make friends with Asquith. Asquith told LG and said that for two years Northcliffe had attacked him in the most disgraceful way. A took no notice of him and his attacks, and now that he had altered his tactics A meant to adopt the same plan and leave him severely alone. LG says that N's vanity is colossal, that he wants to be a Dictator, and that he (LG) does not intend to be dictated to. [. . .]

Referring to the rumours of difficulties at the War Office, LG said the soldiers' view is that it is his duty to find the men, but that after they have been thrown into the cauldron, he has no further responsibility. He added, 'I believe that is not the nation's view. It is not mine, and it is a view I would never accept. I am entitled to inquire how it is that our casualties are so much heavier than those of the French. I am not entitled to say, "You attacked So-and-so; why did you not attack So-and-so?" but I am entitled to consider the general conduct of the campaign. That is one of my duties.'

LG alluded to the articles in *The Times* and *Daily Mail*, and to Northcliffe's statement in a speech which he delivered privately on Tuesday. N is very violent and bitter. [. . .] Everything is black or white. [. . .LG] thinks that Rothermere will be more useful to him than Northcliffe, because R is not so hated by the Liberal Party. 'Nothing,' he said, 'did me so much harm with the Liberal Party as my relations with Northcliffe.' [. . .]

LG this week met Gwynne of the *Morning Post* at the Bath Club. LG said that he cut Gwynne dead. Gwynne then wrote to him and asked him to see Maxse,[10] whom LG invited to breakfast. He describes Maxse as a delightful fellow but a violent fanatic. [. . .]

29 October I am told that LG created an unfavourable impression by taking the LCJ and Colonel Lee with him to France. LG says he is very apprehensive concerning the military position. He fears the Rumanians will be unable to hold the passes. [. . .] Asquith does not like the position. LG is doubtful of the wisdom of the advance on the Somme. The losses have been very serious. [. . .] LG says that there is no truth in the rumour that he has meditated advising the recall of Haig. There is no one to replace him. LG strongly resents Northcliffe's attitude, and says that he is quite unreliable and that his vanity is colossal. Rothermere, his brother, has expressed the same opinion to LG. LG repeated that he does not intend to allow Northcliffe to dictate his policy. [. . .]

LG:[. . .] Even the Almighty formed a Trinity. Northcliffe is a Unitarian. It is a poor sort of religion. [. . .]

LG is keen that the *Daily Chronicle* should be purchased by friends of his. I have had several interviews with David Davies on the subject and have promised to negotiate with Donald, the editor. I believe that Mr Lloyd, the proprietor, is willing to sell. His health is very bad. LG says that he cannot rely on Northcliffe, and made the naive remark that N's support is a doubtful asset for a Radical politician. [. . .] LG has a wonderful faculty for believing what he wants to believe, or what it suits him to believe for the time being. [. . .]

1 November   LG and Lord Burnham to breakfast. The former says that when he criticised the arrangements in connection with Rumania, Northcliffe told his secretary that if LG continued to criticise the Army command, he (N) would have to denounce him, not only in his papers but from his seat in the House of Lords. LG seemed much amused at this threat, and remarked that Northcliffe could begin as soon as he liked. [. . . LG says] our generals lack vision. They are able, industrious, brave and thorough, but have no genius. The question of man-power is becoming very serious. [. . .]

Much talk concerning opinion of General Staff as to function of Minister for War. LG elaborated the views already recorded. He says that his personal relations with Robertson and the staff are quite friendly. Apparently he had a set-to with Robertson some little time ago. Brade tells me that Robertson had quite a good case, but that LG who had a better one made mincemeat of him, I suppose at the Army council. [. . .]

3 November   Brade sent for me hurriedly. He says that LG is furious that the Ministry of Munitions is engaging in a newspaper campaign to secure public support for the reservation of munition workers from military service. [. . .]

5 November   Dined with LG, who told me that he had made an important speech at the War Council this week in which he reviewed the whole situation. Asquith said to Hankey,[11] the Secretary of the Council, that LG's speech was one of the most concise and logical statements he had ever heard – not a word wasted. LG spoke for an hour. The Council have telegraphed to the Allies inviting them to a conference in Paris at the end of this week. Asquith and LG are to represent Gt Britain. [. . .]

19 November [. . .] To dinner with LG as usual. Found him very gloomy.

LG: I am very depressed about the war. Perhaps it is because I am tired. I have not felt so depressed before. I want to go away for a week alone, so that I may think quietly by myself. Things look bad. The Rumanian news is alarming. [. . .]

R: When is the Conference?

LG: We to to Paris on Tuesday. The Conference will probably last four days. I think the time has come when the politicians must exercise more power regarding the appropriation of supplies. The soldiers and officials in each country are too intent on providing for their own requirements. They will not pay due regard to those of their Allies. Russia in particular is neglected. This is a fatal error. We are now at a testing point. [. . .]

We talked of M. Cambon, a close friend of the Marquis [de Chasseloup Laubat, who just arrived].

LG: He is a great man. He had much to do with our coming into the war. He came and wept, and the German Ambassador came and wept – but he wept like a German. He wept tears like German sausages. Cambon wept like an artist.[12] [. . .]

26 November Dined with LG. Found him much preoccupied. [. . .] I told LG that Donald of the *Daily Chronicle* had asked to see the PM and that he hoped to do so tomorrow, when he proposed to tell him that things cannot go on as they are doing, and to suggest that a committee of three or four – Asquith, LG, Bonar Law and Balfour – should be appointed to control the country. The members to be relieved of their departmental duties so that they would be enabled more effectually to exercise a judicial mind on matters brought before them. I said I had long had this idea and was glad Donald was going to put it forward.

LG: No doubt General Robertson has urged him to do so. But I fear it would not work; the Committee would never decide anything. Asquith is too judicial. [. . .]

R: The *Morning Post* have been patting you on the back this week.[13]

LG: Yes. A curious *volte-face*. The Young Tories are at the back of that. They are very dissatisfied, and anxious that I should take charge of affairs.

R: How about Bonar Law?

LG: Max Aitken has just telephoned to say he is coming here to see me at 9.30 p.m. No doubt he is coming from Bonar. [. . .]

R: Donald had tea with Mrs Asquith the other day. She told him that Mr A had been sadly hit by the death of his son,[14] and that never a day passes but that he weeps about him in his bedroom. That looks bad. It seems as if he is breaking, poor man, under the strain.

LG: Yes. There is no doubt that his son's death, followed by recent events in the war, have hit him hard.

At this point Max Aitken arrived and I retired. It is evident that the crisis is serious. Lord Reading is on the scene as is usual on such occasions. LG telephoned him tonight.

29 November   Colonel David Davies, LG's Parliamentary Secretary, tells me that LG is most distressed regarding the position and is threatening to resign. Davies wants to see him and advise him not to do so. D says the situation is most serious.

1 December   LG and Burnham to breakfast. [. . .]

LG:[. . .] Now that Northcliffe has deserted me I shall have to depend on the Dukes. An alliance with Northcliffe is something like going for a walk with a grasshopper. [. . .]

Yes, the prospects are gloomy. We have only just a chance to win the war. We cannot win unless things are changed. If they are not changed I shall leave them (the Cabinet). [. . .]

As LG was leaving I asked him to play golf tomorrow (Saturday). He said pointedly, 'Not tomorrow, but next Saturday.' I understand this to mean resignation or reconstruction!

2 December   Donald says the Prime Minister has asked to see him tomorrow (Sunday). He has never seen the PM before on political business, and thinks the crisis will be settled by a reconstruction of the War Council. I told him that LG had resigned, or would do so tomorrow. He seemed very much surprised.

Today the political situation developed into a crisis. Yesterday LG wrote a letter to the PM, in effect demanding that the War Council should be reduced in number, that LG should be Chairman, that Mr

A should conduct the general business of the Government, and that he should have a veto on the general decisions of the War Council. I have not seen the letter but I gather that this was its purport.

3 December Donald has received a message from the poisonous Le Bas stating that McKenna will resign unless he is included in the War Council. Le Bas asked for an appointment with Donald, who promised to see him this evening. [. . .] I dined at LG's at Walton Heath, but he was unable to come down from London. He had been down to lunch and had returned to see the PM. His resignation was publicly announced,[15] but Mrs LG did not know whether he had actually resigned. During the evening he telephoned that his interview with the PM had been satisfactory, also that the poisonous Le Bas had been going round newspaper offices blackguarding him, LG, and pressing McKenna's claims.

4 December Saw LG at the War Office. Found him packing[16] War Office papers. He says he hears the PM is going back on all he said yesterday, although I understood LG to say that Asquith had confirmed the interview by a letter. What will happen LG does not know. He is determined to insist upon his demands and to resign if they are not granted. I told him I thought he was quite right, and that he need not worry about money if he thought resignation necessary. Lord Derby then came into the room. I said (to LG), 'I hope you are firm.' He answered, 'Firm as a rock.' [. . .]

5 December Asquith has resigned.[17]

6 December Bonar Law has declined to form a Government. The King has sent for LG.
　　LG and Burnham were to dine with me at Queen Anne's Gate. LG arrived an hour late. He looked tired and worn. He said that he and Carson met Bonar Law last night. BL was indisposed to form a Government. LG and Carson urged him to do so. LG offered to serve under him in any capacity. BL ultimately agreed, subject to Asquith and his associates taking office under him. Today Asquith declined. This evening the King called a conference consisting of Asquith, LG, Bonar Law, Balfour and Grey. Balfour got up from his bed to attend. Asquith absolutely declined to serve under Bonar Law. He said that after being Premier he could not accept a subordinate position. LG

thinks Mr A acted badly. The interview was, however, most friendly. This pleased the King, who was evidently pleased to see that Asquith and LG were on such good terms. LG said that his relations with Asquith had always been of the most friendly character. They have never had a quarrel. LG thinks that Balfour was surprised at Asquith's attitude.

LG says that on Sunday Asquith agreed to his proposals with certain modifications, which LG accepted. Bonham Carter, Asquith's secretary and son-in-law, was delighted. Now he [A] says no agreement was reached and that the proposals were only agreed for subsequent consideration. LG says whether A is losing his memory, whether he does not know what he is saying, or whether his statement is open to another construction, he does not know. Bonar Law told LG that subsequently to the interview between LG and Asquith, the latter said to Bonar Law that a settlement had been arrived at. BL cannot understand A's action in repudiating it. All A's best friends, Bonham Carter, Hankey and Eric Drummond,[18] advised A to carry out the arrangement. LG thinks he was persuaded in the other direction by Mrs A, McKenna and Runciman. LG does not know what advice Grey gave. He is terribly nervous and jumpy. Montagu had been acting with LG, so LG says, but his personal friendship for the PM will cause him to follow Mr A. Burnham says that he saw the PM this morning and urged him to serve under Bonar Law. He understood that Mr A would do so. When LG had gone, Burnham told me Asquith had referred to the Press campaign against him and had suggested that LG was responsible for it. Burnham said Asquith was very bitter. Evidently he conceals his feelings from LG. [. . .]

LG has the support of at least eighty Liberals upon whom he can draw in case of need.[19] If he cannot form a Cabinet from amongst the politicians, he will invoke the aid of business men to carry on the war. Should the House of Commons prove impossible, he will go to the country. There are still 7,200,000, voters here, and he thinks he will receive overwhelming support. McKenna is bitterly opposed to him from motives of envy and jealousy. Runciman acts in concert with McKenna, although LG believes he is not activated by similar motives. LG spoke strongly of the imprudence of Northcliffe's leaders in the *Daily Mail* during the last few days. He had not seen him for three months till Monday or yesterday, I forget which, when he implored N to refrain from abusing Asquith and Balfour. LG says that no reliance is to be placed on Northcliffe, and that his brother, Rothermere, tells

LG that Northcliffe will never subordinate his business interests to the national welfare. If he can see a line on the contents-bill and arresting headlines, he will never forego the opportunity.

LG inquired whether he could count on Burnham's support. B replied in the affirmative. Burnham suggested that I should see N and endeavour to persuade him to mitigate his abuse of Asquith and of Balfour, which was calculated to exacerbate the situation and render LG's task more difficult. I replied that I thought such a request might be productive of more harm than good. LG said nothing, but I think agreed with me. As he left I wished him good luck. He replied, 'I shall do my best. The belief of these fellows that I shall fail will be an additional incentive.' He would eat no dinner beyond a plate of soup. From me he was going to see Bonar Law, who had gone to see Arthur Balfour. [. . .]

10 December LG telephoned and asked me to dine as usual. Just in the same simple way. He has not changed. When an official envelope arrived addressed to the 'Prime Minister', he laughed and said, 'I cannot help thinking this has come to the wrong person. . . .' At dinner he was full of fun and kept us in roars of laughter by imitating a speech of Curzon's at the War Council. He again referred to Curzon's great knowledge, which is most valuable, he says. [. . .]

I congratulated LG on his arrangement with the Labour Party,[20] which I said was crucial.

LG: Vital! I made the best speech I have ever made. [. . .] I think I have got a good Ministry. I have done my best to get the right men. Balfour acted well. He will be a great source of strength to a Government which is a National Goverment. I am sorry for some of my friends. They would not have Winston at any price.[21] Had I insisted, the new Ministry would have been wrecked. The same remark applies to Reading. Neither of them has been near me. I suppose they felt that their approaches would have placed me in an awkward position. Then I should have liked to give Dalziel something, but I could not take in a newspaper man; it was impossible. The same remark applies to Rothermere. I told him so. [. . .]

LG: McKenna has ruined the PM. He is responsible for all that has happened. He is a contemptible creature – jealous, small-minded and malignant. We had a scene in the War Council. I could not go on. I said at the Council, 'I hear that one of my colleagues has said that I have been endeavouring to get rid of my Chief of Staff (Robertson) by sending him on a mission to Russia. That is a lie, and the man who said it knows it to be so.' Curzon then said, 'I think you ought in fairness to give the name.' I replied, 'It was the Chancellor of the Exchequer.' McKenna said, 'I?' I (LG) then said, 'Yes, you! Either you or another man is saying what is untrue, and I know which I prefer to believe.' (The other man I (R) understood to be Robertson.) McKenna then collapsed. The PM did not rebuke him. Afterwards he said to me, 'I could not have believed it. It is almost unbelievable.' And yet the PM said not a word in public. That hardened me. I felt I could not go on with benefit to the nation under such circumstances.

Bonar Law has been here today. He is very timid. He is worrying about matters which really give no cause. Difficulties which will arise in forming new governments. You cannot provide for everybody. [. . .] Bonar Law is very worried because no provision has been made for Max Aitken.[22]

R: I am glad Bonar Law will usually lead the House of Commons. That will please the Conservatives.

LG: Yes. We shall have a strong front bench. [. . .] By the way, that wretched creature Le Bas has acted disgracefully. He is a dirty dog. [. . .] I have told the Northcliffes that if they endeavour to wreck the Government, a time will come when I shall have to appeal to the House of Commons to decide whether such conduct can be tolerated. I do not intend to be bullied. The position is serious. I am very worried about the war. [. . .]

R: How about Buckmaster?

LG: He is a snipe. He deserves nothing and will get nothing. I have stipulated. [. . .] We were hard put to it for a Lord Chancellor. What a fool Sam Evans[23] was to quarrel with me. He would have had the Woolsack. We wanted a Liberal, and would in default of a better have appointed Loreburn if he had not been a 'pacifist' Radical. [. . .]

R: Austen Chamberlain and his little coterie are disgruntled. I met him on Saturday. [. . .]

LG said he had told Northcliffe, or sent him word, I don't know which, that if he continued his attacks on members of the Government, he (LG) would be compelled to bring the subject before the House of Commons, who would certainly adopt severe measures. (Walter Long and others have addressed a letter to LG on the matter already.) LG added, 'I have made it clear that I cannot hope to protect him, and that his newspapers may be stopped.'

Referring to Winston, LG said that he had found it impossible to include him in the Government. The Conservatives would not have it, and had LG insisted he could not have formed the Ministry. He asked me to see Winston and explain this, and tell him that he (LG) would endeavour to find some position for him, such as Chairman of the Air Board, when the Report of the Dardanelles Commission had been published.[24] [. . .]

11 December Called upon Winston and gave him my message. Mrs C came in as I was finishing and I had to repeat. Winston made me a little speech. He said that for twelve years he and LG had acted in concert and that he (W) had almost invariably subordinated his views to those of LG, the exception being the dispute on the Naval estimates in 1913. At the Marconi time he (W) had stood loyally by LG, and had debased himself to Northcliffe in order to secure his neutrality. LG had repaid him by bringing about his downfall when the Coalition was established, and now he had passed him by. Winston had determined on the first occasion never to speak to LG again, but had succumbed to his advances. Mrs Winston remarked that LG had said in her presence that he would do his best to atone for what had been done.

'Now,' resumed Winston, 'I don't reproach him. His conscience will tell him what he should do. Give him that message and tell him that I cannot allow what you have said to fetter my freedom of action. I am still a member of the Liberal Party, and an event may happen at any moment which may lead me irrevocably to alter my position.[25] I will take any position which will enable me to serve my country, but I have had enough soft soap and can only judge by actions. Had he stood by me he would have had a loyal and capable colleague whom he could trust. Instead of that he allied himself with associates who are not really in sympathy with him, and who, when he has served their purpose, will desert him without compunction. However, my only purpose is to help to defeat the Hun, and I will subordinate my own feelings so that I may be able to render some assistance.'[26] [. . .]

12 December Called to see LG. Found him suffering from a severe chill, due, as he said, to his having sat in his room at the War Office without a fire. Recounted with discretion my interview with Winston, and suggested that LG should invite him to lunch, which he said he would do. He seemed somewhat distressed at Winston's attitude and said he was unreasonable. Winston had asked me who had objected to his inclusion in the Goverment. I had replied that I did not know. This

I also told LG who remarked that Winston had no right to make such an enquiry. [. . .]

13 December [. . .] Winston telephoned that he feared his message might have seemed minatory, but that this was not his intention. I promised to convey this to LG.

20 December Hartshorn wrote to ask me to tell the PM that the miners had been sitting all day to consider Government proposals to take over mines and that the men are apprehensive that it was suggested to apply the penal sections of the Munitions Act. The miners are to see the PM tomorrow.

21 December[27] Lord Derby asked me to call. He said he wished to consult me as a friend regarding the course to be taken in reference to the military scandal. Sir John Cowans, Mrs Cornwallis West, etc. [. . .] Lord D said that this business had given him great anxiety. [. . .] Called at Downing Street and dictated memorandum for the PM setting out points which miners would make and suggesting course to be adopted. Later called and saw the PM, who said meeting with miners had gone off most satisfactorily, and thanked me for what I had done. While at Downing Street saw Gardiner, editor of the *Daily News*, waiting to see LG. He looked worn. All his ideals have been shattered. He has been wrong all along the line. A nice man, but he has bad judgment.

Christmas Day Lunched and spent afternoon with LG at Walton Heath. I told him that Asquith had offered Donald of the *Daily Chronicle* a knighthood, which he had refused. This had been followed by the offer of a baronetcy, which Donald had also declined. (Donald told me so this morning and showed me Asquith's letter offering the knighthood.) LG said he understood that a knighthood had also been offered to Spender of the *Westminster*, and it was evident that Mr A was making a strong bid for journalistic support. He added, 'Three men helped bring Mr A down – McKenna, Gulland (the Whip) and Spender. They have ruined him.'

R: You saw Gardiner of the *Daily News* on Thursday. I hear that he asked Donald to join him in urging discussion of peace terms. Of course D declined. He is sound on the war. [. . .] I hear that you had a strictly business talk with Gardiner.

LG: Yes, I think he wanted to talk at large, but I restricted the conversation to the Peace Note. He was difficult and said he was of opinion that terms should be discussed. I put the matter to him strongly, and made it plain that I did so, not as Lloyd George, but as Prime Minister. Reluctantly he agreed to write as we desired. When he had given his promise I closed the interview. I knew that he would not break his word. He is not a bad chap, but he has bad judgment and cranky notions. I promised my colleagues to see Gardiner and the representative of the *Manchester Guardian*. The latter, Bone, is I think a pacifist. Those were the two papers we feared. We did not wish the Germans to have anything to quote. [. . .]

R: I see that Max Aitken has got his peerage.

LG (laughing): Yes, my first peer![28] He had a great deal to do with the formation of the Government. He is Bonar's *fidus Achates*.

January–August 1917

Riddell's meetings with Lloyd George inevitably were fewer in the first months of the new government, but the conversations he recorded are packed with interest. The failure of Neville Chamberlain as Director-General of National Service was an early topic. Of greater importance, Lloyd George did not attempt to hide his concern about Winston Churchill and Edwin Montagu, who were dangerous in opposition but anathema to Tory Ministers. On the other hand he displayed obvious satisfaction that the Dardanelles Report would prove to be even more damaging to Asquith than to Churchill. From time to time Lloyd George paused to reflect upon his colleagues in the Ministry and his position in the country, ever mindful that sooner or later an election must come and that he had yet to establish a strong political base. Hence the very real concern over the attitude of militant Nonconformists like Robertson Nicoll on such a matter as state purchase of the liquor trade. On military and diplomatic questions Lloyd George allowed Riddell to learn something of his dissatisfaction with both the Army and Navy chiefs as well as with the Foreign Office, but not until August are Haig and Robertson pinpointed as major obstacles. Sidelights on Lloyd George as Prime Minister are provided by such incidents as Mrs Lloyd George's furious outburst against her husband's leading colleagues and the manner in which Colonel David Davies was dropped from the domestic entourage.

Unable to spend as much time with Lloyd George as he might have wished, Riddell made up for it by talking frequently to other important people. Churchill continued to use him as a confidant, usually to attack Lloyd George or Asquith, the one for excluding him from the new Government, the other for past treatment. Press business accounted for several meetings with Carson at the Admiralty, and there were conversations with such others as Lord Derby, General Robertson, Field-Marshal Lord French, Northcliffe, Robertson Nicoll and Robert Donald. At the same time Riddell continued to be interested in labour problems, and he observed with detachment how Lloyd George took credit for settling a strike of engineers when the credit belonged elsewhere. A fresh source of information for the diaries is now provided by Lloyd George's secretaries, and for the next six years Riddell would learn many details of high politics while waiting to see the Prime Minister. Sometimes these tidbits were amusing as well as instructive, witness the penultimate entry in this chapter.

13 January　Have been busy regarding National Man Power Scheme. Dined with Neville Chamberlain[1] and his Chiefs of Staff. He seems a sensible man, but not a flier. He cannot make up his mind and is afraid to act. [. . .]

14 January　Dined with LG. Donald was there also. LG has taken him into grace again.[2] Wise for many reasons. [. . .]

Donald: I hear that Asquith has been ordered three months' rest. I wonder if he will again take a great part in public life?

LG: I doubt if he will. He has had a trying time.

Donald: Why don't you make him our French Ambassador?

LG: He would not take it. He does not like foreigners.

R: He would make a splendid Lord Chancellor.

LG: Yes, admirable. I would have offered him the position, but did not want to run the risk of offending him.

Donald: He would not have taken it. He declined to serve under Bonar Law. Bonar Law told me so, and that he was convinced that Asquith thought Bonar Law could not go on without him, in which supposition he was correct. Bonar Law and his friends thought him indispensable. Asquith was convinced that you (the PM) would be unable to form a Government, and that the King would have to recall him. Asquith confirmed this when I saw him, and when I inquired what would happen regarding you, Mr PM, he said, striking his hand on the table, 'He will have to come in on my terms!' [. . .]

R: Are you satisfied with Neville Chamberlain? He seems a nice man but not a genius.

LG (looking worried): This is one of the few cases in which I have taken a pig in a poke, and I am not very sure of the pig! [. . .]

27 January　LG came to dine with me at the Golf Club. He spoke of the liquor question. He is dissatisfied with the action of the Central Control Board and thinks that D'Abernon[3] has not been a success as Chairman. LG doubts whether he has been anxious to effect radical changes. LG says that Asquith would never recognise that the drinking habits of the people were a serious hindrance to the conduct of the war. He thinks that probably D'Abernon had a hint not to be too drastic in his methods. [. . .]

1 February   Northcliffe tells me he still thinks the war will be a long business. He says the arrangements for raising the loan have been mismanaged, and made other comments on what he alleged to be the incompetence of the Government. I said they have not yet had much time in which to formulate and execute their plans. With this he did not agree, and says that unless LG displays greater powers of organisation he will be displaced before the war terminates.

4 February   LG spoke at Carnarvon yesterday. I met him at Euston tonight and drove with him to Downing Street. The United States broke off relations with Germany yesterday, and today Wilson's speech to Congress is published. LG's first words were, 'And so he is not going to fight after all! He is awaiting another insult before he actually draws the sword!' [. . .] LG considers that the Foreign Office staff are sadly in need of reorganisation and rehabilitation. He has not a high opinion of Spring Rice,[4] our Ambassador in Washington. [. . .]

He is very dissatisfied with the position in regard to National Service and doubtful about Neville Chamberlain.[5] [. . .]

11 February   Dined with LG at Walton Heath. We talked of the naval and military situation. I inquired whether the time had not arrived when the War Council must sum up and balance the different national requirements, viz. man-power for the army, munitions, shipbuilding and agriculture. Each of these is essential, and neglect of any one of them may be disastrous.

LG: Yes, that is quite true. I fear we are about to enter upon a big fight with the soldiers, who wish to disregard all other branches. [. . .]

We talked of Montagu.

R: He is wirepulling vigorously for a job.

LG: Yes. He is of military age and fears the guns. I have rarely seen a man who fears them more. I am sorry for him.[6] [. . .]

We talked of Winston. [. . .] LG thinks that Winston meditates becoming the Disraeli of the Liberal Party and hopes to recover his position by making eloquent speeches. LG says that Winston is entirely self-centred. The question he always puts is, 'What is the best thing for me to do?', not 'What is the best thing that I can do for the country?' [. . .]

14 February Dined with the Other Club and drove home with Winston. Very bitter. He again said that he did not wish to discuss matters with LG unless the latter had some definite proposal to make. He did not intend to be put off with mealy-mouthed promises and expressions of good will. [. . .] He said that during the war he would not join in an attack upon the Government unless serious occasion for such action arose, but he reserved full liberty of action. I asked him what he thought of Asquith's speech in the House of Commons on the opening of Parliament. He thought it poor. 'At this stage of the war,' he said, 'oratory and rhetoric are useless. The conduct of the Germans has been described a hundred times in every possible combination of words. A speech to be of any value must contain useful suggestions or constructive criticism. Asquith's speech contained neither.'

Winston said that he understood LG's difficulties in forming his government, but that he failed to take the bold course which would have secured for him Winston's support and assistance as a colleague. He had preferred Walter Long and Austen Chamberlain, who had all along been drags on the wheel and had wholly failed to render useful assistance in the prosecution of the war. [. . .] He says [. . .] that the Dardanelles Report will clear him, although 'Mr Cockroach', as he described [Walter] Roch,[7] MP, has made a damaging minority report in which he attacks both Asquith and Winston.

15 February Lunched with Winston at his house. When I arrived he handed me the Dardanelles Report, which had been lent him by LG. After I had skimmed it, he asked my candid opinion. I told him I thought he had come well out of the inquiry, but that the document would be most damaging to Asquith and Kitchener. I felt sure the public would be surprised at the findings, and shocked at the disclosures regarding the conduct of the war. I said that LG would of course publish the Report. Winston replied in the affirmative, but said that Asquith was making great efforts to prevent publication. The evidence is not to be published, as it contains secret matter which cannot be disclosed during the war, including proof that when we stopped the naval operations the Turks had only three rounds of ammunition left. I inquired how Winston thought Fisher had come out of the inquiry. He replied, 'Not well.'[8]. [. . .]

18 February LG called for me and I returned with him for dinner. He referred to the strain on his colleagues and himself. This week has been one of the hardest he has ever experienced. Since he has been PM he has held seventy-five meetings and the War Cabinet have interviewed ninety experts. [. . .]

We talked of the Dardanelles Report. I said, 'It is not good for Winston, but it is bad for Asquith and Kitchener. Winston does not come out white or black, he comes out grey.' LG agreed and said that Mr Asquith has written protesting against the Report being published without the evidence, knowing full well that the evidence cannot be published until after the war. LG intends nevertheless to publish the Report on Monday. LG says that there is an organised attempt to re-establish the Asquith legend [. . .] Carson told LG that having known Mr A for years he has no doubt as to the policy he is pursuing. He is playing a deep game, and at the right moment will endeavour to strike and regain his office. [. . .]

LG: [Runciman] and McKenna formed a disastrous combination. Runciman with his affection for vested interests and McKenna with his favourite doctrine that from a financial point of view British trade must be the first consideration. They forgot that in war there are other things that are essential in order to avoid destruction.

R: How do you stand with your colleagues?

LG: Well, I have Carson, Bonar Law and Henderson. Neither of the two first would be inclined to serve under the other, but both are willing to serve under me. Then I think that Milner and I stand for very much the same things. He is a poor man, and so am I. He does not represent the landed or capitalist classes any more than I do. He is keen on social reform, and so am I. Balfour, again, would rather serve under me than under Bonar Law. I think he likes me. Perhaps he regards me as a brigand but thinks that you must put up with brigands during a war.

R: Have you prepared your speech on the restriction of imports, agriculture and shipbuilding? It will be an epoch-making statement. Incidentally the remnants of the feudal system will be abolished without a word of comment. The royal bird, the pheasant, will be shorn of his sacred rights, the agricultural labourer will have a minimum wage of *25s*, and the landlord will be forbidden to raise his rents.

LG: Yes, and a serious breach will be made in the sacred doctrine of Free Trade by the grant of minimum prices to the farmer for a fixed period. Truly we live in wonderful times!

10 March Called at the Admiralty by appointment to see Sir Edward Carson. Suggested he should issue through me a statement to the editors acquainting them with the seriousness of the position and giving details. He said that he welcomed the suggestion and would prepare and send me a paper. [. . .]

We talked of Asquith and the Dardanelles Report. Carson said that Mr A presided with great dignity at the Cabinet, and that he (Carson) regarded him with feelings of friendship and affection. But Mr A had been a failure during the war, as he had endeavoured to conduct public affairs in the same way as he had done during times of peace. Compromise and finesse were all very well in peace time, but fatal during a war. [. . .]

Winston asked me to call at Cromwell Road. [. . .] He read a letter he had written to LG, complaining of the excision of certain portions of the Dardanelles Report and asked formally for a complete copy of the evidence. He requested me to take the letter with me to Walton, which I did. He said that he now meant to fight and attack Northcliffe. I advised him to leave N alone. An attack would do no good and would only please N and serve his purpose. [. . .]

17 March   Lunched and played golf with LG, the LCJ and Donald; the first game LG has played for about four months. [. . .]

28 March   Dined with Albert Illingworth,[9] the Postmaster-General – a very shrewd man of business. He has a poor opinion of the War Office organisation.

1 April   Dined with LG at Walton. [. . .]

R: If you had an election, how would you stand? Would not most of the sitting Members be returned, probably on the representation that they would support you in the war?

LG: I should make it quite plain to the Liberals and the Labour people that they would have to undertake to support me against Asquith or anyone else, and that I should run candidates against those who were not willing to give such an undertaking. I think those who gave it could be relied upon to support me, and I am told that I could rely on securing the adherence of at least 150.

R: The Nonconformists are very bitter concerning the proposed State purchase of the liquor trade. Robertson Nicoll, Dr Clifford and others are vowing vengeance. Nicoll compared you on Wednesday to Judas Iscariot!

LG: Did he? I see that the *British Weekly* is full of it. It is unfortunate that Astor failed to issue to the Press a full report of the deputation which I saw last week from Scotland. I was asked both by the Prohibitionists and the Labour people to receive a deputation. I saw them together. [. . .]

(At this someone came in and so the conversation was interrupted. LG was perhaps not sorry, as he knows my views and dislikes opposition.)

5 April   Called at Downing Street. [. . .]

LG invited me to go upstairs to dinner. [. . . It] was served in the great dining-room. A wonderful sight. So far as the food, service, and appointments were concerned, it looked as if a small suburban household were picnicking in Downing Street – the same simple food, the same little domestic servant, the same mixture of tea and dinner. And yet with all that, an air of simple dignity and distinction pervaded the room – no affectation, no pretension, nothing mean, nothing ignoble. [. . .]

Called to see Carson at the Admiralty. Discussed form of secret letter to be sent to the Press. He is to revise that drafted by me. He still takes a gloomy view and thinks his colleagues too optimistic. He says the Germans are putting out more submarines than we are destroying, and that if the war continues the results must be very serious. [. . .]

11 May   H. G. Wells's covert attack on the monarchical system has caused much uneasiness at Buckingham Palace. The King and Queen have been badly stage-managed.[10] [. . .]

12 May   Golfed with LG, Reading and Donald at Swinley Forest. LG looked tired, but laughed and joked as usual. He gave an affecting account of his conference with the French. When he arrived in Paris they were in the depths. After his speech at the Conference, Nivelle, Pétain,[11] and the rest shook hands with him and thanked him for what he had said and for the encouragement he had given. 'They are like children,' said LG, 'delightful and wonderful children – brave, brilliant, and resourceful, but children all the same. And that is why I love them as I do. The time has come for someone to point out that France entered this war for the sake of Russia, and that Russia is acting a mean part to leave her in the lurch. I am not sure that I am not the man to say it.'

LG said that the temper of the House of Commons in the secret session was admirable. The naggers kept quiet, as there was no chance of publicity. Winston made an excellent speech.[12] He put his points well. [. . .]

17 May Met General Robertson and Lord Derby at Downing Street. They were waiting to attend the War Council and evidently fretting at the delay. Robertson told me privately that the War Council, and in particular the PM, have too much to do. The arrangements for carrying on the war have improved, but are not yet what they should be. Robertson says the French position is serious and requires constant attention. It is most unsatisfactory that the PM should have to make such frequent journeys to France. Robertson thinks some person of position should be appointed to represent the PM as a sort of liaison officer. At present we have no proper representative in France. [. . .] In my many and varied communications with Buckingham Palace, Ministers and public officials, I have found that the two former are much more courteous and amenable to reason than the latter. No one is more arrogant and pig-headed than a civil servant. The people at Buckingham Palace make mistakes because they do not know or realise the conditions. They are always anxious to do the right thing when it is pointed out.

18 May Dined at the Other Club. General Smuts was elected an honorary member. He was present and made himself very affable. I had a long talk with Winston Churchill. He is to lunch tomorrow with LG at Walton and said he regretted I should not be there. He thinks that LG should endeavour to get Asquith into the Government, but does not know whether A would be willing to join. He thinks also that Smuts should be elected a member of the War Council. He described him as the 'only unwounded statesman of outstanding ability in the Empire'. By 'unwounded' he meant the only one who is fresh and bright, unwounded mentally and physically. Winston spoke in slighting terms of Milner and Curzon and said that LG was fighting the battle practically single-handed. He added, 'He made a terrible mistake in cutting himself adrift from me.' (Yesterday Gen. Robertson described Curzon to me (R) as 'a pompous windbag'.) Winston spoke bitterly of the Tories. He evidently thinks they excluded him from the Government. He looked ill and is rather a pathetic figure.

20 May Dined with LG. Sir James Stevenson of the Ministry of Munitions came to discuss labour questions. LG said he had been on the telephone to Sheffield and had returned a firm answer. The strike was settled yesterday in most other districts. LG spoke strongly regarding the action of the engineers, which he said was due in a great measure to the objection of the younger members to go to the war. Sir James Stevenson and I pointed out that there was much to be said for the men and that LG was wrong in assuming that the trade-union view was unfavourable to the strikers or that it was due to unworthy motives. We urged that the chief causes of unrest and dissatisfaction were: (1) suspicion and distrust of the undertakings by the Government and the capitalist, (2) knowledge that the employers are taking advantage of the war to introduce cheaper labour which they hope to retain after the war, (3) the huge fortunes made by ship-owners and others, (4) the high prices of food and other essentials, (5) interference with trade-union privileges which have been built up after years of agitation.

LG argued strongly that everything must be subservient to the war and that the working classes must be patriotic and trust the Government. He called Sir James Stevenson and me two strikers. [. . .]

23 May Sir James Stevenson lunched with me. He says Addison was furious at the statement that LG had settled the strike. The settlement was effected by Addison. A memorandum for publication was sent to Downing Street for approval. Sutherland, LG's secretary, at once telephoned to the Press saying that LG had settled the strike! Addison reproached LG with this on Monday when LG admitted that Addison had been unfairly treated and promised to make an explanatory statement in the House of Commons, which he did, but LG got the credit for the settlement all the same.[13] [. . .] Sutherland is very adroit and never misses an opportunity. [. . .]

2 June Lunched and golfed with LG, who was full of fun and in very good spirits. [. . .]

Northcliffe has gone to America on a special mission for the Government. LG said, 'Don't you think it a good idea? He was getting unbearable, jumpy and dangerous. It was necessary to get him something to do and I think he will do the job well.' [. . .] Much talk of the appointment of a successor to Lord Devonport[14] as Food Controller. I told LG that the sugar queues were causing grave discontent and that the sugar distribution called for immediate reform. The working classes are angry that their wives and families should be compelled to undergo this trouble and indignity, while the wants of the rich are supplied very much as they were before the war. LG did not appear to know about the queues and said that steps must at once be taken to remedy matters.

3 June Dined with LG. [. . .] Colonel David Davies came to Walton in the hope of seeing LG regarding the position at Salonika, which Davies described as serious. LG said that he really must have a little rest from official business, and that he would only see Davies if he promised not to discuss the Salonika problem. Davies therefore went home in a huff.

Davies is furious that Northcliffe has been sent to America, and says that he (Davies) would like to leave Downing Street and return to the Army.

9 June Lunched with LG at Walton. He said he had just called a Cabinet to consider this morning's air raid on London. He spoke much of Robertson Nicoll's attitude in the _British Weekly_. This is obviously causing him some perturbation. I said, 'Nicoll is angry about your proposals to purchase the drink trade. He thinks you are adopting tricky tactics with the object of involving the nation in a scheme so that retreat will be impossible.'

LG replied that he would come to no decision until after the Committee had reported. The terms might prove quite impossible. Both parties are annoyed. Nicoll and Co. on the one hand, and Astor, the protagonist of purchase, on the other. He did not intend to embark on any scheme which is not essential as a war measure. More beer will now be brewed. That will relieve the situation and thus render the proposals for purchase unnecessary. I had better tell this to Nicoll. It was useless for LG to see him again. When they last met at LG's house at lunch, he saw that Nicoll was excited, so did not argue with him. [. . .]

11 June Dined with LG. The Donalds came. [. . .] Donald said that LG ought to rope Winston into the Government as otherwise he might join Mr A who, Donald thought, was growing in popularity. LG agreed about the roping in, but not about Mr A.

10 July Called upon Mrs LG. She seemed much perturbed and rather angry. She told me that things are going badly, and that 'a change must be made in the people about him', and 'it is quite likely we may find it necessary to leave here'. What she meant I did not care to enquire. [. . .]

14 July Called on Mrs LG again. She referred to what she said on Tuesday. [. . . To LG she had said:] 'You do not govern the country. It is governed by all these devils around you.'[15] [. . .]
   We talked of the resignation of Col. David Davies, MP. The PM was angry with him, and wrote him a letter containing some of David Davies' own phrases which had annoyed the PM. 'The result was,' said LG, 'that poor Davies at once took to his bed. He never thought when he kept on worrying me that his letters might have the same effect.' [. . .]

17 July LG made his speech to the Press – well planned, well phrased, and full of secret information. He asked me to have tea with him afterwards. We discussed forthcoming changes in the Government. The PM said he must have more support. Carson's judgment was good and would be very helpful in the War Council.[16] Geddes[17] would, he thought, do well at the Admiralty, and Winston was coming in also. LG spoke bitterly of Balfour's action regarding Lord Hardinge and said he had threatened resignation if Hardinge's was accepted. [. . .]

19 July Called on Winston at Eccleston Square by arrangement. Told him frankly the position in regard to the Ministry of Munitions, viz. that most of the leading men are in a state of mutiny, that resignations are imminent and that Addison has too long delayed reorganisation. [. . .] He seemed much surprised at the state of affairs, thanked me for the information, and discussed a proposed scheme of re-organisation, which he seemed to regard favourably. [. . .] No one in authority ever criticises the doings of the upper classes. In this respect LG is one of the chief offenders, and as a result is raising up a horde of enemies among the workers. [. . .]

Shortly before Glasgow speech. [. . .] Robertson Nicoll is vehement against LG on the purchase of the liquor trade.He prophesies that this scheme will alienate many of LG's oldest and best friends and perhaps bring the Government down. He says that LG has reached his zenith and that he will now decline. He charges LG with treachery in regard to the drink business.

29 July Spent the afternoon with Winston. [. . .] He spoke bitterly of LG who, he said, had fettered his (Winston's) freedom of action by illusory promises of office.[18] Winston does not accuse LG of doing this intentionally, and regards his action as being due to a fear of the Tories, such as Walter Long. Winston remarked that fate might ordain that LG and he would be opposed in a life-long struggle.[19] At the moment his, Winston's, star was low, but it might rise and he might find himself at the head of a great party in opposition to LG. Winston thinks that LG will remain with the Tories but will be compelled to bow to their will. [. . .]

30 July At LG's suggestion have taken Great Walstead, Lindfield, Sussex, for a month, so that he may get some short holidays and at the same time keep in touch with his work. [. . .]

On Sunday we visited Winston at Lingfield. He had just returned from Dundee and gave us a minute account of his doings. [. . .] Winston read cablegrams from his *friend*[20] Northcliffe, with whom he was now upon terms of intimate association. From them and other documents to which he referred, it appeared that the Americans are doing badly. Their constructional policy is said to be defective and ill-planned. LG agreed, and remarked that the situation in USA was far from satisfactory. [. . .]

2 August Motored with LG to Great Walstead. Found Lord Robert Cecil, Lord Milner and General Smuts there already. Baron Sonnino, the Italian Foreign Minister, arrived shortly afterwards. [. . .]

Afterwards I talked alone with Smuts, who told me that the War Cabinet is snowed under by papers and details, and that some drastic revision of the organisation was necessary. There is no sufficient delegation and Ministers have no time to think out the really great problems of the war. At the end of the week the mind is in a haze owing to the number and complexity of the problems which have arisen. [. . .]

4 August To LG's meeting at the Queen's Hall and then with him to tea at Downing Street. Later motored to Lindfield. He again discussed the American trip, on which he seems very keen. Thinks it essential that attempts should be made to expedite American preparations. I suggested that it might be dangerous for the Prime Minister to be absent for so long at such a time. He agreed, but considered the hastening of the American preparations vital. After the excitement of the speech, he was very tired and went early to bed.

6 August Long talk with LG on the war. He gave me Haig's dispatch to read, which I found very disappointing. Obviously he is not confident about the future. LG says that he (LG) wrote a memorandum a month ago in which he prophesied the practical failure of the recent offensive.

R: There is an uneasy feeling that while we are confidently talking of smashing Germany, there is no evidence of any definite plan likely to lead to victory within a reasonable period, and that meanwhile we are steadily sacrificing ships and lives. That feeling is growing.

LG: I have said, and am still saying, that we must hit the enemy elsewhere. We must formulate new plans. Our soldiers have no imagination. Haig naturally has no eyes for anywhere but his own Front. He wants, very properly, to win the war there, and the soldiers at home, Robertson and the rest, have no genius. They are fine, hard-working men, but they lack the vital spark. [. . .]

12 August Philip Kerr, editor of *The Round Table*, and now one of LG's secretaries, arrived. [. . .]

In the afternoon we motored to Winston's, where I invited Donald of the *Daily Chronicle* to meet us, as LG wanted to see him on the crisis. [. . .]

LG had a long talk with Donald, which he described as 'useful.' [. . .]

13 August [. . .] Life at Great Walstead is very interesting; it brings out all phases of the PM's character. He is a remarkable combination of forces; a poet, an orator and a man of action. His energy, power of work, and power of recuperation are remarkable. He has an extraordinary memory, imagination, and the art of getting at the root of a matter. What the military call the *coup d'oeil*. He possesses every sort of courage, daring, patience, bravery in the face of personal danger and in the face of responsibility – *courage d'esprit* as the French say. He has no respect for tradition or convention. He is always ready to examine, scrap, or revise established theories and practices. These qualities give him unlimited confidence in himself. He has a remarkably quick, alert and logical mind, which makes him very effective in debate. He is one of the craftiest of men, and his extraordinary charm of manner not only wins him friends, but does much to soften the asperities of his opponents and enemies. He is full of humour and a born actor. His oratory has a wide range. On the whole he is a good judge of men. He has an instinctive knowledge of character, often quite uncanny, coupled with a remarkable power of divining the thoughts and intentions of people with whom he is conversing. His chief defects are: (1) Lack of appreciation of existing institutions, organisations, and stolid, dull people, who often achieve good results by persistency, experience, and slow, but sound, judgment. It is not that he fails to understand them. The point is that their ways are not his ways and their methods not his methods. (2) Fondness for a grandiose scheme in preference to an attempt to improve existing machinery. (3) Disregard of difficulties in carrying out big projects. This is due to the fact that he is not a man of detail.[21]

14 August Spent an hour with Lord French at the War Office. He spoke very bitterly of Sir William Robertson. French says that Robertson is anxious to get the whole of the military power into his own hands, that he is a capable organiser but not a great soldier, and that we are suffering from a lack of military genius. Henry Wilson, one of the best brains in the Army, is without a job, and no steps are being taken to ascertain the views of our leading soldiers. [. . .]

Much of this I told LG, who expressed a wish to see French and Wilson. Consequently [. . .] they came to Great Walstead to lunch. [. . .]

After lunch LG had a long conference with French, Wilson and Philip Kerr. What happened precisely I have not heard, but LG remarked several times that in his opinion French is the biggest soldier we have yet produced in the war. Not an organiser, but a soldier.

27 and 28 August Lords Burnham and Reading, M. Thomas, French Minister of Munitions, Philip Kerr, Colonel Hankey, and Professor Mantoux at Gt Walstead. [. . .] LG repeated that the Italians are short of guns and ammunition. He said he had fought to get them supplies, but with poor results. Our staff would not part with any part of the equipment on the Western Front. We talked of one army and one front. We had never had anything approaching that, and our prospects are being seriously imperilled in consequence. The soldiers had got into a groove. The war would never be over unless Robertson and the others could be induced to take a wider point of view. [. . .] LG remarked that the soldiers would take no advice from a civilian. They regarded the war as their prerogative. He referred to the memoranda which he wrote in November 1916 and July 1917. He said that his forecast had unfortunately been completely justified. [. . .]

LG slept for four hours. During the remainder of the day (28th) we all talked steadily about the war. LG, Colonel Hankey, Philip Kerr and I.

LG said that unless the war is conducted on different lines we are certain to lose it, and that unless a change is made it would be better to make the best peace possible. But he was strongly of opinion that new and better methods were available. He read extracts from his minute of July, in which he predicted the failure of the offensive on the Western Front and advocated an Italian offensive. He said that events had unfortunately proved that he was right – indeed, all the prognostications which were set forth in the memoranda prepared by him from time to time have proved correct. He added, 'My warnings and suggestions have, however, been disregarded by the soldiers. Robertson is obstinate as a mule and he has no vision. All his thoughts are concentrated on the Western Front. We are losing the flower of our Army, and to what purpose? What have we achieved? The Italians are doing well – better than was expected. If we support them by sending them 300 guns with the necessary ammunition, we may enable them to break the Austrians and thus achieve a success which might well be the turning-point of the war. I have written urging this, and that we should suspend the offensive on the Western Front. Robertson will not agree. He is a stiff sort of man – unbending. He would rather break. He cannot even bend when it is to his own advantage.' [. . .]

LG: [. . .] While the soldiers have displayed great powers of organisation and marvellous fortitude and courage, they have not shown any vision or initiative. All these great offensives have been failures, and one hesitates to think how many glorious lives have been sacrificed. It is hard to make such a criticism, but it is true. The generals have done their best. They have done all they knew. [. . .]

Milner arrived about 8. LG had a long private talk with him on what had taken place at the Cabinet. The conversation was subsequently continued, LG, Milner, Hankey, Kerr, and self being present. Milner said that Robertson had attended the Cabinet today. He was obviously tired mentally and physically. No doubt sad and disheartened at the breakdown of his plans. It was to be regretted that this discussion had been necessary at the beginning instead of at the end of Robertson's holiday. His manner was quite changed. He was very piano. [. . .]

When LG had gone to bed, I asked Milner what he thought of the dispute. He said he agreed with the PM, but that it was most unfortunate that the PM and Robertson are so antipathetic. They have no confidence in each other. Robertson is suspicious of LG and consequently is not frank and open, and LG underrates Robertson's ability and perhaps overrates his obstinacy. I asked him how Bonar Law regarded the matter. 'In his heart of hearts,' said Milner, 'he agrees, I think, with LG'. [. . .]

29 August Robertson and General Maurice[22] arrived about 11 a.m. LG saw them alone first of all and later with Milner. The interview was of a friendly character. I was in an adjoining room with Hankey and Kerr. The latter laughingly remarked, 'The great bamboozler is now at work; the victim is being covered with saliva.' Hankey retorted, 'But he will find old Wally[23] [*sic*] a tough morsel. In his way he is just as crafty as LG himself.' The PM came out and spoke to us, saying, 'He (Robertson) looked glum when he arrived, but he is in good humour and all is going well.' [. . .] I had a private talk with Robertson, who said [. . .]'He [LG] is too jumpy. He wants to change about too much. If a thing does not do well, he wants to try something else too quickly.' [. . .]

Robertson struck me as a fine, sterling sort of a man with a clear, direct, well-ordered mind, but without much imagination and perhaps erring on the side of obstinacy – not a genius, but a man with a fine brain. No spark of fire, but real good strong stuff. [. . .]

9 September Motored with LG, Mrs LG, Megan, and Philip Kerr to Criccieth. Lunched on the roadside. As we neared our destination the PM began to recite Welsh verses with much emphasis and feeling – all the time holding his wife's hand as if they were a newly married couple. [. . .]

September 1917–March 1918

Britain had now entered the darkest period of the war, immortalised by the word Passchendaele. Russia was torn by revolution, France reeled from her losses, American aid was as yet largely promissory, and a great German offensive in the West could not be long delayed. Riddell saw more of Lloyd George in the next few months than earlier in 1917, and was a fascinated but sympathetic observer of his struggles. These centred on the Prime Minister's battle to exert his authority over the Army chiefs – Robertson, Haig and Derby. Not only did Riddell hear much of Lloyd George's opinions and suspicions of these and other persons, he played the role of go-between when Lord French's aid was invoked against Robertson and Haig. While the war with the generals is the dominant theme in many of the diary entries during these months, Lloyd George's other problems are not overlooked. He continued to suspect Churchill and Montagu of flirting with the Asquithians as a form of insurance should the Government fall, while Beaverbrook's evident disgruntlement posed an added threat to stability. Northcliffe's celebrated public refusal of the Air Ministry elicited some pithy remarks in Riddell's presence, and the Lansdowne letter resulted in the need to pacify an angry Lord Burnham. Lesser matters such as the Cecils' determination to prevent Lloyd George from making off with the Tory party and Sir John Simon's reneging on a promise to defend Lloyd George in a lawsuit provided added material for the diarist.

As in preceding chapters, there is much more in the diaries than what Riddell learnt from conversation with Lloyd George. Dinners at the Other Club revealed something of how a cross section of important people felt about the issues of the moment, with Lloyd George's possible fate an engrossing topic. Rothermere and F. E. Smith had much to say on these occasions. At other times Lord Derby's willingness to talk about his dilemma found in Riddell an interested listener, as did Beaverbrook's reflections upon propaganda and persons. For a short time Riddell had a new interest when Lloyd George put him on a committee to investigate the shortcomings of British propaganda, and he penned some harsh words about Charles Masterman and the system that operated under him. As Riddell shared his feelings with Lloyd George he could claim a measure of credit for the appointments of Beaverbrook and Northcliffe which caused such an uproar in parliamentary circles. The chapter ends on a lighter note, with Lloyd George practising a little harmless deception on J. H. Thomas regarding his intention to attack Asquith in the Commons on relations with the Press.

13 September   An awful day with storms of rain, but LG, Kerr, Megan and I went for a long walk after tea. LG says that the Western offensive looks like being a failure and that he has received a letter from Burnham, who has been in France, telling him that there is much dissatisfaction in the Army on the subject. [. . .]

14 September   [. . .] The situation on the Western Front is unsatisfactory. The offensive seems to have been a failure. LG is now considering what course to take. A fight with the soldiers seems to be imminent.[1] LG thinks that our generals have displayed no great ability, and there are rumours that the detailed arrangements on the Western Front have not been what they should. He has evidently decided to press for a cessation of the Western offensive. He has said on many occasions that he was opposed to it and has prophesied its failure. In view of events he obviously intends to urge his own views upon the soldiers. Whether they will agree remains to be seen. If not, a battle royal is pending. [. . .] LG says that soldiers are not adaptable. The soldier is apt to sneer at the politician, but the latter is far more ready to adapt himself to fresh conditions than the former. If he did not, he would be kicked out. The soldier, on the other hand, has fixity of tenure and his training tends to make him rigid. LG says, as is no doubt the case, that the newspapers are badly informed concerning the war, and that the public are gradually becoming uneasy at the absence of news of a definite success on the Western Front. *The Times* has published an article commenting on the lack of information as to the progress of the campaign. [. . .]

21 September   [. . .] Much talk of the operations in connection with the Western offensive. Both LG and Milner consider the continuation of the offensive a mistaken policy. Asquith has been visiting Haig, and LG and Milner are disposed to believe that the soldiers are preparing to defend their position by engaging the sympathies of the Opposition and the Press. LG and Milner spoke strongly regarding the loss of life involved in a continuation of the offensive and the inadequate results achieved. They say that the soldiers have no plan but to continue to batter the German front on the West, and that they have been holding out the same hopes and making the same promises for the last two years.

22 September   Drove with Lord Milner to Llandudno Junction. He said the soldiers stand well with the public, who do not know the facts and have short memories. That a quarrel with the soldiers would therefore involve an attack which would dishearten our people and hearten the enemy. That he therefore is opposed to any such proceeding and thinks a quarrel unnecessary. He is going to London to see Robertson, and believes that the difference of opinion is capable of amicable adjustment. He thinks that by now the soldiers must recognise the necessity for an alternative policy and that it is inexpedient to continue to rely solely on the Western offensive, which in his opinion should be modified so as to conserve our troops. He fully agrees with LG on the general policy, but is anxious to carry the soldiers with the Cabinet, whereas LG rather favours more aggressive action. He has, however, agreed to adopt Milner's plan. Any breach would involve the appointment of a new Chief of Staff and Commander-in-Chief. This would be difficult, as there are no alternatives.

Hankey, Secretary to the War Council, a very able man of whom LG, Asquith, Milner and other Ministers hold the highest opinion, has been busy here during the past week. He is an indefatigable worker and displays great tact. He is hopeful of a successful issue with the soldiers and has already put matters in train with Robertson. [. . .]

3 October   Lord French asked me to lunch at 34 Lancaster Gate. He said he was anxious to let the PM know three things, but did not like to communicate with him direct. [. . .]

He thinks that Robertson fails to envisage the war as he should. His thoughts are concentrated on the Western Front. He does not realise that our battle line extends from Baghdad to Ostend. He is gradually concentrating power into his own hands, so that he controls the whole of our military affairs and policy. Maurice and the other officers are able men but they are afraid to assert themselves. A large section of leading officers think with French and Wilson regarding strategic questions, but their opinion is never asked. [. . .] He said that he would like to dine with the PM and have a chat with him. [. . .]

I communicated the message and arranged for a dinner at my house.

5 October   The PM and French to dinner. [. . .] The PM regretted that he had not asked French to speak at the Cabinet. He did not know his views and did not want to risk increasing the volume of opposition. French said that if he were asked his views on any subject by the Cabinet, he should say exactly what he thought. He repeated with emphasis what he had said to me about Robertson. [. . .] The PM asked Lord French whether he thought General Allenby[2] was a good soldier and suitable for his Egyptian command. French replied, 'The best man you could get.' [. . .]

[R:] Why does Winston always make such marked reference to Asquith in his speeches?

LG: I think he knows that they mean to attempt to turn me out. I think he wants to keep in with them so that he will not again be out of office. He does not want to burn his boats. [. . .] He is not acting well, but I shall not mention the matter to him. He will have to take care how he handles the public. They have not forgiven or forgotten. He must rebuild his foundations. [. . .]

7 October   Dined with LG. I told him I thought that both the Tories and the Liberals were on the move, and that they were anxiously looking to the time when one party or the other would be able to seize the reins of power. Also that they reckoned on the fact that he had no party. I said, 'They hope to see you suspended between earth and heaven like Mahomet's coffin.' LG agreed, but added, 'They will find that I am not in my coffin yet. They will have to reckon with me when the time comes.' He agreed that Winston and Montagu, who are very thick just now, are endeavouring to secure themselves in the event of a collapse of this Government. Yesterday LG told me that Max Aitken is in a disgruntled mood. Why, LG does not know. He thinks that Max is disappointed that he is unable to exercise more power. [. . .]

15 October   Dined with Sir Howard Frank. [. . .] I walked home with Brade, who says that Robertson is very angry with LG and has been saying that he means to get even with him. Brade does not think he will succeed. [. . .]

18 October   In consequence of representation as to the condition of affairs in South Wales, I (R) suggested to Carson that Smuts should go there to deliver a speech before the miners take their ballot as to whether they should strike as a protest against the Government's recruiting proposals. Carson brought the proposal before the Cabinet, who approved the idea, and Smuts agreed to go.

Winston Churchill addressed editors as to the work of his Department. Before doing so he asked me to call, which I did. He outlined his speech. I made some suggestions and advised him to limit his remarks to three-quarters of an hour. He agreed, but spoke for an hour and a half. [. . .]

19 October Interesting talk with Fisher[3] at the Education Office. He is willing to consider a modification of the clause prohibiting children from working before school hours. He is a very clever man, but his mind is very discursive – perhaps fluid would be a better word. He talks all over a subject like quicksilver.

Long talk with [Sir Arthur] Steel-Maitland,[4] the new Minister of Overseas Trade, and his assistant, Sir William Clark.[5] [. . .]

Have been appointed to act on committee to investigate our propaganda methods. The other members are Burnham, Beaverbrook and Donald, with Carson as Chairman. We have had one meeting. The whole thing is a shocking muddle.[6] The work is being duplicated and the foreign press publicity is being very badly handled. [. . .]

20 October [. . .] Lunched and played golf with LG, Philip Kerr and Donald. LG thinks that the soldiers are trying to make use of Asquith and Co. and that there has been an informal coalition between the two. He says that even Massingham has now adopted this attitude. [. . .] LG agreed that the old parties are moribund. They stand for nothing. The problems which produced them have faded into insignificance. Now there will be a big fight between those who have the stuff and those who want to get it.

21 October Dined with LG. [. . .] We talked of the condition of parties. I said, 'I don't know what is the difference between a Tory and a Liberal nowadays.'

LG: I agree, and that would not be a bad thing to say publicly. [. . .]

I said that the political situation was very peculiar. 'You have no party, no organisation, and no coterie of supporters. You stand almost alone. You ought to make an offensive and defensive alliance with some of the leading men and get an organisation.' He agreed. [. . .]

26 October Attended Propaganda Committee meeting. The whole thing is an unholy mess. The waste and overlapping are scandalous. This after three years of war. But what could be expected of an incompetent creature like Masterman? Unfit to organise a Sunday School, and a jobber of the first water.

27 October   Golfed and lunched with LG. Very full of the Italian disaster.[7] [. . .] As Lord French says, the unexpected is always what happens in war. LG pursued here by Hankey and another officer. After lunch they retired to my room and had a conference. Things look pretty bad.

In discussing the Italian news, LG said, 'This shows once more that the Germans have more brains in their high command than we have. Our generals have kept their eye fixed on the Western Front. They have not visualised the whole battle-field. When the Germans are in difficulties in one arena of war, they suddenly deliver a smashing blow in another. We shall beat them as Napoleon was beaten. He had the brains, but he was fighting the whole world. . . .'

31 October   Saw LG at Downing Street. [. . . He said:] This Italian business has come as a sad blow to our soldiers (Robertson & Co.). They are now quite afraid I shall publish my memoranda and correspondence. As you know, I have been urging action on the Italian Front for nearly four months. You remember what took place at Great Walstead. Gwynne, Editor of the *Morning Post*, has urged me not to publish. He says that the result would be to shake the confidence of the army in its leaders. I don't agree with him. He is the agent of the General Staff. [. . .] The soldiers cannot have it both ways. [. . .] If it should be necessary, I shall let the public know the facts.

8 November   Other Club. Present: Rothermere, Mark Sykes,[8] F. E. Smith, Beaverbrook, Owen Phillips,[9] Garvin, Goulding and others.[10]

Much talk about naval and military position. Rothermere terribly pessimistic. Most of those present calling for the heads of Robertson and Haig. Rothermere said that he had heard that LG and Haig had had a terrible row in Paris and that the latter had sent in his resignation. Someone asked whether Northcliffe would support Haig, and reference was made to the articles written by Northcliffe as to the organisation of the Army in France. Rothermere said, 'My brother has not got the knowledge to criticise any organisation. He does not understand such things!' Rothermere was very violent at LG's neglect to get rid of incompetents, Hardinge, etc. Someone said that Hardinge was kept to prevent Balfour from going. There was a strong chorus of

disapproval about Balfour. Rothermere said that he had been offered
two Cabinet positions which he had refused, as he would not serve in
any Cabinet with Balfour, who was absolutely useless for war purposes
and should have been got rid of long ago.'[11]

The general opinion expressed was that LG's fate was at hand. He
must either insist upon his own policy, or accept responsibility for that
of his military advisers. If he is not satisfied with them, he must get rid
of them. The nation is in a position of extreme peril and this is no time
for mealy-mouthed proceedings. Rothermere said that Derby is entirely in the hands of the soldiers, and that he is a man of no military
ability whatsoever and should be got rid of. It is rumoured that
Rothermere himself wants to be War Minister. [. . .] F. E. Smith told
me privately that he is all for LG and that [. . .] he thinks he is the only
man to carry on the war. All the party tonight agreed with this opinion.

9 November   Sir Reginald Brade confirms the rumour of the quarrel
between LG and Haig in Paris. [. . .]

13 November   Called upon Reginald Brade at the War Office. [. . .]
Discussed LG's Paris speech with Brade who said that difficulties
would occur when some specific proposal was put forward by the new
War Council. Our Staff would object and then the fat would be in the
fire. He thinks that LG and Robertson differ so much temperamentally that trouble is certain to arise, and that Robertson will
probably have to go. [. . .]

15 November   Brade dined with me. He has had a long interview with
LG, who told him that he and Haig had had it out in Paris, but
afterwards went for a walk together and parted the best of friends. LG
cannot make out Robertson's attitude regarding new proposals. He
says that Robertson left Paris forty-eight hours in advance of him and
returned to London to start his Press campaign. Brade tells me of new
proposals for Press censorship, which he had got Cabinet to refer to
the Admiralty, War Office and Press Committee. Brade expects
strong opposition, as proposals involve censorship of all articles
advocating peace. In this I agreed. He is to send me a memorandum
setting forth the proposals.

17 November   Golfed with LG. Referring to his Paris speech he said,
'It was necessary. I had to speak strongly to secure attention both here

and in France and Italy. McKenna & Co. have been rubbing their hands and saying, 'We have got him now!' [. . .]

R: The public are agreed as to the necessity for the allied War Council. Criticism is mainly directed against your observations concerning our operations on the Western Front. [. . .]

We talked of Northcliffe, whose letter announcing his refusal of the Air Ministry is published today.[12]

LG: I did not see the letter until I saw it in the newspapers. You cannot rely on him. He has no sense of loyalty and there is something of the cad about him. You can see it in his face. He is angling for the Premiership. His object is plain. People talk of politicians interfering in military strategy, and quite correctly. [. . .] But it is seldom recognised that politics is a most difficult field of strategy demanding long training and special qualifications. The administration of public affairs cannot be learned in a few months. It takes years of training. The business man is well able to grapple with a definite task, but he is hopelessly at sea when it becomes necessary for him to decide and carry out great questions of public policy.[13]

R: Rothermere is supporting you. He wants you to shed Balfour, Derby and Curzon – perhaps others. He covets the position of War Minister, but Brade tells me he is very nervous about taking responsibility.

LG: He would be overwhelmed in a very short time. He is quite unfitted for such a post.[14] [. . .]

Poole of Lewis & Lewis told me that Sir John Simon had agreed to represent LG in his libel action against the *Daily News* and *Westminster*, although he said that in his opinion the action should not have been brought. He had declined to take any fee. He lunched with LG on the day before the hearing and a consultation was fixed for 6 o'clock. Greatly to Poole's astonishment Simon walked up and down the room declaiming that the action should not have been brought and remarked, 'How can I, on the last day that I will appear at the Bar (he was about to join the Army) appear in court against the *Daily News* and *Westminster?*' Ultimately he said that LG must procure another counsel as he would not act. Poole considers that Simon acted very badly and abandoned his client because he was afraid to offend two powerful Liberal papers.[15] [. . .]

22 November [. . .] The Other Club. F. E. Smith [. . .] spoke very bitterly of Geoffrey Dawson, Editor of *The Times*, who he thinks attacked him unfairly in regard to the recent case as to the Shipping Controller's powers. He said that he would never shake hands again with Dawson, who was a liar. He again referred to the Censorship incident which took place early in the war (October 1914). [. . .] He said that Dawson, then Robinson, came to him before the matter was dealt with in the House of Commons. F. E. Smith wrote out in Dawson's presence what it was agreed that he (F. E.) should say, the object being to shield *The Times*. It was understood that Dawson should not attack F. E., who had agreed to take upon himself the responsibility. F. E. carried out his part of the bargain, but on the day following the debate in the House of Commons, the *Daily Mail* violently attacked him and alleged that he was responsible for the publication of the peccant article. In other words, F. E.'s generosity in taking the blame was used against him. Dawson never wrote to apologise for or explain Northcliffe's conduct.

24 November   LG lunched with me, and we played golf in the afternoon. He said that he only received information concerning Kitchener's attempt to form an Allied Council only just before he went into the House of Commons to make his great speech. He thinks that Mr A would have liked to impugn the statement. [. . .]

LG: Yes. He adopted the wrong tactics. His opening carried no conviction. I am glad the debate took place. It has cleared the air. I am glad I have had an opportunity of crossing swords with Mr A. It had to be, and it is well over. I don't often read the *Spectator* or the *Nation*, but I read them this week. They are amusing reading. Strachey has never forgiven me for calling him a pompous person, and as for Massingham, he is just like a shrieking shrew. [. . .]

R: How did Northcliffe get on at the conference with the Americans?

LG: Not a success; his observations were really very poor. He made the worst sort of show of anyone present. I was surprised and so were all of us. He came to Carson and, referring to Carson's speech in which he castigated Northcliffe unmercifully, remarked, 'Well, I deserved it. I don't complain.' Carson was amazed and told me that he thought N an extraordinary personage. I spoke to N concerning his letter to the newspapers in which he most improperly mentioned that I had offered him the position of Minister for Air. He said he was very sorry and would see Cowdray and apologise. Did you ever see such a man?

Donald (who was lunching with us): Northcliffe has a cruel face, and it has grown coarser and crueller since he has been in America.

LG: Yes, he looks a cruel fellow and would have no mercy if he had you in his clutches. But although it may seem a contradiction, he is a kindly fellow. He has both qualities. To our surprise we have found out that he is not an organiser. His great capacity lies in another direction.

Later, when we were alone, LG told me that he had appointed Rothermere Minister for Air.

We talked of the political situation. He said, 'The Liberals will have to choose whether they are going to follow me or not. There will be a cleavage. I shall have to rely upon the business classes to a great extent. I shall have to organise.' [. . .]

25 November   Dined with LG. [. . .] We spoke of Beaverbrook who is very disgruntled just now. LG thinks he is disappointed that he is not the power behind the throne. He has considerable abilities of a sort and great ambitions which he cannot satisfy. His appearance and reputation (deserved or undeserved) are against him. He is better suited for American politics than those of this country. He would like to be the Colonel House of America [*sic*].[16] [. . .]

27 November   Long private talk with Lord Derby at the War Office. Spoke with much feeling of the death of his son-in-law, Neil Primrose.[17] [. . .] He told me that he had had a hard time during the past ten days. He had been on the point of resignation. He said, 'I am usually charged with impetuosity, but on this occasion I restrained myself, and I think I acted for the best. I should have resigned had not LG made certain alterations in his Allied Council scheme. But he met me very fairly. I like him, and was glad to be able to meet him. The Army Council were on the point of resignation; it was touch and go. I was happily able to be of service in that respect. Had they resigned, I think the Government would have fallen. My resignation would have been an additional blow. I don't say that I could have brought the Government down, but I think my resignation would have shaken them. The scheme was badly managed, and I think LG's Paris speech was a great mistake. The effect upon the Army has been most unfortunate. They have lost confidence in their leaders and in the politicians. A feeling of unrest and anxiety has been caused. I strongly favour the idea of an Allied War Council, but should like to make it a real one. [. . .] The introduction of Harry Wilson[18] may well cause trouble. . . . He has the reputation of being an intriguer, and I think it justified. If he wants to accomplish an object and is frustrated in a direct attack, he will endeavour to secure his object by a devious attack.' [. . .]

2 December   Lord Burnham telephoned to me that he resented Bonar Law's observations concerning the Lansdowne letter, which he said were not justified as it had been passed by a person in high authority. Burnham asked me to let the PM, who had just returned from the first Allied Conference, know this.

3 December   LG had tea with me at Walton Heath. [. . .] We spoke of Lansdowne's letter.[19] LG said he knew nothing about it until he saw it in the newspapers.

R: Did Balfour know of it?

LG: That is what I am wondering. I have my suspicions.

R: I think he did from what Burnham said to me last night.

LG: Burnham is breakfasting with me tomorrow morning. I shall hear all about it then, I expect.

R: Burnham wants me to see him this evening.

LG: [. . .] The letter was ill-advised and inopportune. I have read it again. Lord Lansdowne advocates making a treaty with a nation whom we are fighting because they have broken a treaty. He advocates that the treaty should be enforced by a League of Nations consisting of the nations who are now engaged in attempting to enforce the treaty already in existence. The letter is really a pacifist letter. [. . .] If Balfour has been a party to this, I shall have to consider what course to take. A step of that sort (Lansdowne's) should not be sanctioned or countenanced without the approval of the War Cabinet. It is a serious matter. The advantage of raising the question in the House of Commons would be that Asquith and his followers would have to declare themselves. It is important that they should. [. . .] Northcliffe, who was in Paris, said that had he been in London when the letter was offered to *The Times*, he would have published it accompanied by a stinging leader. I think *The Times* attack on Lansdowne, charging him with being in his dotage, is in bad taste. They are attacking him too brutally. [. . .]

Later, called on Burnham at the *Daily Telegraph*. He said that on Wednesday last Lord Lansdowne came to him in the House of Lords and told him that he had written a letter which *The Times* had declined to publish, as they disagreed with it. He asked Burnham to accept. He said that he (Lansdowne) had informed Arthur Balfour of his intentions and had asked him to read the letter, as he (Lansdowne) had no wish to publish anything that the Foreign Office might regard as harmful. Balfour replied that he was leaving for Paris and that Lansdowne had better show the letter to Hardinge, who had his complete confidence and knew his views. Lansdowne accordingly took the letter to Hardinge, who said that he saw no objection to it, but on the whole thought that publication would be advantageous. Lansdowne said that he had also discussed the letter with Colonel House on several occasions, and that he was favourable to publication. Lansdowne handed the letter to Burnham, who said he would publish it, although he differed with much that Lansdowne had said. After Bonar Law had made his speech condemning the letter, and, as Burnham thinks, impliedly condemning the *Daily Telegraph* for publishing it, Burnham saw him and complained that the Government should have acted in this way in view of Hardinge's approval, which had been a vital factor in Burnham's decision to publish. Bonar Law replied that he was unaware that Balfour and Hardinge had been consulted, and that he regretted if anything he had said in his speech could rightly be construed as a condemnation of the *Daily Telegraph*. Burnham said he was disposed to publish a paragraph stating that publication had been authorised by the Foreign Office. Bonar Law begged him not to do so, and asked him not to tell LG that Balfour and Hardinge had been consulted, as this would only occasion trouble. Burnham declined to agree, and said he should certainly state the facts to LG. Burnham also saw Lord Robert Cecil, who said he was ignorant of the facts concerning Balfour and Hardinge. [. . .]

I suggested that Burnham should take no action beyond stating the facts to LG [. . .] if the Government do not propose to make the facts public, he should ask Bonar Law for a letter stating that publication was quite justifiable in view of Hardinge's consent, and that in abstaining at the request of the Government from making this fact public Burnham was subordinating his own interests to those of the nation. Burnham thanked me and said that he should act on my advice. [. . .] Burnham mentioned that he thought Northcliffe was running the Government, and that Curzon had told him (Burnham) that he had gone into the Cabinet room and found Northcliffe stalking up and down, laying down the law to LG in a loud voice and arrogant manner. [. . .]

Later to Downing Street, when I telephoned on a private telephone to LG, telling him shortly and privately what Burnham had said. He seemed much surprised, although he had anticipated that Balfour was mixed up in the business.

9 December   Lunched with LG at his house at Walton. We talked of peace terms. LG said we should have to secure some territory to compensate us for what we had expended – the greater part of the German Colonies, Palestine and Mesopotamia. France would want Alsace-Lorraine, and the Germans could recoup themselves with a large slice of Russia. The Russians had acted badly and must take the consequences.[20] The time for peace had not arrived, but it would come – he hoped before long.

R: The German position is too strong at the moment. They would want too much. But our position at the end of next year will not be favourable unless the unexpected occurs, which may well happen. We shall have lost more of our shipping, our foreign trade will have disappeared, and our debt will have increased by another 3,000 millions. I don't trust the Americans. Naturally they desire to make America the first nation in the world. At the end of 1918 they will hold all the gold in the world; they will have a huge mercantile fleet, which they have never had before; and they will have opened new markets all over the world, markets which they have been developing while we have been fighting. They resent our command of the seas. Mahan, the American admiral, first enunciated what this means, and it is obvious that the Americans will endeavour to clip our naval wings. Wilson's main purpose is to defeat the Germans, but his subsidiary object is to put Gt Britain in her place. He is a cool crafty fellow, and we shall have to watch that in our efforts to annihilate the Germans we do not annihilate ourselves. One cannot talk publicly like this, but these are factors to be borne in mind.

LG looked thoughtful, but made no reply, beyond saying that he thought Colonel House was a sly old fox. [. . .]

23 December   Arranged for the PM to lunch with me and French on the following day. Dined with the PM at Walton Heath. [. . .] LG said that General Charteris[21] had been called upon to give up his position with Haig. LG thinks that Charteris's views have been wrong and that he has done much harm by disseminating unduly optimistic opinions and prognostications. This was also confirmed by Philip Gibbs.[22] [. . .] LG thinks the military position is serious and that Robertson and Haig have mismanaged matters. He says that Haig is very selfish and will not release a single man, gun, or aeroplane from the Western Front. Haig has always been against reprisals. Why, LG does not know. [. . .]

24 December [. . .] LG and French to lunch at Queen Anne's Gate. [. . .]

I left LG and French to talk in private. When the former had gone French told me that he took a gloomy view of the situation in France and thought it possible that we might have to withdraw altogether, in which case he wanted to know definitely from the PM that he (French) would continue to command in this country. He said that the PM had replied, 'Of course.' French thinks that another twelve months will be a serious thing for us, and that we may emerge from the struggle half-ruined. Both French and LG spoke strongly concerning the British offensive in France. The latter said yesterday that he had stipulated in fixing the man-power arrangements that our casualties should be reduced next year by one half, also that if a suitable man were available it would be well to replace Haig, but that no suitable man had been suggested. He also said that the War Cabinet had taken evidence from the French generals on the subject of casualties which had been very useful in dealing with the man-power question. Pétain had sent the evidence at LG's request. [. . .]

25 December Christmas Day. Dined midday with LG and remained until after 10. [. . .] Eric Geddes telephoned to say that Jellicoe had resigned. LG said, 'It is a good thing, as Jellicoe has lost his nerve. . . .' Although LG did not say so, I gathered that Jellicoe had been asked to resign; but of this I am not sure. [. . .]

LG thinks that much harm is done by publishing harrowing details of air raids, and proposes to issue a regulation prohibiting this.

31 December Dined with LG at Downing Street. [. . . He] said he would now have to reply to the Germans' peace terms, and that after dinner he would get to work. [. . .]

1918

1 January   Winston lunched with me. Talked of peace terms. [. . .]

Winston: We must fight on to a finish. You never know when the Germans will crash. [. . .] I am terribly anxious about the Navy. I know it as no other civilian knows it. Changes are being made which prevent me from sleeping at night. Oliver[23] and Bacon[24] are going. It is madness. They cannot be replaced – particularly Oliver. The position is most serious. I wish I was in Opposition. When the war is over I shall resign. I could not stop with this Government; I would prefer Opposition. While the war is on I must help to the best of my ability, and I was miserable while I was unemployed. Labour is very difficult. [. . .]

5 January   Lunched with LG at Downing Street. Present, Lord Reading, M. Thomas, Mr and Mrs Churchill, J. L. Garvin, M. Mantoux. LG just back from making great speech on our war aims. He said to Reading and me, 'I *went as near peace as I could*.[25] It was the right moment. The time had come to speak definitely.' He explained at lunch that his speech was a counter-offensive against the German peace terms with a view to appealing to the German people and detaching the Austrians. LG spoke with great and unwonted animation and gestures – very graceful. I thought his object was to appeal to Garvin, who took the view that LG's terms, if accepted, would leave the Germans stronger than when they entered the war. Garvin enlarged on the accession to German power in the East and prophesied another war in which Germany would dominate the world. Winston expressed the same opinon. [. . .]

LG stated to us the gist of his speech. I said, 'What about Palestine and Mesopotamia? You are not very clear about them.' He replied, 'Oh, that will have to be worked out hereafter.' This I thought significant. Winston and Garvin both looked very gloomy and thoughtful when the terms were being discussed.

6 January   Dined with LG, who told me that Clemenceau[26] had telegraphed that he entirely agreed with LG's speech. LG regards this as being most important. I described the speech as one of the most epoch-making in the war [. . .] said that it had met with almost universal approval, but no doubt the *Morning Post* and those who think with them will criticise it. LG said that he expected them to do so, but that Clemenceau's letter would place them in a difficulty. [. . .]

We talked of the Naval changes. LG said he had told Sir Eric Geddes that he would support him, and that if he (Geddes) had to go, he (LG) would go too. I told him what Winston had said.

LG: Winston is wrong. Oliver is one of those men who cannot see the wood for the trees and Bacon is incompetent. If there is a row we shall have a secret session, when there will be disclosures that will astonish the House of Commons. Gross negligence and incompetence. [. . .]

11 January Lord French to lunch. He asked my opinion as to an article which he was anxious to write deprecating the criticism by the Army of the Higher Command, and by the Higher Command of the Cabinet. [. . .] I told Lord F that I thought such an article would be most harmful and that it would foster the spirit of distrust and dissatisfaction now existing in the lower ranks. I also pointed out that the article would infringe the salutary rule which he desired to enforce regarding criticism. I advised him to write to the Prime Minister setting forth his views. French replied, 'I think you are right. I am sure you are. I shall act on your advice.' [. . .]

Had tea with Edward Carson. He spoke of the PM. He said, 'He is a wonderful man. How he accomplishes so much and stands so much strain, I do not know. When I look round, I do not see who could replace him. His courage, power of work, power of decision, and urbanity are remarkable. He must possess a marvellous constitution.' Carson told me that he has the feeling that peace is in the air. [. . .]

13 January Dined with LG at Walton. He spoke strongly of the incompetence of the Higher Military Command. He said that he had propounded two questions to them: (1) What are the respective forces of the Central Powers and the Allies? and (2) what plan had they got to end the war? To neither were they able to give any satisfactory answer. Nor had they prepared any definite plan for strengthening our forces by the increased use of mechanical appliances. Their only proposal was more men and still more men. He is convinced that the use of man-power could be economised by the increased use of machine-guns, etc. He had asked Pétain how we could cut down our casualties. Pétain, who is a blunt sort of man, replied, 'By getting better generals!' Our casualties are 48 per cent, while those of the French are only 25 per cent. Auckland Geddes,[27] who had been at Walton Heath today, had told him that the Army recruiting arrangements had been very defective. (I should think that Geddes himself was in a great measure responsible.)

LG inquired whether I thought that Northcliffe would carry on the foreign propaganda satisfactorily. I said, 'Yes. But his appointment might mean a quarrel with Donald.' [. . .]

18 January   [. . .] Drove with LG and Miss Stevenson to Barnes and walked through Richmond Park to Kensington, where we again joined the car and drove to Walton. LG said that he had had a very hard week and was longing for a sleep. He said that he had had a great success in the House of Commons in the secret session. [. . .]

20 January   Dined with LG. [. . .] I referred to the rumours that he (LG) and Asquith might come to an arrangement. They lunched together the week before last to discuss LG's peace terms speech. LG replied that there had been no proposal of that sort. He doubts if Asquith would serve under him, but thinks that from a financial point of view he might like to become Lord Chancellor and lead the House of Lords.

27 January   Dined with LG, who describes Hertling's[28] speech on the peace terms as 'defiant in tone but pacific in intention'. LG thinks the speech clever. I said, 'It all boils down to Alsace-Lorraine and the German colonies, with questions relating to the freedom of the seas looming in the distance.' LG agreed. He said that he always liked reading Bethmann-Hollweg's speeches. He thought them very able – firm and clear. In short, regular hammer-blows. Smuts was with LG today. Just back from France, where he saw Haig, who, he thinks, looks tired and worn. I told LG that yesterday I had called upon Robertson Nicoll, who was now more friendly to him. I said that Nicoll had commented upon the malignant hostility of the McKenna-Runciman faction who foregather at the Reform Club. Nicoll described it as far surpassing anything he had ever known. This bitterness had evidently changed his feeling to LG. I told him that Nicoll had remarked upon the desirability of reuniting LG to his old associates, the Dissenters, and that he thought this would be easy if LG would drop state purchase. LG avowed that he was now paying no attention to this, as he had other things to see to – the conduct of the war, etc. He did not, however, say in terms that he had abandoned the scheme. [. . .]

We then discussed the political situation. LG thinks that the Liberal party in its old form is a thing of the past and cannot be galvanised into life.

He doubts the success of the great efforts now being made by the Liberal organisation, who are very busy indeed in all directions. He thinks that it may come to a fight between him and Henderson, and that all Parties, including Labour, will be split and be reconstituted. I said, 'But you must have candidates. You cannot vote without having someone to vote for.' LG agreed, and said that he had some men coming to see him about the matter tomorrow morning, with the object of forming an organisation. He told me that Guest had accumulated a good deal of money as a party fund, quite a large sum. LG reckons that it will take half a million to fight an election. He said that he proposes to appoint Beaverbrook to succeed Carson as head of the Department of Information, and that Beaverbrook is to appoint Northcliffe to manage foreign propaganda. He asked my opinion. I replied that Beaverbrook's appointment might not be very popular, but that I thought he would do the work well. Northcliffe's appointment would no doubt be severely criticised, and care would be necessary in dealing with Burnham and Donald, with both of whom he was unpopular. Donald in particular might resent the appointment. LG agreed that the plan was open to objection but naively added, 'Northcliffe is anxious for the job.' [. . .]

28 January   Called upon Beaverbrook at the Hyde Park Hotel. He told me that ten days ago LG offered him the Duchy of Lancaster[29] with financial control of the Ministry of Munitions. Beaverbrook discussed the proposal with Winston, and subsequently told LG that Winston's views and his were so much at variance that he (Beaverbrook) had decided to decline the position. Winston had long been a friend of his and he did not wish to break with him, as he would be sure to do under such an arrangement.

Later [John] Buchan[30] had an interview with Beaverbrook at which he (Buchan) expressed anxiety that Northcliffe should succeed Carson as head of the Information department, and that failing this Buchan himself should be appointed. He asked Beaverbrook for his support in these proposals. Beaverbrook told Buchan that he could not support either. No. 1, because Northcliffe's appointment would be most unpopular; and No. 2, because Buchan was unfit for the job. Beaverbrook then had another meeting with Lloyd George, who told him that Northcliffe was anxious for the position but that he could not appoint him for several reasons. LG suggested that Beaverbrook should take the post and appoint Northcliffe, with proper guarantees, as head of foreign propaganda. Beaverbrook said that he would only act if he were invested with ministerial authority. LG then revived the Duchy proposal, but said that B would have to arrange for it. (By this I understand with the present holder.)

Beaverbrook told LG that a friendly arrangement with Northcliffe was vital to his administration, that LG had no party, that he depended upon the Press, and that as he had lost the support of one important section he must secure the support of another. What LG said to this he did not say but he mentioned that LG left him to chat with Northcliffe, who had agreed to act in the capacity described, and had given guarantees as to the manner in which he should perform his duties, loyalty to LG, etc. 'Whether,' said Beaverbrook, 'I can rely on guarantees, I don't know. I expect to lose my life in a deadly scrap with Northcliffe, which is certain to come sooner or later.' Beaverbrook further remarked that there was no reliance to be placed on Northcliffe. I said, 'He will keep his word, but if hard circumstances arise and you disagree he will become your enemy. He has no give and take such as most men display in their dealings with friends and associates.'

B repeated a conversation with LG somewhat as follows:

LG: Recently you have been hostile to my Government. What is the reason?

B: Yes, I have been hostile because you did not carry out the promises which you made when I helped you to form it. For one thing you promised to dismiss Robertson and you have not done so.

LG: Well, if you join my administration (Beaverbrook rolled this word over with much satisfaction) may I rely upon your loyalty?

B: Yes, whole-hearted, and not only when we agree but when we disagree.

LG: That is all right.

Beaverbrook said that he rather favoured accepting LG's offer as he might thus minimise the hostility of powerful persons. I said, 'In the Cabinet?' 'No,' answered B. I then said, 'The King?' 'No,' said B, 'LG told me that he had secured the K's assent. I was referring to you (GAR), Burnham and Donald.' I told him that I should have no objection, but that Burnham and Donald might strongly resent the Northcliffe part of the proposal. Beaverbrook said that he should not tell them until Northcliffe was appointed. I advised him that this would be a mistake and that he should explain to the Committee both individually and collectively what he proposed to do. He said that he thought I was correct. The further discussion was adjourned pending LG's return from France.

Beaverbrook is a strange creature. I found him in a brilliantly lighted room containing a stack of newspapers piled up in one of the corners. The accumulation of weeks. While I was with him he indulged in a conversation on the telephone with Bonar Law. Reading is to dine with him tonight. Guest, the Whip, arrived while I was in the room. It was curious to observe Beaverbrook's manners, or lack of them, when dealing with Guest, who paid him a certain amount of deference, I thought. Beaverbrook lay at full length upon the sofa and hardly spoke. He was very civil to me as he always is. What is the source of his power politically I don't quite know. It may be his friendship with B Law, his ownership of the *Daily Express* which now has the largest circulation of all the morning papers, or his friendship with Rothermere with whom he is very thick. It was amusing to notice his conceit, not perhaps unnatural. He and Guest both expressed themselves as being anxious for the termination of the war on almost any terms. They are both nice fellows, but political adventurers of the deepest dye.

9 February   Charles Russell[31] asked me to invite certain of the Irish Convention delegates to dinner. Called with him to see Horace Plunkett.[32] [. . .] He said he wanted me to tell the PM that an early settlement of the Irish question is absolutely essential. Ireland is prosperous and has the superficial appearance of being quiet and contented. Unfortunately there is a seething mass of rebellion which may break out at any moment. [. . .]

16 February   This has been an exciting week – the military crisis in full blast. Long Cabinet discussions and rumours of resignations. Maurice Hankey rang me up this afternoon and asked me to take him to Walton Heath. Later in the afternoon he arrived with the news of Robertson's resignation. He is to be succeeded by Wilson. Hankey says it was bound to come. Apart from other differences, LG and Robertson are temperamentally in opposition. [. . .] Robertson was very moved. A statement is to be issued this evening. At the Versailles conference it was agreed that the Allied resources should be pooled and placed under the command of a group of generals presided over by Foch. The pool is to be available to repel the German advance at any point which may require special reinforcements. The group of generals are, however, to be controlled by the Versailles military council, on which Wilson was our representative. This plan was agreed to by Robertson. It involved a modification of the Order in Council which prescribes his powers. When the Cabinet came to put the plan into execution, it is said that Robertson objected.[33]

17 February Dined with LG. [. . .]

LG: [. . .] I could not sleep for two nights after the appearance of the wretched articles in the *Daily Mail*,[34] which tied my hands and did endless mischief. Then again, one has to carry one's colleagues along with one; one cannot shed them on the road for lack of patience and persuasion. Derby has been the chief difficulty. He has been resigning twice a day. He has no courage, and funk is often equal to treachery. I can see why they call him 'Genial Judas'. First he sold Robertson; then he sold me; then he resold Robertson; then he resigned and now he wants to know if we really wish him to resign. He is frightened to death of criticism. [. . .] Geddes acted very differently regarding Jellicoe. [. . .] Robertson has acted foolishly. At the Versailles Conference the soldiers had their say. Some of them made long speeches. Robertson agreed to the resolutions.

R: Which, I understand, involved some curtailment of his powers under the Order in Council.

LG: Yes. He raised no objection until we came to carry out the arrangements. Then he objected. We offered him Versailles if he thought that the more important post, but he would not take it, and would not accept his old position with modified powers. Now he says that he has not resigned. Of course he is being backed by Asquith & Co. He, Robertson, has become swollen-headed. [. . .] We shall give him another post, but Haig, who has been here today, refuses to give him command of an army. [. . .] Haig has acted well. He will not resign. He says that he is out to beat the Germans. If he had resigned I should have been in an awkward position. As it is we have to face a very serious crisis, and the Government may fall. This is the first real test we have had; and although I know that the country is with me, I am not sure what line the House of Commons will take.

R: The incident will bring about a coalition with strange bedfellows. The Asquith group and the section of the Tories whose motto is 'The Army, right or wrong'.

LG: Yes, we must be prepared for that. I said to Kerr yesterday, 'Have you packed up? We may be out next week.' He replied, 'No, I have not yet begun to pack!'

R: You are stronger than perhaps you think, but you weaken your-self continually by taking steps to conciliate interests which are not as powerful as they think or as you believe them to be. The remedy is often worse than the threatened disease.

LG: The position is a difficult one, but in this particular matter I have made up my mind to take the fence. Having done so, I feel happier and stronger. Wilson is an abler man than Robertson. Robertson is what you call a safe man. [. . .]

18 February   LG, Kerr and Miss Lindsay Williams, the artist, to lunch with me at Walton Heath.

LG far from well and very preoccupied with his speech for tomorrow. [. . .]

19 February   LG came to lunch. [. . .] He said that Robertson had accepted the Eastern Command, but that no doubt this was only a temporary measure. The Asquithians are in full cry and Robertson is probably hoping to get back. [. . .] It is a pity he [LG] has not cultivated the House of Commons more assiduously of late. He has rather lent himself to the idea that he regards outside influences as more im-portant. For the present the House of Commons is the real arbiter of his destiny. He told me that Lord Robert Cecil is resigning.[35] He came into the Government only with reluctance and has never been happy. Balfour, Bonar Law, Milner and Curzon are all with LG, who says that Milner is a man of first-class courage. Smuts and LG agreed some time ago that Robertson was not the man for the job. Yesterday LG told me that Robertson had written a friendly letter, saying that he (LG) had treated him well. [. . .]

20 February   Reginald Brade who was with the PM on Sunday (the 17th) tells me that Robertson has become very swollen-headed. He has been sitting in Asquith's lap and thought that Mr A would pull him through. He did not see that he was being used as a political pawn. LG's speech yesterday settled the crisis and Mr A was powerless to help Robertson. Mrs Asquith has been cultivating Lady R for all she is worth, and the latter like a foolish woman has allowed herself to be used like a tool. Hankey told me that the Asquiths invited him to lunch on Saturday the 16th, but he thought it wiser not to go as he believed that they wanted information which of course he could not give.

21 February   Long chat with Lord Derby. [. . .]

We talked of the political crisis. Derby is evidently badly rattled. He looks shaken. He said, 'I think the PM wants me to go. I see the first signs in the *Manchester Guardian* today. . . .'

(I did not refer to the *Morning Post* leader of yesterday, in which Lord Derby was charged with deserting Robertson & Co. when the cock crowed, and thus comparing him with the Apostle Peter during another and more celebrated crisis.) [. . .]

24 February   LG made his speech on Monday and wiped the floor with the Opposition. When I arrived this evening, I found him looking very tired. He said, 'I feel miserable, and as if I had been beaten all over. I have had a hard week. The Asquithians are mad. Mr A spoke badly. [. . .] I could see that he knew the game was up. He has been largely responsible for Robertson's conduct. Robertson was led to believe that Mr A would pull him through. His acceptance of the Eastern Command really settled the matter. [. . .]

R: What is to be your relationship to the Conservative Party?

LG: The question of policy would be difficult. I am not going to be dragged at the tail of the Conservative Party. My policy is very similar to that of Randolph Churchill. However we shall see.

2 March   LG lunched with me, and we drove to Ockley to tea. He says that Salisbury[36] and the rest of the Cecils are busily conspiring against him. Balfour and Bonar Law are anxious for a combination with LG, but Salisbury and the others do not want to lose control of the Conservative Party. LG is not sure what line Walter Long intends to take up. [. . .] The old-fashioned badges have ceased to have any meaning.

LG: [. . .] My position at the present time is very difficult. I am not sure of the House of Commons. It is no use being Prime Minister unless you can do what you want to do. It is useless for me to say that I can, because I can't. I have to make compromises all the time in order to conciliate different sections. It is trying to carry on a great war on such conditions. [. . .]

16 March   Golfed with LG and he lunched with me. [. . .]

LG: [. . .] J. H. Thomas[37] (the labour leader) came to see me before I spoke in the debate on Press appointments this week. I thought he came to spy out the land and so I told him that I was going to make a detailed statement concerning Mr A's relations with the Press, as to which I mentioned some particulars to Thomas. Of course I did not intend to do this unless Mr A attacked me, but I did not explain this to Thomas. I am sure that he at once went to inform Mr A & Co. of what I had said, for I saw from Mr A's face that he was feeling anxious and that he desired me to understand that he did not propose to make a violent attack. It was all quite amusing. [. . .]

March–November 1918

The Germans attacked in late March and a badly mauled British army retreated in disorder before the tide turned in favour of the Allies. Never was Riddell so valuable a companion to Lloyd George as during these dark weeks of peril. Saturdays and Sundays invariably found him at Walton Heath with the Prime Minister, who clearly needed a crony and confidant with whom he could relax and think aloud. It was not all about the military situation, either. Churchill was a subject for discussion in light of his disgruntlement at Austen Chamberlain's inclusion in the War Cabinet instead of himself. Then there was the Maurice Debate, with Lloyd George rejoicing over how he had downed 'Old A' (i.e. Asquith). From now until October a recurrent theme was the purchase of the *Daily Chronicle*, for Lloyd George had come to regard Robert Donald as an enemy who must be destroyed and the paper as a necessity for his success at the next general election. The conversations Riddell recorded with Lloyd George and others about this tortuous transaction shed much light, not very flattering, on the relations between politicians and the Press at this time.

Riddell saw less of other leading figures in the closing months of the war, although he noted such things as Lord French's remark that Haig and Robertson should have been court-martialled, then taken on to the Horse Guards Parade and shot. From June until the armistice, as the threat of defeat changed into the prospect of victory, domestic politics became the chief subject of interest in the diaries. Lloyd George's peculiar situation as a Prime Minister without a party led to all sorts of suggestions regarding the political future, some little better than crude attempts to cash in on the leader's popularity. One was a scheme to form the biggest newspaper trust in the country, another an advertising campaign to portray Lloyd George as a bastion against Bolshevism. There were Harmsworth brainstorms to prevent Lloyd George from becoming a Tory puppet. And we get our first glimpse of the ineffable William Sutherland, whose name will always be linked with the seamier side of fund-raising. The diary entries in the weeks leading up to the armistice show how far war aims and peace terms were beginning to put a serious strain on harmonious relations with France and the

United States, Woodrow Wilson in particular. By 11 November little had been settled off the battlefield.

23 March   Black Saturday.[1] Drove to Walton in LG's car. Found him waiting for me. He said, 'I must go back to London at once. The news is very bad. I fear it means disaster. Come with me!' [. . .]

On the way back LG told me that the Germans had broken through our line and that the 3rd and 4th[2] [*sic*] Armies had been defeated. He further said that the arrangement for pooling the British and French reserves had not been carried out – that Haig and Pétain had stuck their heels into the ground and had declined in effect to carry out the scheme. Foch had been here this week. The War Council had asked him about the reserves and found that he had no information. LG believes that Haig had made no preparation for the attack, notwithstanding that he was warned that it would probably take place exactly as it did. Wilson foresaw it. [. . .] LG says that Gough,[3] who commands one of the defeated armies, should have been sent home weeks ago, but Haig and Robertson would not agree. Our arrangements with our generals have been disastrous. We have failed to cashier the incompetent as we should have done.

24 March   Black Sunday.[4] LG went from Walton to London in the afternoon. I dined at his house and awaited his return. He arrived at 10.30 looking very tired. He said again, 'Things look very bad. I fear it means disaster. They have broken through, and the question is what there is behind to stop them. The absence of the reserves is a most serious factor. The French are now bringing up their reserves, but it may be too late. I foresaw this when I made my Paris speech. That was why we formed the Versailles plan, but it has not been acted upon.' [. . .]

(Notwithstanding the news, the PM was firm and cheerful. Although very anxious and much worried, he did not fail to have a good laugh as usual. His courage is remarkable. His work and anxieties are always with him, but he mingles them with bright and amusing conversation which lightens the burden.)

30 March   Easter Sunday. LG and Philip Kerr to lunch. LG says that the news is better, but that he has had an awful week – the most anxious he has ever had. He went to church on Good Friday. When they chanted 'O Lord make haste to save us', he said to himself, 'and You will have to hurry up or You will be too late.'

I congratulated him on the appointment of Foch as Commander-in-Chief of the French and British Armies. He said, 'If I had had my way in appointing a Commander-in-Chief months ago, I think that today things would have been very different.' [. . .]

31 March [Easter Sunday.] Dined with LG. Almost as soon as I arrived the telephone bell rang and a message came through from Lord Reading stating that for the next three months President Wilson would send 120,000 men per month if we would provide the shipping. LG was very excited and said this was the biggest thing he had accomplished during the last week. He insisted on the secretaries taking down the message verbally. He then said, 'At last I have stirred Wilson into action. I sent a message for Reading to read at a dinner at which he was the guest. That had the effect. Wilson is now willing to do anything if I will give him the credit of furnishing the supplies. I don't care who has the credit. We have begged and begged for men but have been unable to get them out of Wilson. These 480,000 will be invaluable. We must publish the joyful news.' [. . .]

During the evening LG again referred to our lack of generalship. He said that our armies are splendid, but that the generals were second-rate men, charged with the performance of a first-rate task. He spoke highly of Plumer,[5] and Harington,[6] his chief of staff. He also spoke well of Byng[7] and Horne.[8]

April [n.d.]   Called upon Lord French at the Horse Guards. He says that the position is very serious – that we may have another Sedan in which we should probably be able to save only some 500,000 men, and that he is making all necessary preparations to repel an invasion. In his opinion there will be no invasion unless we are defeated in France. He considers the position is due to the mismanagement of Robertson and Haig. [. . .] They should have been court-martialled and taken out into that square (pointing to the Horse Guards Parade) and shot. French thinks from Haig's proclamation that he has lost his head. [. . .]

April [n.d.]   Sunday. LG and Kerr called for me and we went for a walk. LG says that the news is better. We are holding our own and giving the French time to come to our help, but the position is very critical. The American generals are acting badly. Pershing[9] wants to keep back his men for the American Army instead of incorporating them with the British troops. It is another case of professional jealousy.

LG thinks Haig's proclamation a mistake; it looks as if he were rattled. [. . .]

April [n.d.]   Wednesday or Thursday. Called at Downing Street. [. . .] LG is glad that Derby is leaving the War Office.[10] He has not done what he should. LG has had to do much of the work of the Secretary of State for War during the past month. I referred to a bitter attack upon LG by Repington in the *Morning Post*. LG said that he had not read it. [. . .]

21 April   Dined with LG at Walton. He says he thinks we are in for a big fight with the Irish, but that we must go through with it. The Sinn Feiners are in league with the Germans. [. . .]

LG says that the Americans are very slow, and that we urgently need their help. Wilson does not seem to realise the urgency, and he is so inaccessible that Reading cannot get an opportunity to explain the situation as it should be explained. It is three weeks ago that the 120,000 men were promised, but so far as LG can discover very few are on the road. While we were talking a long telegram from Reading was communicated over the telephone, in which it was stated generally that the 120,000 men would be provided, but that their disposition must be left to General Pershing, as America would not place the men at the unconditional disposition of General Foch. LG evidently thought this unsatisfactory. [. . .]

I told him of my interview with Winston yesterday, and that I thought him disgruntled and angry that he had not gone into the War Cabinet instead of Chamberlain. LG agreed and added, 'He is on the fence. He wants in the event of the fall of the Government to be able to join Asquith, with whom he is very friendly just now. He thinks that the Tories block his way. He does not see that during the war any Government must be a Coalition Government containing a large proportion of Tories.' LG said that Lord Milner and C. P. Scott of the *Manchester Guardian* had been visiting him during the afternoon. [. . .]

April [n.d.]   Saturday. Drove with LG to Walton. He said that he had to make one of the most difficult speeches he had ever had to make. He had to describe the recent military operations which had been so disastrous, but he could not tell the whole story, as the result would be to depress our troops and give information to the enemy. He could not say, for example, that the decision of the Versailles Conference as to the formation of an army of manoeuvres had not been carried out by Haig and Pétain. He said, referring to the conference he had attended at GHQ this week, 'I left London at 9 p.m. I slept the night at Folkestone. I crossed at 7 a.m., and was back in London at 4 a.m. next morning. I made a strong speech. I was almost brutal in what I said about the conduct of affairs. Haig endeavoured to reply, but he was very feeble. Pétain said nothing.'

April [n.d.]   Sunday. Dined with LG. [. . .] He expects a row with the Irish. They are out to oppose conscription for Ireland by every means in their power and would rather not have Home Rule than Home Rule coupled with conscription.

4 May   Drove down with LG. Called for him at Buckingham Palace, where he had gone to see the King. He asked me what I thought of a statement he had prepared for publication regarding his visit to France. I told him I considered it very good. He then gave his secretary instructions to issue it to the Press so that it would appear in the early editions of the Sunday papers. [. . .]

11 May   Drove down with LG, Mrs LG, Philip Kerr, and F. Guest, the Whip.
    R: Well, you smashed them this week. You had a fine case and made a wonderful speech. (The Maurice debate.)
    LG: Yes, I think we did pretty well. Old A looked very sick. He crouched low down on the bench and kept moistening his lips, a habit of his when excited. He made a great mistake. As he meant to go to a division, he should have continued the debate. As it was, he divided without making any reply. As usual he lacked courage.
    R: And ended up by going into the lobby with all the pacifists and cranks. Hugh Cecil made the only debating speech after you sat down. Were you very tired?
    LG: Tired? I was not very tired when I sat down, but three hours after I was absolutely done and things looked as black as they could. However, I felt better in the morning. [. . .]
    We talked of Donald of the *Daily Chronicle*. LG said that Donald had acted worse than any other editor during the crisis. He asked if I knew the reason. I said there were four possible: (1) That he is endeavouring to procure from the Liberal Party money to purchase the *Daily Chronicle*; (2) That he is anxious to obtain a Privy Councillorship

and thinks that the best method is by attacking LG; (3) That he is actuated by vanity. He thinks that he brought down the last Government by a ratting article which he published and which was repeated by the *Westminster Gazette*, and he may be anxious to repeat his exploit. (4) He may be actuated by personal pique because LG has choked him off calling and telephoning on Sunday.

LG: Well, I wonder which is the correct cause? [. . .] He is an unreliable fellow and a vain creature whose vanity is always likely to lead him astray. [. . .]

12 May Dined with LG. [. . .] He told an amusing story of Rothermere.[11] R has the same failing as Asquith, according to LG. [. . .] LG says Rothermere did the right thing at the Air Ministry, but in the worst possible way. [. . .]

We talked of the attitude of the *Liverpool Post*, which LG considers unfriendly. I said that this was no doubt due to the fact that Jeans,[12] the chief proprietor, considers that he has been overlooked in the matter of honours. It was arranged that I should see him and ascertain if a bargain could be struck.

May [n.d.] Sunday. Dined with LG. [. . .He] spoke of the political intrigues which are on foot against him. 'I can play that game as well as, if not better than, they can – in fact I have done so, but now I am devoting all my thoughts and energy to the war. Nothing else matters. (Then laughing) I don't know about the wisdom of the dove, but I have some of the craftiness of the serpent.'

We talked of the Le Bas scheme to attack LG by means of newspaper articles paid for as ads (the 4/- per inch campaign). LG remarked that Le Bas was both a knave and a fool, as he had spoiled himself by the bombastic letter which he wrote acknowledging the scheme and defending it. [. . .]

7 June Presided at the 91st Anniversary of the Printers' Pension Fund. Record subscription, £16,000. A most successful evening. The PM came and delivered a fine speech and had a wonderful reception. He told me that he had come only to please me, which was very nice of him. He had to leave early. As the car was late he walked part of the way. A large crowd followed him, and he was much amused by a small girl who called out, 'Hullo! Are you Charlie Chaplin?'

8 June LG and P. Kerr lunched with me, and we played golf later, LG going home to have a sleep in the afternoon. [. . .]

LG talked much of the *Daily Chronicle*. He thinks Donald very unreliable and said, as I have heard from several other sources, that negotiations had been on foot to purchase the *Daily Chronicle*, first of all by Beaverbrook and others at the instance of LG, and secondly by the Asquithians. The first negotiations failed and LG believes that the second proved abortive also. LG would like the paper to be bought in his interest, and discussed ways and means.

9 June Dined with LG. [. . .]

We talked of the political situation. I said, 'The Opposition are much more moderate than they were. Perhaps they have had a shock with Maurice and the 4/- per inch campaign, or perhaps they are like a child who is unusually quiet – they are up to some mischief. I have heard that they are looking to a snap division to improve their position. LG said he agreed that the Opposition had been more moderate, and that he too had been speculating as to their next move. I said, 'It is very noticeable that Pringle[13] and Hogge,[14] the skirmishing brigade, have been very silent of late.' LG thinks that the Asquithians may be negotiating with the Irish, and said that Herbert Samuel had recently been in Ireland, LG surmises with the object of endeavouring to come to some arrangement with Dillon[15] & Co. [. . .]

17 June Dined as usual. Much talk about the newspapers and Parliament. [. . .LG] said that Parliament was not required in war-time and was often dangerous. Some of the Members are now putting questions which are conveying information to the enemy.

R: But surely that danger could be surmounted quite easily. Such questions could be suppressed and answered privately, or by reference to a number instead of giving the question itself.

LG: That might be done.

R: Parliament, with all its defects, is the nation's watchdog. Unfortunately the watchdog had allowed himself to be chained up, with the result that the newspapers are performing his functions. [. . .]

LG thinks that before long there must be a general election. We must have a Parliament which represents the views of the people.

Today LG had lunch with Beaverbrook. Montagu was there and Hulton, the newspaper proprietor, who lives near Beaverbrook. What happened I don't know, but it is obvious that political conversations are proceeding. Guest and Beaverbrook are very thick. [. . .] Beaverbrook gets his power from three sources so far as I am able to judge: (1) His influence over Bonar Law; (2) His newspaper connections; and (3) A dominating and intriguing personality. [. . .] LG spoke very favourably of Milner's last speech, which he describes as excellent. He thinks that Milner improves every day. [. . .]

23 June Dined with LG and wife. [. . .] Evidently LG is meditating a national party in which he will endeavour to weld together all the classes. Everyone is to be satisfied. The rich must give to the poor, but the poor must not ask too much. They must be good children. I wonder! What about the huge trusts that are being formed? Will they lead to industrial peace?

We talked of the *Daily Chronicle*. Donald asked me to call upon him today, which I did. He told me an interesting story, casting a curious light on the ways of politicians and journalists. Some months ago Guest, the Whip, with Donald's connivance, approached Lloyd, chief owner of the *Chronicle*, with a view to purchase. The name of the purchaser was given as Lord Leverhulme, who was to be associated with two or three other supporters of Lloyd George. Later Donald discovered that Beaverbrook was the real purchaser and that Leverhulme's name had been used without his sanction. Thereupon Lloyd broke off the negotiations. The price was to have been £450,000 (the existing debentures and preference shares) plus £900,000 for the ordinary shares, making in all £1,350,000, but the tangible assets were to be valued at £750,000. Lloyd declined to see Beaverbrook under any circumstances. Donald continued, 'I don't quite know how far LG was involved in all this, but there is no doubt that he was in the scheme and that he was plotting to hand over the *Daily Chronicle* to Beaverbrook, who is a very dangerous man calculated to do LG serious injury. That,' added Donald, 'is why I am unfriendly to LG. That is why I attack him in the *DC*. I can do what I like with the paper. Mr Lloyd never interferes.' [. . .] This incident was followed by an attempt on the part of Lord Cowdray, Oliver [*sic*] Partington,[16] David Davies and other Liberals to purchase the paper, the real mover being McKenna. Cowdray is bitterly opposed to LG, so Donald says, and he has Lord Murray in his pocket. The negotiations broke down because Donald put forward a scheme which would vest control in the staff, meaning, I assume, in Donald. [. . .]

All this I told to LG with some limitations. He is still violent against Donald, upon whom he says no reliance can be placed, and evidently would prefer to get rid of him altogether. He says you cannot trust him. I said I thought he could be controlled and might be trusted to do justice to the paper commercially. Some men are more loyal to things than to individuals. He loves the *Chronicle*. [. . .]

I said, 'Beaverbrook is a dangerous fellow. He is consumed with ambition and is seeking to secure domination over the Press. He is very close with Rothermere and on friendly terms with Northcliffe. He is busy cultivating Hulton, he owns the *Express*, he is trying, as Minister of Information, to ingratiate himself with the colonial Press whom he has invited to a conference, and if he could get control of the *Chronicle* he would be one of the most powerful men in the Kingdom. He is not a pleasing personality and he has not the gift of speech, but he is clever and energetic and writes well. . . .'

LG agreed. He thinks, however, that Beaverbrook only wants to be the power behind the throne and pull the strings. [. . . He added:] 'Reverting to the newspapers, I admit that the combination you describe would be uncomfortable, but I don't believe that the newspapers have the power they think they possess. A prominent man can always defend himself and often put the newspapers in the wrong. . . .'

30 June   Dined as usual. We had an interesting conversation on the length of the war. [. . .]

We once more discussed a general election. LG said that many of the younger members of the Conservative Party favour an arrangement whereby LG would be placed at the head of a definite party and a definite organisation. His thoughts lie in the same direction, but he sees a difficulty with the Liberals – he feels that he can depend on a certain number of the Liberal members, but the creation of a new party with a new organisation would bring about an absolute and definite split. [. . .]

I have taken Danny, Hurstpierpoint, for the summer for LG and self. We spoke of our doings of last summer. [. . .]

13 and 14 July   At Danny – The 14th (Sunday) a busy and exciting day. LG sent Hankey post-haste to Canterbury to fetch Lord Milner. Urgent telephone messages were also dispatched asking Sir Robert Borden, Smuts and General Wilson to come. Later they arrived, Smuts having travelled from Oxford, Borden from London, and

Wilson from Henley. Wilson brought with him General Radcliffe.[17] Borden and Smuts arrived in the afternoon, Milner in time for dinner, and Wilson and Radcliffe at 9 p.m. [. . .] After dinner, the party assembled in the hall and sat in conference with Hankey and Philip Kerr until after midnight, the subject of discussion being the disposal of the American troops, the major part of which had been placed by Foch in the rear of the French Armies. LG's contention is that this disposition is unfair to the British, who have brought over 600,000 of them, and the result will be to place our Army in a dangerous position should we be attacked. His proposal was to send Borden and Smuts to see Clemenceau. From what I gathered, Milner was averse to any such action on our part. LG seemed dissatisfied with what had taken place at the conference. [. . .]

20 and 21 July   Danny again [. . .]

Last week Mrs LG came to Danny, and this week she and my wife came, also Megan and a friend. In the afternoon, while Kerr and I were out, [Eric] Geddes arrived and had a long talk with the PM. I had a long interview with Geddes at the Admiralty on Tuesday, when he bitterly complained that the Navy does not receive adequate recognition in the Press, with the result that our people and the Allies do not appreciate what has been done. I agreed, but said that the Navy was to blame, and told him of my campaign for publicity and of the letter from Sir Douglas Brownrigg,[18] the Chief Censor, in which he said that the Navy did not want publicity. This rather stumped Geddes, who of course pointed out that this took place before he went to the Admiralty. I said I appreciated that, but he had to suffer. I explained to him what he should do, viz. (1) Take the matter in hand himself [. . .]; (2) Get the PM to make a speech explaining what the Navy has done; and (3) See the editors and make a statement to them. He said he would. [. . .] He gave me a long explanation concerning naval activities, but rather prophesied that the submarine attack may become more acute. [. . .] Geddes is a clear-headed, forcible man – one of the best of the Ministers. He is a business man with drive, knowledge of organisation, and no prejudices in favour of existing methods. [. . .]

29 July[19]   [. . .] We talked much of the forthcoming election. LG is now full of it, and palpitating with energetic enthusiasm. His vitality is wonderful. He is like a skilful prize-fighter in the ring. He is all over the arena, defending here and attacking there.

He says that Henry Norman[20] started life as a cobbler and is very ambitious. 'He has his price,' said LG, 'and is justified in demanding it. [. . .] If Norman does his job, he will be entitled to his peerage. From the cobbler's bench to the House of Lords is a big jump, and I can quite understand the attraction of the prospect to a man like Norman.'

3 August   Much talk of the Cellulose scandal, in which a man named Grant Morden[21] is concerned. He is said to be a Canadian who has wormed his way into Walter Long's confidence and to be financing Bottomley. LG evidently much annoyed about the Cellulose business, but he said very little. He proposes to go to Criccieth for a fortnight's holiday and then return to Danny for September. He often talks of the qualities necessary for a great War Minister – courage, energy, optimism, decision, and so on, and frequently instances Earl Chatham as being the greatest War Minister of modern times. But he never mentions one quality possessed by both Chatham and himself – an indispensable characteristic in a great War Minister, but one fraught with danger in ordinary times. The expense of the war and the measures which he takes never seem to enter into his calculations. He rejoices in the sacrifices and efforts which his spirit and success induce his countrymen to make. In short the question of price never enters into his contemplation. Millions mean nothing to him. The object to be achieved is the only thing that matters. This gives him a great advantage over men who count the cost before they act. He is never hampered by ordinary commercial restraints. [. . .]

12 August   Dined with Mr Waterbury, an American banker. Northcliffe was there, together with Waterbury's two daughters. N very affable. He says that his throat is still troublesome, due to bronchitis. He seemed quite friendly to LG, although the latter has been told that Northcliffe and Rothermere had the idea a short time ago of endeavouring to bring down the Government. Milner told LG this. Personally I doubt the story. LG thinks that Northcliffe is aiming at the Premiership. This I also doubt.

13 and 14 August   Much talk with the PM regarding the forthcoming election. Sir Henry Norman is to organise the campaign. LG says that Norman has written quite a good memorandum. LG absolutely ex-uding energy and enthusiasm. He has a wonderful way of getting things moving; a sort of all-pervading energy. He is going to Criccieth for a few days, after which he returns to Danny, which he has enjoyed very much, so he says. While he is away he is going to read up reconstruction, and prepare his opening speech, which he will make at Manchester.

R: Are you going to deal with Free Trade and Protection?

LG: Only very generally. The time is not yet ripe. [. . .]

R: You will be on safer ground in dealing with the condition of the working classes.

LG: Quite true. The statistics given me by Sir Auckland Geddes are most disquieting. They show that the physique of the people of this country is far from what it should be, particularly in the agricultural districts where the inhabitants should be the strongest. That is due to low wages, malnutrition and bad housing. It will have to be put right after the war. I have always stood during the whole of my life for the under-dog. I have not changed, and am going still to fight his battle. Both parties will have to understand that. We have set up a Committee to consider a programme, and I shall make a strong point, a very strong point, of what I have just said to you. [. . .]

15 August   I met William Sutherland, LG's secretary, at the Carlton. An amusing cynical dog. He was engaged as usual in supping and wining, being entertained to dinner by a Tory magnate who is coming over to LG. A few days ago Sutherland dined with Lord Charles Beresford, who has £100,000 for party purposes and proposes to utilise it for LG's campaign. Sutherland says they want cash. I gave him some likely names, including Sir Howard Spicer,[22] who came to me the other night to say that he and nineteen friends of his can put up £250,000. The Asquithians are busy hunting for cash and the Tories are doing the same, so that notwithstanding all the pious protestations against the party system, it is still in reality as strongly entrenched as before.

17 August   Jack Seely, his wife, and Lord Gainford spent the afternoon with me at Walton. JS as optimistic and flamboyant as ever and as kind and genial. He wanted my opinion on the statement made to him by Stephenson Kent[23] and his people to the effect that the country is on the verge of revolution. I said I did not believe it, and thought that Kent wanted a holiday, being absolutely worn out.

Owing to pressure from me, the Ministry of Munitions have at last set up a decent Press and Publicity Department. Seely said that he and Winston were much obliged for my help. [. . .]

August [n.d.]   LG back from Wales. His return signalised by a strike of the Metropolitan Police, who assembled in great force in Downing Street and assumed a very menacing attitude. This made the occupants feel that they were really face to face with a revolution. The Police came out on the Friday, which prevented LG going to Danny as intended. The strike was settled on the Saturday, so we started in the evening. [. . .]

I congratulated LG on settling the strike.

LG: The whole thing has been disgracefully mismanaged. The terms granted by me had been agreed upon for some time past, but the men had never been told. [. . .]

Later LG spoke of the War Cabinet. He asked would the inclusion of Northcliffe strengthen the Cabinet, and said that he had reason to believe that N was anxious to enter the Cabinet. We all – Sutherland, Miss Stevenson and self – said that we thought N's appointment would be unpopular with the majority of the people, that it would occasion serious animosities, political and otherwise, and that N would be a difficult man to work with, as, if he could not have his way, he would be continually kicking over the traces. LG agreed and said that Arthur Balfour would be more useful, as he had the art of analysing a subject and stating the argument for and against with great power and skill. 'His mind is opposed to action,' said LG, 'but I can decide, and such a discussion is of the utmost value.' Later he remarked that Reading would be more useful than Northcliffe. [. . .]

We had much talk about a general election. LG is strongly in favour of an appeal to the country in November, and commented upon the obvious fear of an election on the part of Henderson and the Asquithians. LG proposes to hold a meeting of the Liberal Party to ascertain who is prepared to support him. He also proposes to make an arrangement with the Tories as to the seats which are to be left to their candidates. He says that the Tories have loyally supported him, and he proposes to be equally loyal to them. He hopes to carry with him 120 of the Liberals. The issue at the election will really be who is to run the war. Is it to be LG, Bonar Law and their associates, or Asquith, McKenna, Runciman and others who act with them? [. . .] He is to make all this plain in his speech at Manchester on September 12th. [. . .]

4, 5 and 6 September Winston Churchill and Rothermere at Danny for the night. [. . .]

We talked, the three of us, about an election. My companions were evidently not keen on it. I said, 'The main argument in favour of it is the necessity for a strong, virile House of Commons that will express the views of the people. [. . .] The House of Commons is their mouthpiece and the natural safety-valve.' This argument seemed to weigh with W and R. [. . .]

LG spoke strongly about Beaverbrook's disloyal conduct in attacking him and the Government in the *Daily Express*.[24] He said he felt so indignant that he doubted if he could bring himself to shake hands with him. Winston counselled soothing Beaverbrook over, and described him as resembling a petulant woman. Afterwards Winston said to me that LG and Beaverbrook were at the parting of the ways, that the latter thought he had not been adequately paid by LG for his services in the crisis, and that unless matters were arranged there was the prospect of a lifelong feud which might be arranged by a little tact. LG said in the presence of Winston and Rothermere that Beaverbrook had been successful beyond his merits. At forty he was a peer and a Minister of State. What more could he expect? 'I am not ungrateful,' said LG. 'I got Beaverbrook these honours in the face of much opposition from his own party. One hundred and thirty Conservatives met to protest. To calm them I had to make one of the most skilful speeches I have ever made. And I also had to appease the King. In standing by Beaverbrook and fighting his battles I consider I paid him any debt I owed him.'[. . .]

On Saturday came a memorandum from Sutherland saying that Rothermere had seen Beaverbrook, who was in a very dangerous mood and likely to resign. Rothermere further said that Beaverbrook had not found his office a bed of roses, that Masterman and Buchan had been too much for him and that he did not know how to get rid of them. Rothermere now urges an early election, as he thinks all sorts of financial scandals will be unearthed and that these will be detrimental to the Government. When LG received this memorandum he sat up and delivered a short oration on Beaverbrook. [. . .]

The controversy is bound up with the proposals to purchase the *Daily Chronicle*, on which transaction LG is very keen. On Thursday night, 4 September, he called me into the garden and told me that Guest had been in treaty for the *Daily Chronicle*, that [Frank] Lloyd wants to sell and that the price is £1,100,000. The profits roughly are about

£200,000 p.a., of which about £130,000 is payable in excess profits duty. It seems that Sir Henry Dalziel now has an option on the paper until October 1. He proposed to borrow £700,000 from a bank, to put £75,000 of his own money into the deal, and the Government were to put in £325,000 of the party funds. The bank, however, wanted the major part of the £700,000 guaranteed. Guest and his solicitor, Balfour of Birchams, had advised against the transaction. This made Dalziel furious. Now a new combination was suggested, consisting of Solly Joel and the Berrys of the *Sunday Times*.[25] LG wanted my advice, which I set out. [. . .] I strongly advised that LG should not be associated with the Joel interest. [. . .] On the Saturday, however, further developments occurred. Andrew Weir[26] and others appeared on the scene as prospective purchasers, and here the matter stands. To return to Beaverbrook, one ground of complaint is that LG has excluded him from the *Chronicle* deal.

September [n.d.]   Called upon Lord Reading. [. . .] Reading sees trouble ahead with America. He says that the Americans mean what they say, and that when they stipulate for no conquests they mean it. We had a long talk regarding an election. R is evidently opposed to it. He described it as very dangerous. [. . .]

21 September   LG returned from Manchester, where he has been laid up for a fortnight with influenza. I dined with him at Downing Street. Bonar Law and Sir William Milligan, LG's Manchester doctor, were there. LG has had a nasty illness which has shaken him a good deal. He was, however, bright and gay as usual. He and Bonar Law talked of our reply to the Austrian Peace Note. (The newspapers were suddenly called together on Sunday evening by the PM's secretary, when they were told confidentially by Sir Eric Geddes, who had been at Manchester with the PM, of the contents of the Note and of the views of the Government.) LG said the American reply was very brusque, and that he thought a more reasoned answer necessary. Bonar Law agreed. LG asked my opinion. I said that for popular consumption in Germany and Austria we might perhaps with advantage recapitulate the effect of the speech in which LG stated our peace terms.

BL: The Germans are bullies, and when you are getting the best of a bully it is often well to be short and peremptory in your replies to his overtures.

LG: On the other hand, the Austrians are getting very sick of the war, and it might be well to let them see what our terms are. [. . .]

Bonar Law said he thought the time had come when he should make a speech to the members of his Party. LG agreed.

BL: But before I speak we must decide upon our policy. We must both speak with the same voice.

LG: Well, next week we can have a talk. [. . .]

22 September [. . .] Much talk with LG about the election. He is drawing up reasons pro and con. He asked me for my views. [. . .] The point [I made] is the necessity for re-establishing the authority of Parliament in the country. He agreed, but said that Bonar Law and Balfour would be frightened by any definite reference to the labour situation and would consider labour unrest as a reason against an election. On the following day LG showed me his memorandum and one which had been prepared by Guest, who arrived (23rd) with Andrew Weir to discuss the *Daily Chronicle* purchase. Weir is now negotiating. He wants [Frank] Lloyd to leave £500,000 in the concern. LG fears that the result may be that the property will be lost.

He is anxious to improve labour conditions, but he is not really in sympathy with labour. As I have always said, he does not understand the point of view of the worker. Just now he is angry about the strikes and keen on putting the strikers into the Army. They stand in the way of the prosecution of the war, and so must be coerced. He says very little concerning the commercial and manufacturing classes who have been, and are, making fortunes out of the war. [. . .] He does not seem to realise that social unrest is certain to occur when millions are working for a pittance and their employers have every luxury.

27 September The foxes come out of the burrows. Lords Murray and Rothermere appeared on the scene yesterday, with the proposal, so I gather from various sources, that there should be a coalition with the Old Gang. Asquith to become Lord Chancellor, Runciman and, I think, Samuel, to enter the Government, together with half a dozen of the younger men all thirsting for office. I am told that Mrs A has started the hare which the said peers are now pursuing. What the PM thinks of this, I don't yet know. Rothermere arrived today with Northcliffe, whom it is hoped to capture. Whether he was willing I have not heard, as it was late when I arrived. I understand that Northcliffe is not supposed to know of the visit of the conspirators yesterday. This may or may not be true. It may be a bit of domestic humbug on the part of Rothermere to dust the eyes of LG and others as to Northcliffe's actual knowledge of and participation in the ramp. Then the LCJ arrived. He was to have come tomorrow, but I understand that LG asked him to come a day earlier. Whether the Chief knows of the plot, I can't say, but he volunteered the information that Margot Asquith had invited him for dinner last night, adding, 'I suppose that I shall be under suspicion.'

Perhaps the Chief is not yet fully primed, but he and Murray have a curious habit of calibrating, as they say in gunnery. [. . .]

The publication of Haig's dispatches was discussed.

Wilson: Haig has agreed to cut out certain portions indicated by Milner.

LG: I don't think that will do. We can have no cuttings out. (Wilson looked rather glum at this.) If the dispatches are published we must publish our reply. We must show that we sent 1,200,000 men to France this year. We must also show that the Cabinet objected to Haig taking over so much of the line. He wants to throw the blame on other people and to conceal that he is a rotten General. That I shall not allow. The difficulty is that if we publish the dispatch and the explanation, we may be giving information to the enemy. [. . .]

27 and 28 September   A great day. Arthur Balfour, Bonar Law and Reading. The two former did not arrive until 9 o'clock, having had a breakdown. Meanwhile LG was making notes as to the topics of discussion. Bonar Law is very broken and obviously on the verge of a breakdown. I had a touching interview with him. [. . .]

LG and I talked of this later.

LG: I don't know what to do with him. There is only one remedy. He has no outside interests and he won't go for a holiday. He does not even care for golf or bridge. He just reads and works and smokes all day. What he really wants is a female companion – someone who will sympathise with him and take him out of himself. [. . .]

After dinner, LG, AJB and Bonar Law retired for a conference, which lasted until 11.30, the subjects being, so I believe, the proposal for a general election, and the Bulgarian peace proposals. I asked LG whether there was to be an election. His answer was not definite. In effect he said, 'Yes, unless peace negotiations alter the position.'

When Bonar Law and AJB came from the room where the conference took place, this after LG had gone to bed, AJB remarked, 'The PM is certainly a very attractive creature.' Bonar Law said, 'When he is keen on anything, he sweeps you along with him and imagines you are in agreement with him, when probably you are not. You may have to show him later plainly that you are not!'

AJB: When he is wrong, he is usually wrong in a more interesting way than other people.

BL: He will only see one side of a question when he has made up his mind. [. . .]

On the morning of the 28th another conference took place. AJB and BL returned to London at 12.30. LG told me later that he may have to go to France for a conference with the Bulgarians, to whom a safe conduct has been offered.

LG: I shall trust no one else. I must go myself. AJB would not be quite the man for the task. It will require handling. The Serbians will be apt to think only of their side of the war. They will want to decimate the Bulgarians now that they have them in their power.

R: That is only natural. So should I if I were a Serbian.

LG: Yes, quite right, so should I! But we must look at the war as a whole. I am disposed to try to get the Bulgarians out of the war. We might be able to get them to attack the Turks. I should like to see that rotten old Empire broken up.

Much talk between LG and Reading on the same subject. Reading pointed out that America is not at war with Bulgaria, but may want a say in the peace negotiations. Bulgaria may, he thinks, ask for American intervention. Reading views the future of our relations with America with grave apprehension. He thinks that the American people are at the beginning of a new era. In the war serious points of difference are continually arising. [. . .]

29 September Talked with LG and Reading regarding the crisis of March. LG bitterly complained of American delays in sending troops. [. . .]

Later I had a long talk with Reading about Anglo-American relations.

R: Why does Wilson always refrain from mentioning LG in his speeches? And also the British effort? It looks ungenerous. It looks as if he wanted to adopt a high-handed, imperious attitude later on.

Reading: The position is very dangerous and difficult. Wilson sits aloft and apart, and he directs and feeds the Press with his views and opinions. One great danger is that we may come to cross-purposes with the Americans, and in particular that LG and Wilson may come to cross-purposes. I think that much might be done by removing minor causes of disagreement, such as the differences regarding the cost of transport of American troops and the alleged profit on the wool. [. . .]

30 September   Robertson Nicoll came down to lunch. [. . .] Later on came Milner, Henry Wilson, Radcliffe the DMO, and Sir Joseph Maclay.[27] After dinner a long conference was held which lasted till a late hour. [. . .]

1 October   [. . .] The *Daily Chronicle* purchase has been completed. LG is to have full control of the editorial policy through Sir H. Dalziel, who will in effect be his agent. The experiment will be interesting.

In the evening, Lord French, Sir Henry Wilson, Sir Rosslyn Wemyss[28] and Hankey arrived for the night. Much talk of Irish conscription. French all for it. And of course Wilson. LG more judicial, but with obvious leanings in favour of enforcing the Act. After dinner an important conference at which I was not present.

3 October   [See Appendix for Northcliffe's letter of 3 October 1918 to Riddell.][29]

10 October   LG back from Paris. Quite fresh after a twelve-hour journey. Sat up talking until nearly 11. [. . .]

LG told me that Wilson had replied to the German Peace Note without consultation with the Allies or the military commanders. Foch says that an armistice would be fatal, as it would enable the Germans to shorten their line without loss, which is just what they want to do.

R: Wilson seems to be a very conceited person.

LG: Yes. Clemenceau calls him Jupiter. Wilson is adopting a dangerous line. He wants to pose as the great arbiter of the war. His Fourteen Points are very dangerous. He speaks of the freedom of the seas. That would involve the abolition of the right of search and seizure, and the blockade. We shall not agree to that. Such a change would not suit this country. Wilson does not see that by laying down terms without consulting the Allies, he is making their position very difficult. He had no right to reply to the German Note without consultation, and I insisted upon a cablegram being sent to him. The position is very disturbing. [. . .]

The *Daily News* and *Westminster* are furious about the purchase of the *Chronicle*. It is amusing to read the *Westminster* declaiming against capitalists purchasing newspapers, considering that it is a subsidised organ, and a bankrupt one at that.[30]

12 October A momentous day. Lunched with Mr and Mrs LG at Walton and then on to Danny. LG not very well. [. . .]

Later Lord Reading arrived for the night. More talk about peace.

LG: It is important that you, Reading, should get back to America to look after our interests there. [. . .] I am not quite sure that it would not be a good thing for Clemenceau or me to make a speech indicating the position in an inoffensive way. The American public would soon understand and would speedily make it clear to Wilson that he must act in accord with the French and British, who have borne the burden of the day. Before you (Reading) go, you must get the facts about Pershing. It is a pity you cannot get them from the French. Pershing is a most difficult, conceited man. Before the recent operations, Weygand, Foch's Chief of Staff, went to him to give him advice. He refused to take it and there was, of course, a scene. Everything happened as Weygand predicted, with the result that the American Army has been quite ineffective. [. . . Pershing] says that America did not enter the war with the same objects as France and Gt Britain, but for independent objects, and therefore wants an independent army. [. . .]

Later LG sat reading Foreign Office papers, occasionally reading extracts aloud and making comments. Some very amusing. For example: 'The Germans are in a serious condition internally. Revolution is imminent if no peace is possible. They have no raw materials. The Kaiser is about to abdicate in favour of his second son.'

LG: That's the British Navy. President Wilson can't claim that!

After LG had gone to bed, the German reply to President Wilson's Note came over the telephone from Downing Street. It was written down and taken to LG by Kerr, who soon returned saying, 'There is awful language going on upstairs, I can tell you! He thinks that the Allies are now in a devil of a mess. Wilson has promised them an armistice.'

R: His note does not say that. It says, 'I will not propose a cessation of hostilities while German armies are on the soil of the Allies.'

Reading: The next sentence, however, refers to the good faith of the discussion depending upon the consent of the Central Powers to evacuate. Does not that mean an armistice to enable them to do so?

R: Wilson may well say, get out as best you can, and when you are out I will make proposals.

Kerr: He can't mean that.

R: Most people read the Note in the sense I indicated.

Reading: It is badly drafted. [. . .]

13 October   Much talk with LG and Reading regarding Wilson's first Peace Note. We walked to the top of Wolstenbury Hill, LG declaiming all the time against Wilson's action in replying without consultation with the Allies, and also in regard to the terms of the Note.

LG: The Germans have accepted the terms, as I prophesied they would. We are in a serious difficulty. Wilson has put us in the cart and he will have to get us out. [. . .]

Reading strongly rebutted LG's contention that Wilson had placed himself in a difficult position.

LG: You are a Wilson man. He can do no wrong! The time is coming when we shall have to speak out. We have borne the heat and burden of the day and we are entitled to be consulted. What do the Fourteen Points mean? They are very nebulous.

Reading disclaimed Wilsonite proclivities and was obviously perturbed at LG's observations. [. . .]

To lunch came A. J. Balfour, Bonar Law, Milner, Winston Churchill and Harry Wilson. Later came Rosslyn Wemyss and Hankey. After lunch a big conference at which I was not present. A. J. Balfour, Hankey and Philip Kerr then set to work to write memoranda expressing the decisions arrived at, each in a separate room. Meanwhile LG and the rest of the party adjourned to the gardens. From subsequent conversation I gathered that the terms of the armistice had been under discussion and that the conference had decided upon demanding unconditional surrender. [. . .]

Before the party broke up it was decided that Sutherland should see the newspapers and explain the position. I told Milner that I had provided Sutherland with a list. [. . .]

15 October   Guest, the Whip, asked me to call upon him at the House of Commons. He explained that he had been unable to arrange for LG to have control of the *Daily Chronicle* for more than ten years. He had proposed 'or for the period of LG's active political life, whichever should be the longer'. The people who had contributed the balance of the money over and above that provided by the party funds would not, however, agree to this alternative. The agreement is to be entered into between the Company that owns the paper and Guest, as Chief Whip, Illingworth, the Postmaster General, and Dudley Ward,[31] the second Whip. It appears that the party funds are vested in Guest and

Illingworth, whom the former describes as LG's trustees. The three persons named are to represent LG and act on his instructions, so that in effect he will control the *Daily Chronicle* for ten years.[32] Guest, who seemed very hipped, said that he supposed LG was satisfied, but that he has never said so. [. . .]

He also told me that he is endeavouring to raise a fund of £3,000,000 or £4,000,000 to purchase other newspapers and thus form the biggest newspaper trust in the country. [. . .] I said I thought such schemes dangerous in the extreme, and that if the public became aware of them the result would be disastrous and would tend to inflame industrial unrest. Guest did not much like this.

He talked much of politics. [. . .] Beaverbrook is a genius for whom a place should be found in the Government [. . .] Beaverbrook can help keep Bonar Law straight. [. . .] He (Guest) saw little of LG and was not in his confidence to any great deal and did not know what he meant to do. [. . .] Violent intrigues are on foot with a view to all sorts of political combinations. [. . .] No principles are involved.

It is merely a question of personalities. Guest, F. E. Smith, Beaverbrook & Co. stand for nothing but the party game. They are not out to accomplish any reform or carry on any policy. Their only object is to keep certain groups together. Winston is evidently busy intriguing.

19 October LG came to tea with me. He, Philip Kerr and I again played a few holes in the twilight. More talk about the German answer not yet issued. Haig is here for consultation. LG thinks he looks worn and is anxious for peace. It seems that he advised LG to make peace some time ago. Haig thinks there is a lot of fight still left in the Germans.

LG: If the Commander-in-Chief is tired out, what must the Army be? If I were the Germans I should want to know whether the Allies are prepared to accept Wilson's Fourteen Points. Of course we are not. We cannot accept No. 2 – freedom of the seas. And there are other questions that will require very careful consideration. It is most unfortunate that Wilson did not consult the French and ourselves before formulating his terms. [. . .]

25 October The First Lord asked me to call and see him. He is just back from America. He says that the President was much surprised to learn what the British Navy had done, and how little had been done by the American Navy. He showed me the figures. The American contribution has been practically nothing, whereas we have had to take off our destroyers and other craft from submarine chasing in order to guard the American troop-ships. Notwithstanding all the promises which have been held out, the Americans have produced very few war craft – the amount quite negligible; but arrangements have now been made which Geddes thinks will ensure increased production, although on a much smaller scale than was originally proposed. On the other hand, our naval shipping construction has been amazing. Geddes showed me the figures. He thinks the Germans have been holding up their submarine campaign during the past month, owing to the peace negotiations. [. . .]

27 October   LG telephoned asking me to lunch at Downing Street. [. . .] Lord Reading to lunch also. They had both been at the Cabinet. Reading very voluble and complimentary to LG about what had happened at the Cabinet. What the subject was I did not ask and was not told. [. . .]

R: I suppose that our policy is to get the Central Powers out of the war one by one. Turkey will go next, I assume, and then Austria?

LG: Yes; when Germany finds herself isolated, she will begin to think with a vengeance.

R: And then for the Fourteen Points!

LG (laughing): Clemenceau says that the Almighty was content with ten, but that ten are not enough for President Wilson, who wants to surpass all records. [. . .]

30 October   [. . .] Mr Higham, the advertising agent, came to see me. He told me that the Election Committee set up by the Whips had decided upon an advertising campaign. The Committee consisted of Guest, Henry Norman, George Younger[33] and Sir William Bull.[34] He further told me that he had written to Northcliffe asking to see him, but that he had declined to do so. I asked Mr Higham to let me see the copy for the advertisements. In short, the advertisement insisted upon the necessity for leadership, particularly as an antidote to Bolshevism, and indicated the necessity for the working classes to work harder and produce more, of course under competent leadership, in order to help pay off the national debt. I told Higham that I thought the advertisement most ill-advised and that it would create the impression that Lloyd George was being financed by the capitalists, who were going to use him as their instrument for the purpose of wangling the working classes [. . .] the publication of such advertising might lose the election. [. . .]

Saw Guest, who told me that the scheme had been abandoned. [. . .] He seemed much upset. [. . .] Guest said that LG was very difficult to work with. It was impossible to satisfy him and he would not come to decisions. 'He never gives me a word of praise,' said Guest, 'and if he is satisfied he does not say so. I have a dog's job!'

It is apparent also that Sutherland, the PM's secretary, is disgruntled. He evidently thinks that what he does is not appreciated, and he will not work with Guest whom he despises. Guest in his turn dislikes Sutherland, I believe. [. . .]

31 October [See Appendix for Riddell's letter of 31 October 1918 to Lloyd George.][35]

5 November LG just back from Paris. He said that he had had a most successful conference. He said, 'We have detached Germany's allies one by one, and now she is alone, and we have sent her some hot pepper in the shape of our armistice terms.' [. . .]

8 November Lunched with Guest at the Ritz. Present: Rothermere, Henry Dalziel, Henry Norman and Col. Sanders.[36] The object to discuss plans for the forthcoming election. [. . .] Rothermere spoke in a very domineering, hectoring way. He said, 'I am sick of the Tory incubus. I will not help and my brother will not help to establish a Government in which LG will be in any way under the control of the Tories. [. . .] My editors have to do what they are told. I run my papers. If an editor will not obey instructions, he is on the doorstep the next day. I do not allow my editors to criticise my policy. They have to do what they are told. That is the modern way of running newspapers.' [. . .]

I was surprised at Rothermere. He said some shrewd things, but talked a great deal of bragadoccio [*sic*] nonsense.[37] LG told me on the following day that Bonar Law had said that he could not understand how a man who talked such nonsense as Rothermere could be so successful in business.

9 November Lord Mayor's Banquet at Guildhall. Took my wife.[38] A remarkable gathering. LG's and Balfour's speeches worthy of the great occasion. Geddes, Lords Weir and Milner very dull, and far too long. LG in great form, smiling and winking at me all the time when anything amusing happened. [. . .]

10 November   Drove with LG, Mrs LG, Megan and Miss Roberts to Walton Heath at 11.15. Before we started LG busy with Bonar Law.

LG: Bonar Law said to me, 'Do you want to go down to history as the greatest of all Englishmen?' I replied, 'Well, I don't know that I do, as I shan't be there at the time. But tell me your prescription! Do you mean retire into private life now that the war has been won?' Bonar said, 'Yes!' He is right. I might take to farming, and just make an occasional appearance on great occasions when I had something important to say. [. . .]

I told LG that I had heard that the Foreign Office had appointed Mair[39] to communicate with the Press regarding the peace negotiations, and that it had been suggested that I should act in that capacity in his place.

LG: A capital idea. Northcliffe wrote proposing that he should act. I told him plainly that I would not agree. We had quite a row. It would not be fair to the other daily papers.

11 November   [No diary entry for this day.]

November 1918–June 1919

Within a few weeks of the armistice Lloyd George won a resounding victory at the 'Coupon' election and then turned his thoughts almost wholly to the peace settlement. During the election campaign Riddell continued to record something of what went on behind the scenes in Downing Street. Various diary entries show that schemes were afoot which reflected little credit on the Prime Minister and his associates. One of these, which received Lord Milner's blessing, consisted of sending one million copies of Rothermere's *Sunday Pictorial* to the troops in France, the intent being to influence their vote. Another saw Rothermere and Hulton agreeing to spend large sums of money to advertise the coalition in their newspapers. But Lloyd George's ambivalence where Northcliffe, Rothermere and Beaverbrook were concerned is very evident, a measure of his uncertainty about his own strength and the power of the Press.

The diaries took a new turn when Riddell was appointed liaison officer between the British delegation and the Press at the Paris conference. In this role he embarked upon a career of his own which marked the beginning of his divergence from Lloyd George. Though they continued to see each other regularly and frequently, it was a more formal kind of relationship than before, sometimes almost adversarial. Riddell discovered that he was a Press man first and foremost, which was not always to the liking of a Prime Minister who was inclining to be autocratic and secretive.

From January to June of 1919 the scene is usually Paris. Riddell's official position as Press liaison officer gave him many opportunities to converse with not only Lloyd George, but others such as President Wilson, Colonel House, Bernard Baruch and W. M. Hughes, as well as Bonar Law, Northcliffe, Lord Birkenhead and Philip Kerr. The great questions were the terms of peace and whether Germany would sign the treaty. Riddell responded to the occasion and recorded many descriptions of people and events that are essential reading to those who would understand the peace conference. Particularly vivid are the initial German response to the terms and the actual signing of the treaty at Versailles. Not quite all the material in the chapter is of this high level of seriousness. There is, for example, an amusing bit which shows Lord Derby as rather less than a brilliant ambassador to Paris. And A. J. Balfour's difficulties with his Cecil cousins get a passing nod.

13 November   The newspapers appointed me to represent the Press at the Peace Conference. In doing so, Lord Burnham made some nice observations which were received with acclamation. He referred to what I had done for the Press during the war, and said that I was the best person to go to Paris, quite apart from my right to the position in view of what I had done already. At the request of the Conference, he wrote a letter to the Prime Minister sending the resolution, and strongly supporting my nomination.

The Prime Minister said he was very gratified that I was going. Northcliffe had proposed that he should act, but the Prime Minister would not agree as the other papers would object to the appointment of a competitor. Northcliffe, however, told me that he would not take the job, and that he would do everything in his power to help me. He rang up quite voluntarily, and both he and his assistant, Sir Campbell Stuart,[1] have been most kind in every way. [. . .] Mr Balfour also said he thought I was the best person to go, and that he was glad the newspapers had asked me to do so. [. . .]

16 November   Drove to Walton with LG, who had made a big speech in the morning to the joint party meeting and had been at the Thanksgiving Service at the Albert Hall in the afternoon. He was very chatty on the journey. Asquith has had an interview with him, with what precise object LG does not know. Asquith referred to the undesirability of LG's candidates fighting Asquith's candidates and threw out a hint of a desire to attend the Peace Conference. The following conversation took place, either at the interview or while Asquith and LG were walking to St Margaret's [for the MPs' Thanksgiving Service on the 11th]. Some event was referred to. LG said, 'No doubt due to mischief makers.'

Asquith: They are always about, and usually appear at the wrong moment!

LG thinks that Asquith referred to the action of McKenna in December 1917 [*sic*].[2] LG again repeated that had not Asquith been badly advised, the split would never have occurred. 'I did not want to be Prime Minister,' he said, 'I only wanted to run the war.'

R: The arrangement would not have worked. It would have come to an end at an early date. You cannot have two engineers responsible for warding off an avalanche.

LG: Perhaps you are right. He would not have had the courage to come to great decisions when there was opposition from Haig and Robertson. He would have funked unity of command.

17 November To dinner at the PM's at Walton. Found Winston there. He had brought his election manifesto for the PM to read.

LG (laughing): I shall take it into the other room so as not to disturb the conversation.

When he returned he said, 'I see you have complimented Mr Asquith upon his ability and sagacity, but (smiling) you have nothing to say about my ability and sagacity!' Winston replied: 'My object is to rope in the Asquith party. . . .'

After dinner. LG to Winston: You and I must run this election. We are the only people who know anything about electioneering. Dear old Bonar has no more idea of it than an old hen. [. . .]

26 November Called upon Sir William Tyrrell[3] at the Foreign Office by appointment, to discuss Press arrangements at the Peace Conference. He showed me a memorandum from our Embassy in Paris in which it was proposed that there should be a censorship of telegrams and letters going to the British and Dominion newspapers. The proposal was to form a Press Bureau in Paris under the charge of a Government official. It was further proposed that the number of correspondents should be limited and that only approved correspondents should be allowed to attend. Further that no Press messages should be permitted except from duly authorised correspondents. I said the Press would strongly oppose any censorship. Sir William Tyrrell replied that there was much to be said for holding the Conference in public. I arranged to bring the question of censorship before the newspaper conference tomorrow.

(They passed a strong resolution against both.)

29 November Met Bonar Law at Downing Street. [. . .] He spoke of Northcliffe's attitude. His papers are not very friendly. I said, 'Have you seen him lately?' Bonar Law replied, 'No. I think the less one sees of him the better.'

30 November Dined with [LG] and Mrs LG at Walton Heath. He had a great reception at Newcastle, but is suffering from a cold. [. . .]

LG: Northcliffe is trying to blackmail me into giving him a seat at the Peace Conference.

R: On what grounds?

LG: Because he thinks he has deserved it. Of course it would be impossible. Such an appointment could not be defended. [. . .] He knows that I do not intend to do what he wants, and he is anxious to pretend he will not take what he knows he cannot get. I told his brother Cecil today, who came no doubt as his brother's envoy, that I did not mean to be treated in this way, and if necessary I shall have to say something in public. I told him that Northcliffe does not seem to realise that if I quarrel with him I shall raise a great accession of support in many quarters, and that I really have little to fear from his opposition, which would be discounted by the fact that I had deemed it necessary to speak plainly concerning him. I say again that I would rather cease to be Prime Minister than be at the beck and call of Northcliffe, Rothermere, Beaverbrook & Co. [. . .] He had the impudence, as you know, to ask that I should tell him what was to be the composition of my Government should I become Prime Minister again.[4] Of course I would never agree to give him information of that sort as a consideration for his support. [. . .]

1 December Asked Sir Howard Spicer to serve on a Committee at the Whips' office charged with supervising the arrangements for election to be held on December 14. At one of the meetings Spicer stated that there was a proposal to send 1,000,000 copies of the *Sunday Pictorial* – an LG number – to France. He produced a letter from Lord Milner saying that the Army authorities would distribute the copies amongst the troops. Spicer said that the proposal emanated from Beaverbrook, who had stated that there would be no difficulty with the Army people. They could easily be squared. The promise of £1,000 to Jack Cowans would do the business. Whether Beaverbrook said this I (R) cannot say. I repeat Spicer's statement. I said that any such distribution would arouse the deepest animosity amongst the other papers, and that it would do the PM more harm than good. According to Spicer, Beaverbrook's statement was made in the presence of the PM and Rothermere, who owns the *Sunday Pictorial*. Later Spicer said that all newspapers were to have the opportunity to send copies to France. Spicer and I saw Milner and Cowans, and it was agreed that so many tons a day should be despatched. I impressed on Milner that all publications must have an equal chance, and to this he agreed.[5]

8 December   The PM telephoned from Beaverbrook's at Leatherhead, asking me to go and see him there. Winston and Rothermere were there also, I heard later. Being out I could not go. Later Philip Kerr arrived and harangued me on the grounds that Beaverbrook and Rothermere had said that I had prevented the sending of a very large number of the *Sunday Pictorial* and other papers to France. [. . .]

Dined with the PM, Philip Kerr and Miss Stevenson. [. . .] Northcliffe very mischievous in his papers, but evidently fears to go bald-headed for LG. Northcliffe wired yesterday to LG saying that he understood the French and Italians had prepared their indemnity claims and enquiring why we had failed to do so. LG replied, 'It is untrue. The Allies are acting together. I wish you would not always be trying to make mischief.'

LG: I think that telegram should be published. I shall have to make a speech on Northcliffe. [. . .]

9 December   I met them [the Whips' committee] with the PM and Rothermere, when they undertook to distribute one hundred tons [of newspapers] per day during the election. [. . .] Milner's letter most imprudent. If it had become public it would have been severely criticised. Beaverbrook is an unscrupulous little devil. These schemes are not necessary. The PM is strong enough without them, to say the least of it.

There was a proposal to spend large sums in advertising the election, but it was abandoned as it was said to be illegal. Rothermere and Hulton agreed to spend £30,000 in advertising the Coalition in connection with their papers. This was carried out.

Christmas Day   Played golf in the morning with LG and then with him to mid-day Xmas dinner, he carving the turkey in great style. After dinner sat and talked for some time and listened to the pianola. LG slept for three hours. [. . .]

We talked of the elections. [. . .] He said that next week he proposes to take a short holiday to consider the reconstruction of the Government. The difficulty is that there are so few men available. He is very doubtful about a Minister of Labour and a Minister of Agriculture. Addison is to do the Housing. He doubts Lord Lee at the Board of Agriculture. He thinks him too unpopular with the landlords. I said, 'Of course you will find a place for Sir Robert Horne.[6] He is a clever fellow.'

LG: Yes, I think I shall put him in the Cabinet. He is an able man. [. . .]

R: Winston is a difficulty.

LG: Yes, a great difficulty.

R: How about the Colonies for him?

LG: There will be nothing doing in that department. It would be like condemning a man to be head of a mausoleum. He would just have to see that it was kept clean.

R: I don't agree. The Colonies will offer many problems. The Office wants bucking up and it would be a splendid thing if the Minister were to make a tour of the Empire.

LG: Yes, I agree about that. The Colonial office might be a good place for Winston.

R: Will Beaverbrook be in the Ministry?

LG: No, I think not. His health is bad. He is clever, but absolutely without scruple of any sort or kind. Not a very desirable sort of politician.

Mrs LG: It is a pity that the PM accepted any assistance from Beaverbrook and Rothermere at the election. I am sure he did not need it. I don't trust them or like their ways. The PM does best when he goes his own way and keeps clear of all these wire-pullers and people who want nothing but to grind their own axe. [. . .]

1919

18 January[7]   Lord Derby sent for me. Called to see him about 10.30. He said that he had not seen the Prime Minister. We discussed the Press situation. [. . .] I said, 'Are you going to the opening of the Peace Conference?' He said, 'No. I have nothing to do with it.' I replied, 'I understand that you have to summon the delegates.' 'What?' said Lord Derby. 'Now I come to think of it, I did receive a communication from the Foreign Office last night.' He opened his box, and there, sure enough, found the letter asking him to summon the delegates today to the Quai d'Orsay at 3 o'clock. [. . .]

Attended opening meeting of Peace Conference. I sat just behind Lloyd George, Arthur Balfour, Bonar Law and Barnes. All the speeches were prepared except those of Clemenceau and Lloyd

George. Owing to a mistake, the latter did not arrive until Poincaré[8] was half way through his speech. [. . .] When LG arrived, Hankey handed him a note saying that he would have to make a speech seconding the motion to make Clemenceau permanent Chairman. Notwithstanding this LG made an admirable speech, which took everybody's fancy. But he was very angry that he had arrived late, and asked me to insert an explanation in the newspapers.

When having tea, I had a chat with President Wilson, who said he thought Poincaré's speech very fine, and that it contained some eloquent passages. I said it was more like an essay than a speech. He said he agreed with this. We talked of the French people. I mentioned the coat-of-arms of the City of Paris – a ship with a Latin inscription underneath: [in English] 'It often rolls but it never sinks.' I said this was emblematic of the French nation. The President said that the motto was new to him, and that he was much interested by it. He agreed that the motto was emblematic of France. We spoke of increased Press representation at the full Conference. I suggested it might be possible to arrange for 30 instead of 15. He said he saw no objection to this and would support the proposal.

January [n.d.] F. E. Smith and Chilcott[9] [. . .] came to my rooms for an hour. The former very gracious and full of his new position [Lord Chancellor]. He called me 'George', talked of our long friendship, and [. . .] mentioned that I might always call him 'F. E.' [. . .] He talked much of his excursions as Censor, and of his case against *The Times*, repeating what he had told me some time ago concerning Geoffrey Robinson [i.e. Dawson], whom he described as a 'dishonest rascal', although he qualified this by saying that Robinson had no power to control Northcliffe's actions – who had attacked F. E. in the *Daily Mail* – as Robinson's undertaking extended only to *The Times*. F. E. is very thick with Beaverbrook. [. . .]

The decline of Lord Reading is noticeable. [. . .] There is evidently a coolness between him and LG. [. . .] It is obvious that personal contact between LG and Wilson has diminished the importance of Reading's position.

22 January Long chat with Bernard Baruch, Head of the United States War Board, and Swope of the *New York World*. Baruch says he is strongly in favour of getting rid of all Government restrictions and he thinks it absolutely necessary that the world should get to work again at once. He strongly urges the early settlement of peace terms with Germany, Austria, etc, or at any rate the settlement of the economic terms, so as to free raw materials, etc. He thinks that the blockade must be raised in whole or in part to enable the Germans to feed themselves by making use of their mercantile credits in the Argentine, etc. He says that Wilson has offered him the Treasuryship of the United States, but that he has declined, as he thinks Wilson's position would be made more difficult if the Treasurer were a mercantile man and a Jew like him, Baruch. He said, 'I want nothing and prefer to get back to civil life.' He is strongly impressed with the intention of the working classes of the world to have more. He says, 'So far as I am concerned, I am prepared to give up voluntarily, through the medium of taxation, a very large part of my income. I am convinced that, unless the wealthier classes take that course, they may have everything taken from them. [. . .]

23 January Hearing that the Americans are issuing semi-official secret announcements as to subjects to be discussed by the Conference, saw LG and urged him to arrange for similar documents to be issued to the British Press. I showed him one of the American *communiqués*. After reading it, he said it was obvious we must do the same and that he would give the necessary instructions. He also said that we have done more in the way of preparations than the Americans. For example, draft proposals regarding the League of Nations have been prepared by Smuts and Lord Phillimore.[10] Wilson is very pleased with these and proposes to make them the basis of the constitution of the League. Then in the matter of labour, we have prepared an elaborate case. [. . .]

25 January Long talk with McCormick and Sheldon of the United States Mission. They confirmed what Baruch had said. They think the delay in settling the economic terms with the enemy most serious, as the effect is to prevent the resumption of industry and commerce in the Allied countries. Merchants will not order goods, and manufacturers will not start new industries until they know what the economic terms with the enemy will be. The subject of raw materials is vital and pressing. Everyone is waiting for a fall in the markets. McCormick and Sheldon said that all restrictions should be removed and that markets should be allowed to resume their natural level. But they say this cannot happen until the peace terms have been settled. McCormick had to go. After he left I had a further talk with Sheldon, who told me that there has been a good deal of friction between Reading and Hoover.[11] [. . .]

26 January   To Amiens by car with the PM and party. Lunched at Foch's old headquarters, a ruined château. LG showed me the room where he lunched with Foch when the latter was residing there. I drove in the same car with Winston, who spoke much of the Bolshevists, against whom he is very bitter. He would like military intervention in Russia by means of British, French and American volunteers. I said the British public would not agree to their Government organising another war in order to interfere with the domestic affairs of Russia. Winston agreed, but said their view might alter. I said I saw no prospect of such a change. [. . .] His conception of the State consists in a well-paid, well-nurtured people, managed and controlled by a Winston or Winstons. [. . .]

He spoke much of LG, whom he described as a delightful companion; a man with unerring judgment, etc. (It was not always thus, but one could hardly expect it.) Winston said what I believe to be true – that he (Winston) never bore malice, and never believed unfriendly things reported to have been said of him by his friends. He thinks that Asquith is done. He missed his tide, and should have become Lord Chancellor when LG formed his first Government. Winston says that LG would beat Asquith at any part of the game any day. Winston says that Asquith was ruined by McKenna, Runciman & Co. 'Perhaps,' said Winston naively, 'it is fortunate that Asquith did not combine with LG. If he had he would no doubt have taken some of his people with him, and there would have been less for me.' [. . .]

30 January   A great disturbance due to an article in the Paris *Daily Mail* suggesting that the British delegates of the Home Government have been kow-towing to Wilson; that they have been giving away the case of the Colonies; that the Colonies resent this and that there is a serious fear of the British Empire breaking up in consequence. Sir Campbell Stuart, who has just been appointed by Lord Northcliffe one of the Directors of the Paris *Daily Mail*, came to see me. He said he thought the article most ill-advised and dangerous, and asked me to ascertain the PM's views on it, also those of President Wilson. Subsequently Montagu Smith, the writer of the article, called. He said that the article was based on information received from three Colonial statesmen – Hughes, Botha and Sir Joseph Ward.[12] He said he had shown them the proof, and they had inserted or suggested the sentence regarding the disruption of the Empire. He also said he had seen Montagu, MP, for an hour and that he had approved the article, and that it has also received the approval of Lord Robert Cecil. Montagu Smith said that these things wanted saying; that he was convinced we were paying too much deference to President Wilson; and that the Colonies would never stand it. He said he had called to see Davies, LG's secretary, and had asked for an interview with LG, but this had been refused. He said he wanted to know what LG's views were and was quite willing to be guided by them. He requested me to see LG and find out what he thought.

Later, attended the Peace Conference, where I saw Botha. I took him into the ante-room and got him some tea. He seemed much perturbed. [. . .]

Later, saw Hughes of Australia, who is at the bottom of the whole thing. [. . .] I said, 'You have made a nice flare-up!' To this he made no direct answer, but began to talk about the Colonial position. [. . .]

Later I met some of the Australian journalists who work with Hughes. They were loud in their admiration of the *DM* article and in their objections to the mandatory principle – quite violent, in fact. Then I saw Montagu, who also complained of the article, although Montagu Smith said that he had approved. Which statement is correct, it is difficult to say.

Later, I saw the PM, who was highly indignant concerning the article. He said it had made his task today very difficult. He also said that President Wilson had protested against the article and the disclosure of information, and had stated that if this sort of thing was repeated, he would break off the Conference and go back to America. I promised to communicate this to Campbell Stuart. The PM was very strong about Northcliffe, and was evidently under the impression that N was at the bottom of the newspaper campaign. [. . .]

1 February Dined with the PM, who gave an amusing account of some of Clemenceau's observations at the Peace Conference. The question of the disposition of Heligoland arose, whereupon Clemenceau remarked, pointing to Wilson, 'He will hand it over to the League of Nations.' When Constantinople was under discussion, Clemenceau said, turning to Wilson, 'When you cease to be President we will make you Grand Turk.'[. . .]

LG says that Reading is not pleased, because he (R) had proposed to act as a go-between between LG and Wilson. 'No go-between is necessary,' said LG. [. . .]

February [n.d.]   Dined with LG. Reading there also. [. . .] R is going to America for a time, and on his return will resume his work in the Law Courts. Obviously he is a disappointed man. The conversation turned on Wilson. LG said he had found him much nicer and had got on with him much better than he expected, whereupon R remarked, 'That is a great satisfaction to me. Nothing is more important than that you two should get on well together.' In saying this he was obviously sincere, but gave me the impression that though glad to see the child of friendship a strong and lusty infant he regretted that the services of the midwife had been so soon dispensed with by the parents.

I drew R's attention to the similarity between Wilson and Chamberlain. He thought Wilson a bigger man than Joe. LG, on the contrary, thought Joe the abler man of the two. [. . .]

8 February   Returned from Paris with LG, family and suite. He slept most of the way to Boulogne. On the way from Dover, after reading *The Times* account of the Polish pogroms, he remarked, 'The Bolshevists have done nothing worse that that! It is a terrible story, which proves that savagery is an incident in most revolutionary movements in such countries.' He referred also to the labour situation in England, and gave me the idea that he viewed the future with grave apprehension. His responsibilities are enough to make the stoutest heart quail. [. . .]

16 February   Dined with LG at Walton. Found him busy dictating cablegrams to [. . .] two of his secretaries.

LG: Winston is in Paris. He is a dangerous fellow. He wants to conduct a war against the Bolsheviks. That *would* cause a revolution! Our people would not permit it. Winston has a very excitable brain. He is able, but may go off at a tangent at any moment. [. . .]

We spoke of the new House of Commons.

LG: It is a curious assembly. Quite different from any other House of Commons I have known. When I was speaking, I felt, as I looked in front of me, that I was addressing a Trade Union Congress. Then when I turned round, I felt as if I were speaking to a Chamber of Commerce. It will be interesting to see how it acts. [. . .] I shall have to make a change at the Board of Trade. Stanley[13] is very weak. Bonar does not want to change for some reason. [. . .]

We also spoke of the industrial situation. I referred to the necessity of releasing raw materials without delay, so that manufacturers could get to work. Now they are afraid to make purchases, as they fear a falling market. [. . .]

We spoke of increasing the death duties.

LG: There is much to be said for that in our present situation, burdened as we are with a colossal debt, which demands for its service a greater revenue than our pre-war taxation. I think it would be a fair thing to take 50 per cent of the larger fortunes as death duties. [. . .]

23 February   Dined with LG. [. . .] We spoke of Lord Robert Cecil.

LG: He has greatly improved his position during the war. He is ambitious, and like the Cecils will seek power wherever he sees a prospect of obtaining it. [. . .] I don't know that he is a very reliable colleague. Arthur Balfour does not know it, but Bob Cecil tried to get him out of the Foreign Office. I declined to be a party to the proposal. AJB told Bonar and me that he could never rely on the Cecils. 'They are my relations,' he said, 'but whenever I have been in a tight place, the three of them have always gone against me.' And what Balfour said is quite true. [. . .]

1 March   Drove with LG to Walton Heath, where we lunched and golfed. [. . .]

Much talk about the labour disputes. LG thought the Labour Conference most interesting. He said that notwithstanding much wild talk, the Conference displayed the sterling common sense of the British people. Referring to his own speech, he said, 'I got them with me during the last five minutes. [Ernest] Bevin,[14] the dock-labourers' representative, saw this. He is a powerful fellow, with a bull neck and a huge voice – a born leader. He got up and tried to remove the impression, but was too violent. He showed no tact. A thing of this sort has to be done in a good-tempered way. But if there is trouble, mark my words! You will hear more of Bevin!' [. . .]

The conversation turned on President Wilson's position in America. LG remarked, 'The Republicans are attacking him in the most un-scrupulous manner. Formerly they attacked him because he was anti-British. Now they are attacking him because he is pro-British. They will stick at nothing to "out" him. I like him. He may be vain, but, as old Clemenceau says, he means well. Now we must get away to the Peace Conference and finish the job up and get the world back to work. Conditions are more settled here at the moment. Paris is now weighing down the scale.'

8 March   While I was seated in the Peace Conference ante-chamber, a cable arrived from Plumer setting forth the parlous condition of the Germans in the occupied territory. This was taken in to LG, who read it to the Supreme War Council, upon whom apparently it made a great impression. The Council decided to victual the Germans, provided they hand over their ships and pay for the food in freight, bills of exchange on other countries, goods or gold. The French strongly opposed this. LG said to me afterwards that the French are acting very foolishly, and will, if they are not careful, drive the Germans into Bolshevism. [. . .] The Americans are very pleased with LG's speech. Baruch said that in Wilson's absence they have no efficient advocate at the Peace conference, and do not make half enough fight upon important questions. All the commercial people, British and American, favour abolishing the blockade and urge an early settlement with Germany so that the world may again get to work. The truth is that five valuable months have been spent in dealing with the less important subjects, including the machinery for governing the world after the war. Wilson's obsession for the League of Nations; our desire to avoid awkward questions, and the French desire for delay are responsible. Meanwhile Mr Lenin has jumped up like a jack-in-the-box and is spreading disease germs all over the world, just as influenza is spread. [. . .]

13 March   Walked home with LG after he had addressed the Press. He said, 'The French demands are absurd. I will not agree to them. I object to any nation having a preference, and the claim will have to be reasonable.' [. . .]

15 March   On my way to the Quai d'Orsay with Lord Burnham I met LG returning in his motor. He looked very tense. Later I called on him. He said Wilson (President) had not attended today's meeting of the Supreme War Council, as he desired further to consider proposed terms of peace with the Germans. LG very angry. He said, 'We shall never get a settlement if we continually re-open what has been decided. Yesterday at our informal Conference at the Crillon we did nothing. Wilson talked for an hour about his League of Nations and his ideals, but we did nothing practical. The position is serious. I am calling a meeting of my colleagues for this evening.' [. . .]

LG: The election[15] is most timely and valuable to me. I am having a great row with the Tories. They want a land bill that will carefully protect the landowner, the lawyer and the surveyor. I have declined to be a party to anything of the sort. [. . .] Unless the Tories agree to what I want, I shall fight the matter out to the end. Bonar is here. I sent for him. It was necessary that I should see him and put the matter to him plainly. Land must be got quickly for housing and other state purposes. Delays will be dangerous. [. . .]

16 March   Drove with LG and party to Soissons and the Chemin des Dames. We lunched *en route* in a wood. After lunch I had quite a long walk with him, the motors catching us up later. He again referred to his quarrel with the Tories and to the advantages of the West Leyton and Liverpool elections. He said, 'I have made it quite clear that I don't intend to play their game. The country is in no mood for delays. I told Bonar that the evidence in the colliery commission proves what I have been saying for years, but no one paid any attention because they thought I was exaggerating. Now the facts are proved by evidence in a legal tribunal. The owners are making a very poor show. They have nothing to say in answer to the charges as to housing conditions, etc. I am not going to be made the landowners' cat's-paw, and unless the Tories accept my bill, I shall take steps to make them accept it.' [. . .]

Much talk about Clemenceau and Wilson. LG said, 'Each lacks and fails to understand the other's best qualities. When Wilson talks idealism, Clemenceau wonders what he means, and, metaphorically speaking, touches his forehead, as much as to say, "A good man, but not quite all there!"' [. . .]

19 March   In the morning golfed with LG and Kerr at St Cloud. Labour situation at home very serious. Wilson, Clemenceau and Orlando want LG to stay here and finish up the Peace Conference, whereas the Cabinet at home wants him to return there for a few days to endeavour to settle the labour question. I asked him what he was going to do. He replied, 'There is only one Person who knows, and He won't say. I shall stay if possible as I think it essential to get this business finished. The Peace Conference will react on Labour.'[. . .]

21 March Great dissatisfaction at slow progress of Peace Conference negotiations. Drove home with LG from the Quai d'Orsay. He said that things were not going well, and again referred to Clemenceau's state of health. [. . .]

LG: I dined with Briand the other night. He says that Clemenceau is losing ground rapidly and that the opposition in the Chamber is growing. Of course that was to be expected. When I decided in December to have an election, I saw there would be considerable dissatisfaction in the country for some time to come, and that it was desirable to have a fresh Parliament. I cannot say that the House of Commons is quite what I should have desired. At the same time, it is a new Parliament, elected to deal with present-day issues, whereas the French Parliament is out of date. [. . .]

24 March LG back from Fontainebleau. I met Harry Wilson, who painted a gloomy picture of the position in the East. He said, 'We are drifting to disaster. I have told the PM that if the Conference don't take charge of affairs, affairs will take charge of them! It is all due to [President] Wilson. . . .'

Later saw Philip Kerr and told him the feelings of dissatisfaction were growing and that a general attack by all sections of the Press might be expected. Strongly urged more publicity. He endeavoured to defend the Conference against the allegations of delay. [. . .I] strongly urged that PM should meet the journalists.

Later, having seen the *communiqué*, in which it was stated that the Council of Ten had been engaged in discussing submarine cables at Teschen, I thought it advisable to let the public know that drastic steps were being taken to conclude terms of peace. I therefore communicated the above information to the Press. The French and American Press did not get the news, and the French were very much annoyed in consequence, particularly as LG had made a strong complaint in the Council that secret information was being handed out by French officials to the French newspapers.

26 March In accordance with my suggestion, LG met the journalists today and made a long statement dealing with various questions, but only one remark need be recorded here. Someone said to him, 'Will the terms be submitted to the Plenary conference?' His reply was, 'I devoutly hope not!'

28 March He is very angry with the Press for criticising alleged delay of the Conference and his views on Polish boundaries. He says that Wickham Steed, Editor of *The Times*, has a personal animus against him because he snubbed him. I said the whole world is asking for peace. They want to get to work. All eyes are turned to Paris. The people do not understand the delays. They do not appreciate the difficulties because they have not been explained. They are nervous and critical. They think civilisation may be shattered.

LG: You really must try to get the papers to be more reasonable. They must not lose their heads. They must remember that we are settling the peace of the world. It is a gigantic task. We must make, if we can, an enduring peace. That is why I feel so strongly regarding the proposal to hand over two million Germans to the Poles, who are an inferior people so far as concerns the experience and capacity for government. We do not want to create another Alsace-Lorraine. The French are now in agreement and so are our people. My views have been grossly misrepresented. That is what I object to.

R: If more information were supplied – not necessarily for publication – these misunderstandings would not be so likely to arise. But it must be remembered that violent antagonisms are necessarily raised by the subjects of discussion and that the various protagonists are all anxious to secure the assistance of the Press and will use every means in their power to do so. [. . .]

LG: [. . .] We are making progress. We are gradually drawing nearer. These attacks in the Press are most harmful.

29 March Dined at the Majestic and afterwards went to look at the dancing. LG, AJB and many others there. [. . .]

Walked home with LG. Still very angry about Press criticism, and that his motives and actions should be misconstrued. Used strong language about some of the journalists and rather indicated that the Press had not been properly handled. He said he rather thought of getting Sutherland to come over, as he was more used to this sort of work than Kerr. I said, 'It is not a question of handling. It is a question of supplying information. Kerr and you are the only two people who have the information, and if you cannot give it out, nothing else will satisfy the Press. Furthermore, you are dealing with questions which raise the most violent international antagonisms, and every nation implicated in the various disputes is endeavouring to make use of the Press as a propaganda agent. The Poles, the Greeks, the Czecho-Slovaks, the Jugo-Slavs, the French are all busy.'

(I might have added that he himself is not inactive in this respect.)[16]

30 March Motored with him [LG] to St Germain and Versailles. [. . .]

Very long talk with LG about the Press. I reiterated that more news should be given out and that secrecy would result in unfavourable criticism. LG agreed that it would be desirable to publish more, but said there were great difficulties, and that premature publication of decisions had led to serious trouble in Germany and Eastern Europe. He added, 'I am sure that if the public and Parliament knew the facts they would support the policy of the Conference. I know Parliament, and I know that if I made a speech explaining the position, they would support the Conference. I believe the public would do the same. There must be reason in a matter of this sort.' I said that while I saw the difficulties, I thought that the Conference would have done well to give more information by agreement instead of allowing it to percolate out through unauthorised and devious channels. Ultimately, after more discussion, it was agreed that LG or Kerr should make a point of seeing me every day for the purpose of giving information. LG said, 'The truth is that we have got our way. We have got most of the things we set out to get. If you had told the British people twelve months ago that they would have secured what they have, they would have laughed you to scorn. The German Navy has been handed over; the German mercantile shipping has been handed over, and the German colonies have been given up. One of our chief trade competitors has been most seriously crippled and our Allies are about to become her biggest creditors. That is no small achievement. In addition, we have destroyed the menace to our Indian possessions.'[17] [. . .]

31 March The Council of Four are meeting at Wilson's house or the Ministry of War. This afternoon I went to the latter for the first time. [. . .] LG full of fun. I drove home with him. He said that he had had a row with the Belgian Minister and that the Belgians were putting forward preposterous claims. He remarked, 'I had to tell him quite plainly that the Belgians had lost only 16,000 men in the war, and that, when all was said, Belgium had not made greater sacrifices than Great Britain. The truth is that we are always called upon to foot the bill. When anything has to be done it is "Old England" that has to do it. If the Rumanians have to be supplied with food and credits have to be given, in the final result England has to stand the racket. It is time that we again told the world what we have done. These things tend to be forgotten. Our policy is quite clear but imperfectly understood. We mean that the French shall have coal in the Saar Valley and that the Poles shall have access to the sea through Danzig; but we don't want to create a condition of affairs that will be likely to lead to another war. We don't want to place millions of Germans under the domination of the French and the Poles. That would not be for their benefit, and what is the use of setting up a lot of Alsace-Lorraines? [. . .]

'Wilson's view is the same as ours. I think you ought to explain the American and British view to the Press.'

1 April   Saw Philip Kerr and told him that the Colonial Ministers are very bitter. They feel they are not being consulted, and doubtless remember the fuss made of them during the war. Strongly urged that LG should invite them to lunch or dinner and explain the position and obtain their support. Later Kerr told me he had seen the PM and this would be done. I told Kerr there is a strong feeling that the heads are not consulted enough before important decisions are arrived at. Consequently there is the danger that LG will not get the support which he ought to have. It is important that he should carry with him the whole of the Delegation. The feeling is growing that the policy is dictated too much by one person without consultation.

5 April   This has been a week of criticism and alarms. The Council of Four has been conducting its deliberations with much secrecy, and the public and the Press have become anxious and critical, the Northcliffe Press and the French papers in particular.

I strongly advised LG to see some of the French journalists and give them interviews, which he has done with good results. I also advised him to instruct Sutherland to see the Editors at home and explain the position to them in person. The correspondents here are too prone to be influenced by all the wire-pullers and intriguers who are swarming in Paris just now. Consequently instructions have been given to Sutherland, and I myself dictated a memorandum informing him of the situation, not with a view to influencing Editors to adopt LG's policy, but so that they may know the facts and form their own opinions. This evening I saw LG in order to procure information for the usual daily statement to the Press. Found him reclining on the sofa.

LG: Well, we have made great progress. We have settled practically all outstanding questions with the exception of that relating to breaches of the Laws of War. We shall begin next week to draft the Peace Treaty. I will make a statement to the Press for publication on Monday evening. I shall have something interesting to say.

R: Will the peace terms be published before they are discussed with the Germans?

LG: No, certainly not! They will be handed to the Germans when they come to Versailles. If the terms were published beforehand, the position of the German Government would be made impossible. The terms might lead to revolution. We shall be very strict about any infraction of this arrangement, and shall punish any paper that publishes the terms before we make them public.

R: You will have to make that clear beforehand. Are you going to make a statement in the House of Commons before you meet the Germans?

LG: I am not sure that I am. In any case, I shall not state the terms. What do you think of the disgraceful attacks upon me in *The Times* and *Daily Mail*? They call me a pro-German. That is a libel. I have a good mind to bring an action. I shall certainly say in public what I think about Northcliffe. His action is due to vanity and spleen. He wanted a seat at the Conference. He did not get it. No one has taken any notice of him. His advice has not been asked about a single subject. I ran the election without him and I beat him. He is full of disappointment and bitterness.

R: I should not bring any action. You are accustomed to say bitter things yourself. [. . .]

LG: I should like to ask him (N) this question, 'By whom would you replace me? Bonar Law and Balfour both agree with me, so they would be equally objectionable.'

R: He is quite entitled to criticise the Conference for delay or silence or for the policy they are adopting regarding any subject, but any person who breaks up the Conference will assume a serious responsibility, as the result would be that we should lose the fruits of the war.

LG: That is quite true. (But I doubt whether he meant to assent to the proposition that criticism is justified. High priests engaged in sacred ordinances never like to be criticised.) [. . .]

9 April Met Walter Long in the street. He complained that Northcliffe is actuated by personal motives and does not base his criticism upon the merits of the case. I said, 'That may be, but politicians have often said that about their critics.'

Drove to Fontainebleau, where I spent the morning with Northcliffe.

We golfed and lunched together. [. . .] He said some remarkable things about President Wilson – somewhat as follows:

'Unless LG and Clemenceau are careful, Wilson will put them in the cart. Wilson is a vain man – his vanity is colossal. I have seen many evidences of it. He is a bluffer, and I agree with Sir William Wiseman,[18] who says he is a gambler. He is a political adventurer and will stick at nothing. [. . .] His power is waning. He is losing his position in America steadily. He is a sentimentalist and will put all the blame for the delay and any defects in the Peace Treaty on LG and Clemenceau.'

He said but little concerning LG. [. . .]

On my return called on LG. Found him curious as to my meeting with Northcliffe. I [. . .] told him sufficient to acquaint him with N's state of mind. LG said that next week he would give N such a dressing-down in the House of Commons that N would not know himself when he had done with him. We again discussed question of publishing draft peace terms.

LG: Publication would be an act of treachery. We shall prosecute. No paper would dare to publish.

R: I do not agree. Any paper that gets the terms – and they will all try to get them – will risk a prosecution. They will risk a fine of £2,000 and many will risk imprisonment. If my hands were not tied, I should do my utmost to get the terms. And remember you are dealing with papers of all nations – not only the British Press. How will you control the Americans, the Italians, the Belgians, the Serbians and so on?

LG: That may be difficult, but it is essential. Neither Clemenceau nor I propose to state the terms in Parliament until the time arrives for ratification. [. . .]

LG spoke of indemnities and I thought his tone very changed. Today he said the Germans would have to pay to the uttermost farthing. He pushed aside economic difficulties and said that if the Germans decline to fulfil their obligations, we can compel them by an economic blockade. This changed attitude may or may not be due to the strong and growing feeling at home on the subject of indemnities. It is interesting to endeavour to analyse LG's mind and actions during the Conference. He has performed a great service by establishing better relations with Wilson, and he has fought our battle with great vigour, courage, skill and dexterity. But it is useless to deny that he has become more autocratic; more intolerant of criticism, and more insistent upon secrecy. Thus he has given Northcliffe his opportunity, which the latter is not using very skilfully, with the result that LG may give him a nasty shock. No four kings or emperors could have conducted the Conference on more autocratic lines. Information has leaked out, and every day I have received a dole from the PM or Kerr on his behalf, which I have passed on to the Press, but there has been no systematic issue of information, and the doings of the Council of Four have been shrouded in mystery. This has had a bad effect upon the public. Delays were inevitable, but the people find them hard to bear in the absence of information as to the reasons. I am afraid that the secrecy has been due in no small measure to LG. Anyway, he has been in sympathy with the policy. He is just as ready as ever to gather information and to consult, and just as charming and kind, but his attitude is rather that of a benevolent autocrat. 'I will decide what is for your good and will see you get it.' [. . .] LG is eager to do his best for his country, but he wants to act in secret without criticism or interference from the public – a sort of mild dictatorship.

11 April To dinner with LG. Present, Bonar Law, his son, Mrs Astor, Kerr, Miss Stevenson.

Much talk of result of Hull election declared today. The Unionist candidate, Eustace Percy, defeated, and huge turnover of votes. BL described this as serious. LG said it showed the people would not have men of this sort.[19] I said it showed that the people were tired of delays in regard to housing, etc. Both LG and BL admitted that the Government had lost ground. [. . .]

BL: The miners are raising troublesome points on the Sankey report. The owners will probably decline to agree to what is asked. That may force us into nationalisation before we are ready.

LG: Well, if it does, that will not be very serious. It has to come. The State will have to shoulder the burden sooner or later. [. . .]

They talked of Winston.

LG: He is a dangerous man. He has Bolshevism on the brain. Now he wants to make a treaty with the Germans to fight the Bolshevists. He wants to employ German troops, and he is mad for operations in Russia.

BL: He is a dangerous fellow. His judgment is bad. He is too impulsive.

The talk turned on the Whips. LG described Fulton[20] as an able Whip – much better than Guest. 'Guest,' said LG, 'is always running Winston and the things in which Winston is interested.' [. . .]

The discussion turned on the telegram sent to LG yesterday by two hundred MPs regarding fulfilment of election pledges as to indemnities.[21]

LG: I think my reply took the right line. I said I was prepared, if need be, for a general election. That made them think.

BL: Yes, the reply was on the right lines. [. . .]

LG: Kennedy Jones is a dirty dog. [. . .]

[BL] without arguing the point clearly showed that he attached grave importance to the message. He went on to urge LG to return to England for a few days. [. . .]

Much talk of [President] Wilson. LG said he thought him more sincere than he had done at first. He talks a lot of sentimental platitudes, but he believes them. He is not a hypocrite nor a humbug. He is sincere. The difference between his point of view and that of old Clemenceau is marked. The old boy believes in none of Wilson's gods and does not understand them. [. . .]

12 April   Today I received from Swettenham of the Press Bureau a copy of a message sent by Tuohy, of the *New York World*, containing a copy of the draft terms of the indemnity. I at once saw LG and A. J. Balfour with it, and pointed out early realisation of my forecast. They were much perturbed and surprised.

17 April   LG in great spirits after his speech in the H of C.[22] [. . .] I said, 'You did not tell the House of Commons much. Most of your speech was occupied with a disquisition on Russia and an attack on Northcliffe!'

20 April   Telephoned message asking me to go with LG and party to Noyon. [. . .]

LG: I have a very important bit of news that we must talk over, but we won't discuss it now. We will deal with it later.

He, Miss Stevenson and I drove together in one car, the others following in three more cars. [. . .]

Meanwhile LG had disclosed his news, viz. a telegram from the Germans stating that they proposed to send messengers to receive the peace terms and take them to Weimar. The Council of Four had replied, stating they would treat only with plenipotentiaries. The question was whether this should be made public. Eventually it was decided to send it out. We decided this at 7.55 p.m. I motored to the

Astoria, five minutes from LG's flat in the rue Nitot. I was fortunate enough to get the Press Bureau in three minutes, and by five minutes past eight the message was in London and being distributed to the newspapers. [. . .]

LG said the result of the message to the Germans might be to bring about the fall of the German Government, and that we were at a critical period of the negotiations. He thought the Germans' reply would show their disposition. If they agreed to send representatives, that would show they were anxious for peace. If they declined to do so, it would show they were indifferent. [. . .]

23 April Great excitement today over President Wilson's public declaration on the Italian situation. I waited for LG at the rue Nitot. When he came in at about 7 o'clock he said, 'Well, the fat is in the fire at last! It is a pity that Wilson sent out the statement so hurriedly. On Sunday he produced it and read it to Clemenceau and me. Meanwhile I have been trying to bring about a settlement. If I had had more time, I think I might have done so. Now it is impossible to say what will happen. The Italians have acted badly. I want you to make it quite clear to the Press that, under the Pact of London, Fiume went to Croatia. We stand by the Treaty. We have told the Italians that we think they are unwise to press for all they are entitled to under it, but that if they insist we shall support them. We have, however, also indicated that we shall insist on the portion of the Treaty relating to Fiume being observed. [. . .] The President read the statement again tonight. He is very pleased with it. Old Clemenceau said it was very good. He is an old dog. He had heard it all before and so had I. The position is very serious.'

R: It seems strange that after all the secrecy that has been observed one of the Plenipotentiaries should appeal, over the head of one of his colleagues, to the peoples of the world, and in particular to the nation represented by that colleague with whom he has a difference of opinion. Which of the Fourteen Points does that come under?

LG only laughed. I dashed off to communicate the information to the newspaper correspondents who had been anxiously waiting for an hour. Later I telephoned a long statement to London. Then I returned to the PM's to dinner. [. . .] LG full of facetious observations concerning the Press and the crisis. He said to me, 'This is a god-send to you. I saw you try to look miserable when I told you what had happened. But it was a poor attempt. You were evidently delighted.' [. . .]

25 April   LG remarked to Kerr: 'Garvin is the only person who understood the inwardness of my speech in the House of Commons. He has a touch of genius, that fellow! Did you read his article in the *Observer?* He saw that the meaning of my speech was a declaration that I intended to pin my faith to democracy.' [. . .]

27 April   Early this morning we started for the Vimy Ridge, visiting Arras *en route*. [. . .]

Dined with him on my return. Henry Wilson there. (President Wilson very unpopular.) Colonel Jackson[23] said, 'There is very strong feeling against him in Paris.' I said, 'Our people are fed up with Wilson. They are tired of playing second fiddle, considering what we have done in the war.'

[Jackson] said that the destination of the German mercantile shipping was settled. That under the arrangement America was to get 600,000 tons, which is double what she has lost. [. . .] I said, 'Surely this is not in accordance with Wilson's declaration that America expects nothing and will get nothing out of the war.' I did not say, but I thought, that the British people would get a shock when they heard of this settlement. [. . .]

Earlier in the day I said to him [LG]: There is no doubt that Wilson feels his unpopularity. He is beginning to try to work the Press in his usual fashion. [. . .]

LG (thoughtfully): He is a cold-blooded fish. When I returned from London the other day, he never congratulated me on my success in the House of Commons. He never said a word, and after the election he never mentioned the matter.

(To me, R, it looks like a battle between two masters of craft. Each thinks that he is cleverer at the game than the other, with the result that each is frequently taken at a disadvantage.) [. . .]

Week ending 3 May   After a hard struggle the Council of Three have agreed to the publication of the peace terms contemporaneously with their being handed to the Germans. This decision has not been openly indicated, but the thing has just happened. This is in the face of LG's persistent avowals that he would not agree to the terms being published until they were actually signed.

I think my contention that the Germans would certainly publish the terms if we did not, and my reminder of what took place when the armistice terms were handed over, however, had their effect. I have also been engaged in fighting for the right of the Press to be present when the peace terms are handed over.

On 2 May I got the papers to pass the annexed resolution, which I presented to the Council of Three on 3 May.

> At a meeting of British correspondents held at the Maison Dufayel on May 2nd, 1919, Sir George Riddell in the Chair, the following resolution was passed:
> 'This meeting of journalists desires strongly to represent to the Peace Conference that it is essential in the interests of the Allied people that accredited correspondents of the Allied Press should be admitted when the Peace Terms are handed to the Germans, so that an adequate report of the proceedings may be supplied to the public.' Among the reasons which may be urged in support of this claim is the fact that the German Delegation comprises a number of journalists who are acting in various capacities, and that the probability is that they will furnish reports to the German Press based upon direct observation of the proceedings. The British correspondents recognise that the accommodation is restricted, but they see no reason why a limited number of correspondents should not be admitted. They wish to make it plain that they do not claim special privileges; they are of opinion that arrangements should be made for the admission of representatives of the Press of all the nations concerned.' [. . .]

I prepared a paper on the Indemnity question, with the object of explaining to editors the technical questions involved. I also obtained one from Mr Keynes, of the Financial Mission. According to him, the Germans can pay not more than two thousand millions. The publication of his paper as issued would have been disastrous.[24] Consequently I deleted a large number of the paragraphs. I issued the two papers to the Press, first showing them to Kerr. [. . .]

4 May Went with LG and party to the woods near Fontainebleau, where we had lunch at the Hôtel du Fôret. I drove with Bonar Law. He said he thought LG had got the better of Wilson. Wilson had had to give up most of his fourteen points.

R: We have got the freedom of the seas relegated to the background, but beyond that I don't see that we have scored so heavily. Of course we have got the German colonies, Mesopotamia and Palestine, and we have got our protectorate of Egypt confirmed. They are big things, but I don't see what else could have happened.

Bonar Law talked much of Northcliffe, and was anxious to know how he took his lathering by LG. Bonar Law said he thought that N was the sort of man who, when tackled, knuckled under. He said that N always left Carson alone. No doubt that was because Carson attacked him. BL said that LG's attack on Northcliffe was very dexterous, but that the speech as a whole was open to serious Parliamentary criticism, had there been anyone to criticise. He then went on to describe what he would have said in reply, pointing out LG's previous alliance with N – the fact that he had appointed him to two offices in his Government and that nothing had occurred warranting LG's change of attitude except the fact that N had had the temerity to disagree with him. I said it might also have been pointed out that LG had told the H of C nothing about the peace negotiations, and that he had diverted the whole of the debate to Russia and N, apparently with the object of avoiding the real questions at issue.

Bonar Law: Yes, I quite agree, but the truth is that nine-tenths of the H of C hate N and were only too glad to see LG go for him.

BL said that after N wrote his letter regarding, I think, the retirement of Lord Cowdray, BL advised LG to attack N. But for some reason LG did not think the time ripe.

BL said he had told LG that the H of C is an amorphous body with no nerves or joints and no real parties, with the exception of the Labour Party, and no objective.

Returning to N, he said that N had remarked that the Press could make or ruin a statesman. BL thought this wrong. He thought that the Press could help to make a statesman, but that when a man had reached a certain position, the Press could not drag him down if he were really competent. I said I agreed. I complimented BL on his management of the H of C. He said he thought that after the Peace the House would not submit to anyone leading it except the PM, and that LG would have to do the job himself. [. . .]

I also said I thought some Ministers resented being sent for as if they were messengers. BL agreed and said that no Minister had ever conducted such a personal Government as LG. [. . .]

He said that Asquith was a nice man to work with, but very tricky, of which he gave instances. He expressed the opinion that, if it had not been for Kitchener, Asquith might have gone right through the war. He added that Kitchener let him down.

I said, 'Yes, but he did great things all the same, and in a measure held Asquith up.'

BL: That is quite true, but in the end K's incompetence ruined Asquith. [. . .]

5 May The Council of Three, in consequence of our resolution, proceeded to Versailles to look at the accommodation. As a result they decided to admit forty-five journalists, including five Germans, ten of the forty to represent Great Britain and the British Dominions. This is another score for the Press. At the end LG played up well and did his best to secure adequate representation. He said that Canada and Australia, having regard to their contributions to the war, were entitled to as much consideration as any of the smaller nations, none of whom had done so much. Wilson, apparently foreseeing difficulties with his own Press, was not very keen on the Dominions being represented, but when LG put the point as to our overseas effort, Clemenceau agreed with him and said that the Dominions were entitled to special representation. Later on Sir Maurice Hankey telephoned to say I was to have an extra seat for myself, which is gratifying considering that I have been the leading critic of the authorities. [. . .] I am off to Versailles in the morning.

7 May When I got up, I said to myself, 'This is going to be one of the most interesting days of my life.' And it was. At two o'clock I started for Versailles, driving through the Bois de Boulogne, St Cloud, and the lovely woods of Versailles. There was nothing to show that this was a momentous day in the world's history. Then suddenly I heard behind me the insistent and prolonged note of a motor-horn. It was Clemenceau in his Rolls-Royce, driving to Versailles at fifty miles an hour, one gloved hand on each knee and 'a smile on the face of the Tiger' that made one feel that the drama was really beginning. He was gone in a flash. [. . .]

The Trianon Palace Hotel has been the headquarters of the Allies throughout the war. It is a great white building standing in beautiful grounds. No less than three different tickets were required to enable me to reach the door. I alighted amidst a crowd of soldiers, officials, photographers and cinema operators. Indeed the combined whirr of the cinema cameras was almost equal to that of a small aeroplane. [. . .]

The journalists were the first to take their places. They sat at the bottom of the room behind the German delegates and facing the head table. Most appropriately they sat on gilded chairs covered with red satin. Five chairs were reserved for the German pressmen, who looked gloomy and ill at ease. [. . .]

At three precisely the Allied delegates began to take their places. In the middle of the top table sat M. Clemenceau, on his right President Wilson, and on his left Mr Lloyd George. Mr Balfour, Mr Bonar Law, Mr Barnes[25] and Sir Joseph Ward were also at the top table, the

remaining places being occupied by the American delegates. M.
Paderewski[26] was one of the last to enter, looking very much like the
representations one sees of the British Lion.

Then there was a pause before the chief attendant announced the
German plenipotentiaries. All eyes were turned to the door half way
down the room on the right of the chairman. In they walked, stiff,
awkward-looking figures, and, as I thought, comparing badly with the
Allied representatives. They all wore morning coats, and were
followed by their secretaries and two interpreters, who sat at a separate
table on the right of the German delegates. As the Germans walked in,
after a moment's hesitation everyone stood up. [. . .]

The Germans being seated, Clemenceau rose and began the proceedings in his usual concise and business-like way. He declared the
Conference open, and delivered a short speech which everyone felt
was absolutely appropriate to the occasion – not a word too much or
too little. He gave no evidence of nervousness and was never at a loss
for a word. As he spoke, one felt that one was in the presence of a great
historic figure – this wonderful old man of seventy-seven – the
spokesman of hundreds of millions of people, but as calm and un-
perturbed as if he were speaking in the Chamber of Deputies. [. . .]

After Clemenceau's speech had been interpreted, he enquired
whether anyone wished to speak. Thereupon Count Brockdorff-
Rantzau[27] put up his hand after the manner of a school-boy and,
remaining seated, began to read his speech, which was interpreted
sentence by sentence, first in French and then in English. [. . .]

The length and tone of the Count's speech were obviously a surprise
to the Allied delegates. We had been told that the proceedings would
be over in five minutes, and that they would be of such a formal
character that it would not be really worth while for the Press to attend.
As it turned out, the proceedings were anything but formal. As the
Count proceeded it was interesting to watch the effect produced on
some of the principal figures in the scene. M. Clemenceau, President
Wilson, and Mr Lloyd George in particular listened most intently. M.
Clemenceau slowly tapped on the table with an ivory paper-knife and
the President toyed, as is his custom, with a pencil in his hand with
which he always seems to be about to make notes, but which he rarely
uses. When the Count uttered some of his most pungent and tactless
remarks, M. Clemenceau turned to Mr Lloyd George and evidently
made biting comments on what was being said. When Mr Lloyd
George is roused or annoyed, he often shows it by moving uneasily in

his seat as if he were about to get up and assault someone. Needless to say on this occasion these signs were not lacking. He too devoted his attention to an unfortunate ivory paper-knife, which was observed to snap and break. . . . President Wilson leaned over and joined in the *sotto voce* conversation. At last the speech and its interpretations were concluded, and Clemenceau abruptly declared the proceedings at an end. The Germans walked slowly out of the room, and after a few minutes were followed by the Allied delegates, the Council of Four proceeding to the conference room in which the Allied Staff have held so many momentous meetings. [. . .]

Much indignation was expressed that Count Brockdorff-Rantzau spoke sitting down. Whether this was an intentional slight, or due to ignorance or physical incapacity, has not yet been disclosed. [. . .]

The proceedings ended at about 4 o'clock. Altogether it was a wonderful afternoon. As a great personage[28] (not British) said to me, as he walked out of the Conference, 'The Germans are really a stupid people. They always do the wrong thing. They always did the wrong thing during the war. They don't understand human nature. This is the most tactless speech I have ever heard. It will set the whole world against them.' [. . .]

After the Conference, while I was waiting in the corridor, LG came out of the room where the Council of Four were sitting, with a paper in his hand, and blackguarded Philip Kerr and two Foreign Office officials for having allowed a paragraph to appear in the Mandatory arrangements. [. . .] LG was absolutely red in the face, and K and the officials looked very upset but said nothing. [. . .]

8 May LG asked me to golf with him, Sir Robert Borden and Philip Kerr. He said: 'Those insolent Germans made me very angry yesterday. I don't know when I have been more angry. Their conduct showed that the old German is still there. Your Brockdorff-Rantzaus will ruin Germany's chances of reconstruction. But the strange thing is that the Americans and ourselves felt more angry than the French and Italians. I asked old Clemenceau why. He said, "Because we are accustomed to their insolence. We have had to bear it for fifty years. It is new to you and therefore it makes you angry."'. [. . .]

9 May A very interesting talk with J. T. Davies and Miss Stevenson. They both say that LG is more difficult during a political crisis than at any other time. At the time of the last election he was the very devil.

10 May   Went to the Hôtel du Fôret, Fontainebleau, with LG and party for the week-end. [. . .] Before we started I called at the rue Nitot, where I waited until LG's arrival from the Conference at the President's house. He brought with him the first German notes on the peace terms. Holding the papers aloft, he said, 'What will you give me for these exclusive?' I replied, '£10,000!' Whereupon, laughing loudly, he thrust them into my hands, saying, 'They are yours on those terms. Take and publish them at once.' [. . .] I went off and cabled the notes to London, of course for general publication, and then we started. [. . .]

11 May   In the morning we walked in the woods and sat and talked. LG told me that the Italians were behaving very badly. He said they had landed troops at Smyrna and sent a fleet there. He said, 'This is a curious commentary on the prophecies of a peaceful, unselfish world!'

LG says [President] Wilson is furious, and that he has every justification for being so. [. . .]

LG told me that Foch was going to the Front to make preparations to invade Germany if the Germans declined to sign, and suggested that I should let the newspapers know this, so that the Germans would get an early hint of what was in store for them.

26 May   Dined with Colonel House and Stannard Baker, head of the American Press Department. [. . .]

House told me that he was trying to get LG to go to America in October to attend the first meeting of the League of Nations. He said that the President and he hoped I would be with LG, and would do my best to persuade him to go. He also expressed the hope that the newspapers would be prepared to hold an all-world Press conference in Washington at the same time, and asked me to propose this to our people and take charge of the arrangements. [. . .]

27 May   Met LG, accompanied by Winston and Hankey, taking a constitutional before going to the meeting at President Wilson's. I walked with them. He said, 'How are things in England?'

R: They are all marking time. You are wanted badly. They all want to know whether the Germans are going to sign and when. I noticed strong indications that the public are losing faith in Parliamentary institutions. There is a strong movement in many quarters for direct action. Parliament does not seem to be interested in itself, and the public certainly are not interested in it. [. . .]

LG: [. . .] I agree that I ought to be back as soon as possible. There is no one there with a drive to get things done.

R: Housing is badly needed.

LG: Yes, if I had been there I could have pushed things forward to much better advantage, but I had to stop here. There was no help for it. [. . .]

28 May Dined with LG. [. . .]

At this juncture the news came through on the telephone from London that the German Note on the Allied terms had been issued by Reuters and published in the London papers. We were furnished with a summary of the Note.

LG: This is a most remarkable proceeding. The terms have not yet been presented to the Allies. It is like writing a letter to a man and publishing it in the newspapers before you send it to him.[29] What an extraordinary people they are! They always do the wrong thing! If the published Note is accurate, it looks as if they meant to sign.

9.30 p.m. – We then went for a short walk. The conversation turned on Asquith. I asked LG what he thought of Mr A's speech. He said, 'I thought it a poor effort – a feeble attempt to reconstitute a great party.' [. . .]

30 May Dined with him [LG]. After dinner we discussed German Peace Note. He said that he had been very busy reading it all the morning, and that it required close attention. I said, 'Official documents that you read in full are not usually so long. This Note is almost as long as a novel.' He and I then counted the words on the first two pages, and estimated the total length at about 65,000 words.

He: The Germans allege that where the principles laid down in the Fourteen Points work in favour of the Allies, they have been applied in preparing the Peace Terms, but where they work in favour of Germany, some other principles have been introduced and acted upon – military strategy or economics, etc. Of course there may be some ground for that argument. [. . .]

I: I suppose the discussion will centre upon Silesia and reparations? Those are the main points.

He: Yes. [. . .]

3 June Much comment in French Press and American papers published in Paris regarding the attitude of the British Empire De-

legation, and LG in particular, on concessions to the Germans. I had a
long talk with Philip Kerr, from whom as a rule, in default of LG, I
receive inspiration for my communications to the Press. Kerr said, 'It
is most desirable that the Press should not comment upon the attitude
of the British Delegation in reference to German concessions.' He
added, 'LG says the public will have to leave the matter to him to deal
with as best he can. If they are not satisfied with him, they will have to
get someone else. It is impossible to discuss these matters in the Press,
as the discussion involves all sorts of questions which cannot be openly
stated for fear of giving the enemy information and for fear of causing
disagreement amongst the Allies. LG is anxious to make the very best
possible Peace and to make it as soon as possible.'

8 June   Spent the day with LG. Before we started he handed me a file
of correspondence, saying, 'Read that and tell me whether you think
the letters ought to be published. They are the letters I wrote about
munitions, before and after Asquith made his speech.[30] I shall be glad
to know what you think.'

After reading them I said, 'They are remarkable documents. I think
they should be made public. They make your position clear.' He said,
'I agree with you. I think they should be published. I must consider the
matter. I was always pressing for action. I objected to the few meetings
held by the War Council. I thought we should meet much oftener, but
Asquith would not agree.' [. . .]

We drove to Pontoise, about thirty miles from Paris, where we had
lunch at a small restaurant. Bonar Law went with us. He and I drove in
one car. [. . .] Bonar Law spoke a good deal about the reply to the
German Peace Note. He thinks that the amount of the indemnity
should be fixed and that the Germans should issue bonds for it,
payable so much per annum – say eight thousand millions payable at
three hundred millions per annum. His ideas are very sound and his
judgment good, but for a constructive policy he lacks the force which
comes from strong conviction and a strong desire to have one's own
way. His attitude towards life is one of negation. He feels that life is a
burden. Nothing matters very much. He said that he had given up
reading serious novels because he found them too exacting. He had
given up playing bridge since his boy's death because it did not occupy
his mind. It had become too mechanical. But he had taken to playing
chess again, because the game demanded concentrated attention. [. . .]

After dinner, while I was in the middle of a very interesting conversation with LG as to the composition of the Cabinet and the state of affairs at home, Eric Geddes arrived. [. . .] LG was referring, before Geddes came, to the paucity of good men available. He says that the Labour men were a complete failure as administrators. [. . .]

10 June Invited newspaper correspondents to dinner to meet LG, who in reply to questions made a statement as to the policy of the Council of Four in regard to alterations in the Treaty. He complained of criticisms. I said that the publication of untruths and half-truths was due to a mistaken policy of silence, and that if the decision of the British Empire Delegation regarding alterations in the Treaty had been communicated privately to the Press much trouble might have been avoided. He answered that perhaps I was right.

13 June Had a little talk with President Wilson while he was having his portrait painted by Sir William Orpen.[31] [. . .]
    ı promised the President that I would give him a *Life of Robespierre* with an inscription in it by LG who had given it to me. This pleased him.
    We talked of Clemenceau. I told him one or two stories of the old man which he had not heard. The President said that he had been reading an account of Clemenceau's philosophy of life, in which he remarked, 'Life consists of the play of unrestrained natural forces' – in other words, the evolutionist's view of sociological development.
    President: If you take that view, I don't see how you can have any hope or incentive to action. [. . .]

17 June Dined with him [LG] – taking Elinor Glyn[32] and Orpen with me. [. . .] At dinner he spoke in strong terms of the stoning of the German delegates by the people of Versailles, and characterised it as a disgraceful episode calculated to do much harm. He said that they were guests and should have been treated as such. He further said that the Conference should not have been held in France. It should have been held in a neutral country. The French Press had acted very badly. I said that the authorities were to blame. The common people had not invited the Germans and could not be expected to control their feelings, considering the abominable way in which the Germans had acted. He did not approve of this, and said I was not doing myself justice and that such a thing could not have happened in our country. [. . .]

22 June   Everyone waiting expectantly for the German reply to the Allied Note. If before 7 o'clock tomorrow night the Germans do not express their willingness to sign, the Allied armies are to march to Berlin. [. . .]

LG: We have also received secret information [. . .] that the Germans are prepared to sign subject to two conditions: 1. That they shall not be held responsible for the war; and, 2. That they shall not be required to give up the persons mentioned in Clause 227 of the Treaty. We shall agree to no conditions, and unless they are prepared to sign unconditionally at one minute past seven tomorrow night the armies will march forward – under the leadership, so far as the British armies are concerned, of that great General who fought such a fine battle on the Home Front in Whitehall (General R).[33]

Immediately we had finished tea, a telephone message came from Clemenceau, asking if he might come and see LG. A reply being sent in the affirmative, Clemenceau arrived in the course of a few minutes. I went into the adjoining room. Soon a message was sent out asking that President Wilson should be invited to come over, as LG was unable to go out. Soon afterwards the President arrived. A little later General Wilson came, and Ian Malcolm[34] also came down from Balfour's flat. [. . .]

It appeared that Clemenceau had been advised that the German reply had been received at Versailles and was on its way to Paris. In due course it arrived. LG and President Wilson sat on it until 8 o'clock, when they adjourned for dinner, resuming their labours at 9. [. . .]

Shortly before 8 o'clock LG came out to me and said, 'The German Note is very much what we thought it would be. We are drawing up our reply. We shall decline to agree to any conditions. The reply will be ready in about an hour and we will then let you have it.' I then telephoned to London stating the position and saying I would send the formal Notes at 10 o'clock.

While I was having my dinner at the Majestic, Sir William Sutherland, one of the Prime Minister's secretaries, brought me the text of the Allied reply and a French translation of the German Note, saying that the English would follow. I dashed down to the Astoria, and telephoned the Allied answer to London. Later the English translation of the German Note arrived in driblets. The last portion, having the pith of the Note, I telephoned to London, sending the full Note by cable, and concluded the whole business by midnight.

23 June This morning early another Note arrived from the Germans asking for 48 hours' further time. The Council met at 9, and replied, declining. At 4.30 in the afternoon news came through from the Villa Majestic that a Note had been received saying that the Germans were willing to sign, but that the Note had not yet been translated. Shortly afterwards this was confirmed by Philip Kerr, who telephoned the news to me. I at once telephoned the information to London – a momentous message, being the first intimation sent that the Treaty was to be signed. Yesterday and today I sent all these telephone messages myself.

24 June Received letter saying that Council of Four had determined, in consequence of my representations, to visit Versailles for making arrangements [for signing the Treaty], and asking me to meet them. Clemenceau in great form. [. . .]

I wanted him to fix the hour for signing the Peace for 11 o'clock, so that the correspondents could get their telegrams off in decent time. He said, 'No, impossible! The function would last five hours. You must have *déjeuner*. If you fix eleven you will get nothing to eat. It must be two o'clock!' [. . .]

I wanted Clemenceau to make some changes in the seating of the journalists – if possible to place the seats on a slightly raised platform. He said this was impossible, but with great energy and decision gave orders that the seats should be brought further forward, directing the operations with his stick. [. . .]

28 June Signing of the Peace.[35] A great sight, but from a spectacular point of view badly arranged. The space allotted to the journalists very much like a bear-garden. The news that the Treaty had been signed was telephoned to London by me and my assistants, two of Reuters' men. [. . .] The room was very hot. I opened the windows in the adjoining room, which improved matters but made the architect of the Château very angry. At the beginning the Press were shut off by a line of soldiers. After some trouble, I got these removed, and prevailed upon the journalists to sit down. After the ceremony, Clemenceau, LG and Wilson went to see the fountains in the grounds, where they were mobbed by the crowd. [. . .] LG said the experience was very unpleasant, particularly as he was feeling none too well. He thought the whole thing badly managed, and that it was disgraceful that people should have been allowed to go up to the Germans in the room where

Peace was signed and ask for their autographs. In the evening I dined with the American Press Association. A very pleasant evening. Elmer Roberts in the chair. [. . . The Conference has brought] about a better understanding between American and British newspaper men. [. . .]

And so ends the most interesting six months of my life. [. . .]

July–December 1919

After the excitement of Paris and Versailles there was the inevitable reaction. Leaders as well as ordinary men and women settled back to the mundane tasks of peace-time. The post-war boom had created a climate of optimism and everything seemed auspicious for a speedy return to normality in domestic affairs. For a few months Riddell's diaries reflect this mood, and in consequence his subjects are diverse and, on the whole, lacking in drama. With one or two exceptions personalities seem of greater moment than policies or programmes. But international affairs could not be thrust completely into the background until the next phase of the conference era. Riddell observed how Lloyd George was growing more critical of the French, Syria being the point of issue. And Winston Churchill, who could not be ignored, was fired up about the Bolshevik menace. Indeed, complained Lloyd George, he had 'got Russia on the brain.' Closer to home, there is little mention of Ireland at this time, but industrial unrest in Britain causes Riddell to reflect critically, though privately, on Lloyd George's attitude towards the working classes. Earlier he had pondered Lloyd George's ability to be a great leader in a situation which called for retrenchment rather than spending on huge schemes.

Party politics account for a number of diary entries, one subject of some importance being the suggestion of a 'Centre Party' under the Prime Minister to supersede moribund Liberalism and diehard Toryism. Here Riddell has reservations about Lloyd George's apparent leaning towards the capitalists. As usual the Press lords – Northcliffe, Rothermere and Beaverbrook – come in for much comment, mostly hostile, and in this connection Riddell grows more suspicious of the activities of William Sutherland. Of incidental interest is the appearance in these pages of such names as Campbell Stuart, Lord and Lady Astor, and Hamar Greenwood, all intent upon becoming important. Nancy Astor's busy tongue already had put her on a level with Margot Asquith. At the end of the year Riddell is elevated to the peerage, although he carefully says nothing about the Palace's hostility to this project of Lloyd George's.

29 June   Off home with the PM, who looks tired and worn. As the train steamed out, he said, 'That's over! There is always a sense of sadness in closing a chapter of one's life. It has been a wonderful time. We do not quite appreciate the importance and magnitude of the events in which we have been taking part.' As the ship steamed out of the harbour at Boulogne, I stood on the deck by his side, as he acknowledged the plaudits of the crowd on the quay. I said, 'Now for the next chapter!' 'Yes,' he replied, 'now for the next chapter!' Later he said that the reactionaries were hard at work. 'If they imagine,' he added, 'that I am going to carry out their policy, they are much mistaken. I shall support the cause of the people, and if it becomes necessary to break with these people, I shall do so. Let me have a fortnight's holiday, and then I will decide what to do.' The news reached us at Folkestone that the King and Cabinet were to meet LG at Victoria. The PM changed his clothes in the train. After doing so, he sat wrapped in deep thought. [. . .]

The PM had a great reception at Victoria, and drove off with the King. I had the honour of stepping out of the train immediately following LG. Something to remember.

10 July   Called at the War Office to see Winston regarding meeting on the Russian situation [. . .] the newspapers being called together by the NPA in the usual way. He wanted to exclude the *Daily Herald*, to whom he had already sent an invitation. I told him that this would be a fatal mistake and would rouse a storm of indignation throughout the country. [. . .] He ultimately agreed to their presence.

I told Winston what I thought of his Russian campaign and that the working classes would not stand for it. He did not like this. [. . .] He is a nice man but dangerous. [. . .] Brade, looking very apprehensive and shaking his head, said, 'He really is a dangerous man. He might land us in awful difficulties.' What Brade referred to, I don't know, but evidently he had had a shock.

12 to 15 July   To Criccieth, to spend a few days with the PM.
Much interesting talk. Hankey told me the last German Note arrived early on the Monday morning. He was awakened by Dutasta [Chief Secretary of the Peace Conference] at about 6 a.m. Together they went to LG's but could make no one hear. Then they went to President Wilson's and succeeded in waking him through the medium of [Admiral] Grayson, his doctor. Wilson got out of bed and said, 'It is

cold here. Come into my bathroom, which is warmer.' This they did and arranged a meeting for 9 o'clock. [. . .]

LG enquired whether Northcliffe was better. [. . .] 'He will have to make up his mind what line he intends to take. If he goes on attacking me, I shall have something more to say about him. [. . .] I don't propose to allow matters to rest. I shall let the public know and fully realise that he is attacking me and my Government for personal reasons.'

I had to return before I had intended and had no opportunity for a private talk, so I heard nothing more of LG's political plans. Evidently he and Winston must have decided upon some joint action, as W, after his return to London from Criccieth, made a carefully prepared speech, proposing the formation of a Central Party, so called. But I heard no details. [. . .]

22 July To lunch at Winston's. Much talk about the coal strike.[1] Both Mr and Mrs W very violent against the colliers. Winston said, 'This is the time to beat them. There is bound to be a fight. The English propertied classes are not going to take it lying down.' I said that there was much to be said for the point of view of the working classes, who had been unfairly treated in the past. Winston said that he was all in favour of good wages and conditions but that the manu-facturing and commercial magnate was indispensable and that the fewer and bigger magnates there are, the better for the world. [. . .]

27 July Dined with LG at his new house at Cobham. He greeted me warmly, saying, 'You will always have a hearty welcome in any house where I am master!' [. . .]

LG told us that he proposed to tour the country in connection with housing. I said, 'Are you quite sure about your organisation? [. . .] Do you think they will deliver the goods?'

He replied, 'I have not yet had time to look into that. It was my intention to take the matter up on my return from Criccieth, but the coal strike supervened. . . .'

3 August This week-end I thought LG seemed quite worn out. It is true he talked with his accustomed vivacity, but underlying it all was a sense of weariness and effort. Also he seemed physically tired, and I noticed that when he got up from a low couch his face flushed up as if the effort were considerable. He has aged greatly during the past six months. [. . .]

Hankey was there. Much talk about the Liverpool police strike. LG very anxious for news and continually asking Hankey to go to the telephone to enquire of Downing Street. LG again referred to his regret at leaving Paris and to the sorrow he felt when he looked out of the window at the rue Nitot and saw President Wilson's house shut up. He said, 'Strangely enough I liked Wilson and was more sorry to leave him than I anticipated. He is more likeable than Clemenceau. Clemenceau is hard.' [. . .]

We had much talk about Northcliffe. [. . .]

R: [. . .] Northcliffe has gone away for two months, leaving Stuart, Caird & Co. in charge.

Stuart is anxious for a rapprochement. He wants LG to adopt and push *The Times* Irish scheme, which is Stuart's idea. [. . .] Stuart is a clever young man, very intelligent, shrewd and suggestive [. . .] with a special aptitude for journalism and a strong nose for political affairs and intrigues, not using the latter word in any malicious sense. A man of the Northcliffe type without his genius, but with more balance and real geniality. Stuart told me that he doubts whether Northcliffe will ever forgive LG or again be on the same terms with him. He says that N's *amour propre* has been sadly hurt. [. . .] He cannot bear the daily strain of regular work. Stuart added, 'N never did any work at the Department of Information. He never presided at a single Committee meeting. He left it all to me.' [. . .]

I told him [LG] what I had said to Stuart.

R: Why is Beaverbrook attacking Winston in the *Express*? I thought they were great friends?

LG: No doubt Beaverbrook, who is an unscrupulous fellow, has combined with Northcliffe. B is attacking Winston for staying in Russia, and *The Times* is attacking him for not stopping there. They hope between them to injure the Government.

(I don't believe a word of this, but LG has got Press attacks and combinations on the brain.)

LG: Our friend William Sutherland does not help me with the Press as he did. He now thinks that he is a great statesman, and wants to have policies of his own. [. . .]

10 August   Visited LG at Cobham, where I found him with Professor Chapman [. . .] and Hankey.

Hankey, by the way, is now an interesting study. For some time past the conviction has been dawning upon him that he is a great man. Now his new honour, coupled with the £25,000 and the praise of two Prime Ministers, has convinced him of the fact.[2] He is a serious little man and takes himself very seriously. I hope the PM will not spoil him. [. . .]

14 August I regard the general position as very unsatisfactory. The Government have no grip on the administration. Waste is raging on all sides, and no attempt is made to put things in order. The truth is that my friend [LG] is worn out and requires a rest. He has lost energy and grip, and buoys himself up with the belief that present-day conditions are inevitable after the war. Naturally he is suffering from the reaction of a great effort and a great victory. It also remains to be seen whether he can be an economist. It will be a new role. He has always hitherto been a spender. He has never considered money. His reputation has been made by his tongue and carrying out great schemes. [. . .] It is a different thing to be called upon to use the knife in order to carry out a humdrum policy which makes no appeal to the emotions. [. . .]

20 August Started for Deauville – quite a merry party. Mr and Mrs LG, Eric Geddes, Sir Hamar and Lady Greenwood,[3] and Captain Ernest Evans. [4] Guest joined us at Southampton. LG in good spirits but evidently very tired.

At breakfast next morning much talk about the House of Commons. LG and Guest very bitter about Lord Robert Cecil.[5] Guest said that during one of the recent debates he was telling some members in the Lobby that the question was whether the Cecils or the members of the House were to control Parliament. Lord R heard him and remarked, 'Well, the Cecils would be better than the Guests!' [. . .]

22 August Long discussion on the Press. Winston described the power of the newspapers as one of the most menacing features of public life. He said that these great instruments are now-a-days controlled [. . .] by organisers who use their power to gratify their own private whims and dislikes. He went on to say that Northcliffe, Rothermere, Beaverbrook and Hulton were quite unscrupulous and unreliable.

All the others expressed agreement (LG, Geddes and Greenwood). LG remarked that the journalists at the Peace Conference had been ignorant and unreasonable, ranting day after day about subjects they did not understand. [. . .]

Geddes: Beaverbrook is an unscrupulous fellow. [. . . He] has pursued me with relentless animosity in the *Daily Express*. [. . .]

Winston: It would be interesting to see how Northcliffe, Rothermere and Beaverbrook could carry on the public business. They would be quite incompetent. They have all tried their hands without conspicuous success.

LG: Quite true.[6] [. . .]

23 August   Kerr arrived from Paris, evidently impressed with the necessity of making concessions to the French in the Eastern Mediterranean. LG angry with the French for their attitude concerning Syria. He said that the Syrians would not have the French, and asked how the Allies could compel them to acccept mandatories who were distasteful. He added, 'I should have to make a public statement of the facts.' His attitude to the French has changed greatly since the end of 1918. He continually refers to their greed. [. . .]

25 August   LG full of publicity schemes to counteract the newspapers. House to house distribution of his last speech, etc. Guest much perturbed at LG's criticism, so J. T. Davies tells me. [. . .]

28 August   [. . .] Long talk with Geddes alone after the others had gone to bed. He has been very moody and irritable during the past two days. Now he explained the reason. That he was sick of being kept hanging about; that LG had not kept his promise to him although he fully recognised LG's inability to do so. [. . .]

30 August   [. . .] Mrs Astor very fierce on the subject of Winston and Russia. She said, 'Why not send him to carry on the Russian campaign? He could call for volunteers and raise the necessary funds.'

I said he might become Czar. This greatly amused LG. Mrs Astor treated us to dramatic descriptions of how Winston would conduct himself in his new role. It is amusing to note the jealousies of most Ministers and their wives of their colleagues. This is specially noticeable among the lesser lights like the Astors and Greenwoods. They are all pushing hard for place and position.

Sir William Sutherland and Rothermere seem to be trying to torpedo the Government. It is a peculiar position. Sir William Sutherland represents the PM with the Press and in Parliament, and at the same time he is carrying on a secret campaign against the Government.

He wants promotion, and unless he gets it will be serious danger to the PM and his colleagues. This week Rothermere is attacking Bonar Law.

Long talk between LG and General Bridges,[7] who has been in Russia. The General strongly urges that we should continue to support the anti-Bolshevists and continue to occupy Armenia. LG said this was impossible and that we could not bear the expense. He told the General that the French and Americans will do nothing, although they are loud in their declamations in favour of action. 'The poor old British Empire,' he said, 'is asked to do everything and gets not a word of thanks in return.' The General looked disappointed, but had nothing to say in answer. [. . .]

General Bridges said that the League of Nations ought to take charge of the Russian situation and Armenia.

LG: They will do nothing of the sort. The League, I am sorry to say, is a humbug and a sham. One of its main objects was the reduction of armaments, yet what do we find? America, the protagonist of the League, is about to increase her navy and army to an enormous extent. The League is to apply to every nation but America. The League is not to interfere with American affairs, but America is to have a voice in the affairs of Europe. A strange position! [. . .]

1 September Mrs Astor said Lord Lansdowne was very ill and probably dying.

LG: He acted with great courage in writing his celebrated letter. I did not agree with him, but it was a plucky thing to do. The result was that he deposed himself from the very influential position he held as leader of the Unionist Party in the House of Lords, and incurred the hatred and contempt of a large section of his friends and followers. What is more, before he wrote his letter he circulated a paper to the Cabinet, in which he said what he afterwards repeated in his letter. Asquith, McKenna and others who were saying practically the same thing because they were convinced that we could not go on after Christmas, 1917, had not the courage to support Lansdowne in the Cabinet. He was the only one who had the courage of his convictions, and I admire the old boy for it. As he made his statement publicly, I feel at liberty to refer to what took place in the Cabinet. [. . .]

2 September LG: [. . .] I don't mind saying that it went much against the grain to have to propose £100,000 for Haig,[8] considering how he acted on this and other occasions. [. . .]

4 September   The Greenwoods and Mrs Astor are hating each other like the members of a Christian Government. Both parties paying court to the PM in the most ardent and unblushing way. Very amusing to see. No wonder that Kings and Prime Ministers grow to think they are divinities. [. . .]

He [LG] spoke of Northcliffe to me when alone. He said, 'I have fought a good many people who have tried to down me and I have always defeated them. McKenna, Donald, Gardiner, Massingham and others. I think Northcliffe will suffer the same fate.'

7 September   LG told me that AJB had complimented him today on his administration, and said that he, AJB, had recently warned some of his Unionist colleagues that they could not hope to form a Government that would last a month, and that LG was the only man capable of leading a coalition. 'B has always been very kind to me,' said LG. 'I like him and am glad to see him looking so well. The younger Conservatives are with me, and as soon as I can get things a bit more clear I shall be able to get on without the Vincent Caillards, Trevor Dawsons, Dudley Dockers, etc, who see the knife at their throats and who know I am not in sympathy with them.'[9]

8 September   The capitalist party have been trying to nobble him [LG] unsuccessfully. His leanings are towards the professional view of life, but he is shrewd enough to see the trend of public opinion. A capitalist movement is on foot for propaganda among the working classes. A large fund is being raised for the purpose, and it looks as if Guest, the Whip, is implicated in the scheme. He is a nice man, but a pure political adventurer without any political principles. He lives with a fast set, and does not perceive the incongruity of urging economy upon the nation while he himself comes over here with a team of polo ponies and lives the life. He is very kind-hearted and generous, and did well in the war, but has no ardent desire to change a very pleasant world.

9 September   Arrival of Bonar Law and his daughter. Poor man! He looks gloomy as usual, as well he may considering the unfounded attacks upon him by Rothermere, William Sutherland & Co. His loyalty to LG is remarkable. [. . .]

10 September   Long talks with Bonar Law and Guest regarding LG's proposals to form a new party consisting of the Conservatives, a section of the Liberals and the Lloyd Georgeites. The suggestion is that the organisations should be amalgamated. Guest said he saw great difficulties as he did not believe that the Tories would be prepared to hand over their machine and trust themselves to the tender mercies of LG. Guest is a shrewd sort of man with no book knowledge – rather amateurish in his work, but very much on the spot where money is concerned. Guest added that the proposal was to give the party a new name – 'National Democratic,' he thought.[10] Evidently Guest is not keen or sanguine, and always has Winston in mind. [. . .]

Bonar Law told me that he thought it very doubtful whether the Conservatives would be willing to hand themselves over body and soul to LG. He said they were quite prepared to go with him step by step, but that he did not believe that they would agree to scrap their party organisation and give up their powers of defence and offence should he propose something with which they totally disagreed.

12 September   [. . .] We all drove to Evreux, where we lunched. [. . .] I drove from Deauville to Evreux with LG and Miss Stevenson. We talked about the political situation. LG said he thought the time had come for him to strike out on his own account, and that the present situation was very artificial. He said, 'Then those who are for me will declare themselves, and those who are against me will do the same. Then I shall know where I am.' [. . .]

20 September   Drove with LG to Cobham. [. . .]

LG said that he thinks a speaking campaign in the country most important, so that people may know what has been and is being done. He complained that very few of the Ministers make speeches and that the burden of exposition and stimulation is left almost exclusively to him. He said, 'The Ministers say they have not sufficient time, but look what I have to do, and yet I make speeches.' [. . .]

We talked of Winston.

LG: [. . .] I told him that he had got Russia on the brain and that the consequences would be serious. But I don't know what to do with the boy. [. . .]

R: Why is he [Beaverbrook] attacking Winston so viciously?

LG: He says that he strongly disapproves of his proceedings and that he is a public danger. But I rather suspect that they must have had a quarrel of some sort. [. . .]

24 September   Brade dined with me. [. . .] He says that there is a perpetual wrangle between the civilians and soldiers, and that Winston is the most difficult Secretary of War he has ever had to deal with. [. . .]

27 September   A short note on some of the figures moving behind the political scenes may be interesting.

Sir William Sutherland, the PM's Parliamentary secretary and Press manager, is very thick with Rothermere and Beaverbrook. Rothermere has made him a Director of the *Mirror*. It looks as if they were playing a three-handed game. Sutherland has not a good word to say for any member of the Cabinet except LG. They are all duds or worn out. Rothermere expresses the same opinion in his articles. This creates a very bad impression among the public, who are coming to think that the Government consists of one man surrounded by a lot of duffers. Rothermere has devised a new system of publicity. He writes, or has written by Sutherland or someone else, a strong political article. This he advertises in practically every paper in the country, with the result that his views obtain very wide expression. How far Rothermere and Sutherland act with Beaverbrook, it is difficult to say, but they are very close.

Hulton, the proprietor of the *Evening Standard*, *Daily Sketch*, etc, is also very thick with Beaverbrook and to a certain extent is fed by Sutherland.[11] Hulton lives next to Beaverbrook in Surrey and sees a great deal of him. What the game of Rothermere, Beaverbrook and Sutherland is, it is difficult to say. They have no substitute for LG, nor any representatives for the Cabinet. It is difficult to discover the precise relations between Rothermere and Northcliffe. I don't think the former has any influence on the latter politically, although Northcliffe is on very friendly terms with Rothermere's son.

28 September   The great railway strike is in full blast. Dined with LG at Cobham. Present, Sir Eric and Sir Auckland Geddes [and others]. LG seemed worried, as well he might. He said that the men had acted badly in breaking off the negotiations suddenly and prematurely. The country was against them, and they were sure to be beaten. [. . .]

1 October   Strange happenings. For the first time in history the printers in the newspaper offices have objected to print matter of which they disapproved – to wit, attacks on the railway men. This caused consternation amongst proprietors and editors, who held their ground with considerable firmness. [. . .] This movement is more important than it looks, and is capable of quaint developments. One novel feature of the strike is an advertising campaign in which both the Government and the men are stating their case. [. . .]

There can be no doubt that LG was wrong in describing the strike as a Bolshevist movement, as he did in his published message. This has been the key-note of the Government campaign run by Sir William Sutherland and others on the usual party lines of misrepresentation and deception. Use the note that is likely to please and convince. Truth and accuracy are immaterial.

4 October [. . .] I have preserved a very even keel in this [strike] business in the *News of the World*. I believe that the men have a good case, and that the movement is a legitimate effort to obtain justice in the matter of wages. LG with all his powers does not understand or sympathise with working men. His point of view is that of the solicitor or shopkeeper. The general attitude of the upper and middle classes is that 'you must give these fellows a lesson'.

5 October Miss Stevenson telephoned that the strike settled and that LG expected me to dinner as usual. [. . .]

[LG]: 'I am glad the strike is settled. I could have crushed them, but did not want to do it. I said to them, "If there is fighting, it will put the things you and I care for back for years. The nation will turn reactionary. Housing and all those things will not be regarded with the same generous eye." That impressed them very much,' said LG. 'The Commune put back the cause of Labour in France for twenty years. Albert Thomas told me that. [. . .] The railway men have agreed not to strike until September 1920. That breaks up the Triple Alliance. The strike came too soon for the colliers and transport workers. They were not ready. Now we have detached the railway men. I think the result of the strike will have a most salutary influence.' [. . .]

11 October Golfed with LG. [. . .]

We [LG and I] spoke of the miners' claim to nationalisation. LG described their real object as being the appropriation of the mines for their own benefit, and referred to statements made by Hodges, one of their leaders. 'It is not nationalisation that they really want,' said LG, 'it is "guildism" or syndicalism.'

I described my interview this week with Hartshorn, who told me that

the miners are bent on nationalisation and that it is a religion with
them. It is difficult to argue about a religion. A Scottish Colonel who
had commanded a miners' regiment during the war also described his
men's belief in nationalisation as a religion.

'Look here,' said LG after dinner. 'If you were Prime Minister and
you had to make a big speech this week, what would you say?'

R (laughing): Luckily I am not Prime Minister. If I were I think I
should point to the financial position of the country and the necessity
for united effort by all classes for increased production. I should also
indicate the necessity for economy, not only political but individual. I
should also emphasise the importance of reviving Parliament, the
Cabinet, political meetings, and all the ordinary paraphernalia of our
public life. [. . .]

LG: That is not so bad. I have thought of saying several different
things. One thing I thought of saying was that the Press and public
must stop nagging at men holding high positions. If it goes on, I can't
keep some of the most useful Ministers. Eric Geddes is going.[12] He
says he can't and won't stand it.

R: When at Deauville I told you he was on the point of going, but
you would not believe me. [. . .] I doubt the advisability of doing what
you suggest. Why challenge the Press to justify their action? You are
sure to have criticism. You will only intensify it.

LG: There is perhaps a good deal in what you say. [. . .]

18 October Golfed with LG and Guest at St George's Hill. [. . .] I
gave LG today a cheque for £2,750 in an envelope to purchase his
motor. He was very pleased.[13] [. . .]

It is curious that LG always refers to the workers as 'they'. Class
distinction goes deep. LG has the feelings of the solicitor when dealing
with working men. Decent fellows, but unsophisticated, uneducated,
and rather unreasonable on the whole. [. . .]

19 October To dinner with LG as usual (Sunday). Lord Lee was
there. [. . .]

When Lee had gone, LG spoke of Northcliffe thus:

LG: I think the time has come for me to go for Northcliffe again.
[. . .] I must let the public know that there is a personal feud which is
the reason for Northcliffe's continuous attacks. Then the public will
learn how much importance to attach to them. I have some things to
say about Northcliffe that will cut him to the quick and make him

squirm. Then I think I am entitled to enjoy myself a little. I shall enjoy attacking him. [. . .]

26 October To Cobham to dine with LG as usual (Sunday). The new Viscount and Viscountess Astor were there. Neither of them seemed much distressed at the death of the late Viscount, who appeared to be unmourned and unsung. Perhaps he deserved it. [. . .]

[Re. housing.] The whole thing has been mismanaged. Addison is a nice man, a real Radical and well-meaning, but a poor administrator. The result is chaos. [. . .]

He [LG] is very bitter about Northcliffe. I had no chance of a private talk, but I should think LG is considering his future. [. . .]

2 November Dined with LG at Cobham. [. . .]

LG: [. . .] When I spoke in the House of Commons last week it was like going back to the old days. It is a wonderful stimulus to hear the cheers and counter-cheers and to be able to say the things that come into one's mind at the moment.

R: Apart from your speech the division was the most notable event of the Economy debate. It showed that there is and must be a strong line of cleavage between Labour on the one hand and the capitalist and middle classes on the other. The Liberals stand for nothing. In fact they are more conservative than a large section of the Unionists.

LG: What you say is quite true. The same thing occurred to me. The abstention of the Liberals from the division was the most notable event in the history of the country. Many of the young Conservatives, particularly the young officers who have returned from the Front, are most democratic in their views and anxious for reform. The so-called Liberal Party consists mostly of plutocrats like Runciman[14] and Cowdray who have no sympathy whatever with the aspirations of the mass of the people. [. . .]

9 November Dined with LG and Mrs LG at Cobham. [. . .] Earlier in the day I played golf with Seely, who said that unless the Prime Minister would agree to make the Air Ministry a separate Department he should have to resign. [. . .] I told LG that I thought Seely intended to resign if he did not get his way. LG said he would be sorry but there was no alternative. The creation of a new department would no doubt mean more expenditure which could not be faced. He was strongly in favour of a Ministry of Defence to be responsible for the

Army, Navy and Air Force. If this plan were adopted the efforts of the three services would be co-ordinated and they would not be competing against each other. He said he thought there would not be another big war, at any rate for ten years, and that meanwhile we could consolidate our position. [. . .]

20 November   Lunched with Sir Nevil Macready.[15] Long talk about the police. He said he found affairs in a bad state and that the men had much cause for complaint. The barracks were very bad, and the men were poorly paid. Matters are now greatly improved, but he has come to a standstill. [. . .]

26 November   [. . .] Dined at Sir Abe Bailey's.[16] Big party, including the PM, Lord French, Lord Reading, etc. French said that Irish conditions were very bad and that more severe measures would have to be adopted. I asked him what he thought about Home Rule. He replied that Home Rule was an absolute necessity. I asked him what he thought of the Irish Government at Dublin Castle. He said, 'It is as bad as it can be. I don't mean that the system is corrupt, but it is bad. There is no proper control. It is impossible to make a satisfactory alteration under existing conditions.' [. . .]

2 December   Lunched at Downing Street. Present: Mr and Mrs LG, [H.A.L.] Fisher, Minister of Education, and Sir Robertson and Lady Nicoll. [. . .]

LG gave an amusing account of introducing Lady Astor into the House of Commons. He said she would continue a perpetual clatter of conversation walking up the floor of the House. This he and Balfour found most embarrassing, as it is against the rules to talk on the floor of the House. When she got to the table she almost forgot to sign the register owing to her anxiety to engage in conversation with Bonar Law. Then she wanted to have a chat with the Speaker. [. . .]

Fisher said that Lord Robert Cecil had made quite a position for himself in the country by his advocacy of the League of Nations, but this statement did not meet with any response from LG or Nicoll. They both hate the Cecils like poison, except Arthur Balfour whom they love and respect, and who [. . .] seems to dislike his relatives almost as much as LG [does]. [. . .]

7 December   Yesterday was the third anniversary of LG's

appointment as Prime Minister. Tonight I dined at Miss Stevenson's. Present: the Prime Minister, Sir Nevil Macready, Miss Bennett. [. . .]

We had a merry little party and much interesting chat. Yesterday he made a big speech to the Manchester Liberals. He said he had a wonderful reception. The audience stood and applauded for some time. [. . .]

21 December   As customary, to Cobham, where I found Fisher, Minister of Education, and Scott of the *Manchester Guardian*, who had come to see LG about Irish Home Rule at his invitation. LG had been busy dictating his speech, which was being typed in an adjoining room. At dinner LG asked how we thought the proposals would be received. Fisher said that no party in Ireland would be satisfied, but that when the scheme had become *un fait accompli* he thought the Irish would work the scheme. Scott was of the same opinion.

LG: There will be no enthusiasm. I hate my job in the House of Commons tomorrow. The Unionists naturally will not be enthusiastic. Carson will not oppose, but he will be very critical and frigid, and the Nationalists, if they come, will be unfriendly. It is a most unfortunate country. Something awkward always occurs at critical moments in her history. There was the assassination of Lord Frederick Cavendish, there was Parnell's downfall, and now there is this dastardly attack on Lord French.[17] I wish someone else was going to make the speech tomorrow. [. . .] I have a HELL (spelling out the letters) of a task. [. . .]

On Saturday (yesterday) I played golf with LG and Sassoon,[18] MP for Folkestone, and Miss Stevenson. LG said that Lady Astor had remarked that Eric Geddes had a face like a beef trust, and that this was a sample of the gentle sayings by which she ingratiated herself with people with whom she came into contact. Clever but vicious. Much talk about Spen Valley.[19] LG said he devoutly hoped John Simon would be at the bottom of the poll as he deserved. LG told us that the Coalition organisation had been very bad, that nothing had been done until he personally took the matter in hand and sent down some good speakers. [. . .] His energy is wonderful where he is interested. He does things and acts with promptitude. I had tea with Sassoon at his mansion in Park Lane. [. . .] He remarked in course of conversation on the attitude of the working-class, 'In this huge house I occupy only four rooms. Sometimes I ask myself whether the State ought not to take the rest of the house for those who cannot otherwise secure houses.' [. . .] It is a sign of the times that such an idea should have entered a millionaire's brain.

28 December   To Criccieth. On Tuesday, December 22, J. T. Davies asked me to call at Downing Street. When I arrived Miss Stevenson handed me a letter stating that the PM had decided to offer me a peerage.[20] I wrote formally accepting and a letter of thanks to LG at Criccieth, in which I said amongst other things that our friendship had been one of the joys of my life and that many of my happiest hours had been spent with him. When I reached Cricccieth, I thanked him again. [. . .] He said, 'My dear boy, it has been a pleasure to be able to do it for you!' [. . .] He also said that he thought of bringing in a Bill which would allow a member of the House of Commons to attend and speak in the Lords in support of any Bill of which he might be in charge, and vice versa. Then he added, 'I shall attend, and I shall write to Northcliffe telling him that I shall be there and that if he wants to challenge my actions that is the proper place and not from behind the hedge of a newspaper. I shall publish the letter, and people will know what to think if he fails to accept my challenge.' [. . .]

29 December   LG said he thought it a mistake for statesmen to read too many newspapers. (He commits the error himself, if it be an error!) [. . .] If trade becomes brisk and profitable, and if our housing scheme works out satisfactorily, the nation will not pay much attention to newspaper comment. There will be little unemployment, and proper measures must be provided for the support of those who are inevitably unemployed.

R: 200,000 houses will be the best answer the Government can furnish. They will speak for themselves and cannot be ascribed to fortuitous circumstances.

LG: I doubt if we can build 200,000 houses in a year. [. . .]

LG said that Beaverbrook is trying to split the Coalition. 'If he did,' added LG, 'I might say and should say that I found the Tories unsympathetic to the cause of true social reform, and that I meant to take my own line.'

1920

This was a year of promise unfulfilled as the post-war boom petered out and hopes turned sour. An air of unreality hung over affairs both domestic and foreign. The leaders with whom Riddell conversed seemed unsure of their destination and lacking in initiative. Trade refused to return to the pre-1914 pattern and such problems as reparations and exchange rates, to say nothing of Ireland, defied solution. At home industrial unrest threatened the country with massive strikes if not worse things. It was symptomatic that Lloyd George should mention the possibility of his retirement, though in the next instant his mind was busily exploring the idea of a new political party. Riddell now began to discern cracks in the coalition structure. Churchill was a disturbing element as his obsession with Russia and Bolshevism refused to abate, causing Lloyd George to utter strictures upon his waywardness. Lord Birkenhead's professed willingness to shoot the workers if they became unruly scarcely augured well for statesmanlike decisions, and Austen Chamberlain seemed merely inadequate. Riddell also noted that Bonar Law exhibited little enthusiasm for any political realignment that might cut him off from traditional Toryism, yet he was distressed at the quarrel between Beaverbrook and Lloyd George. Outside the ministry Northcliffe as well as Beaverbrook continued to exasperate Lloyd George, a theme frequently repeated in Riddell's pages.

Throughout the year the scene shifted rapidly back and forth between domestic and foreign politics. In January peace discussions were resumed in Paris, Riddell again being at the Prime Minister's elbow as Press liaison officer. The next session was at San Remo in April, where he became more aware of Lloyd George's growing hostility to the French and reflected on Britain's lack of a clear policy. There was some friction between the two men, then and again later, over how publicity for these conferences should be handled. Riddell was also present at the several attempts to co-ordinate Franco-British efforts through a series of meetings at Philip Sassoon's house at Hythe. Brussels was the next formal meeting place of the peace conference, followed by a gathering at Spa, and once more it is evident that Riddell is increasingly out of sympathy with Lloyd George's foreign policy. Something very nearly like an open break occurred in August when the leaders of Britain and Italy met in Lucerne, apparently to bring pressure jointly on France. Lloyd George asked Riddell's opinion of a draft memorandum, and when the latter had the temerity to criticise it the Prime Minister in the presence of others angrily accused him of being pro-French, or by implication anti-Lloyd George. And whilst these things were taking place there was the worsening Russian-Polish situation, which afforded Riddell a number of opportunities to record interesting conversations.

Some diversion from these sombre matters is to be found in one or two anecdotes about royalty, and there is Lloyd George's classic description of Lady Astor as 'a clever, amusing, scheming, thrusting humbug'. But Ireland was a darkening cloud. The closing months of 1920 find Riddell engrossed with the coal strike and seeking ways to mediate. A rather gloomy Christmas Day at Downing Street seemed an appropriate end to this fruitless year.

1 January [. . .] We talked much of the by-elections and Spen Valley in particular. LG is fully convinced that the Coalition will lose Spen Valley, but hopes that Simon will not be successful.[1] I said the lesson of the by-elections is that the lower middle classes are joining hands with Labour, strictly so called. The journalists' union, for example, are federating with the printers. [. . .]

8 January To Paris, to attend resumed Peace Conference. Travelled with LG, Bonar Law, Lord Curzon, Lord Birkenhead, etc. Bonar Law and Curzon congratulated me on my peerage. [. . .]

LG in high spirits, but much obsessed by Northcliffe and his villainies. I said, 'The British public are not fools. They judge by results. You have been ruined by the failure of your housing scheme. If you could wave a magic wand and produce two hundred thousand houses, Northcliffe's criticisms would not matter. [. . .] The Government will have to face the financial position. Houses cannot be built to let at economic rents. All the same, the nation must have houses and unless they get them there will be trouble.' I gave him figures which he did not seem able to refute.

10 January Signing of Protocol and *procès-verbal* ratifying the Treaty. It was interesting to see old Clemenceau going through the ceremony

– the quick way in which he walked round the tables. LG said that after the signing of Protocol, which took place in a private room, Clemenceau had to shake hands with the German delegate. He said to LG, 'I spat on the place in order to commemorate it!'

Dinner with Birkenhead, Bonar Law, etc. Much talk about the political situation, etc. [. . .]

It was generally agreed that unless the Liberals and Conservatives join forces and present a united front, they will find themselves in serious difficulties. Birkenhead was all for this, but Bonar Law said very little, and it is obvious that the older section of the Conservatives are not disposed to give up their organisation and place themselves unreservedly in LG's power. [. . .]

14 January Campbell Stuart [. . .] came to dinner. He said that the dispute between LG and Northcliffe was most unfortunate from a national and journalistic point of view, and that the latter was obsessed by the quarrel and determined to get LG out. This was leading him to give a certain measure of support to the Labour Party. [. . .] He said he had a plan. If the King were to offer N[orthcliffe] the position of Lord Lieutenant of Ireland, he might take it. It would gratify his ambitions and would form a bridge for reconciliation between N[orthcliffe] and LG.[2] [. . .]

15 January I told LG what CS had said. He did not, as I expected, meet the proposal with ridicule. On the contrary, he seemed to be rather favourable. He again mentioned that he was meditating another attack on N. He said that the propaganda work in Germany for which N gained the credit had not been done by his department at all but by the Navy and War Office. He also said that N had spent enormous sums in America and had taken with him a ridiculously large staff. [. . .]

On Monday I had a long talk with Pomeroy Burton, the second largest shareholder in the *Daily Mail*. He told me that N's health is very bad. He said that N is growing very stout and indifferent, although this does not prevent him from bending his mind on the removal of LG & Co. Burton says that he thinks N may be willing to sell his interest in the *Mail* and that he, Burton, is about to offer him two million pounds for it, having arranged the necessary finances. He thought it probable that the offer might be accepted, in which case he should drop the attacks on LG & Co. and make the leading feature of the policy an attempt to bring about a better understanding between Gt Britain and the USA. He told me this in strict confidence. [. . .] I should doubt whether N would be prepared to sell out. But one never knows. It was surprising that Burton ever managed to secure a holding in the *Mail.* [. . .]

Long interview with Derby. [. . .] He said that the quarrel between LG and Northcliffe was most unfortunate and was doing much harm to Gt Britain. [. . .]

Derby is a peculiar person. Journalists have never had a high opinion of him. They say he is treacherous and a snob. He is always very nice to me in private, but his manner is quite different when I meet him out; which is amusing. I think he rather suspects me of being a bit of a Bolshevik!

22 January The Russian situation. LG has displayed much persistence and sagacity in pursuing the policy which he has un-doubtedly held from the early days of the Conference. The Allies now understand the impossibility of fighting the Bolsheviks in Russia. No nation is prepared to supply troops or money. This week the Con-ference (Clemenceau, LG and Nitti)[3] decided to enter into arrangements with the Russian co-operative societies for the exchange of commodities. Contemporaneously the War Office issued a semi-official statement that a new war was imminent, for which the Allies must be prepared. This caused a great sensation, which was intensified by the arrival of Winston, Walter Long, Henry Wilson and Lord Beatty in Paris.

I directed LG's attention to the War Office statement and asked for an explanation. LG said the statement was unauthorised. Winston and Henry Wilson said the same, but added, 'It is true, nevertheless.' Both Winston and Wilson denied that they knew of the weekly meetings at which information is issued by the War Office to the Press. I told LG, Winston and Wilson that important declarations of this kind should not be made by a junior officer at a private meeting of newspaper reporters. They should be made publicly by some responsible person. Subsequently a sort of denial was issued by the Government. [. . .]

Yesterday I lunched with Campbell Stuart, who said he had a message from Northcliffe for me, viz.: 'Tell Riddell, that if there is a dispute between LG and Winston regarding intervention in Russia, I shall support the Prime Minister.' Campbell Stuart attached great importance to this message. I communicated it to LG, who was, of course, much interested and began to speculate as to the meaning and intention. He surmised that Northcliffe was anxious for a rapprochement and regarded this as the first olive branch. I doubted if so much importance could be attached to the message and suggested that Northcliffe was honestly apprehensive of Winston's policy. LG however would not accept this explanation. The wish is often father to the thought. Evidently he would welcome an arrangement. Such is politics. Your enemy of today is your friend of tomorrow.

While in Paris I saw a good deal of the Lord Chancellor (F.E.) – an interesting study. Very clever and brilliant, but drinks too much. Far more than is good for him. [. . .] He has some wild political notions. He said if the Labour people show signs of revolution, we must shoot. Shooting is the right method to repress such agitations. The trade unions are tyrannical. We made a great mistake to permit them to maintain Members of Parliament. [. . .]

24 January Played golf with LG at St George's Hill. This was what he said about Russia:

LG: Winston is an extraordinary fellow. He was very troublesome while we were in Paris. I had to handle him very firmly. [. . .] He tried to shout me down. He is a wild, dangerous fellow. To secure his own ends he becomes quite reckless. He is indifferent to the risks involved. He would sacrifice men and money. He did the same in the Dardanelles. I have never known any man so self-centred. That is what tells against him. He thinks of himself before he thinks of his job. [. . .] Now he is changing his views on Russia. [. . .] I am glad I have crushed his Russian schemes. I don't believe that India is in any danger. When Russia was well equipped the Russians could not cross the mountains.

R: The chief danger is Bolshevist propaganda.

LG.: Yes, but you can't keep ideas out of a country by a military cordon. They will percolate somehow. You must take other steps to counteract such attempts. [. . .]

31 January Golfed with LG and Sassoon at Burnhill. Miss Stevenson also. LG in very good form. He says that he thinks Asquith's return for Paisley would be bad for the country, as it would give fresh life to the Asquithian party, which should join up with other constitutional forces. [. . .]

1 February Dined with LG. Only Miss Stevenson there. After dinner he said: [. . .] 'I am faced with a serious crisis and must make up my mind how to act. I have told Bonar Law that I am not going on like this. We are losing by-election after by-election. There is no proper political organisation in the country and no enthusiasm. . . .

'Now there are three courses open for me:

'First to retire. I say, "I have won the war. I have made the Peace. I have started the reconstruction. I am prepared to go on supporting the policy which I have initiated but I want a rest. I have held office for fourteen years. That is a long time for any man to hold office." That would put me in a very strong position. [. . .]

'My second course would be to resign and organise the coalition Liberals into a stronger party. I should lead them in the House of Commons and that too would give me a strong position.

'My third course is fusion – I mean fusion between the two branches of the coalition. There is much to be said for that. Bonar Law and Arthur Balfour favour it. Bonar of course hates to do anything, but he sees the imperative necessity and so he is prepared to act. [. . .]

'It might be necessary for us to shed some of the most reactionary members of our party – some of the hard commercial men who have no bowels of compassion for the mass of the people – men who look upon workers as nothing more than producers of goods. I will never stand for that. I told Bonar Law so, and, to do the Conservatives justice, I don't believe they care for these people any more than I do. I told Bonar my views, and that while for some reasons I should like to retire, for others I felt bound to go on as a matter of loyalty to our people. Of course all the younger Conservatives are strongly in favour of fusion – men like Horne, Worthington-Evans,[4] etc. [. . .]

'Have you seen the pamphlet written by Chiozza Money[5] for the Paisley election? It is a remarkable document. I have it here (reading). You will see that he advises Labour not to vote for Asquith for the purpose of turning me out. In effect he says, "We prefer Labour to Lloyd George, but we prefer Lloyd George to Asquith." That is a remarkable pronouncement. You will see also that he says that the Tories and propertied classes are not quite sure about me, but they have no doubts about Asquith. They are quite right there. Asquith would rather be shot than do anything to which the propertied classes would really object.'

12 February   Peace Conference resumed in London. At the request of the newspapers I re-started my Paris conferences with the Press.

13 February   While I was waiting at Downing Street, LG came out of the Cabinet where the Peace Conference had been sitting. He said, 'On Sunday I am going to play golf. I must have some fresh air. There is no valid reason why I should not play. Everybody else does, and I see no reason why I should submit myself to a self-denying ordinance. So on Sunday we will have a game. It will be my first game in England on a Sunday – quite a momentous occasion! I may be damned spiritually!'

R: The trouble is that we won't know until a later date, when it will be too late.

LG: Well, I must just take my chance!

14 February   Had a chat with LG in the Cabinet Room. The Conference sat until 7.15p.m. [. . .] Bonar Law came in. I told him the joke about Addison being LG's illegitimate son. He was much amused and told me a story about Beaverbrook. Recently the *Daily Express*, Beaverbrook's paper, published an exclusive article regarding Barnes's retirement. Bonar Law said someone went from the Government to Beaverbrook and asked him where he got the information. Beaverbrook replied, 'Will you undertake not to divulge the source if I tell you?' 'Yes!' was the answer. 'Well,' said Beaverbrook, 'We got it from Barnes's mistress!' The point of the story is that Barnes is the last word in stodgy respectability.[6]

15 February   Golfed with LG at St George's Hill. [. . .]

We again discussed the proposal to form a new party. [. . .]

LG: [. . .] I had the Liberal Ministers down to Cobham this week – Addison, Shortt,[7] Fisher, Gordon Hewart,[8] Kellaway[9] and Macnamara. Fisher and Shortt were strongly against anything being done at present. They said action was premature. Gordon Hewart took the same view until he heard my case. Then he veered over to my way of thinking. Addison and Macnamara, who know much more about electioneering than the other three, and Kellaway, were all for immediate action. [. . .]

R: Yes, I think you want action now.

LG: It is difficult to know what to do. [. . .] But this is certain. We must be on the move. We cannot let things remain as they are. [. . .]

We talked much of the Paisley election. LG thinks Asquith will get in, but that this will be unfortunate, as it will help re-establish the 'Wee Frees'.[10] He thinks that Asquith will make very little difference in the House of Commons. [. . .]

29 February   Golfed and spent the day with LG. Much talk of the political situation, which grows more and more perplexing. Mr Asquith elected this week for Paisley by a large majority, and the 'Wee Frees' consequently much elated and full of fight. At Wrekin, Palmer,[11] a candidate run by Bottomley, at the head of the poll.

R: You will have to take more active steps to form your new party. The coalition are like an army with brilliant leaders but no organisation or proper team work. The Conservatives don't support the Liberal candidates and vice versa.

LG: Yes, we have no proper side. Something must be done. I am taking measures. [. . .] I agree that the position is unhealthy. Constant defeats at by-elections are disheartening to everyone and the party lose enthusiasm. The members feel that they are not properly supported. I saw Beaverbrook last Sunday. He agrees that a new party must be formed, and half promised his support, but I can't trust him. He is a strange fellow. [. . .] I can't quite make out [what he wants]. I think he only wants power. He wants to be in things. He wants to be consulted. . . .

R: [. . .] [Northcliffe] regards the *Daily Express* with aversion. He is jealous of the items of news they get from Government circles. He looks upon Beaverbrook as a rival. He despises, but in his heart fears him and his paper, which is making headway. [. . .] Any bargain with Beaverbrook will be like money lent from day to day. You will be liable to have the loan called in at any moment. [. . .]

LG: [. . .] Another trouble is that our Whips' Office is badly managed. [. . .] I am strongly disposed to appoint Sutherland as Whip.[12] He knows the work, he is energetic and is a keen politician. [. . .]

6 March   Spent the morning with LG and lunched with him at Cobham. We walked on the heath at the back of his house for an hour. He spoke of Russia. He strongly favours peace with the Russian Government. He said he had advocated this in Paris in February 1919. [. . .] He expects that the representatives of the Russian Government will arrive in England at an early date to make arrangements regarding trade with Russia. [. . .]

We discussed Winston in connection with Russia.

LG: I saved him from a nasty fall in October last but he does not thank me. He thinks that I have destroyed his policy. He admits that Denikin has failed as I prophesied he would, but he says that if I had used my power I could have made his campaign a success. Winston is wrong there but that is what he says. [. . .]

LG said that the *Daily Express* has published the Peace Conference memorandum on high prices which has been kept very secret. He described these frequent premature disclosures by the *Express* as being disgraceful, and speculated as to the source of their information. I replied that Bonar Law must be privy to what was done, but LG denied this. Perhaps LG knows more about the source than he admits. He and Bonar Law could easily stop the leakage if they wished to do so. I said very little but thought a lot. The *Express* correspondent is always hanging about 10 Downing Street.

7 March Golfed with LG, returning to lunch and then on to Walton Heath to tea. . . . Much talk of the political situation. The Liberal candidates at Stockport, Freddy Guest and others came to lunch to discuss the course to be adopted owing to the dispute between the two parties in the constituency. It seems that Lord Salisbury has written a letter advising the Conservatives not to support a Lloyd George candidate. Consequently the political situation is becoming more and more complicated. LG very angry at an attack upon him and his policies in the *Observer*.[13]

R: No doubt Lady Astor is at the back of it. She is a schemer.

LG: Yes – a dangerous schemer. She is trying to force my hand to give her husband high office for which he is not suited and for which he has given no justification. [. . .] She is very angry just now because I have made Philip Sassoon my Parliamentary secretary. The other day she and Miss Stevenson had quite a row about it. There is a great rivalry between Sassoon and the Astors for the Prince of Wales, who shows a preference for the former. That makes Lady A very mad. [. . .] She is a clever, amusing, scheming, thrusting humbug. [. . .]

(The newspaper attacks are evidently causing him much concern. Notwithstanding all his worries he is cheerful and seems well. He has wonderful powers of sleep. Last night he went to bed early and slept all night. This morning after breakfast he slept again for an hour, and in the afternoon for two hours. [. . .])

20 and 21 March Long talks with LG on the political situation. He said, 'Was there any stage at which I could, with honour, have broken up the Coalition and thrown over my Conservative colleagues? I cannot think of one. Now I should like some rest. For many reasons I should like to resign and take a good long holiday. But I feel there is work for me to do. Fate, Providence, or what you will, has ordained me for the purpose. It is my destiny and I must fulfil it.'

(The truth is that he enjoys the life, arduous though it may be. The business man who has made all the money he really wants still labours on. He often feels tired and weary and comes to regard himself as a sort of business patriot. The same thing applies to statesmen. As a general rule they stay on because they like the life, but they think the reason is undiluted patriotism. Human motives are so mixed that it is impossible to analyse them.)

LG says he thinks Asquith intends to go slow. He does not seem aggressive. He intends to bide his time in the hope that the Tories will get sick of LG and then combine with Mr A. LG added, 'In the House of Commons the other night Mr A was very polite, especially when he saw me taking notes. He has no stomach for a real fight. He never had. He does not want me to begin to attack him.' LG says that Bonar Law and the Conservatives are behind him (LG). The sympathies of some of them may not be in favour of LG's schemes, but they do what he wants, which is the important thing. [. . .]

The telephone rang. The secretary at Downing Street to speak to LG.

LG (returning): A revolution has broken out in Germany. That may change everything. It is a military rising and may be royalist. Strangely the Bolsheviks in Russia sent us warning that a revolution would take place in Germany. The Bolsheviks were asked to assist the re-volutionary party but declined, as they said it was not part of their game to help to re-establish a monarchy in Germany.

LG said the French had helped to bring about the revolution by making and enforcing demands which had made the position of the German Government impossible. [. . .]

LG [. . .] is angry that the *Observer*, owned by the Astors, has been attacking the Government. He intends to tell Astor that either he must leave the administration or that the attacks must cease. [. . .]

27 March [. . .] Golfed with LG, Reading and Sassoon at Walton Heath. LG and I thought Reading looked older. He seems to have lost some of his wonderful spring and vitality. He told me that he sees a good deal of Asquith. He says that Mr A talks as well as ever and greatly enjoys his social life. I enquired what was his plan of action. Reading doubted whether he had any thought-out plan. He thinks that Mr A is pushed forward by his women folk. Had he failed at Paisley, he would have given up the fight most probably, but his victory has put fresh heart into him. [. . .]

I drove to Cobham and dined with LG and his wife in the evening.

He said that Mr Asquith does not relish the fight which he sees may take place between him and LG. [. . .]

I notice that LG is steadily veering over to the Tory point of view, although no doubt they will not relish some of his doings. He constantly refers to the great services rendered by captains of industry and defends the propriety of the large share of profits they take. He says one Leverhulme or Ellerman[14] is worth more to the world than say 10,000 sea captains or 20,000 engine drivers, and should be remunerated accordingly. He is also at heart opposed to the claims of Labour, and would like to fight the working classes if he dared. He knows they do not trust him and he dislikes their independent spirit. He wants to improve the world and the condition of the people, but wants to do it in his own way. [. . .]

I believe LG is honestly convinced that Socialism is a mistaken policy. [. . .] I have observed this conviction growing upon him during the past four years. His point of view has entirely changed. [. . .]

LG said that Wickham Steed of *The Times* had become very friendly with Mr A (I had heard this elsewhere). 'But never mind,' said LG, 'I shall beat Asquith.' [. . .]

10 April Left for San Remo with LG to attend the Peace Conference. I to represent British Press as before. [. . .]

In the course of another conversation, LG remarked, 'What the country needs today is a great religious movement. All classes are too selfish and greedy. They are not thinking of the country. They are thinking only of themselves.' [. . .]

LG says Montagu is keen to become Viceroy of India, and is working hard to accomplish his desire. LG does not approve. He said that Montagu is a pushing Jew. [. . .]

Many talks with Curzon – a most complicated and interesting personality – pompous, but witty and amusing, and well-informed. [. . .]

19 April Peace Conference opened formally. Many rumours concerning fresh disputes between the French on the one hand and the British and Italians on the other. Long talks with LG, P Kerr and Hankey. All very critical of the French, their view being that the military party, headed by Foch, are struggling hard to force Millerand[15] to take up the position that if France's allies will not support her in military measures to coerce the Germans, France should act on her own account. Many rumours are current as to French intentions. Some say that the French wish to occupy and exploit Ruhr coalfields, as they are now satisfied that the Germans will pay nothing by way of indemnity. [. . .] Regarding Germany and France, the time has come when we must decide what course we are going to take. The French, and Foch in particular, see clearly, and have a definite plan of action. We have none. We can no longer shirk a decision. We must decide whether we intend to compel the Germans by force, or a show of force, to perform their obligations or whether we intend to treat them as friends and brothers, the latter alternative involving, in some measure, waiving certain parts of the Peace Treaty. LG asked me to ascertain for him what the French view was. From Adam of *The Times* and others in touch with the French, I obtained confirmation of the rumours stated above. [. . .] I communicated this to LG. [. . .]

23 and 24 April   A terrible hullaballoo about the Anglo-French situation. Intensified rumours of disagreement between LG and Nitti on the one hand and Millerand on the other. It is said that LG and Nitti proposed that the Germans should be sent for with a view to a conference. *The Times* writes in a mad style. I invited LG to meet the British Press at dinner and subsequently arranged for him to meet the American Press. At the dinner he said in effect that he did not regard the Germans as contumacious but thought the German Government weak and unable to enforce its commands. He compared it to a paralysed body. He also indicated his fears of a French military policy. At the same time it is obvious that he is trimming his sails for an arrangement with the French. He feels that public opinion will not tolerate any breach in the alliance. [. . .]

24 April   History of Publicity at San Remo.
    On the first day of the Conference I went with LG to the Villa de Vachan, where a preliminary discussion was to take place. After the meeting, Hankey came on to the terrace with the draft *communiqué* as to the day's proceedings written in pencil. The last clause read, 'A daily *communiqué* will be issued, but beyond this no information as to the proceedings of the Conference will be published,' or words to that effect. I said, 'I have no right to speak, but I venture to describe that as a most ill-advised statement. The rule will not be kept, and the Conference will once more become a laughing-stock.' LG and Curzon

were there. I reminded them of what took place at the first Conference in 1919. LG and Hankey were not pleased at my intervention, but eventually the offending words were deleted, Hankey muttering, as they were struck out, 'Whether the words go in or not, there is the resolution which they have just passed.' Later I told the correspondents of the resolution, and that I proposed to make a strong protest. Later I saw LG and told him that the French and Italians would not follow the rule and that the British journalists would be compelled to secure their information from foreign sources. I also said that I felt strongly disposed to cable the Newspaper Proprietors' Association suggesting that the newspapers should recall their correspondents as a protest.

LG said he thought Kerr might give me information as he did on previous occasions. When I repeated this to Hankey, he was very disgusted but said little. He, however, remarked, 'LG made the proposal, and now he is the first to break it.' And then Hankey shrugged his shoulders. The truth is that LG and Hankey are both strongly averse to publicity except when it suits their purposes. As each day has passed LG has become more communicative for Press purposes – more and more eager to explain that there is no difference between him and the French. The resolution of a week ago has been observed by no one and has proved a complete farce.

Millerand and LG had a long, satisfactory interview this morning at the Hôtel Royal. They are to prepare a joint declaration making recommendations to the Conference. Both parties ascribe all the trouble to the newspapers! Little is said concerning the fundamental difference between the points of view which led to the discussion. [. . .] Whatever may be LG's views today, there is no doubt that when he arrived here he was very anti-French. That is, suspicious of French military tendencies and designs, and pleased at having given the French what he called a lesson in regard to the Ruhr incident. I told Hankey, Kerr, Miss Stevenson and J. T. Davies that nothing must be done to impair the French alliance. LG knows my views and is not pleased. They do not suit his book.[16] [. . .]

15 May To Hythe, to attend a conference between British and French missions. Chief British representatives, LG and Austen Chamberlain. Chief French representatives, Millerand and Marsal, French Minister of Commerce.

The conference took place at Sir Philip Sassoon's house at Lympne.

He entertained the party. The French arrived on Friday evening and left midday on Sunday. The French have been very busy working the English Press to support the French claim for priority in respect of devastated areas. I telephoned informing Kerr and LG of this. I said that the Government Press arrangements in connection with foreign affairs require reorganisation. The Press will not take a line from Downing Street, as they always suspect political motives. By tradition the cue should come from the Foreign Office, and journalists are glad to hear the FO point of view. The FO people say they are not kept informed and do not themselves know what the Government point of view is. Whether this is due to Curzon's neglect to inform them, or whether he does not always know the PM's mind, I cannot say, but the result is deplorable. On this occasion the French have carefully primed not only their own, but the British newspapers, whereas we have done nothing to explain the Government attitude on the subjects to be discussed at the conference. Kerr agreed, and said he had arranged in future to keep the FO Press Department informed. [. . .]

Derby is much shrewder than appears – very observant, a good judge of character, and an intriguer of the first water. A proclivity which is aided by his bluff John Bull manner. He has been seeing Northcliffe, Wickham Steed, and others of the tribe, with a view to impressing upon them the inadvisability of continuing to attack the PM. [. . .] I think his intervention is having some effect. [. . .]

In the afternoon, LG, Bonar Law, Austen Chamberlain, Hankey and Kerr had a conference with General Malcolm,[17] who holds a sort of roving commission for the British Government in Berlin.

LG (to Malcolm): You had better let the Germans know what our view is. They must disarm and they must pay. But subject to that we are in favour of rehabilitating Germany. In fact Germany must be rehabilitated if she is going to pay. [. . .]

An amusing comedy has been in progress – viz. a fight between Lady Astor and Philip Sassoon for possession of LG and the Prince of Wales. At the moment the honours rest with Sassoon. Miss S[tevenson] wrote to Lady A commiserating with her on the attack upon her in *John Bull* regarding the Divorce Bill. Lady A replied, 'I had fully expected a letter from the PM sympathising with me and supporting me.' [. . .]

23 May   At Cobham to dinner. LG better but still rather shaky. The strain has told on him at last and he needs rest. He was at a Cabinet

Meeting during the week. He said it was a difficult Cabinet and he had
to attend. He showed me a dispatch sent by Curzon. [. . .] The tone of
the dispatch had made LG very angry. He described it as a pompous
and dangerous document and said he should speak strongly to Curzon
about it. LG again referred to the Poles. I told him I had spent an hour
with Prince Sapieha, the Ambassador. LG prophesied that the Poles
would suffer a severe defeat and said it would do them good, as they
have become swollen-headed and a danger to Europe.

30 May Dined with LG at Cobham. Present: Lord and Lady Lee,
Lord Dawson,[18] Miss Stevenson and Captain Evans. Much talk of
Lenin and Krassin the Russian representative whom LG is to meet
tomorrow. LG said that Lenin is the biggest man in politics. He had
conceived and carried out a great economic experiment. It looked as if
it were a failure. If it was, Lenin was a big enough man to confess the
truth and face it. He would modify his plans and govern Russia by
other methods. In his (LG's) opinion, Communism was doomed to
failure as it ignored some of the most important qualities of human
nature. At the time it had to be tried and he did not object to the
experiment so long as it was not tried here! The British working
classes did not really believe in the Russian experiment but they did
not wish it to be interfered with. They regarded it as a democratic
movement which should have fair play from all democracies. The
innate feeling of the Britisher is that foreigners, and especially
Russians, are queer devils who engage in all sorts of queer
practices. [. . .]
  We spoke again of the Poles. LG still thinks they will be beaten. He
told us that in Paris in December the Polish delegation brought him a
large map in which they indicated the territories they regarded as
essential to Poland. 'A most preposterous claim,' said LG. 'The Poles
have quarrelled with all their neighbours, and they are a menace to the
peace of Europe.' When Pathek, the Prime Minister of Poland, came
to see him, LG warned him of the dangers of offensive measures
against Russia and that Gt Britain could not give the Poles its support.
This LG thought it well to repeat in writing. [. . .]

2 June To reception at Bonar Law's – occasion, marriage of his
daughter to Sykes,[19] the flying man. [. . .] Miss Bonar Law is a nice
unaffected girl. On the whole the presents struck me as rather measly.
  Afterwards went into No 10. LG appeared, looking very spick and

span and apparently quite recovered from his illness. Lord Derby was there, having just returned from the Derby, where his horse ran second. He said that he was going to see Northcliffe as to a fund for bringing over French soldiers as visitors to Gt Britain – 'Not a political visit!' he remarked. LG looked very funny, and said, 'He (Northcliffe) is a damned scoundrel! He is doing his best to make mischief between France and Gt Britain, and has been trying to do so for months past. I don't mind what he says about home politics, but when it comes to stirring up international strife, that is another matter!' [. . .] His anger against Northcliffe is growing.

6 June To dinner with LG at Cobham as usual. Lord St Davids[20] and General Tudor[21] were there. Tudor is now head of the police force in Ireland – General Macready's head man. Tudor seems determined and capable, but told me that the life is wearing. [. . .] He told the PM he thought martial law a necessity and that otherwise it would be impossible to convict. LG was very emphatic upon the necessity for strong measures. He said, 'When caught *flagrante delicto* you must shoot the rebels down. That is the only way.' [. . .]

11 June Lord French called. We had a long talk about Ireland. He said he had been a good deal rattled but was better now. The life was very fatiguing – worse than active service. It was not realised that there was an Irish Army with regular divisions, battalions, companies, etc. We were endeavouring to cope with the situation by police measures – quite unsuitable. He had urged that the country should be placed under martial law, but the Cabinet would not agree. The Prime Minister was not favourable. [. . .] If the position were recognised and if the Irish were met by a proper military force, the whole agitation would be crushed in a few months. [. . .] It was absurd to think that the British Army could not quell such an insurrection if given proper powers. He said it was an underground conspiracy.[. . .]

12 June Lunched with Winston, who said he thought the country was quieter than it had been for years.[. . .]

As usual he was violent against the Bolsheviks. He described the Prime Minister as a wonderful man. He said, 'It is extraordinary that we have been able to work together on such terms of personal friendship notwithstanding the divergence of our views regarding Russia. . . .' (I think it most extraordinary. R) [. . .]

13 June   Dined with LG at Cobham as usual. [. . .]

We talked of Lenin's letter to the Labour Party, which LG described as an insane document. I said, 'It looks to me as if Lenin were becoming a bit rattled.' LG agreed. He said the negotiations with Krassin were not making good progress, and thought that Lenin's letter might make matters more difficult. [. . .]

20 June   To Hythe. Another conference at Lympne between LG, Austen Chamberlain, Millerand and the French Minister of Finance. Foch and Henry Wilson summoned at the last moment regarding the Turkish position – very serious, Kemal Pasha[22] being on his hind legs. Venizelos[23] also in attendance. It was decided to give him a free hand with the Turks. [. . .] The position of the French is curious. They had an armistice with Kemal which they asked him to renew, but apparently he declined. In any case it is said that the French troops will not fight against the Turks, so that if the Greeks have bitten off more than they can chew, it will be Gt Britain, as usual, that will have to come to the rescue. [. . .]

As usual, everything wrapped in mystery – 'Hush!' being the order of the day. But as usual everything leaked out. [. . .]

21 June   Crossed to Bolougne. LG had a good reception by the French, who were more demonstrative than on any former occasion – no doubt all arranged by Millerand, who seems genuinely anxious to bring about a good understanding between the two countries. We returned home on the following day, Tuesday. The proceedings at this conference were more formal than usual. I had very little chance of a talk with LG alone. [. . .]

26 June   Went to Cobham in the morning to golf with LG. [. . .] Only Miss Stevenson there. [. . .]

We spoke of the situation in Turkey. I said, 'Do you think it was wise to give Smyrna to the Greeks?'

LG: I have no doubt about it. You must decide whom you are going to back. The Turks very nearly brought about our defeat in the war. It was a near thing. You cannot trust them and they are a decadent race. The Greeks, on the other hand, are our friends, and they are a rising people. We want to be on good terms with the Greeks and Italians. You cannot trust the French altogether. Who knows but some day they may be opposed to us? I have been in the House of Commons for thirty years, and during that time the French have often been within an ace of declaring war upon us. We must secure Constantinople and the Dardanelles. You cannot do that effectively without crushing the Turkish power. Of course the military are against the Greeks. They always have been. They favour the Turks. The military are confirmed Tories. It is the Tory policy to support the Turks. They hate the Greeks. That is why Henry Wilson, who is a Tory of the most crusted kind, is so much opposed to what we have done. [. . .]

1 July till about 9 July   To Brussels with LG and party to the Peace Conference. [. . .]

It is evident that Austen Chamberlain's days as Chancellor of the Exchequer are numbered. Publicly he is much criticised, and has a knack of getting into awkward positions and continually changing his ground.[24] He is to be succeeded by Sir L. Worthington-Evans, a solicitor whom I have known for many years – a capable, pushing sort of man of the practical type – rather on the common side, and lacking the culture which leading ministers possess.[25] Quite a new type for a first-class position.

On Friday night, July 2, I dined at the Palace, the party consisting of the chief members of the delegations. [. . .]

Very *important interview* [26] (5 July). Saw LG specially regarding publicity and told him most emphatically that more information must be given out. I said that unless this were done there would be all sorts of lying rumours, and that the public were growing sick and tired of secrecy which was only half secrecy.

Philip Kerr supported me in my view.

LG: Well, there is a good deal in what you say. Of course, the French and Belgians will give out a lot of stuff.

R: We know from experience what they will do. The Conference always adopts the wrong policy. The members swear themselves to secrecy. One or more nations always break the vow, and at the end of the Conference everyone breaks it.

LG: Well, this time at any rate the British will give out everything.

P. Kerr: When Riddell and I get a free hand we are not bad publicity agents for the British Empire.

As a result of this conversation I was enabled for the first time in the history of Peace Conferences to furnish the newspaper correspondents with full and accurate accounts of the proceedings. Some of the information I got from LG himself, and the remainder from Kerr, who

attended the meetings and took notes which he afterwards communicated to me. It was thus, in effect, possible for me to give a full and
accurate report to the Press twice a day. This entirely altered the usual
Peace Conference atmosphere. Very few misrepresentations were
published, and the newspapers and public were pleased and satisfied.
All through the Peace Conferences till now LG has taken the wrong
view of publicity. He always wants to negotiate in secret and does not
recognise that this is impossible in these days, when every public
function is surrounded by myriads of reporters and when every public
man and official, including LG himself, when it suits him, is anxious to
use the Press to advance his own plans and policy. I have thrown my
meetings open to American journalists and day by day I have communicated in my own words the doings of the Peace Conference to
150 millions of people. The British and American journalists entertained me to dinner and said some nice things. [. . .]

I had a curious interview with Wickham Steed, the Editor of *The
Times*. When I first met him he said that he was going to Spa to play
golf, that he did not intend to do any work, but would be in the
neighbourhood. Not a word of truth in it. Pure bluff! As there does not
happen to be a golf course within a hundred miles. He is a nice man,
but jumpy and inaccurate. [. . .]

In a day or two Lord Derby arrived. Soon after his arrival he took
me aside and said, 'I am going to make another attempt to bring about
a reconciliation between the PM and Northcliffe. If I were a private
individual, and LG and Northcliffe had a quarrel, it would be of no
interest to me, except as a matter of gossip. I should say, "Let them
fight it out!" But, holding the position I do, and knowing as I do that
the attitude of the Northcliffe press is doing the country the most
serious injury on the Continent, I feel it my duty to attempt to put an
end to this intolerable state of affairs. [. . .] I think the matter might be
adjusted if Northcliffe were promised a certain position.'[27] [. . .]

10 July Stinnes, the German capitalist, upset the Conference by
saying he intended to speak as a matter of right, and that people who
were not suffering from the disease of victory would appreciate his
point of view and what he had to say. He also made an impertinent
reference to the employment of black troops.

LG said to me as we walked away, 'Today we have seen a real
specimen of the jack-boot German. I wish I were going to reply this
afternoon instead of Millerand. I think perhaps I can do the insolent

business better than he can. I should say something that would annoy
Mr Stinnes!'

Millerand in reply made a dignified speech in which he said there
was no desire to chastise the Germans, and that if they performed the
Treaty they would again be received into the family of nations. These
sentiments did not meet with the approval of the French Press, and
there is a terrible hullabaloo in Paris. LG is very pleased about the
Conference, which was his idea. He says it has shown the advantages
of discussion as compared with notes. [. . .]

12 July   Dined with LG, Sassoon, Kerr and Miss Stevenson in LG's
private room. [. . .]

Later I had a long talk with P. Kerr and arranged that he should see
the Press in my absence. He spoke much of LG's policy and relations
with the Foreign Office. He said the latter had no conception of policy
in its wider sense and did not understand in the least what LG was
driving at. [. . .]

I said that Gt Britain was seriously handicapped because our Press
are not adequately informed of the trend of our foreign policy. [. . .] I
told Kerr, as I had told Curzon, that the papers will not take a line
from Downing Street. Traditionally they are accustomed to receive
information on foreign affairs from the FO, and would pay attention to
what the FO told them. In the old days, when newspapers were fewer
and only three or four of them dealt exhaustively with foreign affairs,
the information was given out by some of the officials who kept in close
touch with the Press and who were themselves dealing with the matters
involved. Today there are so many new papers and so many subjects
requiring comment that this scheme is impossible. I said that in my
opinion the time had come when a competent journalist should be
employed for the purpose – one who would keep in touch with
Downing Street, the Foreign Secretary and the heads of the various
departments at the Foreign Office and keep the Press advised as to the
trend of our policy. [. . .]

18 July   Dined at Cobham with LG, Miss Stevenson and Megan. At
dinner LG very preoccupied and irritable. . . .

LG: Public life is becoming almost impossible for any decent man.
Unless they take care they will drive all decent people out of it. Public
men are maligned and abused as if they were criminals. All sorts of
base motives are imputed to them. I have been at Spa working twelve

and fourteen hours a day under trying conditions – eating bad food and sitting in stifling rooms. I am represented as having been on a joy-ride. Such attacks are scandalous, and I sometimes feel that I will resign and regain my independence.

Several times during the evening, as we sat there in the dusk, LG alluded to the expected reply from the Soviet Government regarding the cessation of hostilities against the Poles. He was evidently very excited and telephoned two or three times to ascertain if the Russian cable had arrived. The conduct of international affairs is a great game. LG was just as eager about this message as a lover awaiting a telegram. He said, 'Much depends on the Soviet reply. If they make peace, they will place the Germans entirely in our hands.' [. . .]

At about 9.30 a telephone message arrived saying that the Russian telegram, 2,400 words, had come. LG dashed into the house to hear it and shortly returned saying that the message was too long to read over the telephone, but the gist of it was that, while the Russians did not admit the right of any nation or group of nations to intervene in the dispute between Russia and Poland, they would grant an armistice if the Poles asked for one, as there was nothing they desired more than peace. [. . .]

LG said he was disposed to give this exclusive to the *Daily Telegraph*. [. . .] He said he was anxious to make the *Daily Telegraph* the Government organ so as to counteract the influence of *The Times*. Later at LG's request I telephoned to the *Daily Telegraph* telling them of the Russian reply. [. . .]

LG says that Worthington-Evans is not altogether a success. LG thinks him too crude.

22 July   The Other Club. Sat next to Winston. Very depressed regarding the Polish situation. He said, 'The Bolsheviks are fanatics. Nothing will induce them to give up their propaganda and endeavours to create a communistic world.' He prophesies that they will attempt the formation of a Soviet Government in Poland and later on endeavour to accomplish their purpose in Germany. 'It may well be,' he continued, 'that Gt Britain and France will have to call upon the Germans for their assistance.' [. . .]

'No man [Churchill went on] can stand the strain the PM is bearing at the present time. He really ought to hand over the international questions to the Foreign Secretary. At present the PM is conducting the business of the Foreign Office with the assistance of Philip Kerr –

a nice man, but I distrust him. I don't like his point of view. I don't think that any man who does not hold a leading position in the State should be permitted to exercise so much influence on important questions of policy. I told him so the other night. I said to him, "What responsibility have you got? And what have you done to justify your position? You have never fought an election, you have never assumed the risks of public life, you have no real responsibility. If things go wrong, others have to take the consequences. All that you have to do is to walk out of Downing Street. They are formulating schemes which affect the lives of millions and the destinies of the world, and all this is done behind the scenes."' [. . .]

I think there is some justice in these criticisms. Kerr has been invaluable to the PM and is an able person. [. . .]

23 July   To dine with the Lord Chancellor at the House of Lords, where he entertained the King and sixty other guests. [. . .] I sat next to Winston, who was particularly agreeable. He told me that although he had had many disagreements with LG, he was very fond of him, and would always be prepared to stand by him in a pinch. He dilated at length on the Bolshevik danger to civilisation. He said, 'What I foresaw has come to pass. Now they are invading Poland, which they mean to make a jumping-off ground for propaganda in the rest of Europe. They will make peace with the Poles and endeavour to form a Soviet Government in Poland. The Bolsheviks are fanatics. Nothing will turn a fanatic from his purpose. LG thinks he can talk them over and that they will see the error of their ways and the impracticability of their schemes. Nothing of the sort! Their view is that their system has not been successful because it has not been tried on a large enough scale, and that in order to secure success they must make it world-wide.' [. . .]

24 July   Golf with LG at St George's Hill. [. . .] He said, 'I have put up a big bluff. It has come off! If it had not come off it would have been awkward. Everyone thought from my speech in the House of Commons that we intended to make war for Poland. I never intended anything of the sort, and only used the threat in order to compel the Russians to grant the Poles an armistice. . . .'

25 July   Dined with Mr and Mrs LG at Cobham. Lord and Lady Lee and Lord Dawson were there. Directly I arrived LG told me that the

Bolshevists had agreed to attend a conference in London. He said, 'The *Nation* and all that crew have been rejoicing because the Bolshevists had rejected my overtures. This is a great occasion. The Russians wish the leading Allies to attend, and, if it were necessary, to summon all the small nations whose territories abut on Russia, so that a general discussion on peace may take place. I am very pleased.' [. . .]

LG again referred to the misdeeds of *The Times* newspaper and to the injury which it was doing. [. . .] LG's idea evidently is that he can weaken *The Times* by contributing special political intelligence of high importance to the *Telegraph*. [. . .]

31 July   Lunched at Cobham with LG, Miss Stevenson and Captain Evans. [. . .] LG much incensed against Beaverbrook, whom he described as an unreliable little cad. He said that Bonar Law had asked him (LG) to make friends with Beaverbrook, which he had tried to do. He had dined with him several times, but notwithstanding that Beaverbrook had made friendly protestations, he had at once attacked the Government. [. . .]

8 August   To Hythe for another conference. The principal figures LG, Millerand, Foch, Henry Wilson and Beatty. Strong divergence between British and French views concerning Poland – almost sole subject for discussion. [. . .] On Sunday the Bolshevist reply to our Note proposing a conference in London was eagerly awaited. When it arrived it was deemed unsatisfactory, inasmuch as the Russians insisted upon direct negotiations with the Poles. It was evident to me that the Bolshevists do not intend to make peace with the Poles through the Allies, that they intend to press forward their military measures against Poland and to prosecute their propaganda campaign in all countries with the object of establishing Soviet Governments. [. . .]

9 August   The Conference at Hythe concluded. LG said that no statement was to be made to the Press except that a unanimous decision had been arrived at, subject, in the case of Gt Britain, to the approval of Parliament, he having given an undertaking that Parliament would be consulted. I, however, succeeded in eliciting details from various sources, and was able to give the correspondents a detailed statement. It is obvious that there is a serious difference between the French and British points of view regarding Poland. Foch took me on one side and enquired through an interpreter what was the position in Gt Britain on the Polish question. I told him that the people were in favour of Polish independence but would not engage in another war.

Foch: They do not understand. They would do so if the newspapers would properly explain the situation. It is serious. If Poland falls, Germany and Russia will combine. You will have a worse position than in 1914. [. . .]

The Conference broke up with a strangely unreal air. One felt that the real feelings of those who had taken part in it were not openly expressed. Foch said what he meant, it is true, but I am not sure about the others. Everyone looked more than he said, except perhaps LG who probably thought more than he showed. [. . .]

14 August   The trade unions have appointed a direct action committee to stop the war. A very important movement. LG's bluff, as he calls it, has not bluffed the Russians, but it has bluffed our people at home [and] given the Labour leaders their chance for saying what it suits them to say. [. . .]

18 August   To Lucerne with LG and party. [. . .] LG said he wanted a holiday amongst the mountains and was absolutely bent on Switzerland. No doubt he is fond of mountains, but I think his real reason is that he is very angry with the French, and is anxious to meet Giolitti, the Italian Prime Minister, in order to make a combination with him on the Russian and Polish questions. LG's antipathy to the French very marked, and dates from the beginning of the Peace Conference in Paris, when he was furious at the attacks by the French papers. [. . .]

22 August   Conference took place at the villa, under the trees in the garden. [. . .]

In the morning LG, Giolitti and Hankey agreed provisionally on a memorandum to be issued to the Press dealing with the Russian and Polish questions, the document having been previously prepared by LG and Hankey. Before lunch LG handed me the draft and asked me what I thought of it. It began by stating that the Governments of Gt Britain and Italy thought it desirable to make a statement concerning their policy. I said I thought the memorandum undesirable and dangerous in its present form, that it would accentuate difficulties between France and ourselves, and might lead to the reorientation of world power, with France and America on one side, and Gt Britain, Italy, Greece and the rag-tag and bobtail of Europe on the other.

LG was very angry and strongly controverted my views. He also charged

me with being pro-French. He continued the discussion at lunch-
time, which made things rather awkward, particularly as the servants
were present. I said, 'You asked my opinion, and I gave it. I may be
wrong, but those are my views.'

LG: Why should not Gt Britain and Italy state their policy? Gt
Britain and France have met on several occasions without Italy. Why
should not Gt Britain and Italy meet without France?

R: [. . .] This is the first time that a public statement of policy of this
sort has been issued. As the subject is under discussion and you have
asked my opinion, I think it right to say that there is a strong feeling
that we are devoting too much time to international and not enough to
home affairs. We cannot be the arbiters of Europe. We have no power
to enforce our decisions, and the result of our continued interference
is that we make enemies all round. [. . .]

Hankey came to me afterwards and said he was glad I had spoken as
I did, adding, 'You never did a better piece of work, and LG after you
had gone said he was glad you had stated your views, as it was well to
hear the other side. Owing to what you had said, I (Hankey) succeeded
in getting him to hold over the memorandum until the following day,
so that we all might sleep on it.'[28]

23 August   The memorandum redrafted, mainly with reference to the
Bolshevik terms, and also no doubt having regard to the Polish military
successes, which have entirely changed the aspect of affairs.

LG evidently very disappointed with the action of the Bolsheviks.
He is still keen on making peace with them. [. . .]

30 August   [. . .] Lunched with [Kerr] and A. J. Balfour. [. . .] We
talked of Mrs Asquith's reminiscences,[29] which AJB described as a
disgusting exhibition and inaccurate. [. . .]

About 1 September   Coal strike negotiations in full blast. Dined with
Hartshorn, who told me that there is a strong feeling amongst the
miners in favour of a strike. That they are very angry at the contumely
showered upon them by the Press, that they believe this is due to the
Board of Trade, and that unless Sir Robert Horne is careful he will get
the miners into such a state of mind that they will strike just to show
their independence. He said that Horne had been unsympathetic and
unapproachable.

The next day I cabled the purport of this to the PM at Lucerne.

Subsequently Horne asked me to call. He said that he thought a strike imminent and outlined the Government preparations to meet it. I said I thought the strike would be avoided, but that I did not believe the miners would be firm in their demand to prescribe the price of coal. Consequently the dispute would resolve itself into a wage question, which would be settled by some sort of compromise as usual. I said the contents-bills would be, 'Lloyd George settles another strike.' Evidently Horne did not like this. I told him the miners thought he was too much in league with the masters. [. . .] He protested that he had no leaning towards the proprietors. [. . .]

14 September   Lunched with Inverforth at the Ministry of Munitions. [. . . He] gave me some remarkable particulars as to the chaos which had prevailed at the Ministry [of Munitions] during the war. Money was poured out and all sorts of improvident arrangements made. [. . .]

15 September   Dined with Hartshorn, Brace, Sir Joseph Hewitt[30] and [Sir Andrew] Duncan, the Coal Controller, at the Hotel Russell. Sir J. Hewitt entertained the party.

Very long discussion. Brace and Hartshorn read the proposals which they had made at the Miners' Executive today and which had been accepted. In effect, these eliminated the claim to fix the price of coal, emphasised the claim for *2s* increase in wages, and proposed machinery to increase the output, the fall in which had seriously perturbed the miners' leaders. Ultimately I suggested that the question of wages, output, etc, should be referred to a Joint Committee of masters and men. Everyone agreed to this .[. . .]

16 September   Lunched with Lord Lee,[31] who is very anxious to be appointed Viceroy of India. He had written me a long letter proposing this, and indicating that he was anxious to hand over Chequers at once to the Prime Minister, which he would be able to do if he were appointed Viceroy. I said to Lee, 'Why not approach the Prime Minister yourself?' He replied, 'I don't care to do that, but should like you to read him my letter.' I said I thought it a mistake to mix Chequers up with the Viceroyalty, as it rather looked as if he were offering a bribe, and that the effect might be to antagonise the PM. [. . .]

Later I saw him [LG] at Downing Street. He said he would not think of appointing Lee, who would not be suitable. I sent Lee a message, telling him what the PM had said. [. . .]

By the way, I have forgotten to record what Curzon told me about the Queen's Monshee.[32] After the death of John Brown, she became very much attached to an Indian Monshee who was continually in attendance upon her. He saw all the private correspondence and papers, and I think Curzon said the Queen wrote him a number of letters. When she died the Government were very much afraid that the Monshee would make use of the documents in his possession and make trouble, but he acted honourably and handed over everything that he had. He was sent back to India and given a job, which he is still enjoying, I think. Curzon said the relations between Victoria and the Monshee were very curious. [. . .]

1 October Spent the evening with Hartshorn, Brace and the Coal Controller [Sir Andrew Duncan]. The two former very disgruntled because, having fought the fight, the Government would give them no assistance, and had insisted upon 248,000,000 tons as the datum line for the *2s* advance, whereas Brace and Hartshorn had insisted upon 244,000,000 tons. They said they would not support the proposals, which are to be balloted amongst the miners. I made a strong appeal to the Coal Controller to modify the figures, which he agreed to do, but not to the extent demanded by Brace and Hartshorn. It was rather a painful interview. Brace and Hartshorn have no doubt achieved great things by defeating Smillie's attempt to induce direct action. [. . .]

The interview took place in Sir J. Hewitt's room, but he was not there. However, his absence did not interfere with the supply of lubricants.

2 October Saw LG and discussed with him what had happened on the previous evening. He said that the Coal Controller had no authority to make any change in the figures, and that he was surprised to hear he had made such promises. Therefore the ballot will go forward on the figures as originally stated. The chances are that the miners will accept, but the Government are running risks. [. . .] It is unfortunate that the Government have not seized this opportunity to endeavour to convince the miners of their good will, etc. [. . .]

Later. We had some talk about the threatened coal strike.[33] LG evidently apprehensive. He is not in touch with the Labour point of view, and has no real sympathy with Labour. His outlook is that of a benevolent capitalist. He has much more sympathy with the middle classes than he has with the working classes. . . . The truth is that they are too strong and independent and won't let him have his own way. [. . .]

16 October   Golfed with LG and Miss S at St George's Hill. Much talk about the coal strike. I said it was a great pity no settlement had been arrived at, and that if the strike continued serious complications would arise with the other unions. I also prophesied a settlement.

LG and Miss S did not take my view, and expressed the opinion that there was bound to be a row. It had got to come. [. . .]

17 October   Dined with LG at Cobham. Sir Arthur Crosfield[34] and his wife were there. Again much talk about the strike. LG said it was time for a lesson. The trouble was bound to come . These sentiments were heartily applauded by Sir Arthur Crosfield.

I said I doubted whether the Government quite realised what a strike meant and that it looked as if the railway men and transport workers would support the colliers. [. . .]

During the week, strike in full blast. Several interviews with Hartshorn and Brace. As I anticipated, efforts are now being made to arrive at a settlement. Secret meetings have been taking place between LG, Brace, Hartshorn and Hodges. I have been taking an active part in some of the discussions between the miners' leaders and the officials.

23 October   Golfed with LG, Eric Geddes and Sassoon at St George's Hill. The PM very anxious about the strike, as the railway men have threatened to come out tomorrow night. Before we started, numerous telephone calls from Bonar Law and Horne, asking LG to come to town. He, however, determined on having his game of golf, and gave instructions over the telephone as to what should be done. It was decided to write a letter to the miners, saying that the Government were still willing to negotiate. [. . .]

The Northcliffe Press today are out for a settlement of the strike and certain sections of the employers have told the Government that an early settlement is essential.

LG very critical about Northcliffe's actions, which he says make negotiations of this sort very difficult. He said, 'What is Northcliffe at? Is he veering over to the Labour Party?' [. . .]

Referring again to Northcliffe, LG said, 'Has he really been ill?' I said, 'Yes, he has had a swelling in his neck which has had to be removed.'

LG remarked, 'He has also got a swollen head. It is a pity they did not remove that too!'[35] [. . .]

We returned to Cobham for tea, and I afterwards drove to London with LG. We had a long chat. Evidently he was very uncomfortable about the strike situation. [. . .]

5 November Went to France with Lord Midleton[36] and other members of the War Memorials Commission to consider the sites and forms of memorials. [. . .] Simpson, President of the RIBA, said that old Lord Bryce had some funny habits. One of them was to stick his pipe in the fly of his trousers when he was not using it. [. . .]

11 November Campbell Stuart came to see me. [. . .] I told him [. . .] of my interview with Northcliffe.[37]

CS agrees with my views, and doubts whether anything in the nature of a formal reconciliation is possible. CS repeated that Wickham Steed is more violent than Northcliffe. Last night at the Guildhall after LG's speech, Wickham Steed was almost trembling with rage. He said, 'It is the speech of a politician, unworthy of the occasion.' [. . .]

13 November Spent the day with LG at Trent Park, Sassoon's place. LG much interested in my interview with Northcliffe. LG very angry with the French, and again repeated that France is anxious to resume her position as military dictator of Europe. He admitted, however, that Foch is an honest patriot who believes there will be another war, and that the French must be prepared for it. He again discussed the old question of the Rhine boundary and explained the reasons which had led him, Clemenceau and Wilson to decide in favour of the arrangements defined by the Treaty in preference to the adoption of Foch's plan of placing the bridgeheads over the Rhine in the possession of the French. LG repeated his old argument about the creation of another Alsace-Lorraine. I said that I did not believe the French people were unfriendly to us and that when in France my colleagues and I had received the greatest kindness on all hands. This, however, did not convince LG, who is very anti-French just now. [. . .]

14 November Again spent the day at Trent Park with the PM. Played golf with him and the American Ambassador, to whom LG put many questions regarding the state of public affairs in America and American public men.

There was much talk as to the position President Wilson will occupy in history. [. . .]

LG said he felt sure Wilson would occupy a great place in history. Neither he (LG) nor Clemenceau in connection with the Peace Conference had done any special thing which could be ear-marked as his work, whereas, for better or worse, Wilson had advocated an idea which had been embodied in the League of Nations. The League might fail, but it would be an historic fact. Davis agreed with this. [. . .]

20 November Spent the week-end at Lympne with LG. [. . .] The party consisted of LG, Mrs Rupert Beckett,[38] Miss Stevenson and myself. [. . .]

LG said the whole tendency of the world was reactionary. People wished to be let alone. They did not want remedial legislation. This he regretted, being a Liberal. He thought there would be a revulsion later on in favour of reform, and that in this country we should forestall this by passing legislation for the benefit of the people. He said the present state of feeling was the natural aftermath of the war, and that the action of the Bolsheviks had contributed to produce this effect. [. . .]

Mrs Beckett told an amusing story about the Welsh investiture [of the Prince of Wales]. It was a very hot day and the Queen looked tired and miserable. Mrs Beckett heard the King say to her, 'I say, cheer up, May! Or else they will again be saying that I have been beating you!' At the time there were all sorts of ridiculous stories circulating as to the King drinking, ill-treating the Queen, etc. The Queen smiled and at once cheered up.

On Sunday LG and I spent several hours alone together. He said that Bonar Law was pressing him to make it up with Beaverbrook, but that he had declined unless Beaverbrook apologised for having said that LG had conspired against a colleague (Chamberlain). LG had said that B was a cad, and apparently this had been repeated by Winston, who had also indiscreetly and erroneously recounted a conversation regarding Mrs Rupert Beckett's son-in-law, one Markham. [. . .]

On Monday morning, just as LG started to town, he said, 'Have you seen the *Express*? There is a most unscrupulous attack upon us in regard to our Irish policy. Beaverbrook suggests that we should withdraw from Ireland. I think I shall have to go for him in the House. I don't believe that the British people would tolerate such pusillanimous conduct!'

27 November Played a few holes with LG and Sassoon. [. . .] LG told me there was very little difference between the English and French policies regarding Constantine's[39] return. Neither nation was prepared to take naval or military action, and both recognised that the Greeks were entitled to select their own rulers. The proposal is to tell them that the Allies do not approve of the appointment of Constantine, and that if he is appointed they will not regard Greece in the same friendly spirit as they otherwise would. Having regard to Constantine's record, there will be a feeling of suspicion and uneasiness which will be calculated to interfere with amicable relations between the Allies and the Greeks. [. . .]

We had another talk about B[eaverbrook]. LG said that BL had been to him yesterday, and had again asked him to make up the quarrel and to meet B at dinner. BL had repeated that his relations with B were such that the situation was very difficult. LG was his friend and colleague, and if B was attacking him, it made matters very unpleasant. LG again told BL that he did not feel he could meet B unless he apologised for charging him (LG) with unworthy conduct in attacking a colleague. BL said that B did not put the same construction on what he had published as LG did. LG had replied that this was not equivalent to an apology. LG went on to say that he did not feel he could meet a man who had treated him badly and upon whom he could not rely. He had told BL that he hated personal quarrels and had always avoided them. BL however had remarked, 'If this quarrel develops, it will be very unpleasant for me [BL] to have to choose between you [LG] and B.' [. . .]

11 December Talked of Chamberlain as Chancellor of the Exchequer. LG said, 'He is very good in the House of Commons – a good Parliamentary speaker, but he is not a man to deal with stormy times. He has no initiative. He has no idea of adopting new measures and taking bold courses. . . .'

18 December Week-end at Trent Park with LG, Lord Dawson, Mrs Rupert Beckett and Miss Stevenson. [. . .]

LG gave a graphic account of a dinner which he had attended at Bonar Law's. Beaverbrook, Hamar Greenwood and, I think, one or two more were present.

LG: I went determined to do all the talking. Someone said, 'Who would be the best Viceroy for Ireland when the Home Rule Bill comes into force?' I at once replied, 'Northcliffe, the most eminent Irishman living. He has all the qualities for the post. He would not do at a time like this, but he would do well in the role of the great pacifier. He is energetic and can make himself very pleasant, and he is a man with big ideas. Furthermore, he has no history at the back of him which would tend to dim his efforts. He would come fresh to the task.' When I said this, I saw Beaverbrook's jaw drop. He expected to hear me run Northcliffe down and could not believe his ears. BL said, 'Whose leg are you pulling now?' I said, 'No one's! I am perfectly serious!' [40] [. . .]

We talked about the present naval programme, the subject of much discussion.

LG: [. . .] You must not push too hard. It would be a great mistake for the country to engage in a big ship-building programme at the moment. Naval construction is in a fluid state. We must ascertain how best we can spend our money. We cannot afford to enter into direct competition with America. [. . .]

[LG also] said, 'The League of Nations is the greatest humbug in history. They cannot even protect a little nation like Armenia. They do nothing but pass useless resolutions.' [. . .]

21 December   [. . .] At night as I was going to the House of Lords I met the Attorney-General [Sir Gordon Hewart], Beaverbrook and Chilcott. The AG and Chilcott asked me to go to the Lord Chancellor's room where we sat and talked for an hour. F.E. was very gracious. [. . .]

We then talked of Paris. F.E. said that when he went there in January 1919 he stood lower than he had ever done since he had been Chancellor. He knew that he was wrong in going to Paris without the PM's permission, but he did it for the best and the PM had no right to treat him as he had. He refused to see him and never invited him to dinner. [. . .] The breach had been healed long ago. . . . [Beaverbrook insisted that LG had been deliberately ungracious. When Riddell questioned this, Beaverbrook became very violent.]

The conversation then turned off on to other topics, but Beaverbrook's virulence was obvious. Evidently he hates LG and [. . .] I think he hates me too. The other three men were evidently very uncomfortable. [. . .]

Christmas Day   Spent the afternoon and dined with the PM at Downing Street. Rather a gloomy proceeding, strongly impregnated with the atmosphere of the offices downstairs. [. . .]

The PM was in fairly good spirits, but the festivity had an unnatural air. [. . .]

1921

Like the coalition Government itself, Riddell's diaries by now are exhibiting a loss of momentum. His growing estrangement from Lloyd George over major policy matters cannot be disguised, and the number of conversations with the Prime Minister is barely half that of two years earlier. Foreign issues continue, as in 1920, to account for many of the entries. German reparations caused difficulties with the French, who were bent on occupying the Ruhr, and Riddell in his capacity as Press liaison officer was present at many meetings between the leaders of France and Britain as they wrestled with this problem. And just as he questioned the wisdom of risking a quarrel with the French, so too Riddell could not share Lloyd George's pro-Greek proclivities in the face of rising Turkish nationalism. He continued to listen, but said little. A new opportunity arose in the autumn with the proposal that a disarmament conference should be held in Washington. Lloyd George decided not to go and he did not wish Riddell to go either. At this stage, however, Riddell saw his own importance increasing and that of Lloyd George diminishing, so he went to the Washington Conference in November. His work there was sufficiently valuable for A. J. Balfour, leader of the British delegation, to press Downing Street to direct him to stay longer than he intended.

A number of disparate entries about personalities provide rather more colour. Riddell witnessed an interesting ceremony early in the year when Lord and Lady Lee turned Chequers over to the nation, and at Easter there is an unusually revealing picture of a house party where the principal guest was the Prince of Wales. A published story about an intrigue against Lloyd George in which Churchill and Birkenhead were alleged to be the chief plotters brought fervent denials and assertions of loyalty from the Lord Chancellor. Lloyd George remained sceptical, however. When Sir Robert Horne was appointed Chancellor of the Exchequer Churchill's loyalty was further suspect for he coveted the place and did not hide his soreness. Another of the supposed plotters against Lloyd George was Beaverbrook, and when Bonar Law retired from the Government Mrs Lloyd George hazarded that this was due as much to Beaverbrook as to Law's health.

Throughout the year Lloyd George's animus towards Beaverbrook – 'an unreliable, poisonous little man' – becomes more marked. Another thread that appears repeatedly in Riddell's pages is Northcliffe's increasingly irrational behaviour and the consequent turmoil amongst his staff. The source of much of this information was Campbell Stuart, by no means a disinterested party. As always Riddell is keenly interested in the miners and includes some useful entries about the colliery discussions. The Irish negotiations of September round out the list of domestic subjects.

1 January   At Lympne, with LG, Winston, Sir Wm Sutherland and Miss Stevenson. Sir Hamar and Lady Greenwood came on Sunday. LG and Winston in great form. Sutherland brought with him gramophone records of speeches made by Harding,[1] the American President-elect, and other American politicians. We all sat round and listened to the speakers' nasal platitudes delivered through the gramophone horn. The interjections of the PM and Winston, shouted into the horn as the speeches progressed, most amusing. [. . .]

LG said that Harding's speech on American naval aspirations made him feel that he would pawn his shirt rather than allow America to dominate the seas. If this was to be the outcome of the League of Nations propaganda, he was sorry for the world and in particular for America. [. . .]

Much talk about Ireland. LG said that the Home Rule Act was the most important measure the Government had passed, and that he thought de Valera[2] recognised this. He had returned to Ireland, first, because he felt that the militant Sinn Feiners had been beaten, and second, because he was anxious to capture the Irish Parliament and be in a position to say, 'Look what we compelled them to give you!' [. . .]

Winston expressed himself as being strongly in favour of granting the fullest financial concessions to the Irish. He said it would be worth it, as the Irish question was doing us much injury abroad. [. . .]

Much talk about Ireland after Hamar Greenwood's arrival. He said the time had not arrived for a settlement. He was pushing on with the arrangements for holding the Irish Parliaments. He hoped that when the elections were held, Ireland would be in such a state that the electors would be able to record their votes without fear or favour. He also hoped that independent candidates would come forward in the South and that a representative Parliament would be elected. [. . . He added,] 'If we effect a premature settlement we may lose the benefit of all we have done. Ireland has been terrorised. We must free her from the terror. There are already signs that the Irish people are breathing more freely.'

8 January At Chequers. The PM's house-warming party.[3] Invited by Lord and Lady Lee after consultation with Mrs LG, J. T. Davies and others. Davis, the American Ambassador, and his wife, Reading, Milner, Sir Hamar and Lady Greenwood, Robert Horne, Lord and Lady Lee, the PM and Megan were there or imminent when I arrived about 7 o'clock. Mrs LG arrives tomorrow morning from North Wales. [. . .]

After dinner Lee made a speech of some length. He commenced by referring to the Spanish custom of saying to guests, 'Everything here is yours,' without of course meaning it. He said that on this occasion he could make the statement with perfect sincerity. In future, the house and its contents, dear as they were to Lady Lee and himself, would be the property of the Prime Minister and his successors. The final deed of gift was ready and would be signed after dinner. [. . .]

In replying to Lee, the PM thanked him and Lady Lee for their self-sacrifice and abnegation. [. . .] He spoke of the trials and tribulations of public life, and in particular of Prime Ministers. He said he had read the lives of many Prime Ministers, all of whom thought their burdens almost insupportable. He thought he was justified in saying that the task of a Prime Minister at the present time was far more onerous than that of any of his predecessors. He referred to the violence and malignity of the Press, which he said made life almost intolerable, and made public men feel that they must turn round and claw their adversaries. (Suiting the action to the word, he turned round and made a very tiger-like claw, no doubt directed at Northcliffe & Co.) [. . .]

After dinner Lee and Lady Lee signed the deed of gift, of which I was one of the witnesses, and signed their names in the Visitors' Book with an inscription, which was well done. After the deed was signed, Lee handed it to me and asked me to send it to the Secretary of the Trust. [. . .]

I went for a walk with Milner, who told me he was tired out and determined to have a rest. He thinks that most of the Ministers are tired, but that most of them have not worked as long as he has done. [. . .]

22 January Golfed with LG at Coombe Hill. [. . .]

We talked of the vacancies in the Cabinet. LG said it was very difficult to find men to fill them, there were so few of outstanding ability. [. . .]

Talked with LG about German reparations. The Foreign Office yesterday issued a statement that the Germans had accepted the proposal for the payment of one hundred and fifty millions per annum, and that the prospects of the Conference were therefore bright. LG said the real difficulty was fixing the total sum, that the French did not want to fix this as they did not want to inform the French public of the true position of affairs, that is that the sum receivable will be much less than the French imagine and the French public have been led to believe. In other words the Government do not want to let the French public know that they will have to bear a great part of the cost of the war themselves. The British Government, on the other hand, think there can be no effective settlement until the total has been fixed. LG expects a big fight on this point. [. . .]

23 January Travelled to Paris with the British Mission – LG, Curzon, etc. LG said that the six months he spent in Paris in 1919 was the happiest and most interesting period of his life. He had no doubt about that. [. . .]

25 January Dined with LG. Long talk about reparations. He said the French would not face the facts and persisted in saying that Germany must pay so much in cash without indicating how the payment could be made without ruining her own trade. [. . .] All France is seething with this question. The French politicians are full of promises, but the public do not understand the position, which has never been explained to them.

Yesterday the Conference after a long discussion referred the questions relating to the breaches of the naval, military and air clauses to experts to be presided over by Foch. Foch has now changed his mind regarding the air possibilities and has made a report, in which he says that the German aerial menace is more deadly than ever in its potential means of destruction, and that unless steps are taken to prevent the Germans from manufacturing aircraft they may at any minute destroy the *moral* of a nation by a sudden attack. [. . .]

Henry Wilson is very clear-headed. He is fully convinced that we shall have a war with America within the next twenty years.[4] He said it is bound to come. [. . .]

26 January A long talk on financial matters [. . .] with Worthington-Evans, who [. . .] is to be the new Minister of War. It was amusing to see him stalking up and down the room as he talked, very full of himself and exuding success and old brandy at every pore. He is certainly a capable man, and, as I have said before, quite a new thing in Ministers. [. . .] Dined with LG, Auckland Geddes, Hankey, Philip Kerr, Miss Stevenson and J. T. Davies.

Owing to the meagre character of the information given out on Monday, Tuesday and Wednesday [I] made strong representations as to importance of more complete disclosure of the doings of the Conference. I pointed out that the French and British publics were misinformed as to the attitude of the PM and the British representatives, and that Paris was therefore full of false rumours and poison gas. I also showed, by producing Havas messages, that French officials were not only giving out more information, but were selecting that which suited them, and were indicating to the French Press what line it should take. [. . .]

It was arranged that on the following day Kerr should attend the Conference and take full notes so as to be in a position to supply me with an adequate report of the proceedings. The PM said there had been an agreement that nothing should be published beyond a bare statement of the decisions arrived at. I said that if this was the agreement it had not been acted upon, and that if the French were not giving out information the Italians or Belgians were doing it. [. . .]

27 January Philip Kerr attended the Conference as arranged and made full notes. In the evening he and I prepared reports of the speeches made by LG and Briand – speeches of vital importance. The publication of these entirely altered the whole atmosphere of Paris and London. I drove back from the Conference with LG, who said he thought it undesirable to publish quite all that he had said, as the effect might be to bring about the downfall of the Briand Government. [. . .]

In preparing our report, Kerr and I toned down LG's observations somewhat, but their purport was evident. [. . .]

28 January Friday was a hectic day. The Conference did not sit, but the whole time was occupied in private conversations between the committee appointed by the Conference to report upon reparations, etc. LG, Briand and other members of the Conference. At last a conclusion was arrived at. [. . .]

I got full details of the proposed settlement from Worthington-
Evans and D'Abernon and communicated them to the Press. There
was a general feeling of exhilaration at the settlement. LG asked me to
dine with him, but I was unable to do so, as the British and American
Press were entertaining me to dinner – a very pleasant function at
which kind and complimentary things were said concerning my work
and especially what I had done for the Americans, who had no one to
represent them.

Elmer Roberts, Head of the Associated Press of America, gave me a
most thoughtful and lucid account of the situation between Gt Britain
and America – a subject on which he is very well informed. He regards
future possibilities as serious. [. . .] He therefore thought it vital that
the newspapers should be careful not to stir up bad feelings between
the two countries as he was afraid they were doing, and that every
effort should be made by the British Government to come to some
arrangement which would obviate the friction which he had described.
I asked him to write down what he had said, as I was anxious to give the
paper to the PM and Auckland Geddes. [. . .]

29 January   I went to the Quai d'Orsay where I had tea with the
delegates. After tea we went to the Salon d'Horloge, where the
agreement was signed. Everyone looked much relieved, but the truth is
that the whole thing is a bit of eye-wash to save Briand's face and to
meet LG's objection to making the German burden too heavy. Under
the Paris agreement I reckon that the Germans during the next five
years will pay much less than they would have paid under the Boulogne
agreement,but Briand cannot face a fixed sum, and LG will not agree
to the figure demanded by the French – hence the percentage
arrangement. International agreements and international politics are
strange things. Sometimes one thinks that the world is not run on
realities but on fictions suitable for immediate consumption. [. . .]

15 February   Important interview with Kerr and Sir William Tyrrell at
the Foreign Office, regarding forthcoming conferences – on the 21st
regarding Turkish questions, and on the 28th with the Germans. The
publicity arrangements are to be on the same lines as at the Continental conferences, but Vansittart,[5] Curzon's secretary, is to be
associated with Kerr, so that the FO will be kept in touch. We
discussed the permanent relations of the FO with the Press. We all
agreed that the existing arrangements were most unsatisfactory and

that, as a result, British newspapers were being used by foreign Governments to advocate their respective views; while on the other hand, the British case was not being represented. Tyrrell said that before and during the war the FO arrangements had worked satisfactorily. For a long period he himself had provided the Press with information. Since the Peace there had been no proper channel of information except at the Conferences when Philip Kerr had supplied me with information and had seen certain journalists in order to furnish them with the official view.

Tyrrell further said it was impossible for anyone to perform this task satisfactorily unless he was in the closest touch with the Foreign Secretary. It was essential that the person charged with this duty should have intimate knowledge of what was being done and of the Foreign Secretary's state of mind from day to day and hour to hour. The Private Secretary was the only person who had this information. I said that the Press would not accept a policy from individuals. This was contrary to tradition. But they would pay attention to the FO view. For that reason it was most important that there should be a well-informed and recognised medium of communication. [. . .] Tyrrell and Kerr agreed and the latter said it was essential that the new system should be set up immediately, so that it would be in working order when the FO resumed full control of foreign affairs. Therefore it was agreed that Vansittart should work with Kerr and that the statements for the Press should be supplied by the two jointly. [. . .]

LG is overburdened and the sooner the administration of foreign affairs reverts to the Foreign Office the better. For the past two years the work has been mainly done by Lloyd George, Philip Kerr, Sir Maurice Hankey and his staff. The FO has become more or less a cypher. [. . .] The truth is that during the conferences Hankey and his staff have in a great measure superseded the Foreign Office.

19 February To Chequers. Long talk with LG. Much excited as to the Cardigan election, in which [Ernest] Evans, his secretary, is opposing Llewelyn Williams.[6] The result expected every minute when I arrived. Mrs LG has been working like a Trojan in the constituency, delivering fifty-eight speeches in a fortnight. While LG and I were walking in the park, Mrs LG came running out breathless, to tell him that Evans had won by a majority of 3,500. He was delighted and said that if the result had been the other way it would have been a serious personal set-back. He warmly embraced Mrs LG, bestowing several hearty kisses upon her and telling her that she had won the election. [. . .]

Much talk about newspapers as usual. LG said that he heard that Hulton was not only seriously ill but financially embarrassed by heavy overdrafts, etc. He said that he thought Beaverbrook was very anxious to get hold of the Hulton business, which would be a calamity. LG had sent a message to Hulton of a discreet character telling him that if he wanted financial assistance LG would provide it.

He said, 'Guest has done remarkably well. We have got ample funds in the coffers, and they could not be better spent than in this way.' He said that Beaverbrook was trying to stir up trouble all the time and that he was a dangerous person. [. . .]

21 to 25 February   A great week in one way. Kerr and I have really pulverised secret diplomacy, and by hook or crook have succeeded in extracting and publishing all that happened at the Greco-Turkish Conference [at St James's Palace]. [. . .]

I have also secured a victory in getting a fine room for the Press in the Palace itself and tea for the Press.

1 March   Meeting with the Germans at Lancaster House to discuss Reparations. I stood in the Gallery adjoining the Conference Room, the door of which was open, so I heard von Simons's[7] speech and the translations. The speech was tactless and ill-advised, and made a very bad impression. When LG came out, he said to me, 'What a people they are! They always do the wrong thing! Their proposals are absurd. They have done their best to alienate the sympathies of those who were in favour of moderation. I shall give them Hell for this. We are not going to be jack-booted by the Germans!'

Kerr gave me a detailed account of the speech, from which I prepared the statement issued to the Press.

4 March   Meeting with the Turks and the Greeks at St James's Palace. They did not meet each other in the Conference Room, but we all had tea together, and there were no indications of any ill-feeling. The Greeks declined the proposal of the Conference to appoint a Commission. The Turks accepted it. I asked LG what was to happen next. He said, 'They are Orientals. We are going to let matters simmer for a bit, but I shall see the Turkish and Greek representatives informally.' [. . .]

10 March   The Conference [with the French] was held in Bonar Law's room at the House of Commons. They began late as LG was speaking in the House of Commons. I arrived about 7.30 and found him storming up and down his room next to Bonar Law's, loudly complaining that he had been deserted by his secretaries and that no arrangements had been made for dining the Conference. He said, 'Just think of it! Here am I with all these responsibilities and no one to help me! It is scandalous I should be left to arrange for a dinner!' Then he went and gazed moodily out of the window. Meanwhile the Conference was going on in the next room. On going downstairs I found that arrangements had been made. [. . .] LG asked me to dinner. I dashed down to St James's Palace, gave the Press an account of the proceedings and then returned [to the House of Commons]. [. . .]

17 March[8]   LG came to me today and said, 'We have sent for Foch. You had better let the Press know. It will put the fear of God into the Germans. You can say that we have sent for him so that we can consult him about the enforcement of the Treaty – say the sanctions.'

19 March   To Chequers. [. . .] Nothing very special happened worth recording, except that I noticed that LG's attitude to the working classes has changed in a measure. Notwithstanding his speech about the danger of Communism, he is much more sympathetic than he was. [. . .]

27 March (Easter Sunday)   The Prince of Wales came down. It was a curious party. *Dramatis Personae*: the Prince of Wales; Sir Philip Sassoon, wealthy young Jew; Lloyd George, formerly village boy, now Prime Minister, at one time advocate of the working classes and antagonist of millionaires; Lady Ribblesdale, wealthy American, with dress down to her middle, heavily powdered and painted, rather apprehensive of modern-day movements; Macdonald, dilettante member of the aristocracy; Gubbay, shrewd commercial Jew – a very nice little man, with mind chiefly intent upon income tax; Mrs Gubbay, clever Jewess with philosophy of life all worked out; Evelyn Fitzgerald, genial stockbroker and man of the world, secretary to Jack Cowans during the war, great man with the ladies; Miss Stevenson, with her wonderful history – descended from French officer who was Legion of Honour when serving under Napoleon I, began life as a teacher in a small school; Sir Robert Horne, political adventurer and son of a

Presbyterian minister; Dudley Ward, grandson of the late Lord Esher, with long descent, rowed in university boat; Mrs Dudley Ward, daughter of Nottingham lace manufacturer, now moving in the highest society – a clever, perceptive sort of woman, but outwardly childish and frivolous, always on the move, always singing, dancing, smoking, talking or playing tennis. The PoW and Sassoon very thick with her, but the true inwardness of the ménage I don't pretend to understand.[9]

He [LG] has appointed Sassoon a trustee of the National Gallery, which has given the latter much pleasure. He came to see me on the Thursday and asked me to get into touch with the newspapers, so as to prevent adverse criticism. I spoke to one or two of the Editors including Steed of *The Times*, who made some facetious observations. [. . .] Nothing vicious appeared. [. . .]

The PM spent much time sleeping or in his own room. Nothing very exciting took place in the way of conversation. [. . .]

3 April   Burnham arrived. He, LG and I went for a walk and subsequently had tea together. Much talk of the coal strike and labour situation.

I congratulated Burnham on the arrangement he had arranged for the school teachers.[10] He told us they were much happier now, and that increased remuneration had done much to soften their feelings. Burnham strongly criticised the economy campaign in regard to education. He said that it was absurd, and that Rothermere and his satellites were ignorant of the facts and very shortsighted.

LG strongly agreed with this. He paid Burnham compliments about the *Telegraph* on its sanity, and on the amount of reading matter. [. . .]

Much talk of Ireland.

Burnham and I both agreed that it would be difficult for the PM to see Collins,[11] particularly as it would be necessary to give him a safe conduct. [. . .]

Burnham: Do you really think you are getting these people under?

LG: It is difficult to say. [. . .] Shrewd observers say it will take twelve months. The question is whether the people of this country are prepared to go on for twelve months. [. . .] I see no alternative but to fight it out. [. . .] A republic at our doors is unthinkable. [. . .]

In the evening, long quiet chat with LG. [. . .]

LG: I should not mind going out now, provided I did not go out discredited. I would not mind going out on some question on which I feel strongly. A question of this sort is about to arise on the Railway Bill. [. . .]

5 April   Lunched with Vernon Hartshorn, who gave me an account of the points in dispute. He put a very different face on the pumping situation. He explained that the masters had given the safety-men notice and posted notices on the pits stating that any man who went on working did so on the new terms. Of course the men would not do this pending a settlement.

I drove off to Downing Street and dictated a memorandum to Sylvester,[12] the new secretary, defining the points in difference, and repeating what Hartshorn had said. I saw the PM and explained the matter to him. He told Sylvester to send the memorandum to him at the House of Commons. LG much surprised to learn that the movement is not one of extremists, but that the men at the back of it are old-fashioned miners like Hartshorn, Stephen Walsh,[13] Tom Richards,[14] etc. The PM said, 'We will do anything that can be done, except resume control and subsidise the mines.' [. . .]

17 April   To Chequers. Mrs LG, Megan and Miss Cazalet. [. . .]

Mrs LG told me that she thought Bonar Law's illness had been accentuated by his difficulties with Beaverbrook. The position was becoming intolerable for BL. It was difficult for him to continue working with LG when Beaverbrook was making covert attacks upon him. She said, 'No doubt Bonar Law was ill, but I wonder whether he would have resigned had it not been for Beaverbrook?'

22 April   To Lympne, arriving at 9.30. LG, Sir Philip Sassoon and Miss Stevenson. Much talk about the miners' dispute.

I said that the Board of Trade and Coal Control Department had badly bungled matters. Their information had been wrong. They had thought that the miners were bluffing. Consequently they had let the nation slip over the precipice. The dispute should have been settled before decontrol. I thought Horne and Bridgeman[15] had handled the matter badly.

LG agreed. He said he did not know that the dispute was serious until it was too late to take action. He said that Hartshorn had had dinner with him on the previous evening. He had told him that the miners were very angry with Horne and much disliked him. [. . .] LG said that Bridgeman was quite inadequate for the position, but that Bonar Law had insisted upon his appointment. [. . .] Strong about the order of precedence. [. . .]

A long talk about the Conference tomorrow.

LG: I have received a protest against the proposed occupation of the Ruhr, signed by Asquith, Lord Robert Cecil and Barnes, and there is a strong feeling in the provincial Press. The French are anxious to enter the Ruhr at all costs, I am afraid. [. . .] I support the Paris terms. The Germans will have to carry them out. The French are now talking of tearing them up and making fresh demands. I cannot agree to that. [. . .]

LG then sent for the German Note regarding French reparations, just received. He said, 'You might let the Press know about this. In fact there is no reason why you should not let them have a copy if you like.'

After reading the document through, to see that it contained nothing that should not be disclosed, he gave it to me, and I telephoned the contents to London – three-quarters of a column of *The Times*. [. . .]

24 April   After the morning Conference on Sunday I walked up and down the terrace with LG and Philip Kerr.

LG: The French are most unbusinesslike. They have got no plan. I had to ask Berthelot[16] to draw up a document setting forth what they wished to do, and I had to supplement this by a scheme prepared by our own people who were working at it until twelve last night.

I told LG that I was not at all sure that the French were unbusinesslike. I thought it was their plan of action to be indefinite. They want to get into the Ruhr. They don't want to be tied up by any conditions. Too much definition probably does not suit their purpose. LG had said that the French talked nothing but platitudes. I remarked that platitudes might best serve their purpose at the moment.

In the event nothing definite was settled. Everything stands over for the Supreme Council on Saturday. [. . .]

LG said that Winston is very disgruntled. He thinks he should have had the Chancellorship. Beaverbrook is endeavouring to stimulate his dissatisfaction. Beaverbrook's great fear is that LG will have an early election and thus secure himself in power for some time to come. [. . .]

I hear that Philip Kerr is going to the *Daily Chronicle*. LG discussed this project with me some time ago. I mentioned the matter to Kerr, who did not deny that I was right. He is to be succeeded by Sir Edward Grigg,[17] who has been secretary to the Prince of Wales and was formerly on *The Times*. I said to Kerr that the old order was changing and would never be revived. LG's relations with his staff were tending to become more formal. I have had a pleasant association with Kerr. We have done good work together. A clever, honourable, high-minded man, although rather fantastic in some of his ideas. He said that LG is becoming a real autocrat, and that none of the Ministers really pulls his weight in the Cabinet. They are all superior clerks. Kerr has the highest opinion of LG's ability, and regards him as a sort of superman. [. . .]

5 May   A very busy week. The Conference started on Saturday and continued day by day until today, on several occasions sitting until very late. On the last day we finished at midnight.

It was interesting to watch the by-play of the various interests. Sir Alfred Mond was one of the strongest advocates for enforcing strict terms against the Germans, Winston taking the opposite line. Mond said to me, 'I know the Germans, there is only one way to deal with them. You must hit them over the head. I have no patience with Winston and the others who are anxious to treat them lightly, etc, etc.' [. . .]

It was obvious from what I heard that the French are bent on occupying the Ruhr if they can, by hook or by crook. They hate the Germans; they have no faith in them; they believe that at the first opportunity they will seek revenge; and the French think that in default of any guarantee for the future their best plan is to smash Germany while they have the chance. [. . .]

LG was very anxious to get the Americans back into the Conference. He said, 'That would help me to manage the French. At present my position is very difficult. The French want to take a course which in my opinion would cause another conflagration. It is difficult for me, single-handed, to withstand them. The Americans will be valuable allies.'

14 May   To Chequers. [. . .] We [LG and R] had a long chat before dinner. He said that Winston is very angry that Horne has been appointed Chancellor of the Exchequer, and that he should not be surprised if Winston resigned, with a section of the Conservatives who are tired of the LG régime because they think it too democratic. Winston might try to lead them and form a combination with Birkenhead. [. . .]

[LG said:] I think Beaverbrook is influencing Hulton. The *Evening Standard* have not been very friendly. I shall make the position quite clear to Hulton. When he got his baronetcy he wanted to have the remainder appointed to his son, who is illegitimate. I found great difficulty doing this. The Palace are very sticky about such things and I have been unable to find any precedent. I shall tell him quite plainly that if he attacks me I shall take no further trouble.[18] I have no doubt Beaverbrook has told him that if he wants to get this thing done he had better attack me. But he is mistaken. [. . .]

15 May   Had a long talk with Horne. He expressed surprise that the miners were so unfriendly towards him. I told him that he had made Hartshorn an enemy by declining to listen to his advice, and that the miners were under the impression that he, Horne, was strongly in favour of the masters, for one reason because they believed he was on the point of becoming engaged to Lady Markham,[19] the big colliery owner. [. . .] Horne said that he had been brought up with colliers, that his father, a Scotch minister in a mining village, had always championed their claims, and that his brother had worked in a coal mine as an ordinary collier, gradually rising to the position of colliery manager. [. . .]

Hodges and other miners' leaders are expected here tomorrow. LG told me that he had no wish to starve the miners into submission, and that he is anxious to make a settlement that will satisfy them and thus avoid further disputes. [. . .]

Lady Markham arrived for the occasion. Rather unfortunate from the point of view of the colliery negotiations. The next morning a message came from Hodges and Co. to say they were not coming. The PM at once said that he thought they had been frightened off by seeing in the newspapers the names of the party at Chequers, and that evidently they thought the scene was being prepared for them. [. . .]

13 June   To Chequers. [. . .] Saw LG. He said, speaking at large, 'I cannot get into touch with Addison. He is under the impression that he is a popular hero, whereas in fact he is nothing of the sort.' From this observation I gathered that Dr Addison is going to be thrown to the wolves. [. . .][20]

23 June   Evan Williams, President of the Coal Owners' Association, and Hartshorn came to lunch. Had a long talk extending over two hours. Friendly, but Hartshorn evidently very bitter at the failure of the strike. Evan Williams spoke in a very fair way. They both agreed that unless masters and men are prepared to co-operate to re-establish the industry, the results are likely to be very serious. [. . .]

24 June [. . .] Saw Miss Stevenson at Downing Street. Asked her concerning the story of an intrigue against LG. She said it was quite true – that LG knew what had been going on. The article in the *Manchester Guardian* [21] was well informed. They wondered who wrote it. Evidently the writer had inside information. The parties to the intrigue had been Winston, Birkenhead, Beaverbrook, McKenna and, they thought, Addison. The plot was to prevail upon LG to resign on the grounds of his health and to appoint Winston PM. This, however, resolved itself into a scheme to appoint Birkenhead. The change led to the defection of Winston and the break-up of the cabal. LG had been well informed. [. . .] Birkenhead had written a letter to the PM disclaiming the intrigue, but LG had evidence that the letter was inaccurate.[22] [. . .]

9 July To Chequers with Hankey. A big party in connection with the Imperial Conference. The Overseas Premiers were there with their wives., [. . .]

10 July [. . .] My wife and I went to lunch with Lord Burnham [at Hall Barn,] where there was a large party, including the American Ambassador and Sir Campbell Stuart of *The Times*.

LG telephoned to say he would come over to Hall Barn to see the Ambassador, but the latter said he would prefer to go to Chequers. He told my wife that a momentous public announcement would be made today or tomorrow regarding the suggested Conference between Gt Britain, America, Japan and China concerning Eastern affairs and disarmament. We left Burnham's at about 4 o'clock. The Ambassador sent a message by me to LG saying that he would start for Chequers immediately his despatches arrived. When I got to Chequers I found the party having tea under the trees. [. . .]

In due course the Ambassador arrived with his wife at about 7 o'clock. LG at once went off with him for a private confab. They both returned looking very elated. Dinner was served on the lawn with Chinese lanterns spread about among the trees. [. . .] Before dinner LG took me aside to explain that President Harding was about to convene a Conference [on the limitation of armaments] and that the announcement was to be sent out tonight by the American Government. He said the idea had originated in the Imperial Conference, and that he, on behalf of the Conference, had addressed letters to the United States, Japan and China asking for their views. It was important that, while President Harding should not be robbed of the honour of acting with promptitude, the public both here and in America should appreciate the part which had been played by the British Empire. It was arranged that I should communicate with the newspapers. Grigg drew up a short memorandum which I issued through the Press Association and subsequently I rang up the London morning newspapers for the purpose of explaining the position to them and of warning them that they might expect to receive later on the announcement from the American Government. [. . .] I was busy telephoning until nearly 11.30 p.m. Meanwhile Grigg and Hankey were busy preparing the PM's statement for the House of Commons on the following day.

Altogether an interesting and historic day. [. . .]

13 July   Violent articles in *The Times* today against LG and Curzon, suggesting that the former is the most mistrusted man in the world, and that the latter's haughty bearing makes him unsuitable for international conferences. *The Times* contends that neither LG nor Curzon should be permitted to attend the conference regarding Far Eastern affairs and disarmament.

I lunched with Northcliffe and sat next to Andrew Caird, who referred to the articles which he described as futile and objectionable. [. . .]

Later Northcliffe rang me up and asked me to inform the PM that he, Northcliffe, strongly disappoved of these articles, which he said had been written by a wild Irishman who had been censured. N asked me to represent to the PM that he should refrain from making fun of *The Times* and said that *The Times* staff have no sense of humour. [. . .]

17 July   Dined with Campbell Stuart at his house. [. . .] Stuart had not heard of N's conversation with me. He said it was not true that the article had been written by an Irishman. It had been written or inspired by Steed, who is absolutely obsessed with hatred and distrust of LG. Stuart says that Steed has been in virtual control of *The Times* for the past twelve months, and that N has had very little to do with the policy of the paper. Ultimately N felt so strongly about this particular article that Stuart thinks that Steed would have lost his job had it not been for Curzon's action in boycotting *The Times*, which brought about a revulsion of feeling on the part of N. Stuart thinks, however, that Steed will talk N over, and that the result will be that Steed will be at

Washington when the Conference takes place, and that he may be a thorn in LG's side. [. . .]

One day in week commencing July 18   Met LG at Downing Street. We spoke about the Washington Conference. He said, 'Of course you will go for the papers.' I replied, 'Yes.' He then went on to say that the Imperial Conference had had a meeting that morning, and that he, Smuts, Hughes and Massey[23] did not intend to allow the British Empire to take a back seat. Gt Britain had won the war. She had made enormous sacrifices in men and money, and they were quite determined that she should not be overshadowed by America. 'At the next Conference with the French,' said LG, 'I mean to say that it was a pity we did not come into the war in the fourth year instead of the first. Then we should have been properly appreciated. [. . .] I don't mean to see the old country put into the background. [. . .] Hughes, Massey and Smuts quite agree with me.'

26 July   Lunched with Campbell Stuart. [. . .] He said things have developed very seriously at *The Times*. Long, the foreign editor, was going. [. . .] Last night Northcliffe cabled an article from America [. . .] but CS has ordered it out of *The Times* and the other editions of the *DM*. Marlowe, the editor of the latter, is away. Sutton agreed to this course, provided CS took the lead, which he had no hesitation in doing, as he thought the article most ill-advised and dangerous. He said, 'This may mean that I shall lose my job. It is unheard of that an article cabled by Northcliffe should not be inserted. [. . .]'

28 July   Saw LG at Downing Street. With reserves gave him an account of what transpired with Campbell Stuart.
    LG had read the article. He said that the Attorney-General advised him that it was a seditious libel. If Northcliffe had been here he would have prosecuted him, but doubted the wisdom of prosecuting people who were not really responsible. Therefore he proposed to bring a civil action for libel against the *Daily Mail*. [. . .] LG said he is not going to the Supreme Council meeting.
    LG: In the minds of the French these meetings have developed into a sort of Dempsey-Carpentier engagements. I am always supposed to be getting the best or trying to get the best of the French champion for the time being. They have put up Clemenceau, Millerand, Leygues, Briand, etc, and it is always represented that I am getting in a knock-

out blow. The consequence is that the French representatives are afraid to be reasonable because they fear it will again be said that I have defeated them. Our people do not regard the meetings in this way, and, so far as I am concerned, my only object is to make the best possible arrangements in the interests of all concerned. The whole thing is most unfortunate. [. . .]

31 July To Chequers. Much talk of the Northcliffe-Steed incident. [. . .] LG considers that Northcliffe and Steed have done themselves an enormous amount of harm, and said it was a serious thing to have two wild men gyrating round the world making poisonous statements concerning their own country. He said 'It has always been the same since January 1919. I offended Steed's vanity by declining to take his advice, and he is a bitter, fanatical enemy.'

He said, 'I had a bit of fun with Winston. Beaverbrook printed the article in the *Express* – a dirty trick. I told Winston, who is thick with Beaverbrook, that the Law Officers had advised that the article was a seditious libel, and that we should probably proceed against the *Mail* and *Express*. This made Winston look very thoughtful. I have no doubt that he communicated what I had said to Beaverbrook, because during the next few days the *Express* contained laudatory articles about me. Beaverbrook cannot be trusted. He is an unreliable, poisonous little man, and I would rather go into opposition than co-operate with him. He is certain to do you in.' LG is going to the Conference in Paris. He told me the French have urgently desired him to go, as they think that, unless he does so, it will be thought that there is rift between Gt Britain and France. [. . .]

2 August The Lord Chancellor asked me to see him in his private room at the House of Lords.

I congratulated him on his speech on Lord Crewe's motion that the Government business should be postponed to an autumn session – defeated by 124 to 79.

F.E.: I hope you will tell the PM that I made a good speech and did my utmost for the Government. I really think that if I had not spoken as I did the results might have been different. [. . .] I want you to tell the PM this because a number of mischievous people are putting about the report that I am caballing against him. It is an absolute untruth. All my interest lies in supporting him. [. . .] I should like to see him go to America and make a great success of the Conference and then go to the country on his return. I should like to see him win the election and remain in power for three or four years or as long as he wanted to remain. After that I should feel that my time had come. You can tell him that secret intrigue is foreign to my nature. What I have to say, I say openly. Furthermore, I am loyal to my friends and I am loyal to him. I want you to tell him all this and to remove from his mind any feeling which may have been engendered by false and malicious reports that I have been caballing against him. [. . .]

7 August With LG, Curzon and Robert Horne to Paris, to attend meeting of the Supreme Council. I to represent the Press as usual. American journalists very insistent that I should go. On my arrival all the newspaper men, British and American, gave me a hearty welcome.

LG in great form on the journey, and we had an amusing lunch. Curzon is first-rate company, and I never find him pompous. [. . .]

Our mission very anti-French regarding the Silesian question, which is the main point for discussion. LG vows he will not give way, and the French are equally insistent on their point of view. Everyone in Paris very excited and the gloomiest apprehensions are expressed regarding the probability of a rupture. [. . .]

7 August (cont'd) [24] Philip Kerr's duties have been taken over by Sir Edward Grigg, who proves more easy to deal with than Kerr. Grigg gives me practically a verbatim report of the proceedings. [. . .] It looks as if there will be a deadlock over Silesia. LG is still very pro-Greek and much elated at the Greek military successes. He said we always regarded the Turk as a first-class fighting man but even here he has broken down. LG told me he believes the Greeks will capture Constantinople, and he evidently hopes they will. He induced the Council to declare neutrality and was careful [to say], when informing me of this, that neutrality would not prevent British nationals from assisting the Greeks with money and munitions. Evidently the era of peace has not yet arrived. [. . .]

11 and 12 August Day of great interest. LG in conference with Briand all the morning. At lunch he went off to Rambouillet to lunch with the President. [. . .] On his return there was a further conference, and later it was announced that LG was returning to England on the following morning, owing to the Irish Question. The announcement caused enormous excitement, particularly as I understood in the first instance that the whole mission were going, which proved to be an error.

On Friday morning there was a further conference, after which I saw LG. [. . .] He said, 'The Silesian question is to be referred to the League of Nations. What do you think of that?' I thought he was joking, but he assured me he was serious. I came out and made the announcement to some of the newspaper people, all of whom greeted it with derision. But later on I made the announcement formally. [. . .]

19 August Lunched with Lord Lee at the Admiralty. [. . .]

He is very concerned about the Washington Conference. [. . . He] is most anxious that LG should go to Washington, or, failing that, Arthur Balfour. Of course he wants to go himself. [. . .] He told me quite privately that Beatty is very difficult to get on with, and that the relations between them are very strained. [. . .]

26 August [. . .] LG said he had had some quite nice friendly talks with Asquith lately. Asquith agreed with him that Briand had made a mistake to take office. [. . .]

29 August Went on with LG and Mrs LG to Blair Atholl, where we remained until Wednesday, when we motored to Inverness. The Duke and Duchess most kind and hospitable. [. . .]

The Duchess is a most talented person and a very hard worker. She is a brilliant pianist and has composed some excellent music. She is also a member of the Education Authority and several other local bodies. Although she has such artistic qualities, she has a legal mind and is, I think, one of the cleverest women I have ever met. We had a long talk about rating, and she astonished me by her knowledge of legal technicalities. She is said to be an eloquent speaker. LG strongly urged her to go into the House of Commons, and she seems disposed to take his advice.[25] [. . .]

1 to 6 September From Inverness we motored to Gairloch.

We found that the Sinn Fein representatives were already there with De Valera's reply. J. T. Davies was despatched to the hotel to fetch them to the house, and in about a quarter of an hour they arrived, walking up the carriage drive, one on each side of J.T. [. . .] They handed the reply to LG, and were out of the house in a few minutes. [. . .]

LG handed me the reply and asked me what I thought of it. I said, 'It looks as if they want a conference, but desire to show a bold front to their followers.' I added that I thought the letter showed they did not intend to insist upon a republic, but to suggest some other method of government involving Irish freedom, with a link between Gt Britain and Ireland.

LG did not agree with this, and said he thought they intended to fight. [. . .]

During Friday, Saturday, Sunday and Monday, everyone was busily engaged discussing the Irish Question, including Macready, who arrived in a destroyer. LG proposed holding a Cabinet at Dingwall to consider the Government's answer. I said this would be a mistake, and suggested Inverness, the capital of the North, with which LG agreed. [. . .]

At Gairloch LG was very full of plans for dealing with Ireland should the conference break down. I told him privately that while I was convinced that 95 per cent of the British public were strongly in favour of enforcing the maintenance of the union between Gt Britain and Ireland, they would not be prepared to support anything in the nature of devastation. [. . .] They would not be prepared to combat outrage with outrage. [. . .]

6 September [. . .] After the Cabinet meeting, LG sent for me and gave me the material for a statement to the Press. He would not give me the contents of the letter, as he said they were to be kept secret until they reached the hands of the Sinn Feiners. I asked him whether his colleagues and the officials could be relied upon to keep secrecy. He said, 'Of course they can. I won't tell you about the letter now, because I will tell you about it tomorrow.' I made my statement to the Press and returned to the hotel. Within ten minutes one of the newspaper men told me privately what the contents of the letter were, and it was obvious from what was published in various papers on the following morning that a copy of the letter must have been given out or shown to a journalist. In addition, information as to what took place must have been supplied by some person at the Cabinet. [. . .]

8 September To Brahan Castle to get a copy of reply for distribution to the Press. Found the PM and Winston in conclave. I told them that the note had escaped. They were much surprised and expressed strong views. They wanted to know what I thought of the letter. I said, 'Very good but not as clear as it might have been for the ordinary man, and I think, the introduction of the word "tribalism" doubtful.' The PM said it was a difficult letter to write. [. . .]

13 September   The Irish delegates arrived with De Valera's letter. LG was out fishing. [. . .] They came to Flowerdale [where LG was staying] at about 6 o'clock and handed him the letter in the secretaries' room. He brought it into the drawing-room and, after reading it, handed it to Grigg and me and asked our opinion of it. We both said that the letter was most unsatisfactory, inasmuch as it insisted upon the Irish delegates being received at the Conference as representatives of an independent nation. That admission would establish a point in favour of the Irish which the Cabinet were determined not to concede, as they were only prepared to enter the Conference on the basis of Ireland remaining a part of the British Empire.

LG: That is just my opinion. I shall tell them to treat the letter as not having been delivered and to take it back to De Valera and explain to him and his colleagues that they have made a mistake in writing such a letter and had better redraft it. [. . .]

The delegates then set off for Inverness, where J.T. Davies is staying. We telegraphed to him asking him to arrange for the Irish delegates to get through on the telephone to Dublin, which they succeeded in doing at about 1 o'clock in the morning. But meanwhile the letter had been disclosed, so that the die was cast and the letter became a *fait accompli*.

15 September   LG and Grigg busy drafting an answer to De Valera's last letter. Grigg asked me to look through the draft, in which I suggested one or two alterations, of which LG appoved. By this time the correspondence had developed into a telegraphic controversy which nearly wrecked the small Gairloch post-office. But it is only fair to say that the local postmistress rose to the occasion and did the work extremely well.

On the Friday afternoon a further letter arrived by telegraph from De Valera. On the Saturday LG replied by telegram. Later De Valera sent another letter, the reply to which was drafted on the Sunday. [. . .]

Meanwhile another letter had arrived from De Valera. As this was to be the final declaration by the Government, the draft was a matter of serious consideration. Its terms were discussed at length by the Ministers present at Gairloch. Birkenhead arrived in [Sir R. P.] Houston's yacht.[. . .] Several draft letters were prepared and placed side by side on the same piece of paper. Ultimately the final draft was evolved and sent out to the Cabinet for their approval. [. . .]

Much talk about Washington. Winston strong that LG should go. Incidentally A. J. Balfour came under notice. LG said he heard that AJB was dominating the League of Nations. Winston said, that if you wanted nothing done, AJB was undoubtedly the best man for the task. There was no one to equal him.

The Ministers evidently did not enjoy Gairloch and presented a somewhat disconsolate appearance. [. . .]

14 October Sir Campbell Stuart and Sir Harold Boulton[26] [. . .] lunched with me. [. . .]

Campbell Stuart told me that Wickham Steed had been very difficult since his return, and that he departs for America on 5 November with Mme Rose.[27] He says that Steed is very thick with Beatty, who has given him (Steed) an account of Beatty's interview with the King prior to his departure for Washington. He also said that Stamfordham had written a very friendly letter to Steed since his return, acknowledging a memorandum which Steed had sent to him regarding the state of affairs in America, and that Steed had read this letter at *The Times'* conference. CS predicted a tremendous row at Washington, as he has heard that Lee and Beatty are on bad terms. Consequently Steed will no doubt be putting forward the Beatty point of view. [. . .]

16 October To Chequers – the PM, Mrs LG, Olwen and Megan. [. . .]

He had been busy dictating his unemployment speech – a long business. He said his intention was to go to Washington, but that it was impossible to say what might happen between now and the date of sailing. Much depended on the Irish Conference. Honestly he could not say any progress had been made. His experiences during the discussion with De Valera had been repeated. He could get nothing definite. The delegates were impossible people. They came to the point, but would not come to decisions. He really could not say why. He could not say whether they did not want to do so, or whether they were afraid to do so. Secret advices from Ireland stated that there was a schism in the ranks of the Sinn Feiners. The moderate section wanted a settlement, whereas the gunmen did not. Arthur Griffith[28] was no doubt the leader, but unfortunately he had no power of expression. It was difficult to understand what he said. He spoke rather like John Rowland (formerly the PM's secretary – a clever, but incoherent, Welshman).[29] Michael Collins was undoubtedly a considerable person. LG thinks that during the next fortnight the Irish Conference will come to a termination one way or another. He said that if a settlement is reached he may have to stay to get it through the House of Commons, as there may be considerable opposition.

We talked of Washington. I said that Beatty and Wickham Steed were [. . .] rather thick. [. . .] I also told the PM what he did not know – namely that Lee and Beatty were at daggers drawn. [. . .] LG said that he had always thought Beatty unsuitable for his position. [. . .] He is fond of the limelight.

We spoke of Henry Wilson. I said he is very disgruntled just now. He is angry about Ireland and the state of the world generally, which of course he ascribes to the 'little Frocks'.[30] I referred to a speech which I had heard Wilson make the other night at the Guildhall.

LG: Yes, he is very difficult. I am not sorry he is going. His time is up in January.[31] [. . .]

21 October Lord Lee sent for me regarding the *Daily Telegraph* correspondent at Washington. Repington is going for the *Telegraph*. Lee said that he could not be trusted; that he had shown that he could not keep a confidence; and that it was a serious thing that the *Daily Telegraph* should be represented by such a man. [. . .]

23 October Went to Cliveden to lunch with Lord and Lady Astor. The PM, Mrs LG, Grigg, Philip Kerr and others were present. [. . .]

Lady A is an extraordinary person in her way. She has completely captured the 'Round Table' set, who were there in strong force. Grigg, Philip Kerr, Brand,[32] and later Geoffrey Dawson. [. . .]

LG in talking of the group remarked, 'It is a very powerful combination – in its way perhaps the most powerful in the country. Each member of the Group brings to its deliberations certain definite and important qualities, and behind the scenes they have much power and influence.'

30 October To Chequers to lunch. [. . .]

Much talk with the PM about Ireland. I am booked to sail in the *Aquitania* on Saturday. Both he and Sutherland not in favour of my going. The PM said that anything may happen shortly, and that he thought I should be more useful here than in America. He thought the Washington Conference would open with a great blare of trumpets, that the papers would be full of reports for a week or so, and then that the proceedings would begin to lose interest. [. . .]

LG: In the course of the next few days I may have to come to a vital decision. The points are these. It looks as if the Sinn Feiners will accept the sovereignty of the King, that they will agree to remain as part of the British Empire, and will also agree to give us all the facilities we want for the Navy, but they will demand Tyrone and Fermanagh, and that the Customs, Excise, etc, and the Post Office shall be controlled by the over-riding Parliament, instead of by the Northern and Southern Parliaments. The Ulster people will never agree and the question will then arise whether the English people are prepared to fight in order to support them. [. . .] There is no doubt that in principle, the country is hardening against the Sinn Feiners, but the point is whether people are prepared to give effect to their principles. [. . .]

31 October When talking with Robert Donald about the Life of Sir Edward Cook, just issued, Donald told me that he had got rid of Cook from the *Daily Chronicle* at the instigation of LG. At that time a big political fight was on, and Cook was writing the leaders for the *Chronicle*. LG said that Cook had no fire in his belly. [. . .]

Donald made some caustic observations about the *Daily Chronicle* under its present régime. He said, 'This is the first instance of a great newspaper being run in the interests of and on the instructions of the Prime Minister. Philip Kerr is nothing more nor less than the PM's agent.'

3 November Called at Downing Street. Found LG seated in Miss Stevenson's room. I explained that, having made arrangements with the Press to represent them at the American Conference, I had no alternative but to fulfil my engagement and was starting on the *Aquitania* on Saturday.

LG: I am sorry you are going, but it cannot be helped. I think under the circumstances you have no alternative.

R: When will you come to Washington?

LG: Perhaps never. Things look very awkward. Bonar Law has come out as the advocate of Ulster. Whether he thinks he sees his opportunity to become Prime Minister or whether he is solely actuated by a conscientious desire to champion the cause of Ulster I don't know, but I can hardly bring myself to believe that he would desire to supplant me. [. . .]

I am not going to continue the Irish war if a settlement is possible. I shall resign, and the King will have to send for someone else. [. . .] Sinn Fein are prepared to accept allegiance to the Crown and to agree that Ireland shall remain part of the Empire, subject to Tyrone and Fermanagh being joined to Southern Ireland or, at any rate, to a plebiscite, and subject also to the Irish fiscal, postal and telegraphic arrangements being relegated to a central Parliament to be elected on the basis of population. If the matter can be settled on those lines, I am not prepared to continue civil war. [. . .]

The position is very precarious, and it is giving me a lot of worry. In fact, I have been more worried about it than I have in regard to any matter since the war troubles in the Spring of 1918. They are all impossible people. Both sides are equally unreasonable. However, we shall see what we shall see.

5 November   Sailed on the *Aquitania* for the Disarmament Conference at Washington. A pleasant voyage. [. . .]

12 November   Attended opening of [Disarmament] Conference and heard [Secretary] Hughes's speech proposing naval reductions. A remarkable occasion. [. . .]

Lunched with A. J. Balfour, who was most gracious. Hankey also pleasant. Balfour told us that Hughes had been with him for two hours on the previous afternoon, that he had said he intended to make an important statement of policy. [. . .] Balfour and Hankey expressed themselves as being most favourably impressed with Hughes's proposals, which AJB described as bold and statesmanlike. [. . .]

15 November   [. . .] The relations between Lee and Beatty are strained. Lee loud in his complaints of Beatty's conduct. They are hardly on speaking terms. Lee says that this is entirely Beatty's fault, and that he, Lee, is determined to give him no opening for resignation. [. . .] Dined with Auckland Geddes[33] and wife. Geddes rather perturbed about the Lee–Beatty situation. [. . .]

By arrangement with Preston, who looks after the Press at the Navy Building, I visited an American elementary school and said a few words to the children. An interesting experience. Every day the children salute the American flag and make a sort of oath to it. In my honour, they sang the American National Anthem. Then the head teacher, a very nice woman, said, 'Now the children will sing the British National Anthem.' To my surprise they sang 'Rule Britannia'! [. . .]

1 December   Spent half an hour with President Harding – a fine up-standing sort of American – very much like the mayor of a provincial town who has been promoted to some high office, a typical local politician of the superior sort – closely in touch with the views of the common people, and with a clear, simple mind which enables him to go to the heart of a subject. All this accompanied by a good deal of unction and commonplace. [. . .]

12 December   I had taken my passage on the *Aquitania* for tomorrow, but the Delegation passed a resolution urging me to stay. This was cabled to London with the result that LG sent me a long telegram urging me to stop on public grounds.

Consequently I agreed to stop for another ten days. Arthur Balfour, Geddes, Hankey and Lee all said very nice things.[34] [. . .]

16 December   Called to see Lee. [. . .] He said that on the whole he was satisfied with the settlement, but there were several points which might and should have been settled differently. He said that AJB had completely ignored him; that he, Lee, had not been present at any of the meetings; and that AJB had declined to regard him as First Lord of the Admiralty, saying that he was simply a delegate. [. . .]

22 December   Started for home [. . .] after a very strenuous six weeks. [. . .] The American Press treated me remarkably well and the American newspapers were full of my doings.

23 December   [. . .] There is a good deal of misconception about this Conference. The Americans are keen on settling naval matters, but are far keener on establishing good relations with China, which they regard as the best outlet for their goods, etc. In Paris President Wilson fought hard for the Chinese and was much perturbed at the decisions arrived at. In Washington the air is permeated with China. The Chinese case was prepared by Americans, and every effort is being made to ingratiate America with the Chinese. The American Government were very keen on settling the Anglo-American-Japanese question. Japan is a big problem. I hope the new arrangement will work well. She is our friend, and has based her new régime on British lines, but she is likely to become a serious trade rival.

January–October 1922

The last ten months of the coalition ministry were one long diminuendo, occasionally punctuated by arresting bursts of sound. Though Riddell's visits to Downing Street and Churt were steadily growing fewer, he continued to find interesting material for his diary, some of it from Lloyd George, some from J. T. Davies and others. Always to the fore is the question of the Prime Minister's political future. At one moment he is prepared to turn the helm over to Austen Chamberlain or Bonar Law, at another he seems to be bracing himself for a hard fight to retain his place. By the end of July he is saying he will be guided by events. To resign or not to resign did not become an obsession, for there were many other problems to occupy Lloyd George's mind during these months. The long years of jousting with Northcliffe finally ended, but not before Lloyd George thought of pacifying him with an honour, possibly even an earldom. Northcliffe's insanity and approaching death made the future of *The Times* a subject of widespread interest. This intrigued Riddell greatly, and with Campbell Stuart's aid he observed with a newspaperman's delight the manoeuvres for control. Lloyd George was but one of many who cast covetous eyes upon *The Times*, for, as he explained to Riddell, 'I want to get out and am looking for a soft place on which to fall.' But as with Queen Elizabeth I, one cannot always be sure that Lloyd George meant what he said or said what he meant. Meanwhile the living Beaverbrook and Rothermere provided Riddell with subjects to replace the dying Northcliffe, and his pen does not spare either.

In the final analysis it was foreign affairs and the honours controversy that brought Lloyd George down. Though Riddell was present at the Cannes Conference in January and witnessed the celebrated Briand golf match, we learn little that is new. He did not attend the Genoa Conference in May, contenting himself with some reflections upon the unenthusiastic reception accorded Lloyd George on his return. Riddell's long-standing conviction that the British Government had backed the wrong horse in the Graeco-Turkish conflict was confirmed by the summer's events, and he took gloomy satisfaction in writing that the policy had proved disastrous. Nor did he hide his feelings from Lloyd

George, who sourly dubbed him 'Riddell Pasha' in return. Concurrently serious trouble was brewing at home over the sale of honours and Tory hostility. J. T. Davies treated Riddell to some entertaining details about the working of the honours system and various recipients – Northcliffe, Samuel Waring, Archibald Williamson, Moynihan the surgeon, Hildebrand Harmsworth – but more important is Lloyd George's stated determination to expose past transactions rather than submit tamely to allegations about his own régime. This threat availed him little, for the damage was done and his fall had become inevitable.

3 January Lunched with Campbell Stuart [. . .who] thinks [. . .] Beaverbrook [. . .] is trying to influence the Northcliffe press, which Birkenhead has unwisely said he has in his pocket. Beaverbrook is playing a double game. He pretends to be working with Rothermere against the Government; he pretends to be working with LG; and also pretends to be working with Birkenhead. But according to CS, he is selling the lot! [. . .]

7 January The PM cabled urging me to go to Cannes, where I arrived this morning. Found LG at the golf club. He gave me a warm reception and congratulated me on what he called my 'American victories' [. . .] He said he wished to have a chat with me about the election. Later I told him my views. I said the country was against an election. Things were bad. An election would disturb trade. Everyone was busy scratching for a living. There was no question on which the country was anxious to express an opinion. The coalition would no doubt return with a reduced majority, but LG's reputation would suffer, as people would say that the election was a piece of political gerrymandering. I said, 'You will suffer now and in history. [. . .]'

LG told me that Briand and Bonomi, the Italian Prime Minister, were coming to lunch at the golf club, and that he intended to take them out to play golf. In due course the event happened and created a tremendous sensation. Neither Briand nor Bonomi had ever touched a golf club, and their efforts were of course quaint. All the party roared with laughter, but poor Briand was helping to dig his own grave. LG was jubilant over his experiment, and said it would help to relieve the tension. In fact, on one round he had one or two little political chats with Briand and his entourage. I think LG's object was to create good feeling, he having had quite a row with Briand on the first day of the Conference regarding an interview which Briand had given to a

Belgian paper. Personally I thought the golf experiment a great mistake, and that it would be misunderstood and tortured by the Press. France is very much concerned about the position, and the incident had the appearance of a music-hall farce. Things turned out as I believed they would. Briand's position in France was very shaky, and the golf match – so-called – helped to do the trick. [. . .]

12 January   On Thursday morning I went to the Villa Valetta [where LG was staying]. Briand arrived. Curzon was there already – also Grigg and Vansittart. LG came downstairs very cheery, and the delegates went into conference. [. . .] LG, Briand & Co. settled down to business, the purpose being to settle an *aide mémoire* drawn up by LG and Grigg, setting out more or less the statement made by LG to Briand at their first meeting at Cannes on the previous Friday. This was to have been issued to the Press on the previous day and had been given to me for the purpose. I told La Bassée, the Havas representative, that I was about to issue it. In a few minutes, Briand, accompanied by Loucheur, came to me in the hall of the Carlton Hotel in an excited state, begging me not to issue the document until he had seen it. I agreed, and arranged for Grigg to let Briand have the document immediately, which he did. When Briand saw it he objected to certain phrases, and in particular to the reference to Tangier without further explanation. The result was that the issue was postponed in order that Briand might confer with LG on the document on the following morning. Hence the interview at the Villa Valetta. After a prolonged discussion, in the course of which changes were made in the document, LG came out of the room and made the dramatic announcement that Briand was returning to Paris to interview his Cabinet and face the Chamber. [. . .]

When LG first said that Briand was returning to Paris, Vansittart, Sylvester and I thought he was joking, but soon ascertained that he meant what he said. [. . .]

It subsequently transpired that Briand had received that morning a telegram from Millerand criticising the proposals in reference to Genoa, reparations and the proposed Anglo-French guarantee. Briand's prognostications, however, were not verified. He did not return, and on the following day when Rathenau, the German, was actually on his legs speaking in the Conference, a message arrived stating that Briand had resigned. The news soon spread round the council chamber, and LG, who was in the chair, adjourned the Conference for tea.[. . .] LG said, 'We shall finish with Rathenau and then we shall go home this evening.' This we did, starting at 7 o'clock and arriving at Paris at 2.30 on Saturday.

Later Poincaŕe, Briand's successor, called on LG at the British Embassy. [. . .]

On LG's return from the interview with Poincaŕe, I saw him. The interview lasted about an hour and a half. He said, 'Poincaŕe is a fool!' He repeated this two or three times, most emphatically. 'He actually proposed that there should be a military convention between Gt Britain and France, defining the size of the respective armies and other military details. I told him plainly that our people would never agree to anything of the sort, and that if this was insisted upon, our offer of the guarantee would be withdrawn. He also talked in a foolish way about reparations. He said in effect that he did not believe in conferences and that reparations questions should be settled by the Commission. He did not seem to know that they had no power to distribute the money received in the event of the full payments not being made. Nor did he seem to appreciate the impossibility of arriving at an agreement about a matter of this sort by despatches and correspondence. Generally speaking, the interview was most unsatisfactory. Nothing was settled and I really don't know where he is – and wonder whether he knows!'

28 and 29 January   Played golf with LG at Beaconsfield. Then with him to Chequers. Had some remarkable talk with him on Saturday evening and after dinner on Sunday.

He referred bitterly to an article by Lovat Fraser in the *Sunday Pictorial*, in which it was stated that we want a more austere, high-minded Prime Minister, a man who stays at home and who does not gad about Europe in *trains de luxe* with golf clubs, etc. [. . .He continued:] Then who are these people to attack me? Rothermere is separated from his wife and infatuated with some girl. He wanted to get a divorce so that he could marry her, but Beaverbrook and other friends – so-called – advised him against it. Lovat Fraser is given to the bottle. Nice people, these, to talk about the austere life! I could deal them a shrewd blow. [. . .]

We talked of the prospects of the election.

LG: I put Labour down at 180, and the Wee Frees at 100. That would give 280 out of 617, which I think will be the membership of the House of Commons, after striking off the Irish Vote except Ulster.

Fifty-seven would be a very narrow majority. The truth is that the position turns on the Conservatives. [. . .]

We then talked of Northcliffe.

LG: I wonder whether it would be possible to effect a settlement with him. I have got a Knighthood of St Patrick at my disposal. Beaverbrook wants it, and Grigg wants it for Abercorn.[1] I intended it for Carson, but of course I cannot give it to him in view of his present attitude. I might give it to Northcliffe if one felt that one could rely on him, but I cannot forget that he sold me over the Air Ministry. [. . .] I have beaten him all along the line, and there is really no reason why he and I should not be friends.[2]

R: I think what he would like would be an earldom.

LG: Well, it might be done. [. . .]

We then returned to the discussion of the course he should take. Ultimately he said, 'Well I think the best course is to wait until Parliament meets. Then we shall see the real attitude of the Conservatives. If they want me to go on, I will. If they don't, I shall retire and write my book.' [. . .]

He spoke strongly about Lord Grey,[3] whose attack on his policy he bitterly resented. [. . .]

3 February   Lunched with Winston with whom I had a long private chat. He says he is very busy and that the Prime Minister has put an enormous amount of work on his shoulders. He likes the work and is not afraid of accepting responsibility which relieves LG.

Winston said that the Irish situation was very awkward. He intended to propose arbitration regarding the boundary question, as he thought this the only way out. But he added that everyone in Ireland seemed to be unreasonable. The Irish will not recognise that they, like every other civilised people, must adopt reasonable methods for settling differences.

He told me that he had been in favour of an election in February and thought that LG had missed his market. I said that I understood that LG had offered to resign in favour of Chamberlain and had offered to support him, but that the latter had declined the proposal.

Winston laughed and replied, 'I doubt whether it was put in in that direct way. There are different ways of putting a proposition. You can put it in such terms as to ensure a negative answer.' [. . .]

12 February   On Sunday motored to Chequers, arriving in the afternoon. Had a long private talk with LG. Very interesting. This is what he said: 'My position is quite plain. I don't care whether I go or not. In fact I would rather be out of it. [. . .] I have told Chamberlain and Bonar Law that I am willing to give up and support either of them, provided they carry out my policy on two points: (1) that they give effect to the Irish settlement if it is going to be settled; and (2) that they give effect to my policy for the pacification of Europe. Chamberlain, as I have said, is not prepared to accept the responsibility. Bonar Law is a strange fellow. . . .'

R: Did Bonar show any disposition to take the Premiership himself?

LG: It was interesting to see him. He kept taking up the crown and trying it on his head, and then when he felt it was a crown of thorns, he put it down again. And then he took it up again.

R: A great deal will depend upon Arthur Balfour. [. . .]

LG: [. . .] It will be interesting to know what line he is going to take. He may wish to become Prime Minister. If he does, I shall support him. [. . .] I am in agreement with Birkenhead and Chamberlain. They wanted me to see AJB and endeavour to secure his support, but I declined. I shall do nothing to influence him. He must do just as he thinks best. [. . .]

(Yesterday I had a very illuminating conversation with Worthington-Evans, whose attitude towards LG has evidently changed. Obviously he is groping about for another leader, but cannot see one. He said, however, that if AJB would take the position, the Party would rally round him to a man. He doubted whether he would.)

19 February [. . .] Chequers on Sunday afternoon. When I arrived LG met me at the door with Geddes and Horne. He took them out for a walk, and afterwards had a long private discussion on the Geddes Report. Meanwhile Mr and Mrs Philip Snowden[4] arrived – very nice people. Snowden asked LG what he thought of the Labour victory at Manchester.[5] LG said he had expected it and that he anticipated others. He asked Snowden to what he ascribed the Labour success. Snowden replied, 'To the threat in the Geddes Report to interfere with education. . . .'[6]

LG (looking at Geddes and Horne): That is just what I have been telling you. Your educational proposals may appeal to the upper class, but they do not appeal to the people, and even Riddell here is a violent antagonist.

R: I strongly object to the teachers' salaries being cut down. The result will be to turn them into Bolsheviks. The salaries may have been raised to a high level but a man always resents having his salary reduced. I look upon adequate payment for teachers as an insurance.

Horne expressed himself very strongly in favour of carrying out the report, saying, 'Why should school teachers have a higher rate of pay than country parsons or country lawyers?'

R: Because they are more useful members of the community, and because if you do not pay them properly they can do more harm. If you don't take care, you will have the next generation inculcated with ideas prejudicial to the stability of the country.

Horne looked at Geddes sorrowfully, but made no further reply. [. . .]

21 February Long talk with Commander Chilcott, Birkenhead's quondam ally – but apparently they are not so friendly as they were. He said that Birkenhead had taken to drink again, and that it would certainly overwhelm him. He also said that Birkenhead and others had been engaged in a conspiracy against the Prime Minister, and that all the details were set forth in a letter which he, Chilcott, had from Birkenhead.[7] [. . .]

25 February To Lympne, arriving about 5 o'clock. LG came back at about 8 o'clock from Boulogne, where he had been meeting Poincaré – their second meeting. [. . .]

I asked LG whether the interview had been satisfactory. He said, 'Well, we got all we wanted. . . .'

On Sunday he remained in bed until lunch-time. He seemed very preoccupied. After lunch we had some music. While this was going forward, LG went to the writing-table, obtained a bundle of notepaper and sat down by the fire busily writing in pencil. He covered sheet after sheet, notwithstanding the music. Later in the evening he sent for me to go to his bedroom and then handed me the result of his labours to read. His notes had been transcribed by Miss Stevenson. They consisted of a long letter to Chamberlain in which he set forth that he views the present political situation with alarm. He thought that in the interests of the country and those of Europe it would be a calamity if the House of Commons were split into a number of sections. What England and the world needed was a strong homogeneous Government in Gt Britain. Unless she had such a Government she could not continue to perform the services to humanity that she is now performing. He outlined what had been done by the Government and what they were hoping to do. He said that he had already offered Chamberlain and Bonar Law to retire in favour of either of them and to give his successor his support. He now repeated the offer and strongly urged that it should be accepted. He asked my opinion on the letter. I said I thought he was taking the right course. [. . .]

If Chamberlain or Bonar Law accepted his proposal, well and good. If not, then he, LG, could reply that if he were going on, it would be necessary that he should have united support. In short the letter was a step in the direction of a fused party. [. . .]

2 March To Coombe Hill with LG and Grigg. We found Guest waiting for us.

The political crisis in full blast. LG evidently very tired. [. . .]

LG: [. . .] Not only have I to carry the leaders with me but we must stop the dry rot that is taking place in the constituencies. Younger acted badly, and no doubt, during my absence at Cannes, Chamberlain completely lost his head. Had he taken a strong line with Younger he might have controlled him. But he did not – he was wobbly, and now we are paying the penalty.[8] [. . .]

4 March On Saturday I received a message asking me to go to Chequers. I arrived with McCurdy,[9] the Whip, whom I drove down, at about 7.30.

LG extremely cheerful and bright – brighter than I have seen him for some time. Whether this was due to Chamberlain's speech or to over-excitement, I don't know. [. . .]

After dinner, LG took McCurdy and me upstairs into the Long Gallery, saying he wished to have a political talk. When we were seated he began by saying that he had read McCurdy's memorandum, which he thought very good. He agreed that three courses were open – (1) for him to resign, (2) putting the matter in the inverse order to that adopted by McCurdy – to insist on the formation of a national or centre party, and (3) to continue on the faith of assurances by the leaders of the Conservative Party. Then he said, 'Now, Riddell, what is your view?'

R: I doubt whether it will be possible for you to continue under existing conditions, notwithstanding the assurances received from Chamberlain and the others. Fresh troubles are certain to develop. At present you reign, but don't rule. [. . .] If you don't object to giving up office, then it would be best to take the plunge [and resign. . . .]

McC: Winston made a speech today advocating a National Party.

LG: Yes, he is strongly in favour of it. And so is Birkenhead.

5 March   We went for a walk – LG, McCurdy and I. Much more talk about the political situation. LG went to London at 3 o'clock, to attend the party dinner.

7 March   When at Downing Street found LG seated in Miss Stevenson's room with his feet up. [. . .]

He said it was impossible to keep anything secret. It had been agreed at the dinner on Sunday night that letters should be written to Younger and McCurdy, and it had been agreed that these should be kept secret. The information, however, appeared in the Press on Monday morning and must have been given away by someone present at the dinner. [. . .]

Long and interesting interview with Campbell Stuart. [. . .]

Northcliffe has given CS his power of attorney and absolute control of *The Times*, *Daily Mail* and *Evening News*. It seems that when Northcliffe returned he made unfavourable reflections on the *Mail* and the *News* with the result that Marlowe, Editor of the *Mail*, resigned. CS strongly protested and urged N to make it up with Marlowe, to whom N apologised, whereupon Marlowe withdrew his resignation. CS says that N is anxious to get rid of Evans.[10] [. . .] Evans, however, is a tough personage who says what he thinks and is not afraid of N or anybody else.

23 March   To Criccieth, where I arrived at midday on Friday, returning on Monday with the PM and others. [. . .]

Much talk with the PM about the political situation, which has been further complicated by Winston's attitude towards the Bolsheviks. He declines to agree to the political recognition of the Soviet, and may resign if LG insists. This might bring about a complete smash-up of the Government. LG had a long talk with McCurdy. He was to speak to Winston at Northampton on the Saturday. LG carefully instructed McCurdy what to say to Winston and J. T. Davies was busy telephoning to London to secure that Winston should not commit himself in his speech on Saturday. [. . .]

We came back on the Monday by special train, and LG at once plunged into the political maelstrom. The form of the Genoa resolution was settled, and, so far as could be gathered, Winston was appeased and the Cabinet's unity maintained.

It is quite clear to me that LG means to hold on as long as he can. He does not mean to resign or to ride for a fall. But all his hopes are concentrated on Genoa. He looks to the Conference to restore his star to the zenith. He told me that he believed that Lenin and Co. had seen the error of their ways, and were anxious to approximate to normal economic methods. [. . .]

[. . .] At Genoa he hopes to secure a treaty of peace. [. . .] LG's Greek policy has proved a disastrous failure, but he did not refer to it, and I did not bring the subject up.

6 April   Lunched with LG. He is anxious for me to go to Genoa, but there are difficulties. Northcliffe & Co. are violently opposed to my going, and N has intimated that in his opinion it is not right that I should go, as I should only be representing a section of the Press and not the whole of it as heretofore. [. . .]

Northcliffe returns today, and on his arrival Burnham and I are to see him about the affairs of the NPA generally – Northcliffe's action in regard to Labour having caused serious difficulties. [. . .]

I had an interesting conversation with JTD, who strongly deplores LG's rapprochement with Rothermere and Beaverbrook. Miss S holds the same view, but says that the PM, being assailed in other quarters, has to make use of them. J. T. says that LG met Rothermere on the ship, and suggested that he should go to Genoa, which he did. LG seems to have had the idea that Rothermere would give him his support, but reference to the Rothermere papers does not justify this optimism. Openly they are not so violent against LG, but in a quiet insidious way they are critical of his policy and doing their best to destroy it. J. T. told me that the only result so far as he could see of the Rothermere rapprochement was that he, J. T., got a letter from Rothermere, saying that LG had arranged with him to confer a baronetcy on Hildebrand Harmsworth,[11] and that he had asked Rothermere to communicate this fact to J. T. What an amazing story! If this comes about, an honour will have been extorted for almost every member of the Harmsworth family. [. . .]

A great deal of secret Cabinet matter has leaked out into the *Daily Express*. It appears under the initials of James, their correspondent. LG is continually complaining about this, but I am sure the information is supplied by JTD. In fact I have tackled him on the subject, and while he did not admit the allegation, he did not deny it. Whether he acts as agent for LG in order to curry favour with Beaverbrook, or whether he supplies the information to James for some consideration, I don't know. But it is curious that since I raised the point with J. T., the paras.

have stopped. But this may be due to LG's absence in Genoa. One never knows! [. . .]

Sir Samuel Waring[12] is working hard for a peerage and has showered gifts upon most people at 10 D St. J.T. confided to me that he was trying to push him through this time, and that he did not think it well to charge him too much, as if Waring's financial position were shaky and the facts were to come out hereafter they would not look so bad.

20 May   To meet the PM at Victoria on his return from Genoa. A big crowd on the platform and outside the station, but I thought the former not very representative or enthusiastic. Perhaps this was due to its being Saturday and a very hot evening. There was no real cordial Parliamentary support. [. . .]

I had a long chat with Austen Chamberlain. [. . .] He said, 'Northcliffe has been the best friend LG has had at the Conference. His action has created public sympathy for LG amongst people who are strongly opposed to his policy.' [. . .]

21 May   To Philip Sassoon's at Trent to meet LG, who had not arrived when I got there at about 1 o'clock. He came about 4. I found Bonar Law. [. . .]

I was much interested in BL. It is quite evident that he is hankering for power. Many men who give up a position are, after retirement, more jealous of their late colleagues than they were while in the saddle. I think this is Bonar's state of mind. [. . .] He is critical, and while not having the dash to seize the crown, he sits in judgement on the King [i.e. LG] and would like to depose him and wear the crown himself.[. . .]

BL went off before dinner. LG said that as usual he was in a gloomy state. 'Things were very bad.' LG added, 'I countered him saying, "Yes, Bonar, but they will be very much worse! They are always growing worse!" He did not know what to say to that. His gloom always reacts on me by making me more cheerful' [. . .]

3 June   LG and J. T. Davies arrived. The latter told me some very interesting things, to wit: Waring has got a peerage. J. T. says that his peerage and baronetcy have cost him, 'one way or another,' £100,000. [. . .]

J. T. says they have done well this time with honours. Everyone has had to pay up – whatever his qualifications. Archibald Williamson,[13] who has strong political claims, £50,000; Moynihan,[14] the surgeon, £10,000, etc, etc. [. . .]

Referring to Hildebrand Harmsworth's baronetcy, J. T. said that he (J. T.) had written to Rothermere asking him how he was going to pay for it. Rothermere replied, 'I shall shortly begin to pay in meal and malt.' [. . .]

[Riddell waxed critical of the latest Harmsworth honour.] LG did not quite know what to say to this, but of course he did not like it. [. . .] On the whole I think he is more self-centred than he was, and less tolerant of criticism. It is not surprising, considering the position which he holds and the adulation showered upon him. [. . .]

Criccieth: 4 June [. . .] I omitted to say that in talking about Hildebrand Harmsworth's title LG said, 'By the way, which Harmsworth is it?' To which I replied, 'The one who drinks.' That rather surprised him. Caird tells me that Hildebrand is a decadent of the worst type – the worst of all the Harmsworths [. . .]

Mrs LG told me that she had received an anonymous letter saying that Shakespeare,[15] one of the PM's secretaries, was engaged in an enterprise which would shortly land him in the same position as Crawshay-Williams[16] – a former secretary of LG's – to wit, the Divorce Court, and that the lady was the wife of an MP. Mrs LG handed this to the PM, who, according to J. T., took up a very high moral tone [. . .] which was rather amusing.[17] I have had a pleasant little holiday. Both Mr and Mrs LG are admirable hosts. They give one plenty of freedom. [. . .]

11 June [. . .] Andrew Caird telephoned asking me to see him 'on a matter of almost national importance'. He came to Walton Heath. He tells me that Northcliffe has gone out of his mind, he believes.[18] [. . .]

17 June Played golf with LG at St George's Hill. [. . .] He talked much about Northcliffe's serious illness, and speculated as to what would become of his papers if he gave up. LG said, 'In that case I must get friends of mine to acquire *The Times*, otherwise it might get into the hands of Beaverbrook or someone else who would make things difficult.'[19] LG said that if the reports concerning Northcliffe were true, it was a tragic business, and that he felt sorry to see him end in this way. [. . .]

On my way home I called upon Hulton at his house in Leatherhead. [. . .] He also talked much about Northcliffe, and said that he had heard that he had gone off his head. To my surprise Hulton spoke in bitter and rather contemptuous terms of Beaverbrook, who I thought was a friend of his. [. . .] Hulton said that he could not understand Beaverbrook. One day he was all for LG, and the next bitterly opposed to him. He implied that Beaverbrook was an unscrupulous fellow, and said quite plainly that he had acted in a disgraceful way in his transactions with Frank Lloyd, and that if he, Hulton, had treated Lloyd in the way that Beaverbrook had done, he could not again show his face in Fleet Street. [. . .]

24 June   LG and Worthington-Evans came to Walton Heath to play golf, arriving for lunch. LG evidently very depressed about Henry Wilson's assassination. . . .[20]

I asked LG whether it was true there was to be an election at an early date. He said, 'No, but it is an easy rumour to set about. Why should there be an election till next year?' I told him that [Robert] Donald had met Bonar Law at Beaverbrook's and that BL had expressed his intention of returning to politics whole-heartedly. He said, 'You must be one thing or the other.' He added that he intended to support LG and that between them they could sweep the country. [. . .]

2 July   To Chequers. LG and I had some talk about American political finance. The wherewithal is provided by the great interests.

LG: [. . .] I am not going to bind myself to the cart-tail of a lot of capitalists. It may be unpleasant to take the money of one plutocrat in exchange for an honour, but when all is said, nothing very serious happens. Whereas if a political party is financed by great trade interests, who want something for their money, the result is certain to be very serious, as no public question would be considered on its merits. [. . .]

8 July   Played golf with LG and Miss Stevenson at St George's Hill. He said that he had heard bad news of Northcliffe, and that he thought he was not likely to recover. LG had had an interview with Rothermere. [. . .]

We then talked of the Honours controversy. [. . .]

LG: [. . .] I shall make it quite plain that if there is to be an enquiry, it will have to begin with Lord Salisbury's administration, or at any rate with Arthur Balfour's. Sir George Younger tells me that Lord Northcliffe, for example, gave £200,000 for his peerage, £100,000 of which went to Mrs Keppel and £100,000 to King Edward. And there are several other cases such as those relating to Michelham and Wandsworth[21] which would be strange reading. I don't defend the system, but I have done merely what other Prime Ministers have done, and I am going to make it clear that if I am going down, I am going to bring the temple down with me. I am not going to be sacrificed by people and the descendants of people who have been engaged in carrying on precisely the same system. [. . .]

20 July A pleasant dinner at Lord Dawson's. [. . .] Poole of Lewis & Lewis, who was at the dinner, told me that the PM had had him down to Chequers and that LG was anxious to get hold of *The Times*. [. . .]

Everyone in *The Times* is most anxious as to what will happen in the event of Northcliffe's death. No one seems to know what he has done. Amongst other things, the Harmsworth group all say that Campbell Stuart's day is over. [. . .]

22 July To Chequers, where I remained until Monday morning. Sir Auckland and Lady Geddes, Sir Eric Geddes. [. . .]

Much talk about trade conditions. Mond and [Eric] Geddes very interesting. The PM most anxious for facts that would confirm his opinion that Germany is on the verge of bankruptcy. Not getting these from Mond and Geddes, he did not pursue the subject. [. . .]

LG to Geddes: What do you think of the political situation?

Geddes: Very difficult. I should have an election as soon as possible. Things are going against the Government and I should get out! You want a holiday. I should leave the other people to it.

LG: Well, what do you think, Riddell?

R: Generally speaking I agree. But it is difficult to get out at the moment without being charged with running away from an awkward situation, because there is no doubt that the atmosphere just now is not good. Genoa cannot be regarded as an unqualified success, and the Honours controversy has left a nasty taste, although nothing specific has occurred.

LG: The atmosphere is bad. It would be impossible to go out now, much as I should like to do so. [. . .] I am tired and no wonder! I have had seventeen years' continuous work, but I am not going to lay myself under the charge of deserting my friends when they were in a tight place.

Geddes: I think the Conservatives would like Chamberlain to have his opportunity.

LG: Well, I am quite willing. The question is whether he wants his opportunity.

Geddes: Then there is Bonar Law.

LG: But he could not with decency step in front of Chamberlain. [. . .]

29 July   To Churt, LG's new house high up among the heather. [. . .] The joint production of Tilden, the architect, and Miss Stevenson – the latter in full charge and very busy. [. . .]

We talked of his political future. It is clear that he has not made up his mind what he wants to do. Indeed, he said plainly that he 'shall be guided by events'. He is feeling the constant strain, but does not wish to relinquish the position. He is preparing for a retreat (building the house at Churt and arranging to write books), but is also arranging to carry on the fight. The Whips' Office is to be reorganised. This week the Dissenters have been mobilised at a lunch, and generally speaking, I doubt if he will go until he is turned out or thinks it impossible to carry on. [. . .]

We talked much of the future of *The Times*. LG says that Rothermere tells him that Northcliffe's fortune amounts to some five millions, and that the death duties will reach some two millions. To meet these his newspaper interests will have to be sold and *The Times* will be the first to go, as it is losing some £3,000 per week. Rothermere does not believe that Marlowe, Caird, etc, will be able to carry on the *Mail* successfully. They have not got the flair. LG holds the same opinion. [. . .]

LG asked whether I would advise him to get up a syndicate to buy *The Times*. He said that Beaverbrook, Rupert Beckett and others are after it. I replied that from that point of view it would be as well to get together the money to purchase it. By so doing he would prevent it from becoming an enemy newspaper, but he need be under no illusions. If he secured good men to run *The Times* – men equal to the job – they would run their own policies more or less. They would not be 'tame seals'. I reminded him of his dissatisfaction with the *Daily Chronicle*. Nothing is ever right. He admitted all this, but said, truly enough, that it would be intolerable to be under Beaverbrook's lash. I told him that the chief difficulty would be to make *The Times* pay. It is easier to acquire newspapers than it is to manage them. [. . .]

LG much perturbed at the death of Scott Dickson,[22] the Scottish LCJ.[23] He says that Robert Horne will want the job, as he covets it above all things and wishes to leave politics because there is a split between the Tories and LG. He will not want to desert the latter, but on the other hand could not well desert his party. [. . .] From this observation I gather that all is not well in the Coalition and that LG foresees trouble ahead. [. . .] LG says the Tories are becoming more and more anxious for their own Government. [. . .]

September [n.d.] To Churt. LG, Sir Robert Horne, Sir E. Grigg, Miss Stevenson, J. T. Davies and Shakespeare. [. . .]

Politics is a strange business. Greenwood says he is sick of it.[24] Horne is anxious to escape to the Bench. Shortt ditto. Gordon Hewart gone already. [. . .]

I had an interesting talk with Horne about his future. [. . .] He thinks that Winston might do well as Chancellor, although he has economic views which Horne considers dangerous. He says that Winston is disloyal to the PM and that LG knows this. [. . .]

Horne told me (Grigg and Shakespeare being present) that he is going to America in October regarding the British debt. He regards the mission as very awkward. Congress has so tied the hands of the American Government that he does not see what he can hope to accomplish. [. . .]

R: Many leading Americans are strongly in favour of remitting all war debts, but the American people are not.

Horne: I agree. Taft[25] put it well. He said the people of the Middle West visualise a man called Uncle Jonathan sending shiploads of gold coins to England which the English spent. Now they want to see a man called John Bull return those coins.

2 September Played golf with LG, Horne and Grigg. [. . .]

LG much interested in *The Times* position. He did not tell me so, but I ascertained that he spent last week-end at Beaverbrook's. The Lord Chancellor and Winston were also there. [. . .]

I had dinner with LG on the previous Friday evening, when I told him privately about Northcliffe's wills, much to his surprise. Poole, the solicitor who is acting for LG in his negotiations to acquire *The Times*, was also at dinner. [. . .]

Things have gone very badly with the Greeks and evidently LG is much perturbed. [. . .]

4 September   [. . .] I explained the position in regard to the Northcliffe wills and the sale of *The Times*.

LG: The position is this. I want to get out and am looking for a soft place on which to fall. At the moment I don't see it. However, I want to get control of *The Times*. That would give me great power and would enable me to compel the Conservatives to pay due regard to my views and policies. They attach great importance to the attitude of *The Times*. Therefore I am anxious that no stone should be left unturned to enable me to acquire the paper.

Grigg says the PM really wants a holiday. To outward appearance he seems well, but he has lost his power of initiative. It is difficult to get him nowadays to devise fresh expedients. Grigg thinks strongly that he should resign as soon as possible and take a rest. [. . .]

Apart from other questions, the political situation is most complicated. There is a strong movement in the Conservative Party for a Conservative leader. On the other hand, Chamberlain and the Lord Chancellor are anxious to go on as before. [. . .] One thing is certain – there is going to be an early election – perhaps as early as October. LG is seeing the Liberals at Churt this week, and in November the Conservatives have their annual meeting. The Lord Chancellor and Winston are strongly in favour of an early election. [. . .]

To revert to the political situation, things have not gone well for LG. Greece, America's attitude in regard to our debt, the situation with France and the situation with Russia, are all awkward problems on the wrong side of the ledger. [. . .]

I have been in close touch with Campbell Stuart, just back from Canada, Caird and others. There is little, I might almost say no, regret at Northcliffe's death in his entourage. They all appear to be on the scramble, and Rothermere appears to be the chief scrambler. [. . .] All sorts of people are nibbling at *The Times*, including the Prime Minister, the Lord Chancellor, Rothermere, Beaverbrook, Ellerman, and others. Chilcott mysteriously told me that he had got the necessary funds which were to be provided by one of the big oil groups who are anxious for journalistic power, but who are prepared to support the PM. When, however, he found that the whole of Northcliffe's interests were not to be acquired, but only *The Times*, which shows a heavy loss, he cooled off. [. . .]

15 September   Dined with the PM at Downing Street. Mrs LG and Hankey. Much talk about *The Times*. LG now says that for financial reasons he does not think it worth while to interest himself in the purchase. He thinks it will be difficult to get people to invest in a property which shows such a heavy loss. [. . .] Much talk about the Turkish situation, which is deplorable. Smyrna is in flames and the civilian population (non-Turkish) in a horrible predicament. Kemal Pasha, completely victorious, is dictating to Europe. Never was any policy so disastrous as that of which LG has been the chief protagonist. [. . .] Venizelos was one of LG's idols.

When I arrived at Downing Street, LG was with Winston, whose strident voice was reverberating through the house. [. . .]

As we sat down to dinner, LG poured himself out a small glass of brandy, saying, 'I am tired and have had a hard day.' Beyond this he gave no sign of anxiety or distress at the situation. His courage is remarkable and he shows to best advantage when encountering 'dreadful odds'. Many of his policies are not happy, but when called upon to face a crisis, he is splendid.

After dinner, he and Hankey went through and settled the draft naval and military instructions to the forces in the Near East decided upon by the Cabinet. LG loud in his denunciations of Curzon, who had left the office at 7.30 and gone into the country. He says that Curzon's health is still bad and that he is quite unfitted to hold his position. [. . .]

24 September   To Churt with Grigg. [. . .] The PM outwardly in good spirits but obviously anxious concerning the Turkish situation, which is in a critical phase. [. . .] I ascertained that LG, Birkenhead and Winston lunched today with Beaverbrook at his Putney residence, the two latter [*sic*] reporting that Max was getting out of hand. What happened I do not know, except that Beaverbrook published a letter on the Sunday (25 September) saying that as he was not in agreement with the Government's policy he would say nothing about his experiences in Constantinople [. . .] or his views on the Eastern question.

This is a curious business. Things have come to a strange pass when the PM, Lord Chancellor and Minister for Dominions deem it necessary to kow-tow to a Canadian adventurer in order to secure the support of his papers! [. . .]

I said to LG, Horne and Grigg on Monday morning that it looked as if we were drifting into another war. If Kemal does not observe the injunction to refrain from entering the neutral zones, it means fighting, and no one can tell where the conflict will end. [. . .]

LG, who spoke in a very subdued and lowly manner, quite contrary to his usual style, said, 'The position is most serious. . . . You say (alluding to a remark of mine) that the country will not stand for a fresh war. I disagree. The country will willingly support our action regarding the Straits by force of arms if need be.' [. . .]

Horne was full of fight in regard to the Turks, but strangely did not seem to know the details of all that has happened since November 1918. He described the PM as more anti-Turk than pro-Greek and said that LG was living in the past – in the days of Gladstone – and that he (Horne) often thought this when he heard him speak on the subject. I said that LG was both anti-Turk and pro-Greek. Venizelos, I told Horne, had captivated LG, [President] Wilson and Philip Kerr. Horne was much interested, and said that threw a flood of light on the situation.

LG and I talked of Grant Morden, the MP and Canadian adventurer, who, they tell me, has sold out of Odhams, the company which owns *John Bull*, and with Donald, late of the *Chronicle*, has purchased the *People* – a strange combination, Grant Morden being a hanger-on of the Conservative Party, and Donald, in his old days, a violent Radical of the old-fashioned type. [. . .]

13 October Lunched with LG, who is evidently not well pleased at our attitude on the Eastern question, concerning which we have been in strong opposition to him. However, he turned the matter off by greeting me as 'Riddell Pasha', and saying that it was to be expected that the *News of the World* would be in favour of polygamists. [. . .]

He said the political situation was dubious and he thought the crash was coming. [. . .]

15 October[26] Quiet dinner with J. T. Davies, who told me funny things. [. . .] He says that they have plenty of money for the forthcoming election but have had to refund certain amounts collected from two baronets made some time ago, who have become, or are about to become, bankrupt. [. . .]

The Northcliffe group admit that he paid £100,000 for his baronetcy, which went to Mrs K[eppel], and £100,000 for his peerage, which went to King E[dward]. This confirms what LG says.[27]

I have had many talks with CS, Howard F[rank] and others concerning *The Times*. Walter[28] has now got his option to purchase Northcliffe's shares, which must be offered to him at a price. Rothermere is anxious to buy the shares. CS is determined that he shall not, and says that he and Walter have got the money to buy them. Meanwhile they have purchased Ellerman's shares and CS has got an agreement as Managing-Director for two years. [. . .]

I had a long talk with Wickham Steed, who confirmed what CS had told me. Steed says that he had a terrible time with Northcliffe, who several times took out a loaded revolver. Steed said, 'I sat on several occasions looking directly down the barrel. I had an awful time with him. I did not sleep for thirty-two hours. . . .'

CS says that he has got Lady N[orthcliffe] on his side. [. . .]

October 1922–September 1934

The last chapter is little more than a series of post-scripts, with the final entry, an anecdote about Lord Derby and the Queen, coming but a few weeks before Riddell's death. The *raison d'être* for the diaries vanished with Lloyd George's resignation, and entries become sporadic and disjointed. One or two have a touch of pathos, for example the scene at Downing Street when Lloyd George returned from the Palace, no longer Prime Minister of Britain. Though Riddell incurred Lloyd George's anger anew by using the *News of the World* to support Bonar Law at the 1922 general election, old habit was too strong and they continued to see something of each other over the next few months. Invariably such meetings proved difficult, barbed remarks were exchanged, and neither man can have regretted the end of a long and interesting association. Perhaps Riddell was a fair- weather friend, as Beaverbrook suggested. The fact that the latter did not hide this opinion may account for some of the sharp things about Beaverbrook that appear in the diaries nearly to the end.

In other spheres Campbell Stuart continued to keep Riddell informed about *The Times*, and anecdotes about Lord Rothermere and his son do little to improve the image of the Harmsworths. There were conversations with Birkenhead about the last days of the coalition, followed some months later by talks with Sir Robert Horne and A. J. Sylvester about Baldwin succeeding Bonar Law. Thereafter Riddell was reduced to snippets from such others as Lord Curzon, Bernard Baruch and Robert Vansittart, and the diaries conclude lightly on a royal note.

19 October At 4.15 this afternoon, Miss Stevenson telephoned to say that the PM had gone to Buckingham Palace with his resignation. The [Tory] Party Meeting took place today, and decided by a large majority against the Coalition.[1]

Later I called and found LG seated by the fire in Miss Stevenson's room with a small notebook in his hand, busy thinking over the speech which he is to make at Leeds on Saturday.

R: Well, the die is cast!

LG: Yes, and I am glad of it. One could not go on under the circumstances. [. . .]

R: Shall we have an election?

LG: That all depends on Bonar.

R: Will he be able to form a Cabinet?

LG: That remains to be seen. I don't think he likes the position.

R: Do you remember a cartoon in *Punch* which showed Lord John Russell knocking hard at a door which the footman had thrown open? Lord John had run away round the corner, and was wondering whether he had done well to knock.

LG: That quite sums up the situation. That is what Bonar is thinking to-night! [. . .]

Then he got up and walked about the room and put out his hand. I said, 'It has been a wonderful time!' He said, 'Yes!' (shaking hands with me heartily). 'We have had a wonderful time together!' And then he walked away into the Cabinet Room.

J. T. Davies told me that the PM had promised him the vacant Directorship of the Suez Canal Company, but at the last minute agreed to give it to Horne. J. T. very much upset. He said that he had been relying on it, and that if it were diverted he would be left in the cart. He said that LG had tried to talk him out of it, but that he had declined to waive his rights.

20 October   At the luncheon to the Prince of Wales at the Guildhall, J. T. Davies took me aside and, with a beaming face, said that he got his Suez Canal Directorship. [. . .]

1 November   Campbell Stuart came to see me and stayed about three hours. He gave me a dramatic account of the acquisition of *The Times* by Walter and J. J. Astor. He said that Rothermere had been doing his utmost to get the paper, but that he, CS, had circumvented him. At the last moment he found that Sir Robert Hudson,[2] Lady Northcliffe's friend, was working with Rothermere, for whom Sir Charles Russell was acting as solicitor. CS went to see Hudson. While there he inadvertently heard Hudson talking on the telephone to Sir Charles Russell. From their conversation he gathered that Russell was anxious to find out whether Walter had the money to exercise his option. Consequently Hudson returned and begged to question Stuart as to Walter's intentions. Stuart, being warned by the telephone conversation, led Hudson to think that Walter had not been able to get more than a million pounds. The result was that Rothermere put in an offer of £1,350,000.

When the matter came before the judge he required Rothermere to enter into a firm contract to buy at this price, subject to Walter's option. Then he said, 'Does Mr Walter wish to exercise his option?' Walter's lawyer jumped up and said quietly, 'Yes, please! I am ready with the deposit now!' This took Rothermere & Co. completely by surprise. As they came out of the court, Charles Russell said to Campbell Stuart, 'Well, you have done us! You have been very clever about it.' Campbell Stuart is of course highly delighted about it, and says he will go down to history as the man who saved *The Times* and placed it in good custody in the interests of Britons.[3] [. . .]

He says that Steed will have to go, and that the preliminary steps have been taken. [. . .] Stuart's idea is to manage the business part of *The Times* himself, and also to act as Managing Editor, leaving the Editor to deal with questions of policy, etc. [. . .]

3 November   Spent a couple of hours with Wickham Steed and Mme Rose at their flat, when they told me the story from another angle. According to them, various members of *The Times* editorial [staff] set to work to find millionaires to join in purchasing *The Times*. Freeman, I think it was, suggested J. J. Astor. Steed gave me the names of the other millionaires who were to act in concert – I think, but I am not sure, the Duke of Westminster, Lord Derby, Duke of Sutherland and Lord Inchcape. Steed continued, 'Up to a certain point we were all acting in concert – Walter, Campbell Stuart, and the others. Then at the last moment Stuart rushed the claim. He had Walter completely under his thumb and the two then made private arrangements with Astor. [. . .] Steed went on to say that Walter had sent for him after the deal had been completed and had told him that under the new conditions it was thought better to appoint another Editor. Steed said that he was not surprised. [. . .] He does not know who the new Editor is going to be. *The Times* are going to give him a pension for life and want to keep him on the staff as a writer. [. . .] It was a most interesting interview.

4 November   Miss S rang up to say that LG would like me to dine with him at Vincent Square tonight (Saturday). He has not been pleased with my attitude with reference to Eastern affairs. He did not greet me with his customary jollity, but made the singular remark as he shook hands – he does not usually shake hands – 'Still cheeky, I suppose?', evidently referring to some humorous observations I had made about him at the Press Club Dinner on the previous Saturday, these having been widely reported. [. . .]

[Later.] The conversation turned on Rothermere. LG said eagerly that R was coming over to him. I said, 'I don't know that that will do you much good. The British people won't have any dictator. They would not be dictated to by Lord Northcliffe, and they won't be dictated to by Rothermere.'

LG could see that I was thinking that they would not be dictated to by him. I said, 'Northcliffe was your best friend. Your stock has been going down ever since he died. His attacks helped you.'

LG: Well, I have lots of other friends. [. . .]

15 November Much talk of a combination between the Bonar Lawites and the Asquithians. McKenna spent Sunday with Beaverbrook at Cherkley Court. No doubt Bonar Law & Co. are anxious to fortify themselves with new blood. If they could secure Grey, McKenna and Runciman, they would be a source of strength for administrative purposes. [. . .]

16 November The day after the election.

Long chat with Burnham at the *DT* Offices. He told me that when he arrived back from Geneva on the Saturday he found that Bonar Law had been telephoning asking to see him. On the Sunday, Burnham called and had a long chat with Bonar Law. He [BL] denied there was an intrigue against LG and ascribed recent events to the action of the party machine in the constituencies. For various reasons, the local party leaders had become sick of LG and determined to get rid of him. [. . .]

Bonar said he wished to consult Burnham about Rothermere, who called upon him and first demanded as a condition of his support an undertaking to withdraw from Palestine and Mesopotamia. To this Bonar replied that he was quite willing to look into the figures, but that he could give no undertaking and that regard must be paid to our obligations. Rothermere said that this was most unsatisfactory, and then went on to say that under the circumstances he should withdraw his support from Bonar Law unless he was prepared to give him a step in the peerage. Bonar asked, 'What are you now?' He replied, 'A Viscount.'

Bonar: I suppose you wish to be made an Earl?

Rothermere: Yes.

Bonar: I am afraid I cannot gratify you. But it had been my intention to give your son,[4] who is a promising young man, a minor post, where he could learn the business of administration.

Rothermere said very little more, but promised to send his son to see Bonar.

When Esmond [Harmsworth] arrived he said that he had come to suggest that he should be appointed Under-Secretary for India.

Bonar: Do you understand what that means? It means you would have to reply in the House of Commons to all Indian questions. Such a thing would be impossible. You have not the experience. [. . .]

What happened then Burnham did not say explicitly, but I gathered that like the rich young man in the Scriptures, Esmond went away sorrowful at the injustice of being unable to purchase a seat in the Kingdom of Heaven. [. . .]

Stuart says that the relations between Bonar Law and Beaverbrook are mysterious. The Central Conservative Office people called on Stuart the other morning, and told him that they were much disturbed at Beaverbrook's predominance with BL and suggested an article in *The Times* on the subject. CS said that this was not the policy of *The Times*. [. . .]

18 November To Churt for the week-end. Found LG in wonderful form, laughing and carrying on like a boy. [. . .]

Much talk about the elections. LG. quoted figures to show that while the Conservatives have not half the votes, they have three-fifths of the members. He made great play with this. [. . .]

The change in the atmosphere since he has been out of office is amazing. Now he is working like a little dynamo to break up the Conservative Party by bringing the more advanced section to his flag, to join up with the 'Wee Frees', and to detach the more moderate members of the Labour Party – this with the object of forming a Central Party of which he will be leader. [. . .]

On Monday we played golf at Hindhead. LG played remarkably well. And he seemed remarkably well. On Saturday I thought him very jumpy, which was not surprising considering the efforts he has made during the past three weeks. He wrote out the first of his articles with his own hand. This he did before he got up. He is evidently very bitter against Bonar Law, Curzon, etc, and talked in the most bitter manner of the latter, who, he said, was responsible for what had happened in Turkey, as he had neglected during the past ten or twelve months to take advantage of opportunities for settlement.[5] [. . .]

We had a long talk about Rothermere. I told LG without disclosing the source of my information what Burnham and Campbell Stuart had told me.

LG: But you have not heard all the story. It was a private conversation and Bonar would have been guilty of a gross breach of confidence if he had referred to it in public. Furthermore he did not say that he had spent more than four hours with this young cub trying to square him and his father. What a preposterous thing for a Prime Minister to do when forming his Cabinet! He did not say that he had offered young Harmsworth the Under-Secretaryship of Foreign Affairs – a much more important position than the Under-Secretaryship of the India Office. I regard it as a much more serious offence to appoint an incompetent person to great public office than to advance a man a step in the peerage.[6] After all, what does an Earldom matter? Whereas the appointment of this youth to such an office might have done the country irreparable injury. [. . .]

21 November Campbell Stuart came to see me and tells me that the negotiations for getting rid of Steed and appointing Geoffrey Dawson as Editor of *The Times* are progressing. [. . .]

November [After the election] Recent events have been badly managed. LG, Birkenhead and Winston have played into Beaverbrook's hands. By associating with him they have invested him with a power which otherwise he did not possess. He has deluded them and led them into a quagmire. What his relations with Birkenhead are, it is difficult to say. There are subterranean influences, the details of which are not apparent. [. . .]

It is obvious that LG was trying to secure Bonar's support through Beaverbrook and failed. LG said to me that he did not understand the relations between Birkenhead and Beaverbrook, and he was glad that he himself had never become entangled with Beaverbrook financially, although Beaverbrook had attempted to establish such relations. [. . .]

1923

11 January Arrived at Algeciras. For business reasons it was difficult to get away,[7] but I felt bound to pay LG a visit. For one thing I wanted to see him, and for another because if I did not go it would look as if he were deserted by his friends now that he was no longer in office. His greeting was cordial but not effusive, and it was obvious that he was still resentful regarding my policy during the election and my opposition to his pro-Greek schemes. [. . .]

[In conversation Riddell remarked that the British people, unlike LG, were not prepared to treat the French as if they were our enemies and the Germans our friends.]

LG did not much like this, but countered by saying during one of our conversations (we had many) on the same subject that the present Government had precisely the same view as the last, and were just as antagonistic to the French. I denied the truth of the latter part of this statement, and added, perhaps foolishly, that even politicians had no monopoly of wisdom, as shown by recent events in the East and elsewhere. This made LG much annoyed. He remarked, 'Nor news-paper proprietors any monopoly of wisdom.' [. . .]

13 January   We started for Seville, where we arrived at about 8 o'clock. [. . .]

LG obviously much pleased by the attention of the Archbishop and Cardinals. He is like a pretty woman who has been absolutely the rage and who is being somewhat neglected. Even the smallest attentions are gratifying, whereas in other times they would have been disregarded or treated as a matter of course. [. . .]

In the evening we had somewhat of a set-to about the French. LG let out what I had long suspected as being the basic cause of his aversion to the French. He said, 'How did they treat us when we went to Paris for the Conference in 1919?. . .' The French foolishly and ungratefully treated the Americans with more respect that they did the British. Wilson had a gold chair, for example, whereas LG did not, and Wilson was asked to address the Senate and Congress [*sic*] and received all sorts of public attentions, whereas LG was virtually ignored. [. . .] The occurrences mentioned were only symptoms of what the French really had at heart – viz. the cultivation of American friendship in preference to that of Britain, who had made many sacrifices in the joint interest. [. . .]

15 January   We returned to Algeciras, going part of the way by train. I saw Megan had been crying. She intimated that she had had a terrible row with her father, with whom she was not on speaking terms, but did not disclose the cause, except to intimate that he had been very irritable.[8] LG came into the railway carriage, but soon disappeared into the next compartment, evidently not caring to remain in the same carriage as his daughter. In fact he seemed very short with everybody except Mrs LG. [. . .]

We lunched on the way back. LG still seedy and irritable. During lunch he took from his pocket the draft of an article written in pencil and in a low voice, but with much unction, read it out, ostensibly to Miss Cazalet, but obviously so that I should hear it. It contained most bitter references to the French. [. . .]

16 January J. T. told me that LG has received a telegram stating that the *Daily Telegraph* had declined to publish one of his articles owing to his anti-French bias. I was not surprised.

The Birkenheads arrived. [. . .] I asked him whether it was necessary for himself, Chamberlain and other Conservative leaders to resign after the Carlton Club meeting, and whether it would not have been better for the Government to ask for a vote of confidence and, if refused, to have gone to the country. He replied that the Conservative leaders had no alternative but to resign. He thought, however, that the Government should have asked for a vote of confidence before the meeting at the Carlton Club. I asked, 'Why did they not do so?' To which he answered that LG was afraid of the honours question, and that he thought some resolution about this would have been tacked on to the vote. He added that LG had been very perturbed about the honours, and that he had never seen him so much worried about anything. This confirmed what Hamar Greenwood told me. Birkenhead said that too many peerages had been granted and that the proposal to give Robinson[9] a peerage was a terrible error. Waring also should never have been made a peer. He thought there had been some very curious proceedings in regard to honours, and that LG suspected this and was therefore most apprehensive. [. . .]

He spoke much of Ireland and Turkey, which he said were the proximate cause of the Government's downfall. He asked why LG had been so pro-Greek. I gave an explanation to the effect already stated in my diary. B described the policy as most disastrous. Regarding Ireland, Birkenhead said that while the Conservative Party were unable actively to oppose the settlement, they had been displeased with it and thought that he and Chamberlain had sold the pass. [. . .]

17 January I spent a couple of hours talking with LG and Mrs [LG]. His manner today was quite different. He seemed to be much more settled in his mind. He was busy upon his article for the *Daily Chronicle*, etc. He read portions to me and asked my opinion. I strongly urged him to cut down his references to the French. The article as prepared included some of the pungent matter I heard him read on the previous day. He discussed my points, and eventually in a great measure adopted my suggestions by striking out the inflammatory portions, the chief being a suggestion that Britain was an honest and France a dishonest nation. [. . .]

LG and I and Mrs had a long talk about LG's political future. [. . .] LG said his difficulty was that if he organised his own party, that would tend to intensify the differences between him and the Conservatives and the Asquith Liberals. He said he did not propose to go to the House of Commons much this session. [. . .]

LG and I went for a longish walk, during which he discussed the situation in the Ruhr at length. He said that Bonar Law had not managed things well in regard to France, that he ought not to have broken with Poincaré. [. . .]

25 February   To Churt for the night. [. . .]

LG spoke much of the Mitcham [by-]election, and seemed delighted at the appearance of the independent Conservative candidate. I said I thought he had been put up by Rothermere, and that it was most undesirable that newspaper proprietors should be putting forward Parliamentary candidates. I said I did not understand what Rothermere was after. [. . .] LG strongly disagreed with what I had said as to the action of newspaper proprietors. [. . .] I have a shrewd suspicion that although Rothermere is so anti-German and pro-French, he and LG are working together against Bonar Law. I was very much struck by LG's general attitude. He is evidently bitter and disappointed and inclined to give rein to the reckless side of his make-up. [. . .] He was quite friendly, but obviously much nettled by my disagreement with his policies. [. . .]

2 April   To Churt to spend the day with LG. He seemed well but looked rather thin and drawn.[. . .] He said he had given up playing golf. [. . .]

He was much more gracious and friendly than when we were in Spain, but it was clear that the iron had entered into his soul and that he was resentful of the way in which he had fallen into the background. [. . .]

He held out gloomy prospects for the future, saying that Labour would move forward gradually by increasing the levies upon wealth, and by carrying out public services at the expense of the richer classes. [. . .] He said, 'Asquith and I have no money. Why should we come out to defend these people?. . .'

This interview left me with a strange feeling. It is apparent that LG's one desire is to get back at all costs. [. . .] After eight years, practically the leading man in the world, he has now sunk back into a position of comparative insignificance, for the time being at any rate. He gets very little mention in the Press; he is surrounded by malicious enemies. [. . .]

I am becoming very slack in keeping my diary, and think I shall abandon it altogether before long.

6 May To Churt for tea and dinner.

LG said that he thought Bonar was done, and that his health was bad. He said that Bonar should never have taken the position, and that he was a terrible failure. I did not assent to this but I thought it wiser to say nothing. [. . .]

29 May Long interview with S[ylvester] who tells me that Baldwin's[10] selection was due in a great measure to J.C.C. Davidson,[11] Bonar's late secretary, who strongly feared Curzon's appointment. By manipulation Davidson succeeded in getting representations in favour of Baldwin placed before Stamfordham, who was much impressed and consequently nominated him. Davidson exercises much power, but Beaverbrook has been busy, although S is not sure as to the extent of his influence. [. . .] He says that McKenna has been asked to join the Government, owing to Bonar's intervention. During the settlement of the American debt Bonar was advised by McKenna, who strongly objected to the Baldwin settlement. Bonar took his line, but the only supporter he had in Cabinet was Lloyd-Graeme.[12] [. . .]

S[lyvester] is to leave Downing Street and to become Deputy-Clerk of the Privy Council, in which capacity he will be second to Hankey once more. Beaverbrook evidently wants to curry favour with him. I have always had a suspicion that Beaverbrook or one of his satellites was in close touch with J. T. D[avies], from whom the *Express* obtained its inspiration, supposed to be due to Beaverbrook's relationship with Bonar Law. I fancy Beaverbrook was anxious to play the same game with S. Beaverbrook is a bluffer. For example: Sir James Dunn[13] told

Hamar Greenwood that when he received his baronetcy Beaverbrook invited him to lunch and explained that the honour was due to his intervention, and that he had been working for it for a long time. As Dunn had drawn his cheque, he knew the facts, and remarked to Hamar Greenwood, 'What I objected to was the implication that I could be bluffed in this way.'

From talking to Horne, I could see that Beaverbrook is playing the same game in regard to Baldwin – the confidence trick. He tells Horne & Co. that he is all powerful with Baldwin if he likes. They take him at his own valuation and repose their confidences in him. He then goes to Baldwin, no doubt, and says that he, Beaverbrook, is all powerful with these other people. He then establishes the relationship of a go-between. [. . .]

30 May   Robert Horne had lunch with me. He says that Baldwin strongly pressed him to join the Government. [. . .] Horne said, however, that he could not accept office without Chamberlain and strongly urged his inclusion in the Government. [. . .] He [Baldwin] was anxious to include Chamberlain, but was prevented by representations from some of the 'Die-Hards'.[14] [. . .] Horne had lunch with Winston the other day and asked him where he stood politically. He replied, 'I am what I have always been – a Tory Democrat. Force of circumstances has compelled me to serve with another party, but my views have never changed, and I should be glad to give effect to them by rejoining the Conservatives.' [. . .]

10 September   Long talk with Barney Baruch, the American, at the Ritz Hotel. He wired asking me to have tea with him. He began by complimenting me on my work at the Washington Conference, saying that I had done more for Britain than anyone present at the Conference by giving the Press a British tinge. [. . .]

He gave a dramatic account of an interview between him and President Wilson, who is a close friend.

Wilson, placing his paralysed arm on the table beside him, said in slow but firm accents, 'Perhaps it was providential that I was stricken down when I was. Had I kept my health I should have carried the League. Events have shown that the world was not ready for it. It would have been a failure. Countries like France and Italy are un-sympathetic with such an organisation. Time and sinister happenings may eventually convince them that some such scheme is required. It may not be my scheme. It may be some other. I see now, however, that my plan was premature. The world was not ripe for it.'

Baruch said that the incident was so pathetic that he could only say in reply, 'Well, Mr Wilson, you did what you thought was for the best!' [. . .]

13 November [. . .] Spent nearly an hour with Lord Curzon. [. . .] We spoke of the Greco-Turkish policy. Curzon said, 'LG was responsible. He was bent on it. He had interviews behind my back with Venizelos, Stavridi and others. He seemed to be in Venizelos' pocket. [. . .] He made a fatal speech which led to the destruction of the Greek Army. The Turks at once attacked them. When the true history is written, the story will prove amazing. It was a disastrous business.'

I also had a long talk with Vansittart, Curzon's secretary, who expressed gloomy views concerning the European situation, saying that France was now the only European power that counted. Poincaré was a disagreeable man, but courageous and obstinate. His policy was definite and capable of execution, whereas ours was necessarily nebulous. I also had a few words with Eyre Crowe[15] on the staircase. He confirmed what Vansittart had said [. . .] and then left, looking like an undertaker.

11 April 1924 [Riddell talked with Sir George Graham, who had been visiting the King.] The King remarked of the new Labour Government: 'Well, one cannot imagine Queen Victoria getting on with a Labour Government.' And then, with just a trace of emotion, 'Or my father, adaptable as he was. Times change, and I suppose I have changed with them.'[16]

[The last diary entries, fourteen in number, are in 1933 and 1934. They consist of brief notes of conversations with such figures as Sir John Simon, Lord Davies, Lord Macmillan, Sir Robert Bruce and others, but are of little interest. The diaries close with this anecdote, written on 28 September 1934, a few weeks before Riddell's death:]

After a strenuous pilgrimage with the Queen at an exhibition, Lord Derby, in an exhausted state, remarked to a friend of mine, 'If I had a horse with legs like the Queen's, I could make a fortune.'

Notes

Introduction

1 A recent check of one hundred books on this period of British history – biographies, memoirs, monographs – reveals that fully nine-tenths of them contained references to Riddell, and the great majority quoted from one or more of his published volumes.

2 Published by Ivor Nicholson & Watson, London.

3 9 June 1933.

4 Published by Victor Gollancz, London.

5 *Times Literary Supplement*, 16 November 1933.

6 Published by Country Life, London.

7 Beaverbrook to Riddell, 30 May 1933, and Riddell to Beaverbrook, 1 June 1933. House of Lords Record Office. Beaverbrook Papers, BBK C/276.

8 Public Trustee to editor, 11 November 1982.

9 For much of the following information on Riddell I am indebted to the News Group Newspapers Ltd who granted me permission to read an unpublished biography by Stafford Somerfield.

10 Others in this category amongst Riddell's contemporaries were Asquith, Balfour, Lloyd George and Rosebery. For different reasons Bonar Law and Ramsay MacDonald could also be grouped with them.

11 Many important people lived in Queen Anne's Gate, among them Lord Haldane, Lord Fisher, St Loe Strachey and Edwin Montagu.

12 Bernard Darwin, *James Braid* (London, 1952), p. 171.

13 Bernard Falk, *Five Years Dead. A Postscript to 'He Laughed in Fleet Street'* (London, 1937), p. 259.

14 6 December 1934.

15 *More Pages*, p. 17.

16 Quoted in Stephen Koss, *The Rise and Fall of the Political Press in Britain. Volume Two: The Twentieth Century* (London, 1984), p. 103.

17 In *Intimate Diary* (p. 154) Riddell changed this to read: 'When I arrived I was handed a letter stating that the PM had decided to advise His Majesty to give me a peerage. . . .'

18 Published by Cassell, London.

19 P. 145.

20 A. J. P. Taylor (ed.) *Lloyd George. A Diary by Frances Stevenson* (London, 1971), p. 294.

21 From Stafford Somerfield's unpublished biography. This interview with Countess Lloyd George seems to have been in 1953.

22 For example, as late as 24 March 1922 Lloyd George was writing to Frances Stevenson: 'Riddell arrived this morning. [. . .] I am jolly glad

he is here.' A. J. P. Taylor (ed.), *My Darling Pussy. The Letters of Lloyd George and Frances Stevenson, 1913–41* (London, 1975), p. 41.
23 House of Lords Record Office. Lloyd George Papers, G/16/12/1–7.

1908–1911

1 The first paragraph of this first entry was an unimportant anecdote about the publisher Sir George Newnes (1851–1910).
2 John Morley (1838–1923), Liberal statesman, Secretary for India, 1905–10, Lord President of Council, 1910–14, created Viscount Morley of Blackburn.
3 Sir William Harcourt (1827–1904), Liberal statesman.
4 This should be 'President of Board of Education'.
5 This has been described a number of times, recently in John Grigg, *Lloyd George: The People's Champion, 1902–1912* (London, 1978), p. 182. The incident was more serious than Riddell's words suggest.
6 Incorrectly dated October 30 in *More Pages*, p. 4
7 John Alfred Spender (1862–1942), editor of *Westminster Gazette*, 1896–1922.
8 Joseph Chamberlain (1836–1914), Radical, later Unionist, statesman.
9 Edward Alfred Goulding (1862–1936), Unionist MP, created Baron Wargrave.
10 John Michael Fleetwood Fuller (1864–1915), Liberal MP.
11 See Riddell's comment of 19 April 1912, p. 394, n. 24.
12 Henry William Massingham (1860–1924), editor of the *Nation*, 1907 – 23.
13 Alfred Moritz Mond (1868–1930), Liberal, later Conservative MP, First Commissioner of Works, 1916–21, Minister of Health, 1921–2, created Baron Melchett.
14 Riddell tried to soften this in *More Pages*, p. 18, by adding: 'Of course this was only intended as a joke. There is no question of Winston's loyalty and devotion to Mr A.'
15 At this time Neil Primrose (1882–1917), son of a former Prime Minister, was twenty-nine years old and a Liberal MP. Churchill was then thirty-six.
16 Later Riddell changed his opinion on this. See, for example, the entry of 7 March 1915.
17 This appears to have been a clumsy attempt at 'Delcassé', after the French statesman who was forced to resign as a result of German pressure. Possibly Riddell meant *déclassé*, although this seems unlikely.
18 James Ramsay MacDonald (1866–1937), Labour MP and later Prime Minister.
19 Charles Silvester Horne (1865–1914), Liberal MP and leading Congregationalist minister.
20 John Edward Bernard Seely (1868–1947), Unionist, then Liberal, MP, Under-Secretary for Colonies, 1908–11, Under-Secretary for War,

1911–12, Secretary for War, 1912–14, Under-Secretary for Munitions, 1918–19, Under-Secretary for Air, 1919, created Baron Mottistone.
21 Lord Charles Beresford (1846–1919), Admiral and enemy of Lord Fisher, Unionist MP, created Baron Beresford.
22 William John Braithwaite (1875–1938), civil servant.
23 Emmeline Pankhurst (1858–1928), suffragette leader.

1912

1 John Elliott Burns (1858–1943), Labour and Liberal MP, President of Local Government Board 1905–14, President of Board of Trade 1914.
2 Walter Hume Long (1854–1924), Conservative MP, President of Local Government Board 1915–16, Colonial Secretary 1916–19, First Lord of Admiralty 1919–21, created Viscount Long of Wraxall.
3 John William Hills (1867–1938), Unionist MP, Financial Secretary to Treasury 1922–3.
4 Percy Holden Illingworth (1869–1915), Liberal MP, Chief Whip 1912–15.
5 Waldorf Astor (1879–1952), Unionist MP, 2nd Viscount Astor.
6 The strike began on 1 March and ended on 11 April.
7 Robert Smillie (1857–1940), Labour MP and miners' leader.
8 Vernon Hartshorn (1872–1931), Labour MP and miners' leader.
9 Randall Thomas Davidson (1848–1930), Archbishop of Canterbury 1903–28.
10 George Rankin Askwith (1861–1942), industrial arbitrator, created Baron Askwith.
11 Harold Spender (1864–1926), Liberal journalist, brother of J. A. Spender.
12 Philip Whitwell Wilson (1875–1956), author and journalist, former Liberal MP.
13 Arthur Henderson (1863–1935), Labour MP and statesman, President of Board of Education 1915–16, Paymaster-General 1916, Minister without Portfolio 1916–17.
14 Riddell's italics.
15 Sydney Charles Buxton (1853–1924), Liberal Minister, Postmaster-General 1905–10, President of Board of Trade 1910–14, Governor-General of South Africa 1914–20, created Earl Buxton.
16 Hubert Llewellyn Smith (1864–1935), civil servant, Permanent Secretary, Board of Trade 1907–19.
17 See also Riddell's letter to Lloyd George of 16 March 1912, printed in John Grigg, *Lloyd George. From Peace to War. 1912–1916* (London, 1985), p. 22.
18 Riddell added nine more lines in *More Pages*, p. 46, which do not appear in the manuscript.
19 Enoch Edwards (1852–1912), Labour MP and miners' leader.
20 Michael Hicks Beach (1837–1916), Conservative statesman, created Earl St Aldwyn.

21   James Louis Garvin (1868–1947), editor of *Observer* 1908–42, editor of *Pall Mall Gazette*, 1912–15.
22   Kennedy Jones (1865–1921), newspaperman of *Daily Mail* school.
23   Harold Harmsworth became Lord Rothermere in 1914 when Asquith was Prime Minister.
24   Cyril Arthur Pearson (1866–1921), newspaper proprietor, founder of St Dunstan's for the blind.
     On 19 April Riddell had written in his diary: 'I also hear that C. A. Pearson is practically blind. A tragic history. Newnes dead at 58, insolvent and a drunkard. Northcliffe an old man at 46 with shattered nerves. Kennedy Jones and Pearson also done at 46. This does not say much for the policy of hustle advocated by Northcliffe, Pearson, Kennedy Jones & Co.'
25   This refers to Lord Burnham and his son Harry Lawson, owners of the *Daily Telegraph*.
26   Robert Threshie Reid (1846–1923), Liberal Minister, Lord Chancellor 1905–12, created Earl Loreburn.
27   At this point in the manuscript is a copy of a telegram from Riddell to Lloyd George, dated 19 June 1912: 'Please put me down privately for a thousand. [. . .] Good luck to the poor man's champion.'
28   William Wedgwood Benn (1877–1960), Liberal, later Labour, MP, Junior Whip 1910–15, created Viscount Stansgate.
29   Harry Gosling (1861–1930), Labour MP and trade union leader.
30   Elizabeth Asquith (1897–1945) was then fifteen years old.
31   Charles Edward Henry Hobhouse (1862–1941), Liberal Minister, Under-Secretary for India 1907–8, Financial Secretary to Treasury 1908–11, Chancellor of Duchy of Lancaster 1911–14, Postmaster-General 1914–15.
32   George Earle Buckle (1854–1935), editor of *The Times* 1884–1912.
33   Thomas Marlowe (1868–1935), editor of *Daily Mail* 1899–1926.
34   Alfred George Gardiner (1865–1936), editor of *Daily News* 1902–19.
35   Ralph D. Blumenfeld (1864–1948), editor of *Daily Express* 1904–32.
36   It is clear from the manuscript that this is 'Cassell', not 'Carson' as in *More Pages*, p. 80. 'Edward' should read 'Ernest'. The wealthy Cassell (1852–1921) had been a great friend of Edward VII. It is highly unlikely that Sir Edward Carson should have been with Asquith on such an occasion in the year 1912.
37   The 'prominent member' is not identified in the manuscript.
38   Christabel Pankhurst (1880–1958), daughter of Emmeline Pankhurst.
39   Some other future marquess must have been intended. The 16th Marquess of Winchester succeeded to the title in 1899 and died in 1962. The 17th Marquess was only seven years old at this time.
40   In *More Pages*, pp. 91–2, Riddell made the contents of this letter appear to be an ordinary diary entry.
41   First mention of the house, 'Cliftondown', that Riddell built for Lloyd George at Walton Heath.
42   Frederick Sleigh Roberts (1832–1914), supreme commander in South Africa 1899, field-marshal, created Earl Roberts.

43 A significant comment, foreshadowing Lloyd George's advocacy of conscription in 1915.
44 Alfred Lyttelton (1857–1913), Unionist MP and former Colonial Secretary.
45 Megan Lloyd George (1902–66), later Liberal, then Labour, MP. The 'dead daughter' refers to Mair, Lloyd George's favourite child, who died in 1907 at age seventeen.

1913

1   The medical profession had vigorously opposed National Insurance.
2   Ellis Jones Griffith (1860–1926), Liberal MP, Parliamentary Under-Secretary for Home Office 1912–15.
3   Francis Knollys (1837–1924), private secretary to Edward VII and George V, created Viscount Knollys.
4   Sir Henry Campbell-Bannerman (1836–1908), Liberal statesman, Prime Minister 1905–8.
5   First mention of Marconi in the diaries.
6   Riddell was introduced to Mrs Pankhurst on 4 September 1916 and took the opportunity to tease her a little about this incident.
7   John Satterfield Sandars (1853–1934), former private secretary to A. J. Balfour.
8   On this day Lloyd George appeared before the Marconi Committee.
9   William Waldegrave Palmer (1859–1941), Unionist Minister, President of Board of Agriculture 1915–16, 2nd Earl of Selborne.
10 Andrew Caird (1870–1956), newspaperman under Northcliffe.
11 Andrew Carnegie (1839–1919), Scottish-born American industrialist and philanthropist.
12 Prince Louis of Battenberg (1854–1921), First Sea Lord 1912–14, Admiral of the Fleet, created Marquess of Milford Haven, father of Earl Mountbatten of Burma.
13 Lord Hugh Cecil (1869–1956), Unionist MP, created Baron Quickswood.
14 Lloyd George and McKenna were born in 1863.
15 Riddell's italics.
16 Louis Botha (1862–1919), Boer general, Prime Minister of South Africa 1910–19.
17 Whittaker Wright was a company promoter who was sentenced to penal servitude in 1904 for issuing a fraudulent balance sheet. He committed suicide before being gaoled.
18 I.e. the Land Campaign.
19 Cecil Chesterton, editor of *New Witness*, had been sued for libel by Godfrey Isaacs, brother of Rufus Isaacs. Chesterton lost.
20 Sir Albert Spicer (1847–1934), Liberal MP.
21 James Falconer (1856–1931), Liberal MP.
22 Frederick Handel Booth (1867–1947), Liberal MP.
23 Riddell had noted on 20 June that Lloyd George was 'full of beans and jollity'.
24 John St Loe Strachey (1860–1927), editor and proprietor of the *Spectator* 1898–1925.

25 Robert Offley Ashburton Crewe-Milnes (1858–1945), Liberal Minister, Secretary for India 1910–15, Lord President of Council 1915–16, President of Board of Education 1916, created Marquess of Crewe.
26 Augustine Birrell (1850–1933), Liberal Minister, Chief Secretary for Ireland 1907–16.
27 Riddell's italics. This passage was heavily underlined in the diary.
28 Joseph Devlin (1871–1934), Irish Nationalist MP.
29 Joseph Albert Pease (1860–1943), Liberal Minister, Chief Whip 1908–10, Chancellor of Duchy of Lancaster 1910–11, President of Board of Education 1911–15, Postmaster-General 1916, created Baron Gainford.
30 Lewis Harcourt (1863–1922), Liberal Minister, First Commissioner of Works 1905–10 and 1915–16, Colonial Secretary 1910–15, created Viscount Harcourt.

January–July 1914

1   On New Year's Day.
2   This was intended as a warning to Lloyd George. See John Grigg, *Lloyd George. From Peace to War. 1912–1916*, p.136.
3   A significant comment on Churchill's state of mind.
4   Charles Prestwich Scott (1846–1932), editor of *Manchester Guardian* 1872–1929, owner from 1905.
5   Riddell added an amusing little story: 'McKenna said that Lord Charles Beresford hated him like poison and that for a long time he (McK) and his wife used to receive most objectionable anonymous letters which they were certain came from Lady B, who on one occasion when alone in the Ladies' Gallery at the H of C put out her tongue at Mrs McK.' When McKenna was First Lord of the Admiralty he worked closely with Lord Fisher, which explains Beresford's attitude.
6   Riddell added: 'I am not quite sure regarding McKenna's feelings towards him. Simon no doubt would like to clear him out of the way as a possible rival for the premiership. They are each only about 40 years of age!'
7   Riddell first wrote 'damned', then struck it out in favour of 'very'.
8   I.e. from the Estimates.
9   Perhaps with reason. Churchill had attended a private dinner of Conservative leaders on 8 December 1912.
10 Masterman had to stand for re-election upon entering the Cabinet in January. He lost his seat for Bethnal Green and was defeated again later at Ipswich.
11 Sir Lewis Namier, who worked on propaganda under Masterman during the war, remarked to me (ed.) many years ago on Masterman's chronic slovenly appearance.
12 Theodore Roosevelt (1858–1919), President of the United States 1901–9, early advocate of American intervention on Allied side.
13 Woodrow Wilson (1856–1924), President of the United States 1913–21.
14 Riddell's italics.

15 The famous Buckingham Palace Conference.
16 William Graham Greene (1857–1930), Permanent Secretary at Admiralty 1911–17, Secretary at Ministry of Munitions 1917–20.
17 Reginald Herbert Brade (1864–1933), Permanent Secretary at War Office 1914–20.
18 George Mark Watson Macdonough (1865–1942), Director-General of Military Intelligence 1916–18, Adjutant-General to the Forces 1918–22, Lieutenant-General.
19 Obviously the last three sentences of this paragraph were added later.

August 1914–May 1915

1 Lloyd George also dined at Queen Anne's Gate on the eve of forming his wartime administration, 6 December 1916.
2 William Lygon (1872–1938), Liberal Minister, Lord President of the Council 1910 and 1914–15, First Commissioner of Works 1910–14, 7th Earl Beauchamp.
3 Thomas Mackinnon Wood (1855–1927), Liberal Minister, Under-Secretary for Foreign Affairs 1908–11, Financial Secretary to Treasury 1911–12 and 1916, Secretary for Scotland 1912–15, Chancellor of Duchy of Lancaster 1916.
4 In *War Diary*, p.6, Riddell told a story about Sir John French phoning to ask who was to command the expeditionary force. This is not in the manuscript.
5 The colourful story in *War Diary*, p. 9, about Lord Kitchener pointing to F. E. Smith at this dinner and announcing that he was to be the Press Censor does not appear in the manuscript.
6 A more prosaic account of these events than that which appeared in *War Diary*, p. 10.
7 Incorrectly dated 19 August in *War Diary*, p. 14.
8 For later comments by F. E. Smith on this incident, see entries for 23 March 1917 and (n.d.) January 1919.
9 The famous Queen's Hall speech.
10 Since the Marconi affair. Murray had been in South America in the meantime.
11 Charles Richard John Spencer-Churchill (1871–1934), 9th Duke of Marlborough.
12 The sinking of the three British cruisers *Aboukir*, *Cressy* and *Hogue*.
13 Riddell's italics.
14 Hedley Francis Le Bas (1868–1926), publisher.
15 Stanley Brenton Von Donop (1860–1941), Master-General of the Ordnance, 1913–16, Major-General.
16 This refers to the agitation against the First Sea Lord, Prince Louis of Battenberg, on account of his German origins.
17 I.e. persons of German birth who were not naturalised British subjects.
18 William Hesketh Lever (1851–1925), soap manufacturer and former Liberal MP, created Viscount Leverhulme.
19 Horatio George Gilbert Parker (1862–1932), novelist and Unionist MP.

20   Maurice Bonham Carter (1880–1960), Private Secretary to Mr Asquith 1910–16.
21   This transaction was never completed. The owner, W. W. Astor, turned the *Observer* over to his son Waldorf. The *Pall Mall Gazette* was sold separately to Davison Dalziel, and later it passed to Sir Henry Dalziel.
22   Hardinge Stanley Gifford (1823–1921), former Conservative Lord Chancellor, created Earl of Halsbury.
23   The Constitutional Conference of 1910.
24   Henry Charles Keith Petty-Fitzmaurice (1845–1927), Conservative statesman, former Governor-General of Canada and Viceroy of India, Minister without Portfolio 1915–16, 5th Marquess of Lansdowne.
25   Henry Hughes Wilson (1864–1922), Director of Military Operations 1910–14, Chief of Imperial General Staff 1918–22, Field-Marshal.
26   Frederick Edward Guest (1875–1937), Liberal MP, Treasurer of Household 1912–15, Secretary for Air 1921–2.
27   John William Gulland (1864–1920), Liberal MP, Chief Whip 1915–16.
28   Thomas James Macnamara (1861–1931), Liberal Minister, Parliamentary and Financial Secretary to Admiralty 1908–20, Minister of Labour 1920–2.
29   George Compton Archibald Arthur (1860–1946), Private Secretary to Lord Kitchener 1914–16, Assistant Director of Military Operations 1916–18.
30   John Maynard Keynes (1883–1946), economist, created Baron Keynes.
31   Riddell's italics. Presumably Fisher meant 'mouse'.
32   The 'matter' here was the excessive optimism of the Press.
33   Cecil Bisshopp Harmsworth (1869–1948), Liberal MP, Parliamentary Under-Secretary for Home Affairs 1915, Under-Secretary for Foreign Affairs 1919–22, brother of Lords Northcliffe and Rothermere.
34   Harmsworth, like Asquith, had been a Liberal Imperialist in the old days.
35   At the time Riddell did not think this was the reason for McKenna leaving the Admiralty. See entry for (n.d.) November 1911.
36   The battle of Festubert had been portrayed as a victory, whereas in fact it was a failure for British arms.
37   Of 29 March.
38   Frank Athelstan Swettenham (1850–1946), colonial administrator, Joint Director of Press Bureau 1915–18.
39   Edward Tyas Cook (1857–1919), newspaperman, Joint Director of Press Bureau 1915–18.
40   A reference to Asquith's convivial habits.
41   Archibald Philip Primrose (1847–1929), Liberal statesman, Prime Minister 1894–5, 5th Earl of Rosebery.
42   Riddell's italics.
43   Valentine Williams (1883–1946), journalist with *Daily Mail*.
44   Joseph Jacques Césaire Joffre (1852–1931), Commander-in-Chief of French Army 1914–16.
45   Of 20 April, when Asquith, on the strength of Kitchener's assurance, spoke confidently about the supply of ammunition to the front.

46　It is not clear what Kitchener meant by 'American intervention'.
47　Charles à Court Repington (1858–1925), Lieutenant-Colonel, military correspondent of *The Times* 1904–18, later with *Morning Post*, then *Daily Telegraph*.
48　Brinsley John Hamilton FitzGerald (1865–1931), ADC and Private Secretary to Sir John French 1914–15.

May–December 1915

1　Michael Bolton Furse (1870–1955), Bishop of Pretoria 1909–20, close friend of Geoffrey Robinson, editor of *The Times*. Riddell described Furse as 'an ecclesiastic about 6 ft 6 in tall, with voice and language to match. [. . .] LG told me that the Bishop used oaths like us ordinary mortals.'
2　Arthur Knyvet Wilson (1842–1921), First Sea Lord 1910–11; at Admiralty during war, Admiral of the Fleet.
3　Lloyd George further remarked that 'Winston has been intolerable, or rather he was during the first few months. If the PM was late he would not talk to anyone but Kitchener. The little dogs were not worth his notice. I am afraid he is angry with me just now. He came up to me in quite a menacing way and said I can see you don't mind what is going to happen to me, or something to that effect. I replied you are quite mistaken. We all have our ups and downs and must make the best of them. . . .'
4　Fisher had a somewhat Oriental appearance, which gave rise to stories about his antecedents.
5　Riddell may have begun to suspect that Northcliffe was already showing signs of insanity.
6　This appeared on 10 June.
7　Edouard Percy Cranwill Girouard (1867–1932), Director-General of Munitions Supply 1915–17.
8　James Stevenson (1873–1926), businessman, at Ministry of Munitions 1915–18, Surveyor-General of Supply, War Office, 1919–21, created Baron Stevenson.
9　Wife of Sir J. Herbert Lewis (1858–1933), Liberal MP and friend of Lloyd George's. He was Parliamentary Secretary to Local Government Board 1909–15, and to Board of Education 1915–22.
10　Riddell's italics.
11　Edward Hulton (1869–1925), newspaper proprietor, owner of *Daily Sketch*.
12　In view of the fact that Riddell himself had been the guilty party in a divorce suit. He seems to have feared that Hulton knew this.
13　Riddell's italics.
14　Frank Hodges (1887–1947), miners' agent, later Labour MP.
15　Because of Von Donop's German-sounding name. This occasion suggests that Churchill's determination to shun Lloyd George was short-lived.
16　Churchill meant the Northcliffe newspapers.
17　Riddell's italics.
18　Howell Arthur Gwynne (1865–1950), editor of *Standard* 1904–11, and *Morning Post* 1911–37.

19 Arthur Pole Nicholson (1869–1940), Parliamentary correspondent for *The Times* 1908–13; for *Daily News* 1914–19; and for *Daily Chronicle* 1920–3.
20 Josiah Clement Wedgwood (1872–1943), Liberal, later Labour, MP, created Baron Wedgwood.
21 George Cave (1856–1928), Unionist Minister, Solicitor-General 1915–16, Home Secretary 1916–19, Lord Chancellor 1922–4 and 1924–8. Created Viscount Cave.
22 Robert Vernon Harcourt (1878–1962), Liberal MP.
23 Ivor John Caradoc Herbert (1851–1933), Liberal MP, created Baron Treowen.
24 This refers to the conversation of 5 January 1915, when Guest wanted to know if he had a chance of becoming Chief Whip after Percy Illingworth's death. Riddell told him that being Winston Churchill's cousin was an impediment.
25 Philip Kerr (later Lord Lothian) was meant.
26 The 'small matter' was some detail about Le Bas' humble origins and early employment which Riddell had divulged to the Press. (See Introduction.)
27 Howard Frank (1871–1932), estate agent, served at War Office and Ministry of Munitions during war.
28 There is a curious ambiguity here. Presumably Northcliffe meant 'a public exposure in my newspapers of the state of affairs'.
29 When Sir William Lever sued Northcliffe's Amalgamated Press Limited for libel in 1907.
30 This may have been on the 30th. It is not clear from the manuscript.
31 Riddell's italics.
32 John Howard Whitehouse (1873–1955), anti-war Liberal MP.
33 It is not clear why Riddell excised Brade's name in the manuscript. The entry for 14 November identified him.
34 Churchill resigned the Duchy of Lancaster on 12 November, after Asquith excluded him from the new War Committee.
35 An oblique tribute to Asquith, who was acting as Secretary for War in Kitchener's absence.
36 This incident is described at greater length in *The History of The Times*. Vol. IV, Part 1 (London, 1952), p. 283, and Part 2 (London, 1952), Appendix II, G, pp. 1069–70.
37 Kitchener did return to the War Office, but with his powers further reduced. The new CIGS, Sir William Robertson, assumed control of military strategy.

January–July 1916

1 Where Lloyd George experienced a rebuff on Christmas Day 1915. A meeting of workers at St Andrew's Hall, Glasgow, shouted him down when he tried to appeal to their patriotism.
2 Robert Munro (1868–1955), Liberal Minister, Lord Advocate 1913–16, Secretary for Scotland 1916–22, created Baron Alness.
3 Riddell did not share his suspicions with the reader, but he seems to imply that the Cabinet leak was Lloyd George.

4   Henry Wickham Steed (1871–1956), Foreign Editor of *The Times* 1914–19, editor, 1919–22.
5   Robert Leicester Harmsworth (1870–1937), Liberal MP, brother of Lords Northcliffe and Rothermere.
6   George Croydon Marks (1858–1938), Liberal MP, created Baron Marks. Riddell excised Marks' name in *War Diary*, p. 156. It is not clear why.
7   George Nathaniel Curzon (1859–1925), Conservative statesman, Lord Privy Seal 1915–16, President of Air Board 1916, Lord President of Council 1916–19, Foreign Secretary 1919–24, created Marquess Curzon of Kedleston.
8   William Morris Hughes (1864–1952), Prime Minister of Australia 1915–23.
9   By his speech in the House of Commons on 7 March calling for Fisher's return and, by inference, his own.
10   Riddell's italics.
11   In fact there was more compromise than Riddell's words here suggest. See correspondence in Northcliffe Papers, British Library, Add. MS 62170, ff. 158–60.
12   Robert Laird Borden (1854–1937), Prime Minister of Canada 1911–20.
13   A remarkably shrewd forecast, considering the gulf between Lloyd George and Bonar Law at this time.
14   Christopher Addison (1869–1951), Liberal, later Labour, MP, Parliamentary Secretary to Board of Education 1914–15, to Ministry of Munitions 1915–16, Minister of Munitions 1916–17, Minister of Reconstruction 1917–19, Minister of Health 1919–21, Minister without Portfolio 1921, created Viscount Addison.
15   Theobald von Bethmann Hollweg (1856–1921), Chancellor of Germany 1909–17.
16   Asquith.
17   Reading.
18   Arthur John Bigge (1849–1931), private secretary to King George V 1901–31, created Baron Stamfordham.
19   John Thomas Davies (1881–1938), private secretary to Lloyd George 1912–22.
20   Basil Zaharoff (1850–1936), international financier and armaments king.
21   A bitter attack by A. G. Gardiner, which took the form of an open letter to Lloyd George, printed in the *Daily News* and *Star* on 22 April.
22   George Geoffrey Robinson (1874–1944), editor of *The Times* 1912–19 and 1922–41. Assumed surname of Dawson in 1917.
23   David Davies (1880–1944), wealthy Liberal MP, created Baron Davies.
24   First mention that Lloyd George might form his own party.
25   Bonar Law was on friendly terms with the editor of the *Glasgow Herald*, Robert Bruce.
26   'Cliftondown'.
27   Thomas Power O'Connor (1848–1929), journalist and Irish Nationalist MP.
28   Geoffrey Howard (1877–1935), Liberal MP, junior whip 1915–16.
29   Arthur Hamilton Lee (1868–1947), Unionist MP, Parliamentary Secretary to Ministry of Munitions 1915–16, Director-General of Food Production 1917–18, Minister of Agriculture 1919–21, First Lord of

Admiralty 1921–2, created Viscount Lee of Fareham. Riddell had the strange idea that Lee, whose father was a Church of England clergyman, was Jewish.

30 John Edward Redmond (1856–1918), MP and leader of the Irish Nationalist Party.
31 Lloyd George meant that Asquith and other Liberal ministers hoped to see him come a cropper over Ireland.
32 John Rushworth Jellicoe (1859–1935), commanded Grand Fleet, 1914–16, First Sea Lord 1916–17, Admiral of the Fleet, created Earl Jellicoe.
33 The Battle of Jutland.
34 Riddell changed this in *War Diary*, p. 187 to read: 'Poor Kitchener has been drowned. I feel very grieved. We got on well. He was a great man, but very uneven.'
35 It would be more accurate to say that Lloyd George had had an inconclusive discussion with Asquith about the War Office.
36 But in fact Lloyd George accepted the War Office without securing any diminution of General Robertson's powers as CIGS.
37 Apparently this refers to the *Daily Chronicle* leading article of 29 March 1915.
38 First mention of Lloyd George's interest in acquiring a newspaper to support him.
39 Charles Solomon Henry (1860–1919), wealthy Liberal MP.

July–December 1916

1 Editor's italics.
2 David Beatty (1871–1936), commanded First Battle Squadron 1913–16, commanded Grand Fleet 1916–18, First Sea Lord 1919–27, Admiral of the Fleet, created Earl Beatty.
3 Edwin Montagu.
4 Some strongly anti-semitic remarks followed.
5 But he told Frances Stevenson, who wrote in her diary on 26 July: 'Of all the Cabinet worms, I think Montagu is the wormiest' (*Lloyd George. A Diary by Frances Stevenson*, pp. 109–10).
6 Frances Stevenson (1888–1972), private secretary and mistress to Lloyd George, later Countess Lloyd George of Dwyfor.
7 William Sutherland (1880–1949), private secretary to Lloyd George, Coalition Liberal MP and Whip, Chancellor of Duchy of Lancaster 1922.
8 The famous 'Knock-out Blow' interview of 29 September.
9 Charles Hardinge (1858–1944), Permanent Under-Secretary at Foreign Office 1906–10 and 1916–20, Viceroy of India 1910–16, created Baron Hardinge of Penshurst.
10 Leopold James Maxse (1864–1932), editor of *National Review*.
11 Maurice Pascal Alers Hankey (1877–1963), Secretary to Committee of Imperial Defence 1912–38; to War Council 1914–15; to Dardanelles Committee 1915; to War Committee 1915–16; to War Cabinet 1916–18; to Cabinet 1919–38, created Baron Hankey.
12 This refers to the visits the two ambassadors paid to the Foreign Office on the eve of war.

13 Article in *Morning Post* of 23 November, praising instead of criticising Lloyd George.

14 Raymond Asquith (1878–1916), killed in action.

15 In *Reynolds' Newspaper* of this day, a popular journal owned by Sir Henry Dalziel who is frequently described as a crony of Lloyd George's.

16 'Packing' was changed to 'reading' in *War Diary*, p. 227. This altered the meaning considerably.

17 Up to this point in the crisis Riddell's diary entries are very thin.

18 James Eric Drummond (1876–1951), private secretary to Mr Asquith, later Secretary-General to League of Nations, 16th Earl of Perth.

19 The estimates of the support Lloyd George enjoyed amongst Liberal back benchers were generously inflated, thanks largely to that incurable optimist, Dr Addison.

20 Lloyd George's meeting with Labour leaders on 7 December. Unkindly but accurately described as the 'doping séance'.

21 These two sentences are badly worded. Lloyd George meant that leading Unionists insisted upon the exclusion of Churchill. And of Northcliffe also, although Lloyd George does not mention it here.

22 Aitken's curious hold over Bonar Law was evident at other times also. See, for example, Mrs Lloyd George's comments of 17 April 1921 on the reasons for Bonar Law's resignation from the coalition ministry.

23 Samuel Evans (1859–1918), former Liberal MP, Solicitor-General 1908–10.

24 This was the second time Lloyd George funked a difficult encounter with Churchill. Sir Max Aitken had been charged with this same task on 6 December.

25 Churchill seems to have imagined that Asquith was about to resign the leadership of the Liberal Party and that he would step into the former Prime Minister's shoes.

26 Churchill then switched the conversation to Northcliffe's delinquencies.

27 This entry appears to be under the wrong date. The celebrated affair concerning improper influence on military personnel erupted in August 1916 and was buried by the end of November. Possibly Derby was referring to the problem of reassigning Cowans, the Quartermaster-General, to other duties.

28 Lloyd George's last peers, whose names appeared in the resignation honours list of 10 November 1922, by contrast were quite uncontroversial.

January–August 1917

1 Arthur Neville Chamberlain (1869–1940), Director-General of National Service 1917, Prime Minister, 1937–40.

2 By asking Donald to assist with propaganda work.

3 Edgar Vincent (1857–1941), former Unionist MP, Chairman, Central Control Board 1915–20, created Viscount D'Abernon.

4 Cecil Spring-Rice (1859–1918), Ambassador to United States 1912–18.

5 Chamberlain lingered on in this office until August 1917. Henceforth he and Lloyd George were enemies.
6 Lloyd George added that Montagu was 'a self-seeking, scheming Jew who thinks of nothing but his own advancement'.
7 Walter Francis Roch (1880–1965), Liberal MP.
8 Riddell dined that evening with Brade, who said there was more to the story than the Dardanelles Report revealed. For example, the Commissioners could not take into account how Churchill would badger Kitchener late at night when the old soldier was dead tired.
9 Albert Holden Illingworth (1865–1942), Liberal MP, Postmaster-General 1916–21, created Baron Illingworth.
10 In a letter to *The Times* on 21 April, Wells had spoken of 'an alien and uninspiring Court'. The King remarked spiritedly: 'I may be uninspiring, but I'll be damned if I'm an alien.'
11 French generals.
12 So effective was Churchill that Lloyd George determined to bring him into the ministry, and did so a few weeks later.
13 And continued to get the credit in many subsequent accounts.
14 Hudson Ewebanke Kearley (1856–1934), former Liberal MP, Food Controller, 1916–17, created Viscount Devonport.
15 Her anger was prompted by the Mesopotamia scandal and the way important people were trying to shield each other from blame.
16 Lloyd George was not revealing the true reason to Riddell. In fact Carson had been a failure at the Admiralty and it was necessary to kick him upstairs.
17 Sir Eric Geddes.
18 This almost certainly is misdated. Churchill would hardly have spoken in such a fashion on the morrow of becoming Minister of Munitions. Possibly 'June 29' was intended.
19 This recalls the Max Beerbohm cartoon in *The Tatler* of 26 April 1911, entitled 'The Succession' (i.e. to Asquith). Churchill is saying, 'Come, suppose we toss for it, Davey.' Lloyd George replies, 'Ah, but, Winsey, would either of us as loser abide by the result?'
20 Riddell's italics.
21 This is a later assessment by Riddell, inserted at this point. There is no diary entry for 13 August. The sentence about 'courage, patience, bravery in the face of personal danger' was excised in *War Diary*, p. 256.
22 Frederick Barton Maurice (1871–1951), Director of Military Operations at War Office 1915–18, Major-General.
23 This should read 'Wully', Robertson's nickname.

September 1917–March 1918

1 This was the beginning of Lloyd George's great battle with Robertson, Haig and Derby.
2 Edward Henry Allenby (1861–1936), commanded 3rd Army 1915–17, commanded Egyptian Expeditionary Force 1917–19, Field Marshal, created Viscount Allenby of Megiddo.

3   Herbert Albert Laurens Fisher (1866–1940), historian and Liberal Minister, President of Board of Education 1916–22.
4   Arthur Steel-Maitland (1876–1935), Unionist MP, Parliamentary Under-Secretary for Colonies 1915–17, Secretary, Department of Overseas Trade, 1917–19.
5   William Henry Clark (1876–1952), Comptroller-General of Commercial Intelligence Department, Board of Trade, 1916–17, Comptroller-General of Department of Overseas Trade 1917–28.
6   As a result of rivalry between the Foreign Office and the official propaganda department at Wellington House under Charles Masterman.
7   At Caporetto, where the Italians were heavily defeated.
8   Mark Sykes (1879–1919), Unionist MP, co-author of 'Sykes-Picot Agreement' of 1916.
9   Owen Cosby Phillips (1863–1935), Liberal, later Conservative, MP, created Baron Kylsant.
10 It is significant that Churchill, a regular diner, was absent, although he was in London. At this time he did not wish to be identified with any particular group.
11 But in a few weeks Rothermere accepted the post of Air Minister, although Balfour was Foreign Secretary.
12 On Northcliffe's return from his mission to the United States, Lloyd George discussed with him the possibility of becoming Air Minister, though no formal offer was made. Northcliffe then proceeded to publish a letter announcing his refusal. Lloyd George was somewhat embarrassed. The incumbent, Lord Cowdray, was infuriated and never forgave Lloyd George.
13 But Lloyd George had been strong for businessmen in high office when he became Prime Minister, witness such appointments as Lord Devonport, Lord Rhondda and Neville Chamberlain.
14 Yet he appointed Rothermere to be Air Minister on 26 November 1917.
15 This solves the little mystery of Simon's withdrawal from the case. Possibly he had talked to leading Asquithians after agreeing to defend Lloyd George and concluded that by doing so he might damage his prospects with the official Liberal party.
16 Presumably he meant 'the Colonel House of Britain'. House was President Wilson's personal representative to the Allied Governments.
17 Killed in action in Palestine.
18 General Sir Henry Wilson.
19 Letter of 29 November 1917 to the *Daily Telegraph*, urging a negotiated peace.
20 All of this, save for the part about France wanting Alsace-Lorraine, was excised in *War Diary*, p. 298.
21 John Charteris (1877–1946), Chief of Intelligence to General Haig. Brigadier-General.
22 Philip Gibbs (1877–1962), war correspondent for *Daily Chronicle*.
23 Henry Francis Oliver (1865–1965), Chief of Admiralty War Staff 1914–17, commanded First Battle Squadron 1918, Admiral of the Fleet.
24 Reginald Hugh Bacon (1863–1947), Vice-Admiral commanding Dover Patrols 1915–18.

25 Riddell's italics.
26 Georges Clemenceau (1841–1929), Prime Minister of France and Minister of War 1917–20.
27 Auckland Campbell Geddes (1879–1954), Unionist Minister, Minister of National Service, 1917–18, President of Local Government Board 1918–19, President of Board of Trade 1919–20, Ambassador to United States 1920–4, created Baron Geddes.
28 Georg von Hertling (1843–1919), Chancellor of Germany 1917–18.
29 The present holder of this post was Sir Frederick Cawley, a Liberal MP, who received a peerage (Baron Cawley) on making way for Beaverbrook.
30 John Buchan (1875–1940), author and Unionist MP, later Governor-General of Canada, created Baron Tweedsmuir.
31 Charles Russell (1863–1928), solicitor.
32 Horace Curzon Plunkett (1854–1932), Irish Unionist politician.
33 Riddell added some comments in *War Diary*, p. 312, which do not appear in the manuscript.
34 Lloyd George may have been referring to the *Daily Mail* article of 13 October 1917, which was headed 'Ministerial Meddling Means Military Muddling', and established the tone for what followed.
35 Cecil did not resign until a fortnight after the Armistice, and then over a minor matter concerning the Church in Wales.
36 James Gascoyne-Cecil (1861–1947), Unionist peer, 4th Marquess of Salisbury.
37 James Henry Thomas (1874–1949), Labour MP and trade union leader.

March–November 1918

1 Riddell's italics.
2 This should read '5th'.
3 Hubert de la Poer Gough (1870–1963), commanded Fifth Army 1916–18, General.
4 Riddell's italics.
5 Hubert Charles Onslow Plumer (1857–1932), commanded 2nd Army 1915–17 and 1918, commanded Italian Expeditionary Force 1917–18, Field-Marshal, created Viscount Plumer.
6 Charles Harington (1872–1940), Deputy-Chief of Imperial General Staff 1918–20, commanded Army of Black Sea 1920–1 and occupation forces in Turkey 1921–3, General.
7 Julian Hedworth George Byng (1862–1935), commanded 3rd Army 1917–19, Field-Marshal, created Viscount Byng of Vimy.
8 Henry Sinclair Horne (1861–1929), commanded First Army 1916–19, General, created Baron Horne.
9 John Joseph Pershing (1860–1948), Commander-in-Chief of American Army in Europe 1917–19, General.
10 On 18 April Milner became War Secretary in succession to Derby, and Chamberlain, who in opposition had become a dangerous critic of Lloyd George, entered the War Cabinet.

11 As follows: 'With plenty of liquor on board he [Rothermere] remarked: "Readingsh [*sic*] greatest Jew since Jesus Christ – that's what I think – greatest Jew since Jesus Christ!"'

12 Alexander Gregor Jeans (1849–1924), Managing-Director of *Liverpool Post*, he received a knighthood before the year was out.

13 William Mather Rutherford Pringle (1874–1928), Liberal MP.

14 James Myles Hogge (1873–1928), Liberal MP.

15 John Dillon (1851–1927), Irish Nationalist MP.

16 Oswald Partington (1872–1935), Liberal MP, 2nd Baron Doverdale.

17 Percy Pollexfen de Blaquière Radcliffe (1874–1934), Director of Military Operations at War Office 1918–22, General.

18 Douglas Egremont Robert Brownrigg (1867–1939), Chief Censor at Admiralty 1914–18, Vice-Admiral.

19 This may have been 28 July. It is unclear in the manuscript.

20 Henry Norman (1858–1939), Liberal MP, Liaison Officer at Ministry of Munitions 1916–18.

21 Grant Morden (1880–1932), Unionist MP.

22 Howard Spicer (1872–1926), papermaker.

23 Stephenson Hamilton Kent (1873–1954), Director-General, Munitions Labour Supply.

24 On 29 August 1918, when the *Daily Express* in a leading article entitled 'Some Questions on a General Election' demanded to know Lloyd George's programme on key issues such as Tariff Reform, Ireland and the Welsh Church.

25 Solly Joel (d. 1931) was a financier. The Berrys were the future Lords Camrose (1879–1954) and Kemsley (1883–1968).

26 Andrew Weir (1865–1955), shipowner, Minister of Munitions 1919–21, created Baron Inverforth.

27 Joseph Paton Maclay (1857–1951), shipowner, Minister of Shipping 1916–21, created Baron Maclay.

28 Rosslyn Erskine Wemyss (1864–1933), First Sea Lord 1917–19, Admiral of the Fleet, created Baron Wester Wemyss.

29 Only about one-quarter of this letter appeared in *War Diary*, pp. 365–6.

30 Lloyd George's comment.

31 William Dudley Ward (1877–1946), Liberal MP and former Junior Whip.

32 Riddell added: 'Guest said that a debate was to take place in the House of Commons that night regarding the *Daily Chronicle*. . . . (In the debate Sir Henry Dalziel stated in precise terms that he alone controls the policy of the *DC* – a curious statement in view of the facts.)'

33 George Younger (1851–1929), Unionist MP and chairman of party organisation, created Viscount Younger of Leckie.

34 William Bull (1863–1931), Unionist MP.

35 Riddell included only a fraction of this letter in *War Diary*, p. 377, and made it appear to be a diary entry.

36 Robert Arthur Sanders (1867–1940), Unionist MP, Parliamentary Under-Secretary for War 1921–2, Minister of Agriculture 1922–4, created Baron Bayford.

37 Leo Amery was also at this luncheon. He commented on the newspaper proprietors present: 'I felt I was in a real den of thieves when they once started talking.' And of Rothermere: 'A more perfect specimen of the plutocratic cad it would be hard to imagine' (*The Leo Amery Diaries*, eds. John Barnes and David Nicholson, London, 1980, p. 242).
38 This was unusual. Riddell rarely took his wife anywhere.
39 Presumably this was G. H. Mair of the *Manchester Guardian*.

November 1918–June 1919

1   Campbell Stuart (1885–1972), publisher, Deputy Director of Propaganda in Enemy Countries 1918.
2   This of course should read '1916'.
3   William George Tyrrell (1866–1947), Assistant Under-Secretary for Foreign Affairs 1919–25, created Baron Tyrrell.
4   Churchill made the same demand on 7 November.
5   The story of this attempted transaction came out in a much more innocuous form in *Intimate Diary*, pp. 3–4.
6   Robert Horne (1871–1940), Unionist Minister, Minister of Labour 1919–20, President of Board of Trade 1920–1, Chancellor of Exchequer 1921–2, created Viscount Horne of Slamannan.
7   The Allied leaders were now gathered in Paris.
8   Raymond Poincaré (1860–1934), President of the French Republic 1913–20.
9   Warden Stanley Chilcott (1871–1942), Unionist MP.
10 Walter George Frank Phillimore (1845–1929), Lord Justice of Appeal 1913–16, created Baron Phillimore.
11 Herbert Hoover (1874–1964), Chairman of Commission for Relief in Belgium 1914–19, President of the United States 1929–33.
12 Joseph George Ward (1856–1930), Prime Minister of New Zealand 1906–12 and 1928–30, New Zealand representative in Imperial War Cabinet.
13 Albert Henry Stanley (1874–1948), Unionist Minister, President of Board of Trade 1916–19, created Baron Ashfield.
14 Ernest Bevin (1881–1951), Labour leader and later Cabinet Minister, General Secretary of Transport and General Workers' Union 1921–40.
15 The Liberal defeated the Coalition Unionist candidate in the West Leyton by-election on 14 March. The same thing happened at Central Hull on 11 April.
16 Riddell added this comment later.
17 It is not clear what Lloyd George meant by the last sentence.
18 William George Eden Wiseman (1885–1962), banker, Chief Adviser on American Affairs to British Delegation in Paris 1918–19. Wiseman's name was excised in *Intimate Diary*, p. 47.
19 Presumably this was a reference of the fact that Percy was a younger son of the Duke of Northumberland.
20 Riddell meant 'Wilson', i.e. Leslie O. Wilson, the Unionist Chief Whip.

21 The so-called 'Lowther Telegram', after the chief organiser, Colonel Claude Lowther, a diehard Unionist MP.
22 On the 16th, when he demolished Northcliffe with a devastating attack.
23 Francis Stanley Jackson (1870–1947), Unionist MP, Financial Secretary to War Office 1922–3.
24 Keynes soon made his views known in *The Economic Consequences of the Peace (1919)*.
25 George Nicoll Barnes (1859–1940), Labour Minister, Minister without Portfolio in War Cabinet 1917–20.
26 Ignace Jean Paderewski (1860–1941), Polish pianist, composer and statesman. Premier of Poland 1919.
27 Ulrich Brockdorff-Rantzau (1869–1928), German Foreign Minister 1919.
28 The 'great personage' was President Wilson.
29 Evidently Lloyd George was reminded of Northcliffe's conduct in the Air Ministry affair of late 1917.
30 Apparently this refers to Asquith's Newcastle speech of 20 April 1915. It is curious that Lloyd George's mind should have been on such a matter at this time.
31 William Orpen (1878–1931), artist and portrait painter.
32 Elinor Glyn (d. 1943), prolific writer of romantic fiction.
33 A nasty crack at Field-Marshal Sir William Robertson.
34 Ian Zachary Malcolm (1868–1944), Unionist MP.
35 Riddell's italics.

July–December 1919

1 Which lasted from mid-July to mid-August.
2 The new honour was the GCB, and the £25,000 was a Parliamentary grant for services during the war.
3 Hamar Greenwood (1870–1948), Liberal, later Conservative, MP, Parliamentary Under-Secretary for Home Affairs 1919, Secretary, Overseas Trade Department 1919–20, Chief Secretary for Ireland 1920–2, created Viscount Greenwood.
4 Ernest Evans (1885–1965), private secretary to Lloyd George 1918–20. Liberal MP.
5 For attacking the Coalition and its ways.
6 It appears that the politicians were trying to get a rise out of Riddell, the only newspaper proprietor present. When this gathering dispersed Riddell had a long talk with Lloyd George and Frances Stevenson about the Harmsworths, in particular their lack of manners. Lloyd George described them as 'an unattractive family. Vulgar and coarse.'
7 George Tom Molesworth Bridges (1871–1939), member of British Mission to USA 1917–18, Lieutenant-General.
8 The parliamentary grant made to Haig in recognition of his services as Commander-in-Chief.
9 Three leading capitalists who were not highly regarded.

10   Guest forgot that the name 'Coalition National Democratic Party' had been used by the handful of Labour men who supported Lloyd George at the 'Coupon Election' of 1918.
11   But see Riddell's diary entry for 17 June 1922, when Hulton disabused him of this idea.
12   In fact Geddes remained at the Board of Trade until March 1920.
13   At this point in the manuscript is the following note, typed separately: 'This was due to a suggestion from Miss Stevenson, who said that Ministers were no longer to use Government motors, and that LG would have to acquire one for himself. He said he would like to have the one he was using, which would cost about £3,000, and that it would be nice if I were to make him a present of it. This was subsequently confirmed by J. T. D[avies].'
14   This refers to Sir Walter (later Baron) Runciman, the great shipowner who was the father of the Liberal ex-Minister Walter Runciman.
15   Cecil Frederick Nevil Macready (1862–1946), Adjutant-General to the Forces 1916–18, Commissioner of Metropolitan Police 1918–20, GOC in C, Forces in Ireland 1920–2.
16   Abe Bailey (1864–1940), South African mine-owner.
17   On 19 December there was a Sinn Fein attempt to ambush the Viceroy, Lord French, but the attackers were repulsed and French was unharmed.
18   Philip Albert Gustave David Sassoon (1888–1939), wealthy Unionist MP.
19   The forthcoming by-election in this Yorkshire constituency.
20   In *Intimate Diary*, p. 154, Riddell gave a rather different phrasing from the manuscript: 'When I arrived I was handed a letter stating that the PM had decided to advise His Majesty to give me a peerage, in recognition of my public work.'

1920

1   Labour won the seat, Sir John Simon came second, the Coalition candidate ran third.
2   See entry for 18 December 1920, when Lloyd George startled Bonar Law, Beaverbrook and several others with this suggestion.
3   Francesco Saverio Nitti (1868–1953), Prime Minister of Italy 1919–20.
4   Laming Worthington-Evans (1868–1931), Unionist MP, Parliamentary Secretary to Ministry of Munitions 1916–18, Minister of Blockade 1918, Minister of Pensions 1919–20, Minister without Portfolio 1920–21, Secretary for War 1921–2 and 1924–9.
5   Leo Chiozza Money (1870–1944), Liberal MP, Parliamentary Secretary to Ministry of Shipping 1916–18.
6   Riddell excised the names of Addison and Barnes in *Intimate Diary*, p. 168.
7   Edward Shortt (1862–1935), Liberal MP, Chief Secretary for Ireland 1918–19, Home Secretary 1919–22.
8   Gordon Hewart (1870–1943), Liberal MP, Solicitor-General 1916–19,

Attorney-General 1919–22, Lord Chief Justice of England 1922–40, created Viscount Hewart.

9 Frederick George Kellaway (1870–1933), Liberal MP, Parliamentary Secretary to Ministry of Munitions 1916–21, Secretary, Department of Overseas Trade 1920–1, Postmaster-General 1921–2.

10 The Independent Liberals who were followers of Asquith, as distinct from the Coalition Liberal supporters of Lloyd George.

11 Charles Palmer (1869–1920) was formerly editor of the *Globe*. Horatio Bottomley (1860–1933) was the notorious proprietor of *John Bull*.

12 To replace the Coalition Liberal Chief Whip, F. E. Guest.

13 Garvin, the editor, had become estranged from Lloyd George because of the Peace Treaty and the Irish situation. Relations improved by early 1922.

14 John Reeves Ellerman (1862–1933), shipowner and large shareholder in *The Times*.

15 Alexandre Millerand (1859–1943), President of the French Republic 1920–4.

16 The increasing frequency of such remarks is a measure of Riddell's growing disenchantment with Lloyd George's foreign policy.

17 Neill Malcolm (1869–1953), British Military Mission to Berlin 1919–21, Major-General.

18 Bertrand Dawson (1864–1945), physician-in-ordinary to Kings Edward VII, George V and Edward VIII, created Viscount Dawson of Penn.

19 Frederick Hugh Sykes (d. 1954), Chief of Air Staff 1918–19, Major-General.

20 John Wynford Philipps (1860–1938), financier and former Liberal MP, created Viscount St Davids.

21 H. Hugh Tudor (1871–1965), Major-General, Chief of Police, Ireland, 1920.

22 Mustapha Kemal (1880–1938), Turkish nationalist leader, ruler of Turkey 1922–38.

23 Eleutherios Venizelos (1864–1936), Prime Minister of Greece 1910–15, 1917–20, 1924, 1929–32 and 1933.

24 Chamberlain, however, continued as Chancellor of the Exchequer until March 1921.

25 The remark about culture is curious, considering such ministers as Bonar Law, Eric Geddes, Hamar Greenwood, etc.

26 Riddell's italics.

27 This suggests that Derby had the same idea as Campbell Stuart about Northcliffe for Lord Lieutenant of Ireland.

28 This occasion, noted by various writers, did not mark a break in relations between Lloyd George and Riddell. But it probably ensured that the old intimacy would never be resumed.

29 The first volume of Margot Asquith's *Autobiography*, just published.

30 Joseph Hewitt (1865–1923), colliery owner.

31 Lee's name was excised in *Intimate Diary*, p. 237.

32 A reference to the Munshi Abdul Karim, whom she had employed as a confidential secretary.

33   Which began on 1 April and continued to 4 July.
34   Arthur Henry Crosfield (1865–1938), manufacturer and former Liberal MP.
35   Such asperity suggests the degree of Lloyd George's weariness.
36   St John Brodrick (1856–1942), former Conservative Secretary for War. Created Earl of Midleton.
37   In Paris, between 5 and 10 November. Northcliffe was 'much perturbed about the state of Ireland' but said nothing about the dispute with Lloyd George.
38   Mrs Rupert Beckett, wife of Hon. Rupert Beckett (1870–1955), chairman of the *Yorkshire Post*.
39   Constantine I (1868–1923), King of Greece 1913–17 and 1919–22.
40   Lloyd George indulged in some further leg-pulling about the Black and Tans, also to Beaverbrook's amazement.

1921

1   Warren Gamaliel Harding (1865–1923), President of the United States 1920–23.
2   Eamonn De Valera (1882–1975), Sinn Fein leader.
3   When Lord and Lady Lee turned Chequers over to the nation as a country home for Prime Ministers.
4   Apparently Riddell considered this a good example of Wilson's clear-headedness.
5   Robert Gilbert Vansittart (1881–1957), clerk in Foreign Office, later Permanent Under-Secretary, created Baron Vansittart.
6   Llewellyn Williams (1867–1922), Liberal MP.
7   Walter von Simons, German Foreign Minister 1920–1.
8   Not 18 March, as given in *Intimate Diary*, p. 285.
9   Riddell modified this passage considerably in *Intimate Diary*, p. 286. Doubtless he guessed the nature of the relationship between the Prince of Wales and Mrs Dudley Ward.
10   The so-called 'Burnham Scales'.
11   Michael Collins (1890–1922), Sinn Fein leader.
12   A. J. Sylvester, Private Secretary to Lloyd George.
13   Stephen Walsh (1859–1929), Labour MP, Parliamentary Secretary to Ministry of National Service 1917 and to Local Government Board 1917–19.
14   Tom Richards (1859–1931), Labour MP and miners' leader.
15   William Charles Bridgeman (1864–1935), Unionist MP, Parliamentary Secretary to Ministry of Labour 1916–19, to Board of Trade 1919–20, to Mines Department 1920–2, Home Secretary 1922–4, created Viscount Bridgeman.
16   Philippe Berthelot (1866–1934), French Foreign Minister.
17   Edward William Macleay Grigg (1879–1955), private secretary to Lloyd George 1921–2, created Baron Altrincham.
18   Beaverbrook had suggested to Lloyd George on 4 June that the remain-

der of Hulton's baronetcy should be given to his illegitimate son, and to his son's heirs, adding that the Lord Chancellor (Birkenhead) had said there would be no difficulty if the Prime Minister approved. (House of Lords Record Office. Lloyd George Papers, F/4/6/3.) But the baronetcy became extinct on Hulton's death.

19 Widow of Sir Arthur Markham, a Liberal MP at the time of his death in 1916.
20 This was correct. Addison had been reduced from Minister of Health to Minister without Portfolio in April 1921, and resigned, or was forced out, in July.
21 Of 23 June.
22 Despite Birkenhead's fervent protests, the alleged intrigue was not altogether without substance.
23 William Ferguson Massey (1856–1925), Prime Minister of New Zealand 1912–25.
24 August 7, not 8 or 9 as in *Intimate Diary*, p. 311.
25 The Duchess of Atholl was a Conservative MP from 1923 to 1938, and Parliamentary Secretary to the Board of Education 1924–9.
26 Harold Boulton (1859–1935), writer of songs.
27 Steed's mistress of many years.
28 Arthur Griffith (1872–1922), Sinn Fein leader.
29 Rowland's name was excised in *Intimate Diary*, p. 329.
30 'Frocks' was Wilson's favourite term for politicians.
31 I.e. as Chief of the Imperial General Staff.
32 Robert Henry Brand (1878–1963), banker, created Baron Brand.
33 At this time Geddes was Britain's Ambassador in Washington.
34 A rather florid version of this appeared in *Intimate Diary*, p. 343. But in fact Balfour had cabled Lloyd George to make a personal appeal to Riddell to stop on in Washington, as his assistance was 'almost essential'. (Lloyd George Papers, F/43/7/20.)

January–October 1922

1 James Albert Edward Hamilton (1869–1953), 3rd Duke of Abercorn.
2 He did not give the Knighthood of St Patrick to Northcliffe and they did not become friends.
3 I.e. Viscount Grey of Fallodon, the former Foreign Secretary, and not Earl Grey, his cousin.
4 Philip Snowden (1864–1937), Labour MP and later Chancellor of the Exchequer, created Viscount Snowden.
5 Labour won the Clayton division with a turnover of nearly 8,000 votes.
6 A part of the so-called 'Geddes Axe' to cut Government spending.
7 Apparently a reference to the alleged conspiracy of the previous summer. See diary entries for 24 June and 2 August 1921.
8 Sir George Younger, the Conservative Party organiser, had come out strongly against an early election. This effectively killed Lloyd George's chances of appealing to the country at this time.

9   Charles Albert McCurdy (1870–1941), Liberal MP, Parliamentary Sec-
     retary to Ministry of Food 1919–20, Food Controller 1920–1, coalition
     Liberal Chief Whip 1921–2.
10   Walter J. Evans, editor of the *Evening News* for many years. Evans retired
     shortly after this.
11   Hildebrand Aubrey Harmsworth (1872–1929), brother of Lords
     Northcliffe and Rothermere, former proprietor of the *Globe*.
12   Samuel James Waring (1860–1936), merchant, created Baron Waring.
13   Archibald Williamson (1860–1931), Liberal MP, created Baron Forres.
14   Berkley George Andrew Moynihan (1865–1936), surgeon, created Baron
     Moynihan of Leeds.
15   Geoffrey Hithersay Shakespeare (1893–1980), private secretary to Lloyd
     George 1921–3, later Liberal MP.
16   Eliot Crawshay-Williams (1879–1962), former Liberal MP.
17   Amusing in light of Lloyd George's relationship with Frances Stevenson.
18   On 31 May Riddell had a visit from a staff member of *The Times* who told
     him of the problems at Printing House Square and the evidence that
     Northcliffe was going mad.
19   First mention of Lloyd George's interest in acquiring *The Times*.
20   Wilson was gunned down by two Irishmen on the steps of his Eaton
     Square house on 22 June 1922.
21   Herbert Stern (1851–1919), financier, created Baron Michelham of
     Hellingly. Sydney James Stern (d. 1912), financier, created Baron
     Wandsworth.
22   Scott Dickson (1850–1922), former Unionist MP, Lord Justice Clerk of
     Scotland 1915–22.
23   This should be 'LJC', i.e. Lord Justice Clerk.
24   Greenwood told Riddell privately that 'he had spent £2,000 of his own
     money while Chief Secretary, but that there was no prospect of a refund
     and that LG up to now had neglected to fulfil his promises'.
25   William Howard Taft (1857–1930), Chief Justice of the United States
     and former President (1909–13).
26   This may have been 12 October. It is not clear from the manuscript.
27   This was not quite what Lloyd George had said. See diary for 8 July.
28   John Walter (1873–1968), Chairman of *The Times* 1910–23.

October 1922–September 1934

1   The famous Carlton Club meeting of Conservative MPs.
2   Robert Arundell Hudson (1864–1927), later married Northcliffe's widow.
3   Another version has it that Stuart was tricked by the telephone call.
4   Esmond Cecil Harmsworth (1898–1978), publisher, 2nd Viscount
     Rothermere.
5   This was hardly fair, considering how Lloyd George had treated Curzon.
6   Yet Lloyd George had made Cecil Harmsworth Parliamentary Under-
     Secretary for Foreign Affairs in early 1919, a post he retained until the fall
     of the coalition.

7 Riddell was being disingenuous here. During the previous fourteen years business reasons had seldom, if ever, kept him from being at Lloyd George's side if the opportunity offered.

8 This may have been the occasion when Megan learnt the truth of her father's relationship with Frances Stevenson.

9 Sir Joseph Robinson, a South African financier of dubious reputation.

10 Stanley Baldwin (1867–1947), Conservative Minister, Financial Secretary to Treasury 1917–21, President of Board of Trade 1921–2, Chancellor of Exchequer 1922–3, later Prime Minister, created Earl Baldwin of Bewdley.

11 John Colin Campbell Davidson (1889–1970), private secretary to Bonar Law, later Conservative Minister, created Viscount Davidson.

12 Philip Lloyd-Greame (1884–1972), name changed to Cunliffe-Lister, Unionist MP, Parliamentary Secretary to Board of Trade 1920–1, Secretary, Overseas Trade Department 1921–2, President of Board of Trade 1921–2 and 1924–9, created Earl of Swinton.

13 James Hamet Dunn (1875–1956), Canadian industrialist, widow married Lord Beaverbrook.

14 In this context the term meant those Conservatives who had determined to have nothing further to do with Lloyd George and his associates.

15 Eyre Crowe (1864–1925), Permanent Under-Secretary at Foreign Office 1920–5.

16 Not quite as worded in *Intimate Diary*, p. 413.

APPENDIX A

(Sir George Riddell to Sir William Robertson Nicoll)

Confidential

10 August 1912

My dear William,

I had a long chat on Thursday morning with the Master of Elibank. He seemed to be very depressed and not very well. I said to him, 'I hope this bombshell is not due to anything serious in connection with your health.' He replied, with some hesitation, 'No, nothing serious, but I need a rest.' And it was evident from his manner that his health was causing him considerable anxiety. He then went on to say, 'My retirement is due to the combined action of two causes – my health and the state of the affairs of my family. My father has recently made over to me the family estates, which are heavily encumbered. I have been looking into matters, and find them much worse than I anticipated. I feel it to be my duty to my brothers and myself to devote my attention for two or three years to the management of our property. I have been thinking the matter over for some time. My original intention was to take a Colonial Governorship and to allow the rents to accumulate with a view to the redemption of the charges, but this would have been a slow business and I should have been exiled for five years from all my friends. I might have taken a Government department, with a seat in the Cabinet, but such an appointment would have left me no time for my private affairs and would have involved a heavy strain upon my mental and physical powers.

'A short time ago, my old friend Lord Cowdray suggested to me that I should join his firm. I saw that this was a unique opportunity which would enable me to secure the conditions which were rendered necessary by the state of my health and my private affairs. I saw the Prime Minister, who had known for some time past that some change was necessary. I took his opinion and he advised me to accept the offer. Now that the decision has been made, I feel that the giving up of this Office (he waved his hand and looked sadly round the room) will be a terrible wrench, but I hope to resume my active political work at no distant date, and I shall look forward to the time.'

He also said, and he was not very explicit and I did not care to ask

417

him to explain himself, that there was a secret reason of a private and personal character connected with his affairs which was known to his colleagues and intimates – the Premier, LG, Winston and Grey. He mentioned this at the beginning of the interview but whether it was one of the two reasons above mentioned, or a third, I could not discover. He spoke with considerable emotion. As I was leaving, he said to me, 'You and I have been very good friends. We have done a good many things together, we must not get out of touch with each other; we may be able to do other things in the future.' I said, 'The Presbytery sat last night in sackcloth and ashes.' He smiled sadly and said, 'Now that I shall be more free, I hope the Presbytery will allow me to come and dine sometimes.' I said we should be honoured. I told him that you had gone to Scotland and I asked him whether I might send you a note indicating what he had said as to the reasons for his retirement. He said, 'By all means. You can repeat our private conversation to him.' And thus the interview terminated.

There may be something behind the scenes, but there is no doubt that the poor man is ill and that the family affairs are in a bad way. He implied that unless matters are righted he and his two brothers will have very little. This is all the news I can get for you at the moment. I may hear something further before long, in which case I will communicate it. I hope you had a pleasant journey.

Sir W. Robertson Nicoll

Yours very faithfully,

Lumsden, Aberdeenshire

George A. Riddell

APPENDIX B

(Lord Northcliffe to Sir George Riddell)

Private

3 October 1918

My dear Riddell,

I did not wish to send that message to the meeting about the Red Cross, but Mr Herbert Brown, England's champion beggar, who has raised £995,000 for the Red Cross out of farmers alone (and farmers be hard parties) stood over me while I did it – in order that the City of London Red Cross should get a start.

I was very sorry to miss you at Danny, which must have reminded you not a little of Sutton Place. I was describing it to my Lady, and she was especially interested in the stone-paved garden, which was looking delightful that sunny morning.

The Old Gang are trying to lay hold of the legs of the Prime Minister and drag him down, and drag him down they will unless he realises his position. Because he often comes face to face with the little people in the Government, he seems to think that they have some standing in the country. At last week's Albert Hall Italian gathering, Walter Long rose and spoke for some time, and no one among the ten thousand in the hall knew who he was. He was followed by Austen Chamberlain, and at the end of five minutes, the mob, losing their patience and their manners, effectively silenced him. It was a pathetic sight. Do not let the Prime Minister be fooled.

I should be very glad to help him, and my Paris *Daily Mail*, which now has a daily circulation of 320,000 among the soldiers, could, I think, win the election, if I go over there and work; but I am not going to work for the return of the Old Gang. Asquith, I understand, is very hard up, and I think he might be made Lord Chancellor, though the few people to whom I have mentioned the matter seemed outraged by the idea.

My exact position may be summed up in the following words:

'I do not propose to use my newspapers and personal influence to support a new Government, elected at the most critical period in the history of the British nations, unless I know definitely and in writing and can consciously [*sic*] approve, the personal constitution of that Government.'

I have only just seen the photographs of *The Times* lunch. Apparently my staff were afraid to show it to me. You use the work 'hard-bitten' – most of then look to me like hard-drinking!

Sir George Riddell, Bart.

Yours sincerely,
Northcliffe

APPENDIX C

(Sir George Riddell to Lloyd George)

Private & Personal

31 October 1918

My dear Prime Minister,

Mr Higham, the advertising agent, came to me yesterday with the first instalment of the Coalition advertising, which it was proposed to insert in the next issue of the Sunday newspapers. I took strong exception to it. In my mind it created the impression that the capitalists had put up a big fund to jockey the working classes, and that they are using you as an instrument. Furthermore, the advertisement contained what I thought to be a most injudicious reference to Bolshevism. There is no object in advertising the Bolshevists, of whom happily there are very few. I am sure that if you had seen the advertisement you would have agreed with me. I told Guest what I thought and understand that the copy has now been stopped, so assume that the advertisement is to be re-written.

The first public notice in connection with the Election is of vital importance. We all think you will win, hands down, if your friends do not queer your pitch by ill-advised action. I am rather suspicious of the advertising campaign. I am not at all sure that the British people like paid advertisements of this sort. But if there is to be a campaign, as apparently there is, the judicious writing of copy is of the first importance. Northcliffe rang me up this morning to say that Higham had asked to see him, and that he had declined, as he (Northcliffe) did not intend to take any political hints from advertising agents. This attitude is symptomatic and prophetic.

Hoping that you are flourishing, and with every good wish for the success of your wonderful mission.

Ever yours, and very hurriedly, to catch a train.

PS What I think about the advertising is that it is useless to create wrong impressions. You are not being run by the capitalists or by anybody else except Lloyd George, and it is a great mistake that the people should be led to think that you are. Most of us, with some brilliant exceptions of course including yourself, have sufficient sins to account for, without being placed under wrongful suspicion. I am seeing to that matter for you and hope to report progress on your return. I am lunching tomorrow with a mutual friend with a tail – Scotch and Welsh mixed.

PS II   I think the election arrangements will want very careful watching, or there will be trouble.

APPENDIX D

Names excised in Riddell's published volumes (in italics within square brackets)

More Pages From My Diary

p.30   (2 December 1911) 'Distinguished Lady Orator [*Lady Dysart*]: The Insurance Bill would destroy the beautiful intimacy between master and maid.'

p.33   (12 December 1911) 'When Cecil Rhodes died, another South African millionaire [*Abe Bailey*] was supposed to be endeavouring to take his place. . . .'

p.56   (28 April 1912) 'L. G. spoke in angry terms about a question by a Tory MP [*Ian Malcolm*] as to a Labour man's [*J. Pointer*] assertion that MPs [*H. H. Asquith* and *George Wyndham*] appear in the House the worse for drink.'

p.60   (11 May 1912) 'A leading Liberal [*George Lambert*] told me that his people owed much to one of Murray's predecessors [*G. Whiteley*], who found the coffers empty and got in £500,000.'

p.72   (23 June 1912) 'A House of Lords official told me a tragic story about an unhappy peer [*10th Duke of St Albans*] who was attacked by a terrible disease which caused him to mortify. [. . .] Another prominent person told me a quaint story about a lunatic peer [*11th Duke of St Albans*] who thought he was Charles II.'

p.92   (1 October 1912) 'During an angry dispute with a policeman [*Count Herbert Bismarck*], who thinks himself no end of a swell, remarked, 'Do you know who I am? I am [*Count Herbert Bismarck*]!' The policeman responded, 'That may explain, but does not excuse, your conduct!'

p.94   (23 October 1912) 'When Lord Balcarres described to Nicoll the Philistinish furniture and decoration in a North Country House [*Joseph Chamberlain's*] he had been visiting, he remarked, "They rose up and smote you forcibly every time you looked at them."'

p.117   (19 January 1913), 'Edward Grey lost his watch at a conference. He said to [the *Bulgarian*] delegate. 'I cannot think what has become of my watch!' A few days later this delegate brought him the missing watch. 'Where did you get it?' asked

Sir Edward. 'I got it from a colleague [the Servian delegate],' was the reply. 'How did he get it?' asked Sir Edward. 'I don't know,' was the answer. 'He does not know I have taken it from him!'

p.120   (8 February 1913) 'L. G.: 'Yes, but the task of waiting for dead men's shoes is an ungrateful one. I remember that [*Lawson Walton*] held on because he heard that [*Lord Loreburn's*] heart was weak and that [*Samuel Evans*], another aspirant for [*Lord Loreburn's*] job, used to look at [*Lawson Walton*] (who was himself very ill) to see if he was shrinking any further!'

War Diary

p.74   (10 April 1915) L. G. says that [*Sir John Simon*] worries too much about small points. If you were buying a large mansion he would come to you and say, 'Have you thought that there is no accommodation for the cat?'

p.86   (13 May 1915) 'Long talk with [*Sir Stanley Buckmaster*] who told me he had written me a strong letter in reply to one from me criticising certain of the arrangements at the [Press] Bureau.'

p.114   (31 July 1915) 'L. G. gave me his reasons for parting with [*Sir Percy Girouard*]. LG says he is too erratic.'

p.156   (17 February 1916) 'The preliminary announcment that [*Sir George Croydon Marks*] is to succeed him [Lord Murray, as head of the Labour Department at Munitions] has roused a storm in the Department.'

p.247   (1 April 1917) 'LG: Yes, [*Halsey*] is a first class man [at the Admiralty], I think. I have been much impressed by him.'

p.347   (17 August 1918) 'He [Seely] wanted my opinion on the statement made to him by [*Stephenson Kent*] and his people to the effect that the country is on the verge of revolution.'

Intimate Diary of the Peace Conference and After

p.47   (9 April 1919) '[Lord Northcliffe]: 'Wilson [i.e. President] is a vain man –his vanity is colossal. I have seen many evidences of it. He is a bluffer, and I agree with [*Sir William Wiseman*] who says he is a gambler.'

p.57   (23 April 1919) 'Do you remember the cynical remark, 'If you want to succeed in politics, you must keep your conscience well under control'? Somebody said, 'Well, that would not give [*Winston Churchill*] much trouble.'

p.168   (14 February 1920) 'Well,' said Beaverbrook, 'we got it from [*Barnes's*] mistress!' The point of the story is that [*George Barnes*] is the last word in respectability.'

p.237   (16 September 1920) 'Lunched with [*Lord Lee*], who is very anxious to be appointed Viceroy of India.'

p.280   (19 February 1921) 'LG remarked, "Worthington-Evans said to [*Count Sforza*] a foreigner, who is probably a Jew, and whom Evans evidently regarded as such, 'Scotland, my boy! Scotland's no place for your people! Even they cannot make a living there!'"

p.134   (26 August 1921) 'A troublesome person [*Sir William Peterson*] wished at the final dinner to make a speech about LG but was vigorously assailed by Sir Harry Brittain. . . .'

p.328   (16 October 1921) 'He spoke rather like [*John Rowland*] a clever, but incoherent, Welshman.'

p.401   (15 January 1923) 'In the evening B told an amusing story about one of his first cases – a breach of promise case tried before a dignified old judge [*Mr Justice Wills*].'

Index

Churchill, Winston 138, 162–6, 178ff.,
  388; as Home Secretary 19–24; as
  First Lord 25–119; as Minister of
  Munitions 201–49; as Secretary for
  War 255–332; as Colonial
  Secretary 342–75
Clark, Sir William 202, 405n.5
Clemenceau, Georges 1, 212–13, 240–1,
  244, 253ff., 268ff., 327–8, 406n.26
Clifford, Dr J. 143, 187
Collins, Michael 340, 354, 412n.11
conscription, *see* National Service
Constantine I, King 328–9, 412n.39
Cook, Sir Edward 104, 355, 398n.39
Cowdray, Lord, 208, 229, 292, 295
Crawshay-Williams, Eliot 369, 414n.16
Crewe, Marquess of 68, 90, 396n.25
Crosfield, A.H. 326, 412n.34
Crowe, Eyre 389, 415n.15
Curzon, Lord 129–30, 137, 148, 170,
  177, 189, 209, 309, 325, 346, 375,
  382–3, 389, 401n.7

D'Abernon, Lord 183–4, 403n.3
Daily Chronicle 9, 71, 75–7, 99, 142–3,
  161, 163, 172, 222, 228–30, 235ff., 372
Dalziel, Sir Henry 33, 101,130, 149, 177,
  236, 240
Davidson, J.C.C. 387, 415n.11
Davidson, Randall, Archbishop of
  Canterbury, 34, 393n.9
Davies, David 154, 170–2, 174, 182,
  191–2, 229, 401n.23
Davies, J.T. 89, 152, 367–9, 376, 379,
  387, 401n.19
Davies, Willie 21
Dawson, Sir Bertrand 313, 411n.18
Dawson, Geoffrey *see* Robinson, Geoffrey
Derby, Lord 113, 133ff., 150, 180, 204,
  207, 218, 220, 225, 252, 302, 312, 314,
  317, 389
De Valera, Eamonn 332, 350ff., 412n.2
Devlin, Joseph 72, 155, 396n.28
Dickson, Scott 373, 414n.22
Dillon, John 228, 407n.15
Dissenters 20, 81, 87, 89, 93, 102, 143–4,
  187
Donald, R. 9, 21, 32–3, 43, 47, 58, 60,
  66–8, 71, 79, 91, 96, 99, 103, 120, 124,
  128–9, 161, 173, 180, 183, 191, 194,
  226–30, 355, 376
drink question 104–5, 107–10, 183–4,
  187–8, 191–2
Drummond, James E. 176, 403n.18
Duncan, Sir Andrew 324–5
Dunn, Sir James 387–8, 415n.13

Edward VII, King 64–5, 371, 376
Edwards, Enoch 39, 393n.19

Elibank, Master of, *see* Murray, A.
Ellerman, Sir John 309, 411n.14
Evans, Ernest 287, 337, 409n.4
Evans, Samuel 178, 403n.23
Evans, Walter J. 366

Falconer, James 67, 395n.21
First World War 88–246; *1914* 91ff.;
  1915 101ff., 109, 111, 129, 132–4;
  1916 145–7, 154, 168, 171, 186;
  1917 191ff.; *1918* 223; naval
  warfare 91, 93, 97, 158, 164, 188;
  peace conferences 247–82, 287,
  300ff., 367, 388
Fisher, H.A.L. 202, 296–7, 305, 405n.3
Fisher, Lord 23, 28, 93–4, 100, 110, 112,
  117, 119, 148, 157, 185
FitzGerald, Brinsley 112, 117, 399n.48
Foch, F. 217, 223–4, 231, 240, 276,
  309–10, 315, 321–2, 327, 334
Frank, Howard 131, 400n.27
Fraser, Lovat 361
French, Sir John 47, 56–7, 81–2, 98–100,
  106–12, 118, 120, 126, 165, 195, 200–
  1, 211, 213, 224, 296–7, 314
Fuller, John M.F. 22, 392n.10
Furse, Michael 114, 399n.1

Gardiner, A.G. 47, 58, 180–1, 394n.34
Garvin, J.L. 42–3, 66,90, 212, 270,
  394n.21
Geddes, Auckland 214, 356, 406n.27
Geddes, Sir Eric 192, 213, 231, 236,
  243–4, 287–8, 294, 363–4, 371–2
George V, King 4, 13, 48, 70, 81, 93–4,
  157, 168, 175–6, 188, 284, 328, 389
Gibbs, Philip 211, 405n.22
Giolitti, Giovanni 322
Girouard, P. 123, 399n.7
Glyn, Elinor 1, 279, 409n.32
Gosling, Harry 45–6, 394n.29
Gough, Sir Henry 223, 406n.3
Goulding, E.A. 22, 392n.9
Greene, William Graham 85, 136,
  397n.16
Greenwood, Hamar 287, 332–3, 385,
  388, 409n.3
Grey, Sir Edward 21–2, 27–8, 41, 46, 50,
  54, 60, 62, 68, 71–2, 77, 87–8, 95–6, 99,
  121, 170, 175, 362
Griffith, Arthur 353–4, 413n.28
Griffith, Ellis 54, 131, 395n.2
Grigg, Sir Edward 342, 346, 349, 352,
  360, 374, 412n.17
Guest, F.E. 98, 124, 130–1, 217, 229,
  235, 237, 242–5, 267, 287ff., 307,
  398n.26
Gulland, J.W. 99, 180, 398n.27
Gwynne, H.A. 130, 171, 203, 399n.18

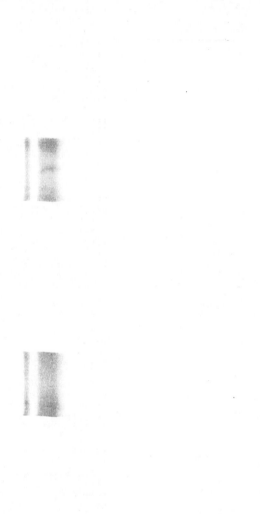